# A SPARROW FALLS
&
# THE DIAMOND HUNTERS

Wilbur Smith was born in Central Africa in 1933. He was educated at Michaelhouse and Rhodes University. He became a full-time writer in 1964 after the successful publication of *When the Lion Feeds*, and has since written thirty novels, all meticulously researched on his numerous expeditions worldwide. His books are now translated into twenty-six different languages.

Also by Wilbur Smith

## THE COURTNEYS
When the Lion Feeds
The Sound of Thunder
Birds of Prey
Monsoon
Blue Horizon
The Triumph of the Sun

## THE COURTNEYS OF AFRICA
The Burning Shore
Power of the Sword
Rage
A Time to Die
Golden Fox

## THE BALLANTYNE NOVELS
A Falcon Flies
Men of Men
The Angels Weep
The Leopard Hunts in Darkness

## THE EGYPTIAN NOVELS
The Seventh Scroll
River God
Warlock
The Quest

*Also*

The Dark of the Sun
Shout at the Devil
The Sunbird
Eagle in the Sky
The Eye of the Tiger
Cry Wolf
Hungry as the Sea
Wild Justice
Elephant Song

# WILBUR SMITH

# A SPARROW FALLS

# &

# THE DIAMOND HUNTERS

p 631

PAN BOOKS

A *Sparrow Falls* first published 1977 by William Heinemann Ltd.
First published in paperback 1978 by Pan Books.
*The Diamond Hunters* first published 1971 by William Heinemann Ltd.
First published in paperback 1972 by Pan Books.

This omnibus first published 2008 by Pan Books
an imprint of Pan Macmillan Ltd
Pan Macmillan, 20 New Wharf Road, London N1 9RR
Basingstoke and Oxford
Associated companies throughout the world
www.panmacmillan.com

ISBN 978-0-330-45796-5

1 3 5 7 9 8 6 4 2

A CIP catalogue record for this book is available from
the British Library.

Typeset by SetSystems Ltd, Saffron Walden, Essex
Printed and bound in Great Britain by
Mackays of Chatham plc, Chatham, Kent

# A SPARROW FALLS
# &
# THE DIAMOND HUNTERS

# A SPARROW FALLS

This book is for my wife and the jewel
of my life, Mokhiniso, with all my love and
gratitude for the enchanted years that I have been
married to her

A sky the colour of old bruises hung low over the battlefields of France, and rolled with ponderous dignity towards the German lines.

Brigadier-General Sean Courtney had spent four winters in France and now, with the eye of a cattleman and a farmer, he could judge this weather almost as accurately as that of his native Africa.

'It will snow tonight,' he grunted, and Lieutenant Nick van der Heever, his orderly officer, glanced back at him over his shoulder.

'I shouldn't wonder, sir.'

Van der Heever was heavily laden. In addition to his service rifle and webbing, he carried a canvas kitbag across his shoulder, for General Courtney was on his way to dine as a mess guest of the 2nd Battalion. At this moment the Colonel and officers of the 2nd Battalion were completely unaware of the impending honour, and Sean grinned in wicked anticipation at the panic that his unannounced arrival would create. The contents of the kitbag would be some small compensation for the shock, for it included half a dozen bottles of pinch bottle Haig and a fat goose.

Nevertheless, Sean was aware that his officers found his informal behaviour and his habit of arriving suddenly in the front lines, unannounced and unattended by his staff, more than a little disconcerting. Only a week before, he had overheard a field telephone conversation on a crossed line between a major and a captain.

'The old bastard thinks he's still fighting the Boer War. Can't you keep him in a cage back there at H.Q.?'

'How do you cage a bull elephant?'

'Well, at least warn us when he's on his way—'

Sean grinned again and trudged on after his orderly officer, the folds of his great-coat flapping about his putteed legs and, for warmth, a silk scarf wrapped around his head beneath the soup-plate shape of his helmet. The boards bounced under his feet and the gluey mud sucked and gurgled beneath them at the passing weight of the two men.

This part of the line was unfamiliar, the brigade had moved in less than a week previously, but the stench was well remembered. The musty smell of earth and mud, overladen with the odour of rotting flesh and sewage, the stale lingering whiff of burned cordite and high explosive.

Sean sniffed it and spat with distaste. Within an hour he knew he would be so accustomed as not to notice it, but now it seemed to coat the back of his throat like cold grease. Once again he looked up at the sky, and now he frowned. Either the wind had shifted into the east a point or two, or they had taken a wrong turning within the maze of trenches, for the low cloud was no longer rolling in the direction that fitted with the map that Sean carried in his head.

'Nick!'

'Sir?'

'Are you still right?'

And he saw at once the uncertainty in the young subaltern's eyes as he looked back.

'Well, sir—'

The trenches had been deserted for the last quarter of a mile, not a single soul had they passed in the labyrinth of high earthen walls.

'We'd better take a look, Nick.'

'I'll do it, sir.' Van der Heever glanced ahead along the trench, and found what he was looking for. At the next intersection a wooden ladder was fastened into the wall. It

2

reached to the top of the sand-bagged parapet. He started towards it.

'Careful, Nick,' Sean called after him.

'Sir,' the young man acknowledged, and propped his rifle before swarming upwards.

Sean calculated they were still three or four hundred yards from the front line yet, and the light was going fast. There was a purple velvet look to the air beneath the clouds, not shooting light at all, and he knew that, despite his age, van der Heever was an old soldier. The glance he took over the top would be swift as a meerkat looking out of its hole.

Sean watched him crouch at the top of the ladder, lift his head for a single quick sweep and then duck down again.

'The hill is too much on our left,' he called down.

The hill was a low, rounded mound that rose a mere hundred and fifty feet above the almost featureless plain. Once it had been thickly forested, but now only the shattered stumps stood waist-high and the slopes were dimpled with shell craters.

'How far is the farm house?' Sean asked, still peering upwards. The farm house was a roofless rectangle of battered walls that stood foursquare facing the centre of the Battalion's sector. It was used as a central reference point for artillery, infantry and aircorps alike.

'I'll have another look,' and van der Heever lifted his head again.

The Mauser has a distinctive cracking report, a high and vicious sound that Sean had heard so often as to be able to judge with accuracy its range and direction.

This was a single shot, at about five hundred yards, almost dead ahead.

Van der Heever's head snapped backwards as though he had taken a heavy punch, and the steel of his helmet rang like a gong. The chin-strap snapped as the round helmet spun high in the air and then dropped to the floorboards in the bottom of the trench and rolled on its rim into a pool of grey mud.

Van der Heever's hands remained locked closed on the top rung of the ladder for a moment, then the nerveless fingers opened, and he tumbled backwards, falling heavily into the bottom of the trench with the skirts of his great-coat ballooning around him.

Sean stood frozen and disbelieving, his mind not yet accepting the fact that Nick was hit, but, as a soldier and a hunter, judging that single shot with awe.

What kind of shooting was that? Five hundred yards in this murky light; one fleeting glimpse of a helmeted head above the parapet; three seconds to set the range and line up, then another instant of time to sight and fire as the head bobbed up again. The Hun that fired that shot was either a superb marksman with reflexes like a leopard – or the flukiest sniper on the western front.

The thought was fleeting and Sean started forward heavily and knelt beside his officer. He turned him with a hand upon the shoulder and felt the sickening slide in his guts and the cold grip on his chest.

The bullet had entered at the temple and exited behind the opposite ear.

Sean lifted the shattered head into his lap, removed his own helmet and began to unwind the silk scarf from around his head. He felt a desolation of loss.

Slowly he wrapped the boy's head into the scarf, and immediately the blood soaked through the thin material. It was a futile gesture – but it served to keep his hands occupied and detract from his sense of helplessness.

He sat on the muddy floorboards, holding the boy's body, his heavy shoulders bowed forward. The size of Sean's bared head was accentuated by the thick curls of dark wiry hair shot through with splashes and strands of grey that sparkled frostily in the fading light. The short thick beard was laced with grey as well, and the big beaked nose was twisted and battered-looking.

Only the black curved eyebrows were sleek and unmarked, and the eyes were clear and dark cobalt blue, the eyes of a much younger man, steady and alert.

Sean Courtney sat for a long time holding the boy, and then he sighed once, deeply, and laid the broken head aside. He stood up, hefted the kitbag on to his own shoulder, and set off along the communications trench once again.

At five minutes before midnight, the Colonel commanding the 2nd Battalion stooped through the blackout curtains that screened the entrance to the mess, and beat the snow from his shoulders with a gloved hand as he straightened.

The mess had been a German dugout six months before, and was the envy of the brigade. Thirty feet below ground level, it was impregnable, even to the heaviest artillery barrage. The floor was of heavy timber boarding and even the walls were panelled against the damp and the cold. A pot-bellied stove stood against the far wall, glowing cheerfully.

Gathered about it in a half circle of looted armchairs sat the off-duty officers.

However, the Colonel had eyes only for the burly figure of his General, seated in the largest and most comfortable chair closest to the stove, and he shed his great-coat as he hurried across the dugout.

'General, my apologies. If I'd known you were coming – I was making my rounds.'

Sean Courtney chuckled and rose ponderously from the

chair to shake his hand. 'It's what I would expect of you, Charles, but your officers have made me very welcome – and we have kept a little of the goose for you.'

The Colonel glanced quickly about the circle and frowned as he saw the hectic cheeks and sparkling eyes of some of his younger subalterns. He must warn them of the folly of trying to drink level with the General. The old man was steady as a rock, of course, and those eyes were like bayonets under the dark brows, but the Colonel knew him well enough to guess that he had a full quart of Dimple Haig in his belly, and that something was troubling him deeply. Then it came to him. Of course –

'I'm terribly sorry to hear about young van der Heever, sir. Sergeant-Major told me what happened.'

Sean made a gesture of dismissal, but for a moment the shadows darkened about his eyes.

'If I'd only known you were coming up into the line this evening, I would have warned you, sir. We have had the devil of trouble with that sniper ever since we moved up. It's the same fellow, of course – absolutely deadly. I've never heard of anything like it. Dreadful nuisance when everything else is so quiet. Only casualties we've had all week.'

'What are you doing about him?' Sean asked harshly. They all saw the flush of anger darken his face, and the Adjutant intervened swiftly.

'I've been on to Colonel Caithness at 3rd Battalion, and we did a deal, sir. He has agreed to send us Anders and MacDonald—'

'You got them!' The Colonel looked delighted. 'Oh I say, that's excellent. I didn't think Caithness would part with his prize pair.'

'They came in this morning – and the two of them have been studying the ground all day. I gave them a free hand, but I understand they are setting up the shoot for tomorrow.'

The young Captain who commanded 'A' Company

pulled out his watch and studied it a moment. 'They are going out from my section, sir. As a matter of fact, I was going to go down and give them a send-off, they will be moving into position at half past twelve. If you'll excuse me, sir.'

'Yes, of course, off with you, Dicky – wish them good luck from me.' Everybody in the brigade had heard of Anders and MacDonald.

'I'd like to meet that pair.' Sean Courtney spoke suddenly, and dutifully the Colonel agreed.

'Of course, I'll come out with you, sir.'

'No, no, Charles – you've been out in the cold all night as it is. I'll just go along with Dicky here.'

T he snow came down thickly out of the utter darkness of the midnight sky. It damped down the night sounds in its thick muffling cloak, muting the regular bursts of a Vickers firing at a hole in the wire on the battalion's left.

Mark Anders sat wrapped in his borrowed blankets and he bowed his head to the book in his lap, adjusting his eyes to the yellow wavering light of the candle-stump.

The rise in temperature that accompanied the first fall of snow and the changed quality of sound entering the small dugout awakened the man who slept beside him. He coughed, and rolled over to open a chink in the canvas curtain beside his head.

'Damn,' he said, and coughed again, the harsh hammering sound of a heavy smoker. 'Damn it to hell. It's snowing.' Then he rolled back to Mark. 'You still reading?' he demanded roughly. 'Always with your nose in a bloody book. You'll ruin your shooting eyes.'

Mark lifted his head. 'It's been snowing for an hour already.'

'What you want all that learning for?' Fergus MacDonald was not so easily distracted. 'It won't do you no good.'

'I don't like the snow,' said Mark. 'We didn't reckon on the snow.'

The snow complicated the task ahead of them. It would cover the ground out there with a sensitive mantle of white. Anybody moving out from the trench into no-man's-land would leave tracks that the dawn light would instantly betray to an observant enemy.

A match flared and Fergus lit two Woodbines and passed one to Mark. They sat shoulder to shoulder, huddled in their blankets.

'You can call off the shoot, Mark. Tell 'em to shove it. You're a volunteer lad.'

They smoked in silence for a full minute before Mark replied.

'That Hun is a bad one.'

'If it's snowing, he probably won't be out tomorrow. Snow will keep him in bed also.'

Mark shook his head slowly. 'If he's that good, he'll be out.'

'Yes.' Fergus nodded. 'He's that good. That shot he made last evening – after lying up all day in the cold, then five hundred yards if it was an inch, and in that light—' Fergus cut himself off, and then went on quickly, 'But you're good also, lad. You're the best, boy.'

Mark said nothing, but carefully pinched out the glowing tip of the Woodbine.

'You're going?' Fergus asked.

'Yes.'

'Get some sleep then, lad. It's going to be a long day.'

Mark blew out the candle flame as he lay back and pulled the blankets over his head.

'You get a good sleep,' Fergus said again. 'I'll wake you in plenty of time,' and he resisted the paternal urge to pat the thin bony shoulder under the blanket.

The young Captain spoke quietly with one of the sentries on the forward firing step, and the man whispered a reply and pointed with his chin along the darkened trench.

'This way, sir.' He went on down the boards, swaddled in clothing so that he had the shape of a bear, and Sean towered head and shoulders above him as he followed.

Around the next revert, through the soft curtains of falling snow, there was the subdued red glow of a brazier from the shallow dugout in the side of the trench. Dark figures squatted close about it, like witches at a sabbat.

'Sergeant MacDonald?' One of the figures rose and stepped forward.

'That's me.' There was a cocky, self-assured tone to the reply.

'Is Anders with you?'

'Present and correct,' said MacDonald, and one of the other figures rose from the circle about the brazier and came forward. He was taller, but moved with grace, like an athlete or a dancer.

'You are ready, Anders?' the Captain went on, speaking in the soft half-whisper of the trenches, and MacDonald replied for him.

'The lad is fighting fit, sir.' He spoke with the proprietary tone of the manager of a prize-fighter. It was clear that the boy was his property, and that ownership gave him a distinction he would never have achieved on his own.

At that moment another flare burst high overhead, a brilliant white and silent explosion of light, softened by the snow.

Sean could judge a man like he could a horse. He could pick the rotten ones, or the big-hearted, from the herd. It was a trick of experience and some deeper inexplicable insight.

In the light of the flare his eyes flickered across the face of the older Sergeant. MacDonald had the bony undernourished features of the slum-dweller, the eyes too close set, the lips narrow and twisted downwards at the corners. There was nothing to interest Sean there and he looked at the other man.

The eyes were a pale golden brown, set wide, with the serene gaze of a poet or a man who had lived in the open country of long distant horizons. The lids were held wide open, so that they did not overlap the iris, leaving a clear glimpse of the clean white about the cornea so that it floated free like a full moon. Sean had seen it only a few times before, and the effect was almost hypnotic, of such direct and searching candour that it seemed to reach deep into Sean's own soul.

After the first impact of those eyes, other impressions crowded in. The first was of the man's extreme youth. He was nearer seventeen than twenty, Sean judged – and then saw immediately how finely drawn the boy was. Despite the serenity of his gaze, he was stretched out tight and hard, racked up with strain close to the snapping point. Sean had seen it so often in the past four years. They had found this child's special talent and exploited it ruthlessly, all of them – Caithness at 3rd Battalion, the ferrety MacDonald, Charles, Dicky and, by association, himself. They had worked him mercilessly, sending him out time and again.

The boy held a steaming tin mug of coffee in one hand, and the wrist that protruded from the sleeve of his coat was skeletal, and speckled with angry red bites of body lice. The neck was too long and thin for the head it supported, and the cheeks were hollow, the eye-sockets sunken.

'This is General Courtney,' said the Captain; and as the light of the flare died, Sean saw the eyes shine suddenly with a new light, and heard the boy's breath catch with awe.

'Hello, Anders, I've heard a lot about you.'

'And I've heard about you, sir.' The transparent tones of

hero-worship irritated Sean. The boy would have heard all the stories, of course. The regiment boasted of him, and every new recruit heard the tales. There was nothing he could do to prevent them circulating.

'It's a great honour to meet you, sir.' The boy tripped on the words, stuttering a little – another sign of the terrible strain he was under – yet the words were completely sincere.

The legendary Sean Courtney, the man who had made five million pounds on the goldfields of the Witwatersrand and lost every penny of it in a morning at a single coup of fortune. Sean Courtney, who had chased the Boer General Leroux across half of Southern Africa and caught him at last after a terrible hand-to-hand fight. The soldier who had held Bombata's ravaging Zulu impis at the gorge and then driven them on to the waiting Maxims, who had planned with his erstwhile enemy Leroux and helped build the Charter of Union which united the four independent states of Southern Africa into a single mighty whole, who had built another vast personal fortune in land and cattle and timber, who had given up his position in Louis Botha's Cabinet and at the head of the Natal Legislative Council to bring the regiment out to France – it was natural the boy's eyes should shine that way and his tongue trip, but still it annoyed Sean. At fifty-nine I'm too old to play the hero now, he thought wryly – and the flare went down, plunging them back into the darkness.

'If there's another mug of that coffee,' said Sean. 'It's bloody cold tonight.'

Sean accepted the chipped enamel mug and hunkered down close to the brazier, cupped the mug between his hands, blowing on the steaming liquid and sipping noisily, and after a moment the others followed his example hesitantly. It was strange to be squatting like old mates with a General and the silence was profound.

'You're from Zululand?' Sean asked the boy suddenly, his

ear had picked up the accent, and without waiting for a reply went on in the Zulu tongue, 'Velapi wena? Where are you from?'

The Zulu language came naturally and easily to Mark's lips though he had not spoken it for two years. 'From the north beyond Eshowe, on the Umfolosi River.'

'Yes. I know it well. I have hunted there.' Sean changed back to English. 'Anders? I knew another Anders. He rode transport from Delagoa Bay back in '89. John? Yes, that's it. Old Johnny Anders. Any relation? Your father?'

'My grandfather. My father's dead. My grandfather has land on the Umfolosi. That's where I live.' The boy was relaxing now. In the brazier glow, Sean thought he saw the lines of strain around his mouth ironing out.

'I didn't think you'd know poor folk, like us – sir.' Fergus MacDonald spoke with cutting edge in his voice, leaning forward towards the brazier with his head turned towards him so that Sean could see the bitter line of his mouth.

Sean nodded slowly. MacDonald was one of them then. One of those who were intent on the new order – trade unions and Karl Marx, Bolsheviks who threw bombs and called themselves comrades. Irrelevantly he noticed for the first time that MacDonald had ginger hair, and big golden freckles on the backs of his hands. He turned back to Mark Anders.

'He taught you to shoot?'

'Yes, sir.' The lad grinned for the first time, warmed by the memory. 'He gave me my first rifle, a Martini Hendry that blew a cloud of gunsmoke like a bush fire but would throw dead true at a hundred and fifty yards.'

'I've hunted elephant with it. A great rifle,' Sean agreed, and suddenly across an age difference of forty years they were friends.

Perhaps, for Sean, the recent death of that other bright young man, Nick van der Heever, had left an aching gap in his life, for now he felt a flood of paternal protection for the youngster. Fergus MacDonald seemed to sense it also, for he cut in like a jealous woman.

'You'd best be getting ready now, lad.' The smile was gone from Mark's lips, the eyes were too calm, and he nodded his thin neck stiffly.

Fergus MacDonald fussed over the lad, and once again Sean was reminded of a trainer preparing his fighter in the dressing-room. He stripped off the heavy, voluminous great-coat and the battle-dress jacket. Over the long woollen full-length underwear went a woollen shirt and two knitted jerseys. A woollen scarf around the throat.

Then a mechanic's boiler-suit which covered the layers of clothing in a single neat skin that would not snag, or flutter in a breeze to draw an enemy eye. A woollen balaclava over the head, and a leather airman's helmet, and Sean saw the reason. The British steel helmet had a distinctive brim, and anyway was no protection from a Mauser bullet.

'Keep your nut down, Mark, me boy.'

Knitted mittens with fingers cut out, and then thick loose gloves over them.

'Keep the old fingers working, lad. Don't let them stiffen up on you.'

A small leather shoulder bag that slung comfortably under the left armpit.

'Ham sandwiches with plenty of mustard, chocolate and barley sugar – just the way you like it. Don't forget to eat, keep you warm.'

Four full clips of .303 cartridges, three slipped into the thigh pockets of the boiler-suit – and one into the special pocket sewn into the forearm of the left sleeve.

'I waxed each round myself,' Fergus announced mainly for the benefit of the listening General. 'They'll slide in like—' and the simile was crude and obscene, meant to show Fergus' scorn of rank and class. But Sean let it pass easily, he was too interested in the preparations for the hunt.

'I won't show Cuthbert until the sun is right.'

'Cuthbert?' Sean asked, and Fergus chuckled and indicated a third figure that lay quietly at the back of the dugout. It was the first time Sean had noticed him and Fergus chuckled again at his puzzled expression and reached out to the reclining figure.

Only then Sean realized it was a dummy, but in the light of the brazier the features were realistic and the helmeted head rode at a natural angle on the shoulders. The model ended abruptly at the hips and below it there was only a broom handle.

'I'd like to know how you are going to do it?' Sean addressed the question to young Mark Anders, but Fergus replied importantly.

'Yesterday the Hun was shooting from low on the northern slope of the hill. Mark and me worked out the angles of the two shots he made and we've got him pegged to within fifty yards.'

'He may change position,' Sean pointed out.

'He'll not leave the north slope. It's in shadow all day, even if the sun comes out. He will want to shoot from shade into light.' Sean nodded at the logic of it.

'Yes,' he agreed, 'but he may shoot from a stand in the German line.'

And Mark answered quietly, 'I don't think so, sir. The lines are too far apart here' – the German line ran across the crest of the hill – 'he'd want a shorter range. No, sir, he's shooting from close in. He makes a stand in no-man's-land, probably changes it every day – but each time he comes close as he can get to our lines while still staying in the shadow.' The boy had not tripped on a single word now that his mind had locked on to the problem. His voice was low and intense.

'I picked out a good stand for the lad, just beyond the farm house. He can cover the whole of the northern slope at less than two hundred yards. He'll move out now and settle in while it's still dark. I'm sending him out early. I want him to make his move before the Hun. I don't want the lad walking on top of the bastard in the dark.' Fergus MacDonald took over from Mark with an air of authority. 'Then we both wait until the light is good and clean, then I start working with Cuthbert here,' he patted the dummy and chuckled again. 'It's damned difficult to give him a nice natural look, like some stupid rooky sticking his head up to take a first look at France. If you let the Hun get too long a look at him, then he'll tumble to the trick, but if you make it too quick, he won't get a chance for a shot. No, it's not easy.'

'Yes, I should imagine,' Sean murmured wryly, 'that it's the most dangerous and difficult part of the whole thing.' And he saw the deadly expression flit across Fergus Mac-Donald's face before he turned to Mark Anders.

'Another mug of coffee, lad – and then it's time to be getting on. I want you in place before the snow stops.'

Sean reached into the breast of his great-coat and brought out the silver flask that Ruth had given him on the day the regiment sailed.

'Put some fangs in the coffee.' He offered the flask to Mark.

The boy shook his head shyly. 'No thank you, sir. Makes me see squiff.'

'Don't mind if I do, sir.' Fergus MacDonald reached swiftly across the brazier. The clear brown liquid glugged freely into his own mug.

The Sergeant-Major had sent out a patrol before midnight to cut a lane through the wire in front of 'A' Company.

Mark stood at the foot of the trench ladder and changed his rifle from the right hand; another flare burst overhead and in its light Sean saw how intent the boy was on his task. He pulled back the bolt of the rifle, and Sean noted that he was not using the standard No. 1 short Lee-Enfield, which was the work-horse of the British army, but that he favoured the American P.14 which also fired the .303 calibre but had the longer barrel and finer balance.

Mark stripped two clips of ammunition into the magazine and closed the bolt, levering a round of carefully selected and waxed ammunition into the breach.

In the last light of the flare he looked across at Sean, and nodded slightly. The flare died and in the darkness that followed Sean heard the quick light steps on the wooden ladder. He wanted to call 'good luck' after the boy, but suppressed the whim and instead patted his pockets for his cheroot case.

'Shall we get on back, sir?' the Captain asked quietly.

'Off with you,' growled Sean, his voice gruff with the premonition of coming tragedy. 'I'll stay on a while.' Though he could give no help, somehow it seemed like deserting the boy to leave now.

Mark moved quickly along the line that the patrol had laid to guide him through the wire. He stooped to keep contact with the line in his left hand, and he carried the P.14 in his right. He lifted his feet carefully, and stepped lightly, trying not to scuff the snow, trying to spread his weight evenly on each foot so as not to break the crust.

Yet every time a flare went up, he had to fall face

forward and lie still and huddled, a dark blot in the electric glare of light against the sheet of white, screened only by the persistently falling veils of snow. When he scrambled up in the darkness and moved on, he knew he left a disturbed area of snow. Ordinarily it would not have mattered, for in the barren, shell-churned wilderness of no-man's-land, such light scrabble marks passed unnoticed. But Mark knew that in the first cold light of dawn an unusual pair of eyes would be scrutinizing every inch of the ground, hunting for just this kind of sign.

Suddenly, colder than the icy snow-laden air against his cheeks, was the deep chill of loneliness. The sense of vulnerability, of being pitted against a skilled and implacable enemy, an invisible, terrifying, efficient adversary who would deliver instant death at the slightest error.

The latest flare sank and died, and he scrambled to his feet and blundered to the dark, jagged wall of the ruined farm house. He crouched against it, and tried to control his breathing, for this newly conceived terror threatened to smother him. It was the first time it had come upon him. Fear he had known – had lived with it as his constant companion these last two years, but never this terrible paralysing terror.

When he touched the fingers of his right hand to his ice-cold cheek, he felt the tremble in them, and in sympathy his teeth chattered in a short staccato rhythm.

'I can't shoot like this,' he thought wildly, clenching his jaw until it ached and locking his hands together and holding them hard against his groin, 'and I can't stay here.' The ruin was too obvious a stand to make. It would be the first point the German sniper would study. He had to get out of there, and quickly. Back to the trenches. Suddenly his terror was panic, and he lifted himself to begin the crazed flight back, leaving his rifle propped against the ruined wall.

'*Bist du da?*' a voice whispered softly near him in the darkness. Mark froze instantly.

'*Ja!*' The reply was further along the wall and Mark found the rifle with his left hand settling naturally on to the stock and his right curling about the pistol grip, forefinger hooking over the trigger.

'*Komm, wir gehen zurück.*' Close beside Mark, sensed rather than seen in the darkness, passed a heavily laden figure. Mark swung the rifle to follow him, his thumb on the safety-catch ready to slip it. The German stumbled heavily in the treacherous snowy footing, and the wiring tools he carried clanked together. The man cursed.

'*Scheisse!*'

'*Halt den Mund,*' snapped the other, and they moved on back towards the German line above them on the crest of the hill.

Mark had not expected a wiring detail to be out in this weather. His first thought had been for the German sniper, but now his mind leaped forward at this sudden good fortune.

The patrol would lead him through the German wire, and their heavy blundering tracks would hide his own from the sniper.

It was only when he had decided this that he realized with surprise that his panic had passed, his hands were rock steady and his breathing was deep and slow. He grinned without humour at his own frailty and moved forward lightly after the German patrol.

They were a hundred paces beyond the farm house when it stopped snowing. Mark felt the slide of dismay in his chest. He had relied heavily on the snow holding, at least until dawn, but he kept on after the patrol. They were moving faster and more confidently as they neared their own lines.

Two hundred yards below the crest Mark left them to go on alone, and began working his way sideways around the slope, groping his way painstakingly through the heavily staked wire, until at last he recognized and reached the stand that he and Fergus had picked out through binoculars the previous afternoon.

The main trunk of one of the oaks that had covered the hill had fallen directly down the slope, pulling up a great matted tangle of roots from the soft high-explosive-ploughed earth.

Mark crawled among the tangle of roots; selecting the side which would be in deepest shadow from the winter-angled sun, he wriggled in on his belly until he was half covered by them, but with head and shoulders able to turn to cover the full curve of the northern slope ahead of him.

Now his first concern was to check the P.14 carefully, paying particular attention to the vulnerable, high-mounted Bisley-type rear sight to make sure that it had not been knocked or misaligned during the journey across no-man's-land. He ate two of the ham sandwiches, drank a few rationed mouthfuls of sweet coffee and adjusted the woollen scarf over his mouth and nose, for warmth and to prevent the steaming of his breath. Then he laid his forehead carefully against the wooden butt of his rifle. He had developed the knack of instant sleep, and while he slept it snowed again.

When Mark woke in the sickly grey light of dawn, he was blanketed by the fine white flakes. Careful not to disturb them, he lifted his head slowly, and blinked his eyes rapidly to clear them. His fingers were stiff and cold; he worked them steadily in the gloves, forcing warm blood to flow.

He had been lucky again – twice in one night was too much. First the patrol to lead him through the wire and now this thin white coat of natural camouflage to blend his shape with the tangled roots of the oak. Too much luck, the pendulum must swing.

Slowly the darkness drew back, widening his circle of

vision, and as it expanded so the whole of Mark's existence came to centre in those two wide golden brown eyes. They moved quickly in the pattern of search, touching in turn each irregularity and fold, each feature, each object, each contrasting colour or texture of snow and mud and earth, each stump of shattered timber or fallen branch, the irregular rim of every shell hole, looking for shadows where they should not have been, seeking the evidence of disturbance beneath the new thin coat of snow, seeking, searching – for life, literally for life.

The snow stopped again a little before nine, and by noon the sky had lightened and there were holes in the cloud-cover; a single watery ray of sun fell and moved like a searchlight across the southern slope of the hill.

'Right, Cuthbert, let's draw some Hun fire.'

Fergus had marked each of the German sniper's kills on the trench map the Sergeant-Major had loaned him. There were two black spots close to each other in the same section of trench. At those places the parapet was too low for the commanding bulk of the hill that commanded the front line. After five men had been killed at those two spots the parapet had been raised with sand-bags and crudely lettered notices warned the unwary.

'KEEP YOUR HEAD DOWN. SNIPER AT WORK.'

The two black spots were only fifty paces apart, and Fergus guessed that the sniper had achieved his successes here by waiting for a victim to pass down the trench. He would get a glimpse of a head in the first gap, and would be aiming into the second gap with his finger on the hair-trigger as the man passed it. He explained this to Sean Courtney as he made his preparations, for by this time Sean was so intrigued by the hunt that only a major German offensive would have lured him back to his headquarters. During the morning he had spoken to his aide-de-camp over the field telephone, and told them where they could find him in an emergency.

'But make sure it's an emergency,' he had growled ferociously into the headset.

'I'll draw him from south to north,' Fergus explained, 'that will force the bloody Hun to turn away from Mark's stand, it will give the lad an extra second while he swings back towards the ridge.'

Fergus MacDonald was good with the dummy, Sean had to concede it. He carried it two feet higher than natural man height, to compensate for the raised parapet, and he gave it a realistic roll of the shoulders, like a hurrying man as he passed it through the first gap.

Sean, the young Captain and the beefy red-faced Sergeant-Major were waiting with a half dozen other ranks beyond the second gap, watching Fergus come down the boards towards them steadily.

Instinctively they all drew breath and held it as he came up to the second gap, all of them tensed with suspense.

Up the slope of the hill, the Mauser cracked, like a bull-whip on the icy air, and the dummy kicked sharply in Fergus MacDonald's hands.

Fergus jerked it down out of sight, and fell to his knees to examine the neat round hole punched through the papiermâché head.

'Oh shit!' he whispered bitterly. 'Oh, shit all over it!'

'What is it, MacDonald?'

'The bloody Hun – oh, the sodding bastard—'

'MacDonald!'

'He's picked the same stand as my boy.'

Sean did not understand for a moment. 'He's in among the oak trunks, he's sitting right on top of Mark. They picked the same stand.'

The vicious stinging discharge of the Mauser was so close, so high and sharp, that for a few seconds afterwards, Mark's ear-drums buzzed with the mosquito hum of auditory memory.

For seconds he was stunned, frozen with the shock of it. The German sniper was somewhere within twenty feet of where he lay. By some freak of coincidence, he had chosen the same point on the slope as Mark. No, it was no freak of coincidence. With the hunter's eye for ground, both men had selected the ideal position for their common purpose – to deliver swift death from hiding. The pendulum of Mark's fortune had swung to the other end of its arc.

Mark had not moved in the seconds since the Mauser shot, but every sense was heightened by the adrenalin that sang through his veins and his heart beat with a force that seemed to reverberate against the cage of his ribs.

The German was on his left, higher up the slope, slightly behind his shoulder. The left was his unprotected side, away from the tangled oak roots.

He trained his eyes around, without moving his head, and in the periphery of his vision saw another of the fallen oak trunks close by. He did not move for another full minute, watching for the flicker of movement in the corner of his eye. There was nothing, and the silence was awesome and oppressive – until a Spandau fired a shot burst, a mile or more away down the line.

Mark began to turn his head towards the left, as slowly as a chameleon stalking a fly. Gradually the distortion of peripheral vision cleared, and he could sweep the whole of the slope above him.

The nearest oak trunk had been savaged with shrapnel, all the bark was torn away and raw chunks of timber ripped from it. It had fallen across a hollow in the earth, forming a bridge; and although the snow had piled up against it, there was a narrow gap between earth and oak. The gap was perhaps three inches wide at the centre, and Mark could see reflected light from the snow beyond.

At that moment, a minute blur of movement snapped his eyes in his skull. It was a fleeting movement of a mere sixteenth of an inch, but it riveted Mark's attention. He started for fully five seconds, before he realized what he was seeing.

Beyond the screening end of the oak trunk, the very tip of a Mauser barrel protruded. It had been bound with burlap to break the stark outline and to prevent reflection of light off metal – but the cruel little mouth of the muzzle was uncovered.

The German was lying behind the oak log, like Mark his right flank protected, facing half-way from Mark – and less than twenty feet separated them.

Mark watched the tip of the Mauser barrel for ten minutes more, and it did not move again. The German had stillness and patience. Once he had reloaded, he had frozen again into that rigour of watchfulness.

'He's so good that there is no way I can clear the shot,' Mark thought. 'If I move an inch, he'll hear me, and he'll be fast. Very fast.'

To get a clear shot, Mark would have to move back twenty feet or more, and then he would be looking directly into the muzzle of the Mauser; a head-on shot, with the German alerted by his movements. Mark knew he could not afford to give away that much advantage, not against an adversary of this calibre.

The long still minutes crawled by without any break in tension. Mark had the illusion that every nerve and sinew of his body was quivering visibly, but in reality the only movement was in the glove of his right hand. The fingers moved steadily in a kneading motion, keeping supple and warm, and the eyes moved in Mark's skull, swivelling slowly back and forth across the battered trunk of the oak, blinking regularly to clear the tears that tension and the icy air induced.

'What the hell is happening up there?' Fergus MacDonald fretted nervously, peering into the lens of the periscope that allowed the observer to keep well down below the sand-bagged parapet.

'The boy is pinned down.' General Sean Courtney did not remove his own eyes from the other periscope, but swung it slightly, sweeping back and forth across the slope. 'Try the Hun with Cuthbert again.'

'I don't think he'll fall for it again,' Fergus began to protest immediately, looking up with those close-set eyes, rimmed with pink now by the cold and the strain of waiting.

'That's an order, Sergeant.' Sean Courtney's broad forehead wrinkled and the dark brows drew sharply together, his voice growled like an old lion and the dark-blue eyes snapped. The power and presence of the man in this mood awed even Fergus MacDonald.

'Very well, sir,' he muttered sulkily, and went to where the dummy was propped against the firing step.

The lash of the Mauser cracked again, and at the shock Mark Anders' eyelids blinked twice very quickly and then flared wide open. The golden brown eyes stared fixedly up the slope, intent as those of the hunting peregrine.

The instant after the shot, he heard the rattle of the Mauser bolt being drawn back and then thrust forward to reload, and again the tip of the hessian-wrapped muzzle stirred slightly – but then Mark's eyes flicked sideways.

There had been another movement, so fine that it might have gone unnoticed by eyes less keen. The movement had been a mere breath, and it had been in the narrow three-inch gap between the oak trunk and the snow-coated earth. Just that one brief stir and then stillness once more.

Mark stared into the gap for long seconds, and saw nothing. Merely shadow and undefined shape, trickily reflected light from the snow beyond. Then suddenly, he was seeing something else.

It was the texture of cloth, a thin sliver of it in the narrow gap, then his eyes picked up the stitched seam in the grey cloth, bulging slightly over the living flesh beneath.

There was some small portion of the German's body showing through the gap. He was lying close up on the far side of the log, and his head was pointed in the direction from which the muzzle of the Mauser projected.

Carefully Mark proportioned the man's body in his imagination. Using the rifle muzzle as his only reference point, he placed the man's head and shoulders, his trunk and his hips –

'Yes, his hips,' Mark thought. 'That is his hip or upper thigh—' and then there was a change in the light. The sun found a weak spot in the cloud cover overhead and the light brightened briefly.

In the better light, Mark made out a small portion of a German service belt, with the empty loop which should have held a bayonet. It confirmed his guess. Now he knew that the slight bulge in the field grey material was caused by the head of the femur where it fitted into the cup of the pelvic girdle.

'Through both hips,' Mark thought coldly. 'It's a pinning shot, and then there is the femoral artery—' Carefully he began to work the glove off his right hand.

He must roll on his side, and swing the long barrel of

the P.14 through an arc of over ninety degrees, without making the least sound.

'Please, God,' Mark asked silently, and began to make the move. Achingly slowly, the barrel of his rifle swung and, at the same time, he began to transfer his weight on to his other elbow.

It seemed to be a complete round of eternity before the P.14 pointed into the narrow gap below the oak trunk, and Mark was doubled up, straining to keep the barrel bearing from this unnatural position. He could not slip the safety-catch from the rifle before firing; even that tiny metallic snick would alert the German.

He curled his finger on the trigger, and took up the pull, feeling the dead lock of the safety mechanism. He aimed carefully, his head twisted awkwardly, and he began to push the safety-catch across with his thumb, while holding pressure on the hair-trigger. It had to be done smoothly, so as not to pull his aim off the sliver of grey uniform cloth.

The thunder of the shot seemed to bounce against the low grey sky, and the bullet crashed through the tiny gap. Mark saw the impact of it, the rubbery shock of metal into flesh.

He heard the German cry out, a wild sound without form or meaning, and Mark swept back the bolt of the P.14, and reloaded with instinctive dexterity. The next shot blended with the echo of the first, coming so close together that they seemed as one. The jacketed bullet crashed through the gap, and this time Mark saw blood spurt, a bright scarlet spray of it that splattered the snow, turning swiftly to pale pink as it was diluted by the melt of its own heat.

Then there was nothing in the gap, the German had been thrown back by the impact – or had rolled aside. Only the smear of pink stained snow.

Mark waited, a fresh cartridge in the breach of the P.14, turned now to face the oak trunk, tensed for the next shot.

If it had not been a decisive wound, the German would be coming after him, and he was ready for the snap shot.

He felt coldly unemotional, but vitally aware, his every fibre and nerve pitched to its utmost, his vision sharp and bright and his hearing enhanced.

The silence drew out for a while longer – and then there was a sound. For a moment Mark did not recognize it, then it came again. The sound of a man sobbing.

It came stronger now, more hysterical, gut-racking.

'Ach, mein Gott – mein lieber Gott—' the man's voice, pitiful, broken. 'Das Blut – ach Gott – das Blut.'

Suddenly the sound was tearing at Mark's soul, cutting deeply into his being. His hand began to shake, and he felt the tremor of his lips once again. He tried to clench his jaw, but now his teeth were chattering wildly.

'Stop it, oh God, stop it,' he whispered, and the rifle fell from his hands. He pressed his mittened hands to his ears, trying to shut out the terrible sounds of the dying German.

'Please, please,' Mark pleaded aloud. 'Stop it, please.'

And the German seemed to hear him.

'Hilf mir, lieber Gott – das Blut!' His voice was broken by the wet helpless sounds of his despair.

Suddenly Mark was crawling forward, through the snow, blindly up the slope.

'I'm coming. It's all right,' he muttered. 'Only stop it.' He felt his senses swaying.

'Ach mein lieber Gott, ach, meine Mutti . . .'

'Oh Jesus – stop it. Stop it.'

Mark dragged himself around the end of the oak log.

The German was half propped against the log. With both hands he was trying vainly to stem the fountain of bright pulsing arterial blood that flowed through his fumbling fingers. The two bullets had shattered both his hips, and the snow was a sodden mushy porridge of blood.

He turned his face to Mark, and already it was drained of all colour, a shiny greyish white, slick with a fine sheen of perspiration. The German was young, as young as Mark, but swiftly approaching death had smoothed out his features so he seemed younger still. It was the face of a marble angel, smooth and white, and strangely beautiful, with blue eyes in pale blue sockets, a burst of pale golden curls escaping from under the helmet on the smooth pale forehead.

He opened his mouth and said something that Mark did not understand, and the teeth were white and even, beyond the full pale lips.

Then, slowly, the German sagged back against the log still staring at Mark. His hands fell away from his groin and the regular pulsing spurt of blood from the shattered flesh slowed and shrivelled away. The pale blue eyes lost their feverish lustre, and dulled, no longer focused.

Mark felt a thread pull in the fabric of his mind, like silk beginning to tear. It was almost a physical thing – he could hear it beginning to give way inside him.

His vision wavered, the dead German's features seemed to run like melting wax, and then slowly reformed again. Mark felt the tear widening, the silken veil of his reason ripping through; beyond it was a dark and echoing chasm.

The dead German's features went on reforming, until they hardened and Mark was looking into his own face as through a wavering distorted mirror. His own haunted face, the eyes golden brown and terrified, the mouth that was his mouth opened – and a cry came from it that was the despair and the agony of all the world.

The last shreds of Mark's reason whipped away on the tempest of horror, and he heard himself screaming – and felt his feet running under him, but there was only blackness in his head, and his body was light and without weight, like the body of a bird in flight.

The German machine-gunner cocked the Maxim with a single savage wrench on the crank handle, and traversed sharply left, at the same time depressing the thick water-jacketed barrel of the weapon until it pointed directly down the slope below the sand-bagged emplacement towards the British lines.

The single wildly running figure was angling away towards the left, and the gunner pulled the wooden butt of the Maxim into his shoulder and fired a single short traversing burst, aiming a fraction low to counteract the natural tendency to shoot high at a downhill target.

Mark Anders hardly felt the mighty hammer strokes of the two bullets that smashed into his back.

Fergus MacDonald was crying. That surprised Sean, he had not expected it. The tears slid slowly from pink-rimmed eyes, and he struck them away with a single angry movement.

'Permission to take out a patrol, sir?' he asked, and the young Captain glanced uncertainly at Sean over the Sergeant's shoulder.

Sean nodded slightly, a mere inclination of the head.

'Do you think you can find volunteers?' the Captain asked uncertainly, and the red-faced Sergeant answered gruffly.

'There'll be volunteers, sir, the lads have a feeling for what that youngster did.'

'Very well, then – as soon as it's dark.'

They found Mark a little after eight o'clock. He hung in the rusting barbed wire at the bottom of the slope, like a broken doll. Fergus MacDonald had to use a pair of wire-cutters to cut him down, and it took them nearly another hour to get him back to the British lines, dragging the stretcher between them through the mud and slushy snow.

'He's dead,' said General Courtney, looking down at the white drained face on the stretcher in the lantern light.

29

'No, he's not,' Fergus MacDonald denied it fiercely. 'They don't kill my boy that easy.'

The locomotive whistled shrilly as it clattered over the steelwork of the bridge. Silver steam flew high in a bright plume, and then smeared back on the wind.

Mark Anders leaned far out over the balcony of the single passenger carriage and the same wind ruffled the soft brown wing of his hair and a spattering of ash particles from the furnace stung his cheek, but he screwed up his eyes and looked down into the bed of the river as they roared across.

The water flowed down under the dipping reeds, and then met the pylons of the bridge and swirled sullenly, flowing green and strong and full down to the sea.

'Water's high for this time of year,' Mark muttered aloud. 'Grandpapa will be happy,' and he felt his lips tugging up into the unaccustomed smile. He had smiled only infrequently during the past months.

The locomotive hurtled across the steel bridge, and threw itself at the far slope. Immediately, the beat of its engine changed and its speed bled away.

Mark stooped and hefted his old military pack, opened the gate of the balcony and clambered down on to the steel steps, hanging with one arm over the racing gravel embankment.

The train slowed rapidly as the incline steepened and he swung the pack off his shoulder and leaned far out to let it drop as gently as possible on to the gravel. It bounced once and went bounding away down the embankment, crashing into the shrubbery like a living animal in flight.

Then he swung down towards the racing earth himself and, judging his moment finely as the train crested the ridge, he let go to hit the embankment on flying feet, throwing his weight forward to ride the impact and feel the gravel sliding under him.

He stayed upright, and came to a halt as the rest of the train clattered past him, and the guard looked out sternly from the last van and called a reprimand.

'Hey, that's against the law.'

'Send the sheriff,' Mark shouted back, and gave him an ironic salute as the locomotive picked up speed on the reverse slope with explosive grunts of power, the rhythm of the tracks rising sharply. The guard clenched a fist and Mark turned away.

The jolt had hurt his back again and he slipped a hand into his shirt and ran it around under his armpit as he started back along the tracks. He fingered the twin depressions below the shoulder blade and marvelled again at how close one of them was to the bony projections of the spine. The scar tissue had a silky, almost sensuous feel, but they had taken long months to close. Mark shuddered involuntarily as he remembered the rattle of the trolley that carried the dressings, and the impassive almost masculine face of the matron as she stuffed the long cotton plugs into the open mouths of the bullet wounds; he remembered also the slow tearing agony as the bloody dressing was pulled out again with the glittering steel forceps, and his own breathing sobbing in his ears and the matron's voice, harsh and impersonal.

'Oh, don't be a baby!'

Every day – day after day, week after week – until the hot feverish delirium of the pneumonia that had attacked his bullet-damaged lung had seemed a blessed relief. How long had it been – from the V.A.D. Station in a French field with the muddy snow deeply rutted by the ambulances and the burial details digging graves beyond the tented hospital – to the general hospital near Brighton and the dark mists of pneumonia, the hospital ship home down the length of the Atlantic, baking in the airless tropics, the convalescent hospital with its pleasant lawns and gardens – how long? Fourteen months in all, months during which the war which men were already misnaming 'Great' had ended. Pain and delirium had clouded the passage of time, yet it seemed a whole lifetime.

He had lived one life in the killing and the carnage, in the pain and the suffering, and now he was reborn. The pain in his back abated swiftly. It was almost mended now, he thought happily, and he pushed away the dark and terrible memories and scrambled down the embankment to retrieve his pack.

Andersland was almost forty miles downstream, and the train had been behind schedule, it was noon already. Mark knew that he would not make it before the following evening – and strangely, now that he was almost home, the sense of urgency was gone.

He moved easily, falling into that long, familiar stride of the hunter, easing the pack on his back slightly as soon as the newly healed wounds stiffened, feeling the good sweat springing cool on his face and through the thin cotton of his shirt.

Absence of so many years had sharpened his appreciation of the world through which he moved, so that which before had warranted only passing attention became now a new and unfamiliar delight.

Along the banks the dense riverine bush was alive with myriad life. The bejewelled dragonflies that skimmed the surface on transparent wings or coupled in flight, male upon female, his long glittering abdomen arched to join with hers; the hippopotamus that burst through the surface in an explosive exhalation of breath, and stared at Mark upon the bank with pink watery eyes, flicking the tiny ears, and wallowing like a gargantuan black balloon in the green swirling current.

It was like moving through an ancient Eden, before the

coming of man, and suddenly Mark knew that this solitude was what his body and mind needed to complete the healing process.

He camped that night on a grassy bluff above the river, above the mosquitoes and the unpleasant darkness of the thick bush.

A leopard woke him after midnight, sawing hoarsely down in the river bottom, and he lay and listened to it moving slowly upstream until he lost it among the crags of high ground. He did not sleep again immediately, but lay and examined, with the pleasure of anticipation, the day ahead of him.

For every day of the past four years, even the very bad days of darkness and ghosts, he had thought of the old man. Some days it had been only a fleeting thought, on other days he had dwelt upon him as a homesick schoolboy tortures himself with thoughts of home. The old man was home, of course, both the mother and father Mark had never known. Always there from his first vaguest memory to the present, unchanging in his strength and quiet understanding.

Mark felt a deep physical pang of longing, as he recalled clearly a picture of the old man sitting on the hard carved rocker on the wide boarded stoep, the crumpled old khaki shirt, crudely patched and in need of laundering, open at the neck to expose a fuzz of silver-white chest hair; the neck and jowls wrinkled like those of a turkey cock, but burned dark brown and pelted with five days' growth of silver stubble that sparkled like glass chips; the huge moustaches of glistening white, the ends curled with beeswax into fearsome spikes, the wide terai hat pulled low over the bright toffee-coloured humorous eyes. The hat was always in place, sweat-soaked and greasy around the band, but never removed, not even at mealtimes – nor, Mark suspected, in the big brass bed at night.

Mark remembered him pausing from working with the

whittling knife, rolling the quid from one cheek to the other, then letting fly at the old five-gallon Tate and Lyle golden syrup can that was his spittoon. Hitting solidly at ten feet, spilling not a single drop of the dark brown juice, and then continuing the story as though there had been no interruption. And what stories! Stories to start a small boy's eyes popping from their sockets and wake him in the night to peer fearfully under the bed.

Mark remembered the old man in small things, stooping to take up a handful of his rich soil and let it run through his fingers, then wiping them on the seat of his pants with the proud fierce expression on his withered old features. 'Good land – Andersland,' he would say, and nod like a sage. Mark remembered him in the big things, standing tall and skinny beside Mark in thick thorn bush with the big old Martini Hendry rifle bellowing and smoking, the recoil shaking his frail old body as, like a black mountain, the buffalo bull came down upon them, blood mad and crazed with its wounds.

Four years since last he had seen him, since last he had heard news of him. At first he had written, long homesick letters, but the old man could not read nor write. Mark had hoped that he might take them to a friend, the postmistress perhaps, and that they might read them to him and write back to Mark.

It had been a vain hope. The old man's pride would never allow him to admit to a stranger that he could not read. Nevertheless, Mark had continued to write, once every month for all those long years; but only tomorrow he would have his first news of the old man in all that time.

Mark slept again for another few hours, then built up the fire again in the darkness before dawn and brewed coffee. He was moving again as soon as it was light enough to see his feet on the path.

From the escarpment he watched the sun come up out of the sea. There were mountains of cumulus thunder clouds standing tall over the distant sea, and the sun came up behind them so that they glowed with red and roses, wine and deep purples, each cloud etched in outline by brilliant red-gold and shot through with shafts of light.

At Mark's feet the land dropped away into the coastal low-lands, that rich littoral of densely forested valleys and smooth golden grassy hills that stretched to the endless white beaches of the Indian Ocean.

Below where Mark stood, the river tumbled over the edge of the escarpment, leaping in sheets of white and silver from wet black rock to deep dark pools which turned upon themselves in foam like huge wheels, as though they rested before the next wild plunge downwards.

Mark began to hurry for the first time, following the steep path downwards with the same urgency as the river, but it was mid morning before he came out on to the warm and drowsing sweep of land below the escarpment.

The river widened, and became shallower, changing its mood completely as it meandered between the exposed sandbanks. There were new birds here, different beasts in the forest and upon the hills, but now Mark had no time for them. Hardly glancing at the flocks of long, heavy-beaked storks and scimitar-billed ibis on the sandbanks, even when the hadedah ibis rose with their wild insanely ringing shrieks of laughter, he hurried on.

There was a place, unmarked except for a small tumbled cairn at the foot of a huge wild fig tree, that had a special significance to Mark, for it marked the western boundary of Andersland.

Mark stopped to rebuild the cairn among the grey scaly roots that crawled across the earth like ancient reptiles, and while he worked, a flock of fat green pigeons exploded on noisy wings from the branches above him where they had been feeding on the bitter yellow fruit.

When Mark went on beyond the fig tree, he walked with a new lightness and resilience to his step, a new set to his shoulders and a new brightness in his eyes – for he walked once again on Andersland. Eight thousand acres of rich chocolate loamy ground, four miles of river frontage, water that never failed, softly rounded hills covered with thick sweet grass, Andersland, the name the old man had given it thirty years before.

Half a mile further on, Mark was about to leave the river and take a short cut across the next ridge to the homestead, when there was a distant but earth-trembling thud, and immediately afterwards the faint sound of human voices on the still warm air.

Puzzled, Mark paused to listen, and again the thudding sound – but this time preceded by the crackling and snapping of branches and undergrowth. The unmistakable sound of timber being felled.

Abandoning his original intention, Mark kept on down the river, until he emerged suddenly from forest into open country that reminded him at first of those terrible devastated fields of France, torn and ravaged by shell and high explosive until the raw earth lay exposed and churned.

There were gangs of dark men in white linen dhotis and turbans felling the heavy timber and clearing out the undergrowth along the river. For a moment Mark did not understand who these strange men were, and then he remembered reading a newspaper report that Hindu labourers were being brought out in their thousands from India to work for the new sugar cane estates. These were the wiry, very dark-skinned men that worked now like a colony of ants along the river. There were hundreds of them – no, Mark realized that they were in their thousands – and there were oxen teams as well. Big spans of heavy, strong-looking beasts plodding slowly as they dragged the fallen timber into rows for burning.

Not truly understanding what he was seeing, Mark left the river and climbed the slope beside it. From the crest he had a new uninterrupted view across Andersland – and beyond, eastwards towards the sea.

The devastation stretched as far as he could see, and now there was something else to ponder. The land was going to the plough, all of it. The forest and grazing land had been torn out, and the trek oxen moved slowly over the open ground, one team following the next, the rich chocolate earth turning up under the plough shares in thick shiny welts. The cries of the ploughmen and the muted popping of the long trek whips carried to where Mark stood, bewildered, upon the slope of the hill.

He sat down on a boulder and for almost an hour watched the men and the oxen at work, and he was afraid. Afraid for what this all meant. The old man would never let this happen to his land. He had a hatred of the plough and the axe; he loved too deeply the stately trees which now groaned and crackled as they toppled. The old man hoarded his grazing like a miser, as though it were as precious as its golden colour suggested. He would never allow it to be turned under – not if he were alive.

That was why Mark was afraid. If he were alive. For, God knows, he would never sell Andersland.

Mark did not truly want to know the answer. He had to force himself to rise and go down the hill.

The dark turbaned labourers did not understand his questions, but they directed him with expressive gestures to a fat babu in a cotton jacket who strutted importantly from work gang to work gang, snapping at a naked black back with a light cane or pausing to write a laborious note in the huge black book he carried.

He looked up, startled, and then immediately became obsequious in the presence of a white man.

'Good day, master—' He would have gone on, but the shiny acquisitive eyes darted over Mark and they saw how young he was, unshaven, his cheap army issue suit was stained with travel and rumpled from having been slept in. It was obvious he carried his entire worldly possessions in his backpack.

'To tell the truth, we are not needing more men here.' His manner changed instantly, becoming lordly. 'I am being in charge here—'

'Good.' Mark nodded. 'Then you can tell me what these men are doing on Andersland.'

The man irritated him, he had known so many like him in the army – bully those below and lick the backsides of those above.

'Beyond doubt we are making ground clear for sugar.'

'This ground belongs to my family,' said Mark, and instantly the man's manner changed again.

'Ah, good young master, you are from the company at Ladyburg?'

'No, no – we live here. In the house,' Mark pointed at the ridge of the hill, beyond which lay the homestead, 'this is our ground.'

The babu chuckled like a fat dark baby, and shook his head.

'Nobody living here now. Alas! The company owns everything.' And he made a wide gesture that took in the whole landscape from escarpment to the sea. 'Soon everything is sugar, you will see, man. Sugar, sugar.' And he laughed again.

From the ridge the old homestead looked the same, just a green-painted roof of corrugated iron showing above the dark green of the orchard, but as Mark came up the overgrown path past the hen coops, he saw that all the window panes had been removed, leaving blank dark squares, and there was no furniture on the wide stoep. The rocker was gone, and there was a sag to the roof timbers at one end of the veranda; a drainpipe had come loose and hung away from the wall.

The garden had the wild untended look of neglect, the

plants beginning to encroach on the house itself. The old man had always kept it trimmed and neat with the leaves swept up daily from under the trees and the white-painted beehives set up in orderly rows in the shade. Somebody had robbed the hives with brutal carelessness, smashing them open with an axe.

The rooms were bare, stripped of anything of possible value, even the old black wood-burning stove in the kitchen, everything except the Tate and Lyle spittoon on the stoep which lay on its side; its spilled contents had left a dark stain on the woodwork.

Mark wandered slowly from room to empty room, feeling a terrible sense of loss and desolation as the windblown leaves rustled under his feet, and the big black and yellow spiders watched him with myriad glittering eyes from the webs they had spun in the corners and across the jambs of the doorways.

Mark left the house and went down to the small family graveyard, feeling a quick lift of relief when he realized there were no new graves there. Grandmother Alice, her eldest daughter, and her cousin who had died before Mark was born. Still three graves – the old man was not there.

Mark drew a bucket from the well and drank a little of the cold sweet water, then he wandered into the orchard and picked a hatful of guavas and a ripe yellow pineapple. In the backyard strutted a young cockerel who had escaped the plunderers. Mark had to hunt him for half an hour before a stone brought him down off the roof in a squawking flutter of feathers.

Plucked and cleaned, he went into the canteen over the fire that Mark made in the backyard – and while he boiled, Mark had a sudden thought.

He went back into the old man's bedroom and in the far corner, where the big brass bed had once stood, he knelt and felt for the loose board. He prised the single nail that held it down with his clasp knife and then lifted the plank.

He reached down into the opening below and brought out first a thick bundle of envelopes tied with a strip of raw hide. Mark riffled the edge of the pack and saw that not a single envelope had been opened. They were all addressed in his own spiky hand. They had been carefully stored in this hiding place. Yet not all Mark's letters were there. The sequence ended abruptly and Mark, checking the last letter, found it postmarked eleven months previously. Mark felt a choking sensation in the base of his throat, and the sharp sting of tears.

He placed the bundle of letters aside and reached again into the opening to bring out the Mazzawatee tea caddy, with the picture of the grandmother in steel-rimmed spectacles on the lid. It was the old man's treasure-chest.

He carried the can and the bundle of letters out into the backyard, for the late afternoon light was going fast in the unlit rooms. He sat on the kitchen step, and opened the tea caddy.

There were forty gold sovereigns in a leather purse; some of them had the bearded head of Kruger the old president of the South African Republic, the others of Edward and George. Mark slipped the purse into the inner pocket of his jacket and in the fading light examined the rest of the old man's treasure. Photographs of grandmother Alice as a young woman, yellowed and dog-eared with age, a wedding certificate, old newspaper clippings from the Boer War, cheap articles of women's jewellery, the same as those that Alice wore in the photographs, a medal in a presentation case, a Queen's South Africa medal with six bars including those for Tugela, Ladysmith and the Transvaal campaigns, Mark's own school reports from the Ladyburg School and then the diploma from the University College at Port Natal – these the old man valued especially, with the illiterate's awe of learning and the written word. He had sold some of his prize livestock to pay for Mark's education, he rated it that highly. Nothing in the tea caddy, apart from the sovereigns, was of any value, but it had all been precious beyond price to the old man. Carefully Mark re-packed the tin and placed it in his backpack.

In the last light of day Mark ate the stringy cockerel and the fruit, and when he rolled into his blanket on the wooden kitchen floor he was still thinking.

He knew now that the old man, wherever he had gone, had intended returning to Andersland. He would never have left that precious hoard behind unless that had been his intention.

A boot in the ribs brought Mark awake, and he rolled over and sat up, gasping with the pain of it.

'On your feet! Get your arse moving – and keep it going.'

It was not yet fully light, but Mark could make out the man's features. He was clean-shaven with a heavy smooth jaw, and his teeth seemed to have been ground down to a flat even line – very white against the dark suntan. His head was round, like a cannon ball, and gave the impression of vast weightiness, for he carried it low on a thick neck like a heavyweight boxer shaping up.

'Up!' he repeated, and drew back the scuffed brown riding-boot again. Mark came up on his feet and squared to defend himself. He found the man was shorter than he was, but he was stocky and solid, with broad thick shoulders and the same weightiness in his frame. 'This is private property, we don't want tramps hanging about.'

'I'm not a tramp,' Mark started, but the man cut him short with a snort of brusque laughter.

'You with the fancy clothes, and the Rolls parked at the door – you had me fooled for a moment there.'

'My name is Mark Anders,' he said. 'This land belongs to my grandfather – John Anders—'

41

He thought he saw something move in the man's eyes, a change in the set of his mouth, doubt or worry perhaps. He licked his lips, a quick nervous gesture, but when he spoke his voice was still flat and quiet.

'I don't know nothing about that – all I know is this land belongs to the Ladyburg Estates now, and I am the foreman for the company, and neither me nor the company wants you hanging around here,' he paused and settled on his feet, dropping his shoulders and pushing out his heavy jaw, 'and one other thing I know is I like to break a head now and then, and I haven't broken one for God knows a long time.'

They stared at each other, and Mark felt a sudden hot rush of anger. He wanted to take up the man's challenge, even though he realized how powerful and dangerous he was. He had the look of a killer, and the weight and the strength, but Mark felt himself coming into balance, his own shoulders dropping.

His tormentor saw it also and his relish was obvious. He smiled thinly, clenching his jaw around the smile so that the cords stood out in his throat, swaying slightly up on to the balls of his feet. Then suddenly Mark felt revolted and sickened by the presence of violence. There had been too much of it in his life already – and there was no reason to fight now. He turned away and picked up his boots.

The man watched him dress, disappointed perhaps, but ready for further confrontation. When he swung his pack up on to his shoulder, Mark asked, 'What's your name?'

The man answered him lightly, still keyed up for violence. 'My friends call me Hobday,' he said.

'Hobday who?'

'Just Hobday.'

'I won't forget it,' said Mark. 'You've been a real brick, Hobday.' He went down the steps into the yard, and fifteen minutes later when Mark looked back from the ridge where the Ladyburg road crossed on its way northwards, Hobday was still standing in the kitchen yard of Andersland, watching him intently.

F red Black watched Mark come up the hill. He leaned against the rail of the dipping tank and chewed steadily on his quid of tobacco, stringy and sunblackened and dry as a stick of chewing tobacco himself.

Although he was one of John Anders' cronies, and had known Mark since he was a crawler, it was clear he did not recognize him now. Mark stopped fifteen paces off and lifted his hat.

'Hello, Uncle Fred,' Mark greeted him, and still it was a moment before the older man let out a whoop and leapt to embrace Mark. 'God, boy, they told me you'd got yourself killed in France.'

They sat together on the rail of the cattle pen, while the Zulu herd boys drove the cattle below them through the narrow race, until they reached the ledge from which they made the wild scrambling leap into the deep stinking chemical bath, to come up again, snorting fearfully, and swin, nose up, for the slope ramp beyond.

'He's been dead almost a year – no, longer, over a year now – lad, I'm sorry. I never thought to let you know. Like I said, we thought you were dead in France.'

'That's all right, Uncle Fred.' Mark was surprised that he felt no shock. He had known it, accepted it already, but there was still the grief that lay heavy on his soul. They were both silent for a longer time, the old man beside him respecting his grief.

'How did he—' Mark hesitated over the word, 'how did he go?'

'Well, now.' Fred Black lifted his hat and rubbed the bald pink pate lovingly. 'It was all a bit sudden like. He went off to poach a little biltong with Piet Greyling and his son up at Chaka's Gate.' Vivid memories crowded back for Mark. Chaka's Gate was the vast wilderness area to the north where the old man had taught him the craft of the hunter. Years before, back in 1869, it had been declared a hunting reserve but no warden had been appointed, and the men of northern Natal and Zululand looked upon it as their private hunting reserve.

'On the fifth day, the old man did not come back into camp. They searched for him another four days before they found him.' He paused again and glanced at Mark. 'You feeling all right, boy?'

'Yes, I'm all right.' Mark wondered how many men he had seen die, how many he had killed himself – and yet the death of one more old man could move him so. 'Go on, please, Uncle Fred.'

'Piet said it looked like he had slipped while he was climbing a steep place, and he had fallen on his rifle and it had gone off. It hit him in the stomach.' They watched the last ox plunge into the dip, and Fred Black climbed stiffly down from the pole fence. He held the small of his back for a moment. 'Getting old,' he grunted, and Mark fell in beside him as they started up towards the house.

'Piet and his boy buried him there. He wasn't fit to bring back, he'd been in the sun four days. They marked the place and made a sworn statement to the magistrate when they got back to Ladyburg.'

Fred Black was interrupted by a cry and the sight of a female figure racing down the avenue of blue gum trees towards them – slim and young, with honey brown hair in a thick braid bouncing on her back, long brown legs and grubby bare feet beneath the skirts of the faded cheap cotton skirt.

'Mark!' she cried again. 'Oh Mark!' But she was close before he recognized her. She had changed in four years.

'Mary.' The sadness was still on Mark, but he could not

talk further now. There would be time later. Even in the sadness, he could not miss the fact that Mary Black was a big girl now, no longer the mischievous imp who once had been below his lordly notice when he had been a senior at Ladyburg High School.

She still had the freckled laughing face and the prominent, slightly crooked front teeth, but she had grown into a big, wide-hipped, earthy farm girl, with a resounding jolly laugh. She was as tall as Mark's shoulder and her shape under the thin, threadbare cotton was rounded and full; she had hips and buttocks that swung as she walked beside him, a waist like the flared neck of a vase and fat heavy breasts that bounced loosely at each stride. As they walked, she asked questions, endless questions in a demanding manner, and she kept touching Mark, her hand on his elbow, then grabbing his hand to shake out the answers to her questions, looking up at him with mischievous eyes, laughing her big ringing laugh. Mark felt strangely restless.

Fred Black's wife recognized him from across the yard and let out a sound like a milch cow too long deprived of her calf. She had nine daughters, and she had always pined for a son.

'Hello, Aunt Hilda,' Mark began, and then was folded into her vast pneumatic embrace.

'You're starved,' she cried, 'and those clothes, they stink. You stink too, Marky – your hair, you'll be sitting on it next.'

The four unmarried girls, supervised by Mary, set the galvanized bath in the centre of the kitchen floor and filled it with buckets of steaming water from the stove. Mark sat on a stool on the back veranda with a sheet around his shoulders, while Aunt Hilda sheared him of his long curling locks with a huge pair of blunt scissors.

Then she drove her daughters protesting from the kitchen. Mark fought desperately for his modesty, but she brushed his defence aside.

'An old woman like me, you haven't got anything I haven't seen bigger and better.' She stripped him determinedly, hurling the soiled and rumpled clothing through the open doorway to where Mary hovered expectantly.

'Wash them, child – and you get yourself away from that door.'

Mark blushed furiously and dropped quickly into the water.

In the dusk, Fred Black and Mark sat together on the coping of the well in the yard, with a bottle of brandy between them. The liquor was the fierce 'Cape Smoke' with a bite like a zebra stallion, and after the first sip Mark did not touch his glass again.

'Yes, I've thought about that often,' Fred agreed, already slightly owl-eyed with the brandy. 'Old Johnny loved that land of his.'

'Did he ever speak of selling it to you?'

'No, never did. I always thought he'd be there for ever. Often talked of being buried next to Alice. He wanted that.'

'When did you last see Grandpapa, Uncle Fred?'

'Well, now,' he rubbed his bald head thoughtfully, 'it would be about two weeks before he left for Chaka's Gate with the Greylings. Yes, that's right. He'd been into Ladyburg to buy cartridges and provisions. Pitched up here one night in the old scotch-cart, and we had a good old chat.'

'He didn't say anything then – about selling?'

'No, not a word.'

The kitchen door flew open, spilling yellow lantern light into the yard, and Aunt Hilda bellowed at them.

'Food's up. Come along now, Fred, don't you keep that boy out there, teaching him your evil ways – and don't you bring that bottle into this house. You hear me!'

Fred grimaced, poured the last three inches of dark

brown liquor into his tumbler and shook his head at the empty bottle.

'Farewell, old friend.' He sent it sailing over the hedge, and drained the tumbler like medicine.

Mark was crowded into the bench against the kitchen wall with Mary on one side of him and another of the big buxom daughters on the other. Aunt Hilda sat directly opposite him, shovelling food on to his plate, and loudly berating him if his rate of ingestion faltered.

'Fred needs somebody here to help him now. He's getting old, though the old fool doesn't know it.'

Mark nodded, his mouth so full he was unable to reply, and Mary reached across him for another hunk of homebaked bread that was still warm from the oven. Her big loose breast pressed against Mark and he almost choked.

'The girls don't get much chance to meet nice boys – stuck out here on the farm.'

Mary shifted in her seat, and her upper thigh came firmly against Mark's.

'Leave the lad alone, Hilda, you scheming old woman,' Fred slurred amiably from the head of the table.

'Mary, give Mark some more gravy on those potatoes.' The girl poured the gravy, steadying herself as she leaned over towards Mark by placing her free hand on Mark's leg above the knee.

'Eat up! Mary's done you a special milk tart for afters.'

Mary's hand still rested on his leg, and now it moved slowly but purposefully upwards. Instantly Mark's entire attention focused on the hand and the food turned to hot ashes in his mouth.

'Some more pumpkin, Marky?' Aunt Hilda asked with concern, and Mark shook his head weakly. He could not believe what was happening below the level of the table – and directly in front of Mary's mother.

He felt a rising sense of panic.

As casually as he could in the circumstances, he dropped one hand into his lap, and without looking at the girl, gripped her wrist firmly.

'Have you had enough, Mark?'

'Yes, oh yes, indeed,' Mark agreed fervently, and tried to drag Mary's hand away, but she was a big powerful lass and not easily distracted.

'Clear Mark's plate, Mary love, and give him some of your lovely tart.'

Mary seemed not to hear. Her head was bowed demurely over her plate, her cheeks were flushed bright glowing pink, and her lips trembled slightly. Beside her, Mark writhed and squirmed in his seat.

'Mary, what's wrong with you, girl?' Her mother frowned with irritation. 'Do you hear me, child?'

'Yes, Mother, I hear you.' At last she sighed and roused herself. She stood up slowly and reached for Mark's plate with both hands, while he sagged slightly on the bench, weak with relief.

M ark was exhausted from the long day's march and the subsequent excitement, but though he fell asleep almost instantly, it was a sleep troubled by dreams.

Through a ghostly, brooding landscape of swirling mist and weird unnatural light, he pursued a dark wraith – but his legs were slowed, as though he moved through a bath of treacle, and each pace was an enormous effort.

He knew the wraith that flitted through the mist ahead of him was the old man, and he tried to cry out, but though he strained with open mouth no sound came. Suddenly a small red hole appeared in the wraith's dark back and from it flowed a bright pulsing stream of blood, and the wraith turned to face him.

For a moment he looked into the old man's face, the intelligent yellow eyes smiled at him over the huge spiked moustache, and then the face melted like hot wax and the pale features of a beautiful marble statue came up like a face through water. The face of the young German – at last Mark cried out and fell to cover his face. In the darkness he sobbed softly, until another sensation came through to his tortured imagination.

He felt a slow cunning caress. The sobbing shrivelled in his throat, and gradually he abandoned himself to the wicked delight of his senses. He knew what was coming, it had happened so often in the lonely nights and he welcomed it now, drifting up slowly out of the depths of sleep.

At the edge of his awareness there was a voice now, whispering, crooning gently.

'There now, don't fuss, there now – it's all right now, it's going to be all right. Don't make that terrible noise.'

He came awake gradually, for long moments not realizing that the warm firm flesh was reality. Above him were heavy white breasts, hanging big and heavy to sweep across his chest, white bare skin shining in the moonlight that spilled through the window above his narrow steel bed.

'Mary will make it better,' the voice whispered with husky intensity.

'Mary?' he choked out the name, and tried to sit up, but she pushed him back gently with her full weight on his chest. 'You're mad.'

He began to struggle, but her mouth came down over his, wet and warm and all engulfing, and his struggles abated at the shock of this new sensation. He felt his sense whirl giddily.

Against the rising turmoil within him, was balanced the

terrible things that he knew about women. Those strange and awful things that the regimental chaplain had explained to him, the knowledge that had sustained him against all the blandishments of the bold little *poules* of France and the ladies who had beckoned to him from the dark doorways of London's back streets.

The chaplain had told them how two equally evil terrible consequences came from unlawful union with a woman. Either there was a disease that was without cure, which ate away the flesh, left a rotting hole in a man's groin and finally drove him insane, or there was a child without a father – a bastard to darken a man's honour.

The threat was too much, and Mark tore his mouth free from the girl's sucking hungry lips and the thrusting, driving tongue.

'Oh God!' he whispered. 'You'll have a baby.'

'That's all right, silly,' she whispered in a cheerful husky voice. 'We can get married.'

She shifted suddenly as he lay stunned by this intelligence, and she swung one knee over his supine body, pinning him under the heavy soft cushion of her flesh, smothering him with the fall of bright clinging hair.

'No.' He tried to wriggle out from under her. 'No, this is mad. I don't want to marry—'

'Yes,' there – oh yes.'

For another instant he was paralysed by the feeling of it, and then with a violent wrench he toppled her over. She fell sideways, her hands clutching wildly at his shoulders for an instant before she went over the side of the bed.

The washstand crashed over, and the thud of the girl's big body upon the floorboards echoed through the silent sleeping house.

For a moment afterwards the echoes died, the silence returned and then was split by a chorus of screams from the bedroom of the younger girls across the passage.

'What is it?' bellowed Fred Black, from the big bedroom.

'There's somebody in the house.'

'Get him, Fred, don't just lie there.'

'Where's my shotgun?'

'Help, papa! Help!'

With a single bound, Mary leapt up from the bedroom floor, snatched her nightgown off the chair and swept it over her head.

'Mary!' Mark sat up, he wanted to explain, to try and tell her about the chaplain. He leaned towards her and even in the faint moonlight he could see the fury that contorted her features.

'Mary—' He did not have time to avoid the blow, it came full-armed and flat-handed, smashing into the side of his head with a force that rattled his teeth and starred his vision. She was a big strong girl. When his head cleared, she was gone, but his ear still sang with the sound of a thousand wild bees.

A dusty Daimler lorry pulled up beside Mark as he trudged along the side of the deeply rutted road with thick grass growing along the central hump.

There was a middle-aged man and his wife in the front seat, and he called to Mark.

'Where are you going, son?'

'Ladyburg, sir.'

'Jump in the back, then.'

Mark rode the last twenty miles sitting high on bagged maize, with a coop of cackling hens beside him and the wind ruffling his stiff newly cropped hair.

They rattled over the bridge across the Baboon Stroom, and Mark marvelled at how it had all changed. Ladyburg was no longer a village, but a town. It had spread out as far as the stream itself, and there was a huge new goods yard below the escarpment in which half a dozen locomotives busily shunted trucks heavily laden with freshly sawn timber from the mills, or with bagged sugar from the new factory.

The factory itself was a monument to the town's progress, a towering structure of steel girders and huge boilers. Smoke and steam boiled from half a dozen stacks to form a grey mist that smeared away on the gentle breeze.

Mark wrinkled his nose at the faint stink of it on the wind, and then looked with awe down Main Street. There were at least a dozen new buildings, their ornate façades decorated with scrolls of ironwork, and beautifully intricate gables, stained glass in the main doors and the owner's name and date of construction in raised plaster lettering across the front; but these were all overshadowed by a giant structure four stories tall, crusted with ornamentation like a wedding cake of a wealthy bride. Proudly it bore the legend 'Ladyburg Farmers Bank'. The driver of the truck dropped Mark on the sidewalk in front of it, and left him with a cheery wave.

There were at least a dozen motor vehicles parked among the scotch-carts and horse-drawn carriages, and the people on the streets were well dressed and cheerful-looking, the citizens of a prosperous and thriving community.

Mark knew one or two of them from the old days, and as he trudged down Main Street with his pack slung over one shoulder, he paused to greet them. There was always a momentary confusion until they recognized him, and then, 'But, Marky, we heard – we thought you'd been killed in France. It was in the *Gazette*.'

The Land Deeds Registrar's Office was in the sprawled labyrinth of Government offices behind the Magistrate's Court and Police Station. There had been plenty of time to think on the long journey up from Andersland, and Mark knew exactly what he was going to do, and in what order.

There was a cramped space in the front of the office

with an uninviting wooden bench, and a plain deal counter. There was an elderly clerk with nearsighted eyes behind steel-rimmed spectacles, and a peaked green eyeshade on his forehead. He looked like an ancient crow in his black alpaca jacket with paper guards over his cuffs, and a bony beak of a nose, as he crouched over his desk making a Herculean task of stamping a pile of documents.

He worked on for a few minutes. Mark patiently read the Government notices that plastered the walls, until the clerk looked up at last with the exasperated air of a man interrupted in a labour that might alter the destiny of mankind.

'I'd like to look at a land deed, please sir.'

*A certain piece of extinguished quit-rent land situate in the division of Ladyburg being Erf. No. 42 of Division A of One. The farm known as ANDERSLAND . . . Deed of Transfer passed in favour of Ladyburg Estates Ltd registered at Ladyburg on 1st day of June, 1919. Know all men whom it may concern that DENNIS PETERSEN appeared before me, Registrar of Deeds, he, the said appearer, being duly authorized by a power of attorney executed at Ladyburg on the 12th day of May, 1919, by JOHN ARCHIBALD ANDERS which power was witnessed in accordance with law . . . and that the said appearer declared that his principal had truly and legally sold . . .*

Mark turned to the next document.

*Agreement of Sale of Immovable property That JOHN ARCHIBALD ANDERS, hereinafter known as the Seller, and LADYBURG ESTATES LTD hereinafter known as the purchaser – the Farm known as ANDERSLAND – together with all improvements and buildings, standing crops, implements and livestock – for the consideration of Three Thousand Pounds Sterling –*

> In witness whereof the parties set their hand:
> JOHN ARCHIBALD ANDERS (his mark) X
> For and on behalf of LADYBURG ESTATES LTD —
> DIRK COURTNEY (DIRECTOR)
> As witnesses of the above:—
>     PIETER ANDRIES GREYLING
>     CORNELIUS JOHANNES GREYLING

Mark frowned at the two names. Piet Greyling and his son had accompanied the old man up to Chaka's Gate almost immediately after witnessing the Deed of Sale, and they had found him dead a few days later and buried him out there in the wilderness.

> General Power of Attorney
> in favour of DENNIS PETERSEN.
> I, the undersigned, JOHN ARCHIBALD ANDERS do hereby empower the above-mentioned DENNIS . . . signed
> JOHN ARCHIBALD ANDERS X (his mark) as witness
>     PIETER ANDRIES GREYLING.
>     CORNELIUS JOHANNES GREYLING.

Mark pored over the bundle of stiff legal parchment with its fancy printing and red wax seals with dangling ribbons of watered silk. Carefully he copied out the names of the parties involved in the transaction into his notebook and when he had finished, the clerk who had been jealously watching his precious papers reclaimed them and reluctantly handed over an official receipt for the five-shilling search fee.

The office of the registrar of companies was directly across the narrow lane, and here Mark was received in a different mood. The keeper of this gloomy cavern was a young lady dressed in severe dove-grey jacket and long sweeping skirt which was at odds with her lively eyes and pert air.

The pretty little face, with freckled snub nose, lit with a quick appreciative smile as Mark came in through the door and within minutes she was helping him in a comradely and conspiratorial manner as he perused the memoranda and articles of association of Ladyburg Estates Ltd.

'Do you live here?' asked the girl. 'I haven't seen you before.'

'No, I don't,' Mark answered warily without looking up at her. He was finding it difficult to concentrate on the documents, and he remembered vividly his last encounter with a young girl.

'You're lucky.' The girl sighed dramatically. 'It's so dull here, nothing to do after work in the evenings.' She waited hopefully, but the silence drew out.

The Directors of Ladyburg Estates were Messrs Dirk Courtney and Ronald Beresford Pye, but they held only a single share each, just sufficient to qualify them to act as officers of the company.

The other nine hundred and ninety-nine thousand, nine hundred and ninety-eight ordinary fully paid up five-shilling shares were held by the Ladyburg Farmers Bank.

'Thank you very much,' said Mark, returning the file to the girl while avoiding her frank gaze. 'Could I see the file for Ladyburg Farmers Bank please?'

She brought it promptly.

The one million one-pound shares of the Ladyburg Farmers Bank were owned by three men, all of them Directors of the Company.

| Dirk Courtney: | 600,000 fully paid-up shares. |
|---|---|
| Ronald Beresford Pye: | 200,000 fully paid-up shares. |

Dennis Petersen: 200,000 fully-paid-up shares.

Mark frowned; the web was tangled and intricately woven, the same names again and again. He wrote the names into his notebook.

'My name is Marion, what's yours?'

'Mark – Mark Anders.'

'Mark, that's a strong romantic name. Have you read *Julius Caesar*? Mark Antony was such a strong romantic character.'

'Yes,' agreed Mark. 'He was. How much do I owe you for the search fee?'

'Oh, I'll just forget about that.'

'No, look, don't do that – I want to pay.'

'All right then – if you want to.'

At the door he paused.

'Thanks,' he said shyly. 'You were very kind.'

'Oh, it's a pleasure. If there's anything else – well, you know my name and where to find me.' Then suddenly and unaccountably, she blushed scarlet. To hide it, she turned away with the files. When she looked again, he was gone, and she sighed, holding the files to her plump little bosom.

Mark found the accounts of the old man's estate filed with the Master of the Court almost contemptuously under the heading 'Intestate Estates less than £100'.

On the credit side were listed two rifles and a shotgun, four trek oxen and scotch-cart – sold at public auction to realize eighty-four pounds sixteen shillings. On the debit side were legal and commission fees accruing to one Dennis Petersen – and costs of winding up the estate. The total was one hundred and twenty-seven pounds; the account had been in deficit – a distribution had been made and the estate closed. John Archibald Anders had gone, and left hardly a ripple behind him, not even the three thousand pounds he had been paid for Andersland.

Mark hefted his pack again and went out into the brilliant sunlight of afternoon. A water cart was moving slowly down Main Street drawn by two oxen, its sprinklers pouring fine jets of water into the roadway to lay the thick dust.

Mark paused and inhaled the smell of water on dry earth, and looked across the street at the towering building of the Ladyburg Farmers Bank.

For a brief moment, he touched the idea of crossing and entering, demanding of the men in there what had made the old man change his firm resolve to die and be buried on Andersland, how the money had been paid to him – and what he had done with it.

But the idea passed swiftly. The men who worked in that building were creatures of a different breed from the penniless grandson of an illiterate hard-scrabble farmer. There were orders in society, unseen barriers which a man could not cross, even if he had a university diploma, a military medal for gallantry and an honourable discharge from the army.

That building was the shrine of wealth and power and influence, where dwelt men like giants, like gods. The likes of Mark Anders did not barge in there demanding answers to unimportant questions about an old man of no account.

'Intestate estate less than £100,' Mark whispered aloud, and set off across town, towards the clanking, huffing sounds of the railway goods yard.

'Yes,' agreed the station master, 'Piet Greyling was a mainline loco driver, and his son fired for him – but they threw in their time months ago, back in 1919, both of them.' He rubbed his chin thoughtfully. 'No, I don't know where they were headed, just too damned happy to see them go, I guess. Oh, yes, now I come to think on it, the son did say something about they were going up to Rhodesia. Going to buy a farm, or something,' and the man

57

chuckled. 'Buy a farm! With what, I wonder – wishes and dreams – not on the salary of a loco driver or fireman.'

The board room of the Ladyburg Farmers Bank occupied half of the top floor of the building; one set of floor-to-ceiling windows faced eastwards to catch the cool sea breeze on hot summer days, the other windows faced the tall escarpment. This made a fine backdrop to the town, and gave an interesting aspect to the huge room with its high ornately plastered ceiling where dancing white cherubs bearing bunches of grapes were suspended upside-down, frozen in their endless jollification.

The walls were panelled in dark mahogany that set off the green velvet curtaining with golden corded edges.

The carpet was green also, and thick enough to muffle the hoofs of a cavalry charge. The board room table was of marble with golden ormolu work, vine leaves and nude female figures clambering up the legs, playing harps or dancing demurely.

At one end of the table, a man stood respectfully, a man with the short neck and heavy shoulders of a wrestler. The seat of his khaki breeches was shiny from the saddle, and his boots were dusty from hard riding. He twisted the rim of a slouch hat nervously between his fingers.

Opposite where he stood at the far end of the marble table, another man slouched elegantly in the leather-padded chair. Even seated, it was clear that he was a big man, the shoulders under the expensive British broadcloth were wide and powerful.

However, his head was nicely balanced on these shoulders, a glorious head of lustrous but skilfully barbered hair, dark curls that extended low down on to his cheeks into magnificent sideboards. The strong smoothly shaven chin had the jut and set of a man accustomed to command, a wide determined mouth and perfect white teeth with which he now nibbled thoughtfully at his lower lip. A small frown formed a bird's foot at the bridge of his nose, between the dark intelligent eyes, and one carefully manicured fist supported his chin as he listened quietly.

'Anyway, I thought you might like to know, Mr Courtney,' the speaker ended lamely, and shuffled his dusty boots on the thick carpet. For a long moment there was silence. The man glanced uneasily at the other two gentlemen who flanked Dirk Courtney, but then flicked back to the central figure.

Dirk Courtney dropped his hand into his lap, and the frown cleared. 'I suspect you did the right thing, Hobday.' He smiled slightly, a smile that enhanced his powerful good looks. 'You can rest in the antechamber. The clerk there will find refreshment for you, but I will want to talk to you again later. Wait.'

'Yes, sir, Mr Courtney, sir.' The man crossed to the door with alacrity, and as it closed behind him the two men flanking Dirk Courtney burst out together.

'I told you at the time something like this would happen—'

'But you told us he had been killed—'

'I never liked the idea—'

'Oh, I thought it was going too far this time—'

They spoke across each other, quick breathless outbursts while Dirk Courtney sat with an enigmatic half-smile hovering on his lips, examining with attention the diamond on the little finger of his right hand, turning the big white stone to catch the light from the windows so that it flicked spots of brilliant light across the ceiling high above where he sat.

After a few minutes, the two of them faltered into silence, and Dirk Courtney looked up politely.

'Have you both finished? I found that most helpful, constructive, imaginative.' He looked from one to the other

59

expectantly, and then when they were silent he went on, 'Unfortunately, you are not in possession of all the facts. Here is some more news for you. He arrived in town this morning, and he went straight to the Land Deeds, from there to the Register of Companies, the Master's Office—' There was a fresh outburst of lamentation from his listeners, while Dirk Courtney selected a cigar from the humidor and prepared it carefully, cutting the end with a gold-plated pocket-knife and moistening it between his lips, then he held it poised between thumb and forefinger while he waited for silence again.

'Thank you, gentlemen – but as I was saying, the gentleman in question then went down to the goods yard – and began making inquiries about Greyling and son.'

This time they were silent, exchanging appalled and disbelieving glances, and the silence drew out while Dirk Courtney struck a Swan Vesta and waited for the sulphur to burn off before he lit the cigar.

'It was all your idea,' said Ronald Pye. He was at least thirty years senior to Dirk Courtney. Once prosperously bulging flesh had sagged beneath his expensive waistcoat, his jowls drooped also, like the wattles of a rooster, and his cheeks were mottled with faded freckles and old man's blemishes, little darker liver spots. His hair also had faded and thinned, stained only by residual traces of the fiery ginger it had once been. But his prominent ears stood out from his head, giving him an alert listening look, like a desert fox, and his eyes had a fox's cunning glitter as they watched Dirk Courtney's face.

'Yes,' Dirk Courtney agreed. 'Most ideas around here are mine indeed. That's why the net reserves of the Farmers Bank have increased from one and a half to fifteen million pounds in the ten years since I started contributing my ideas—'

Ronny Pye went on staring at him, regretting bitterly for the ten thousandth time in those ten years that he had ever been tempted to sell control of the bank to this young adventurer, this elegant buccaneer.

God knows, there had been occasion for doubt, for caution, and he had hesitated long enough before accepting the fantastic offer that Dirk Courtney had made. He had known too much of the lad's history, how he had left his home here in Ladyburg in unsavoury circumstances, estranged from his father and family.

Then, years later, he had sauntered into Ronald Pye's office, unannounced and unheralded, and made his offer.

He had seen at a glance that the boy had grown into a hard man, but the offer had been too good to dismiss, and then immediately after, he had begun to hear the dark rumours that followed the man as vultures follow the lion. He should have been warned; the fact that Dirk Courtney could offer six hundred thousand pounds in cash for sixty per cent of the Bank's shares and support the offer with a Bank guarantee from Lloyds Bank of London was, in itself, enough to give substance to the dark rumours. How often does an honest man make that kind of money in a few short years, he asked himself.

In the end the money had tempted Ronny Pye, that and the chance to score over an old enemy, General Sean Courtney. He had delighted in the prospect of setting up the estranged son, setting him up in almost baronial circumstances in the very centre of Courtney country. The delight in doing so had swung the balance, spite and six hundred thousand pounds cash money.

It had been a bad bargain. 'I was against this from the beginning,' he said now.

'My dear Pye, you are against every new idea – on principle. Yet only a week ago you were swooning like a virgin bride over the balance sheet of Ladyburg Estates, and Zululand sugar.'

Dirk stood up from the chair. His full height was imposing. He smoothed his hair lightly with both hands while his cigar was gripped between strong white teeth, then he arranged the folds of his cravat, touching the pearl pin before swinging away and striding to the far wall of the board room.

He drew down the rolled map of Zululand and north Natal that covered half the wall, and stood back from it. The boundary of every farm was marked in large-scale topography. The farms belonging to Ladyburg Estates had been carefully shaded in green chalk. They made an impressive sweep of colour from sea to mountains, a great phalanx of land and natural wealth.

'There it is now, gentlemen – the scheme that you opposed so violently.' He smiled again. 'It was too rich for your watery blood.' The smile faded, and he scowled. When he scowled, the line of the wide mouth became bitter and the set of the lustrous eyes altered, with a mean pinched expression. 'The key to the whole thing was here on the Umfolosi – the water, we had to have it or none of it made sense. One stupid, stubborn, uneducated old bastard – ' he cut it off abruptly, and in a moment his smile was back, the voice tight with excitement. 'It is all ours now, the full south bank of the river, and it's not going to end there!' His spread hands clamped down on the map, hooked like claws. 'Here,' he said, 'and here, and here—' his hands marched northwards greedily.

He swung away from the map, laughing, and cocked his big handsome head at them. 'Look at you,' he laughed. 'It's running down your legs, you're so terrified – and all because I'm making you rich.'

Dennis Petersen spoke now. He was the same age as Ronny Pye, married to his sister, and, but for that connection, he would never have been seated at the ormolu marble table, for he was the least significant of the three men. His features were indefinite and slightly blurred, his body in expensive clothing was pudgy and shapeless, while the colour of his eyes was difficult to fathom.

'What are we going to do?' he asked, and though his hands were clasped in his lap, it seemed that he was actually wringing them plaintively.

'We?' Dirk asked kindly, and crossed to his chair. 'We, my dear Dennis?' he patted the man's shoulder like a father, despite the age difference. 'We aren't going to do a thing. You just go back to your own office now – and I will tell you about it once it's over.'

'Listen, Dirk.' Dennis lifted his chin firmly. 'No more of that – that rough stuff, do you hear?' Then he saw Dirk's eyes and dropped his chin. 'Please,' he mumbled.

Dirk chuckled. 'Off you go and do your sums, both of you, add up the money. Don't worry about a thing.' He helped them from their seats, a hand on each shoulder, and shepherded them towards the door. 'We have a board meeting tomorrow at nine o'clock, Dennis, I will be discussing the new extraction plant at Stanger. I will want the figures, make sure I have them.'

Alone for a moment, Dirk Courtney's face changed and the eyes narrowed. He pressed out the stub of the cigar in the onyx ashtray as he crossed to the door that led to the antechamber.

'Hobday,' he called softly. 'Come in here a moment, please.'

T here are occasions in a hunter's experience when a spoor begins hot and true and then fades. Mark remembered a hunt like that which he and the old man had made up near Chaka's Gate.

'Dead spoor, gone away,' he muttered aloud now, and stood uncertainly in the main street of Ladyburg. There seemed no way that he might find the old man's grave. No way that he could bring the body back and rebury it beside Alice on Andersland.

Less important was the money that the old man had been paid for Andersland. Three thousand pounds. It was a vast fortune in Mark's eyes and it would be good to know what had happened to it. With that amount, he could afford land of his own somewhere.

Then Mark faced the issue he had avoided up until now and admitted that there was just one more faint chance, but he felt his stomach tighten at what he had to do. With a physical effort he steeled himself and set off steadily down the street towards the towering building of the Ladyburg Farmers Bank. He had not reached it before the church clock on the spire at the end of the street sounded the hour, five clear chimes that echoed across the valley, and a dozen bank employees came out in a group through the front door, smiling and chatting gaily in the relief of the day's work ended – while a uniformed guard began closing and locking the solid mahogany doors.

Mark felt a sneaking sense of relief, and he turned away. 'I'll come back tomorrow,' he told himself firmly.

The boarding house behind the church offered dinner and a bed for seven shillings and sixpence, and Mark thought about it for only a moment. The sovereigns that he had from the old man's hoard might have to carry him long and far.

He went on out to the bridge over the Baboon Stroom and climbed down on to the bank, moving upstream to find a place to camp.

There was a fine site, with trees and firewood a quarter of a mile above the bridge, but when Mark went down the bank to the water, he could smell the stink of it before he touched the surface with the canteen; he paused, squatting on his haunches.

There was a thick soapy scum thrown up along the edge, and it had coated the stems of the reeds. For the first time Mark realized that the reeds were dead and brown, and that the water bubbled with sullen beads of gas. He scooped a handful and sniffed at it, then flicked it away with disgust and stood up, wiping his hand on the seat of his pants.

There was a big yellow fish, at least four pounds in weight, its swollen belly upwards and rotting opaque eyes bulging from its head as it floated in the sluggish current, turning gently in the eddy at the edge of the reeds. Mark watched it with a feeling of disquiet, of foreboding, as though that poisoned and rotting carcass had some special significance in his life. He shuddered softly and turned away, climbed the bank again and shouldered his pack.

He made his way upstream, pausing now and then to peer down into the river-bed, until he was opposite the steel structure of the new sugar mill; here the waters of the stream boiled and steamed with wisps of pale gas that hung like mist in the stiff brown reeds. Around the next bend, he came upon the effluent pipe, a six-inch black iron pipe that stuck out over the far side of the bank, from which the hot, steaming discharge poured in a continuous stream.

A change in the breeze carried the acrid chemical stench of it to where Mark stood, and he coughed and turned away.

A hundred yards further upstream, the clear water chuckled through clean strands of green reeds that bowed and swung gracefully on the breeze, and Mark saw the deep waving shape of an eel in the pool beyond, and watched the small black and pink crabs scurrying across the sugar-white sand below the surface.

He found another camp site on the first slope of the escarpment, beside a waterfall and its slowly swirling pool. In the trees above him, the ferns hung like soft green veils, and when he stripped his clothing and went into the pool, the water was a cool and refreshing delight.

He shaved with the old cut-throat, sitting naked on a mossy rock beside the pool. He dried himself on his shirt and then rinsed it out and hung it beside the small bright fire to dry, and while he waited for the canteen to boil he wandered, bare to the waist, on to the open slope and looked down into the valley.

The sun was already touching the rim of the escarpment, and its low rays were ruddy and warm rose. They burnished the iron roofs of the town, and tinted the column of smoke that rose from the chimney stack of the sugar mill to a beautiful golden bronze. The smoke rose tall into the evening sky, for the breeze had dropped in that peculiar stillness and hush of the African evening.

Movement caught his eye, and he blinked to clear his vision.

There was a hunting party in the open land beyond the town. Even at this distance, Mark could tell they were hunters. Four horsemen moving slowly in a group, one with a rifle or shotgun held against his hip, its barrel pointing to the sky as he leaned forward intently in the saddle. The other three were armed also; he could see the guns in the scabbards at their knees, and they also had that intent air of suppressed excitement, the air of the hunter. Ahead of the group was a single figure, a Zulu in ragged cast-off western clothing, but he led the horsemen in the character-istic attitude of the tracker, trotting in that deceptively fast gait of the Zulu, head down, eyes on the ground, carrying a stripped reed in one hand, the tracker's wand to part the grass, or touch the spoor.

Idly Mark wondered what they were hunting, so close to town, and on the bank of that dying and poisoned river, for they were coming along the same trail that Mark had followed to the escarpment.

The light was going swiftly now, the shining beacons of the iron roofs winked out swiftly as the sun went below the crest, but in the last of the light, Mark saw the leader of the group of horsemen rein in his mount and straighten in the saddle. He was a stocky figure, sitting square on his mount. The man looked up towards the escarpment where

Mark stood, then the light was gone and the group became a dark blob against the darkening land.

Vaguely disturbed, and troubled by the day just past, by the cold memories of the old man, by the sadness of that dying river, and at last by that distant figure, Mark crouched over his fire, munching his stew of tinned bully and then sipping his coffee.

When at last he pulled on his coat and rolled into his blanket close beside the fire, he could not sleep. The sense of disquiet seemed to grow rather than abate, and he found himself wondering again what four horsemen could find to hunt on the edge of a busy town. Then he thought again about the way that they had followed his own path along the river, and the disquiet deepened, sleep receded.

Suddenly he remembered how the old man would never sleep beside his cooking fire.

'I learned that when we was a chasing the Boer. A light in the night brings things other than moths – lions, hyenas and men.' He could almost hear the old man's voice saying it, and he rose immediately, with the blanket still around his shoulders, and moved away up the slope fifty yards until he found a hollow filled with dead leaves.

Sleep came at last and the soft skirt of it was falling lightly across his eyes when a Scops owl called in the forest near him; instantly he was fully awake. It was a familiar night sound, but this one had jarred some deep chord in him. The imitation had been clever, but it did not deceive an ear so closely tuned to the sounds of the wild.

Tense and listening, Mark lifted his head slowly and peered down the slope. His fire was a puddle of pink embers and above him the shapes of the trees were dark and fluffy against a crisp sky of white stars.

The owl called again down near the pool, and, at the same moment, Mark heard something move stealthily near him in the darkness, something big and heavy, the brush of footfalls in the dead leaves. Then there was silence again.

Mark strained his eyes and ears into the darkness, but it was impenetrable under the trees.

Far below in the valley, a locomotive whistled three times, the sound carrying clearly in the stillness, and then there was the huff and puff of the train pulling out from the goods yard and settling into a steady rhythmic beat of boiler and tracks.

Mark tried to put that sound beyond his hearing, trying to filter it out so that he could discern the closer softer sounds in the night around him.

Something moved down the slope, he heard the silky soft whisper of it and then he saw movement; outlined against the glowing ashes of his fire, a man's booted legs stepped out of the darkness and halted beside the fire, standing completely still.

Nearer Mark, there was another movement, a stir of impatient feet in dead leaves – and then, unmistakably, the metallic snick of gun-metal as a safety-catch was slipped to the 'fire' position. The sound struck like electricity along Mark's nerve ends, and his breath caught in his throat. It was very close, six feet away, and now he thought he could make out the loom of the man against the stars. He was standing almost on top of Mark's bed in the hollow, staring down at the fire beside the camp.

The man at the fire spoke now, softly, but his voice carried clearly. 'The bastard has gone – he's not here.' He stooped to the pile of dry firewood that Mark had cut and stacked. He threw a piece on to the embers, and sparks flew upwards in a fiery spiral and the branch flamed, throwing out a circle of yellow light.

Then he exclaimed sharply, 'His pack is still here,' and he hefted the shotgun expectantly, glaring into the night.

'Remember, there's a hundred pounds on it.'

The words and the way the man was handling the

shotgun made his intention clear beyond doubt. Mark felt the warm flood of adrenalin rush through his body, and he was poised and quivering with suppressed energy, ready to burst into explosive movement in an instant.

The man near him moved again, and Mark heard the muted tap of metal on metal, the sound of the man's breathing also, hoarse with tension – and then suddenly and with devastating shock, bright white light split the darkness. A lantern beam swivelled and then fastened on Mark's blanket-wrapped crouching form.

In the instant before he moved, Mark saw the shape of the man beyond the dazzle of the light. He carried the lantern in his right hand holding it high, at the level of his head, and the rifle was in his left hand, hanging at the trail.

He was completely unprepared to find Mark lying almost at his feet, and his shout was wild.

'He's here. My God.' He tried to bring up the rifle, but his right hand held the lantern.

'Shoot! Shoot, damn it!' another voice shouted, a voice somehow familiar, and beside Mark the man dropped the lantern and began to swing up the rifle. Mark launched himself straight at him.

He used the man's own momentum, taking the upswing of the rifle; seizing the muzzle of the barrel in one hand and the stock in the other, he smashed the weapon into the man's face with the full weight and force of his body behind it. He heard gristle and bone crunch, while the solid impact of the steel breach striking into the man's face was transmitted through the rifle into his arms, jarring him to the shoulders.

The man went over backwards, with a cry that bubbled with the quick burst of blood into his nose and mouth. Mark bounded over him and ran at the slope.

Behind him there was a chorus of shouts and cries, and then the blam, blam of a shotgun and the double glow of the muzzle flashes. Mark heard the heavy charges of shot slash into the leaves beside him, and something burned his upper arm like the sting of a wild bee.

'The light. Get the light!'

'There he is, don't let him get away.'

A rifle fired three times in quick succession, it sounded like a .303 Lee-Enfield. The bullet hit a rock and howled away into the sky, another thumped into a tree trunk close beside him as he ran.

Mark fell heavily in the dark and felt his ankle go; the pain of it exploded up his leg into his groin and lower belly. He rolled on to his knees, and the beam of the lantern swept over, and then fastened hungrily on him.

'We've got him.'

A fusillade of shots, and a triumphant chorus of shouts. The shot and bullets shattered the air around him, one so close that the whip of it deafened one ear and he threw himself forward at the slope.

The pain in his foot made Mark cry out. It was white-hot shooting agony that burst from his ankle and broke like brilliant phosphorescent surf against the roof of his skull, but he drove himself on, soaked with sweat, swerving as he ran, sobbing and hobbling on the damaged leg.

They were spread out in the bush behind him, and it seemed that the slope was tiring them quickly, men accustomed to riding horseback, for the cries were becoming strained and breathless, edged with worry and the first fear that their quarry might escape them.

Mark was trying to think between the bursts of agony with which each step racked him. He thought to drop into thick cover and lie until they passed him, but they were too close for that, and they had a tracker with them, a tracker who had brought them unerringly to his camp, even in darkness. To lie down now would be surrender – and suicide, but he could not go on much longer. Already the pain was threatening to swamp him, there was a sound in

70

his head like great wings and his vision was starting to break up and star.

.He fell to his knees and vomited, gagging and choking on the acid gall of it, and within seconds the voice of the pursuit was closer and more urgent. He dragged himself up, and the lantern beam caught him squarely; a rifle bullet disrupted the air about his head so that he staggered as he blundered onwards, using the screen of bush to avoid the beam of light. Quite suddenly he felt the ground tilt upwards under his feet sharply.

He lost his footing again, but in the same movement rolled to his feet and stumbled over a lip on to level ground where there was the sudden sugary crunch of gravel under his feet. Three stumbling paces and he came down heavily, his feet knocked out from under him and, as he went down, steel smeared the skin from his outflung forearm.

He lay panting and blinded for long seconds and heard the hunters bay like hounds down the slope. The sound goaded him and he groped with outstretched hands for purchase to push himself on to his feet once more.

He found the cold smooth steel that had tripped him; it trembled like a living thing under his hands. It came to him then that he had climbed the embankment of the railway line and fallen across the rails of the permanent way.

He pushed himself to his knees, and now he heard the deep panting rush in the night; suddenly the whole slope of the escarpment was lit by reflected light that swung dramatically and brightened like daylight as the locomotive he had heard leaving the goods yard in the valley came roaring out of the deep cutting that skirted the steepest part of the escarpment, before crossing the deep gorge of the river.

The long white beam of the lamp struck him like a solid thing and he flung up his arm to shield his eyes and rolled off the rails, crouching down on the gravel on the opposite side to that of his pursuers.

In the light of the locomotive lamp, Mark saw a stocky agile figure come up the embankment at a run. He ducked across the tracks, directly under the roaring throbbing loco. The dazzle of light prevented Mark seeing his face, yet there was something familiar in the way the man moved and held his shoulders.

The engine came thundering down on Mark, and as it drew level a spurt of steam from the driving pistons scalded him with its hot breath. Then it was past and there was just the dark blurred rush of the boxcars above him.

Mark dragged himself upright, balancing on his good foot and struck the streams of sweat from his eyes, peering upwards to judge his moment.

When it came, he almost missed it; his hands were slippery with sweat and the railing was almost jerked from his grip even though the train had lost much of its speed and power on the slope.

The strain in his shoulder shot an arrow of pain along his arm, and he was torn off his feet, swinging against the side of the boxcar while he grappled wildly for a grip with his other hand.

He found purchase and clung on to the side of the boxcar, his feet still free but scrabbling for the footplates – and at that moment hands like steel claws seized his injured ankle, the full weight of a heavy body bore him down, racking him out against the side of the car.

Mark screamed with the unbearable white-hot pain of the grip on his ankle, and it took all his strength and courage to maintain his double grip on the rail.

His body was penduluming, as the man who held him was himself swung off the ground and then came back to skid and run in the loose gravel of the embankment, as though he were driving a dog-sledge.

Mark twisted his head back and judged the white blob

of the man's face and aimed the kick with his free foot, but it was an impossible target. At that instant the sound of the locomotive altered, as it hit the steel of the bridge where it crossed the deep gorge of the river.

The uprights of the bridge sprang out of the rushing corridor of blackness; Mark heard the deadly hiss of the riveted steel girders flit past his head, and at the same moment the grip on his leg was released. He clung with his remaining strength and resolve to the railing of that goods truck, while the train racketed over the bridge and ploughed on steadily up the slope, until it burst at last over the crest on to the level ground of the plateau. It picked up speed sharply, and Mark dragged himself inch by agonized inch up the railing, until at last he tumbled over the side of the open boxcar on to the load of sugar sacks and lay face downwards, sobbing for each breath, while he rode the high storm surf of pain from his leg.

The cold roused him at last. His sweat-sodden coat was turned icy by the rush of night air and he crawled painfully forward towards the shelter of the high steel side of the car. He checked quietly and found with relief that his purse and notebook were still in his pocket.

Suddenly he was aware that he was not alone and fresh panic gripped him.

'Who's that?' he croaked, recoiling quickly into a defensive attitude.

A voice answered quickly in deep Zulu. 'I mean no harm, Nkosi,' and Mark felt a quick rush of relief. A man crouched against the side of the car, out of the wind, and it was clear that he was as alarmed by Mark's presence as Mark had been by his.

'I mean no harm, lord. I am a poor man without the money to pay to ride the steamer. My father is sick and dying in Tekweni, Durban town.'

'Peace,' grunted Mark in the same language. 'I am a poor man also.' He dragged himself into shelter beside the Zulu, and the movement twisted his ankle and he gasped at the fresh pain.

'Hau!' the black man's eyes caught the starlight as he peered at Mark. 'You are hurt.'

'My leg,' Mark grunted, trying to ease it into a more comfortable position – and the Zulu leaned forward and Mark felt his gentle hands on the ankle.

'You are without shoes?' The man was surprised at Mark's torn and bloodied feet.

'I was chased by bad men.'

'Ha,' the Zulu nodded, and Mark saw in the starlight that he was a young man. 'The leg is bad. I do not think the bone is broken, but it is bad.'

He untied the small pack beside him and he took out some article of clothing. Deliberately he began to tear the material into strips.

'No,' Mark protested sharply. 'Do not destroy your clothes for me.' He knew how each article of western clothing, however ragged and threadbare, was treasured.

'It is an old shirt,' said the Zulu simply and began to bind up the swollen ankle skilfully. When he had finished, it felt easier.

'*Ngi ya bone* – I praise you,' Mark told him, and then he shivered violently as the delayed but icy fist of shock clamped down on him; he felt nausea rise in his throat and he shivered again.

The Zulu took the blanket from around his own shoulders and placed it carefully over Mark.

'No. I cannot take your blanket.' The blanket smelled of smoke from a dung fire, and of the Zulu himself – the earthy African tang. 'I cannot take it.'

'You need it,' said the Zulu firmly. 'You are sick.'

'Very well,' Mark muttered, as another shivering fit caught him. 'But it is a large blanket, big enough for two—'

'It is not fitting.'

'Come,' said Mark roughly, and the Zulu hesitated a moment longer before drawing closer and taking up a fold of the woollen blanket.

Shoulder to shoulder, they sat on into the night, and Mark found himself dropping into a haze of exhaustion and pain, for the swollen ankle still beat like a drum. The Zulu beside him was silent, and Mark thought he slept, but as the train slowed after two hours' hard run across the plateau, he whispered quietly,

'This is Sakabula halt. It stops here for to let the other train pass.'

Mark remembered the desolate siding with its double loop of line. No buildings and only a signboard to identify it. He would have lapsed once more into half sleep, but something warned him, a strange sense of danger which he had developed so acutely in France.

He shrugged aside the blanket, and dragged himself up on his knees to peer ahead. The track came into the siding on a gentle curve, and the silver rails glittered in the lamp of the locomotive.

Far ahead was the sign-post of the halt, stark white in the beam from the locomotive, but there was something else. Parked on the track beside the halt was a dark vehicle, a heavy lorry, and its headlights still burned. In the puddle of yellow light Mark made out the dark shapes of waiting men. Alarm jarred his bowels and clutched at his chest with a cold cramping fist.

A motor lorry from Ladyburg could not have reached here ahead of them, but a telegraph message could have alerted—

'I must go,' Mark blurted, and with stiff fingers he hooked a sovereign out of his money belt and pressed it quickly into the Zulu's hand.

'There is no call for—' the man began, but Mark cut him off brusquely.

'Stay in peace.' He dragged himself to the side of the car

furthest from the waiting men, and lowered himself down the steel ladder until he hung just above the tracks.

He waited for the locomotive to slow down, groaning and creaking and sighing steam, and then he braced himself and dropped – trying to take most of his weight on his good leg.

He collapsed forwards as he struck the ground; ducking his head, he rolled on to his shoulders and, drawing up his knees, went down the embankment like a rubber ball.

In the dry pale grass beside the line, he did not rise but dragged himself on elbows and belly to a low dark thorn bush, fifty yards from the rails. Slowly he worked himself under its low spiny branches and lay face down, gritting his teeth against the dull beat of his ankle.

The train had halted with its van level with Mark's hiding place; the guard climbed down, flashing his lantern, while from the head of the train a group of men, each one carrying a lantern, hurried back towards him, searching the open trucks as they came.

Mark could see they were all armed, and their voices carried loudly as they called explanations to the driver and fireman who leaned from the cab of the locomotive.

'What's the trouble?'

'You've got a fugitive from justice aboard.'

'Who are you?'

'We're special constables.'

'Who's the fellow?'

'He robbed a bank—'

'He killed four men in Ladyburg—'

'He jumped your train on the escarpment—'

'Don't take any chances, you fellows, the bastard is a killer—'

They came swiftly down the train, talking loudly and calling to each other to bolster their courage, and at the last moment Mark remembered the Zulu. He should have warned the man, but he had been too concerned with his own danger. He wanted to shout now, warn him to run, but he could not bring himself to do it. The Zulu would be all right, they would not shoot when they saw he was a black, they might slap him around a little and throw him off—

The Zulu darted out from between two of the boxcars from where he had climbed down on to the coupling. He was a dark flitting shape, and somebody yelled a warning. Immediately there was a shot.

Mark saw the dust from the bullet fly in the lamplight, and the Zulu swerved and ran directly out into the open grassland. Half a dozen shots ripped the night, the muzzle flashes were angry red blooms in the night, but the Zulu ran on.

One of the men on the track dropped to his knee, and Mark saw his face white and eager in the light of the torches. He aimed deliberately, and his rifle kicked up sharply.

The Zulu collapsed in the grass without a cry, and they raced forward in an excited pack to gather around his body.

'Oh, Jesus, it's only a black.' There was confused angry discussion and argument for five minutes, and then four of them took an arm and leg each and carried the Zulu between them to the parked lorry.

The black man's head lolled back, almost sweeping the earth, his mouth gaped open and the blood that dripped from it was black as tar in the lamplight and his head swung loosely to the uneven stride of the men who carried him. They lifted him into the back of the lorry.

The north-bound train came thundering through the siding, its whistle shrilling on a high piercing shriek, and then it was gone on its way to Ladyburg.

The men climbed into the lorry and the engine fired, and it moved away with its headlights sweeping sky and earth as it pitched over the bumpy track.

The stationary train whistled mournfully and it began to

roll forward, rumbling slowly over the tracks. Mark crawled out from his hiding-place beneath the bush, and hopped and stumbled after it, catching it just before its speed built up.

He crawled over the sugar bags into the lee of the steel side, and found the Zulu had left his blanket. As he wrapped it around his icy body, he felt the guilt flood over him, guilt for the man's death, the man who had been a friend – then the guilt turned to anger.

Bitter corrosive anger that sustained him through the night as the train rushed southwards.

Fordsburg is a squalid suburb of Johannesburg, three hundred miles from the golden grassy hills of Zululand and the beautiful forested valley of Ladyburg. It is an area of mean cottages, tiny workers' houses of galvanized iron on timber frames, each with a bleak little garden. In some of the gardens there were brave and defiant shows of bright blooms, barbeton daisies, cannas and flaming red poinsettia, but in most of them the bare untended earth, patched with blackjack and khaki-bush, told of the tenants' indifference.

Over the narrow streets and crowded cottages, the mine dumps held majestic sway, towering table-topped mountains of poisonous yellow earth from which the gold had been extracted. The cyanide process of extraction ensured that the earth of the dumps was barren and sterile. No plants grew upon them, and on windy days the yellow dust and grit whipped over the grovelling cottages beneath them.

The dumps dominated the landscape, monument to the antlike endeavours of man, symbols of his eternal greed for gold. The mine headgears were spidery steel structures against the pale cloudless blue of the highveld winter sky. The huge steel wheels on their heights spun endlessly, back and forth, lowering the cages filled with men deep into the earth, and rising again with the ore bins loaded with the gold-rich rock.

Mark made his way slowly down one of the narrow, dusty streets. He still limped slightly, and a cheap cardboard suitcase carried the few possessions he had bought to replace those he had lost on the escarpment.

The clothes he wore were an improvement on the shapeless demobilization suit that the army had given him. His flannels were neatly creased and the blue blazer fitted his good shoulders and narrow flanks, the open-necked white shirt was snowy clean and set off the smooth brown skin of his neck and face.

He reached the cottage numbered fifty-five on the gate, and it was a mirror image of those on each side and opposite. He opened the gate and went up the short flagged path, aware that somebody was watching him from behind the lace curtain in the front room.

However, when he knocked on the front door it was only opened after a delay of many minutes, and Mark blinked at the woman who stood there.

Her dark short hair was freshly combed, and the clothes she wore had clearly been hastily put on in place of dowdier everyday dress. She was still fastening the belt at her slim waist. It was a dress of pale blue with a design of yellow daisies, and it made her appear young and gay, although Mark saw at once that she was at least ten years older than he was.

'Yes?' she asked, tempering the abrupt demand with a smile.

'Does Fergus MacDonald live here?' He saw now that she was good-looking, not pretty, but fine-looking with good bones in her cheeks and dark intelligent eyes.

'Yes, this is Mr MacDonald's house.' There was a foreign inflection in her voice that was intriguing. 'I am Mrs MacDonald.'

'Oh,' he said, taken by surprise. He had known Fergus was married. He had spoken about it often, but Mark had never really thought about his wife before – not as a real flesh and blood woman, and certainly not one like this. 'I am an old friend of Fergus' from the army.'

'Oh, I see—' she hesitated.

'My name's Mark, Mark Anders.' Instantly her attitude changed, the half smile bloomed and lit her whole face. She gave a small gasp of pleasure.

'Mark, of course, Mark.' She took his arm impetuously and drew him over the threshold. 'He has spoken of you so often – I feel I know you so well. Like a member of the family, like a brother.' She still had his arm, standing close to him, laughing up at him. 'Come in, Mark, come in. I am Helena.'

Fergus MacDonald sat at the head of the deal table in the dingy kitchen. The table was covered with sheets of newsprint instead of a cloth and Fergus hunched over his plate, and scowled angrily as he listened to Mark's account of his flight from Ladyburg.

'The bastards, they are the enemy, Mark. The new enemy.'

His mouth was filled with potato and heavily spiced boerewors, thick farmer's sausage, and he spoke through it.

'We are in another war, lad – and this time they are worse than the bloody Hun.'

'More beer, Mark.' Helena leaned across to fill his tumbler from the black quart bottle.

'Thank you.' Mark watched the foaming head rise in his glass, and he pondered Fergus' statement.

'I don't understand, Fergus. I don't know who these men are, I don't know why they tried to kill me.'

'They are the bosses, lad. That's who we are fighting now. The rich, the mine-owners, the bankers, all those who oppress the working man.'

Mark took a long swallow of his beer, and Helena smiled at him from across the table.

'Fergus is right, Mark. We have to destroy them.' And she began to talk. It was strange confusing talk from a woman, and there was a fanatical light in her dark eyes. The words had a compelling power in her clear articulate voice with its lilting accent, and Mark watched the way she used her hands to emphasize each point. They were neat strong hands with gracefully tapered fingers and short nails. The nails were clean and trimmed but the first two fingers of her right hand were stained pale yellow. Mark wondered at that, until suddenly Helena reached across and took a cigarette from the packet at Fergus' elbow.

Still talking, she lit the cigarette from a match in her cupped hands, and draw deeply before exhaling forcibly through pursed lips. Mark had never seen a woman smoke before, and he stared at her. She shook her head vehemently.

'The history of the people's revolt is written in blood. Look at France, see how the revolution sweeps forward in Russia.'

The short dark shining curls danced around her smooth pale cheeks, and she pursed her lips again to drag at the cigarette, and in some strange fashion Mark found the mannish act shocking – and exciting.

He felt his groin clenching, the tight swollen hardening of his flesh, beyond his reason – far beyond his control. His breathing caught with shock and embarrassment, and he leaned back and slipped one hand into his trouser pocket, certain that both of them must be aware of his shameful reaction, but instead Helena reached across the table and seized his other wrist in a surprisingly powerful grip.

'We know our enemy, we know what must be done and how we must do it, Mark.'

Her fingers seemed to burn like heated iron into his flesh, he felt dizzy with the force of it. His voice was hoarse as he forced himself to reply.

'They are strong, Helena, powerful—'

'No, no, Mark, the workers are strong, the enemy are weak, and smug. They suspect nothing, they wallow like hogs in the false security of their golden sovereigns, but in reality they are few and unprepared. They do not know their own weakness – and as yet the workers do not realize their great strength. We will teach them.'

'You're right, lass.' Fergus wiped the gravy from the plate with a crust of bread and stuffed it into his mouth. 'Listen to her, Mark, we are building a new world, a brave and beautiful new world.'

He belched loudly and pushed his plate away, leaving both elbows on the table. 'But first we have to tear down and destroy this rotten, unjust and corrupt society. There will be hard fighting, and we will need good hard fighting men.' He laughed harshly and slapped Mark's shoulder. 'They'll call for MacDonald and Anders again, lad, you hear me.'

'There is nothing for us to lose, Mark.' Helena's cheeks were flushed. 'Nothing but our chains – and there is a whole world to win. Karl Marx said that, and it's one of the great truths of history.'

'Helena, are you,' he hesitated to use the word, 'are you and Fergus – well I mean, you aren't Bolsheviks are you?'

'That's what the bosses, and their minions, the police, call us.' She laughed contemptuously. 'They try to make us criminals, already they fear us. With reason, Mark, we will give them reason.'

'No, lad, don't call us Bolsheviks. We are members of

the communist party, dedicated to universal communism. I'm the local party secretary and shop steward of the mineworkers' union for the boilermakers' shop.'

'Have you read Karl Marx?' Helena demanded.

'No.' Mark shook his head, dazed and shocked, but still sexually excited by her to the edge of pain. Fergus a Bolshevik? A bomb-throwing monster? But he knew he was not. He was an old and trusted comrade.

'I will lend you my copy.'

'Come on, lass,' Fergus chuckled, and shook his head. 'We are going too fast for the lad. He's got a right barmy look right now.' He leaned over and placed an affectionate arm around Mark's shoulders, drawing him close. 'Have you a place to stay, lad? A job? A place to go?'

'No.' Mark flushed. 'I haven't, Fergus.'

'Oh, yes you have,' Helena cut in quickly. 'I have fixed the bed in the other room – you'll stay there, Mark.'

'Oh, but I couldn't—'

'It's done,' she said simply.

'You'll stay, lad.' Fergus squeezed him hard. 'And we'll see about a job for you tomorrow – you're book-learned. You can read and write and figure, it will be easy to fix you. I know they need a clerk up at the pay office, and the paymaster is a comrade, a member of the party.'

'I'll pay you for lodging.'

'Of course you will,' Fergus chuckled again, and filled his glass to the brim with beer. 'It's good to see you again, son,' and he raised his own glass. 'Send down the line for MacDonald and Anders – and warn the bastards we are coming!' He took a long swallow, the pointed Adam's apple bobbing in his throat, then wiped the froth from his upper lip with the back of his hand.

The regimental chaplain had called it the 'sin of Onan', while the rankers had many more ribald terms for it, 'toss the caber' or 'visit Mrs Hand and her five daughters'. The chaplain had warned of the dire consequences that it would bring – failing sight, and falling hair, a palsied shaking hand and at last idiocy and the insane asylum. Mark lay in the narrow iron bed and stared with unseeing eyes at the faded pink rose-pattern wallpaper of the tiny room. It had the musty smell of being long closed, and there was a wash-basin in an iron frame with an enamel basin against the far wall. A single unshaded bulb hung on a length of flex from the ceiling, and the white plaster around it was fly-speckled; even at the moment three drowsy flies sat on the flex in a stupor. Mark swivelled his attention to them, trying to put aside the waves of temptation that flowed up through his body.

Light steps in the passage stopped opposite his bedroom door, and now there was a tap on the woodwork.

'Mark?'

He sat up quickly, letting the single thin blanket fall to his waist.

'May I come in?'

'Yes,' he husked, and the door swung open. Helena crossed to his bed. She wore a gown of light pink shiny material that buttoned down the front; the skirt opened at each step and there was a glimpse of smooth white flesh above her knees.

She carried a slim book in one hand. 'I said I would lend it to you,' she explained. 'Read it, Mark.' She held out the volume.

*The Communist Manifesto* was the title, and Mark took it from her, opening it at random. He bowed his head over the open pages to cover the confusion into which her near presence plunged him.

'Thank you, Helena.' He used her name for the first

time, wanting her to leave and yet hoping she would stay. She leaned over him a little, looking at the open book, and the bodice of her gown fell apart an inch. Mark looked up, and saw the incredibly silky sheen where the beginning of one white breast pressed against the lace that edged the neck of the gown. Swiftly he dropped his eyes again, and they were both silent until Mark could stand it no longer, and he looked up at her.

'Helena,' he began, and then stopped. There was a smile, a secret womanly smile on her lips, lips that were slightly parted and moist in the harsh electric light. The dark eyes were half hooded but glowed again with that fierce fanatical light, and her bosom beneath the pink satin rose and fell with quick soundless breathing.

He flushed a sultry red under the dark tan of his cheeks and he rolled abruptly on to his side, drawing up his knees.

Helena straightened up slowly, still smiling. 'Goodnight, Mark.' She touched his shoulder, fire sprang afresh from her finger-tips and then she turned and went slowly towards the door. The slippery material of the gown slid softly across the tight double rounds of her buttocks.

'I'll leave the light on.' She looked back at him, and now the smile was knowing. 'You'll want to read.'

The Pay Office of Crown Deep Mines Ltd was a long austere room where five other clerks worked at high desks set in a line down one wall. They were mostly men in advanced middle age, two of them sufferers from phthisis, that dreaded disease of the miners in which the rock dust from the drills settled in the lungs, building up slowly until the lung turned to stone and gradually crippled the man. Employment in the mine offices was a form of pension. The other three were grey and drab men, stooped from poring over their ledgers. The atmosphere in the office was quiet and joyless, as in some monastic cloister.

Mark was given charge of the files and personnel R to Z, and the work was dull and repetitive, soon becoming automatic as he calculated overtime and leave pay, made deductions for rent and union fees and struck his totals. It was drudgery, not nearly enough to engage a bright and active young brain, and the narrow confines of the office were a cage for a spirit that was at home in the wide open sweep of sky and veld and had known the cataclysmic universe of the battlefields of France.

On the weekends, he escaped from his cage and rode on an old bicycle for miles into the open veld, following dusty paths along the base of the rocky kopjes on which grew the regal candelabra of giant aloes, their blooms burning in bright scarlet against the clear pale blue of the highveld sky. He sought seclusion, wilderness, secret places far from other men, but it seemed that always there were the barriers of barbed wire to limit his range; the grasslands had gone to the plough, the pale dust devils swirled and danced over red earth from which the harvest had been stripped, leaving the dried sparse stubble of maize stalks.

The great herds of game that once had covered the open grassland to the full range of the eye were long gone, and now small scrub cattle, multi-coloured and scrawny, grazed in mindless bovine herds tended by almost naked black piccaninnies who paused to watch Mark pedalling by, and greeted him with solemnity which turned to wide-eyed pleasure when he returned the greeting in their own language.

Once in a while Mark would start a small grey duiker from its lay and send it bounding and bouncing away through the dry grass with small sharp horns and ears erect, or else catch a glimpse of a springbuck drifting elusive as smoke across the plain, lonely survivors of the long rifles.

Then the delight of their wild presence stayed long with him, warming him on the dark cold ride home.

He needed these times of quiet and solitude to complete the healing process, not only of the Maxim bullet wounds in his back but of the deeper wounds, soul damage caused by too early an exposure to war in all its horror.

He needed this quietness also to evaluate the swift rush of events that filled his evenings and nights in direct contrast to the grey drudgery of his working days.

Mark was carried along by the fanatical energy of Fergus MacDonald and Helena. Fergus was the comrade who had shared with him experience that most men never knew, the stark and terrible involvement of combat. He was also much older than Mark, a paternal figure, filling a deep need in his life. It was easy to suspend the critical faculties and believe; not to think, but to follow blindly wherever Fergus' bitter restless energy led them.

There was excitement and a sense of commitment in those meetings with men like him, men with an ideal and a sense of destiny. The secret meetings in locked rooms with armed guards at the doors, the atmosphere quivering with the promise of forbidden things. The cigarette-smoke spiralling upwards until it filled the room with a thick blue haze, like incense burning at some mystic rite; the faces shining with sweat and the quiet frenzy of the fanatic, as they listened to the speakers.

Harry Fisher, the Chairman of the Party, was a tall fierce man with a heavy gut, the brawny shoulders and hairy muscular arms of a boilermaker, an unkempt shock of coarse wiry black hair laced with strands of silver and dark burning eyes.

'We are the Party, the praetorian guard of the proletariat, and we are not bound by law or the ethical considerations of the bourgeois age. The Party in itself is the new law, the natural law of existence.'

Afterwards he shook hands with Mark, while Fergus

stood by with paternal pride. Fisher's grip was as fierce as his stare.

'You're a soldier,' he nodded. 'We will need you again, comrade. There is bloody work ahead.'

The disquieting presence of the man stayed to haunt Mark long afterwards, even when they rode home in the crowded tramcar, the three of them squeezed into a double seat so that Helena's thigh was pressed hard against his. When she spoke to him, she leaned sideways, her lips almost touching his cheek, and her breath smelling of liquorice and cigarettes, a smell that mingled with the cheap flowery perfume she wore, and the underlying musky warmth of her woman's body.

There were other meetings on the Friday evenings, great raucous shouting gatherings where hundreds of white miners crowded into the huge Fordsburg Trades Union Hall, most of them boozy with cheap brandy, loud and inarticulate and spoiling for trouble. They roared like the crowd at a bull fight as the speakers harangued them; occasionally one of the audience climbed on to his chair to sway there, shouting meaningless confused slogans until his laughing comrades dragged him down.

One of the most popular speakers at these public meetings was Fergus MacDonald; he had a dozen tricks to excite his audience, he probed their secret fears and twisted the probe until they howled half in pain and half in adulation.

'You know what they are planning, the bosses, you know what they are going to do? First they will fragment the trades—'

A thunderous ugly roar, that shook the windows in their frames, and Fergus paused on the stage, sweeping his sparse sandy hair back off his forehead and grinning down at them with his thin bitter mouth until the sound subsided.

'—the trade that took you five years to learn, they will split it up and now there will be three unskilled men to do your job, with only a year's training to learn that fragment, and they will pay them a tenth of the wage you draw.'

A storming roar of 'No!' and Fergus flung it back at them.

'Yes!' he shouted. 'Yes! Yes! And yes again. That is what the bosses are going to do. But that's not all, they are going to use blacks in your jobs, black men are going to take those jobs away from you – black men who will work for a wage that you cannot live on.'

They screamed now, frantic with anger, a terrible anger which had no object on which to focus.

'What about your kids, are you going to feed them on mealies, are your wives going to wear limbo? That's what will happen, when the blacks take your jobs!'

'No!' they roared. 'No!'

'Workers of the world,' Fergus shouted at them, 'workers of the world unite – and keep our country white!'

The bellow of applause, the rhythmic stamp of feet on the wooden floor lasted for ten minutes, while Fergus strutted back and forth across the stage, clasping his hands above his head like a prize-fighter. When at last the cheering faltered, he flung back his head and bellowed the opening line of 'The Red Flag'.

The entire hall came crashing to its feet, and stood at attention to sing the revolutionary song:

> Then raise the scarlet standard high,
> Within its shade we'll live or die.
> Tho' cowards flinch and traitors sneer,
> We'll keep the red flag flying here.

Mark walked home with the MacDonalds in the frosty night, their breathing smoking like ostrich plumes in the lights of the street lamps. Helena walked between the men, a small dainty figure in her black overcoat with rabbit-fur collar and a knitted cap pulled down over her head.

She had slipped a hand into the crook of the elbows of each of them, a seemingly natural impartial gesture, but there was a disturbing pressure of fingers on the hard muscle of Mark's upper arm, and her hip touched his as she skipped occasionally to catch the longer stride of the men.

'Listen, Fergus, what you were saying there in the hall doesn't make sense, you know,' Mark broke the silence, as they turned into the home street. 'You can't have it both ways, workers unite and keep it white.'

Fergus chuckled appreciatively. 'You're a bright lad, comrade Mark.'

'But, I'm serious, Fergus – it's not the way Harry Fisher—'

'Of course not, lad. Tonight I was shovelling up swill for the hogs. We need them fighting mad, we have things to tear down, bloody work to do.' He stopped and turned to face Mark over the woman's head. 'We need cannon fodder, lad, and plenty of it.'

'So it won't be like that?' Mark asked.

'No, lad. It will be a beautiful brave new world. All men equal, all men happy, no bosses – a workers' state.'

Mark tried to control his pricking nagging doubts.

'You keep talking of fighting, Fergus. Do you mean that, literally? I mean, will it be a shooting war?'

'A shooting war, comrade, a bloody shooting war. Just like the revolution in Russia, where comrade Lenin has shown us the way. We have to burn away the dross, we have to soak this earth with the blood of the rulers and the bosses, we have to flood it with the blood of their minions – the petit bourgeois officer's class of the police and military.'

'What will—' Mark almost said 'we' but it would not come to his lips. He could not make that commitment. 'What will you fight with?'

Fergus chuckled again, and winked slyly. 'Mum's the

word, lad, but it's time you knew a little more.' He nodded. 'Yes, tomorrow night,' he decided.

On Saturday there was a bazaar being held in the Trades Hall, a Women's Union fund-raising drive for building the new church. Where the crazed mob had screamed murder and bloody revolution the previous night, now there were long trestle tables set out and the women hovered over their displays of baked and fancily iced cakes, trays of tarts, preserved fruit in jars and jams.

Mark bought a packet of tarts for a penny and he and Fergus munched them as they wandered idly down the hall, stopping at the piles of second-hand clothing while Fergus tried a maroon cardigan and, after careful deliberation, purchased it for half a crown. They reached the top of the hall, and stood beneath the raised stage.

Fergus surveyed the room casually and then took Mark's arm and led him up the steps. They crossed the stage quietly, and went in through a door in the wings, into a maze of small union offices and storerooms, all deserted now on a Saturday afternoon.

Fergus used a key from his watch-chain to unlock a low iron door, and they stooped through it. Fergus relocked behind him, and they went down a narrow flight of steps that descended steeply. There was a smell of damp and earth, and Mark realized that they were descending to the cellars.

Fergus tapped on the door at the bottom of the stairs, and after a moment a single eye regarded them balefully through a peep hole.

'All right, comrade. Fergus MacDonald – a committee member.'

There was the rattle of chains and the door opened. A disgruntled, roughly dressed man stood aside for them. He was unshaven and sullen, and against the wall of the tiny room was a table and chair, still spread with the remains of a meal and the crumpled daily newspaper.

The man grunted, and Fergus led Mark across the room and through another door into the cellars.

The floor was earthen and the arched columns were in raw unplastered brick. There was the stench of dust and rats, stale dank air in confined space. A single bulb lit the centre starkly, but left the alcoves behind the arches in shadow.

'Here, lad, this is what we are going to use.'

There were wooden cases stacked neatly to the height of a man's head in the alcoves, and the stacks were draped with heavy tarpaulin, obviously stolen from the railway yards for they were stencilled SAR & H.

Fergus lifted the edge of one tarpaulin, and grinned that thin humourless smile.

'Still in the grease, lad.' The wooden cases were branded with the distinctive arrow-head and W. D. of the British War Department, and below that the inscription: '6 pieces. Lee-Enfield Mark IV (CNVD)'.

Mark was stunned. 'Good God, Fergus, there are hundreds of them.'

'That's it, lad – and this is only one arsenal. There are others all along the Rand.'

He lifted another tarpaulin, walking on down the length of the cellar. The ammunition cases, with the quick-release catches on the detachable lids that were painted: '1000 rounds .303.'

'We have enough to do the job.' Fergus squeezed Mark's arm, and led him on.

There were racks of rifles now, ready for instant use, blued steel glistening with gun oil in the electric light. Fergus picked out a single rifle and handed it to Mark.

'This one has got your name on it.'

Mark took the weapon, and the feel of it in his hands was terribly familiar.

'It's the only one we've got, but the moment I saw it, I thought of you. When the time comes, you'll be using it.'

The P.14 sniper's rifle had that special balance that felt just right in his hands but made Mark sick in the stomach. He handed it back to Fergus without a word, but the older man winked at him before racking it again carefully.

Like a showman, Fergus had kept the best for last. With a flourish he whipped the canvas off the heavy weapon, with its thick, corrugated water-jacketed barrel, that squatted on its steel tripod. The Maxim machine gun, in its various forms, had the dubious distinction of having killed more human beings than any other single weapon that man's destructive genius had been able to devise.

This was one of that deadly family, the Vickers-Maxim .303 Mark IV.B, and there were boxes stacked beside it. Each containing a belt of 250 rounds. The gun could throw those at 2440 feet per second and at a cyclic rate of 750 rounds a minute.

'How about that, comrade? You asked what we are going to fight with – how will that do for a beginning?'

In the silence Mark could hear faintly, but distinctly, the sound of children's laughter from the hall above them.

Mark sat alone upon the highest crest of the low kopjes that stretched into the west, black ironstone ridges breaking out of the flat dry earth like the crested back of a crocodile surfacing from still lake water.

The memory of the hidden arsenal had stayed with him through the night, keeping him from sleep, so that now his eyes felt gritty and his skin stretched tight and dry across the bones of his cheeks.

Lack of sleep had left him with that remote feeling, a lightness of thought, detached from reality, so now he sat in the bright sunlight like a day-flying owl, and looking like a stranger into his own mind.

He felt a rising sense of dismay as he realized how idly he had drifted along the path that had brought him here to the very brink of the abyss. It had taken the feel of the P.14 in his hands, and the laughter of children to bring him up at the end of a rope.

All his training, all his deepest beliefs were centred on the sanctity of law, on the order and responsibilities of society. He had fought for that, had spent all of his adult life fighting for that belief. Now suddenly he had drifted, out of apathy, to the camp of the enemy; already he was numbered with the legions of the lawless, already they were arming him to begin the work of destruction. There was no question now that it was merely empty rhetoric shouted at gatherings of drunken labourers – he had seen the guns. It would be cruel and without mercy. He knew Harry Fisher, had recognized the forces that drove him. He knew Fergus MacDonald, the man had killed before and often; he would not flick an eyelid when he killed again.

Mark groaned aloud, aghast at what he had let happen to himself. He who knew what war really was, he who had worn the king's uniform, and won his medal for courage.

He felt the oily warmth of shame in his throat, a gagging sensation, and, to arm himself against future weakness of this same kind, he tried to find the reasons why he had been drawn in.

He realized now that he had been lost and alone, without family or home, and Fergus MacDonald had been the only shelter in the cold. Fergus the older comrade of shared dangers, whom he had trusted without question.

Fergus the father figure – and he had followed again, grateful for the guidance, not questioning the destination.

There had, of course, been Helena as well and the hold she had over him, the tightest grip any human could have over another. He had been, and still was, totally obsessed with her. She had awakened his long suppressed and tightly controlled sexuality. Now it was but a breath away from bursting the wall he had built to dam it; when it burst, it might be a force he could not control, and that thought terrified him almost as much as the other.

He tried now to separate the woman from her womanhood, tried to see the person beyond this devastating web she wove around his senses, and he succeeded in as much that he realized that she was not a person he could admire, not the mother he would choose for his children. Also, she was the wife of an old comrade who trusted him completely.

Now he felt he was ready to make the decision to leave, and to carry that resolve through firmly.

He would leave Fordsburg immediately, leave Fergus MacDonald and his dark, cataclysmic schemes. He felt his spirits lighten instantly at the prospect. He would not miss him, nor that drab monastic pay office with its daily penance of boredom and drudgery. He felt the bright young spirit of anticipation flame again.

He would leave Fordsburg on the next train – and Helena. Immediately the flame flickered and his spirit plunged. There was a physical pain in his groin at the prospect, and he felt the cracks open in the dam wall of his passions.

It was dark when he left his bicycle in the garden shed, and he heard voices raised jovially in the house and bursts of laughter. Lights blazed beyond the curtained kitchen windows and when he stepped into the room there were four men at the table. Helena crossed quickly and hugged him impulsively, laughing, with high spots of colour in her cheeks, before taking his hand and leading him to the table.

'Welcome, comrade.' Harry Fisher looked up at Mark with those disturbing eyes and the shock of dark wiry hair hanging on to his forehead. 'You are in time to join the celebration.'

'Grab the lad a glass, Helena,' laughed Fergus, and she dropped his hand and hurried to the cupboard to fetch a glass and fill it with black stout from the bottle.

Harry Fisher raised his own glass to Fergus. 'Comrades, I give you the new member of the Central Committee – Fergus MacDonald.'

'Isn't it wonderful, Mark?' Helena squeezed Mark's hand.

'He's a good man,' growled Harry Fisher. 'The appointment isn't too soon. We need men with Comrade MacDonald's guts.' The others nodded agreement over their stout glasses, the two of them were both members of the local committee of the party; Mark knew them well from the meetings.

'Come, lad.' Fergus made room for him at the table and he squeezed in beside him, drawing all their attention.

'And you, young Mark,' Harry Fisher laid a powerful hairy hand on his shoulder, 'we are going to issue your party card—'

'How about that, lad!' Fergus winked and nudged Mark in the ribs. 'Usually it takes two years or more, we don't let the rabble into the party, but you've got friends on the Central Committee now.'

Mark was about to speak, to refuse the honour he was being accorded. Nobody had asked him, they had taken it that as he was Fergus' protégé, he was for them. Mark was about to deny it, to tell them the decision he had made that day – when that sense of danger warned him. He had seen the guns, if he was not a friend then he was an enemy with a fatal secret. A secret that they could not risk. He had no doubts at all about these men, now. If he was an enemy, then they would see that he never passed that secret on to another man. But the moment for refusal had passed.

'Comrade MacDonald, I have a mission for you. It is urgent – and vital. Can you leave your work for two weeks?'

'I've got a sick mother,' Fergus chuckled. 'When do you want me to go, and what do you want me to do?'

'I want you to leave, say Wednesday, that will give me time to give you your orders and for you to make your arrangements.' Harry Fisher took a swallow of stout and the froth stayed on his upper lip. 'I'm sending you to visit all the local committees – Capetown, Bloemfontein, Port Elizabeth – so that each of them can be co-ordinated.'

Mark felt a guilty lift of relief at the words, there would be no confrontation with Fergus now. He could merely slip away while he was gone on his mission. Then he glanced up and was startled by the gaze that Helena had fastened upon him. She stared at him with the fixed hungry expression of a leopard watching its prey from cover in the last instant before its spring.

Now when their eyes met, she smiled again that secret knowing smile, and the tip of her pink tongue dabbed at her slightly parted lips.

Mark's heart pounded to the point of physical pain and he dropped his eyes hurriedly to his glass. He was to be alone with Helena, and the prospect filled him with dread and a surging passionate heat.

Mark carried Fergus' cheap and badly battered suitcase down to the station, and as they took the short cut across open veld, the thick frost crunched like sugar under their feet, and sparkled in myriad diamond points of light in the first rays of the sun.

At the station they waited with four other members of the party for the southbound mail, and when at last it came, puffing hoarsely, shooting steam high into the frosty air, it was thirty-five minutes late.

'Thirty-five minutes late is almost early for the railways,' Fergus laughed, and shook hands with each of them in turn, slapping their shoulders before scrambling up the steel ladder into the coach. Mark passed his suitcase up through the open window.

'Look after Helena, lad, and yourself.'

Mark stood and watched the train run out southwards, shrinking dramatically in size until the sound of it was a mere whisper fading to nothingness. Then he turned and started up the hill towards the mine just as the hooters began their mournful wailing howl that echoed off the yellow mesas of the dumps, summoning the disorderly columns of men to their appointed labours. Mark walked with them, one in a thousand, distinguished from the others neither in appearance nor achievement. Once again he felt a sense of seething discontent, a vague but growing knowledge that this was not all that was life, not all that he was capable of doing with his youth and energy; and he looked curiously at the men who hurried with him towards the iron gates at the mine hooter's imperious summons.

All of them wore that closed withdrawn look, behind which Mark was convinced lurked the same misgivings as now assaulted him. Surely they also felt the futility of the dull daily repetition – the young ones at least must feel it. The older and greyer must regret it; deep down they must mourn for the long sunny days, now past, spent toiling in endless drudgery for another man's coin. They must mourn the fact that when they went, they would leave no footprints, no ripple on the surface, no monument, except perhaps a few sons to repeat the meaningless cycle, all of them interchangeable, all of them dispensable.

He paused at the gates, standing aside while the stream of humanity flowed past him, and slowly the sense of excitement built up in him, the certainty that there was something, some special and worthwhile task for him to perform. Some special place that waited for him, and he knew he must go on and find it.

He hurried forward, suddenly grateful to Fergus Mac-Donald for placing this pressure on him, for forcing him to face himself, for breaking the easy drifting course he had taken since his flight from Ladyburg.

'You are late, Anders.' The supervisor looked up from his ledgers severely, and each of his juniors repeated the gesture, a long row of them with the same narrow disapproving expressions.

'What have you got to say?'

'I merely called in to clean out my desk,' said Mark smiling, the excitement still on him. 'And to throw in my time.'

The disapproving expressions changed slowly to shock.

It was dusk when Mark opened the back gate of the cottage and went up the short walk to the kitchen. He had walked all day at random, driven on restlessly by a new torrent of energy and exciting thoughts; he had not realized how hungry he was until he saw the lights in the window and smelled the faint aroma of cooking.

The kitchen was deserted, but Helena called through from the front.

'Mark, is that you?' Before he could answer, she appeared in the kitchen door, and leaned one hip against the jamb. 'I thought you weren't coming home tonight.'

She wore the blue dress, and Mark knew now that it was her best, reserved for special occasions, and she wore cosmetics – something that Mark had never seen her do before. There were spots of rouge on her cheeks and her lips were painted, giving new lustre to her usually sallow skin. The short dark hair was new washed, shiny in the lamplight, and brushed back, caught over one ear with a tortoise-shell clasp.

Mark stared at her. Her legs were smooth and sleek in silken stockings, the feet neatly clad in small pumps.

'Why are you staring, Mark?'

'You are—' Mark's voice turned husky, and caught. He cleared his throat. 'You are very pretty tonight.'

'Thank you, sir.' She laughed, a low throaty chuckle, and she did a slow pirouette, flaring the blue filmy skirt above the silken legs. 'I'm glad you like it.' Then she stopped beside him and took his arm. Her touch was a delicious shock, like diving into a mountain pool.

'Sit down, Mark.' She led him to the chair at the head of the table. 'Let me get you a nice beer.' She went to the ice box, and while she pulled the cap on the bottle and poured, she ran on gaily. 'I found a goose at the butcher's – do you like roast goose?'

Saliva poured from under Mark's tongue. 'I love it.'

'With roast potato and pumpkin pie.'

'For that I would sell my soul.'

Helena laughed delightedly, it wasn't one of Mark's usual shy and reserved replies. There was a sense of excitement surrounding him like an aura this evening, echoing her own excitement.

She brought the two glasses, and propped one hip on the table.

'What shall we drink to?'

'To freedom,' he said without hesitation, 'and a good tomorrow.'

'I like that,' she said, and clinked his glass, leaning over him so that the bodice of her dress was at the level of his eyes. 'But why only tomorrow – why can't the good times start right now this minute?'

Mark laughed. 'All right, here's to a good tonight and a good tomorrow.'

'Mark!' Helena pursed her lips in mock disapproval, and immediately he blushed and laughed in confusion.

'Oh no, I didn't mean – that sounded dreadful. I didn't—'

'I bet you say that to all the girls.' Helena stood up quickly. She did not want to embarrass him and break the mood, so she crossed to the stove.

'It's ready,' she announced, 'if you want to eat now.'

She sat opposite him, anticipating his appetite, buttering the thick slices of bread with yellow farm butter and keeping his glass fully charged.

'Aren't you eating?'

'I'm not hungry.'

'It's good – you don't know what you are missing.'

'Better than your other girls cooked for you?' she demanded playfully, and Mark dropped his eyes to his plate and busily loaded his fork.

'There weren't any girls.'

'Oh, Mark, you don't expect me to believe that! A handsome young fellow like you, and those French girls. I bet you drove them mad.'

'We were too busy, and besides—' he stopped.

'Besides what?' she insisted, and he looked up at her, silent for a moment, and then he began to talk. It was suddenly so easy to talk to her, and he was buoyed up with his new jubilant mood and relaxed with the food and drink in his belly. He talked to her as he had never talked to another human being, and she answered him with the frankness of another man.

'Oh, Mark, that's nonsense. Not every woman is sick, it's only the street girls.'

'Yes, I know. I didn't believe every girl, but well, they are the only ones that a man can—' he broke off. 'And the others get babies,' he went on lamely.

She laughed and clapped her hands with delight. 'Oh,

my darling Mark. It's not that easy, you know. I have been married for nine years and I've never had a baby.'

'Well,' Mark hesitated. 'Well, you are different. I didn't mean you, when I said those things. I meant other girls.'

'I'm not sure if that's meant to be a compliment or an insult,' she teased again. She had known he was a virgin, of course. There was that transparent shining innocence that glowed from him, his unpractised and appealing awkwardness in the presence of women, that peculiar shyness that would pass so soon but which now heightened her excitement, rousing her in some perverse way. She knew now why some men paid huge sums of money to despoil innocence; she touched his bared forearm now, delighting in the smooth hardness of young muscle, unable to keep her hands off him.

'Oh, it was a compliment,' Mark answered her hurriedly.

'Do you like me, Mark?'

'Oh, yes. I like you more than I've ever liked any other girl.'

'You see, Mark,' she leaned closer to him, her voice sinking to a throaty whisper. 'I'm not sick, and I'm not going to have a baby – ever.' She lifted her hand and touched his cheek. 'You are a beautiful man, Mark. I liked you from the first moment I saw you coming up the walk like a stray puppy.'

She stood up slowly and crossed to the kitchen door; deliberately she turned the key and flipped up the light switch. The small room was dark, but for the shaft of light from the hallway.

'Come, Mark.' She took his hand and drew him to his feet. 'We are going to bed now.'

At the door to Mark's bedroom she reached up on tiptoe and kissed his cheek lightly, and then without another word she let his hand drop and glided away from him.

Uncertainly Mark watched her go, wanting to call to her to stay, wanting to run after her – and yet relieved that she had gone, that the headlong rush into the unknown had abruptly halted. She reached the door of her own bedroom and went through without looking back.

Torn by conflicting emotions, he turned away and went through into his own room. He undressed slowly, disappointment now stronger than relief, and while he folded his clothing, he listened to her quiet movements in the room beyond the thin wall.

He climbed at last into the narrow iron bed, and lay rigid until he had heard the light switch click next door; then he sighed and picked up the book from his bedside table; he had not yet read it through, but now the dull political text might divert his emotions enough to allow him to sleep.

The latch of his door snapped softly. He had not heard her in the passage, and she stepped into the room. She wore the gown of slippery peach-coloured satin and she had recombed her hair and retouched her cheeks and lips.

Carefully, she closed the door and crossed the room with slow swaying hips under the moving satin.

Neither of them spoke as she stopped by the side of his bed.

'Have you read it, Mark?' she asked softly.

'Not all of it.' He placed the book aside.

'Well, this isn't the time to finish it,' she said, and deliberately opened the gown, slipped it from her shoulders and dropped it over the back of the chair.

She was naked, and Mark gasped. She was so smooth. He had not expected that somehow, and he stared at her as she stood close beside him. Her skin had an olive creaminess, like old porcelain, a sheen that caught the light and glowed. Mark felt his whole body rocked by the exquisite tension of arousal, and he tried feebly to thrust it aside. He tried to think of Fergus, of the trust that had been placed in him.

'Look after Helena, lad, and yourself.'

Her breasts were big for the slimness of her body, already they hung heavily, almost overripe, drooping smooth and round with startlingly large nipples, rosy brown and big as ripe grapes. They swung weightily as she moved closer to him, and he saw that there were sparse dark hairs curling from the puckered aureole around the nipples.

There was hair also curling out in little wisps from under her arms, dark glossy hair – and a huge wild bush of it below the smooth creamy slightly bulging belly.

The hair excited him, so dark and crisp against the pale skin, and he stared at it, transfixed. All thoughts of honour and trust faded, he felt the dam wall inside him creak and strain.

She reached out and touched his bare shoulder, and it convulsed his body like a whip-lash.

'Touch me, Mark,' she whispered, and he reached out slowly, hesitantly, like a man in a trance, and touched with one finger the smooth ivory warmth of her hip, still staring fixedly at her.

'Yes, Mark. That's right.' She took his wrist and slowly drew his hand upwards, so that the tips of his fingers traced featherlike over her flank and the outline of her ribs.

'Here, Mark,' she said, 'and here.' The big dark nipples contracted at the touch of his fingers, changing shape, thrusting out and hardening, swelling and darkening. Mark could not believe it was happening, that woman's flesh could react as swiftly and dramatically as a man's.

He felt the dam break, and the flood came pouring through the breach. Too long contained, too powerful and weighty to resist, it poured through his mind and body, sweeping all restraint before it.

With a choking cry, he seized her around the waist with both arms, and drew her fiercely to him, pressing his face into the smooth soft warmth of her naked belly.

'Oh, Mark!' she cried, and her voice was hoarse and

shaking with lust and triumph, as she twisted her fingers into the soft brown hair and stooped over his head.


The days blurred and telescoped together, and the universe shut down to a tiny cottage in a sordid street. Only their bodies marked the passage of time, sleeping and waking to love until exhaustion overtook them and they slept again to wake hungry, ravenous for both food and loving.

At first he was like a bull, charging with a mindless energy and strength. It frightened her, for she had not expected such strength from that slim and graceful body. She rode with his strength, little by little controlling and directing it, changing its course, and then she began gently to teach.

Long afterwards, Mark would think back on those five incredible days and realize his great good fortune. So many young men must find their own way into the uncharted realms of physical love-making, without guide, accompanied usually by a partner making her own hesitant first journey into the unknown.

'Did you know that there is a tribe in South America, Mark, that have a rule that every married woman must take one young warrior of the tribe and teach him to do what we are doing?' she asked, as she knelt beside him in one of the intervals of quiet between the storms.

'What a shame,' he smiled lazily. 'I thought we were the first two ever to think of it.' He reached out for the pack of Needlepoint cigarettes on the bedside table and lit two of them.

Helena drew upon hers and her expression was fond and proud. He had changed so swiftly and radically in the last few days, and she was responsible for that. This new assurance, this budding strength of purpose. The shyness and reticence were fading. He spoke now in a way that he had never spoken before, calmly and with authority. Swiftly he was becoming a full man – and she had had a hand in it.

Mark believed that each new delight was the ultimate one, but she proved him wrong a dozen times. There were things that, had he heard them spoken of, might have appalled and revolted him, but when they happened the way Helena made them happen, they left only wonder and a sense of awe. She taught him a vast new respect for his own body, as it came at last fully alive, and he became aware of new broad reaches and depths of his own mind.

For five days neither of them left the cottage; then on the sixth day there was a letter brought by a uniformed postman on a bicycle and Mark, who accepted it, recognized immediately Fergus MacDonald's cramped and laboured hand. Guilt hit him like a fist in the stomach; the dream shattered like fragile crystal.

Helena sat at the newspaper-covered table in the kitchen with the now soiled peach gown open to the waist and read the letter aloud, mocking the writer with the inflection of her voice as he reported a string of petty achievements, applause at party meetings where a dozen comrades had gathered in a back room, messages of loyalty and dedication to bring back to the Central Committee, commitment to the cause and promises of action when the time to strike was ripe.

Helena mocked him, rolling her eyes and chuckling when he asked after Mark – was he well and happy, was Helena looking after him properly.

She drew deeply on the stub of the cigarette and then dropped it into the dregs of the coffee cup at her elbow, where it was extinguished with a sharp hiss. This simple action caused in Mark an unnatural reaction of revulsion.

Suddenly he saw her clearly, the sallow skin wrinkled

106

finely in the corners of her eyes as her youth cracked away like old oilpaint; the plum-coloured underlining of the eye sockets, the petulant quirk of her lips and the waspish sting to her voice.

Abruptly, he was aware of the squalid room, with the greasy smell of stale food and unwashed dishes, of the grubby and stained gown and the pendulous droop of the big ivory-coloured breasts beneath the gown.

He stood up and left the room.

'Mark, where are you going?' she called after him.

'I'm going out for a while.'

He scrubbed himself in the stained enamel bath, running the water as hot as he could bear it so that his body glowed bright pink as he towelled himself down.

At the railway booking office he stood for nearly half an hour, reading the long lists of closely printed timetables pasted to the wall.

Rhodesia. He had heard they needed men on the new copper mines. There was still a wilderness up there, far horizons and the great wild game, lakes and mountains and room to move.

He moved to the window of the booking office and the clerk looked out at him expectantly.

'One second-class single to Durban,' he said, surprising himself. He was going back to Natal, to Ladyburg. There was unfinished business there, and answers to search for. An unknown enemy to find and confront.

As he paid for the ticket with the old man's sovereigns, he had a vivid mental picture of the old man on the stoep of Andersland – with his great spiky whiskers and the old terai hat pulled low over his pale calm eyes. Mark knew then that this had been only a respite, a hiatus, in which he had found time to heal and gather courage for the task ahead.

He went back to collect his belongings. There was not much to pack, and he was in a consuming hurry now. As he swept his few spare shorts and clean socks into the cardboard suitcase, he was suddenly aware of Helena's presence, and he turned quickly.

She had bathed and dressed and she stood in the doorway watching him, her expression too calm for the loneliness in her voice.

'You are going.' It was a statement, not a question.

'Yes,' he answered simply, turning to snap the catches on the case.

'I'm coming with you.'

'No. I'm going alone.'

'But, Mark, what about me?'

'I'm sorry, Helena. I'm truly sorry.'

'But don't you see, I love you—' her voice rose in a low wail of despair. 'I love you, Mark darling, you can't go.' She spread her arms to block the doorway.

'Please, Helena. We both knew it was madness. We both knew there was nothing for us. Don't make it ugly now, please let me go.'

'No.' She covered her ears with both hands. 'No, don't talk like that. I love you. I love you.'

Gently he tried to move her from the doorway.

'I have to go. My train—'

Suddenly she flew at him, vicious as a wounded leopard. He was unprepared, and her nails raked long bloody lines across his face, narrowly missing his eyes.

'You bastard, you selfish bastard,' she shrieked. 'You're like all of them,' and she struck again, but he caught her wrists.

'You're all the same, you take – you take—'

He turned her, wildly struggling, and tipped her back on to the unmade bed. Abruptly the fight went out of her and she pressed her face into the pillow. Her sobs followed Mark as he ran down the passage, and out of the open front door.

It was more than three hundred miles to the port of Durban on the coast, and slowly the train huffed up the great barrier of the Drakensberg Mountains, worming its way through the passes until at last it plunged joyously over the escarpment and ran lightly down into the deep grassy bowl of the eastern littoral, dropping less steeply as it neared the sea, and emerged at last into the lush semi-tropical hot-house of the sea-board with its snowy white beaches and the warm blue waters of the Mozambique current.

Mark had much time to think on the journey down, and he wasted most of it in vain regrets. Helena's cries and accusations echoed through his mind while the cold grey stone of guilt lay heavily in the pit of his stomach, whenever he thought of Fergus MacDonald.

Then, as they passed through the town of Pietermaritzburg and began the last leg of the journey, Mark put aside guilt and regret, and began to think ahead.

His first intention had been to return directly to Ladyburg, but now he realized that this was folly. There was an enemy there, a murderous enemy, a hidden enemy striking from cover, a rich enemy, a powerful enemy, who could command a bunch of armed men who were ready to kill.

Mark thought then of those bloody attacks that he and Fergus had made in France. Always the first move had been to identify and mark the enemy, locate where he was lying, find his stance and assess him. How good was he, was his technique rigid, or was he quick and changeable? Was he sloppy, so that the hunters could take risks, or were risks suicidal?

'We got to try and guess the way the bastard's thinking, lad—' was Fergus' first concern, before they planned the shoot.

'I've got to find who he is,' Mark whispered aloud, 'and guess the way the bastard is thinking.'

One thing at least was clear, a hundred pounds was too high a price in blood money for such an insignificant person as Mark Anders, the only thing that could possibly make him significant in any way was his relation to the old man and to Andersland. He had been seen at Andersland by both the Hindu babu and the white foreman. Then he had brazened into the town asking questions, perusing documents. Only then had they come after him. The land was the centre of the puzzle, and he had the names of all the men who had any interest in the sale.

Mark lifted his suitcase down from the luggage rack and, holding it on his lap, hunted for and found his notebook. He read the names: DIRK COURTNEY, RONALD PYE, DENNIS PETERSEN, PIET GREYLING and his son CORNELIUS.

His first concern must be to find out all he could about those men, find out where each was lying, find his stance and assess him, decide which of them was the sniper. While he did this, he must keep his own head well down below the parapet. He must keep clear of enemy country, and enemy country was Ladyburg.

His best base would be Durban city itself; it was big enough to absorb him without comment, and, as the capital of Natal, he would have many sources of information there, libraries, government archives, newspaper offices. He began making a list of all possible sources in the back of the notebook, and immediately found himself regretting bitterly that Ladyburg itself was closed to him. Records in the Lands Office and Company Registers for the district were not duplicated in the capital.

Suddenly he had a thought. 'Damn it, what was her name!' Mark closed his eyes, and he saw again the bright, friendly and cheerful face of the little girl in the Companies office in Ladyburg.

'Mark, that's a strong romantic name—' He could even

110

hear her voice, but the train was sliding into the platform before her name came to him again.

'Marion!' and he scribbled it into the notebook.

He climbed down on to the platform, carrying his case, and joined the jostling throng of travellers and welcomers. Then he set out to find lodgings in the city.

A penny copy of the *Natal Mercury* led him through its small advertisements to a rooming house in Point Road, down by the docks. The room was small, dark and smelled of those gargantuan cockroaches that infest the city, swarming up from the sewers each evening in shiny black hordes, but the rental was only a guinea a week, and he had the use of the lavatory and shower room across the small enclosed yard.

That night he wrote a letter:

Dear Marion,

I don't suppose you remember me, my name is Mark Anders, the same as Mark Antony! I have thought of you often since I was compelled to leave Ladyburg unexpectedly before I had a chance to see you again—

Tactfully he avoided any mention of the research work he wanted undertaken. That could wait for the next letter. He had learned much about women recently, and he addressed the letter simply to 'Miss Marion, Company Registrar's Office, Ladyburg.'

Mark started the following morning at the City Library, walking up Smith Street to the four-storied edifice of the Municipal Buildings. It looked like a palace flanked by the equally imposing buildings of the Royal Hotel and the cathedral, with the garden square neatly laid out in front of it, bright with spring blooms.

He had another inspiration as he approached the librarian's desk.

'I'm doing research for a book I intend writing—'

Immediately the grey-haired lady who presided over the dim halls and ceiling-high racks of books softened her severe expression. She was a book person, and book people love other book people. Mark had the key to one of the reading rooms given him, and the back copies of all the Natal newspapers, going back to the time of the first British occupation, were put at his disposal.

There was immediately a temptation for Mark, voracious reader that he was, to lose himself in the fascination of history printed as urgent headlines – for history had been one of Mark's favourite subjects both at Ladyburg School and at University College.

He resisted the temptation and went at once to the drawers that contained the copies of the *Ladyburg Lantern and Recorder*. The first copies were already yellowing with age and tore easily, so he handled them with care.

The first mention of the name 'Courtney' leapt at him in thick black headlines on one of the earliest copies from 1879.

*Ladyburg Mounted Rifles massacred at Isandhlwana.*
*Colonel Waite Courtney and his men cut down to a man.*
*Blood-crazed Impis on the rampage.*

Mark guessed that this must refer to the founder of the family in Ladyburg; after that the name cropped up in nearly every issue, there were many Courtneys and all of them lived in the Ladyburg district, but the first mention of Dirk Courtney came in 1900.

112

Ladyburg welcomes one of its Favourite Sons.

Hero of the Anglo-Boer War Returns.

Colonel Sean Courtney purchases Lion Kop Ranch.

Ladyburg welcomes the return of one of her favourite sons after an absence of many years. There are very few of us who are not acquainted with the exploits of Colonel Sean Courtney, D.S.O., D.C.M., and all will recall the major role he played in the establishment of the prosperous gold-mining industry on the Witwatersrand . . .

A long recital of the man's deeds and reputation followed, and the report ended,

Colonel Courtney has purchased the ranch Lion Kop from the Ladyburg Farmers Bank. He intends making this his home and will plant the land to timber. Major Courtney is a widower and is accompanied by his ten-year-old son, Dirk.

The ancient report shocked Mark. He had not realized that Dirk Courtney was the son of his old General. The big, bearded, hook-nosed man he had met that snowy night in France, the man whom he had immediately respected and liked – no, more than liked. The man whose vital force and presence, together with his reputation, had roused in him an almost religious awe.

His instant reaction was to wonder if the General himself was in any way involved in the murderous attack he had survived on the escarpment; and the thought disturbed him so that he left the library and went down to the palm-lined esplanade and found a bench overlooking the quiet sheltered waters of the bay, with the great whale-backed mountain of the bluff beyond.

He watched the shipping, as he pondered the tangled

113

web that was centred in Ladyburg, where the hidden spider sat. He knew that his investigations were going to take time. The reading was a slow business and it would be days before he could expect to have a reply to his letter to Marion.

Later, in his dingy room, he counted the remaining sovereigns in his money belt, and knew that living in the city they would not last him long.

He needed a job.

The floor manager had the beer belly and flash clothing that seem always to go with salesmen in the motor industry; Mark answered his questions with extreme politeness and a false cheerfulness, but with despair below the surface.

He had trudged the city for five days, from one faint prospect of work to another.

'Times are hard,' almost every prospective employer told him at the beginning of the interview, 'and we are looking for a man with experience.'

Mark had no time to pursue his quest at the library. Now he sat on the front edge of his chair waiting to thank the man and say goodbye as soon as he was dismissed, but the man went on talking long after he should have closed the interview. He was talking about the salesmen's commission, and how it was so generous that there was plenty for two.

' – if you know what I mean.' The man winked and fitted a cigarette into his ivory holder.

'Yes, of course,' Mark nodded vehemently, having absolutely no idea what the man meant, but eager to please.

'Of course, I'd be looking after you personally. If we came to some sort of arrangement, right?'

'Right,' Mark agreed, and only then did he realize that

the manager was soliciting a kick-back off Mark's commission. He was going to get the job.

'Of course, sir.' He wanted to leap up and dance. 'I'd like to think we were equal partners.'

'Good.' Fifty per cent of Mark's commission was more than the manager had expected. 'Start Monday, nine o'clock sharp,' he said quickly, and beamed at Mark.

Mark wrung his hand gratefully, but as he was leaving the little cubicle of the office the manager called after him.

'You do have a decent suit, Anders, don't you?'

'Of course,' Mark lied quickly.

'Wear it.'

He found a Hindu tailor at the Indian market who ran up a grey three-piece suit overnight, and charged him thirty-two shillings.

'You wear clothes beautiful, sir. Like a royal duke,' the tailor told him, as he pointed Mark at the fly-blown mirror in his fitting-room, standing behind him and skilfully holding a fold of surplus material at the small of Mark's back to give the front of the suit a fashionable drape. 'You will be an extremely first class advertisement for my humble skills.'

'You can drive a car, of course?' the manager, whose name was Dicky Lancome, asked him casually as they crossed the showroom floor to the glistening Cadillac.

'Of course,' Mark agreed.

'Of course,' Dicky agreed. 'Otherwise you wouldn't have applied for a job as a car salesman, would you?'

'Of course not.'

'Hop in then,' Dicky invited. 'And whip us around the block.'

Mark reeled mentally, but his tongue was quick enough to rescue him.

'I'd prefer you to point out the special features first. I've never driven a Cadillac before.' Which was for once the literal truth. He had never driven a Cadillac, or any other motor vehicle, before.

'Righty ho,' Dicky agreed, and as they sped down the Marine Parade with Dicky whistling and tipping his hat to the pretty girls on the sidewalk, Mark watched his every action with wheel and pedal avidly.

Back at the showrooms in West Street, Dicky flicked casually through a bunch of forms.

'If you make a sale, you fill in one of these – and make sure you get the money.' Then he pulled out his watch.

'God, it's late. I've got a desperately important lunch date,' it was a little after eleven o'clock, 'very important client.' Then he dropped his voice, 'Blonde, actually. Smasher!' and he winked again. 'See you later.'

'But what about prices, and that sort of thing?' Mark called desperately after him.

'There is a pamphlet on my desk. Gives you all that stuff. Ta-ta!' and Dicky disappeared through the back door.

Mark was circling the Cadillac uncertainly, utterly engrossed with the pamphlet, muttering aloud as he tried to master the operating instructions and identify the various component parts of the vehicle from the line-drawing and numberated list, when there was a tap on his arm.

'Excuse me, young man, but are you the salesman?' Before him stood an elderly couple, the man dressed in beautifully tailored dark cloth, a carnation in his button-hole and a cane in one hand.

'We would like a drive in the motor vehicle – before we decide,' said the elegant lady beside him, smiling at Mark in a motherly fashion through the light veil that draped down over her eyes from the brimmed hat. The hat was decorated with artificial flowers, and her hair below the brim was washed silver and neatly waved.

Mark felt waves of panic threaten to engulf him. He looked about desperately for an escape, but already the gentleman was handing his wife into the front seat of the Cadillac.

Mark closed the doors on the couple, and ducked behind the machine for one last brief perusal of the operating pamphlet. 'Depress clutch pedal with left foot, engage gear lever up and left, depress accelerator pedal firmly with right foot, release clutch pedal,' he muttered, stuffed the pamphlet into his pocket and hurried to the driver's seat.

The gentleman sat forward in the centre of the back seat, both hands resting on the head of his cane, grave and attentive as a judge.

His wife beamed kindly at Mark. 'How old are you, young man?'

'Twenty, ma'am, almost twenty-one.' Mark pressed the starter and the engine growled, so she had to raise her voice.

'My,' she nodded, 'the same age as my own son.'

Mark gave her a pale and sickly grin, as he silently repeated the instructions in his mind.

'—accelerate firmly.' The engine beat rose to a deafening bellow, and Mark clung to the driving-wheel until the knuckles of both hands blanched with the pressure of his grip.

'Do you live at home?' asked his passenger.

'No, ma'am,' Mark answered and let out the clutch. The back wheels screeched like a wounded stallion, and a blue cloud blew out from behind as the entire machine seemed to rear upwards, and then hurl itself, slewing wildly, towards the street doors, leaving two long black rubber smears across the polished showroom floor.

Mark fought the wheel and the Cadillac swayed and skidded, lined up with the doors at the last possible moment and careered into the street, moving sideways like a crab. A team of horses drawing a passing coach shied out of the path of the roaring machine, and behind Mark the elderly gentleman managed to struggle up into a sitting position again and find his cane.

'Good acceleration!' Mark shouted above the roar of the engine.

'Excellent,' agreed his passenger, his eyes popping in the rear view mirror.

His wife adjusted her flowered hat that had come down over her eyes, and shook her head sadly.

'You young boys! As soon as you leave home you starve yourselves. I could tell you are living on your own – you are as thin as—'

Mark took the intersection of Smith and Aliwal at the charge, but halfway through it a heavily laden lorry lumbered across their front and Mark spun the wheel nimbly. The Cadillac changed direction ninety degrees and ducked into Aliwal on two wheels.

' – as a rake,' said the lady, holding firmly to the door handle with one hand, and with the other to her hat. 'You should come up to the house one Sunday for a decent meal.'

'Thank you, ma'am, that's very kind.'

When Mark stopped the Cadillac against the pavement in front of the showrooms at last, his hand was shaking so feverishly that he had to make a second effort to earth the magneto. He could feel the damp of nervous sweat soaking through the jacket of his new suit, and he had not the strength to let himself out of the cab.

'Incredible,' said the elderly gentleman in the back seat. 'What control, what mastery – I feel quite young again.'

'It was very nice, dear,' his wife agreed.

'We'll take her,' her husband decided impulsively, and Mark could not believe he had heard right. He had made his first sale.

'Wouldn't it be nice if this young man would come to us as a chauffeur. He is such an excellent driver.'

'No, ma'am,' Mark nearly panicked again. 'I couldn't think of leaving my job here – thank you all the same.'

'Jolly good show, old man.' Dicky Lancome folded the two five-pound notes that were his half-share of Mark's commission on the sale of the Cadillac. 'I can see a great future ahead for you.'

'Oh, I don't know,' Mark demurred modestly.

'A great future,' Dicky predicted sagely. 'But just one thing, old man – that suit,' he shuddered gently, 'let me introduce you to my tailor, now that you can afford it. No offence, of course, but that looks like you are on your way to a fancy-dress ball.'

That evening after close of business Mark hurried back to the library for the first time in a week. The librarian welcomed him with a severe expression like a disapproving school ma'am.

'I thought we had seen the last of you – that you had given up.'

'Oh no, by no means,' Mark assured her, and again she softened and handed him the key to the reading-room.

Mark had mapped out a family tree for the Courtneys in his notebook, for it was confusing. There was a brother to Sean, who was also a colonel at the end of the Boer War, but also a holder of the Victoria Cross for gallantry – a distinguished family indeed. This brother, Colonel Garrick Courtney, had gradually become a noted and then a famous author of military history and of biographies of other successful soldiers – beginning with his *With Roberts to Pretoria* and *Buller, a Fighting Soldier* and going on to *Battle for the Somme* and *Kitchener. A Life*. The books were all extensively and glowingly reviewed in the *Lantern*. The author had a single son, Michael Courtney. Prior to 1914, there were references to this son's business activities as managing director of the

Courtney Saw Mills in the Ladyburg district, and his skills as an athlete and horseman in many local meetings. Then 1917 – LADYBURG HERO DECORATED.

Captain Michael Courtney, son of Colonel Garrick Courtney V.C., was awarded the Distinguished Flying Cross for his exploits with the 21st R.F.C. Fighter Squadron in France. Captain Courtney has been credited with five 'kills' of German aircraft, and was described by his commanding officer as a 'courageous and dedicated officer of high flying skills'. Hero, son of a hero.

Then again, within months, a front-page article outlined in a square of heavy black type.

It is with great regret that we report the death in action of CAPTAIN MICHAEL COURTNEY D.F.C. It is believed that Captain Courtney was shot down in flames behind enemy lines and that his executioner was none other than the notorious Baron von Richthofen of bloody reputation. *The Ladyburg Lantern* extends its deepest and sincerest condolences to his father and family. 'A Rose plucked in full bloom.'

The activities of this branch of the family, its triumphs and tragedies, were all reported in detail – and it was the same with the Sean Courtney family for the period from the turn of the century to May of 1910.

Sean Courtney's marriage to Mrs Ruth Friedman in 1903 was described in loving detail, from the bride's dress to the icing on the cake. 'One of the flower girls was Miss Storm Friedman, aged four, who wore an exact replica of her mother's dress. She makes a pretty new sister for Master Dirk Courtney.' Again the mention of the name that truly interested Mark, and he noted it, for it was the last until May 1910.

Colonel Sean Courtney's achievements in politics and business and the more serious fields of recreation filled page after page of subsequent editions; his election to the legislative council of Natal, and later to Prime Minister Louis Botha's Cabinet; he became leader of the South Africa Party in Natal – and was a delegate to Whitehall in London, taking his entire family with him, to negotiate the terms of Union.

Sean Courtney's business interests flourished and multiplied, new sawmills, new plantations, elevation to new offices, the chairman of the first Building Society in Southern Africa, director of Union Castle Shipping Lines, head of the Government Commission on Natural Resources. Chairman of the South African Turf Club, a one hundred and fifty foot luxury yacht built for him by Thesens of Knysna, Commodore of the Royal Natal Yacht Club – but no further mention of Dirk Courtney until May 1910.

*The Ladyburg Lantern and Recorder's* front page of the edition of 12th May 1910.

*The Ladyburg Lantern* takes great pleasure in announcing that its entire paid up share capital has been acquired by Mr Dirk Courtney, who recently returned to Ladyburg after an absence of some years.

Mr Courtney tells us that the intervening years have been spent in travel, gaining both experience and capital. Clearly they were not wasted, for immediately on his arrival home, Mr Courtney purchased a controlling interest in the Ladyburg Farmers Bank for a reputed one million pounds sterling in cash.

Ladyburg and all its inhabitants are sure to benefit enormously by the vast energy, wealth and drive that Mr Dirk Courtney brings to the district.

'I intend taking a close day-to-day interest in all aspects of my companies' operations in Ladyburg,' he said, when asked of his future plans. 'Progress, Growth, Prosperity for All, are my watchwords.'

Mr Dirk Courtney, *The Ladyburg Lantern* salutes you and welcomes you as a notable ornament to our fair community.

A fter that, hardly an edition of *The Lantern* did not contain fawning eulogies of Mr Dirk Courtney – while mention of his father and family was reduced to an occasional small article in the inside pages.

To find news of Sean Courtney, Mark had to turn to the other Natal newspapers. He began with the *Natal Mercury*.

Ladyburg Mounted Rifles Sail for France
General Courtney Takes his Men to War once more.

That jolted Mark, he could remember the sea mist on the bay and the ranks of khaki-clad figures climbing the gangways, each of them burdened by kitbag and rifle. The singing, and the cries of the women, paper streamers and flower petals twisting and falling in gay and gaudy clouds about them, and the sound of the fog horns reverberating mournfully from the bluff. It was so clear in his mind still. How soon he was to follow them, after exaggerating his age to a recruiting sergeant who did not inquire too closely.

Ladyburg Rifles Badly Mauled
Attack fails at Delville Wood
General Courtney: 'I am proud of them.'

Mark felt sudden stinging tears burn his eyelids as he went slowly down the long casualty lists, pausing as he recognized a name – remembering, remembering – lost again in those terrible seas of mud and blood and suffering.

A hand touched his shoulder arousing him, and he straightened up from the reading table, bewildered at his sudden return to the present.

'We are closing now, it's after nine o'clock,' said the young assistant librarian softly. 'I'm afraid you will have to leave now.' Then she peered more closely at him. 'Are you all right? Have you been crying?'

'No.' Quickly Mark groped for his handkerchief. 'It's just the strain of reading.'

His landlady shouted down the stairs to him as he let himself into the hall.

'I've got a letter for you.'

The letter looked as thick as a complete works of William Shakespeare, but when he opened it there were only twenty-two pages, beginning:

My dear Mark,

Of course I remember you so clearly, and I have thought about you often, wondering what ever had become of you – so your welcome letter came as a marvellous surprise –

Mark felt a guilty twinge at the unrestrained joy that her letter voiced.

I realize that we know so little about each other. You did not even know my name!! Well, it is Marion Littlejohn – silly name, isn't it? I wish I could change it (that's not a hint, silly!) and I was born in Ladyburg (I'm not going to tell you when! A lady never reveals her age!) My father was a farmer, but he sold his farm five years ago, and now he works as a foreman at the sugar mill.

The entire family history, Marion's schooling, the names and estates of all her numerous relatives, Marion's hopes, dreams, aspirations – 'I'd love to travel, wouldn't you? Paris, London' – were laid out in daunting detail, much of it in parentheses and liberally punctuated with exclamation and question marks.

Isn't it strange that our names are so similar – Mark and Marion? It does sound rather grand, doesn't it?

Mark had stirrings now of alarm – it seemed he had called the whirlwind when he had merely whistled for a breeze – and yet there was an infectious gaiety and warmth that came through to him strongly, and he regretted that the girl's features were so hazy in his mind. He realized that he might easily pass her in the street without recognizing her.

He replied that night, taking special care with his penmanship. He could not yet blatantly come to the true purpose of his letters, but hinted vaguely that he was considering writing a book, but that it would require much research in the Ladyburg archives, and that as yet he did not have either the time nor the capital to make the journey, and he concluded by wondering if she did not have a photograph of herself that he might have.

Her reply must have been written and posted the same day as his letter was received.

'My dearest Mark—' He had been promoted from 'Dear Mark'.

There was a photograph accompanying the twenty-five pages of closely written text. It was stiffly posed, a young girl in party clothes with a fixed nervous smile on her face, staring into the camera as though it were the muzzle of a loaded howitzer. The focus was slightly misty, but it was good enough to remind him what she looked like, and Mark felt a huge swell of relief.

She was a little plump, but she had a sweet heart-shaped face with a wide friendly mouth and well-spaced intelligent eyes, an alert and lively look about her; and he knew already that she was educated and reasonably well read – and desperately eager to please.

On the back of the photograph he had received further promotion:

> To darling Mark,
> With much love,
> Marion.

Under her name were three neat crosses. The letter was bursting with unbounded admiration for his success as a Cadillac salesman, and with awe for his aspirations to be a writer.

She was anxious to be of help in his researches, he had only to let her know what information he needed. She herself had access to all the Governmental and Municipal archives ('and I won't charge you a search fee this time!'), her elder sister worked in the editorial office of the *Ladyburg Lantern*, and there was an excellent library in the Town Hall building where Marion was well known and where she loved to browse – please would he let her help?

One other thing, did he have a photograph of himself, she would love to have a reminder of him.

For half a crown Mark had a photograph taken of himself at a beachfront open-air studio, dressed in his new suit, and with a straw boater canted at a rakish angle over one eye and a daredevil grin on his face.

> My darling Mark,
> How handsome you are!! I have shown all my friends and they are all quite envious.

She had some of the information he requested, and more would follow.

From Adams Booksellers in Smith Street, Mark purchased a bulky leather-bound notebook, three enormous sheets of cardboard, and a large-scale survey map of Natal and Zululand. These he pinned up on the walls of his room, where he could study them while lying in bed.

On one sheet he laid out the family trees of the Courtneys, the Pyes and the Petersens, all three names associated with the purchase of Andersland on the documents he had seen in Ladyburg Deeds Office.

On one other sheet he built up a pyramid of companies and holdings controlled by the Ladyburg Farmers Bank, and on another he pyramided in the same way the companies and properties of General Sean Courtney's holding company, Natal Timber and Estates Ltd.

On the map he carefully shaded in the actual land holdings of the two groups, red for General Courtney and blue for those controlled by his son, Dirk Courtney Esquire.

It gave him new resolution and determination to continue his search when he carefully shaded with blue the long irregular shape of Andersland, with its convoluted boundary that followed the south bank of the river; and when he had done so and wiped the crayon from his fingers, he was left with the bitter lees of anger in his mouth, a reaffirmation of his conviction that the old man would never have let it go – they would have had to kill him first.

The anger was with him again whenever he filled in another section of the map, or when he lay in bed each night, smoking a last cigarette and studying the blue and red patchwork of Courtney holdings. He smiled grimly when he thought what Fergus MacDonald would say about such wealth in the hands of a single father and son, and then he wrote in the leather-bound notebook any new information that he had accumulated during the day.

He would switch out the light then and lie long awake, and often, when at last he slept, he dreamed of Chaka's

Gate, of the great cliffs guarding the river and the tumbled wilderness beyond the gates, that concealed a lonely grave. A grave unmarked, overgrown now with the lush restless vegetation of Africa – or, perhaps, long ago dug open by hyena or the other scavengers.

One day, when Mark spent his customary evening's study in the library reading-room, he turned first to the recent issues of the *Ladyburg Lantern*, searching through those editions covering the week following his flight from Ladyburg, and he almost missed the few lines on an inside page.

Yesterday, the funeral service was held of Mr Jacob Henry Rossouw at the Methodist Church in Pine Street. Mr Rossouw fell to his death in the gorge of the Baboon Stroom below the new railway bridge while hunting with a party of his friends.

Mr Rossouw was a bachelor employed by the Zulu-land Sugar Co. Ltd. The funeral service was attended by the Chairman of the Company, Mr Dirk Courtney, who made a short but moving tribute at the graveside, once again illustrating his deep concern for even the humblest of the employees of his many prosperous enterprises. 'Greatness shows itself in small ways.'

The date coincided neatly with his escape from the valley. The man might have been one of his hunters, perhaps the one who had caught his damaged ankle as he hung from the goods truck. If he was, then the connection with Dirk Courtney was direct. Slowly Mark was twisting a rope together, but he needed a head for the noose.

Yet, in one direction, Mark felt easier. There seemed to exist a deep rift between father and son, between General Sean Courtney and Dirk. None of their companies over-lapped, none of their directorships interlocked, and each pyramid of companies stood alone and separated. This separation seemed to extend beyond finance or business, and Mark had found no evidence of any contact between the two men at the social level, in fact active hostility between them was indicated by the sudden change in the *Ladyburg Lantern's* attitude to the father, once the son took control of its editorial policy.

Yet he was not entirely convinced. Fergus MacDonald had repeatedly warned him of the perfidious cunning of the bosses, of all wealthy men. 'They will go to any lengths to hide their guilt, Mark, no trick is too low or despicable to cover the stains of honest workers' blood on their hands.'

Perhaps Mark's first concern must be to establish beyond doubt that he was hunting only one man. Then, of course, the next move must be to go back to Ladyburg, to try and provoke another attack – but this time he would be ready for it and have some idea from which direction it would come. His mind went back to the way in which he and Fergus MacDonald had used Cuthbert, the dummy, to draw fire and force the enemy to reveal himself, and he grinned ruefully at the thought that this time he must do Cuthbert's job himself. He felt for the first time a fear he had not known in France before a shoot, for he must go out against something more formidable and ruthless than he had ever believed possible before, and the time was fast approaching.

He was distracted then by another massive epistle from Ladyburg, one that gave him honest cause for delaying direct action.

My dearest darling,
What great news I have for you!! If the mountain will not come to Mohammed, then he (or she!) must go to the mountain. My sister and her husband are going to Durban for four days' holiday, and they have asked me to join them. We will arrive on the fourteenth – and will be staying at the Marine Hotel on the Marine Parade – won't we be posh!

Mark surprised himself by the strength of his pleasure and anticipation. He had not realized the affection that he had slowly accumulated at such long remove for this willing and friendly creature. He was surprised again when he met her, both of them dressed with obvious pains and attention to detail, both in an agony of shyness and restraint under the surveillance of Marion's sister.

They sat on the hotel veranda and stiffly sipped tea, making small talk with the sister while surreptitiously examining each other over the rim of their cups.

Marion had lost weight, Mark saw immediately, but would never know that the girl had almost starved herself to do so in anticipation of this moment; and she was pretty – much prettier than he remembered or than her photograph suggested. More important was her transparent wholesomeness and warmth. Mark had been a lonely boy for most of his life, but more particularly so in these last weeks, living in his small dingy room with only the cockroaches and his plans for company.

Now he reacted to her like a traveller coming in out of the snow-storm responds to the tavern fire.

The sister took her duties as chaperone seriously at first, but she was only five or six years older than Mark, and perceptive enough to be aware of the younger people's attraction for each other and to recognize the essential decency of the boy. She was also young enough and herself so recently married as to have sympathy for them.

'I would like to take Marion for a drive – we wouldn't be gone very long.' Marion turned eyes as soulful and pleading as those of a dying gazelle on her sister.

'Oh please, Lyn.'

The Cadillac was a demonstration model, and Mark had personally supervised while two of the Zulu employees at Natal Motors had burnished its paintwork to a dazzle.

He drove down as far as the mouth of the Umgeni River, with Marion sitting close and proud and pretty beside him.

Mark felt as good as he ever had in his life; dressed in fashionable style, with gold in his pocket, a big shining automobile under him and a pretty adoring girl beside him.

Adoring was the only word to describe Marion's attitude towards him. She could hardly drag her eyes from his face for a moment, and she glowed every time he glanced across at her.

She had never imagined herself beside such a handsome, sophisticated beau. Not even her most romantic daydreams had ever included a shining Cadillac, and a decorated war hero.

When he parked off the road and they picked a path through the densely overgrown dunes down to the river mouth, she clung to his arm like a drowning sailor.

The river was in spate from some upland rainstorm; half a mile wide and muddy brown as coffee, it surged and swirled down to meet the green thrust of the sea in a leaping ridge of white water. Carried down on the brown water were the debris of the flood, and the carcasses of drowned beasts.

A dozen big black sharks were there to scavenge, pushing high up the river, their dark triangular fins knifing and circling.

Mark and Marion sat side by side on a dune overlooking the estuary.

'Oh,' sighed Marion, as though her heart would break, 'we've only got four days together.'

'Four days is a long time,' Mark laughed at her, 'I don't know what we are going to do with it all.'

They spent nearly every hour of it together. Dicky Lancome was most understanding with his star salesman. 'Just show your face here for a few minutes every morning, to keep the boss happy, then you can slip off. I'll hold the fort for you.'

'What about the demonstration model?' Mark asked boldly.

'I'll tell him you are making a sale to a rich sugar farmer. Take it, old chap, but for God's sake, don't wrap it round a tree.'

'I don't know how I'll ever repay you, Dicky, really I don't.'

'Don't worry, old boy, we'll think of a way.'

'I won't ask again, it's just that this girl is really special.'

'I understand.' Dicky patted his shoulder in a paternal fashion. 'Most important thing in life – a likely bit of crumpet. My heart goes out to you, old son. I'll be cheering you on in spirit every inch of the way.'

'It's not like that, Dicky,' Mark denied, blushing fiercely.

'Of course not, it never is. But enjoy it anyway,' and Dicky winked lasciviously.

Mark and Marion – she was right, it did sound rather grand – spent their days wandering hand in hand through the city. She was delighted by its bustle and energy, enchanted by its sophistication, by its culture, its museums and tropical gardens, by its playground beachfront with myriad fairy lights, the open-air concerts in the gardens of the old fort, by the big departmental stores in West Street, Stuttafords and Ansteys, their windows packed with expensive imported merchandise, by the docks with great merchant ships lining the wharf and the steam cranes huffing and creaking above them.

They watched the Indian fishermen running their surf-boats out from the glistening white beach, through the marching lines of green surf to lay their long nets in a wide semi-circle out into deep water. Then Marion hitched up her skirts and Mark rolled his trousers to the knee to help the half-naked fishermen draw in the long lines, until at last a shimmering silver mound of fish lay on the boat, still quivering and twitching and leaping in the sunlight.

They ate strawberry-flavoured icecream out of crisp yellow cones, and they rode in an open rickshaw down the

Marine Parade, drawn by a leaping howling Zulu dressed in an incredible costume of feathers and beads and horns.

One night they joined Dicky Lancome and a languid siren to whom he was paying court, and the four of them ate grilled crayfish and danced to a jazz band at the Oyster Box Hotel at Umhlanga Rocks, and came roaring home in a Cadillac, tiddly and happy and singing, with Dicky driving like Nuvorelli, rocketing the big car over the dusty rutted road, and Mark and Marion cuddling blissfully in the back seat.

In the lobby of the hotel, under the watchful eye of the night clerk who was poised to intercept Mark if he tried for the elevator, they whispered goodnight to each other.

'I have never been so happy in all my life,' she told him simply, and stood on tip-toe to kiss him full on the lips.

Dicky Lancome had disappeared with both Cadillac and lady-friend, probably to some dark and secluded parking place along the sea front, and as Mark walked home alone through the deserted midnight streets, he thought about Marion's words and found himself agreeing. He could not remember being so happy either, but then, he grinned ruefully, it hadn't been a life crowded with wild happiness up to then. To a pauper, a shilling is a fortune.

It was their last day together, and the knowledge weighted their pleasure with poignancy. Mark left the Cadillac at the end of a narrow track in the sugar cane fields and they climbed down to the long white curve of snowy sand beach, guarded at each end by rocky headlands.

The sea was so clear that from the tall dunes they could see deep down to the reefs and sculptured sand banks below the surface. Farther out, the water shaded to a deep indigo blue, that met at last a far horizon piled with a mountainous range of cumulus clouds, purple, blue and silver in the brilliant sunlight.

They walked down barefooted through the crunching sand, carrying the picnic basket that Marion's hotel had prepared for them and a threadbare grey blanket from Mark's bed, and it seemed that they were the only two persons in the world.

They changed into swimming costumes, modestly separating to each side of a dense dark green milk-wood bush, and then they ran laughing into the warm clear water at the edge of the beach.

The thin black cotton of Marion's costume clung wetly to her body, so that it seemed that she were naked, although clothed from mid thigh to neck, and when she pulled the red rubber bathing cap from her head and shook out the thick tresses of her hair, Mark found himself physically roused by her for the first time.

Somehow the pleasure he had taken in her up until then had been that of friendship, and companionship. Her patent adoration had filled some void in his soul, and he had felt protective, almost brotherly towards her.

She sensed instantly, with some feminine instinct, the change in him. The laughter died on her lips, and her eyes went grave and there were shades in them of fear or apprehension – but she turned to face him, lifting her face to him, seeming to steel herself with a conscious act of courage.

They lay side by side on the grey blanket, in the heavy shade of the milk bush, and the midday was heavy and languorous with heat and the murmur of insects.

The wet bathing-suits were cool against their hot skins, and when Mark gently peeled hers away, her skin was damp beneath his fingers, and he was surprised to find her body so different from Helena's. Her skin was clear milky white, tipped with palest pink, lightly sugared with white beach sand, and the hair of her body was fine as silk, light golden brown and soft as smoke. Her body was soft also, with the gentle yielding spring of woman's flesh, unlike the lean hard muscle of Helena's, and it had a different feel to it, a plasticity that intrigued and excited him.

133

Only when she gasped, and bit her lip and then turned her face and hid it against his neck, did Mark realize suddenly, through the mists of his own arousal, that all the skills Helena had taught him were not moving Marion, as they were him. Her body was rigid, and her face pale and tensed.

'Marion, are you all right?'

'It's all right, Mark.'

'You don't like this?'

'It's the first time it's ever happened—'

'We can stop—'

'No.'

'We don't have to—'

'No, Mark, go on. It's what you want.'

'But you don't want it.'

'I want what you want, Mark. Go on. It's for you.'

'No—'

'Go on, Mark, please go on.' And now she looked at him and he saw her expression was pitiful, her eyes swimming with bright tears and her lips quivering.

'Oh, Marion, I'm sorry.' He recoiled from her, horrified by the misery he saw reflected in her expression, but immediately she followed him throwing both arms around his neck, lying half on top of him.

'No, Mark – don't be sorry. I want you to be happy.'

'It won't make me happy – if you don't want to.'

'Oh, Mark, don't say that. Please don't say that – all I want in the world is to make you happy.'

She was brave and enduring, holding him tightly over her, both arms locked around his neck, her body rigid but spread compliantly, and for Mark the ordeal was almost as painful; he suffered for her as he felt the tremble of locked nerves and the small sounds of pain and tension that she tried to keep deep in her throat.

Mercifully for both of them, it was swiftly ended, but still she clung to him.

'Was it good for you, Mark my darling?'

'Oh, yes,' he assured her vehemently. 'It was wonderful.'

'I want so much to be good for you in every way, my darling. Always and in every way, I want to be good for you.'

'It was the best thing in my life,' he told her, and she stared into his eyes for a moment, searching for assurance, and finding it because she wanted it so terribly.

'I'm so glad, darling,' she whispered, and drew his head down on to her damp warm bosom, so soft and pink and comforting. Holding him like that, she began to rock him gently, the way a mother rocks her child. 'I'm so glad, Mark, and it will be better and better. I'll learn, you see if I don't, and I'll try so hard for you, darling, always.'

Driving home slowly in the dusk, she sat proudly next to him on the wide leather seat, and there was a new air about her, an air of confidence and achievement, as though she had grown from child to matron in the space of a few short hours.

Mark felt a rush of deep affection for her. He felt that he wanted to protect her, to keep that goodness and sweetness from souring, to protect her from unhappiness and wanton damage. For a fleeting moment he felt regret that she had not been able to feed that raging madness of his body, and regret also that he had not been able to lead her through the storm to the same peace. Perhaps that would come, perhaps they would find the way together – and if they didn't, well it wasn't that important. The important thing was the sense of duty he felt towards this woman; she had given him everything of which she was capable, and it was his duty now to give back in equal measure – to protect and cherish her.

'Marion, will you marry me?' he asked quietly, and she began to cry softly, nodding her head vehemently through the tears, unable to speak.

Marion's sister, Lynette, was married to a young lawyer from Ladyburg and the four of them sat up late that night discussing the betrothal.

'Pa won't give permission for you to marry before you are twenty-one, you know how Peter and I had to wait.'

Peter Botes, a serious young man, nodded wisely and placed his finger tips together carefully. He had thin sandy hair, and was as pompous as a judge in scarlet.

'It won't do any harm to wait a few years—'

'Years?' wailed Marion.

'You're only nineteen,' Peter reminded her. 'And Mark will need to build up some capital before he takes on the responsibility of a family.'

'I can go on working,' Marion came in hotly.

'They all say that.' Peter waggled his head sagely. 'And then two months later there's a baby on the way.'

'Peter!' His wife rebuked him primly, but he went on calmly.

'And now, Mark, what about your prospects? Marion's father will want to know.'

Mark hadn't expected to present an account of his affairs, and on the spur of the moment he could not be certain if his total worth was forty-two pounds twelve shillings – or seven and sixpence.

He saw them off on the Ladyburg train the next morning, with a long lingering embrace and a promise to write every day, while Marion swore she would work at filling her bottom drawer, and at altering her father's prejudice against early marriage. Walking back from the railway, Mark remembered, for no apparent reason, a spring morning in France coming back out of the line to go into reserve, and his shoulders went back and his step quickened and became springy and elastic once more. He was out of the line, and he had survived – that was as far as he could think at that moment.

D icky Lancome's polished elastic-sided boots were propped on the desk in front of him and fastidiously crossed at the ankles. He looked up from his newspaper, a teacup held in the other hand with little finger extended delicately.

'Hail the conquering hero comes, his weary weapon slung over his shoulder.'

'Oh come on, Dicky!'

' – weak at the knees, bloodshot eye and fevered brow—'

'Any calls?' Mark asked seriously.

'Ah, the giant mind now turns to the more mundane aspects of life.'

'Play the game, Dicky.' Mark riffled quickly through a small pile of messages that awaited him.

'A surfeit of love, a plethora of passion, an overdose of crumpet, a genital hangover.'

'What's this? I can't read your scrawl.' Mark averted his eyes, concentrating on his reading.

'Mark my words, Mark, that young lady has got the brood lust. If you turn your back on her for ten minutes, she will be up the nearest tree building a nest.'

'Cut it out, Dicky.'

'That's precisely what you should do, old boy, unless you can face the prospect of her dropping your whelps all over the scenery.' Dicky shuddered theatrically. 'Never ride in a saloon if you can drive a sports model, old chap, which reminds me,' he dropped the newspaper, checked the watch from his waistcoat pocket, 'I have this important client.' He inspected his glossy boots a moment, flicked them lightly with the handkerchief from his breast pocket, stood up and adjusted the strawbasher on his head and winked at Mark. 'Her husband's gone up country for a week. Hold the fort, old boy, it's my turn now.'

He disappeared through the office door into the show-room, and then reappeared instantly, an expression of horror on his face. 'Oh God, customers! Get after them, Mark my boy, I'm taking the back door,' and he was gone, leaving only the faint perfume of brilliantine lingering on the air.

Mark checked his tie in the sliver of broken mirror wedged in the frame of the window, and adjusted his welcoming smile as he hurried to the door – but at the threshold he stopped as though coming up at the end of a chain. He was listening with the stillness and concentration of a wild gazelle, listening with every fibre and every quivering nerve end to a sound of such aching and penetrating beauty that it seemed to freeze his heart. It lasted only a few seconds, but the sound of it shimmered and thrilled in the air for long seconds afterwards, and only then did Mark's heart beat again, surging heavily against his rib cage.

The sound was the laughter of a girl. It was as though the air around Mark had thickened to honey, for it dragged heavily at his legs as he started forward, and it required a physical effort to draw it down into his lungs.

From the doorway he looked into the showroom. In the centre of the wide floor stood the latest demonstration model Cadillac, and beside it stood a couple.

The man had his back to Mark, and left only the impression of massive size, a towering figure dressed in dark cloth. Beside him, the girl was dainty, almost ethereal, she seemed to float, light and lovely as a hummingbird on invisible wings.

The earth tilted beneath Mark's feet as he gazed at her.

Her head was thrown back to look up at the man. Her throat was long and smooth, balancing the small head with its huge dark eyes and the laughing mouth, small white regular teeth beyond pink lips, a fine bold brow, pale and wide above those haunting eyes – and all of it crowned by a heart-stopping tumble of thick lustrous hair, hair so black that its waves and falls seemed to be sculptured from freshly oiled ebony.

She laughed again, a lovely joyous ripple of sound, and she reached up to touch the man's face. Her hand was narrow, with long tapered fingers, strong capable-looking hands – so that Mark realized that his first impression had been wrong.

The girl was small only in comparison to the man, and her poise heightened the illusion. However, Mark saw now that she was tall, but graceful as a papyrus stem in the wind, supple and slim, with tiny waist and long legs beneath the light floating material of her skirt.

With her fingertips, she traced the jawline of the man; tilting her head on its long swanlike neck, her beauty was almost unbearable, as her huge eyes shone now with love, and the line of the lips was soft with love.

'Oh Daddy, you are an old-fashioned, grumpy old bear.' She spun away from him, lightly as a ballerina, and struck an exaggerated pose beside the huge glistening machine, putting on a comic French accent. '*Regarde! Mon cher papa, c'est très chic—*'

The man growled. 'I don't trust these fancy new machines. Give me a Rolls.'

'Rolls?' cried the girl, pouting dramatically, 'they're so staid! So biblical! Darling Daddy, this is the twentieth century, remember?' Then she drooped like a dying rose in a vase. 'How could I hold my head up among my friends if you force me to ride in one of those great sombre coffins?'

At that instant she noticed Mark standing in the doorway of the sales office, and her entire mien changed, the carriage of head and body, the expression of mouth and eye flowing instantly from clown to lady.

'Pater,' she said softly, the voice cultivated and the eye cool as it flicked over Mark, a steady encompassing sweep from his head to his feet. 'I think the sales person is here.'

She turned away, and Mark felt his heart convulse again at the way her hip swung and pushed beneath the skirt – and he saw for the first time the cheeky, challenging roll of her small rounded backside as she walked slowly around the Cadillac, calm and aloof, not glancing in his direction again.

Mark stared at her, with fascination, all his emotions in upheaval. He had never seen anything so beautiful, so completely captivating in all his life.

The man had turned and was glaring at him angrily. He seemed, as the girl had teased him, to be biblical. A gaunt and towering figure with shoulders wide as the gallows tree and the big fierce head exaggerated in size by the slightly twisted hooked nose and the dark thick bush of beard, shot through with grey.

'I know you, dammit!' he growled. The face had been burned almost black by twenty thousand suns, but there were deep white creases in the corners of his eyes and the skin in a line below the thick curls of his silvering hair was white also, protected by the band of a hunter's hat – or a uniform cap.

Mark roused himself, tearing his eyes off the girl, for the fresh shock of recognition. At the time he could only believe it was some monstrous coincidence – but in the years that followed he would know differently. The threads of their lives were plaited, and intertwined. But in this instant the shock, coming so close on the other, unsettled him and his voice croaked.

'Yes, General Courtney, I am—'

'Don't tell me, goddammit,' the General cut in, his voice like the crack of a Mauser shooting from cover, and Mark felt his spirit quail before the expression on his face; it was the most formidable he had ever confronted.

'I know – the name is right there!' he glowered at Mark. 'I never forget a face.' The tremendous force and presence of the man threatened to swamp him.

'It's a sign of old age, Pater,' said the girl coolly, glancing over her shoulder without smile or expression.

'Don't you say that, girl,' the man rumbled like an active volcano. 'Don't you dare say that.' He took a threatening step towards Mark, the dark brow corrugated and the blue eyes cutting into his soul like a surgeon's knives. 'It's the eyes! Those eyes.'

Mark retreated a hurried step before the limping, mountainous advance, not quite sure what to expect, but ready to believe that Sean Courtney might at any moment lunge at him with the heavy ebony cane he carried, so murderous seemed his anger.

'General—'

'Yes!' Sean Courtney snapped his fingers with a crack like a breaking oak branch, and the scowl smoothed away, the blue eyes crinkling into a smile of such charisma, of such infectious and conspiratorial glee, that Mark had to smile back at him.

'Anders,' he said. 'Anders and MacDonald. Martin? Michael? No, Mark Anders!' And he clenched his fist and struck his own thigh. 'Old, is it? Girl – who said old?'

'Pater, you are a marvel.' She rolled her eyes, but Sean Courtney was advancing on Mark, seizing his hand in a grip that made the bones creak until he recovered himself and squeezed back, matching the big man's grip.

'It was the eyes,' laughed Sean. 'You've changed so much from that day, that night—' and the laughter dried, as he remembered the boy in the stretcher, pale and moribund, smeared with mud and thick drying blood, and heard again his own voice, 'He's dead!' He drove back the image.

'How are you now, my boy?'

'I'm fine, sir.'

'I didn't think you were going to pull through.' Sean peered closely at him. 'I'll grant you seem to have made it with all colours flying. How many did you collect, and where?'

'Two, sir, high in the back.'

'Honourable scars, my boy, we'll compare notes one day.' And then he scowled again, horrendously. 'You got the gong, didn't you?'

'Yes, sir.'

'Good, you never know in this man's army. I wrote the citation that night, but you never know. What did they give you?' Sean smiled his relief.

'The M.M., sir. I got it at the hospital in England.'

'Excellent. That's good!' he nodded, and he let go of Mark's hand, turning to the girl again.

'Darling, this gentleman was with me in France.'

'How nice.' She touched the design on the radiator of the car with one finger, as she drifted past it, not glancing back at them. 'Do you think we might have a drive now, Pater?'

Mark hurried to the back door to hold it open. 'I'll drive,' she said, and waited for him to jump to the driver's door.

'The starter button is here—' he explained.

'Thank you, I know. Sit in the back, please.'

She drove like a man, very fast but skilfully, picking a tight line into the corners and using the gearbox to brake, double declutching with dancing feet on the pedals, and hitting the shift with a quick sure hand.

Beside her the General sat with the set to his shoulders of a younger man.

'You drive too fast,' he growled, the ferocious tone given the complete lie by the fond smile he turned on her.

'And you're an old fusspot, Daddy,' she laughed again; the thrill of it sang in Mark's ears as she hurled the big powerful machine into the next bend.

'I didn't beat you enough when you were young.'

'Well, it's too late now.' She touched his cheek with her free hand.

142

'Don't bank on that, young lady – don't ever take bets on that.'

Shaking his head in mock despair, but with the adoration still glowing in his eyes, the General heaved himself around in the seat and subjected Mark to another dark penetrating scrutiny.

'You don't turn out at the weekly parades.'

'No, sir.'

'It's an hour on Friday evenings – half an hour square-bashing and then a lecture.'

'Yes, sir?'

'Good fun, really. Tremendous spirit, even though we have combined with the other peace-time regiments now.'

'Yes, sir.'

'I'm the Colonel-in-Chief,' Sean chuckled. 'They couldn't get rid of me that easily.'

'No, sir.'

'We have a monthly shoot – good prizes, and a barbecue afterwards.'

'Is that so, sir?'

'We are sending a team to shoot for the Africa Cup this year, all expenses paid. Marvellous opportunity for the lucky lads who get chosen.'

'I'm sure, General.'

Sean waited for more, but Mark was silent. He could not meet the big man's fierce, unrelenting gaze, and he shifted his eyes – catching as he did so the girl's face reflected in the rear-view mirror.

She was watching him intently, with an unfathomable expression – contempt perhaps, dry amusement, maybe, or something else – something much more intriguing or dangerous. For the split part of an instant, their eyes met, and then her head turned away on the tall graceful column of her neck. The dark shining hair was brushed away from the nape, and there at the juncture with pale skin, the hair

143

was fine and silky, a tiny whorl of it like a question mark at the back of her small sculptured ear.

Mark had an almost insane desire to lean forward and press his lips to it. The thought struck like a physical blow in his groin, and he felt the nerves along his spine racked out cruelly. He realized suddenly then, with a shock that made his senses tilt again, that he was in love with her.

'I want to win that cup,' said the General softly, watching him. 'The regiment has never won it before.'

'I've rather had enough of uniform and war, General.' Mark forced his eyes back to meet the General's. 'But I do wish you good luck.'

The chauffeur held the rear door of the Rolls Silver Wraith open, and Sean Courtney lowered himself into the seat beside his daughter. He lifted his right hand in a brief, almost military, salute at the young man on the pavement and the car pulled smoothly away.

The instant they were alone, his daughter let out a girlish squeal of delight and threw both arms around his neck, ruffling his beard and his heart with her kisses.

'Oh, Daddy, darling, you spoil me!'

'Yes, I do – don't I?'

'Irene will turn bright green and curl up like an anchovy. I love you, my kind and beautiful Daddy. Her father has never bought her a Cadillac!'

'I like that lad, he's one of the bright ones.'

'The sales person? I hadn't really noticed.' She released her grip and sat back in the seat.

'He's got heart.' He was silent a moment then, remembering the snow falling silently across a shell-ravaged hill in France. 'He's got the guts and brightness for better things than selling motor cars.' Then he grinned mischievously, looking young enough to be her brother. 'And I'd love to see Hamilton's face when we take the Africa Cup away from him.'

Beside him Storm Courtney was silent, her hand still in the crook of her father's arm while she wondered what had disturbed her about Mark Anders. She decided it was his eyes – those serene yellow eyes, calm but watchful, floating like golden moons.

Involuntarily, Mark braked the big car almost to a standstill before the white gates. They were tall twin columns, plastered and white-washed with the Zulu name in raised letters on each: EMOYENI – it was a lovely haunting name, the place of the wind, and on the crest of the hills above Durban town, it would indeed receive the cool blessing of the sea breezes during the sweltering summer months. The swinging portion of the gate was two racks of heavy cast-iron spears, but they stood open now, and Mark crossed the iron grid which would prevent hooved animals entering or escaping and started up the gentle curve of the driveway, butter yellow flint pebbles carefully raked and freshly watered, set on each side with deep beds of cannas which were now in full bloom. They had been arranged in banks of solid colour, scarlet and yellow and white, dazzling in the bright sunshine, and beyond them were lush lawns of deep tropical green, mown carpet-smooth but studded with clumps of indigenous trees which had obviously been spared for their size or beauty or unusual shape. They were festooned with garlands of lianas, the ubiquitous monkey rope plants of Natal, and even as Mark watched, a small blue-grey vervet monkey dropped lithely down one of the living ropes, and, with its back arched like a cat and its long tail held high in mock alarm, bounded across an open stretch of lawn until it reached the next clump of trees where it shot to the highest branches and chattered insolently at the slowly passing car.

Mark knew from his investigation that this was merely the Courtney town house, the main family home was at Ladyburg, and he had not expected anything like this splendour. And yet why not, he grinned wryly; the man had everything in the world, this was a mere pied-à-terre. He twisted his head to look back. The gates were out of sight behind him now, and there was still no sign of the house ahead. He was surrounded by a fantasy landscape, half wild and yet lovingly groomed and tended, and now he saw the reason for the animal grid at the main gates.

Small herds of semi-domesticated game cropped at the short grass of the lawn or stood and watched the passing car with mild curiosity. He saw graceful golden brown impala with snowy bellies and spindly back-curved horns, a dainty blue duiker as big as a fox terrier with pricked-up ears and bright button eyes; an eland bull with hanging dewlap, thick twisted horns arming the short heavy head, and a barrel body heavy as a pedigree Afrikander bull.

He crossed a low bridge over the narrow neck of an artificial lake. The blue water lotus blooms stood high above their huge round green leaves that floated flat on the surface. Their perfume was light and sweet and nostalgic on the bright warm air, and the dark torpedo shapes of bass hung suspended in the clear water below the sheltering lotus leaves.

On the edge of the lake, a black and white spur-winged goose spread its wings, as wide as the reach of a man's arms, and pressed forward with snakelike neck and pink wattled head, threatening flight at the intrusion; then, thinking better of such effort, it furled the great wings again and waggled its tail, satisfied with a single harsh honk of protest as the Cadillac passed.

The roof of the house showed through the trees ahead now, and it was tiled in candy pink, towered and turreted and ridged, like a Spanish palace. The last curve of the driveway brought Mark out into full view of the building. Before it lay an open expanse of blazing flowerbeds. The colour was so vibrant and so concentrated that it daunted the eye, and was relieved only by the tall soft ostrich feathers of spray that poured high into the air from the fountains set in the centre of four round ponds, parapeted in stone. The breeze blew soft wisps of spray like smoke across the flowerbeds, wetting the blooms and enhancing the already dazzling colour.

The house was two stories high, with random towers breaking the solid silhouette and columns, twisted like candy sticks, ornamenting the entrance and supporting the window lintels; it was painted white, and it shone in the sunlight like a block of ice.

It should have given the impression of solid size and ostentatious display, but the design was so cunning that it seemed light as a French pastry – a gay and happy house, built in a spirit of fun and probably of love. A rich man's gift to a lovely woman, for the feminine touch was every-where evident, and the great masses of flowers, the fountains and peacocks and marble statues seemed right, the only setting for such a structure.

Slowly, awed and enchanted, Mark let the Cadillac roll down the last curve of the driveway, and the light faint cries of female voices caught his attention.

The tennis courts stood at the end of the lawns, and there were women at play, their white dresses sparkling in the sun, their limbs flashing as they ran and swerved and struck at the ball. Their voices and laughter were sweet and melodious in the warm hush of the tropical mid-morning.

Mark left the car, and started across the lawn towards the courts. There were other female figures, also white-clad, that lolled in deck-chairs in the shade of the banyan trees, watching the play and conversing languidly as they sipped at long frosted glasses, waiting their turn on the courts.

None of them noticed Mark until he was on the edge of their group.

'Oh, I say, girls.' One of them turned quickly in her chair, and appraised Mark with eyes suddenly no longer bored, but clear blue and acquisitive. 'A man! We *are* in luck.'

Instantly the other three changed, each reacting differently: one exaggerating her indifferent and indolent loll in the low chair, another tugging at her skirt with one hand and pushing at her hair with the other, smiling brightly and sucking in her tummy.

They were all young and sleek as cats, glossy with youth and health and that elusive but unmistakable aura of wealth and breeding.

'And what is your pleasure, sir?' asked the one with blue eyes. She was the prettiest of the four, with fine pale golden hair in a halo around the small neat head and good white teeth as she smiled.

Mark felt discomforted under their stares, especially when the speaker turned further in her chair, and slowly uncrossed and crossed her legs, managing to give Mark a flash of white silk panties under the short skirt.

'I am looking for Miss Storm Courtney.'

'God,' said the smiler. 'They all want Storm – why don't any of them ever want me?'

'Storm!' The blonde called out to the court.

Storm Courtney was about to serve, but the call distracted her and she glanced across. She saw Mark and her expression did not change, her attention switched back to the game. She threw the ball high and swung overhand at it, the stroke fluid and controlled. The racket twanged sharply, and the movement threw her white cotton skirt high against the back of her thighs. Her legs were beautifully moulded, slim ankles and gently swelling calves, knees marked only by symmetrical dimples.

She spun lightly and caught the return of the ball, a long lightly tanned arm flashing in a full sweep, and the ball leapt from the racket in a white blur; again her skirt kicked up and Mark shifted slightly on his feet, for the earth had tilted again.

She ran back to the baseline, short neat steps on those long narrow feet, head thrown back to follow the high parabola of the lobbing ball against the blue of the sky. Her dark hair seemed to glow with the metallic sheen of a sunbird's wing as she judged her stroke, and then her whole body went into it, power uncoiling along those long beautiful legs, driven up from tensed and rounded buttocks under the light cotton skirt, through the narrow waist, along young hard back muscles and exploding down through the swinging right arm.

The ball hummed like an arrow, flashed low across the net and kicked a white puff of dust from the baseline.

'Too good!' wailed her opponent despairingly, and Storm laughed, gay and triumphant, and came back to the high fence to pick up the spare balls from the gutter.

'Oh Storm, there's a gentleman here to see you.' The blonde called again, and Storm flipped up a ball with the tip of her racket and the side of her foot, bouncing it once on the turf of the court and then catching it in her free hand.

'Yes, Irene,' she answered lightly. 'I know. He's only a sales person. Ask him to wait by the car until I'm ready to deal with him.'

She had not looked at Mark again, and now she turned away. 'Forty – love,' she called gaily, and ran back to the baseline. Her voice had a music and lilt that did nothing to sweeten the sudden flare of anger which made Mark's jaw set grimly.

'If you are a sales person,' Irene murmured, 'then you

149

can sell me something some time. But right now, darling, I suggest you do what Storm says – otherwise we will all know about it.'

When Storm came to where he waited, she was flanked by the other girls, like maids in waiting attending a princess, he thought, and he felt his resentment fade as he watched her. You could forgive somebody like that, somebody so royal and lovely and heart-achingly beautiful – you could forgive them anything.

He stood attentive, waiting for her, and he realized then how tall she was. The top of that glossy head reached to his chin, almost.

'Good morning, Miss Courtney. I have brought your new Cadillac, and all of us at Natal Motors wish you much joy and enjoyment.' It was a little speech he always used when making a delivery, and he spoke it with all the warmth and charm and sincerity which had made him in so few months the star salesman of Natal Motors.

'Where are the keys?' Storm Courtney asked, and for the first time looked at him directly. Mark realized that her eyes were that dark, almost black, blue like the General's. There was no question who her father was.

She opened them a little wider, and in the sunlight they were the colour of polished sapphires or the blue of the Mozambique current, out in the deep water at noon.

'They are in the car,' he answered, and his voice sounded strange in his own ears, as though it came from a distance.

'Get them,' she said, and he felt himself start to move, to hurry to her bidding. Then something like that sense of danger he had known and developed in France warned him. Her expression was neutral, completely unconcerned, as though she found the effort of talking directly to him was wasted, just one of these tiresome moments in an otherwise important march of events. Yet the warning was clear as the chime of a bell in his head, and only then he saw something else move in her eyes, something dangerous

150

and exciting like the shape of a leopard hunting in the shadows. A challenge, perhaps, a dare – and suddenly he knew clearly that no daughter of Sean Courtney would be reared to such natural arrogance and rudeness. There was a reason, some design in her attitude.

He felt a lightness of mind, that kind of special madness which had driven away fear of consequence so often in moments of peril or desperate enterprise, and he grinned at her. He did not have to force the grin, it was natural and devilish and challenging.

'Certainly, Miss Courtney. Of course I'll get them, just as soon as you say please.'

There was an audible communal gasp from the girls around her, and they stilled with awed delight, their eyes darting to Storm's face and then back to Mark's.

'Say please to the nice man, Stormy.' Irene used the patronizing voice for instructing young children, and there was a delighted burst of giggles from the others.

For one unholy instant something burned in the girl's dark blue eyes, something fierce that was not anger. Mark recognized the importance of that flash; although he did not truly know the exact emotion it betrayed, yet he knew it might affect him. Then it was gone and in its place was true unfeigned anger.

'How dare you!' Storm's voice was low and quivering, but her lips were suddenly frosty white as the blood drained away. The anger was too swift, too strong for the occasion, out of all proportion to the mild exchange, and Mark felt a reckless excitement that he had been able to reach her so deeply. He kept the grin mocking and taunting.

'Hit him, darling,' Irene teased, and for a moment Mark thought she really might.

'You keep your silly mouth shut, Irene Leuchars.'

'Oh la la!' Irene gloated. 'Temper!'

Mark turned casually away, and opened the driver's door of the Cadillac.

'Where are you going!'

'Back to town.' He started the engine, and looked out of the window at her. There was no doubt now that she was the most beautiful creature he had ever seen. Anger had rouged her cheeks, and the fine dark hair at her temples was still damp from her play on the courts. It was plastered against the smooth skin in tiny curls.

'That is my car!'

'They'll send somebody else up with it, Miss Courtney, I'm used to dealing with ladies.'

Again the wondering gasp and burst of giggles.

'Oh, he's a darling!' Irene clapped her hands in applause, but Storm ignored her.

'My father will have you fired.'

'Yes, he probably will,' he agreed. Mark thought about that solemnly for a moment, then he nodded and he let out the clutch. He looked back in the mirror as he took the first bend in the driveway and they were still standing in a group staring after him in their white dresses, like a group of marble statues. 'Nymphs Startled by Satyr' was a fitting title, he thought, and laughed with the reckless mood still on him.

'Jesus,' Dicky Lancome whispered, clutching his brow with horror. 'What made you do it?' He shook his head slowly, wonderingly.

'She was damned rude.'

Dicky dropped his hands and stared at him aghast. '*She* was rude to *you*. Oh my God, I don't think I can stand much more. Don't you realize that if she was rude to you, you should be grateful? Don't you know that there are thousands of peasants like us who go through their entire lives without being insulted by Miss Storm Courtney?'

'I was not going to take that,' Mark explained reasonably, but Dicky cut in.

'Look, old bean, I've taught you all I know, and you still know nothing. Not only do you take it, but if Miss Courtney expresses a desire to kick your fat stupid arse, the correct reply is "Certainly, ma'am, but first let me don fresh bags lest I soil your pretty foot!"'

Mark laughed, the reckless mood still there but fading, and Dicky's expression became more lugubrious.

'That's right, have yourself a good laugh. Do you know what happened?' and before Mark could answer he went on, 'A summons from on high, the ultimate, the Chairman of the Board himself. So the boss and I dash across town – fear, trepidation, cautious optimism – are we to be fired, promoted, congratulated on the month's sale figures? And there is the Board, the full Board mind you, looking like a convention of undertakers who have just been informed of the discovery of Pasteur's vaccine—'

Dicky stopped, the memory was too painful, and he sighed heavily. 'You didn't really tell her to say "please", did you?'

Mark nodded.

'You didn't really tell her she was not a lady?'

'Not directly,' Mark protested. 'But I did imply it.'

Dicky Lancome tried to wipe his face off with one hand, starting at the hairline and drawing the palm of his hand down slowly to his chin.

'I've got to fire you, you know that, don't you?'

Mark nodded again.

'Look,' said Dicky. 'I tried, Mark, I really did. I showed them your sales figures, I told them you were young, impulsive – I made a speech.'

'Thank you, Dicky.'

'At the end of the speech, they almost fired me also.'

'You shouldn't have stuck your neck out for me.'

'Anyone else – you could have picked on anyone else, old chap, you could have punched the mayor, sent abusive letters to the king, but why in the name of all holy things did you have to pick on a Courtney?'

'You know something, Dicky?' and it was Dicky's turn silently to shake his head.

'I loved it – I loved every moment of it.'

Dicky groaned aloud, as he took out his silver cigarette case and offered it to Mark. They lit their cigarettes, and smoked in silence for a few moments.

'So I am fired, then?' Mark asked at last.

'That's what I have been trying to tell you for the last ten minutes,' Dicky agreed.

Mark began to clear out the drawers in his desk, then stopped and asked impulsively. 'Did the General – did General Courtney make the demand for my head?'

'I have no idea, old chap – but sure as hell it was made.'

Mark wanted to believe that it had not been the General. It was too mean a gesture from such a big man. He could imagine the General bursting into the showroom, brandishing a horse-whip.

The man who could take such revenge for a small flash of spirit, might be capable of other things – like killing an old man for his land.

The thought sickened Mark, and he tried to thrust it aside.

'Well, then, I suppose I'd better be getting along.'

'I'm sorry, old bean.' Dicky stood up and offered his hand, then looked embarrassed. 'You all right for the filthy lucre? I could let you have a tenner to tide you over.'

'Thanks, Dicky, but I'll be all right.'

'Look,' Dicky blurted out impulsively. 'Give it a month or so, time for the dust to settle, and then if you haven't got yourself fixed, come and see me. I'll try and sneak you in again through the back door – even if we have to write you up on the paysheet under an assumed name.'

'Goodbye, Dick, and thanks for everything. I really mean that.'

'I'm going to miss you, old chap. Keep your head down below the parapet in future, won't you?'

The pawn shop was in Soldiers Way, almost directly opposite the railway station. The front room was small and overcrowded with a vast array of valuables, semi-valuables and rubbish left here by the needy over the years.

There was a melancholy about the racks of yellowing wedding dresses, in the dusty glass cases of old wedding rings, engraved watches, cigarette cases and silver drinking flasks – all given in love or respect, each with its own sad story.

'Two pounds,' said the pawnbroker, after a single glance at the suit.

'It's only three months old,' Mark said softly. 'And I paid fifteen.'

The man shrugged and the steel-framed spectacles slid down his nose.

'Two pounds,' he repeated, and pushed the spectacles up with a thumb that looked grey and dusty as his stock.

'All right – and what about this?'

He opened the small blue case, and showed the bronze disc nestled in a nest of silk, pinned by its gay little ribbon of white and red and blue. The Military Medal for gallantry displayed by non-commissioned officers and other ranks.

'We get a lot of those – not much call for them.' The man pursed thin lips. 'Twelve pounds ten,' he said.

'How long do you keep them before you sell them?' Mark asked, suddenly reluctant to part with the scrap of metal and silk.

'We keep 'em a year.'

The last ten days of constant search for employment had depleted Mark's resources of cash and courage.

'All right,' he agreed.

The pawnbroker wrote the ticket, while Mark wandered into the back reaches of the shop. He found a bundle of old military haversacks and selected one; then there was a rack of rifles, most of them ancient Martinis and Mausers, veterans of the Boer war – but there was one among them that stood out. The woodwork was hardly marked, and the metal shone smooth and oily, no scratches or pitting of rust, and Mark picked the weapon off the rack and the shape and feel of it brought memories crowding back. He thrust them aside. He would need a rifle where he was going, and it was sensible to have one he knew so well. Fate had put a P.14 there for him, and damn the memories, he decided.

He slipped the bolt from the breech and held the barrel to the light from the doorway, peering into the mouth of the breech. The bore of the barrel was unmarked, the rifling described its clean glistening spirals, again without fouling or pitting. Somebody had cared well for the weapon.

'How much?' he asked the pawnbroker, and the man's eyes turned to lifeless pebbles behind his steel-rimmed spectacles.

'That's a very good rifle,' he said, 'and I paid a lot of money for it. There's a hundred rounds of ammunition goes with it also.'

Mark found he had gone soft in the city; his feet ached within the first five miles and the straps of rifle and haversack cut painfully into his shoulders.

The first night he lay down beside the fire and slept as though he had been clubbed. In the morning he groaned at the effort of sitting upright, the stiffness was in his legs and back and shoulders.

The first mile he hobbled like an old man, until his muscles began to ease, and he was going well by the time he reached the rim of the escarpment and started down into the coastal lowlands.

He kept well away from Andersland, crossing the river five miles upstream. His clothing and rifle and pack were balanced on his head as he waded through a shallow place between white sandbanks, and he dried naked in the sun, sprawled out like a lizard on a rock, before he dressed again and headed north.

The third day, he settled into the long swinging hunter's stride, and the pack rode lightly on his back. The going was hard, the undulating folds of the ground forced him to climb and then descend, taxing every muscle, while the thick thorn scrub made him weave constantly to find a way through, wasting time and almost doubling the distance between point and point. Added to this, the grass was dried and seeding. The seeds were sharp as spears and worked easily through his woollen socks into his flesh. He had to stop every half hour or so to dig them out – but still he made thirty miles that day. In the gathering dusk he crossed another of the countless ridges of higher ground. The distant blue loom of Chaka's Gate almost blended with darkening clouds of evening.

He camped there that night, sweeping a bed on the bare ground below an acacia thorn tree and eating bully beef and maize porridge by the light of the fire of acacia wood that burned with its characteristic bright white flame and smell of incense.

General Sean Courtney stood at the heavy teak sideboard, with its tiers of engraved glass mirrors and displays of silver plate. In one hand he held the ivory-handled carving fork and in the other the long Sheffield knife.

He used the knife to illustrate the point he was making to the guest-of-honour at his table.

'I read it through in a single day, had to stay up until after midnight. Believe me, Jan, it's his best work yet. The amount of research – quite extraordinary.'

'I look forward to reading it,' said the Prime Minister, nodding acknowledgement to the author of the work under discussion.

'It's still in manuscript. I am not entirely satisfied yet, there is still some tidying up to do.'

Sean turned back to the roast and, with a single practised stroke of the blade for each, cut five thin slices of pink beef rimmed with a rind of rich yellow fat.

With the fork he lifted the meat on to the Rosenthal porcelain plate and immediately a Zulu servant in a flowing white kanza robe and red pillbox fez carried the plate to Sean's place at the head of the long table.

Sean laid the carving-knife aside, wiped his hands on a linen cloth, and then followed the servant to the table and took his seat.

'We were wondering if you might write a short foreword for the book,' Sean said, as he raised a cut crystal glass of glowing red wine to the Prime Minister, and Jan Christiaan Smuts inclined his head on narrow shoulders in an almost birdlike gesture. He was a small man, and the hands laid before him on the table were almost fragile; he had the mien of a philosopher, or a scholar, which was not dispelled by the neat pointed beard.

Yet it was hard to believe that he was small. There was a vital force and awesome presence about him that belied the high, rather thin voice in which he replied,

'Few things would give me as much pleasure. You do me honour.'

He seemed to bulk huge in his chair, such was the power of character he commanded.

'I am the one who is honoured,' Colonel Garrick Courtney replied gravely from across the table, bowing slightly – and Sean watched his brother fondly.

'Poor Garry,' he thought, and then felt a guilty stab. Yet it seemed so natural to think of him in those terms. He was frail and old now, bowed and grey and dried out, so that he seemed smaller even than the little man opposite him.

'Have you a title yet?' asked Jan Smuts.

'I have thought to call it *The Young Eagles*. I hope you do not find that too melodramatic for a history of the Royal Flying Corps.'

'By no means,' Smuts contradicted him. 'I think it excellent.'

'Poor Garry,' Sean thought again. Since Michael had been shot down, the book filled the terrible gap that his son's death had left; but it had not prevented him from growing old. The book was a memorial to Michael, of course, an act of great love – 'This book is dedicated to Captain Michael Courtney D.F.C., one of the Young Eagles who will fly no more.' Sean felt the resuscitation of his own grief, and he made a visible effort to suppress it.

His wife saw the effort, and caught his eye down the length of the table. How well she knew him after all these years, how perfectly she could read his emotions, she thought, as she smiled her sympathy for him, and saw him respond, the wide shoulders squaring up and heavy bearded jaws firming as he smiled back at her.

Deftly she changed the mood. 'General Smuts has promised to walk around the gardens with me this afternoon, Garry, and advise me on planting out the proteas he brought me from Table Mountain. You are also such a knowledgeable botanist. Will you join us?'

'As I warned you, my dear Ruth,' said Jan Smuts in that ready, yet compelling voice, 'I do not give much hope for their survival.'

'Perhaps the leucadendrons,' ventured Garry, 'if we find a cool, dryish place?'

'Yes,' agreed the General, and immediately they fell into an animated discussion. She had done it so skilfully, that she seemed to have done nothing.

S ean paused in the doorway of his study and ran a long lingering gaze over the room. As always, he felt a glow of pleasure at re-entering this sanctuary.

The glass doors opened now on to the massed banks of flowers, and the smoking plumes of the fountain, yet the thick walls ensured that the room remained cool even in the sleepy hush of midday.

He crossed to the desk of stinkwood – dark and massive and polished, so that it shone even in the cool gloom – and he lowered himself into the swivel chair, feeling the fine leather stretch and give under his weight.

The day's mail was neatly arranged on a silver salver at his right hand, and he sighed when he saw that, despite the careful screening by the senior clerk down at the city Head Office, there were still not much less than a hundred envelopes awaiting him.

He delayed the moment by swinging the chair slowly to look once again about the room. It was hard to believe it had been designed and decorated by a woman – unless it was a woman who loved and understood her man so well that she could anticipate his lightest whim and fancy.

Most of the books were bound in dark green leather, and stamped on their spine in gold leaf with Sean's crest. The exceptions were the three ceiling-high shelves of first editions with African themes. A dealer in London, and another in Amsterdam had *carte blanche* instructions from Sean to search for these treasures. There were autographed first editions by Stanley, Livingstone, Cornwallis Harris, Burchell, Munro and almost every other African explorer or hunter who had ever published.

The dark panelled woodwork between the book shelves was studded with the paintings of the early African artists; the Baines glowed like rich gems in their flamboyant colours and naïve, almost childlike, depiction of animal and countryside. One of these was set in an intricately carved frame of Rhodesian redwood and engraved, 'To my friend David Livingstone, from Thomas Baines.'

These links with history and the past always warmed Sean with pleasure, and he fell into a mild reverie.

The deep carpeting deadened her footsteps, but there was the light perfume on the air that warned Sean of her presence, and he swung his chair back to the desk. She stood beside his chair, slim and straight as a girl still.

'I thought you were walking with Garry and Jan.'

Ruth smiled then, and seemed as young and beautiful as when he had first met her so many years before. The cool gloom of the room disguised the little lines at the corners of her eyes and the light streaking of silver in the dark hair drawn back from her temples and caught with a ribbon at the back of her neck.

'They are waiting for me, but I slipped away for a moment to make certain that you had all you wanted.' She smiled down at him, and then selected a cigar from the silver humidor and began to prepare it.

'I will need an hour or two,' he said, glancing at the pile of mail.

'What you really need, Sean, is an assistant.' She cut the cigar carefully, and he grunted.

'You can't trust any of these young people—' and she laughed lightly as she placed the cigar between his lips.

'You sound as old as the prophets.' She struck a Vesta

and waved it to clear the sulphur before she held it to the tip of the cigar. 'It's a sign of old age to mistrust the young.'

'With you beside me, I'll be young for ever,' he told her, still awkward with a compliment after all these years and she felt her heart swell with her love, knowing the effort it had required.

She stooped quickly and kissed his cheek, and with a speed and strength that still astonished her, one of his thickly muscled arms whipped around her waist and she was lifted into his lap.

'You know what happens to forward young ladies – don't you?' He grinned at her, his eyes crinkling wickedly.

'Sean,' she protested, in mock horror. 'The servants! Our guests!' She struggled out of his embrace with the warmth and wetness of his kiss still on her lips, together with the tickle of his whiskers and the taste of his cigar, and rearranged her skirts and her hair.

'I'm a fool.' She shook her head sorrowfully. 'I always trust you.' And then they smiled at each other, lost for a moment in their love.

'My guests,' she remembered suddenly, a hand flying to her mouth. 'May I set the tea for four o'clock? We'll have it down at the lake. It's a lovely day.'

When she had gone, Sean wasted another minute staring after her through the empty doorway into the gardens. Then he sighed again, contentedly, and drew the silver salver of mail towards him.

He worked quickly, but with care, pencilling his instructions at the foot of each page and initialling them with a regal 'S.C.'

'No! – but tell them politely. S.C.'

'Let me have the previous year's figures of purchase – and delay the next shipment against bank guarantee. S.C.'

'Why did this come to me? Send it to Barnes. S.C.'

'Agreed. S.C.'

'To Atkinson for comment, please. S.C.'

The subjects were as diverse as the writers – politicians, financiers, supplicants, old friends, chancers, beggars – they were all there.

He flicked over a sealed envelope and stared at it for a moment, not recognizing the name or the occasion.

'Mark Anders Esq., Natal Motors, West Street, Durban.'

It was written in the hand that was so bold and flourishing that nobody could mistake it for any other but his own, and he remembered sending the letter.

Somebody had written across the envelope, 'Left – no forwarding address – return to sender.'

Sean clamped the cigar in the corner of his mouth and slit the flap with a Georgian silver paper-knife. The card was embossed with the regimental crest.

The Colonel-in-Chief and the officers of the Natal Mounted Rifles request the pleasure of *MARK ANDERS ESQ.* at a regimental reunion dinner to be held at the Old Fort . . .

Sean had written in the boy's name in the blank space, and at the end of the card, 'Do try to come. S.C.'

Now it was returned, and Sean scowled. As always, he was impatient and frustrated by even the slightest check in his plans. Angrily he tossed both card and envelope at the wastepaper bin, and they both missed, fluttering to the carpet.

Surprisingly, even to himself, his mood had altered, and though he worked on, he fumed and gruffed now over his correspondence and his instructions became barbed.

'The man is a fool or a rogue or both – under no circumstances will I recommend him to a post of such importance, *despite* the family connection! S.C.'

After another hour, he had finished and the room was hazed with cigar smoke. He lay back in the chair and stretched voluptuously like an old lion, then glanced at the wall clock. It was five minutes short of four o'clock, and he stood up.

The offending card caught his eye again, and he stooped quickly and picked it up, reading it again as he crossed the room, tapping the stiff cardboard thoughtfully on the open palm of his hand as he limped out heavily into the sunlight and across the wide lawns.

The gazebo was set on a constructed island in the centre of the lake with a narrow causeway joining it to the lawns.

Sean's household and guests were gathered there already, sitting about the table in the shade under the crazily contrived roof of the gazebo with its intricate cast-iron work painted with carnival colours. Already a host of wild duck had gathered about the tiny island, quacking loudly for pieces of biscuit and cake.

Storm Courtney saw her father coming across the lawns, and she let out one small excited squeak, leapt from the tea table and flew down the causeway to meet him before he reached the lake.

He lifted her easily, as though she were still a baby, and when he kissed her, she inhaled the smell of him. It was one of the lovely smells of her existence, like the smell of rain on hot dry earth, or horses, or the sea. He had a special perfume like old polished leather.

When he lowered her, she took his arm and pressed close to him, matching her light quick step to his limp.

'How was your lunch appointment?' he asked, looking down on her shining lovely head, and she rolled her eyes and then squinted ferociously.

'He is a very presentable young man,' Sean told her sternly. 'An excellent young man.'

'Oh, Daddy, from you that means he is a weak-minded bore.'

'Young lady, I would like to remind you that he is a Rhodes scholar, and that his father is the Chief Justice.'

'Oh, I know all that – but, Daddy, he just hasn't got zing!'

Even Sean looked for an instant nonplussed. 'And what, may I ask, is "zing"?'

'Zing is indefinable,' she told him seriously, 'but you've got zing! You're the zingiest man I know.'

And with that statement Sean found all his fatherly advice and disapproving words gone like migrating swallows, and he grinned down at her, shaking his head.

'You don't really believe that I swallow all your soft soap, do you?'

'You'll never believe it, Daddy, but Payne Bros. have got in twelve actual Patou Couture models – they're absolutely exclusive – and Patou is all the rage now—'

'Women in savage, barbaric colours, driven mad by those machiavellian scheming monsters of Paris,' growled Sean, and Storm giggled delightedly.

'You are a scream, Daddy,' she told him. 'Irene's father has told her she may have one of them – and Mr Leuchars is a mere tradesman!'

Sean blinked to hear the head of one of the largest import houses in the country so described.

'If Charles Leuchars is a tradesman – what, pray, am I?' he asked curiously.

'You are landed gentry, a Minister of the Crown, a General, a hero – and the zingiest man in the world.'

'I see,' he could not help but laugh, 'that I have a position to uphold. Ask Mr Payne to send the account to me.'

She hugged him again, ecstatically, and then for the first time noticed the card he still held in his hand.

'Oh,' she exclaimed. 'An invitation!'

'Not for you, my girl,' he warned her, but she had taken it from his hand, and her face changed as she read the name. Suddenly she was quiet and subdued.

'You are sending that to that – sales person.'

He frowned again, his own mood altering also. 'I sent it. It was returned. He has left, without a forwarding address.'

'General Smuts is waiting to talk to you.' With an effort she recaptured the smile and skipped beside him. 'Let's hurry.'

'It's serious, old Sean. They are organized, and there is no question but that they are seeking a direct confrontation.' Jan Christiaan Smuts crumbled a biscuit between his fingers, and tossed it to the ducks. They squabbled noisily, splashing in the clear water and chattering their broad flat bills as they dipped for the scraps.

'How many white workers will they lay off?' Sean asked.

'Two thousand, to begin with,' Smuts told him. 'Probably four thousand, all in all. But the idea is to do it gradually, as the blacks are trained to replace them.'

'Two thousand,' Sean mused, and he could not help but imagine the wives, and the children – the old mothers, the dependents. Two thousand wage-earners out of work represented much suffering and misery.

'You like it as little as I do.' The shrewd little man had read his thoughts; not for nothing did his opponents call him 'slim Jannie', or 'clever Jannie'. 'Two thousand unemployed is a serious business,' he paused significantly. 'But we will find other employment. We need men desperately on the railways and on other projects like the Vaal-Harts irrigation scheme.'

'They will not earn there the way they do in the mines,' Sean pointed out.

'No,' Jan Smuts drew out the negative thoughtfully, 'but should we protect the income of two thousand miners, at the cost of closing the mines themselves?'

'Surely it is not that critical?' Sean frowned quickly.

166

'The Chairman of the Chamber of Mines assures me that it is – and he has shown me figures to support this view.'

Sean shook his head, half in incredulity and half in anguish. He had been a mine-owner himself once – and he knew the problem of costs, and also the way that figures could be made to speak the language their manipulators taught.

'You know also, old Sean, you especially – how many others depend for life on those gold mines.' It was a hard probing statement, with a point like a stiletto. The previous year, for the first time, the sales of timber pit-props from Sean's sawmills to the gold mines of the Transvaal had exceeded two million pounds sterling. The little General knew it as well as he did.

'How many men are employed by Natal Sawmills, old Sean, twenty thousand?'

'Twenty-four thousand,' Sean answered shortly, one blond eyebrow lifted quizzically, and the Prime Minister smiled softly before going on.

'There are other considerations, old friend – that you and I have discussed before. On those occasions, it was you who told me that to succeed in the long term, our nation must become a partnership of black man and white, that our wealth must be shared according to a man's ability rather than the colour of his skin – not so?'

'Yes,' Sean agreed.

'It was I who said we must make haste slowly in that direction, and now it is you who hesitate and baulk.'

'I also told you that many small steps were surer than a few wild leaps, made under duress, made only with an assegai at your ribs. I said, Jannie, that we should learn to bend so that we might never have to break.'

Jannie Smuts turned his attention back to the ducks, and they both watched them distractedly.

'Come, Jannie,' Sean said at last. 'You mentioned other

reasons. Those you have given me so far are good but not deadly urgent and I know you are politician enough to save the best until the end.'

Jannie laughed delightedly, almost a giggle, and leaned across to pat Sean's arm. 'We know each other too well.'

'We should,' Sean smiled back at him. 'We fought each other hard enough. They both sobered at mention of those terrible days of the civil war. 'And we had the same tutor, God bless him.'

'God bless him,' echoed Jan Smuts, and they remembered for a moment that colossus Louis Botha, warrior and statesman, architect of Union, and first Prime Minister of the new nation.

'Come,' Sean insisted. 'What is your other reason?'

'It is quite simple. We are about to decide who governs. The duly elected representatives of the people, or a small ruthless band of adventurers who call themselves trade union leaders, representatives of organized labour – or quite simply international communism.'

'You put it hard.'

'It is hard, Sean. It is very hard. I have intelligence facts that I shall lay before the first meeting of the Cabinet when Parliament reconvenes. However, I wanted to discuss these with you personally before that meeting. I need your support again, old Sean. I need you with me at that meeting.'

'Tell me,' invited Sean.

'Firstly, we know that they are arming, with modern weapons, and that they are training and organizing the mineworkers into war commandos.' Jan Smuts spoke quickly and urgently for nearly twenty minutes, and when he had finished he looked at Sean.

'Well, old friend, are you behind me?'

Bleakly Sean looked out into the future, seeing with pain the land he loved once more torn by the hatred and misery of civil war. Then he sighed.

'Yes,' he nodded heavily, 'I am with you, and my hand on it.'

'You and your regiment?' Jan Smuts took the big bony hand. 'As a Minister of the Government and as a soldier?'

'Both,' Sean agreed. 'All the way.'

Marion Littlejohn read Mark's letter, sitting on the closed seat of the office toilet, with the door locked, but her love transcended her surroundings, discounted even the hiss and gurgle of water in the cistern suspended on its rusty downpipe above her head.

She read the letter through twice, with eyes misty and a tender smile tugging uncertainly at her lips, then she kissed his name on the final page and carefully folded it back into its envelope, opened her bodice and nestled the paper between her plump little breasts. It made a considerable lump there when she returned to the main office and the supervisor looked out from his glass cubicle and made a show of consulting his watch. It was an acknowledged, if unwritten, rule in the Registrar's office that calls of nature should be answered expeditiously, and in no circumstances should the answer occupy more than four minutes of a person's working day.

The rest of the day dragged painfully for Marion, and every few minutes, she touched the lump in her bodice and smiled secretively. When at last the hour of release came, she hurried down Main Street and arrived breathless just as Miss Lucy was closing the doors of her shop.

'Oh, am I in time?'

'Come in, Marion dear – and how is your young man?'

'I had a letter from him today,' she announced proudly, and Miss Lucy nodded her silver curls and beamed through the silver steel frames of her spectacles.

'Yes, the postman told me.' Ladyburg was not yet such a

large town that it could not take an intimate interest in the affairs of all its sons and daughters. 'How is he?'

Marion prattled on, flushing and shiny-eyed, as she inspected once again the four sets of Irish linen sheets that Miss Lucy was holding for her.

'They are beautiful, dear, you can really be proud of them. You'll have fine sons between them.' Marion blushed again.

'How much do I still owe you, Miss Lucy?'

'Let's see, dear – you've paid off two pounds and six-pence. That leaves thirty shillings balance.'

Marion opened her purse and counted its contents carefully, then after a mental struggle reached a decision and laid a shiny golden half sovereign on the counter.

'That leaves only a pound.' She hesitated, flushed again, then blurted out, 'Do you think I might take one pair with me now? I would like to begin the embroidery work.'

'Of course, child,' Miss Lucy agreed immediately. 'You have paid for three already. I'll open the packet.'

Marion and her sister Lynette sat side by side on the sofa. Each of them had begun at one side of the sheet and their heads were bent together over it, the embroidery needles flicking in the lamplight as busily as their tongues.

'Mark was most interested in the articles I sent him on Mr Dirk Courtney and he says that he feels Mr Courtney will have a prominent place in the book—'

Across the room, Lyn's husband worked head down over a sheath of legal documents spread on the table before him.

He had lately affected a briar pipe, and it gurgled softly with each puff. His hair was brilliantined and brushed down to a polish with a ruler-straight parting of white scalp dividing it down the middle.

'Oh, Peter,' Marion exclaimed suddenly, her hands stilling and her face lighting. 'I have just had a wonderful idea.'

Peter Botes looked up from his papers, a small frown of annoyance crinkling the serious white brow, a man interrupted at his labour by the silly chatter of woman.

'You do so much work for Mr Courtney down at the bank. You've even been up to the big house, haven't you? He even greets you on the streets – I've seen that.'

Peter nodded importantly, puffing at the pipe. 'Yes, Mr Carter has often remarked that Mr Courtney seems to like me. I think I will be handling the account more and more in the future.'

'Oh, darling, won't you speak to Mr Courtney and tell him that Mark is doing all this work for his book on Ladyburg, and that he is ever so interested in Mr Courtney and his family—'

'Oh, come now, Marion.' Peter waved the pipe airily. 'You can't expect a man like Mr Courtney—'

'You might find he is flattered to be in Mark's book – please dear. I know Mr Courtney will listen to you. You might find he likes the idea – and it will reflect credit on you.'

Peter paused thoughtfully, weighing carefully the value of impressing the womenfolk with his importance and influence against the dread prospect of speaking on familiar terms with Mr Dirk Courtney. The thought appalled him. Dirk Courtney terrified him and in his presence he affected a fawning, self-effacing manner which was, he realized, part of the reason why Dirk Courtney liked to work with him; of course, he was also a painstaking meticulous lawyer, but the main reason was his respectful attitude. Mr Courtney liked respect from his underlings.

'Please, Peter, Mark is going to so much trouble over this book. We must try and help him. I was just telling Lynette that Mark has taken a month's leave from his job

171

to go on an expedition up to Chaka's Gate, just to gather facts for the book.'

'He's gone to Chaka's Gate?' Peter looked mystified, and removed the pipe from his mouth. 'What on earth for? There is nothing up there but wilderness.'

'I'm not sure,' admitted Marion, and then quickly, 'but it's important for the book. We must try and help him.'

'What exactly do you want me to ask Mr Courtney?'

'Won't you ask him to meet Mark, and sort of tell him his life story in his own words. Imagine how that would be in the book.'

Peter swallowed once. 'Marion, Mr Courtney is a busy man, he can't—'

'Oh please.' Marion jumped up and crossed the room to kneel beside his chair. 'Pretty please, for my sake!'

'Well,' he mumbled, 'I'll mention it to him.'


Peter Botes stood like a guardsman beside the head seat of the long ormolu table, bending stiffly from the waist only when it was necessary to turn the page.

' – and here please, Mr Courtney.'

The big man in the chair dashed a careless signature across the foot of the document, hardly glancing at it and without interrupting his conversation with the other fashionably dressed men further down the table.

There was a strong perfume hanging about Dirk Courtney; he wore it with the panache of a cavalry officer's cloak, and Peter tried in vain to identify it. It must be terribly expensive, but it was the smell of success, and he made a resolution to acquire a bottle of whatever it was.

' – and here again, please, sir.'

He noticed now at close range how Dirk Courtney's hair was shining and cut longer at the temple, free of brilliantine and allowed to curl into the sideburns. Peter would wash the brilliantine from his own hair tonight, he decided, and let it grow out a little longer.

'That is all, Mr Courtney. I'll have copies delivered tomorrow.'

Dirk Courtney nodded without glancing up at him, and, pushing back his chair, he stood up.

'Well, gentlemen,' he addressed the others at the table, 'we should not keep the ladies waiting,' and they all laughed with that lustful, anticipatory laugh, their eyes gleaming like those of caged lions at feeding time.

Peter had heard in detail of those parties that Dirk Courtney held out at Great Longwood, his big house. There was gaming for high stakes, sometimes dog-fighting — two matched animals in a pit, ripping each other to ribbons of dangling skin and flesh — sometimes cock-fighting, always women — women brought in closed cars from Durban or Johannesburg. Big city women and Peter felt his body stir at the thought. Introductions to the parties were limited to men of importance or influence or wealth, and during the weekend that the revels continued, the grounds were guarded by Dirk Courtney's bully boys.

Peter dreamed sometimes of being invited to one of those parties, of sitting across the green baize table from Dirk Courtney and casually drawing towards him the multi-coloured pile of ivory chips without removing the expensive cigar from his lips, or of sporting among the rustling silks and smooth white limbs — he had heard of the dancers, beautiful women who disrobed as they danced the Seven Veils, and ended mother-naked while the men roared and groped.

Peter roused himself almost too late. Dirk Courtney was across the room, ushering his guests ahead of him, laughing and charming, flashing white teeth from the swarthy handsome face, a servant standing ready with his overcoat, chauffeurs waiting with the limousines in the street below

– about to depart into a realm about which Peter could only speculate in disturbing erotic detail.

He hurried after him, stammering nervously.

'Mr Courtney, I have a personal request.'

'Come, Charles,' Dirk Courtney did not look at Peter, but smilingly laid a friendly arm across one of his guests' shoulders. 'I trust you are in better luck than last time, I hate to take a friend's money.'

'My wife's sister has a fiancé, sir,' Peter stumbled on desperately. 'He's writing a book about Ladyburg, and he would like to include an account of your personal experience—'

'Alfred, will you ride with Charles in the first car.' Dirk Courtney buttoned his coat, and adjusted his hat, beginning to turn towards the door, just a slight crease to his brow showing his annoyance at Peter's importunity.

'He is a local man,' Peter was almost in tears of embarrassment, but he went on doggedly, 'with a good war record, you might remember his grandfather John Anders—'

A peculiar expression came over Dirk Courtney's face, and he turned slowly to look directly at Peter for the first time. The expression struck instant terror into him. Peter had never before seen such burning malevolence, such merciless cruelty on a man's face before. It was only for an instant – and then the big man smiled. Such a smile of charm and good fellowship that Peter felt dizzy with relief.

'A book about me?' He took Peter's arm in a friendly grip above the elbow. 'Tell me more about this young man. I presume he is young?'

'Oh yes, sir, quite young.'

'Gentlemen.' Dirk Courtney smiled apologetically at his guests. 'Can I ask you to go ahead of me. I will follow shortly. Your rooms are prepared, and please do not feel you have to await my arrival before sampling the entertainment.'

174

Still holding Peter's arm, he led him courteously back into the huge board room to a seat in one of the leather chairs by the fireplace. 'Now, young Master Botes, how about a glass of brandy?' and Peter watched bemused as he poured it with his own hands, big strong hands, covered with fine black hair across the back and with a diamond the size of a ripe pea on the little finger.

With each step northwards, it seemed to Mark that the great bastions of Chaka's Gate changed their aspect gradually, from silhouettes smoked blue with distance until the details of the living rock came into focus.

The twin bluffs faced each other in almost mirror image, each towering a thousand sheer feet but deeply divided by the gorge through which the Bubezi River spilled out on to the coastal lowlands of Zululand and then meandered down a hundred and twenty miles into a maze of swamp and lagoon and mangrove forest, before finally escaping through the narrow mouth of the tidal estuary. The mouth sucked and breathed with the tide, and the ebb blew a stain of discoloured water far out into the electric blue of the Mozambique Current, a brown smear that contrasted sharply with the vivid white rind of sandy beaches that stretched for a thousand miles north and south.

If a man followed the course of the Bubezi up through the portals of Chaka's Gate, as Mark and the old man had done so often before, he came out into a wide basin of land below the main escarpment. Here, among the heavy forests, the Bubezi divided into its two tributaries, the White Bubezi that dropped in a series of cataracts and falls down the escarpment of the continental shield – and the Red Bubezi, which swung away northwards following the line of the escarpment up through more heavy forest and open grassy glades until at last it became the border with the Portuguese colony of Mozambique.

In the flood seasons of high summer, this tributary carried down with it the eroding laterite from deposits deep in Mozambique; turning to deep bloody red, it pulsed like a living artery, and well earned its name, the Red Bubezi.

Bubezi was the Zulu name for the lion, and indeed Mark had hunted and killed his first lion on its banks, half a mile below the confluence of the two tributaries.

It was almost noon, when at last Mark reached the river at the point where it emerged from the gorge between the gates. He reached for his watch to check the time and then arrested the gesture. Here time was not measured by metal hands, but by the majestic swing of the sun and the eternal round of the seasons.

He dropped his pack and propped the rifle against a tree trunk; the gesture seemed symbolic. With the weight from his shoulders, the dark weight on his heart seemed to slip away also.

He looked up at the rock cliffs that filled half the sky above him, and was lost in awe as he had been when he looked up at the arched stone lattice-work of the Henry VII chapel in Westminster Abbey.

The columns of rock, sculptured down the ages by wind and sun and water, had that same ethereal grace, yet a freedom of line that was not dictated by the strict rules of man's vision of beauty. The cliffs were painted with lichen growth, brilliant smears of red and yellow and silvery grey.

In cracks and irregularities of rock grew stunted trees; hundreds of feet above their peers, they were deformed and crippled by the contingencies of nature as though by the careful skills of a host of Japanese Bonsai gardeners, and they twisted out at impossible angles from the face of the cliff, holding out their branches as if in supplication to the sun.

The rock below some narrow ledges was darkened by the stain of the urine and faeces of the hydrax, the fluffy rock rabbits, which swarmed from every crack and hole in the cliff. Sitting in sleepy ranks, on the very edge of the drop, sunning their fat little bodies and blinking down at the tiny figure of the man in the depth of the gorge.

Following the floating wide-pinioned flight of a vulture, Mark watched it swing in steeply, planing and volleying its great brown wings to meet the eddy of the wind across the cliff face, reaching forward with its talons for a purchase as it pulled up and dropped on to its nesting ledge a hundred and fifty feet above the river, folding its wings neatly and then crouching in that grotesque vulturine attitude with the bald scaly head thrust forward, as it waddled sideways along the rim of its huge shaggy nest of sticks and small branches built into the rockface.

From this angle Mark could not see the chicks in the nest, but clearly he recognized the heaving motions of the bird as it began to regurgitate its cropful of rotten carrion for its young. Gradually a sense of peace settled like a mantle over Mark, and he sat down, his back against the rough bole of a fever tree, and slowly, without sense of urgency, he selected and lit a cigarette, drawing the smoke with an unhurried breath and then letting it trickle out through his nostrils, watching the pale blue tendrils rise and swirl on the lazy air.

He thought perhaps that the nearest human being was forty miles distant, the nearest white man almost a hundred – and the thought was strangely comforting.

He wondered at the way in which all man's petty striving seemed insignificant in this place, in this vast primeval world – and suddenly he thought that if all men, even those who had known nothing but the crowded ratlike scrambling of the cities, could be set down in this place, even for a brief space of time, then they might return to their lives cleansed and refreshed, their subsequent strivings might become less vicious, more attuned to the eternal groundswell of nature.

Suddenly he grunted, his reverie shattered by the burning needle sting in the soft of his neck below the ear, and he slapped at it with open palm. The small flying insect was stunned, its carapace too tough to be crushed, even by a blow that heavy. It fell spinning and buzzing into Mark's lap, and he picked it up between thumb and forefinger, examining it curiously, for it was many years since last he had seen one.

The tsetse fly is slightly larger than the house fly, but it has a sleeker more streamlined body, with transparent wings veined in brown.

'The saviour of Africa,' the old man had called it once, and Mark repeated the words aloud as he crushed it between his fingers. It burst in a bright liquid red explosion of the blood it had sucked from his neck. He knew the bite would swell and turn angry red, all the subsequent bites would react in the same way, until swiftly his body rebuilt its immunity. Within a week he would not even notice their stings, and the bite would cause less discomfort that that of a mosquito.

'The saviour of Africa,' the old man had told him. 'This little bastard was all that saved the whole country being overrun and over-grazed with domestic animals. Cattle first, and after cattle the plough, and after the plough the towns and the railway tracks.' The old man had chewed slowly, like a ruminating bull in the light of the camp fire, his face shaded by the spread of the terai hat.. 'One day they will find some way to kill him, or something to cure the sleeping sickness – the nagana – that he carries. Then the Africa we know will have gone, lad.' He spat a long honey-brown spirt of juice into the fire. 'What will Africa be without its lonely places and its game? A man might as well go back and live in London town.'

Looking with new eyes and new understanding at the majestic indigenous forest around him, Mark saw in his imagination what it might have been like without its tiny brown-winged guardians; the forests chopped out for firewood, and cleared for ox-drawn cultivation, the open land grazed short and the hooves of the cattle opening the ground cover to begin the running ulcers of erosion, the rivers browned and sullied by the bleeding earth and by man's filth.

The game hunted out – for its meat and because it was in direct competition to the domestic animals for grazing. For the Zulu, cattle was wealth, had been for a thousand years, and wherever cattle could thrive, they came with their herds.

Yet it was ironic that this wilderness had had another guardian, apart from the winged legions, and that guardian had been a Zulu. Chaka, the great Zulu king, had come here long ago. Nobody knew when, for the Zulu does not measure time as a white man does, nor record his history in the written word.

The old man had told Mark the story, speaking in Zulu which was fitting for such a story, and his old Zulu gunbearer had listened and nodded approvingly, or grunted a correction of fact; occasionally he spoke at length embroidering a point in the legend.

In those days there had lived here in the basin a small tribe of hunters and gatherers of wild honey, so they called themselves Inyosi, the bees. They were a poor people but proud, and they resisted the mighty king and his insatiable appetite for conquest and power.

Before his swarming impis, they had withdrawn into the natural fortress of the northern bluff. Remembering the story, Mark raised his eyes and looked across the river at the sheer cliffs.

Twelve hundred men and women and children, they had climbed the only narrow and dangerous path to the summit, the women carrying food upon their heads, a long dark moving file against the rock wall, they had gone up into their sanctuary. And from the summit the Chief and his warriors had shouted their defiance at the king.

Chaka had gone out alone and stood below the cliff, a tall and lithe figure, terrible in the strength of his youth and majesty of his presence.

'Come down, oh Chief, receive the king's blessing and be a chief still – under the sunshine of my love.'

The Chief had smiled and called in jest to his warriors around him, 'I heard a baboon bark!' Their laughter rang against the rock cliffs. The king turned and strode back to where his impis squatted in long patient ranks, ten thousand strong.

In the night Chaka picked fifty men, calling each softly by name. Those of great heart and fearsome reputation. And he had told them simply, 'When the moon is down, my children, we will climb the cliff above the river,' and he laughed that low deep laugh, the sound of which so many had heard as their last sound on this earth. 'For did not that wise chief call us baboons – and the baboon climbs where no man dares.'

The old gunbearer had pointed out to Mark in daylight the exact route that Chaka had taken to the top. It needed binoculars to trace the hairline cracks and the finger-wide ledges.

Mark shuddered now, retracing the route with his eyes, and he remembered that Chaka had led that climb without ropes, in the pitch darkness after the moon, and carrying his shield and his broad-bladed stabbing spear strapped on his back.

Sixteen of his warriors had slipped and fallen during the climb, but such was the mettle of the men that Chaka had chosen that not one of them had uttered a sound during that terrible dark plunge, not a whisper of sound to alert the Inyosi sentries until the final soft thud of flesh on rock down below in the gorge.

In the dawn, while his impis diverted the Inyosi by skirmishing on the pathway, Chaka had slipped over the rim of the cliff, regrouped his remaining warriors and – thirty-five against twelve hundred – carried the summit with a single shattering charge, each stab of the great blades crashing through a body from chest to spine, and the withdrawal sucking the life blood out in a gushing burst of scarlet.

'Ngidhla! I have eaten,' roared the king and his men as they worked, and most of the Inyosi threw themselves from the cliff top into the river below, rather than face Chaka's wrath. Those who hesitated to jump were assisted in their decision.

Chaka lifted the chief of the Inyosi with both hands high above his head, and held him easily as he struggled.

'If I am a baboon – then you are a sparrow!'

He roared with savage laughter. 'Fly, little sparrow, fly!' and he hurled the man far out into the void.

For once they spared not even the women nor the children, for among the sixteen Zulus who had fallen from the cliff during the climb were those whom Chaka loved.

The old gunbearer had scratched in the debris of the scree face below the cliff and showed Mark in the palms of his hand chips of old bone that might have been human.

After his victory on the summit, Chaka had ordered a great hunt in the basin of the two rivers.

Ten thousand warriors to drive the game, and the hunt had lasted four days. They said that the king alone with his own hands had slain two hundred buffalo. The sport had been such that afterwards he had made the decree:

'This is a royal hunting ground, no man will hunt here again, no man but the king. From the cliffs over which Chaka threw the Inyosi, east to the mountain crests, south and north for as far as a man may run in a day, and a night, and another day, this land is for the king's hunt alone. Let all men hear these words, tremble and obey.'

He had left a hundred men under one of his older indunas to police the ground, under the title of 'keeper of the king's hunt', and Chaka returned again and again, perhaps drawn to this well of peace to refresh and rest his tortured soul with its burning crippling craving for power. He had hunted here, even in that period of dark madness while he mourned his mother Nandi, the Sweet One. He had hunted here nearly every year until at last he had died beneath the assassin's blades wielded by his own brothers.

Probably nearly a century later, the legislative council of Natal, sitting in solemn conclave, hundreds of miles distant from the cliffs of Chaka's Gate, had echoed his decree and proclaimed the area reserved against hunting or despoliation, but they had not policed the Royal Hunt as well as had the old Zulu king. The poachers had been busy over the years, with bow and arrow, with snare and pit, with spear and dog pack, and with high-powered rifled weapons.

Perhaps soon, as the old man had predicted, they would find a cure for the nagana or a means of eradicating tsetse fly. A man-made law would be repealed, and the land given over to the lowing, slow-moving herds of cattle and to the silver-bright blade of the plough. Mark felt a physical sickness of the stomach at the prospect, and he rose and set off along the scree slope to let the sickness pass.

The old man had always been a creature of habit, even to the clothes he wore and his daily rituals of living. He always camped at the same spot when he travelled a familiar road or returned to a place he had visited before.

Mark went directly to the old camp site above the river

junction in the elbow of the main river course, where flood waters had cut a steep high bank and the elevated ground above it formed a plateau shaded by a grove of sycamore fig trees, with stems thick as Nelson's column in Trafalgar Square and the cool green shade below them murmurous with the sound of insects and purple doves.

The hearth stones for the camp fire were still there, scattered a little and blackened with soot. Mark built them back into the correct shape.

There was plenty of firewood, dead and fallen trees and branches, driftwood brought down by the floods and cast up on the high watermark on the bank.

Mark drew clear water from the river, put the billy on to boil for tea, and then, from the side pocket of the pack, brought out the sheath of paper, held together by a clasp and already much fingered and a little tattered, that Marion had sent him.

'Transcript of the evidence from the coroners' inquiry into the death of JOHN ANDERS ESQUIRE of the farm ANDERSLAND in the district of LADYBURG.'

Marion Littlejohn had typed it out laboriously during her lunch hours, and her lack of skill with the machine was evident in the many erasures and over-types.

Mark had read it so many times before that he could almost repeat the entire text from memory, even the irrelevant remarks from the bench.

Mr Greyling (Snr): We was camped there by the Bubezi
   River, Judge –
Magistrate: I am not a judge, sir. The correct form of
   address to this Court is Your Worship.

But now he began again at the beginning, searching carefully for some small clue to what he was seeking that he might have overlooked in his previous readings.

But always he came back to the same exchange.

Magistrate: Will the witness please refer to the deceased as 'the deceased' and not 'the old man'.

Mr Greyling (Snr): Sorry, your worship. The deceased left camp early on the Monday morning, he says like he's going to look for kudu along the ridge. It would be a little before lunchtime we hears a shot and my boy, Cornelius, he says – 'Sounds like the old man got one' – beg your pardon, I mean the deceased.

Magistrate: You were still in camp at that time?

Mr Greyling (Snr): Yes, Your Worship, my boy and me, we was cutting and hanging biltong – we didn't go out that day.

Mark could imagine the butchering of the game carcasses, the raw red meat hacked into long strips, soaked in buckets of brine, and then festooned on the branches of the trees – a scene of carnage he had witnessed so often before. When the meat had dried to black sticks, like chewing tobacco, it was packed into jute sacks for later carriage out on the pack donkeys. The wet meat dried to a quarter of its weight, and the resulting biltong was highly prized through Africa and commanded such a high price as to make the poaching a lucrative trade.

Magistrate: When did you become concerned by the deceased's absence?

Mr Greyling: Well, he didn't come into camp that night. But we weren't worried like. Thought he might have been spooring up a hit one, and slept up a tree.

Further on in the evidence was the statement:

Mr Greyling (Snr): . . . Well, in the end we didn't find him until the fourth day. It was the assvogels – beg pardon, the vultures – that showed us where to look. He had tried to climb the ridge at a bad place, we found where he had slipped and the gun was still under him. It must have been that shot we heard – we buried him right there, you see he wasn't fit to carry – what with the birds and the sun. We put up a nice cross, carved it myself, and I said the Christian words.

Mark refolded the transcript, and slipped it back into the pack. The tea was brewing and he sweetened it with thick condensed milk and brown sugar.

Blowing on the mug to cool it, and sipping at the sweet liquid, he pondered what he had gleaned. A rocky ridge, a bad place, within sound of gunshot of where he now sat, a cairn of stones, probably, and a wooden cross, perhaps long ago consumed by termites.

He had a month, but he wondered if that was time enough. On such slim directions it was a search that could take years, if luck ran against him.

Even if he was succcessful, he wasn't yet sure what he would do next. The main concern that drove him on was merely to find where the old man lay. After that he would know what to do.

He worked the ridges and the rocky ground on the south bank first. For ten days he climbed and descended the rugged rim of the basin, hard going against the grain of the natural geological formations, and at the end of that time he was lean as a greyhound, arms and face burned to the colour of a new loaf by the sun and with a dark crisp pelt of beard covering his jaw. The legs of his pants were tattered by the coarse, razor-edged grass and by the clumps of aptly named wait-a-bit thorns, that grabbed at him to delay his progress.

There was a rich treasure of bird life in the basin, even

in the heated hush of midday, the air rang with their cries – the fluting mournful whistle of a wood dove or the high piping chant of a white-headed fish eagle circling high overhead. In the early morning and again in the cool of the evening, the bush came alive with the jewelled flash of feathers – the scarlet breast of the impossibly beautiful Narina Trogon, named long ago for a Hottentot beauty by one of the old travellers, the metallic flash of a sunbird as it hovered over the pearly fragrant flowers of a buffalo creeper, the little speckled woodpeckers tapping furiously with heads capped in cardinal red, and, in the reeds by the river, the ebony sheen of the long floating tail feathers of the Sakabula bird. All this helped to lighten the long weary hours of Mark's search, and a hundred times a day he paused, enchanted, to watch for a few precious moments.

However, of the larger animals he saw very little, although their sign was there. The big shiny pellets of kudu dung scattered along their secret pathways through the forest, the dried faeces of a leopard furry with baboon hair from its kill, the huge midden of a white rhinoceros, a mountain of scattered dung accumulated over the years as this strange animal returned to the same place daily to defecate.

Pausing beside the rhinoceros midden, Mark grinned as he remembered one of the old man's stories, the one that explained why the rhinoceros was so fearful of the porcupine and why he always scattered his own dung.

Once, long ago, he had borrowed from the porcupine a quill to sew up the tear in his skin caused by a red-tipped mimosa thorn. When the job was done the rhinoceros had held the quill between his teeth as he admired his handiwork, but by accident he swallowed the quill.

Now, of course, he runs away to avoid having to face the porcupine's recriminations – and he sifts each load that he drops, to try and recover the missing quill.

The old man had a hundred yarns like that one to

delight a small boy, and Mark felt close to him again; his determination to find his grave strengthened, as he shifted the rifle to his other shoulder and turned once more to the rocky ridge of the high ground.

On the tenth day, he was resting in the deep shade at the edge of a clearing of golden grass, when he had his first good sighting of larger game.

A small herd of graceful pale brown impala, led by three impressively horned rams, emerged from the far side of the clearing. They fed cautiously; every few seconds they froze into perfect stillness with only the big scooplike ears moving as they listened for danger, and their wet black noses snuffing silently.

Mark was out of meat, he had eaten the last of the bully the previous day, and he had brought the rifle for just this moment – to relieve a diet of mealie porridge – yet he found himself strangely reluctant to use it now, a reluctance he had never known as a boy. For the first time, he looked with eyes that saw not just meat but rare and unusual beauty.

The three rams moved slowly across the clearing, passing a hundred paces from where Mark sat silently, and then drifted away, pale shadows, into the thorn scrub. The does followed them, trotting to keep up, one with a lamb stumbling on long gawky legs at her flank, and at the rear of the troop was a half-grown doe.

One of her back legs was crippled, it was withered and stunted, swinging free of the ground and the animal was having difficulty keeping up with the herd. It had lost condition badly; bone of rib and spine showed clearly through a hide that lacked the gloss and shine of health.

Mark swung up the P.14 and the flat crack of the shot bounced from the cliffs across the river, and startled a flock of white-faced duck into whistling flight off the river.

Mark stooped over the doe as she lay in the grass and touched the long curled lashes that fringed the dark swimming eye. There was no reflex blink, and the check for life was routine only. He knew the shot had taken her in the centre of the heart, an instantaneous kill.

'Always make the check.' The old man's teachings again. 'Percy Young would tell you that himself if he could, but he was sitting there on a dead lion he had just shot, having a quiet pipe, when it came to life again. That's why he isn't around to tell you himself.'

Mark rolled the carcass and squatted to examine the back limb. The wire noose had cut through the skin, through sinew and flesh, and had come up hard against the bone as the animal struggled to break out of the snare. Below the wire the leg had gangrened and the smell was nauseous, summoning a black moving wad of flies.

Mark made the shallow gutting stroke, deflecting the blade upwards to avoid puncturing the gut. The belly opened like a purse. He freed the anus and vagina with the deft surgeon strokes, and lifted out bladder and bowel and gut in one scoop. He dissected the purple liver out of the mass of viscera, cut away the gall bladder and tossed it aside. Grilled over the coals, the liver would make a feast for his dinner. He cut away the rotten, stinking hind leg, and then he carefully wiped out the stomach cavity with a handful of dry grass. He cut flaps in the skin of the neck. Using the flaps of skin as handles, he hefted the whole carcass and lugged it down to the camp by the river. Cut and salted and dried, he now had meat for the rest of his stay. He hung the strips of meat high in the sycamore fig to save them from the scavengers who would surely visit the camp during his daily absences, and only when he had finished the task, and he was crouching over his fire with the steaming mug in his hand, did he think again of the snaring wire that had crippled the impala doe.

He felt an indirect flash of anger at the person who had set that noose, and then almost immediately he wondered why he should feel particular anger at the trapper, when a dozen times he had come across the old abandoned camps of white hunters. Always there were the bones, and the piles of rotting worm-riddled horns.

The trapper was clearly a black man, and his need was greater than that of the others who came in to butcher and dry and sell.

Thinking about it, Mark felt a despondency slowly overwhelm him. Even in the few short years since he had first visited this wilderness, the game had been reduced to but a small fraction of its original numbers. Soon it would all be gone – as the old man had said, 'The great emptiness is coming.'

Mark sat at his fireside, and he felt deeply saddened at the inevitable. No creature would ever be allowed to compete with man, and he remembered the old man again.

'Some say the lion, others the leopard. But believe me, my boy, when a man looks in the mirror, he sees the most dangerous and merciless killer in all of nature.'


The pit had been built to resemble a sunken water reservoir. It was fifty feet across and ten feet deep, perfectly circular, plastered and floored in smooth cement.

Although there were water pipes installed and its position on the first slope of the escarpment above Ladyburg was perfectly chosen to provide the correct fall to the big gabled house below, yet it had never held water.

The circular walls were white-washed to gleaming purity, and the floor was lightly spread with clean-washed river sand and neatly raked.

Pine trees had been planted to screen the reservoir. A twelve-stranded barbed wire fence enclosed the whole plantation, and there were two guards at the gate this evening, tough, silent men who checked the guests as the cars brought them up from the big house.

There were forty-eight men and women in the excited, laughing stream that flowed through the gate, and followed the path up among the pines to where the pit was already starkly lit by the brilliant glare of the Petromax lanterns suspended on poles above it.

Dirk Courtney led the revellers. He wore black gaberdine riding breeches and polished knee-length boots to protect his legs from slashing fangs, and his white linen shirt was open almost to the navel, exposing the hard bulging muscle of his chest and the coarse black body hair which curled from the vee of the neck. The sleeves of the shirt were cut full to the wrist, and he rolled a long thin cheroot from one corner of his mouth to the other without touching it, for his arms were around the waists of the women who flanked him, young women with bold eyes and laughing painted mouths.

The dogs heard them coming and bayed at them, leaping against the padded bars of their cages, hysterical with excitement as they tried to reach each other through the gaps, snarling and snapping and slavering while the handlers attempted to shout them into silence.

The spectators lined the circular parapet of the pit, hanging over the edge. In the merciless light of the Petromax, the faces were laid bare, every emotion, every stark detail of the blood lust and sadistic anticipation was revealed – the hectic colouring of the women's cheeks, the feverish glitter of the men's eyes, the shrillness of their laughter and the widely exaggerated gesturing.

During the early bouts, the small dark-haired girl beside Dirk screamed and wriggled, holding her clenched fists to her open mouth, moaning and gasping with fascinated, delighted horror. Once she turned and buried her face against Dirk's chest, pressing her body, trembling and shuddering, against him. Dirk laughed and held her around the waist. At the kill she screamed with the rest of them and her back arched; then Dirk half lifted her, as she sobbed breathlessly, and supported her to the refreshment table where there was champagne in silver buckets and sandwiches of brown bread and smoked salmon.

Charles came to where Dirk sat with the girl on his lap, feeding her champagne from a crystal glass, surrounded by a dozen of his sycophants, jovial and expansive, enjoying the rising sense of tension for the final bout of the evening when he would match his own dog, Chaka, against Charles' animal.

'I feel bad, Dirk,' Charles told him. 'They have just told me that your dog is giving almost ten pounds.'

'That mongrel of yours will need every pound, Charles, don't feel bad now – keep it for later, when you'll really need it.' Dirk was suddenly bored with the girl, and he pushed her casually from his lap, so that she almost lost her balance and fell. Piqued, she settled her skirts, pouted at Dirk and when she realized he had already forgotten her existence, she flounced away.

'Here.' Dirk indicated the chair beside him. 'Do have a seat, Charles old boy, and let's discuss your problem.'

The crowd drew closer around them, listening eagerly to their banter, and braying slavishly at each sally.

'My problem is that I should like a small wager on the bout, but it does seem most unsporting to bet against a light dog, like yours.' Charles grinned as he mopped his streaming red face with a silk handkerchief, sweating heavily with champagne and excitement and the closeness of the humid summer evening.

'We all know that you make your living betting on certainties.' Charles was a stock-broker from the Witwatersrand. 'However, the expression of such noble sentiment does you great credit.' Dirk tapped his shoulder with the hilt of his dog-whip, a familiar condescending gesture that made Charles' grin tighten wolfishly.

'You will accommodate me then?' he asked, nodding and winking at his own henchmen in the press of listening men. 'At even money?'

'Of course, as much as you want.'

'My dog Kaiser, against your Chaka, to the death. Even money, a wager of—' Charles paused and looked to the ladies, smoothing the crisp little moustache with its lacing of iron grey, drawing out the moment. 'One thousand pounds in gold.' The crowd gasped and exclaimed, and some of the listeners applauded, a smattering of handclaps.

'No! No!' Dirk Courtney held up both hands in protest. 'Not a thousand!' and the listeners groaned, his own claque shocked and crestfallen at this loss of prestige.

'Oh dear,' Charles murmured, 'too strong for your blood? Name the wager then, old boy.'

'Let's have some real interest – say ten thousand in gold.' Dirk tapped Charles' shoulder again, and the man's grin froze over. The colour faded from the scarlet face, leaving it blotched purple and puffy white. The small acquisitive eyes darted quickly around the circle of laughing applauding faces, as if seeking an escape, and then slowly, reluctantly returned to Dirk's face. He tried to say something, but his voice squeaked and broke like a pubescent boy.

'Ah, and what exactly does that mean?' Dirk inquired with elaborate politeness. Charles would not trust his voice again, but he nodded jerkily and tried to resurrect his cheeky grin, but it was crooked and tense and hung awkwardly on his face.

Dirk carried the dog under his right arm, enjoying the hard rubbery feel of the animal's compact body, carrying its fifty-pound weight easily, as he dropped lightly down the steps to the floor of the pit.

Every muscle in the dog's body was strained to a fine

tension, and Dirk could feel the jump and flutter of nerves and sinew, every limb was stiff and trembling, and the deep crackling snarls kept erupting up the thick throat, shaking the whole body.

He set the dog down on the raked sand, with the leash twisted securely around his left wrist, and as the dog's paws touched ground he lunged forward, coming up short against the leash so hard that Dirk was almost pulled off his feet.

'Hey, you bastard,' he shouted, and pulled the animal back.

Across the pit, Charles and his handler were bringing down Kaiser, and it needed both their strength for he was a big dog, black as hell, and touched with tan at the eyes and chest, a legacy of the Dobermann Pinscher in his breeding.

Chaka saw him, his lunges and struggles became wilder and fiercer, and the snarls sounded like thick canvas ripping in a hurricane.

The timekeeper called from the parapet, lifting his voice above the excited buzz of the watchers.

'Very well, gentlemen, bate them!'

The two owners set them at each other with cries of 'Sick him up, Kaiser!' and 'Get him boy. Kill! Kill!' but held them double-handed on the leash, driving them into a madness of frustration and anger.

On the short leash, the Dobermann weaved and ducked, leggy for a fighting dog, with big shoulders dropping back to lower quarters. He had good teeth, however, and a threatening gape, enough to lock the teeth into the killer grip at the throat. He was fast too, swinging and weaving against the leash, barking and thrusting with the long almost snake-like neck.

Chaka did not bark, but the thick barrel of his chest vibrated to the deep rolling snarls and he stood foursquare on his short legs. He was heavy and low in silhouette, Staffordshire bull terrier blood carefully crossed with mastiff, and his coat was coarse and brindled gold on black. The head was short and thick, like that of a viper, and when he snarled, his upper lip lifted back in deep creases revealing the long ivory yellow fangs and the dark pink gums. He watched the other dog with yellow leopard eyes.

'Bate them! Bate them!' yelled the crowd above, and the owners worked the leashes like jockeys pushing for the post, pointing the animals at each other and driving them on.

Dirk slipped a small steel implement from his pocket, and dropped on his knee beside his dog. Instantly the animal swung on him with gaping jaws but the heavy muzzle caged his fangs. His saliva was beginning to froth, and it splattered the spotless linen of Dirk's shirt.

Dirk reached behind the dog and stabbed the short spur of steel into his flesh, a shallow goading wound at the root of his testicles, just enough to break the skin and draw a drop of blood – the animal snarled on a newer higher note, slashing sideways, and Dirk goaded him again, driving him further and further into the black fighting rage. Now at last he barked, a series of almost maniacal surges of sound from his straining throat.

'Ready to slip,' shouted Dirk, struggling to manage his animal.

'Ready here!' Charles panted across the pit, his feet sliding in the sand as Kaiser reared chest high.

'Slip them!' yelled the timekeeper, and at the same instant, both men slipped muzzle and leash and studded collars, leaving both animals free, and unprotected.

Charles turned and scrambled hurriedly out of the pit, but Dirk waited extra seconds, not wanting to miss the moment when they came together.

The Dobermann showed his speed across the pit, meeting Chaka in his own ground, bounding in on those long legs, leaning forward so the sloping back was flattened in his run.

He went for the head, slashing open the skin below the eye in a clean sabre-stroke of white teeth, but not holding.

Chaka did not go for a hold either, but turned at the instant of impact; using his shoulder and the massive strength of his squat frame, he hit the bigger dog off-balance, breaking his charge, so that he spun away and would have gone over but the white-washed wall caught him, and saved him – for Chaka had turned neatly to catch him as he fell.

Now, however, Kaiser was up and with a quick shift of weight he was in balance again – and he cut for the face mask, missing as the small brindled dog ducked, catching only the short cropped ear and splitting it, so that blood flew in black droplets to splatter the sand.

Again Chaka hit with the shoulder, blood streaming from cheek to ear, as he put his weight into the charge. The bigger dog reared out, declining to meet shoulder with shoulder and as he came over he went for a hold – but the crowd screamed as they saw his mistake.

'Drop it! Drop it!' howled Charles, his face purple as an over-ripe plum – for his dog had got into that thick loose skin padded with fat between the shoulder, and he growled as he worried it.

'Work him, Chaka. Work him!' howled Dirk, balancing easily on the narrow parapet above them. 'Now's your chance, boy.'

Locked into his grip the Dobermann was holding too high, his neck and head up and off-balance. As he worried the hold, it gave and pulled like rubber, not affording purchase or leverage to throw his weight across and bring down the brindled terrier.

The smaller dog seemed not even to feel the grip, although a small artery had ruptured, sending a fine spurt of blood dancing into the lantern light like a pink flamingo's feather.

'Drop it,' screamed Charles again in agony, wringing his hands, sweat dripping from his chin.

'Belly him! Belly him!' exhorted Dirk, and his dog twisted under the big dog's chest, forcing him higher so that his front paws were off the ground, and he hit him in the belly, gaping wide and then plunging his yellow eye teeth full into the bare, shiny dark skin below the ribs.

The Dobermann screamed and dropped his shoulder hold, twisting out violently so that Chaka's fangs tore out of his belly hold, ripping out a flap of stomach-lining through which wet purple entrails bulged immediately – but he beat the terrier's try for the throat, jaw clashing into open snarling jaw, and teeth cracked together, before they spun off and circled.

Both heads were masks of blood now, eyelids blinking rapidly, the eyeballs smeared with flying blood from wound and bite, the fur of the faces plastered with black blood, blood filling the mouths and turning the exposed teeth pink, trickling from the corners of the jaw, staining the froth of saliva bright rose red.

Twice more they came together, each charge initiated by the smaller squatter Chaka, but each time the Dobermann avoided the solid contact of chest to chest for which Chaka's instincts dictated that he must keep trying. Instead, Chaka received two more slashes deeply through the brindled skin, into the flesh, down to white bone, so that when his next charge carried him to the wall he left a broad thick smear of red across the white-wash before turning to attack again.

The Dobermann was humped up from the belly wound, arching his back to the agony of it, but fast and lithe still, not trying for another hold since that fool's hold at the shoulder, but cutting hard and deep and keeping off his opponent like a skilled boxer.

Chaka was losing too much blood now, and as he circled again he lolled his tongue for the first time, frothy saliva discoloured with blood dripping from it, and Dirk swore aloud at this sign of weakness and imminent collapse.

Big Kaiser attacked again now, cutting in sharply as though for the throat and then turning in a low dark streak for another weakening flank cut. As he hit, Chaka turned into him steeply, and snapped at his lean belly again, reaching low and with fortune taking a hold on the bulging entrails that showed in the open flap of the wound.

Instantly the terrier went stiff on his forelegs, and hunched his neck, bringing his chin down on to his chest to hold the grip. The Dobermann's charge carried him on and his entrails were pulled out of him, a long thick glistening ribbon in the lantern light – and the women screamed, high with anguished delight, while the men roared.

Chaka crossed the bigger dog's rump now, still holding his guts, and tangled his back legs in the slippery rubbery pink tubes that hung out of the stomach cavity, so that he stumbled off-balance – and the terrier lunged forward, hitting him solidly with the chest, knocking him into the air so he dropped onto his back, screaming and kicking.

Chaka's follow-up was so instinctive, so natural to his breed, that it was swift as the flash of a striking adder and he had his killing hold – locked deep and hard into the throat, bearing down with the solid bone of his jaws, snuffling and working his head on the short hunched neck until his long eye teeth met in the Dobermann's windpipe.

Dirk Courtney jumped down lightly from the parapet; his laugh was pitched unnaturally high and his face was darkened to a congested sullen red as he whipped off his dog, and turned the carcass of the Dobermann with the toe of his boot.

'A fair kill?' he laughed up at Charles, and the man glowered down at him a moment before shrugging acknowledgement of defeat and turning away.

197

Dicky Lancome sat with the voice-piece of the telephone set on the desk in front of him and the ear-piece held loosely to his cheek, trapped there by a hunched shoulder while he trimmed his fingernails with a gold-plated penknife.

'What can I say, old girl, except that I am desolate, but then Aunty Hortense was rich as that fellow that turned everything to gold, that's right Midas, or was it Croesus, I just cannot give her funeral a miss, you do understand? You don't?' and he sighed dramatically, as he returned the penknife to his waistcoat pocket and began to thumb through the address book for the other girl's number. 'No, old girl, how can you say that? Are you certain? Must have been my sister—'

It was almost noon on Saturday morning and Dicky had the premises of Natal Motors to himself. He was making his domestic arrangements for the weekend on the firm's telephone account before locking up, and finding some wisdom in the admonition against changing mounts in midstream.

At that moment he was distracted by the crack of footsteps on the marbled floor of the showroom, and he swivelled his chair for a glimpse through the door of his cubicle.

There was no mistaking the tall figure that strode through the street doors, the wide shoulders and thrusting bearded jaw, the dark glint of eyes like those of an old eagle.

'Oh, Lord preserve us,' Dicky breathed, his guilty conscience delivering a heavy jolt into his belly. 'General Courtney,' and he let the ear-piece of the telephone drop and dangle on its cord, while he slid forward stealthily from his chair and crawled into shelter below his desk, knees drawn up to his chin.

He could imagine exactly why General Courtney was

calling. He had come to discuss the insult to his daughter in person, and Dicky Lancome had heard enough about the General's temper to want to avoid joining this discussion.

Now he listened like a night animal for the stalk of the leopard, cocking his head for the sound of further footsteps and bating his breath to a shallow cautious trickle, in order not to disclose his hiding-place.

The ear-piece of the telephone still dangled on its cord, and now it emitted the high-pitched distorted voice of an irate female. Without leaving the cover of the desk, he reached out to try and muffle the ear-piece, but it dangled tantalizing inches beyond his fingertips.

'Dicky Lancome, I know you are there,' squawked the tinny voice, and Dick wriggled forward another inch.

A hand, in size not unlike that of a bull gorilla, entered Dicky's field of vision, closed on the ear-piece, and placed it in Dicky's outstretched fingers.

'Please allow me,' said a deep gravelly voice from somewhere above the desk.

'Thank you, sir,' whispered Dicky, trying not to draw too much attention to himself even at this stage. For want of anything better to do, he listened respectfully to the ear-piece.

'It is no good pretending not to be listening,' said the female voice. 'I know all about you and that blonde hussy—'

'I expect you need this,' said the deep voice from on high, and the hand passed the mouthpiece of the telephone down into his hiding-place.

'Thank you, sir,' Dicky whispered again, uncertain as to which emotion dominated him at that moment, humiliation or trepidation. He cleared his throat and spoke into the telephone.

'Darling, I have to go now,' he croaked. 'I have an extremely important client in the shop.' He hoped that the touch of flattery might sweeten the coming encounter. He broke the connection and crawled out unwillingly on his hands and knees.

'General Courtney!' He dusted himself down and smoothed his hair, assembled his dignity and salesman's smile. 'We are honoured.'

'I hope I did not interrupt you in anything important?' Only the sapphire twinkle in the heavily browed eyes betrayed the General's amusement.

'By no means,' Dicky assured him, 'I was—' he looked around wildly for inspiration, 'I was merely meditating.'

'Ah!' Sean Courtney nodded. 'That explains it.'

'How can I be of service to you, General?' Dicky went on hurriedly.

'I wanted to find out about a young salesman of yours – Mark Anders.' Dicky's heart was struck by black frost again.

'Don't worry, General, I fired him myself,' Dicky blurted out. 'But I tore a terrible strip off him first. You can be sure of that.' He saw the General's dark beetling brows come together and the forehead crease like an eroded desert landscape, and Dicky nearly panicked. 'He won't get another job in this town, count on it, General. I have put the word out – the black mark – he's properly queered around here, he is.'

'What on earth are you talking about, man?' the General rumbled, like an uneasy volcano.

'One word from you, sir, was enough.' Dicky found that the palms of his hands were cold and slippery with sweat.

'From me?' The rumble rose to a roar and Dicky felt like a peasant, looking fearfully up the slopes of Vesuvius. 'What did I have to do with it?'

'Your daughter,' choked Dicky, 'after what he did to your daughter.'

'My daughter?' The huge voice subsided to something that was close to a whisper, but was too cold and intense.

200

It was a fiercer sound than the roar that preceded it. 'He molested my daughter?'

'Oh God no, General,' Dicky moaned weakly. 'No employee of ours would raise a finger to Miss Storm.'

'What happened? Tell me exactly.'

'He was insolent to your daughter, I thought you knew?'

'Insolent? What did he say?'

'He told her she did not conduct herself like a lady. She must have told you?' Dicky gulped, and the General's fearsome expression melted. He looked stunned and bemused.

'Good God. He said that to Storm? What else?'

'He told her to use the word "please" when giving orders.' Dicky couldn't meet the man's eyes and he lowered his head. 'I'm sorry, sir.'

There was a strangled growling sound from the General, and Dicky stepped back quickly, ready to defend himself. It took him seconds to realize that the General was struggling with his mirth, gales of laughter that shook his chest – and when at last he let it come, he threw back his head and opened his mouth wide.

Weak with relief, Dicky essayed a restrained and cautious chuckle – in sympathy with the General.

'It's not funny, man,' roared Sean Courtney, and instantly Dicky scowled.

'You are much to blame – how can you condemn a man on the whim of a child?' It took Dicky a moment to realize that the child in question was the gorgeous, head-strong, darling of Natal society.

'I understood that the order came from you,' stammered Dicky.

'From me!' The laughter stopped abruptly, and the General mopped at his eyes. 'You thought I would smash a man because he was man enough to stand up to my daughter's tantrums? You thought that of me?'

'Yes,' said Dicky miserably, and then quickly, 'No,' and then hopelessly, 'I didn't know, sir.'

Sean Courtney took an envelope from his inside pocket, and looked at it thoughtfully for a moment.

'Anders believed, as you did, that I was responsible for his dismissal?' he asked soberly now.

'Yes, sir. He did.'

'Can you contact him? Will you see him again?'

Dicky hesitated, and then steeled himself and took a breath. 'I promised him his job back at the end of the month – after we had gone through the motions of dismissal, General. Like you, I didn't think the crime deserved the punishment.'

And Sean Courtney looked at him with a new light in his eye, and a grin lifting the corner of his mouth and one eyebrow.

'When you see Mark Anders again, tell him of our conversation – and give him this envelope.' Dicky took the envelope, and as the General turned away, he heard him mutter darkly, 'And now for Mademoiselle Storm.' Dicky Lancome felt a comradely pang of sympathy for that young lady.


It was almost noon on a Saturday morning and Ronald Pye sat in the back seat of the limousine, stiffly as an undertaker in his hearse, and his expression was as lugubrious. He wore a three-piece suit of dark grey cloth and a high starched collar with stiff wings; gold-rimmed spectacles glittered on his thin beaky nose.

The chauffeur swung off the main Ladyburg road into the long straight avenue that led up to the glistening white buildings of Great Longwood on the lower slopes of the escarpment. The avenue was lined with cycads that were at least two hundred years old, thick-stemmed palm-like plants each with a golden fruit the size of a hogshead, like a monstrous pine cone, nestled in the centre of the graceful fronds. Dirk Courtney's gardeners had scoured the country-side for a hundred miles in each direction to find them, and had lifted them, matched them for size and replanted them here.

The driveway had been smoothed and watered to keep down the dust, and parked in front of the house were twenty or thirty expensive motor cars.

'Wait for me,' said Ronald Pye. 'I won't be long,' and as he alighted, he glanced up at the elegant façade. It was an exact copy of the historic home of Simon van der Stel, the first Governor of the Cape of Good Hope, which still stood at Constantia. Dirk Courtney had his architects measure and copy faithfully every room, every arch and gable. The cost must have been forbidding.

In the hall, Ronny Pye paused and looked about him impatiently, for there was nobody to welcome him, although he had been specifically invited – perhaps summoned was a better word – for noon.

The house was alive; there were women's voices and the tinkling bells of their laughter from deep in the interior, while closer at hand the deeper growl of men punctuated by bursts of harsh laughter and voices raised to that reckless, raucous pitch induced by heavy drinking.

The house smelled of perfume and cigar smoke and stale alcohol, and Ronny Pye saw empty crystal glasses standing carelessly on the priceless rosewood hall table, leaving rings of damp on the polished surface – and an abandoned pair of pearly rose women's silk cami-knickers were draped suggestively over the door handle that led to the drawing-room.

While he still hesitated, the door across the hall opened and a young woman entered. She had the dazed, detached air of a sleep-walker, gliding silently into the room on neatly slippered feet. Ronny Pye saw that she was a young girl, not much more than a child, although her cosmetics had run and smeared. Dark rings of mascara gave her a haunted consumptive look, and her lipstick was spread so that her mouth looked like a bruised and overblown rose.

Except for the slippers on her small feet, she was stark naked and her breasts were immature and tender, with pale unformed nipples, and snarled dishevelled tresses of pale blonde hair hung on to her shoulders.

Still with slow, drugged movements, she took the knickers from the door handle, and stepped into them. As she pulled them to her waist she saw Ronny Pye standing by the main door, and she grinned at him – a lopsided depraved whore's smile on the smeared and inflamed lips.

'Another one? All right, come along then, love.' She took a step in his direction, tottered suddenly and turned away to grab at the table for support, the painted doll's face suddenly white and translucent as alabaster, then slowly she doubled over and vomited on the thick silken expanse of woven Qum carpet.

With an exclamation of disgust, Ronny Pye turned away, and crossed to the doors that led into the drawing-room.

Nobody looked up as he entered, although there were twenty people or more in the room. They were gathered intently about a solid round gaming-table of ebony with ivory and mosaic inlay. The tabletop was scattered with poker chips, brightly coloured ivory counters, and four men sat at the table, each holding a fan of cards to his chest, watching the figure at the head of the table. The tension crackled in the room like static electricity.

He was not surprised to see that one of the men at the table was his brother-in-law. He knew that Dennis Petersen regularly attended the soirées at Great Longwood, and he thought briefly of his pliant dutiful sister and wondered if she knew.

'The man has drawn us all in,' Ronny thought bitterly, glancing at Dennis and noticing his bleary, inflamed eyes, the nervous drawn white face. 'At least I have withstood this, this final filthy degradation. Whatever other evils he has led me into, I have kept this little shred of my self respect.'

'Well, gentlemen, I have bad news to impart, I'm afraid,' Dirk Courtney smiled urbanely. 'The ladies are with me,' and he spread his cards face up on the green baize. The four queens in their fanciful costume stared up with wooden expressions, and the other players peered at them for a moment, and then one at a time, with expressions of disgust, discarded their own hands.

Dennis Petersen was the last to concede defeat, and his face was stricken, his hand shook. And then with a sound that was almost a sob, he let his cards flutter from his fingers, pushed back his chair and blundered towards the door.

Halfway there, he stopped suddenly as he recognized the gaunt forbidding figure of his brother-in-law. He stared at him for a moment, the lips still trembling, blinking his bloodshot eyes; then he shook his head as though doubting his senses.

'You here?'

'Oh yes,' Dirk called from the table where he was gathering and stacking the ivory chips. 'Did I forget to mention that I had invited Ronald? Forgive me,' he told the other players, 'I will be back in a short while.' He stood from the table, brushed away the clinging hands of one of the women, and came to take the elbows of Ronald Pye and his brother-in-law in a friendly grip, and to guide them out of the drawing-room, down the long flagged passage to his study.

Even at midday, the room was cool and dark, thick stone walls and heavy velvet drapes, dark wooden panelling and deep Persian and Oriental carpeting, sombre smoky-looking oil paintings on the panelling, one of which Ronald Pye knew was a Reynolds, and another a Turner, heavy chunky furniture, with coverings of chocolate-coloured leather – it was a room which always depressed Ronald Pye. He always thought of it as the centre of the web in which he and his family had slowly entangled themselves.

Dennis Petersen slumped into one of the leather chairs, and after a moment's hesitation, Ronald Pye took the one facing him and sat there stiffly, disapprovingly.

Dirk Courtney splashed single malt whisky into the glasses that were set out on a silver tray on the corner of the big mahogany desk, and made a silent offer to Ronald Pye, who shook his head primly.

Instead, he carried a glass of the glowing amber liquor to Dennis who accepted it with trembling hands, gulped a mouthful and then blurted thickly,

'Why did you do it, Dirk? You promised that nobody would know I was here, and you invited—' he glanced across at the grim countenance of his brother-in-law.

Dirk chuckled. 'I always keep my promises – just as long as it pays me to do so.' He lifted his own glass. 'But between the three of us there should be no secrets. Let's drink to that.'

When Dirk lowered his glass, Ronald Pye asked, 'Why did you invite me here today?'

'We have a number of problems to discuss – the first of which is dear Dennis here. As a poker player, he makes a fine blacksmith.'

'How much?' Ronald Pye asked quietly.

'Tell him, Dennis,' Dirk invited him, and they waited while he studied the remaining liquor in his glass.

'Well?' said Ronald Pye again.

'Don't be shy, Dennis, me old cocky diamond,' Dirk encouraged him. Dennis mumbled a figure without looking up.

Ronald Pye shifted his weight in the leather chair, and his mouth quivered. 'It's a gambling debt. We repudiate it.'

'Shall I ask one or two of the young ladies who are my

guests here to go down and give your sister a first-hand account of some of the other little tricks Dennis has been up to? Did you know that Dennis likes to have them kneel over—'

'Dirk, you wouldn't,' bleated Dennis. 'You're not going to do that—' and he sank his face into his hands.

'You will have a cheque tomorrow,' said Ronald Pye softly.

'Thank you, Ronny, it really is a pleasure to do business with you.'

'Is that all?'

'Oh no,' Dirk grinned at him. 'By no means.' He carried the crystal decanter across to Dennis and recharged his glass. 'We have another little money matter to discuss.' He filled his own glass with whisky and held it to the light. 'Bank business,' he said, but Ronny Pye cut in swiftly.

'I think you should know that I am about to retire from the Bank. I have received an offer for my remaining shares, I am negotiating for a vineyard down in the Cape. I will be leaving Ladyburg and taking my family with me.'

'No,' Dirk shook his head, smiling lightly. 'You and I are together for ever. We have a bond that is unbreakable. I want you with me always – somebody I can trust, perhaps the only person in the world I can trust. We share so many secrets, old friend. Including murder.'

They both froze at the word, and slowly colour drained from Ronald Pye's face.

'John Anders and his boy,' Dirk reminded them, and they both broke in together.

'The boy got away—'

'He's still alive.'

'Not for much longer,' Dirk assured them. 'My man is on the way to him now. This time there will be no further trouble from him.'

'You can't do it,' Dennis Petersen shook his head vehemently.

'Why, in God's name? Let it be.' Ronald Pye was begging now, suddenly all the stiffness going out of his bearing. 'Let the boy alone, we have enough—'

'No. He has not left us alone,' Dirk explained reasonably. 'He has been actively gathering information on all of us and all our activities. By a stroke of fortune I have learned where he is and he is alone, in a lonely place.'

They were silent now, and while he waited for them to think it out, Dirk flicked the stub of his cheroot on to the fireplace and lit another.

'What more do you want from us, now?' Ronald asked at last.

'Ah, so at last we can discuss the matter in a businesslike fashion?' Dirk propped himself on the edge of the desk and picked up an antique duelling pistol that he used as a paper weight. He spun it on his finger as he talked. 'I am short of liquid funds for the expansion programme that I began five years ago. There has been a decline in sugar prices, a reduction in the Bank's investment flow – but you know all this, of course.'

Ronald Pye nodded cautiously. 'We have already agreed to adapt the land purchases to our cash flow, for the next few years at least. We will be patient.'

'I am not a patient man, Ronny.'

'We are short two hundred thousand a year over the next three years. We have agreed to cut down,' Ronald Pye went on, but Dirk was not listening. He twirled the pistol, aimed at the eye of the portrait above the fireplace and snapped the hammer on the empty cap.

'Two hundred thousand a year for three years is six hundred thousands of sterling,' Dirk mused aloud, and lowered the pistol. 'Which is by chance exactly the amount paid by me to you for your shares, some ten years ago.'

'No,' said Ronald Pye, with an edge of panic in his voice. 'That's mine, that's my personal capital, it has nothing to do with the Bank.'

208

'You've done very nicely with it too,' Dirk congratulated him. 'Those Crown Deep shares did you proud, an excellent buy. By my latest calculations, your personal net worth is not much less than eight hundred thousand.'

'In trust for my family, my daughter and my grand-children,' said Ronny, his voice edged with desperation.

'I need that money now,' Dirk spoke reasonably.

'What about your own personal resources?' Ronald Pye demanded desperately.

'Stretched to their limit, my dear Ronald, all of it invested in land and sugar.'

'You could borrow on—'

'Oh, but why should I borrow from strangers, when a dear and trusted friend will make the loan to the Ladyburg Farmers Bank? What finer security than that offered by that venerable institution? A loan, dear Ronald, merely a loan.'

'No.' Ronald Pye came to his feet. 'That money is not mine. It belongs to my family.' He turned to his brother-in-law. 'Come. I will take you home.'

Smiling that charming, sparkling smile, Dirk aimed the duelling pistol between Dennis Petersen's eyes.

'Stay where you are, Dennis,' he said, and snapped the hammer again.

'It's all right,' said Ronald Pye to Dennis. 'We can break away now. If you stick with me.' Ronald was panting a little, and sweating like a runner. 'If he accuses us of murder, he accuses himself also. We can prove that we were not the planners, not the ones who gave the orders. I think he is bluffing. It's a chance we will have to take to be rid of him.' He turned to face Dirk now, and there was the steel of defiance in his eyes. 'To be rid of this monster. Let him do his worst, and he damns himself as much as he does us.'

'How well conceived a notion!' Dirk laughed delight-edly. 'And I do really believe that you are foolish enough to mean what you say.'

'Come, Dennis. Let him do his worst.' Without another glance at either of them, Ronald Pye stalked to the door.

'Which of your grandchildren do you cherish most, Ronny, Natalie or Victoria?' Dirk asked, still laughing. 'Or, I imagine, it's the little boy – what's his name? Damn! I should know the brat's name – I am his godfather.' He chuckled again, then snapped his fingers as he remembered. 'Damn me, of course, Ronald, like his granddaddy. Little Ronald.'

Ronald Pye had turned at the door and was staring across the room at him. Dirk grinned back at him, as though at some delicious joke.

'Little Ronald,' he grinned, and aimed the pistol at an imaginary figure in the centre of the open carpet, a diminutive figure it seemed, no higher than a man's knee. 'Goodbye, little Ronald,' he murmured, and clicked the hammer. 'Goodbye, little Natalie.' He swung the pistol to another invisible figure and snapped the action. 'Goodbye, little Victoria.' The pistol clicked again – the metallic sound shockingly loud in the silent room.

'You wouldn't—' Dennis' voice was strangled, 'you wouldn't—'

'I need the money very badly,' Dirk told him.

'But you wouldn't do that—'

'You keep telling me what I wouldn't do. Since when have you been such a fine judge of my behaviour?'

'Not the children?' pleaded Dennis.

'I've done it before,' Dirk pointed out.

'Yes, but not children – not little children.'

Ronald Pye stood at the door still. He seemed to have aged ten years in the last few seconds, his shoulders had sagged and his face was grey and deeply lined, the flesh seemed to have fallen in around his eyes, sagging into loose folds.

'Before you leave, Ronny, let me tell you a story you have been desperate to hear for twelve years. I know you have spent much time and money trying to find out already. Return to your chair, please. Listen to my story and then you are free to go – if you still want to do so.'

Ronald Pye's hand fell away from the door handle, and he shambled back and dropped into the leather chair as though his limbs did not belong to him.

Dirk filled a spare glass with whisky and placed it on the arm of his chair, within easy reach – and Ronny did not protest.

'It's the story of how a nineteen-year-old boy made himself a million pounds in cash, and used it to buy a bank. When you have heard it, I want you to ask yourself if there is anything that boy would *not* do.' Dirk stood up and began to pace up and down the thick carpeting between their chairs like a caged feline animal, lithe and graceful, but sinister also, and cruel; and he began to speak in that soft purring voice that wove a hypnotic web about them, and their heads swung to follow his regular measured pacing.

'Shall we call the boy Dirk, it's a good name – a tough name for a lad who was thrown out by a tyrannical father and set out to get the things he wanted his own way, a boy who learned quickly and was frightened of nothing, a boy who by his nineteenth birthday was first mate of a beaten-up old coal-burning tramp steamer running dubious cargos to the bad spots of the Orient. A boy who could run a ship single-handed and whip work out of a crew of niggers with a rope end, while the skipper wallowed in gin in his cabin.'

He paused beside the desk, refilled his glass with whisky and asked his audience, 'Does the story grip you so far?'

'You are drunk,' said Ronald Pye.

'I am never drunk,' Dirk contradicted him, and resumed his pacing.

'We will call the steamer *L'Oiseau de Nuit* – "The Bird of Night", though, in all truth, it's an unlikely name for a stinking old cow of a boat. Her skipper was Le Doux – the sweet one – again a mild misnomer,' and Dirk chuckled reminiscently, and sipped at his glass. 'This merry crew discharged a midnight cargo in the Yellow River late in the summer of '09 and next day put into the port of Liang Su for a more legitimate return cargo of tea and silks.

'From the roadstead, they could see that the outskirts of the town was in flames, and they could hear the crackle of small arms fire. The basin was empty of shipping, just a few sampans and one or two small junks, and the fear-crazed population of the city was crowding the wharf, screaming for a berth to safety.

'Hundreds of them plunged into the basin and swam out to where "The Bird of Night" was hovering. The mate let two of them come aboard and then turned the hoses on the others, driving them off, while he learned what was happening.' Dirk paused, remembering how the pressure of the solid jets of water had driven the swimmers under the filthy yellow surface of the basin, and how the others had wailed and tried to swim back. He grinned and roused himself. 'The Communist war-lord, Han Wang, was attacking the port and had promised the rich merchants an amusing death in the bamboo cages. Now the mate knew just how rich the merchants of Liang Su really were. After consulting the captain, the mate brought "The Bird of Night" alongside the wharf, clearing it of the peasant scum with steam hoses and a few pistol shots, and he led an armed party of lascars into the city to the guild house where the Chinese tea merchants were gathered, paralysed with terror and already resigned to their fate. Another whisky, Ronny?'

Ronald Pye shook his head, his eyes had not left Dirk's face since the tale began, and now Dirk smiled at him.

'The mate set the passage money so high that only the very richest could afford to pay it, two thousand sovereign a head – but still ninety-six of them came aboard "The Bird of Night", each staggering under the load of his possessions. Even the children carried their own weight, boxes and bales and sacks – and while we are on the subject of children, there were forty-eight of them in the party, all boys of course, for no sane Chinaman would waste two thousand pounds on a girl child. The little boys ranged from babes to striplings, some of them of an age with your little Ronald.' Dirk paused to let it register, then, 'It was a close run, for as the last of them came aboard, the mate cast off from the wharf and Han Wang's bandits burst out of the city and hacked and bayoneted their way on to the wharf. Their rifle-fire spattered the upper works, and swept "The Bird of Night's" decks, sending her newly boarded passengers screaming down into the empty holds, but she made a clear run of it out of the river and by dark was pushing out into a quiet tropical sea.

'Le Doux, the captain, could not believe his fortune – almost two hundred thousand sovereigns in gold, in four tea chests in his cabin, and he promised young Dirk a thousand for himself. But Dirk knew the value of his captain's promises. Nevertheless, he suggested a further avenue of profit.

'Old Le Doux had been a hard man before the drink got to him. He had run slaves out of Africa, opium out of India, but he was soft now, and he was horrified by what his young mate suggested. He blasphemed by praying to God and he wept. "Les pauvres petits," he slobbered, and poured gin down his throat until after midnight he collapsed into that stupor that Dirk knew would last for forty-eight hours.

'The mate went up on to the bridge and sounded the ship's siren, shouting to his passengers that there was a government gunboat overtaking them, and driving them from the open deck back into the holds. They went like sheep, clutching their possessions. The mate and his lascars battened down the hatches, closing 'em up tight and solid. Can you guess the rest of it?' he asked. 'A guinea for the correct solution.'

Ronald Pye licked his dry grey lips, and shook his head.

'No?' Dirk teased him. 'The easiest guinea you ever missed – why, it was simple. The mate opened the seacocks and flooded the holds.' He watched them curiously, anticipating their reactions. Neither of his listeners could speak, and as Dirk went on, there was a small change in his telling of it. He no longer spoke in the third person. Now it was 'we' and 'I'.

'Of course, we couldn't flood to the top, even in that low sea she might have foundered, and rolled on her back. There must have been a small airspace under the hatch, and they held the children up there. I could hear them through the four-inch timbers of the hatch. For almost half an hour they kept up their howling and screaming until the air went bad and the roll and slosh of the water got them, and when at last it was all over and we opened the hatches, we found that they had torn the woodwork of the underside of the covers with their fingers, ripped and splintered it like a cage full of monkeys.'

Dirk turned to the empty chair nearest the fireplace and sank into it. He swilled the whisky in his right hand and then swallowed it. He threw the crystal glass into the empty fireplace and it exploded into diamond fragments. They were all silent, staring at the glass splinters.

'Why?' whispered Dennis huskily at last. 'In God's name, why did you kill them?'

Dirk did not look at him, he was lost in the past, reliving a high tide in his life. Then he roused himself and went on, 'We pumped out the hold, and I had the lascars carry all the sodden sacks and bales and boxes up into the saloon. God, Ronny, you should have been there. It was a sight to drive a man like you mad with greed. I piled it all up on the saloon table. It was a treasure that had taken fifty cunning men a lifetime to accumulate. There was gold in coin and bar, diamonds like the end of your thumb, rubies to choke a camel, emeralds – well, the merchants of Liang Su were some of the richest in China. Together with the passage money, the loot came to just over a million in sterling—'

'And the captain, Le Doux, his share?' Ronald Pye asked; even in his horror his accountant's mind was working.

'The captain?' Dirk shook his head and smiled that light, boyish smile. 'Poor Le Doux, he must have fallen overboard that night. Drunk as he was, he would not have been able to swim – and the sharks were bad out there in the China Sea. God knows that with the water full of dead Chinese, there was enough to attract them. No, there was only one share, not counting a token to the lascars. Two hundred pounds for each of them was a fortune beyond their wildest dreams of avarice. That left a million pounds for a night's work. A million before the age of twenty.'

'That's the most terrible story I've ever heard.' Ronald Pye's voice shook like the hand that raised the glass to his lips.

'Remember it when next you have naughty thoughts of leaving Ladyburg,' Dirk counselled him, and leaned across to pat his shoulder. 'We are comrades – unto death,' he said.

For Mark the allotted days were running out swiftly. Soon he must leave the valley and return to the world of men, and a quiet desperation came over him. He had searched the south bank and the steep ground above it, now he crossed to the north bank and started there all over again.

Here, for the first time, he had warning that he was not the only human being in the valley. The first day he came across a line of snares laid along the game trails that led down to drinking-places on the river. The wire used was the same as that he had found on the gangrened leg of the crippled impala doe, eighteen-gauge galvanized mild steel wire, probably cut from some unsuspecting farmer's fence.

Mark found sixteen snares that day and tore each out, bundled the wire and hurled it into one of the deeper pools of the river.

Two days later, he came across a log deadfall, so cunningly devised and so skilfully set that it had crushed a full-grown otter. Mark used a branch to lever the log clear and drew out the carcass. He stroked the soft, lustrous chocolate fur and felt again the stirring of his anger. Quite unreasonably, he was developing a strange proprietary feeling for the animals of this valley, and a growing hatred for anyone who hunted or molested them.

Now his attention was divided almost equally between his search for his grandfather's grave and for further signs of the illegal trapper. Yet it was almost another week before he had direct sign of the mysterious hunter.

He was crossing the river each morning in the dawn to work the north bank. It might have been easier to abandon the camp under the fig trees, but sentiment kept him there. It was the old man's camp, their old camp together, and in any case he enjoyed the daily crossing and the journey through the swampland formed in the crotch of the two rivers. Although it was only the very edge of this watery world that he moved through, yet he recognized it as the very heart of this wilderness, an endless well of precious water and even more precious life, the last secure refuge of so many creatures of the valley.

He found daily evidence of the big game on the muddy paths through the towering stands of reed and papyrus, which closed overhead to form a cool gloomy tunnel of living green stems. There were Cape buffalo, and twice he heard them crashing away through the papyrus without a glimpse of them. There were hippopotamus and crocodile but they spent the days deep in the dark reed-fringed lakelets and mysterious lily-covered pools. At night he often woke and huddled in his blanket to listen to their harsh grunting bellows resounding through the swampland.

One noonday, sitting on a low promontory of rocky wooded ground that thrust into the swamp, he watched a white rhinoceros bring its calf out of the sheltering reeds to feed on the edge of the bush.

She was a huge old female, her pale grey hide scarred and scratched, folded and wrinkled over the massive pre-historic body that weighed at least four tons, and she fussed over the calf anxiously, guiding it with her long slightly curved nose horn; the calf was hornless and fat as a piglet. Watching the pair, Mark realized suddenly how deeply this place had touched his life, and the possessive love he was developing for it was reaffirmed.

Here he lived as though he was the first man in all the earth, and it touched some deep atavistic need in his spirit. It was on that same day that he came upon recent signs of the other human presence beyond Chaka's Gate.

He was following one of the faint game paths that skirted another ridge, one of those that joined the main run of ground into the slopes of the escarpment, when he came upon the spoor.

It was barefooted, the flat-arched and broad soles of feet that had never been constricted by leather footwear. Mark went down on his knees to examine it carefully. Too big for a woman, he knew at once.

The stride told him the man was tall. The gait was slightly toe-in and the weight was carried on the ball of the foot, the way an athlete walks. There was no scuff or drag of toe on the forward swing, a high lift and a controlled transfer of weight – a strong, quick, alert man, moving fast and silently.

The spoor was so fresh that at the damp patch where the man had paused to urinate, the butterflies still fluttered in a brilliant cloud for the moisture and salt. Mark was very close behind him, and he felt the hunter's thrill as, without hesitation, he picked up and started to run the spoor.

He was closing quickly. The man he was following was unaware. He had paused to cut a green twig from a wild loquat branch, probably to use as a tooth pick, and the shavings were still wet and bleeding.

Then there was the place where the man had paused, turned back on his own spoor a single pace, paused again, almost certainly to listen, then turned abruptly off the path; within ten more paces the spoor ended, as though the man had launched into flight, or been lifted into the sky by a fiery chariot. His disappearance was almost magical, and though Mark worked for another hour, casting and circling, he found no further sign.

He sat down and lit a cigarette, and found he was sweaty and disgruntled. Although he had used all his bushcraft to come up with his quarry, he had been made to look like an infant. The man had become aware of Mark following, probably from a thousand yards off, and he had jinked and covered his spoor, throwing the pursuit with such casual ease that it was a positive insult.

As he sat, Mark felt his ill-humour harden and become positive hard anger.

'I'll get you yet,' he promised the mysterious stranger aloud, and it did not even occur to him what he might do, if he ever did come up with his quarry. All that he knew was that he had been challenged, and he had taken up the challenge.

The man had the cunning of – Mark sought for a simile, a properly disparaging simile – and then grinned as he found a suitable one. The man had the cunning of a jackal, but he was Zulu so Mark used the Zulu word 'Pungushe'.

'I'll be watching for you, Pungushe. I'll catch you yet, little jackal.'

His mood improved with the insult, and as he crushed out his cigarette, he found himself anticipating the contest of bush skills between himself and Pungushe.

Now whenever Mark moved through the wilderness, part of his attention was alert for the familiar footprints in the soft earthy places or for the glimpse of movement and the figure of a man among trees. Three times more he cut the spoor, but each time it was cold and wind-eroded, not worth following.

The days passed in a majestic circle of sky and mountain, of sun and river and swamp, so that time seemed without end until he counted on his fingers and realized that his month was almost run. Then he felt the dread of leaving, a sinking of the spirits such as a child feels when the moment of return to school comes at the end of an idyllic summer holiday.

That night he returned to the camp below the fig tree with the last of the light, and set his rifle against the stem of the tree. He stood a moment, stretching aching muscles and savouring the coming pleasure of hot coffee and a cheerful fire, when suddenly he stooped and then dropped to one knee to examine the earth, soft and fluffy with leaf mould.

Even in the bad light, there was no mistaking the print of broad bare feet. Quickly, Mark looked up and searched the darkening bush about him, feeling an uneasy chill at the knowledge that he might be observed at this very moment. Satisfied at last that he was alone he backtracked the spoor, and found that the mysterious stranger had searched his camp, had found the pack in the tree and examined it contents, then returned them carefully, each item to its exact place and replaced the pack in the tree. Had Mark not seen the spoor in the earth he would never have suspected that his pack had been touched.

It left him disquieted and ill at ease to know that the

man he had tracked and followed had been tracking and probably watching him just as carefully – and with considerably greater success rewarding his efforts.

Mark slept badly that night, troubled by weird dreams in which he followed a dark figure that tap-tapped with a staff on the rocky dangerous path ahead of him, drawing slowly away from Mark without looking back, while Mark tried desperately to call to him to wait, but no sound came from his straining throat.

In the morning he slept late, and rose dull and heavy-headed to look up into a sky filled with slowly moving cumbersome ranges of dark bruised cumulus cloud that rolled in on the south-east wind from off the ocean. He knew soon it would rain, and that he should be going. His time had run, but in the end he promised himself a few last days, for the old man's sake and his own.

It rained that morning before noon, a mere taste of what was to come, but still a quick cold grey drenching downpour that caught Mark without shelter. Even though the sun poured through a gap in the clouds immediately afterwards, Mark found that the cold of the rain seemed to have penetrated his bones, and he shivered like a man with palsy in his sodden clothing.

Only when the shivering persisted long after his clothes had dried, did Mark realize that it was exactly twenty-two days since his first night under the fig tree, and his first exposure to the river mosquitoes.

Another violent shivering fit caught him, and he realized that his life probably depended now on the bottle of quinine tablets in the pack high in the branches of the fig tree, and on whether he could reach it before the malaria struck with all its malignance.

It was four miles back to camp and he took a short route through thick thorn and over a rocky ridge, to intersect the path again on the far side.

By the time he cut the path, he was feeling dizzy and

light-headed, and he had to rest a moment. The cigarette he lit tasted bitter and stale, and as he ground the stub under his heel he saw the other spoor in the path. In this place it had been protected from the short downpour of rain by the dense spreading branches of a mahoba hoba tree. It overlaid his own outward spoor, moving in the same direction as he had, but the thing that shocked him was that the feet that had followed his had been booted, and shod with hob-nails. They were the narrower elongated feet of a white man. There seemed in that moment of sickness on the threshold of malaria to be something monstrously sinister in those booted tracks.

Another quick fit of shivering caught Mark, and then passed, leaving him momentarily clear-headed and with the illusion of strength, but when he stood to go on, his legs were still leaden. He had gone another five hundred yards back towards the river when a day-flighting owl called on the ridge behind him, at the point where he had just crossed.

Mark stopped abruptly, and tilted his head to listen. A tsetse fly bite at the back of his neck began to itch furiously, but he stood completely still as he listened.

The call of the owl was answered by a mate, the fluting hoot-hoot, skilfully imitated, but without the natural resonance. The second call had come from out on Mark's right, and a new chill that was not malaria rippled up his spine as he remembered the hooting owls on the escarpment above Ladyburg on that night so many months ago.

He began to hurry now, dragging his heavy almost disembodied legs along the winding path. He found that he was panting before he had gone another hundred yards, and that waves of physical nausea flowed upwards from the pit of his belly, gagging in his throat as the fever tightened its grip on him.

His vision began to break up, starring and cracking like shattered mosaic work, irregular patches of darkness edged in bright iridescent colours, with occasional flashes of true vision, as though he looked out through gaps in the mosaic.

He struggled on desperately, expecting at any moment now to feel the spongy swamp grass under his feet and to enter the dark protective tunnels of papyrus which he knew so well, and which would screen him and direct him back to the old camp.

An owl hooted again, much closer this time and from a completely unexpected direction. Confused, and now frightened, Mark sank down at the base of a knob-thorn tree to rest and gather his reserves. His heart was pounding against his ribs, and the nausea was so powerful as almost to force him to retch, but he rode it for a moment longer and miraculously his vision opened as though a dark curtain had been drawn aside, and he realized immediately that in his fever blindness he had lost the path. He had no idea where he was now, or the direction in which he was facing.

Desperately he tried to relate the angle of the sun, or slope of the ground, or find some recognizable landmark, but the branches of the knob-thorn spread overhead and all around him the bush closed in, limiting his vision to about fifty paces.

He dragged himself to his feet and turned up the rocky slope, hoping to reach high ground, and behind him an owl hooted – a mournful, funereal sound.

He was blind and shaking again when he fell, and he knew he had torn his shin for he could feel the slow warm trickle of blood down his ankle, but it seemed unrelated to his present circumstances, and when he lifted his hand to his face, it was shaking so violently that he could not wipe the icy sweat from his eyes.

Out on his left, the owl called again, and his teeth chattered in his head so that the sound was magnified painfully in his ears.

Mark rolled over and peered blindly in the direction of

the hooting owl, trying to force back the darkness, blinking the sweat that stung like salt in his eyes.

It was like looking down a long dark tunnel to light at the end, or through the wrong end of a telescope.

Something moved on a field of golden brown grass, and he tried to force his eyes to serve him, but his vision wavered and burned.

There was movement, that was all he was sure of – then silent meteors of light, yellow and red and green, exploded across his mind, and cleared, and suddenly his vision was stark and brilliant, he could see with unnatural almost terrifying clarity.

A man was crossing his flank, a big man, with a head round and heavy as a cannon ball. He had a wrestler's shoulders, and a thick bovine neck. Mark could not see his face. It was turned away from him, yet there was something dreadfully familiar about him.

He wore a bandolier over his shoulder, over the khaki shirt with military-style button-down pockets, and his breeches were tucked into scuffed brown riding-boots. He carried a rifle at high port across his chest, and he moved with a hunter's cautious, exaggerated tread. Mark's vision began to spin and disintegrate again.

He blundered to his feet, dragging himself up the stem of the knob-thorn, and one of the sharp curved thorns stabbed deeply into the ball of his thumb; the pain was irrelevant and he began to run.

Behind him there was a shout, the view-halloo of the hunter, and Mark's instinct of survival was just strong enough to direct his feet. He swung away abruptly, changing direction, and he heard the bullet a split second before the sound of the shot. It cracked in the air beside his head like a gigantic bull-whip, and after it, the secondary brittle snapping bark of the shot.

'Mauser,' he thought, and was transported instantly to another time in another land.

Some time-keeping instinct in his head began counting the split instants of combat, tolling them off even in his blindness and sickness, so that without looking back he knew when his hunter had reloaded and taken his next aim. Mark jinked again in his stumbling, unseeing run and again the shot cracked the air beside him, and Mark unslung the P.14 from his shoulder and ran on.

Suddenly he was into trees, and beside him a slab of bark exploded from a trunk, torn loose by the next Mauser bullet in a spray of flying fragments and sap, leaving a white wet wound in the tree. But Mark had reached the ridge, and the instant he dropped over it, he turned at right angles, doubled up from the waist and dogged away, seeking desperately in the gloom for a secure stance from which to defend himself.

Suddenly he was deafened by a sound as though the heavens had cracked open, and the sun had fallen upon him – sound and light so immense and close that he thought for an instant that a Mauser bullet had shattered his brain. He dropped instinctively to his knees.

It was only in the silence that followed that he realized lightning had struck the ironstone ridge close beside him, and the electric stench of it filled the air around him, the rumbling echo of thunder still muttered over the blue wall of the escarpment and the huge bruised masses of cloud had tumbled down out of the endless blue vault of the sky to press close against the earth.

The wind came immediately, cold and swiftly rushing, thrashing the branches of the trees above him, and when Mark dragged himself to his feet again, it billowed his shirt and ruffled his hair, inducing another fit of violent shivering. It seemed the sweat on his face had been turned instantly to hoarfrost; in the rush of the wind, an owl hooted somewhere close at hand, and it began to rain again.

In the rain ahead of Mark, there was the gaunt, tortured

shape of a dead tree. To his fever-distorted eyes it had the shape of an angry warlock, with threatening arms and twisted frame, but it offered a stance, the best he could hope for at this exposed moment.

For a few blessed moments, the darkness behind his eyes lightened and his vision opened to a limited grey circle.

He realized that he had doubled back and come up against the river. The dead tree against which he stood was on the very brink of the sheer high bank. The river had undercut its roots, killing it, and in time would suck it into the flood and carry it away downstream.

At Mark's back, the river was already high and swift and brown with rain water, cutting off any retreat. He was cornered against the bank while the hunters closed in on him. He knew there were more than one, the owl calls had been signals, just as they had on the escarpment of Ladyburg.

Mark realized that perhaps his only hope was to separate them, and lead them unsuspecting on to his stance, but it must be quick, before the fever tightened its hold on his sense.

He cupped one hand to his mouth and imitated the sad, mournful call of the Scops owl. The he leaned back against the tree and held the rifle low across one hip. Off on the right his call was answered. Mark did not move. He stood frozen against the tree trunk, only his eyes swivelled to the sound and his forehead creased in his effort to see clearly. Long minutes drew out, and then the owl hoot came, even closer at hand.

The rain came now on the wind, driving in at a steep angle, ice-white lances of slanting rain, tearing at the bush and open grassland beneath it, hammering into Mark's face with sharp needles that stung his eyelids, and yet cleared his vision again so that he could see into the swirling white veils of water. Carefully Mark cupped his mouth and hooted the owl call, bringing his man closer.

'Where are you?' a voice called softly. 'Rene, where are you?'

Mark swivelled his eyes to the sound. A human figure loomed out of the sodden trees, half obscured by the sheets of falling rain.

'I heard your shots – did you get him?' He was coming towards Mark, a tall lean man with a very dark brown sunscorched face, deeply lined and wrinkled around the eyes, with a short scraggy growth of grizzled hair covering his jowls.

He carried a Lee-Metford rifle at the trail in one hand, and a rubber ex-army gas-cape draped over his shoulders, wet and shiny with rain, a man past the prime of his life, with the dull, unintelligent eyes and the coarse almost brutal features of a Russian peasant. The face of one who would kill a man with as little compunction as he would slit a hog's throat.

He had seen Mark against the dead tree trunk, but the swirling rain and the bad light showed him just the dark uncertain shape, and the call of the owl had lulled him.

'Rene?' he called again, and then stopped, for the first time uncertain, and he squinted into the teeming rain with those flat expressionless eyes. Then he swore angrily, and tried to bring up the Lee-Metford, swinging it across his belly and wiping the safety-catch across with one calloused thumb. 'It's him!' He recognized Mark, and the dismay was clear to see on his face.

'No,' Mark warned him urgently, but the rifle barrel was coming up swiftly, and Mark had heard the metallic snick of the safety-catch and knew that in an instant the man would shoot him down.

He fired with the P.14 still held low across his hip, the man was that close, and the shot crashed out with shocking loudness.

The man was lifted off his feet, thrown backwards with the Lee-Metford spinning from his hands, hitting the rocky ground with his shoulder blades, his heels kicking and drumming wildly on the earth and his eyelids fluttering like the wings of trapped butterflies.

The blood that streamed from his chest soaked into the sodden material of his shirt and was diluted immediately to a paler rose pink by the hammering raindrops.

With a final spasm, which arched his back, the man subsided and lay completely still. He seemed to have shrunk in size, looking old and frail, and his lower jaw hung open, revealing the pink rubber gums of a set of tobacco-stained false teeth. The rain beat into the open staring eyes, and Mark felt a familiar sense of dismay. The cold familiar guilt of having inflicted death on another human being. He had an irrational desire to go to the man, to give him succour, though he was far past any human help, to try to explain to him, to justify himself. The impulse was fever-born and carried on wings of rising delirium; he was at the point now where there was no clear dividing line between fantasy and reality.

'You shouldn't have,' he blurted, 'you shouldn't have tried, I warned you, I warned—' He stepped out from the shelter of the dead tree trunk, forgetting the other man, the man that his senses should have warned him was the most dangerous of the two hunters.

He stood over the man he had killed, swaying on his feet, holding the rifle at high port across his chest.

Hobday had missed with his first three shots, but the range had been two hundred or more and it was up-hill shooting, with intervening bush and tree and shrub, snap shooting at a running, jinking target, worse than jump-shooting for kudu in thick cat bush – a slim swift human shape. He had fired the second and third shots in despair, hoping for a lucky hit before his quarry reached the crest of the ridge and disappeared.

Now he could follow only cautiously, for he had seen the rifle strapped on the boy's back, and he might be lying up on the ridge – waiting his chance for a clear shot. He used all the cover there was, and at last the sheets of falling rain, to reach the rocky crest, at any moment expecting retaliatory fire, for he had shown his own hand clearly. He knew the boy was a trained soldier. He was dangerous and Hobday moved with care.

His relief when he reached the crest was immense, and he lay there on his belly in the wet grass with the reloaded Mauser in front peering down the reverse slope for a sign of his quarry.

He heard the owl hoot out on his left, and frowned irritably. 'Stupid old bastard!' he grunted. 'Pissing himself with fright still.' His partner needed constant reassurance, his old nerves too frayed for this work, and he used no judgement in timing his contact calls. The damned fool! He must have heard the shots and known the critical stage of the hunt was on, yet here he was, calling again, like a child whistling in the dark for courage.

He brushed the man from his thoughts and concentrated on searching the rainswept slope, until he froze with disbelief. The owl call had been answered, from his left, just below the crest.

Hobday came up on his feet. Crouching low, he worked swiftly along the crest.

He saw solid movement in the grey, wind-whipped scrub and dropped into a marksman's squat, drawing swift aim on the indistinct target, blinking the rain out of his eyes, waiting for a clean shot and then grunting with disappointment as he recognized his own partner, bowed under the glistening wet gas-cape, moving heavily as a pregnant woman in the gloom beneath the rain cloud and dense overhead branches.

The man paused to cup his hand over his mouth and call the mournful owl hoot again, and the bearded hunter grinned. 'Decoy duck,' he whispered aloud, 'the stupid old dog!' and he felt no compunction that he was going to let his ally draw fire for him. He watched him carefully, keeping well down on the skyline, the silhouette of his head and shoulders broken by the low bush under which he crouched.

The old man in the gas-cape called again, and then waited listening with his head cocked. The reply called him on, and he hurried forward into the wind and the rain, drawn on to his fate. Hobday grinned as he watched. One share was better than two, he thought, and wiped the clinging raindrops off the rear sight of the Mauser with his thumb.

Suddenly the old man checked and began to swing up the rifle he carried, but the shot crashed out and he went down abruptly in the grass. Hobday swore softly, bitterly, he had missed the moment, had not been able to place the spot from which the shot had been fired. Now he waited with a finger on the trigger, screwing up his eyes against the rain, less certain of himself, feeling a new awe and respect for his quarry, and the first tingle of fear. It had been a good kill, that one, leading the old man right in close, calling him up as though he were a hungry leopard coming to the bleat of a duiker horn.

Then suddenly the bearded hunter's doubts were dispelled, and for an instant he could hardly believe his fortune. Just when he had been steeling himself for a dangerous and long-drawn-out duel, his quarry stepped out into the open from the cover of a twisted dead tree trunk on the bank of the river, a childlike, ridiculously artless act – an almost suicidal act, so ingenuous that for a moment he feared some trap.

The young man stood for a moment over the corpse of the man he had killed. Even at this range, it seemed as though he swayed on his feet, his face very pale in the weak grey light but the khaki of his shirt standing out clearly against the back lighting from the surface of the river.

It needed no fancy shooting, the range was less than a

hundred and fifty yards and for an instant Hobday held his aim in the centre of the boy's chest, then he squeezed off the shot with exaggerated care, knowing that it was a heart shot. As the rifle pounded back into his shoulder and the brittle crack of the Mauser stung his eardrums, he watched the boy hurled backwards by the shock of the strike and heard the bullet impact with a jarring solid thud.

Mark never even heard the Mauser shot for the bullet came ahead of the sound. There was only the massive shock in the upper part of his body, and then he was hurled backwards with a violence that drove the air from his lungs.

The earth opened behind him, and as he fell, there was the sensation of being engulfed in a swirling vortex of blackness – and he knew for just a fleeting moment of time that he was dead.

Then the icy plunge into the swirling brown current of the river caught him and shocked him back from the edge of blackness. The water engulfed his head and he had the strength to kick away from the muddy bottom. As his head broke the surface, he dragged precious air into his crushed burning lungs and realized that he held the P.14 in both hands still.

The wooden stock of the rifle was directly in front of his eyes, and he saw where the Mauser bullet had smashed into the wood and then flattened against the solid steel of the breech block.

The bullet was squashed to a misshapen lump, like a pellet of wet clay hurled against a brick wall. The rifle had stopped it dead, but the tremendous energy of impact had driven the P.14 into his chest, expelling the air from both lungs and hurling him backwards over the bank.

With enormous relief, Mark let the rifle drop into the muddy bottom below him, and was swept away by the current into a swirling nightmare of malaria and rain and raging brown water. Slowly the darkness overwhelmed him, and his last conscious thought was the irony of being saved from death by rifle shot to be immediately drowned like an unwanted kitten.

The water came up over his mouth again, he felt it burn in his lungs and then he was gone into nothingness.

There can be few terrors like those of a mind tortured by malaria fever, a mind trapped in an endless nightmare from which there is no escape, never experiencing the relief of waking in the sweat of terror and knowing it was only delirium.

The nightmares of malaria are beyond the creation of the healthy brain, they are unremitting and they are compounded by a consuming thirst. The thirst as the body burns its strength and fluid in the heat of the conflict, a cycle of attack no less terrible for its regular familiar stages: icy chills that begin the cycle, followed by burning Saharan fevers that rocket the body heat to temperatures so high that they can damage the brain, and that are followed by the great sweat, when body fluid streams from every pore of the victim's body, desiccating him and leaving him without the strength to lift head or hand while he awaits the next round of the cycle to begin, the next bout of icy shivering chill.

There were semi-lucid moments for Mark between the periods of heat and cold and nameless terror. Once, when the thirst burned so that every cell of his body shrieked for moisture and his mouth was dry and swollen, it seemed that strong cool hands lifted his head and bitter liquid, bitter but cold and wonderful, flooded his mouth and ran like honey down his throat. At other times in the cold, he pulled his own grey woollen blanket close around his shoulders and the smell of it was familiar and well-beloved – the smell of woodsmoke and cigarette and his own body smell. Often he heard the rain and crash-rumble of thunder, but always he was dry, and then all sound faded and he was swept away on the next cycle of the fever.

He knew it was seventy-two hours after the first chilling onslaught that he came once again fully conscious. The malaria is that predictable in its cycle that he knew when it was to within a few hours.

It was late afternoon and Mark lay wrapped in his blanket on a mattress of fresh-cut grass and aromatic leaves. It was still raining, a steady grey relentless downpouring from the low pregnant cloudbanks that seemed to press against the tree-tops – but Mark was dry.

Above him was a low roof of rock, a roof that had been blackened over the millennium by the wood fires of others who had sought shelter in this shallow cave; the opening of the shelter faced north-west, away from the prevailing rain-bearing winds, and just catching the last glimmerings of light from where the sun was sinking behind the thick cloud cover.

Mark lifted himself with enormous effort on one elbow and looked about him, bemused. Propped against the rock wall near his head was his pack. He stared at it for a long time, puzzled and completely bewildered. His last coherent memory had been of engulfing icy waters. Closer at hand was a round-bellied beer pot of dark fire-baked clay, and he reached for it immediately, his hands shaking not only from weakness but from the driving need of his thirst.

The liquid was bitter and medicinal, tasting of herbs and sulphur, but he drank it with panting grateful gulps until his belly bulged and ached.

He lowered the pot then and discovered beside it a bowl of stiff cold maize porridge, salted and flavoured with some wild herb that tasted like sage. He ate half of it and then fell asleep, but this time into a deep healing sleep.

When he awoke again, the rain had stopped and the sun was near its zenith, burning down through the gaps and soaring valleys of the towering cloud ranges.

It required an effort, but Mark rose and staggered to the opening of the rock shelter. He looked down into the flooded bed of the Bubezi River, a roaring red-brown torrent in which huge trees swirled and tumbled on their way to the sea, their bared roots lifted like the crooked arthritic fingers of dying beggars.

Mark peered to the north and realized that the whole basin of swamp and bush had been flooded, the papyrus beds were submerged completely under a dull silver sheet of water that dazzled like a vast mirror, even the big trees on the lower ground were covered to their upper branches, and the higher ridges of ground and the low kopjes were islands in the watery waste.

Mark was still too weak to stay long on his feet, and he staggered back to his bed of cut grass. Before he slept again he pondered the attack, and the disquieting problem of how the assassins had known he was here at Chaka's Gate; somehow it was all bound up with Andersland and the death of the old man in the wilderness here. He was still pondering it all when sleep overtook him.

When he awoke, it was morning again, and during the night somebody had replenished the beer pot with the bitter liquid and the food bowl with stiff porridge and a few fragments of some roast flesh, that tasted like chicken but was probably iguana lizard.

The waters had fallen dramatically, the papyrus beds were visible with their long stems flattened and the fluffy heads wadded down by the flood, and the trees were exposed, the lower ground drying out; the Bubezi River in the deep gorge below Mark's shelter had regained some semblance of sanity.

Mark was suddenly aware of his own nudity, and of the stink of fever and body wastes that clung to him. He went down to the water's edge, a long slow journey during which he had to pause often to regain his strength and for the dizziness to stop singing in his ears.

He bathed away the smell and the filth and examined the dark purple bruise where the Mauser bullet had smashed the P.14 into his chest. Then he dried in the fierce glare of the noon sun. It warmed the last chills of the fever from his body – and he climbed back up to the shelter with a spring and lightness in his step.

In the morning he found that the beer pot and food bowl had disappeared, and he sensed somehow that the gesture was deliberate and carried the message that, as far as his mysterious benefactor was concerned, he was able to fend for himself again, and that he had begun to outlive his welcome.

Mark gathered his possessions, finding that all his clothing had been dried out and stuffed into the canvas pack. His bandolier of ammunition was there also and the bonehandled hunting knife was in its sheath, but his food supply was down to one can of baked beans.

He opened it and ate half, saved the rest for his dinner, left the pack in the back of the shelter, and set out for the far side of the basin.

It took him almost two hours to find the killing ground, and he recognized it at last only by the dead tree with its twisted arthritic limbs. The ground here was lower than he had imagined, and had been swept by the flood waters; the grass was flattened against the earth, as though brilliantined and combed down, some of the weaker trees had been uprooted and swept away and, in the lower branches of the larger stronger trees, the flood debris clung to mark the high-water level.

Mark searched for some evidence of the fight, but there was none, no body nor abandoned rifle, it was as though it had never been . . . Mark began to doubt his own memory until he slipped his hand into the front of his shirt and fingered the tender bruising.

He searched down the track of the waters, following the direction of the swept grass for half a mile. When he saw vultures sitting in the trees and squabbling noisily in the scrub, he hurried forward, but it was only a rhino calf, too young to have swum against the flood, drowned and already beginning to putrefy.

Mark walked back to the dead tree and sat down to smoke the last cigarette in his tin, relishing every draw, stubbing it out half-finished and carefully returning the butt to the flat tin with its picture of the black cat – and the trade mark 'Craven A'.

He was about to stand when something sparkled in the sunlight at his feet, and he dug it out of the still damp earth with his finger.

It was a brass cartridge case, and when he sniffed at it, there was still the faint trace of burned cordite. Stamped into the base was the lettering 'Mauser Fabriken. 9 mm' and he turned it thoughtfully between his fingers.

The correct thing was to report the whole affair to the nearest police station, but twice already he had learned the folly of calling attention to himself while some remorseless enemy hunted him from cover.

Mark stood up and went down the gentle slope to the edge of the swamp pools. A moment longer he examined the brass cartridge case, then he hurled it far out into the black water.

At the rock shelter he hefted his pack on to his shoulders, bouncing from the knees to settle the straps. Then, as he crossed to the entrance, he saw the footprints in the fine cold ash dust of the fire. Broad, bare-footed, he recognized them instantly.

On an impulse he slipped the sheathed hunting knife off his belt, and laid it carefully exposed in an offertory position at the base of the shelter wall; then, with a stub of charcoal from the dead fire, he traced two ancient symbols on the rock above it – the symbols that old David had told him stood for 'The-bowed-slave-who-bears-gifts'. He hoped Pungushe, the poacher, would come again to the rock shelter and that he could interpret the symbols and accept the gift.

On the slope of the south butt of Chaka's Gate, Mark paused again and looked back into the great sweep of wilderness, and he spoke aloud, softly, because he knew that if the old man were listening, he would hear, no matter how low the voice. All he had learned and experienced here had hardened his resolve to come to the truth and to unravel the mystery and answer the questions that still hid the facts of the old man's death.

'I'll come again – some day.' Then he turned away towards the south, lengthening his stride and swinging into the gait just short of a trot that the Zulus call 'Minza umhlabathi' – or 'eat the earth greedily'.


The suit felt unfamiliar and confining on his body, and the starched collar was like a slave's ring about Mark's throat, the pavement hard and unyielding to his tread and the clank of the trams and the honk and growl and clash of train and automobile were almost deafening after the great silences of the bush, and yet there was excitement and stimulation in the hurrying tide of human beings that swirled around him, strident and colourful and alive.

The tropical hot-house of Durban town encouraged all growth of life, and the diversity of human beings that thronged her streets never failed to intrigue Mark; the Hindu women in their shimmering saris of gaudy silk with jewels in their pierced nostrils and golden sandals on their feet; the Zulus, moon-faced and tall, their wives with the conical ochre headdresses of mud and plaited hair that they wore for a lifetime, bare-breasted under their cloaks, big stately breasts fruitful and full as those of the earth mother, to which their infants clung like fat little leeches, and the short leather aprons high on their strong glossy dark thighs swinging as they walked; the men in loincloths muscled and dignified – or wearing the cast-off rags of Western clothing with the same jaunty panache and self-conscious assurance that the mayor wore his robes of office; the white women, remote and cool and unhurried, followed by a servant as they shopped or encapsuled in their speeding vehicles; their men in dark suits and the starched collars better suited to the climes of their native north, many of them yellowed with fever and fat with rich foods as they hurried about their affairs, their faces set in that small perpetual frown, each creating for himself an isolation of the spirit in the press of human bodies.

It was strange to be back in the city. Half of Mark's soul hated it while the other half welcomed it, and he hurried to find the human company for which he had sometimes hungered these long weeks just past.

'Good God, my dear old sport.' Dicky Lancome, with a red carnation in his button-hole, hurried to meet him across the showroom floor. 'I am delighted to have you back. I was expecting you weeks ago. Business has been deadly slow, the girls have been ugly, tiresome and uncooperative; the weather absolutely frightful – you have missed nothing, old son, absolutely nothing.' He held Mark off at arm's length and surveyed him with a fond and brotherly eye. 'My God, you look as though you've been on the Riviera, brown as a pork sausage but not as fat. God, I do declare you've lost weight again—' and he patted his own waistcoat which was straining its buttons around the growing bulge of his belly. 'I must go on a diet – which reminds me, lunch-time! You will be my guest, old boy, I insist – I absolutely insist.'

Dicky began his diet with a plate piled high with steaming rice, coloured to light gold and flavoured with saffron; over this was poured rich, chunky mutton curry, redolent with Hindu herbs and garnished with mango chutney, ground coconuts, grated Bombay Duck and half a dozen other sauces, and as the turbaned Indian waiter offered him the silver tray of salads, he loaded his side plate enthusiastically without interrupting his questioning.

'God, I envy you, old boy. Often promised myself that. One man against the wilderness, pioneer stuff, hunting and fishing for the pot.' He waved the waiter away and lifted a quart stein of lager beer to salute Mark. 'Cheers, old boy, tell me all about it.'

Dicky was silent at last, although he did the curry full justice, while Mark told him about it – about the beauty and the solitude, about the bushveld dawn and the starry silent nights, and he sighed occasionally and shook his head wistfully.

'Wish I could do it, old boy.'

'You could,' Mark pointed out, and Dicky looked start-led. 'It's out there now. It won't go away.'

'But what about my job, old boy? Can't just drop everything and walk away.'

'Do you enjoy your job that much?' Mark asked softly. 'Does peddling motorcars feed your soul?'

'Hey?' Dicky began to look uncomfortable. 'It's not a case of enjoying it. I mean nobody really enjoys having to work, do they? I mean it's just something one does, you know. One is lucky to find something one can do reasonably well where one can earn an honest coin, and one does it.'

'I wonder,' Mark mused. 'Tell me, Dicky, what is most important, the coin or the good feeling down there in your guts?'

Dicky stared at him, his lower jaw sagging slightly, exposing a mouthful of half-masticated rice.

'Out there, I felt clean and tall,' Mark went on, fiddling with his beer stein. 'There were no bosses, no clients, no hustling for a commission. I don't know, Dicky – out there I felt important.'

'Important?' Dicky swallowed the unchewed curry

noisily. 'Important? Hey now, old boy, they're selling rakes like you and me on the street corners at ninepence a bunch.' He washed down the rice with a swallow of beer, and then patted the froth from his upper lip with the crisp white handkerchief from his breast pocket. 'Take an old dog's advice, when you say your prayers at night give thanks that you are a good motorcar salesman, and that you have found that out. Just do it, old son, and don't think about it, or it will break your heart.' He spoke with an air of finality that declared the subject closed, and stooped to open his brief case on the floor beside his chair. 'Here, I've something for you.'

There were a dozen thick letters in Marion Littlejohn's neat feminine hand, all in blue envelopes, a colour which she had explained in previous letters indicated undying love; there was also an account for a disputed twelve and sixpence which his tailor insisted Mark had underpaid; and there was another envelope of marbled paper, pale beige and watered expensively, with Mark's name blazoned across it in a peremptory, arrogant hand – and no address.

Mark singled it out and turned it over to examine the crest, thickly crusted in heavy embossing that stood out on the flap.

Dicky watched him open it and then learned forward to read it unashamedly, but Mark saved him the effort and flipped it across to him.

'Regimental dinner,' he explained.

'You'll just make it,' Dicky pointed out. 'Friday the 16th.' Then his voice changed, imitating a regimental sergeant-major. 'Two oh hundred hours sharpish. Dress formal and R.S. bloody V.P. Take your dressing from the right, you lucky blighter, your guinea has been paid by your Colonel-in-Chief – Lord Muck-a-Muck General Courtney his exalted self. Off you go, my boy, drink his champagne and steal a handful of cigars. Up the workers, say I.'

'I think I'll give it a miss,' murmured Mark, and placed

Marion's letters in his inside pocket, to prevent Dicky reading those also.

'You've gone bush-crazy, the sun touched you, old boy,' Dicky declared solemnly. 'Think of those three hundred potential owners of Cadillacs sitting around one table, pissed to the wide, and smoking free cigars. Captive audience. Whip around the table and peddle them a Cadillac each while they are still stunned by the speeches.'

'Were you in France?' Mark asked.

'Not France.' Dicky's expression changed. 'Palestine, Gallipoli and suchlike sunny climes.' The memory darkened his eyes.

'Then you'll know why I don't feel like going up to the old fort to celebrate the experience,' Mark told him, and Dicky Lancome studied him across the loaded table. He had made himself a judge of character, of men and their workings. He had to be a good judge to be a good salesman, so he was surprised that he had not recognized the change in Mark sooner. Looking at him now, Dicky knew that he had acquired something, some new reserve of strength and resolution the likes of which few men gathered about them in a lifetime. Suddenly he felt a humility in Mark's presence, and although it was tinged with envy, the envy was without rancour. Here was a man who was going somewhere, to a place where he would never be able to follow, a path that needed a man with a lion's liver to tread. He wanted to reach across the table and shake Mark's hand and wish him well on the journey, but instead he spoke quietly, dropping the usual light and cavalier façade.

'I wish you'd think about it, Mark. General Courtney came to see me himself—' and he went on to tell him of the visit, of Sean Courtney's anger when he had heard that Mark had been discharged at his daughter's behest. 'He asked for you to be there especially, Mark, and he really meant it.'

Mark showed his invitation at the gates, and was passed through the massive stone outer fortifications.

There were fairy lights strung in the trees along the pathway that led through the gardens of the old fort, giving the evening a frivolous carnival feeling at odds with the usual atmosphere this bastion had known from the earliest British occupation, through siege and war with Dutch and Zulu; many of the Empire's warriors who had paused here on their occasions.

There were other guests ahead of and behind him on the pathway, but Mark avoided them, feeling self-conscious in the dinner-jacket he had hired from the pawnbroker when he retrieved his decorations. The garment had the venerable greenish tinge of age, and was ventilated in places by the ravages of moths. It was too tight across the shoulders and too full in the belly, and it exposed too much cuff and sock, but when he had pointed this out to the pawnbroker, the man had asked him to finger the pure silk lining and had reduced the hire fee to five shillings.

Miserably he joined the file of other dinner-jacketed figures on the steps of the drillhall, and when his turn came, he stepped up to the reception line.

'So!' said General Sean Courtney. 'You came.' The craggy features were suddenly boyish, as he took Mark's hand in a grip that felt like tortoise-shell, cool and hard and calloused. He stood at the head of the reception line like a tower, broad and powerful, resplendent in immaculately cut black and crisp starched white with a gaudy block of silk ribbons and enamel crosses and orders across his chest. With a twitch of an imperial eyebrow, he summoned one of his staff.

'This is Mr Mark Anders,' he said. 'You remember the old firm of Anders and MacDonald, 1st brigade?'

'Indeed, sir.' The officer looked at Mark with quick

interest, his eye dropping from his face to the silk ribbons on his lapel and back to his face.

'Look after him,' said General Courtney, and then to Mark, 'Get yourself a drink, son, and I'll talk to you later.' He released Mark's hand and turned to the next in line, but such was the magnetism and charm of the big man that after the brief contact and the few gruff words, Mark was no longer the gawky stranger, callow and awkward in cast-off clothes, but an honoured guest, worthy of special attention.

The subaltern took his charge seriously and led Mark into the dense crowd of black-clad males, all of them still subdued and self-conscious in their unaccustomed finery, standing in stiff knots, although the waiters moved among them bearing silver trays laden with the regiment's hospitality.

'Whisky, is it?' asked the subaltern, and picked a glass from one of the trays. 'All liquid refreshment tonight is with the General's compliments,' and took another glass for himself. 'Cheers! Now let's see – 1st brigade—' and he looked around. 'You must remember Hooper, or Dennison?'

He remembered them and others, dozens of them; some were vaguely familiar features, just shades at the edge of his memory, but others he knew well, had liked, or disliked, and even hated. With some he had shared food, or passed a cigarette butt back and forth, with others he had shared moments of terror or exquisite boredom; the good ones, the workers, the cowards and the shirkers and the bullies were all there – and the whisky came endlessly on silver trays.

They remembered him also; men he had never seen in his life came up to him. 'You remember me, I was section leader at D'Arcy Wood when you and MacDonald—' And others, 'Are you *the* Anders, I thought you'd be older somehow – your glass is empty,' and the whisky kept coming on the silver trays – and Mark felt tall and clever, for men listened when he talked, and witty, for men laughed when he jested.

They sat at a table that stretched the full length of the hall and was covered with a damask cloth of dazzling white; the regimental silver blinked like heliographs in the candle-light, and now it was champagne cascading into crystal glass in showers of golden bubbles. All around, the comradely uproar of laughter and of raised voices – and each time Mark lowered his glass, there was a turbaned figure at his side and a dark hand poising the green bottle over his glass.

He sagged back in his chair with his thumbs hooked in his armpits and a black cigar sticking a foot out of his mouth, 'Hear! Hearing!' and 'Quite righting!' the after-dinner speakers, as owlish and wise as the best of them, exchanging knowledgeable nods of agreement with his neighbours, while the ruby port smouldered in his glass.

When the General rose from his centre seat at the cross piece of the table, there was an audible stir in the company which had become heavy and almost somnolent with port and long meandering speeches. They grinned at each other now in anticipation, and though Mark had never heard Sean Courtney speak, he sensed the interest and recharged enthusiasm and he sat up in his chair.

The General did not disappoint them; he started with a story that left them stunned for a moment, gasping for breath, before they could bellow with laughter. Then he went at them in a relaxed easy manner that seemed casual and natural, but using words like a master swordsman using a rapier, a jest, an oath, a solid' piece of good sense, something they wanted to hear, followed immediately by something that disturbed them, singling out individuals for praise or gentle censure.

'Third this year in the national polo championships, gentlemen, an honour which the regiment carried easily last year – but a certain gentleman seated at this board has chosen to ride for the sugar planters now, a decision which it is his God-given right to make, and which I am certain not one of us here would condemn,' and Sean Courtney paused, grinning evilly and smoothing his whiskers, while the entire company booed raucously and hammered the table with their dessert spoons. The victim flushed to vivid scarlet and squirmed in the cacophony.

'However, good news and great expectations for the Africa Cup this year. By dint of adroit sleuthing, it has been discovered that dwelling in our very midst—' and the next moment the entire hall was slapping palm to palm, a great thunder of sound, and heads were craning down to Mark's end of the table, while the General nodded and beamed at him, and when Mark slumped down quickly in his seat and tried to make his lanky frame fold like a carpenter's ruler, Sean Courtney called, 'Stand up, son, let them get a look at you.'

Mark rose uncertainly and bobbed his head left and right, and not until later did it occur to him that he had been skilfully manoeuvred into accepting their applause, that in doing so, he was committed. It was the first time he witnessed from a front-row seat the General handling the destiny of a man and achieving his object without apparent effort.

He was pondering this, a little muzzily, as he steered for the safe base of the next lamp post. It would, of course, have been wiser and safer to accept the offer made to him by one of the rickshaw drivers at the gates of the fort, when he had reeled out into the street two hours after midnight. However, his recent unemployment and extravagant expenditure on fancy clothing had left him no choice as to his means of transport. He faced now a walk of some three miles in the dark, and his progress was erratic enough to make it a long journey.

He reached the lamp-post and braced himself just as a

black Rolls-Royce stopped beside him and the back door swung open.

'Get in!' said the General, and as Mark tumbled ungracefully into the soft leather seat, an iron grip steadied him.

'You are not a drinking man.' It was a statement, not a question, and Mark had to agree.

'No, sir.'

'You've got a choice,' said the General. 'Learn, or leave it alone completely.'

Sean had waited for almost half an hour, the Rolls parked under the banyan trees, for Mark to appear through the gates, and he had been on the point of abandoning the evening and giving his driver the order to return to Emoyeni when Mark had tottered out into the street, brushed away the importunate rickshaw drivers and set off like a crab along the pavement, travelling further sideways than forward.

The Rolls had crept silently along behind him with the headlights dark, and Sean Courtney had watched with a benevolent smile the young man's erratic progress. He felt a gentle indulgence for the lad and for himself, for the odd little quirks and whims with which he still surprised himself occasionally. At sixty-two years of age, a man should know himself, know every strength and be able to exploit it, know every weakness, and have built a secure buttress against it.

Yet here he was, for no good reason that he could fathom, becoming more and more emotionally involved with a young stranger. Spending time and thought for he was not sure what end.

Perhaps the boy reminded him of himself at the same age, and now he thought about it, he did detect beneath the warm glow of champagne in his belly the nostalgia for that troubled time of doubt and shinning ambition when a boy stood on the threshold of manhood.

Perhaps it was that he admired – no, cherished was a

better word – cherished special quality in any animal. A fine horse, a good dog, a young man, that excellence that horsemen might call 'blood', or a dog-handler 'class'. He had detected it in Mark Anders, and as even a blood horse might be damaged by bad handling or a class dog spoiled, so a young man who had the same quality needed advice and direction and opportunity to develop his full capability. There was too much mediocrity and too much dross in this world, Sean thought, so that when he found class, he was drawn strongly to it.

Or perhaps again – and suddenly he felt that terrible black wave of mourning sweep over him – or perhaps it is simply that I do not have a son.

There had been three sons: one had died before he had lived, still-born in the great wilderness beyond the Limpopo River. Another had been borne by a woman who was not his wife and the son had called another man father. Here Sean felt the melancholy deepen, laden with guilt; but this son was dead also, burned to a charred black mass in the flimsy machine of wood and canvas in which he had flown the sky. The words of Garry's dedication to his new book were clear in Sean's mind. 'This book is dedicated to Captain Michael Courtney, D.F.C., one of the Young Eagles who will fly no more.' Michael had been Sean's natural son, made in the belly of his brother's wife.

The third son lived still, but he was a son in name only and Sean would have changed that name had it been within his power. Those ugly incidents that preceded Dirk Courtney's departure from Ladyburg so many years before, among them casual arson and careless murder, were nothing compared to the evil deeds he had perpetrated since his return. Those close to him knew better than to speak the name 'Dirk Courtney' in his hearing. Now he felt the melancholy change to the old anger, and to forestall it, he leaned forward in his seat and tapped the chauffeur's shoulder.

'Pull up beside him,' he said, pointing to Mark Anders.

'What you need is fresh air,' Sean Courtney told Mark. 'It will sober you up or make you puke, either of which is desirable.'

And by the time the Rolls parked at the foot of West Street pier, Mark had, by dint of enormous mental effort, regained control of his eyes. At first, every time he peered at the General beside him, he had the nauseous certainty that there was a third eye growing in the centre of his forehead, and that he had multiple ears on each side of his head, like ripples on the surface of a pond.

Mark's voice had at first been as uncontrolled, and he had listened with mild disbelief to the odd blurred sounds with which his lips had replied to the General's questions and comments. But when he frowned with the effort, and spoke with exaggerated slowness and articulation, it sounded vaguely intelligible.

However, it was only when they walked side by side down through the loose sand to the edge of the sea where the outgoing tide had left the sand hard and wet and smooth, that he began to listen to what the General was saying and it wasn't tea-party talk.

He was talking of power, and powerful men, he was talking of endeavour and reward, and though his voice was rumbling and relaxed, yet it was like the purr of an old lion who has just killed, and would kill again.

Somehow Mark sensed that what he was hearing was of great value, and he hated himself for the alcohol in his veins that slowed his mind and haltered his tongue. He fought it off actively.

They walked down along the glistening strip of wet smooth sand, that was polished yellow by the sinking glow of the late moon; the sea smelt of salt and iodine, a crisp antiseptic smell, and the little breeze chilled him so that he shivered even in his dinner jacket. But soon his brain was keeping pace with that of the burly figure that limped beside him, and slowly a sense of excitement built up within him as he heard things said that he had only sensed deep in some secret place of his soul, ideas that he recognized but that he had believed were his alone.

His tongue lost its drag and blur and he felt suddenly bright as a blade, and light as the swallow that drinks in flight as it skims the water.

He remembered how he had at one time suspected that this man might have been responsible in some way for the loss of Andersland, and the old man's death. But now those suspicions smacked almost of blasphemy, and he thrust them aside to throw all his mind into the discussion in which he found himself so deeply involved.

He never did suspect until long afterwards how important that single night's talk would be in his life, and if he had known perhaps his tongue would have seized up solid in his mouth and his brain refused to keep peace, for he was undergoing a rigorous examination. Ideas thrown at Mark seemingly at random were for him to pick up and carry forward or to reject and leave lying. Every question raked his conscience and bared his principles, and gradually, skilfully, he was forced to commit himself on every subject from religion to politics, from patriotism to morals. Once or twice the General chuckled, 'You're a radical, did you know that? But I suppose I was at your age – we all want to change the world. Now tell me what do you think about—' and the next question was not related to the one that preceded it. 'There are ten million black men in this country, and a million whites. How do you think they are going to be able to live together for the next thousand years?' Mark gulped at the enormity of the question, and then began to talk.

The moon paled away in the coming of the dawn, and Mark walked on into an enchanted world of flaming ideas and amazing visions. Though he could not know it, his excitement was shared. Louis Botha, the old warrior and statesman, had said to Sean once, 'Even the best of us gets old and tired, Sean, and when that happens, a man should have somebody to whom he can pass the torch, and let him carry it on.'

With a suddenness that took them both by surprise, the night was passed, and the sky flamed with gold and pink. They stood side by side, and watched the rim of the sun rise from the dark green sea and climb swiftly into the sky.

'I have needed an assistant for many years now. My wife hounds me,' Sean chuckled at the hyperbole, 'and I have promised her I will find one, but I need somebody quick and bright and trustworthy. They are hard to find.' Sean's cigar was long dead and horribly chewed. He took it from his mouth and examined it with mild disapproval before tossing it into the creeping wavelets at his feet. 'It would be a hell of a job, no regular hours, no set duties, and, God knows, I'd hate to work for me, because I am a cantankerous, unsympathetic old bastard. But on the other hand one thing I'd guarantee – whoever took the job wouldn't die of boredom, and he'd get to learn a thing or two.'

He turned now, thrusting his head forward and staring into Mark's face. The wind had ruffled his beard, and he had long ago stripped off his black tie and thrust it into a pocket. The golden rays of the rising sun caught his eyes and they were a peculiarly beautiful shade of blue.

'Do you want the job?' he demanded.

'Yes, sir,' Mark answered instantly, dazzled by the prospect of an endless association with this incredible man.

'You haven't asked about the money?' growled Sean.

'Oh, the money isn't important.'

'Lesson one.' Sean cocked a beetling black eyebrow over the amused blue twinkle of his eye. 'The money is always important.'

The next time Mark entered the gates of Emoyeni was to enter a new life, an existence beyond any he had ever imagined; and yet, in all the overpowering new experience, even in the whirl of having to adjust to new ideas, to the daunting procession of visitors and endless new tasks, there was one moment that Mark dreaded constantly. This was his next meeting with Miss Storm Courtney.

However, he would never know if it had not been carefully arranged by General Courtney, but Storm was not at Emoyeni on Mark's first day, nor during the days that followed, although the memory of her presence seemed everywhere in the portraits and photographs in every room, especially the full-length oil in the library where Mark spent much of his time. She was dressed in a full-length ivory-coloured dress, seated at the grand piano in the main drawing-room, and the artist had managed to capture a little of her beauty and spirit. Mark found the tantalizing scrutiny which the portrait directed at him disconcerting.

Quickly a relationship was established between Mark and the General, and during the first few days, the last of Sean's misgivings were set at rest. It was seldom that the close proximity of another human being over an extended period of time did not begin to irritate Sean, and yet with this youngster he found himself seeking his company. His first ideas had been that Mark should be taught to deal with day-to-day correspondence and all the other time-consuming trivia, leaving Sean a little more leisure and time to devote to the important areas of business and politics.

Now he would drift through into the library at odd times to discuss an idea with Mark, enjoying seeing it through younger and fresher eyes. Or he might dismiss his chauffeur and have Mark drive the Rolls out to one of the sawmills, or to a board meeting in the city, sitting up front beside him on the journey and reminiscing about those days in France, or going further back to the time before Mark was born, enjoying Mark's engrossing interest in talks of gold-prospecting and ivory-hunting in the great wilderness beyond the Limpopo River in the north.

'There will be an interesting debate in the Assembly today, Mark. I am going to give that bastard Hendricks hell on the Railway budget. Drive me down, and you can listen from the visitors' gallery.

'Those letters can wait until tomorrow. There's been a breakdown at the Umvoti Sawmill, we'll take the shotguns and on the way back try and pick up a couple of guineafowl.

'Drillhall at eight o'clock tonight, Mark. If you aren't doing anything important—' which was a command, no matter how delicate the phrasing, and Mark found himself sucked gently back into the ranks of the peacetime regiment. He found it different from France, for he now had powerful patronage. 'You are no use to me as third rank marker. You're getting to know the way I work, son, and I want you at hand even when we are playing at soldiers. Besides,' and here Sean grinned that evil, knowing grin, 'you need a little time for range practice.'

At the next turn-out, still not accustomed to the speed with which things happened in the world ruled by Sean Courtney, Mark found himself in the full fig of Second Lieutenant, including Sam Browne cross-strap and shining single pips on his shoulders. He had expected antagonism, or at least condescension from his brother officers, but found that when he was placed in command of range drill, he was received with universal enthusiasm.

In the household Mark's standing was not at first clear. He was awed by the mistress of Emoyeni, by her mature beauty and cool efficiency. She was remote but courteous for the first two weeks or so, referring to him as 'Mr Anders', and any request was preceded by a meticulous 'please' and followed by an equally punctilious 'thank you'.

When the General and Mark were at Emoyeni for the midday meal, Mark was served by one of the servants from a silver tray in the library, and in the evenings, after he had taken his leave from the General, he climbed on the elderly Ariel Square Four motorcycle he had acquired, and clattered off down the hill into the sweltering basin of the city to his verminous lodgings in Point Road.

Ruth Courtney was watching Mark with an even shrewder eye than her husband had used. Had he in any way fallen short of her standards, she would have had no compunction in immediately bringing all her influence to bear on Sean for his dismissal.

One morning while Mark was at work in the library, Ruth came in from the garden with an armful of cut flowers.

'Don't let me disturb you.' She began to arrange the flowers in the silver bowl on the central table. For the first few minutes she worked in silence, and then in a natural and friendly manner, she began to chat to Mark, quietly drawing from him the details of his domestic arrangements – where he slept and ate, and who did his laundry, and secretly she was appalled.

'You must bring your laundry up here, to be done with the household washing.'

'That's very kind of you, Mrs Courtney. I don't want to be a nuisance.'

'Oh nonsense, there are two dhobi wallahs with nothing else to do but wash and iron.'

Even Ruth Courtney, one of the first ladies of Natal, still a renowned beauty as a matron well past forty years of age, was not immune to Mark's unstudied appeal. To his natural charm was added the beneficial effect his coming had upon her own man.

Sean seemed younger, more lighthearted in these last weeks, and watching it, she realized that it was not only the burden of routine work that had been lifted from him. The boy was giving him back a little of that spirit of youth, that freshness of thought, that energy and enthusiasm for the things of life that had gone slightly stale and seemed no longer quite worth the effort.

It was their custom to spend the hour before bed in Ruth's boudoir, Sean lounging in a quilted dressing-gown, watching her brush out her hair and cream her face, smoking his last cigar, discussing the day's events while he enjoyed her still slim lithe body under the thin silk of her nightdress, feeling the slow awakening of his own body in anticipation of the moment when she would turn from watching him in the mirror and rise, holding out one hand to him, and lead him through into the bedroom, to the huge four-poster bed under the draped and tasselled velvet canopy.

Three or four times in the weeks since Mark's arrival in the household, Sean had made a remark so radical, so unlike his usual old-fashioned conservative self, that Ruth had dropped the silver hairbrush into her lap and turned to stare at him.

Each time he had laughed self-consciously and held up a hand to prevent her teasing. 'All right, I know what you're going to say, but I was discussing it with young Mark.' He would chuckle again. 'That boy talks a lot of good sense.'

Then one evening, after Mark had been with them just over a month, they had sat in companionable silence for a while when Sean said suddenly, 'Young Mark, doesn't he remind you of Michael?'

'I hadn't noticed – no, I don't think so.'

'Oh, I don't mean in looks. It's just something about the way he thinks.'

Ruth felt the old crushing regret welling up within her like a cold dark tide. She had never given Sean a son. It was the only true regret, the only shadow on all their sunlit years together. Her shoulders sagged now, as though under the burden of her regret, and she looked at herself in the mirror, seeing the guilt of her inadequacy in her own eyes.

Sean had not noticed, had gone on blithely, 'Well, I can hardly wait until February. It's going to break Hamilton's heart to hand over that big silver mug. Mark's changed the whole spirit of the team. They know they can win now, with him shooting number one.'

She had listened quietly, hating herself for not being able to give him what he had wanted so badly, and she glanced down at the little carved statue of the God Thor on her dressing-table. It had stood there all these years since Sean had given it to her, a talisman of fertility. Storm had been conceived in the height of a raging electrical thunderstorm, and had been named for it. He had joked that it needed thunder and had given her the little godlet.

'A fat lot of help you were,' she thought bitterly, and looked up at her own body under the silk in the mirror.

'So good to look at, and so damned useless!' She did not usually curse, it was a measure of her distress. Lovely as it was, her body would not bear another child. All it was good for now was to give him pleasure. She stood up abruptly, her nightly ritual incomplete, and she crossed to where he sat and removed the cigar from his lips, crushing it out deliberately in the big glass ashtray.

Surprised, he looked up at her, about to ask a question, but the words never reached his lips. Her eyelids were half hooded, they drooped languorously, and her lips pouted slightly to reveal the white small teeth, and there were spots of hectic colour on her high beautifully moulded cheekbones.

Sean knew this expression and the mood it heralded. He felt his heart lurch and then begin to pound like an animal in the cage of his ribs. Usually their loving was a thing of depth and mutual compassion, a thing grown strong and good over the years, a complete blending of two persons, symbolic of their lives together – but once in a rare while, Ruth would droop her eyelids and pout that way with the colour in her cheeks, and what followed was so wild and wanton and uncontrolled that it reminded him of some devastating natural phenomenon.

She pushed one slim pale hand into his gown, and long nails raked lightly across his stomach so that his skin was instantly tingling and alive, and she leaned forward and with the other hand twined her fingers into his beard and twisted his face up to her and kissed him full on the lips, thrusting a sharp pink tongue deep into his mouth.

Sean let out a growl, and seized her, trying to draw her down into his lap and at the same time pulling open the bodice of her nightdress so that her small pointed breasts fell free, but she was quick and strong, twisting out of his grip, the ivory and pink sheen of her skin glowing through the transparent silk of her gown and her bared breasts joggling delightfully as she flew on long shapely legs into the bedroom, her laughter mocking and goading and inviting.

The following morning, Ruth cut an armful of crimson and white carnations and carried them into the library where young Mark Anders was at work. He stood up immediately and as she replied to his greeting, she studied his face. She had not truly realized how handsome he was, and she saw now that it was a face that would age well. There was a good bone structure and a proud strong nose. He was one of those lucky ones who would improve with the addition of a few wrinkles and lines around the eyes, and a little silver in the hair. That was a long way off, however; now it was the eyes that demanded attention.

'Yes,' she thought, looking into his eyes. 'Sean is right. He has the same strength and goodness that Michael had.'

She watched him surreptitiously as she worked at her flower arrangement, deliberately picking the words as she began to chat to him, and when she had completed the flower bowl, she stood back to admire her work and spoke without looking at him.

'Why don't you join us for lunch on the terrace, Mark?'

and the use of his name was deliberate, both of them very conscious of it as it was spoken. 'Unless you'd prefer to continue eating here.'

Sean glanced up from his newspaper as Mark came out on to the terrace, but his expression did not change as Ruth waved Mark to the seat opposite him and he immediately plunged back into the paper and angrily read out the editorial to them, mocking the writer by his tone and emphasis before crumpling the news-sheet and dropping it beside his chair.

'That man's a raving bloody idiot – they should lock him up.'

'Well, sir,' Mark began delicately.

Ruth sighed a silent breath of relief for she had not consulted Sean on the new luncheon arrangements, but the two of them were instantly in deep discussion, and when the main course was served, Sean growled, 'Take care of the chicken, Mark, and I'll handle the duck,' so that the two of them were carving and arguing at the same time, like members of the same family, and she covered her smile with her table napkin as Sean ungraciously conceded a debating point to his junior.

'I'm not saying you are right, of course, but if you are, then how do you account for the fact that—'

And he was attacking again from a different direction, and Ruth turned to listen as Mark adroitly defended himself again; as she listened, she began to appreciate a little more why Sean had chosen him.

It was over the coffee that Mark learned at last what had become of Storm Courtney.

Sean suddenly turned to Ruth. 'Was there a letter from Storm this morning?' When she shook her head he went on, 'That damned uppity little missy must learn a few manners – there hasn't been a letter in nearly two weeks. Just where are they supposed to be now?'

'Rome,' said Ruth.

'Rome!' grunted Sean. 'With a bunch of Latin lovers pinching her backside.'

'Sean!' Ruth reprimanded him primly.

'Beg your pardon.' He looked a little abashed, and then grinned wickedly. 'But she's probably putting it in the correct position for pinching right at this moment, if I know her.'

That night when Mark sat down to write to Marion Littlejohn, he realized how the mere mention of Storm Courtney's name had altered his whole attitude to the girl he was supposed to marry. Under the enormous workload which Sean Courtney had dropped casually on his shoulders, Mark's letter to Marion was no longer a daily ritual, and at times there were weeks between them.

On the other hand, her letters to him never faltered in regularity and warmth, but he found that it was not really the pressure of work that made him keep deferring their next meeting. He sat now chewing the end of his pen until the wood splintered, seeking words and inspiration, finding it difficult to write down flowery expressions of undying love on every page; each empty page was as daunting as a Saharan crossing, yet it had to be filled.

'We will be travelling to Johannesburg next weekend to compete in the annual shooting match for the Africa Cup,' he wrote, and then pondered how to get a little more mileage out of that intelligence. It should be good for at least a page.

Marion Littlejohn belonged to a life that he had left behind him when he passed through the gates of Emoyeni. He faced this fact at last, but was none the less dismayed by the sense of guilt the knowledge brought him, and he tried to deny it and continue with the letter but images kept intruding themselves – and the main of these was a picture of Storm Courtney, gay and sleek, glitteringly beautiful and as unobtainable as the stars.

The Africa Cup stood almost as high as a man's chest on a base of polished ebony. The Emoyeni houseboys had polished it for three days before they had achieved the lustre that General Courtney found acceptable, and now the cup formed the centre-piece of the buffet table, elevated on a pyramid of yellow roses.

The buffet was set in the antechamber to the main ballroom, and both rooms overflowed with the hundreds of guests that Sean Courtney had invited to celebrate his triumph. He had even invited Colonel Hamilton of the Cape Town Highlanders to bring his senior officers by Union Castle liner, travelling first class, as the General's guests to attend the ball.

Hamilton had refused by means of a polite thank-you note, four lines long, without counting the address and the closing salutation. The cup had been in the Cape Town Castle since it had been presented by Queen Victoria in the first year of the Boer War, and Hamilton's mortification added not a little to Sean Courtney's expansive mood.

For Mark it had been the busiest period he had known since coming to Emoyeni. Ruth Courtney had come to place more and more trust in Mark, and under her supervision he had done much of the work of preparing the invitations and handling the logistics of food and liquor.

Now she had him dancing with all of the ugly girls who would otherwise have sat disconsolately along the wall, and at the end of each dance, the General summoned him with an imperious wave of his cigar above the heads of his guests to the buffet table where he had taken up a permanent stance close to the cup.

'Councillor, I want you to meet my new assistant – Mark, this is Councillor Evans. That's right, Pussy, this is the young fellow who clinched it for us.'

And while Mark stood, colouring with embarrassment, the General repeated for the fifth or sixth time that evening a shot by shot account of the final day's competition when the two leading regiments had tied in the team events, and the judges had asked for an individual re-shoot to break the deadlock.

'A crosswind gusting up to twenty or thirty miles an hour, and the first shoot at two hundred yards—'

Mark marvelled at the intense pleasure this trinket gave the General. A man whose fortune was almost beyond calculation, whose land could be measured by the hundred square miles, who owned priceless paintings and antique books, jewellery and precious stones, houses and horses and yachts – but none of them at this moment as prized as this glittering trifle.

'Well, I was marking myself,' the General had taken enough of his own good whisky to begin acting out his story, and he made the gesture of crouching down in the bunker and looking up at the targets, 'and I don't mind telling you that it was the worst hour of my life.'

Mark smiled in agreement. The Highlander marksman had matched him shot for shot. Each of them signalled as a bulls-eye by the flags of the markers.

'They both shot possibles at two hundred yards, and then again at five hundred yards, it was only at the thousand-yard targets that young Mark's uncanny ability to judge the crosswind—' By this time, Sean's audience was cow-eyed with boredom, and there were still ten rounds of deliberate and another ten of rapid fire to hear about. Mark sensed panic signals across the ballroom and he looked up.

Ruth Courtney was beside the main doors of the ballroom and with her was the Zulu butler. A man with warrior blood in his veins and the usual bearing of a chief, now he was grey with some emotion close to fear and his expression was pitiable as he spoke rapidly to his mistress.

Ruth touched his arm in a gesture of comfort and dismissal, and then turned to wait for Mark.

As he hurried to her across the empty dance floor he could not help but notice again how much mother resembled daughter. Ruth Courtney still had the figure of an athletic young woman, kept slim and firm and graceful by hard riding and long walking, and only when he was close to her were the small lines and tiny blemishes in her smooth ivory skin apparent. Her hair was dressed high on her head, scorning the fashionable shorter cut, and her gown had a simple elegance that showed off the lines of her body and the small shapely breasts. One of her guests reached her before Mark did, and she was relaxed and smiling while Mark hovered close at hand until she excused herself and Mark hurried to her.

'Mark.' Her worry showed only in her eyes as she looked up at him towering above her, but her smile was light and steady. 'There is going to be trouble. We have an unwelcome visitor.'

'What do you want me to do?'

'He is in the entrance hall now. Please, take him through to the General's study, and stay with him until I can warn my husband and send him to you. Will you do that?'

'Of course.'

She smiled her thanks, and then as Mark turned away she stopped him with a touch.

'Mark, try to stay with them. I don't want them to be alone together. I'm not sure what might happen.' Then her reserve cracked. 'In God's name why did he have to come here – and tonight when—' She stopped herself then, and the smile firmed on her lips, steady and composed, but they both knew that she had been going to say, 'Tonight when Sean has been drinking.'

Mark now knew the General well enough to share her concern. When Sean Courtney was drinking, he was capable of anything – from genial and expansive bonhomie to dark, violent and undirected rage.

'I'll do what I can,' he agreed, and then, 'Tell me, who is it?'

Ruth bit her lower lip, the strain and worry clear on her

face for a moment before she checked herself, and her expression was neutral when she replied.

'It's his son – Dirk – Dirk Courtney.'

Mark's own shock showed so clearly that she frowned at him.

'What's wrong, Mark? Do you know him?'

Mark recovered quickly. 'No. I have heard of him, but I don't know him.'

'There is bad blood, Mark. Very bad. Be careful.' She left him and drifted quietly away across the floor, nodding to a dowager, stopping to exchange a word and a smile, and then drifting on to where Sean Courtney still held court in the buffet room.

Mark paused in the long gallery, and looked at himself in one of the tall gilt-framed mirrors. His face looked pale and strained, and when he smoothed his hair, his fingers were trembling slightly.

Suddenly he realized that he was afraid; dread was like a heavy weight in his bowels, and his breathing was cramped and painful.

He was afraid of the man he was going to meet. The man that he had stalked so long and painstakingly, and who he had come to know so well in his imagination.

In his mind he had built up an awesome figure, a diabolic figure wielding great and malignant power, and now he was consumed by dread at the prospect of meeting him face to face.

He went on down the gallery, his footsteps deadened by the thick pile of the carpet, his eyes not seeing the art treasures that adorned the panelled walls, for a sense of imminent danger blinded him to all else.

At the head of the marble staircase, he paused and leaned out with one hand on the balustrade to look down into the entrance hall.

A man stood alone in the centre of the black and white checkered marble floor. He wore a black overcoat, with a short cape hanging from the shoulders, a garment which enhanced his size.

His hands were clasped behind his back, and he balanced on the balls of his feet with head and jaw thrust forward aggressively, an attitude so like that of his father that Mark blinked in disbelief. His bare head was a magnificent profusion of dark curls which were shot by the overhead candelabra with sparkling chestnut highlights.

Mark started down the wide staircase and the man lifted his head and looked at him.

Mark was struck instantly by the man's fine looks, and then immediately afterwards by his resemblance to the General. He had the same powerful jaw, and the shape of his head, the set of his eyes and the lines of his mouth were identical, yet the son was infinitely more handsome than the father.

It was the noble head of a Michelangelo statue, the beauty of his David and the magnificent strength of his Moses, yet for all his beauty he was human, not the implacable monster of Mark's imagining, and the unreasonable fear released its grip on Mark's chest, and he could smile a small welcoming smile as he came down the steps.

Dirk watched him without blinking or moving, and it was only when Mark reached the checkered marble floor that he realized how tall the man was. He towered three inches over Mark, and yet his body was so well proportioned that its height did not seem excessive.

'Mr Courtney?' Mark asked, and the man inclined his head slightly without bothering to reply. The diamond that clasped the white silk cravat at his throat flashed sullenly.

'Who are you, boy?' Dirk Courtney asked, and his voice had the depth and timbre to match his frame.

'I am the General's personal assistant.' Mark did not let the disparaging form of address ruffle his polite smile, though he knew that Dirk Courtney was his senior by less than ten years. Dirk Courtney ran an unhurried glance from his head to his shoes, taking in the cut of Mark's evening dress and every other detail in one casual sweep before dismissing him as unimportant.

'Where is my father?' He turned to adjust his cravat in the nearest mirror. 'Does he know I've been waiting here for almost twenty minutes?'

'The General is entertaining, but he will see you presently. In the meantime, will you care to wait in the General's study? If you will follow me.'

Dirk Courtney stood in the middle of the study floor and looked about him. 'The old boy is keeping grand style these days.' He smiled with a flash of startlingly white teeth and then crossed to one of the studded leather armchairs by the stone fireplace. 'Get me a brandy and soda, boy.'

Mark swung open the dummy-fronted bookcase, selected a Courvoisier Cognac from the orderly ranks of bottles, poured some into a goblet, squirting soda on top of it, and carried it to Dirk Courtney.

He sipped the drink and nodded, sprawling in the big leather chair with the insolent grace of a resting leopard, and then once again he surveyed the room. His gaze, checking at each of the paintings, at each of the items of value which decorated the room, was calculating and thoughtful, and he asked his next question carelessly, not really interested in the answer.

'What did you say your name was?'

Mark stepped sideways, so that his view of the man's face was uninterrupted, and he watched carefully as he replied.

'My name is Anders – Mark Anders.'

For a second the name had no effect, then it struck Dirk and a remarkable transformation passed over his features. Watching it happen, Mark's fear was regenerated in full strength.

When he had been a lad, the old man had snared a marauding leopard in a heavy steel spring-tooth trap, and when they had walked up to the site the following morning, the leopard had charged them, coming up short against the heavy retaining chain within three feet of Mark and with its eyes almost on a level with his own. He had never forgotten the terrible blazing malevolence in those eyes.

Now he was seeing the same expression, an emotion so murderous and unspeakably evil that he drew back involuntarily.

It lasted only an instant, but it seemed that the entire face changed, from extravagant beauty to grotesque ugliness and back to beauty in the time it takes to draw breath. Dirk's voice, when he spoke, was measured and controlled, the eyes veiled and the expression of polite indifference.

'Anders? I've heard the name before—' He thought for a moment, as though trying to place it, and then dismissed it as unimportant, his attention returning to the Thomas Baines painting above the fireplace – but in that instant Mark had learned with complete certainty that the vague, unformed suspicions he had harboured so long were based on hard cold fact. He knew now beyond any doubt that something evil had happened, that the sale of Andersland and the old man's death and burial in an unmarked grave were the result of deliberate planning, and that the men who had hunted him on the Ladyburg escarpment and again in the wilderness beyond Chaka's Gate were all part of a design engineered by this man.

He knew that at last he had identified his adversary, yet to hunt him down and bring him to retribution was to be a task that might be beyond his capability, for the adversary seemed invincible in his strength and power.

He turned away to tidy the pile of documents on the General's desk, not trusting himself to look again at his enemy, lest he betray himself completely.

Already he had exposed himself dangerously, but it had been necessary, an opportunity too heaven-sent to allow to pass. In exchange for exposing himself he had forced his enemy to do the same, he had forced him into the open, and he counted himself the winner in the exchange.

There was another factor now that had made his exposure less than suicidal. Whereas before he had been friendless and alone, now he was protected by his mere association with Sean Courtney.

If they had succeeded that night on the Ladyburg escarpment or again at Chaka's Gate, it would be the unimportant passing of a rootless vagrant; now his death or disappearance would rouse the immediate attention of General Courtney, and he doubted if even Dirk Courtney could afford that risk.

Mark looked up quickly from the papers, and Dirk Courtney was watching him again, but now his expression was neutral and his eyes were hooded and guarded. He began to speak, but checked himself as they heard the heavy dragging tread in the passage and they both turned expectantly to the door as it was flung open.

Sean Courtney seemed to fill the entire doorway, the top of the great shaggy head almost touching the lintel and the shoulders wide as the cross-trees of a gallows as he leaned both hands on the head of his cane and glared into the room.

His eyes went immediately to the tall elegant figure that rose from the leather armchair, the craggy sun-browned features darkening with blood as he recognized him.

The two men confronted each other silently, and Mark found himself a fascinated spectator, as he followed intuitively the play of emotions, the reawakening of the memory of ancient wrongs – and of the elemental love and affection of son for father and father for son that had long ago been strangled and buried, but were now exhumed like some loathsome rotting corpse, more horrible for once having lived and been strong.

'Hello, Father,' Dirk Courtney spoke first, and at the sound of his voice, the rigidity went out of Sean's shoulders, and the anger out of his eyes to be replaced by a sense of sadness, of regret for something that once had value but was lost beyond hope, so his question sounded like a sigh.

'Why do you come here?'

'Can we speak alone – without strangers?' Mark left the desk and crossed to the door, but Sean stopped him with a hand on the shoulder.

'There are no strangers here. Stay, Mark.' It was the kindest thing that anybody had ever said to Mark Anders, and the strength of the affection he felt for Sean Courtney at that moment was greater than he had ever felt for another human being.

Dirk Courtney shrugged, and smiled for the first time, a light faintly mocking smile.

'You were always too trusting, Father.' Sean nodded as he crossed heavily to the chair behind his desk.

'Yes, and who should remember that better than you.'

Dirk's smile faded. 'I came here hoping that we might forget, that we might look for forgiveness from each other.'

'Forgiveness?' Sean asked, looking up quickly. 'You will grant me forgiveness – for what?'

'You bred me, Father. I am what you made me—'

Sean shook his head, denying it, and would have spoken, but Dirk stopped him.

'You believe I have wronged you – but I *know* that you have wronged me.'

Sean scowled. 'You talk in circles. Come to the point. What do you want that brings you uninvited to this house?'

'I am your son. It is unnatural that we should be parted.' Dirk was eloquent and convincing, holding out his hands in a gesture of supplication, moving closer to the massive figure at the desk. 'I believe I have the right to your consideration—' he broke off and glanced at Mark. 'God damn it, can't I speak to you without this gawking audience?'

Sean hesitated a moment, was on the point of asking Mark to leave, and then remembered the promise he had made to Ruth only minutes before. 'Don't let him be alone with you for a moment, Sean. Promise me you will keep Mark with you. I don't trust him, not at all. He is evil, Sean, and he brings trouble and unhappiness – I can smell it on him. Don't be alone with him.'

'No.' He shook his head. 'If you have something to say, get it over with. If not, go, and leave us in peace here.'

'All right, no more sentiment,' Dirk nodded, and the role of the supplicant dropped from him. He turned and began to stride up and down the study floor, hands thrust deep into the pockets of his overcoat. 'I'll talk business, and get it over with. You hate me now, but when we have worked together – when I have shared with you the boldest and most imaginative venture this land has ever known – then we will talk again of sentiment.'

Sean was silent.

'As a business man now and as a son later. Do you agree?'

'I hear you,' said Sean, and Dirk began to talk.

Even Mark could not but stand in admiration of Dirk Courtney's eloquence, and the winning and persuasive manner in which he used his fine deep voice and his magnificent good looks; but these were theatrical tricks, well rehearsed and stagey.

What was spontaneous was the burning, almost fanatical glow of commitment to his own ideas which radiated from him as he talked and gestured. It was easy to believe him, for he so clearly believed himself.

Using his hands and his voice, he conjured up before his father a vast empire, endless expanses of rich land, thousands upon thousands of square miles, a treasure the like of which few men had ever conceived, planted to cotton and sugar and maize, watered by a gigantic dam that would hold back an inland sea of sweet, fresh water – it was a dream quite breathtaking in its scope and sweep.

'I have half of the land already,' Dirk paused and cupped his hands with fingers stiff and grasping as the talons of an eagle, 'here in my hands. It's mine. No longer a dream.'

'And the rest of it?' Sean asked reluctantly, swept along on the torrent against his will.

'It's there – untouched, ripe, ready.' Dirk paused dramatically. 'It is as though nature had designed it all for just this purpose. The foundations of the dam are there, built by God as though as a blessing.'

'So?' Sean grunted sceptically. 'Now you are an instrument of God's will, are you? And where is this empire he has promised you?'

'I own all the land south of the Umkomo River, that is the half I have already.' He stopped in front of the mahogany desk and leaned forward with his hands on the polished wood, thrusting a face that glowed with the aura of a religious fanatic towards Sean Courtney.

'We will build a dam between the cliffs of Chaka's Gate and dam the whole of the Bubezi Valley, a lake one hundred and sixty miles long and a hundred wide – and we'll open the land between there and the Umkomo River and add it to the land I already own in the south. Two million acres of arable and irrigated land! Think of that!'

Mark stared at Dirk Courtney, utterly appalled by what he had just heard, and then his gaze switched to Sean Courtney, appealingly, wanting to hear him reject the whole monstrous idea.

'That's tsetse belt,' said Sean Courtney at last.

'Father, in Germany three men, Dressel, Kothe and Rochl, have just perfected and tested a drug called Germanin. It's a complete cure for tsetse-borne sleeping-sickness. It's so secret still that only a handful of men know about it,' Dirk told him eagerly, and then went on, 'Then we will wipe out the tsetse fly in the whole valley.'

'How?' Sean asked, and his genuine interest was evident.

'From the air. Flying machines spraying pythagra extract, or other insect-killers.'

It was a staggering concept, and Sean was silent a moment before he asked reluctantly, 'Has it been done before?'

'No,' Dirk smiled at him. 'But we will do it.'

'You've thought it out,' Sean lay back in his chair and groped absently in the humidor for a cigar, 'except for one little detail. The Bubezi Valley is a proclaimed area – has been since the time of Chaka, and most of the other ground between the Bubezi and Nkomo Rivers is either tribal trust land, Crown land or forestry reserve.'

Dirk Courtney lifted a finger at Mark. 'Get me another brandy, boy.' Mark glanced at the General. Sean nodded slightly, and there was silence again while Mark poured the brandy and brought the glass to Dirk.

'You trust him?' Dirk asked his father again, indicating Mark with his head as he accepted the glass.

'Get on with it, man,' snapped Sean irritably, not bothering to answer the question. Dirk saluted his father with the cut-glass tumber and smiled knowingly.

'You make the laws, Father, you and your friends in the Cabinet and in the Provincial Assembly, and you can change them. That's your end of the bargain.'

Sean had drawn a swelling chestful of cigar smoke as Dirk spoke, and now he let it trickle out so that his head was wreathed in drifting blue smoke as he replied.

'Let's get this clear. You put up the money and I force through Parliament legislation repealing the proclamation of these lands we need between Nkomo and the Bubezi Rivers?'

'And the Bubezi Valley,' Dirk cut in.

'And the Bubezi Valley. Then I arrange that some front company gets control of that land, even if it's only on a thousand-year ground rental?'

Dirk nodded. 'Yes, that's it.'

'What about the cost of the dam and the new railroad to the dam – have you got that type of capital?' Mark could hardly believe what he was hearing, that Sean Courtney was haggling over the assets of the nation, treasures that had been entrusted to him as a high representative of the people. He wanted to shout out, to lash out at them as they schemed. The deep affection he had felt moments before turned slowly to a deep sense of outrage and betrayal.

'Nobody has that type of capital,' Dirk told him. 'I've had my people work out a rough estimate, and there will be little change left out of four million pounds. No individual has that sort of money.'

'So?' Sean asked, the wreaths of cigar smoke drifted away from his head and it seemed to Mark that he had aged suddenly. His face was grey and haggard, the deep-set eyes turned by a trick of the light into the dark empty eye-sockets of a skull.

'The Government will build them for us,' and Dirk chuckled richly, as he resumed his pacing. 'Or rather, they'll build dam and railway for the nation. To open up valuable natural resources.' Dirk chuckled again. 'And imagine the prestige of the man that shepherds these measures through Parliament, the man who brings progress and civilization into the wilderness.' He picked up the brandy glass and tossed off half the contents. 'It would all be named after him – the Sean Courtney Dam perhaps?'

'It sounds impressive.'

'A fitting monument, Father,' Dirk lifted the glass to his father.

'But what of the tribal lands, Dirk?' Sean used his son's name for the first time, Mark noticed, and glanced sharply at him.

'We'll move the blacks out,' Dirk told him casually. 'Find a place for them in the hills.'

'And the game reserves?'

'Good God, are we going to let a few wild animals stand in the way of a hundred million pounds?' He shook the handsome head of curls in mock dismay. 'Before we flood the valley, you can take a hunting safari there. You always did enjoy the hunt, didn't you? I remember you telling me about the big elephant hunts in the old days.'

'Yes,' Sean nodded heavily. 'I killed a lot of elephant.'

'So, Father, we are agreed then?' Dirk stopped once more before Sean, and there was for the first time an anxious air, a small frown of worry puckering his bold high forehead. 'Do we work together?'

Sean was silent for seconds longer, staring at the blotter on his desk-top, then he raised his head slowly and he looked sick and very old.

'What you have told me – the sheer size of it all – has taken me completely by surprise.' He spoke carefully, measuring each word.

'It's big and it's going to take guts,' Dirk agreed. 'But you have never been frightened before, Father. You told me once, "If you want something, go out and get it – for one thing is sure as all hell, nobody is going to bring it to you."'

'I am older now, Dirk, and a man grows tired, loses the strength of his youth.'

'You're as strong as a bull.'

'I want time to think about it.'

'How long?' Dirk demanded.

'Until,' Sean faltered, and thought a moment, 'until after the next parliamentary sessions. I will need to speak to people, examine the feasibility of the whole idea.'

'It's too long,' Dirk scowled, and suddenly the face was no longer beautiful, the eyes changed, coming together into a mean ferrety look.

'It's the time I need.'

'All right,' Dirk agreed, and thrust the scowl aside, smiling down at the massive seated figure. He began the gesture of putting out his right hand, but Sean did not look up and instead he thrust the hand back into his overcoat pocket.

'I am neglecting my guests,' said Sean softly. 'You must excuse me now. Mark will see you out.'

'You will let me know?' Dirk demanded.

'Yes,' said Sean heavily, still not looking up. 'I will let you know.'

Mark led Dirk Courtney down to the front doors, and he felt feverish with anger and hatred for him. They walked in silence, side by side, and Mark fought the wild, dark and violent impulses that kept sweeping over him. He hated him for having tarnished the man he had respected and worshipped, for having smeared him with his own filth. He hated him for the old man and for Andersland, and for the dreadful but unknown deeds he had ordered, and he hated him for what he was about to do to that beloved land beyond Chaka's Gate.

At the front doors, Dirk Courtney took his hat from the table and adjusted it over his eyes as he studied Mark carefully.

'I am a good friend to have,' he said softly. 'My father trusts you, and I am sure he confides in you. You would find me grateful and generous, and I am sure that, since you overheard our conversation, you will know what small items of information might interest me.'

Mark stared at him. His lips felt numb and cold, and his whole body trembled with the effort it took to control himself. He did not trust his own voice to speak.

Dirk Courtney turned away abruptly, not bothering with his reply and he strode lightly down the front steps into the night.

Mark stared after him long after he disappeared. There was the crackling snarl of a powerful engine, the crunch of gravel under spinning wheels, and the twin beams of headlights swept the garden, and were gone.

Mark's feet kept pace with the furious rush of his anger, and he was almost running when he reached the General's study. Without knocking, he pushed open the door.

Words threatened to explode out of him – bitter condemnation, accusation and rejection – and he looked to the General's desk, but it was empty.

He was going to warn the General that he would use any means to expose the foul bargain that had been proposed that evening, he was going to voice his disillusion – his horror that Sean Courtney had even listened to it, let alone given it serious thought and the half-promise of his support.

The General stood at the window, his back to the room and the wide square shoulders slumped. He seemed to have shrunk in size.

'General,' Mark's voice was harsh, strident with his anger and determination, 'I am leaving now – and I won't be coming back. But before I go, I want to tell you that I will fight you and your son—'

Sean Courtney turned into the room, his shoulders still drooped and his head held at a listening angle, like that of a blind man, and Mark's voice trailed away, his fury evaporating.

'Mark?' Sean Courtney asked, as though he had forgotten his existence, and Mark stared at him, not believing what he was seeing – for Sean Courtney was weeping.

Bright tears had swamped and blinded his eyes and streamed down the lined and sun-seared cheeks, clinging in fat bright droplets to the coarse curls of his beard. It was one of the most distressing sights Mark had ever witnessed, so harrowing that he wanted to turn away from it – but could not.

'Get me a drink, son.' Sean Courtney crossed heavily towards his desk and one of his tears fell to the starched snowy front of his dress shirt, leaving a wet mark on the material.

Mark turned away, and made a show of selecting a glass and pouring whisky from the heavy decanter. He drew the simple act out and when he turned back Sean Courtney was at his desk.

He held a crumpled white handkerchief in his hand that had damp patches on it, but although his cheeks were dry now, the rims of his eyelids were pink and inflamed and the marvellous sparkling blue clarity of his eyes was dulled with swimming liquid.

'Thank you, Mark,' he said as he set the glass on the desk in front of him. Sean did not touch the glass but stared at it, and when he spoke his voice was low and husky.

'I brought him into the world with my own hands, there was no doctor, I caught him in my own hands still wet and warm and slippery – and I was proud. I carried him on my shoulder, and taught him to talk and ride and shoot. There are no words to explain what a man feels for his first-born son,' Sean sighed, a broken gusty sound. 'I mourned for him once before, I mourned him as though he was dead, and that was many years ago.' He drank a little of the whisky and then went on softly, so softly that Mark could hardly hear the words. 'Now he comes back and forces me to mourn him again, all over again.'

'I am sorry, General. I thought – I believed that you were going to – bargain with him.'

'That thought dishonours me.' Sean did not raise his voice nor his eyes. 'Leave me now, please Mark. We'll talk about this again at some other time.'

At the door Mark looked back, but the General was not aware of his presence. His eyes were still misty, and seemed to stare at a far horizon. Mark closed the door very softly.

Despite Sean Courtney's promise to discuss Dirk Courtney's proposition again, long weeks went by without even the mention of his name. However, though the life at Emoyeni seemed to continue in its busy round, yet there were times when Mark entered the panelled and book-lined study to find the General brooding darkly at his desk, beak-nosed and morbid as some roosting bird of prey, and he withdrew quietly, respecting his melancholy, knowing he was still in mourning. Mark realized it would take time before he was ready to talk.

During this period there were small changes in Mark's own circumstances. One night, long after midnight, Sean Courtney had entered his dressing-room, to find the lights were still on in the bedroom and Ruth propped on her pillows and reading.

'You shouldn't have waited up for me,' he told her severely. 'I could have slept on the couch—'

'I prefer you here.' She closed the book.

'What are you reading?' She showed him the title.

'D. H. Lawrence's new novel, *Women in Love*.'

Sean grinned as he unbuttoned his shirt. 'Did he teach you anything?'

'Not yet, but I'm still hoping.' She smiled at him, and he thought how young and lovely she looked in her lace nightdress. 'And you? Did you finish your speech?'

'Yes.' He sat to remove his boots. 'It's a masterpiece – I'm going to tear the bastards to pieces.'

'I heard Mark's motorcycle leaving a few minutes ago. You kept him here until midnight.'

'He was helping me look up some figures and searching Hansard for me.'

'It's awfully late.'

'He's young,' grunted Sean. 'And damned well paid for it.' He picked up his boots and stumped through into the dressing-room, the limp more noticeable now that he was in his stockinged feet. 'And I haven't heard him complain yet.'

He came back in his night-shirt and slipped into bed beside her.

'If you are going to keep the poor boy to these hours, it's not fair to send him back to town every night.'

'What do you suggest?' he asked, as he wound his gold hunter and then placed it on the bedside table.

'I could turn the gate-keeper's cottage into a flat for him. It wouldn't need much, even though it's been deserted for years.'

'Good idea,' Sean agreed casually. 'Keep him on the premises so I can really get some work out of him.'

'You're a hard man, General Courtney.' He rolled over and kissed her lingeringly, then whispered in her ear.

'I am glad you noticed.'

She giggled like a bride and whispered back, 'I didn't mean that.'

'Let's see if we can teach you something that Mr Lawrence could not,' he suggested.

The cottage, once it was repainted and furnished with discards from the big house, was by Mark's standards palatial, and marvellously free of vermin and cockroaches. It was less than half a mile from the main house, and his hours became as irregular as those of his master, his position each day more trusted and naturally integrated into the household. His duties came to cover the entire spectrum from speech-writing and researching, answering all correspondence that was not important enough for the General's own hand, operating the household accounts, to merely sitting quietly sometimes when Sean Courtney needed somebody to talk to, and acting as a sounding board for arguments and ideas.

Yet there was still time for his old love of reading. There were thousands of volumes that made up the library at Emoyeni and Mark took an armful of them down to the cottage each evening and read until the early hours, devouring with omnivorous appetite history, biography, satire, political treatise, Zane Grey, Kipling and Rider Haggard.

Then suddenly there was a new spirit of excitement and upheaval in Emoyeni as the next session of Parliament approached. This meant that the household must uproot itself, and move almost a thousand miles to Cape Town.

Lightly Ruth Courtney referred to this annual political migration as the 'Great Trek', but the description was justified, for it meant moving the family, fifteen of the senior servants, three automobiles, a dozen horses, all the clothing, silver, glassware, papers, books and other incidentals that would be necessary to sustain in the correct style a busy social and political season of many months, while General Courtney and his peers conducted the affairs of the nation. It meant also closing Emoyeni and opening the house in Newlands, below the squat bulk of Table Mountain.

In the middle of all this frantic activity, Storm Courtney arrived home from the grand tour of the British Isles and the Continent on which she and Irene Leuchars had been chaperoned by Irene's mother. In her last letter to Ruth Courtney, Mrs Leuchars had admitted herself to be both physically and mentally exhausted. 'You will never know, my dear, the terrible weight of responsibility I have been under. We have been followed across half the world by droves of eager young men – Americans, Italians, Frenchmen, Counts, Barons, sons of industrialists, and even the son of the dictator of a South American Republic. The strain was such that at one period I could bear it no longer and locked both girls in their room. It was only later that I discovered they had escaped by means of a fire escape and danced until the following morning at some disreputable *boite de nuit* in Montparnasse.' With the tact of a loving wife, Ruth refrained from showing the letter to Sean

Courtney and so he prepared to welcome his daughter with all the enthusiasm of a doting father, unclouded by awareness of her recent escapades.

Mark was for once left out of the family preparations and he watched from the library window when Sean handed his wife into the Rolls. He was dressed like a suitor in crisply starched fly-away collar, a gay silk cravat, dark blue suit with white carnation in the button-hole and a beaver tilted jauntily over one eye; his beard was trimmed and shampooed and there was a merry anticipatory sparkle in his eyes, and he twirled his cane lightly as he went round to his own seat.

The Rolls purred away, almost two hours ahead of the time when the mailship was scheduled to berth at No. 1 wharf. It was followed at a respectful distance by the second Rolls which would be needed for the conveyance of Storm Courtney's baggage.

Mark lunched alone in the study and then worked on, but his concentration was broken by the imminent arrival of the returning cavalcade, and when it came, he hurried to the windows.

He caught only a glimpse of Storm as she left the car and danced up the front steps hand in hand with her mother. They were followed immediately by the General, his cane snapping a staccato beat off the marble as he hurried to match their swiftness; on his face he wore an expression that tried to remain severe and stern but kept breaking into a wide beaming grin.

Mark heard the laughter and the excited murmur of the servants assembled to greet her in the entrance hall, and Storm's voice giving a new sweet lilt to the cadence of the Zulu language as she went to each of them in turn.

Mark returned to his open books, but did not look down at them. Instead he was savouring that one glimpse he had of Storm.

She had grown somehow lovelier; he had not believed

it possible, but it had happened. It was as though the divine essence of young womanhood had been distilled in her, all the gaiety and grace, all the warmth and smoothness, the texture of skin and silken hair, the perfect moulding of limb and the delicate sculpturing of feature, the musical lilt of her voice, clear as the ring of crystal, the dancing grace of her movements, the very carriage of the small perfect head on bare brown shoulders.

Mark sat bemused, acutely aware of the way in which the whole huge house had changed its mood since she entered it, had become charged with her spirit, as though it had been waiting for this moment.

Mark had excused himself from dinner that evening, not wanting to intrude on the family's first evening together. He intended going down to the drill-hall for the weekly muster, and afterwards he would dine with some of the other young bachelor officers. At four o'clock, he left the house through a side entrance and went down to the cottage to bath and change into his uniform.

He was thundering out of the gates of Emoyeni on the Ariel Square Four when he remembered that the General had asked for the Railway report to be left on his desk. In the distraction of Storm's arrival, he had forgotten it, and now he swung the heavy machine into a tight turn and tore back up the driveway.

In the paved kitchen yard he pulled the motorcycle up on its stand, and went in through the back door.

He was standing at the library table with the report in his hands, glancing through it quickly to check his own notations, when suddenly the latch on the door clicked. He laid aside the report and turned just as the door swung open.

This close, Storm Courtney was lovelier still. She was three quick light paces into the room before she realized she was not alone, and she paused, startled, poised with the grace of a gazelle on the point of flight.

One hand flew to her mouth, and her fingers were delicately tapered with long nails that gleamed like pink mother of pearl. She touched her lips with the tip of one finger; the lip trembled slightly, wet and smooth and glistening, and her eyes were huge and a dark fearful blue. She looked like a little girl, frightened and alone.

Mark wanted to reassure her, to protect her from her own distress, to say something to comfort her, but he found he could not move or speak.

He need not have worried, her distress lasted only a fleeting beat of time, just long enough for her to realize that the source of her alarm was a tall young man, dashing in the dress uniform he wore, a uniform that set off the slim graceful body, a uniform emblazoned with badges of courage and of responsibility.

Subtly, with barely a shadow of movement, her whole poise changed. The finger on her lip now touched one cheek with an arch gesture, and the trembling lip stilled and parted slightly into a thoughtful pout. The huge eyes, no longer fearful, almost disappeared behind drooping lids, and then examined Mark critically, lifting her chin to look up into his face.

Her stance changed also, one hip thrusting forward an inch, the twin mounds of her breasts lifting and pressing boldly against the gossamer silk of her bodice. The tender taunting line of her lips was enough to make Mark's breath catch in his throat.

'Hello,' she said. Her voice, although low and throaty, bounced the word off Mark's heart, drawing it out into two syllables that seemed to hang in the air seconds later.

'Good evening, Miss Courtney,' he answered her, surprised that his voice came out level and assured. It was the voice that triggered her memory, and the blue eyes flew wide as she stared at him. Slowly her surprise turned to angry outrage. The eyes snapped sparks and two bright scarlet blotches of crimson burned suddenly on the smooth, almost waxy perfection of her cheeks.

'You?' she asked incredulously. 'Here?'

'I'm afraid so,' he agreed, and her consternation was so comical that he grinned at her, his own misgivings evaporating. Suddenly he felt relaxed and at his ease.

'What are you doing in this house?' She drew herself up to her full height, and her manner became frostily dignified. The full effect was spoiled by the fact that she had to look up at him, and that her cheeks still burned with agitation.

'I am your father's personal assistant now,' and he smiled again. 'However, I am sure you will soon become reconciled to my presence.'

'We will see about that,' she snapped. 'I shall speak to my father.'

'Oh, I was led to understand that you and the General had already discussed my employment – or rather my unemployment.'

'I—' said Storm, and then closed her mouth firmly, the colour spreading from her cheeks down her throat as she remembered with sudden acute discomfort the whole episode. The humiliation was still so intense that she felt herself wilting like a rose on a summer's day, and a small choke of self-pity constricted the back of her throat. It was enough that it had happened, that instead of her father's unquestioning support – something she had been accustomed to since her first childhood memories – he had told her angrily that she had acted like a spoiled child, that she had shamed him by misusing his power and influence, and that the shame had been made more intense by the way she had used it without his knowledge, by sneaking behind his back, as he put it.

She had been frightened, as she always was by his anger, but not seriously disturbed. It was almost ten years since he had last lifted a hand to her.

'A true lady shows consideration to all around her, no matter what their colour or creed or station.'

She had heard it often before, and now her fear was turning to irritation.

'Oh, la-di-da, Pater! I'm not a child any more!' she flounced. 'He was insolent, and anyone who is insolent to me will damned well pay for it.'

'You have made two statements there,' the General noted with deceptive calm, 'and both of them need correction. If you are insolent, then you will get back insolence – and you *are* a child still.' He rose from his chair behind the desk, and he was huge, like a forest oak, like a mountain. 'One other little thing, ladies do not swear, and you are going to be a lady when you grow up. Even if I have to beat it into you.'

As he took her wrist, she suddenly realized with a sense of incredulous dismay what was about to happen. It had not happened since she was fourteen years of age, and she had believed it would never happen again.

She tried to pull away, but his strength was enormous, and as he lifted her easily under one arm and carried her to the leather couch, she let out her first squeal of fear and outrage. It changed swiftly to real anguished howls as he positioned her carefully across his lap and swept her skirts up over her head. Her pantaloons were of blue *crêpe de Chine* with little pink roses decorating the target area, and his palm, horny and hard, snapped over the tight double bulge of her buttocks with a sharp rubbery crack. He kept it up until the howling and kicking subsided into heart-racking sobs, and then he lowered her skirts and told her quietly, 'If I knew where to find him, I'd send you to apologize to that young man.'

Storm remembered that threat, and felt a moment of panic. She knew her father was still quite capable of making her apologize even now, and she nearly turned and rushed out of the library. It required a supreme effort once more to draw herself up and lift her chin defiantly.

'You are right,' she said coldly. 'The hiring and firing of my father's servants is not a subject with which I should concern myself. Now, if you would kindly stand aside—'

'Of course, forgive me.' Still smiling, Mark bowed extravagantly and made way for her to pass.

She tossed her head and swished her skirts as she passed him and, in her agitation, went to the wrong shelves. It was some little time before she realized that she was studying intently a row of bound copies of ten-year-old parliamentary white papers, but she would not admit her mistake and humiliate herself further.

Furiously she pondered her next sally, picking and discarding half a dozen disparaging remarks before settling on, 'I would be obliged if in future you would address me only when it is absolutely necessary, and right at this moment I should like to be alone.' She spoke without interrupting her perusal of the white papers.

There was no reply, and she turned haughtily. 'Did you hear what I said?' Then she paused.

She was alone, he had gone silently and she had not even heard the click of the latch.

He had not waited to be dismissed, and Storm felt quite dizzy with anger. Now a whole parade of brilliant and biting insults came readily to her lips, and frustration spiced her anger.

She had to do something to vent it, and she looked around for something to break – and then remembered, just in time, that it was Sean Courtney's library, and everything in it was treasured. So instead, she racked her brain for its foulest oath.

'Bloody Hell!' She stamped her foot, and it was entirely inadequate. Suddenly she remembered her father's favourite.

'The bastard,' she added, rolling it thunderously around her tongue as Sean did, and immediately she felt better. She said it again and her anger subsided, leaving an extraordinary new sensation.

There was a disturbing heat in that mysterious area between navel and knees. Flustered and alarmed, she hurried out into the garden. The short glowing tropical dusk gave the familiar lawns and trees an unreal stage-like appearance, and she found herself almost running over the spongy turf, as though to escape from her own sensations.

She stopped beside the lake, and her breathing was quick and shallow, not entirely from her exertions. She leaned on the railing of the bridge and in the rosy light of sunset her reflection was perfectly mirrored in the still pearly waters.

Now that the disturbing new sensation had passed, she found herself regretting that she had fled from it. Something like that was what she had hoped for when –

She found herself thinking again of that awkward and embarrassing episode in Monte Carlo; goaded on by Irene Leuchars, teased and tempted, she had been made to feel inadequate because she lacked the experience of men that Irene boasted of. Chiefly to spite Irene, and to defend herself against her jibes, she had slipped away from the Casino with the young Italian Count and made no protest when he parked the Bugatti among the pine trees on the high-level road above Cap Ferrat.

She had hoped for something wild and beautiful, something to bring the moon crashing out of the sky and to make choirs of angels sing.

It had been quick, painful and messy – and neither she nor the Count had spoken to each other on the winding road down to Nice, except to mutter goodbye on the pavement outside the Negresco Hotel. She had not seen him again.

Why she thought of this now she could not understand,

and she thrust the memory aside without effort. It was replaced almost instantly with a picture of a tall young man in a handsome uniform, of a cool mocking smile and calm penetrating gaze. Immediately she was aware of the warmth and glow in her lower belly again, and this time she did not attempt to fly from it, but continued leaning on the bridge, smiling at her darkening image in the water.

'You look like a smug old pussy cat,' she whispered, and chuckled softly.

Sean Courtney rode like a Boer, with long stirrups, sitting well back in the saddle with legs thrust out straight in front of him and the reins held loosely in his left hand, the black quirt of hippo-hide dangling from its thong on his wrist so that the point touched the ground. His favourite mount was a big rawboned stallion of almost eighteen hands with a white blaze and an ugly unpredictable nature that only the General could fathom; but even he had to use an occasional light cut with the quirt to remind the beast of his social obligations.

Mark had an English seat, or, as the General put it, rode like a monkey on a broomstick, and he added darkly,' After only a hundred miles or so perched up like that, your backside will be so hot you could cook your dinner on it. We rode a thousand miles in two weeks when we were chasing General Leroux.'

They rode almost daily together, when even the huge rooms of Emoyeni became confining, and the General started to fret at the caging of his big body; then he would shout for the horses.

There were thousands of acres of open ground still backing the big urban estates, and then beyond that there were hundreds of miles of red dirt roads criss-crossing the sugar-cane fields.

As they rode, the day's work was continued, with only the occasional interruption for a half mile of hard galloping to charge the blood, and then the General would rein in again and they would amble on over the gently undulating hills, knee to knee. Mark carried a small leather-bound notebook in his inside pocket to make notes of what he must write up on their return, but most of it he carried in his head.

The week before the departure to Cape Town had been filled with the implementation of details and of broad policies, the winding up of the domestic business of the provincial legislative council before beginning on the national business of Parliament, and, deep in this discussion, their daily ride had carried them further than they had ridden together before.

When at last the General reined in, they had reached the crest of a hill, and the view before them spread down to the sea, and away to the far silhouette of the great whale-backed mountain above Durban harbour. Directly below them, a fresh scar had been torn in the earth, like a bold knife stroke through the green carpet of vegetation, into the red fleshy earth.

The steel tracks of the permanent way had reached this far, and as they sat the fidgeting horses, the loco came huffing up to the railhead, pushing the track carrier ahead of it under its heavy load of steel.

Neither of them spoke, as the tracks were dumped with a faint clattering roar, and the tiny antlike figures of the tracklaying gang swarmed over them, man-handling them on to the orderly parallel rows of timber sleepers. The tap of the swinging hammers began then, a quick rhythmic beat as the fishplates were spiked into place.

'A mile a day,' said Sean softly, and Mark saw from his expression that he was thinking once again of another railroad far to the north, and all that it betokened. 'Cecil Rhodes dreamed of a railway from Cairo to Cape Town –

and I believed once that it was a grand dream.' He shook his beard heavily. 'God knows, perhaps we were both wrong.'

He turned the stallion's head away and they walked back down the hill in silence except for the jingle of harness and the clip of hooves. They were both thinking of Dirk Courtney, but it was another ten minutes before Sean spoke.

'Do you know the Bubezi Valley, beyond Chaka's Gate?'

'Yes,' said Mark.

'Tell me,' Sean ordered, and then went on, 'It is fifty years since I was last there. During the war with the old Zulu king Cetewayo, we chased the remains of his impis up there, and hunted them along the river.'

'I was there only a few months ago. Just before I came to you.'

Sean turned in the saddle, and his black brows came together sharply.

'What were you doing there?' he demanded harshly.

For an instant Mark was about to blurt out all his suspicions – of Dirk Courtney, of the fate that had over-taken the old man, of his pilgrimage to find the grave and to fathom the mystery beyond Chaka's Gate. Something warned him that to do so would be to alienate Sean Courtney completely. He knew enough about him now to realize that although he might accuse and even reject his own son, he would not listen to nor tolerate those accusations from someone outside the family, particularly if those accusations were without substance or proof. Mark put the temptation aside and instead he explained quietly,

'My grandfather and I went there often when I was a child. I needed to go back – for the silence and the beauty, for the peace.'

'Yes.' The General understood immediately. 'What's the game like there now?'

'Thin,' Mark answered. 'It's been shot out, trapped and hunted. It's thin and very wild.'

'Buffalo?'

'Yes, there are some in the swamps. I think they graze out into the bush in the night but I never saw them.'

'In 1901 old Selous wrote that the Cape buffalo was extinct. That was after the rinderpest plague. My God, Mark, when I was your age there were herds of ten and twenty thousand together, the plains along the Limpopo were black with them,' and he began to reminisce again. It might have been boring, an old man's musty memories, but he told it so vividly that Mark was carried along, fascinated by the tales of a land where a man could ride with his wagons for six months without meeting another white man.

It was with a sick little slide of regret, of something irretrievably lost, that he heard the General say, 'It's all gone now. The railway line is right through to the copper-belt in Northern Rhodesia. Rhodes Column has taken the land between the Zambesi and the Limpopo. Where I camped and hunted, there are towns and mines, and they are ploughing up the old elephant grounds.' He shook his head again. 'We thought it would never end, and now it's almost gone.' He was silent and sad again for a while. 'My grandchildren may never see an elephant or hear the roar of a lion.'

'My grandfather said that when Africa lost its game, he would go back and live in old London town.'

'That's how I feel,' Sean agreed. 'It's strange but perhaps Dirk has done something of great value for Africa and for mankind.' The name seemed to choke in his throat, as though it was an effort to enunciate it – and Mark was silent, respecting that effort. 'He has made me think of all this as never before. One of the things that we are going to do during this session of Parliament, Mark, is to make sure that the sanctuary in the Bubezi Valley is ratified, and we are going to get funds to administer it properly, to make sure that nobody, ever, turns it into a sugar cane or cotton field, or floods it beneath the waters of a dam.' As he spoke, Mark listened with a soaring sense of destiny and commitment. It was as though he had waited all his life to hear these words.

The General went on, working out what was needed in money and men, deciding where he would lobby for support, which others in the Cabinet could be relied on, the form which the legislation must take, and Mark made a note of each point as it came up, his pencil hurrying to keep pace with the General's random and eclectic thoughts.

Suddenly, in full intellectual flight, the General broke off and laughed aloud. 'It's true, you know, Mark. There is nobody so virtuous as a reformed whore. We were the great robber barons – Rhodes and Robertson, Bailey and Barnato, Duff Charleywood and Sean Courtney. We seized the land and then ripped the gold out of the earth, we hunted where we pleased, and burned the finest timber for our camp fires, every man with a rifle in his hand and shoes on his feet was a king – prepared to fight anybody, Boer, Briton or Zulu, for the right of plunder.' He shook his head and groped in his pockets before he found his cigars. He laughed no longer, but frowned as he lit the cigar. The big stallion seemed to sense his mood, and he crabbed and bucked awkwardly. Sean rode him easily and quirted him lightly across the flank. 'Behave yourself!' he growled, and then when he quieted Sean went on, 'The day that I met my first wife, only thirty-two years ago, I hunted with her father and her brother. We rode down a herd of elephant and between the three of us we shot and killed forty-three of them. We cut out the tusks and left the carcasses lying. That's over one hundred and sixty tons of flesh.' Again he shook his head. 'Only now am I coming to realize the enormity of what we did. There were other things – during the Zulu wars, during the war with Kruger, during Bombata's rebellion in 1906. Things I don't even like to remember. And now perhaps it's too late to make amends. Perhaps also it's just the way of growing old that a man regrets the passing of the old ways. He initiates change when he is young and then mourns that change when he grows old.'

Mark was silent, not daring to say a word that might break the mood. He knew that what he was hearing was so important that he could then only guess at the depths of it.

'We must try, Mark, we must try.'

'Yes, sir. We will,' Mark agreed, and something in his tone made the General glance across at him, mildly surprised.

'This really means something to you.' He nodded, confirming his statement. 'Yes, I can see that. Strange, a young fellow like you! When I was your age all I ever thought about was a quick sovereign and a likely piece of—' He caught himself before he finished, and coughed to clear his throat.

'Well, sir, you must remember that I had my full share of destruction at an earlier age than you did. The greatest destruction the world has ever known.' The General's face darkened as he remembered what they had shared together in France. 'When you've seen how easy it is to tear down, it makes the preservation seem worth while.' Mark chuckled ruefully. 'Perhaps I was born too late.'

'No,' said the General softly. 'I think you were born just in time,' and he might have gone on, but high and clear on the heat-hushed air came the musical cry of a girl's voice, and instantly the General's head went up and his expression lightened.

Storm Courtney came at the gallop. She rode with the same light lithe grace which marked all she did. She rode astride, and she wore knee-high boots with baggy gaucho pants tucked into the tops, a hand-embroidered waistcoat in vivid colours over a shirt of white satin with wide sleeves, and a black wide-brimmed vaquero hat hung on her back from a thong around her throat.

She reined in beside her father, laughing and flushed, tossing the hair out of her face, and leaning out of the saddle to kiss him, not even glancing at Mark, and he touched his reins and dropped back tactfully.

'We've been looking for you all over, Pater,' she cried. 'We went as far as the river – what made you come this way?'

Coming up more sedately behind Storm on a bay mare was the blonde girl whom Mark remembered from that fateful day at the tennis courts. She was more conventionally dressed than Storm in dove-grey riding breeches and tailored jacket, and the wind ruffled the pale silken gold of her cropped hair.

While she made her greetings to the General, her eyes kept swivelling in Mark's direction and he searched for her name and remembered she had been called Irene – and realized she must be the girl who had been Storm's companion on the grand continental tour. A pretty, bright little thing with a gay brittle style and calculating eyes.

'Good afternoon, Miss Leuchars.'

'Oh la!' She smiled archly at him now. 'Have we met?' Somehow her mare was kneed away from the leading pair, and dropped back beside Mark's mount.

'Briefly, yes, we have,' Mark admitted, and suddenly the china-blue eyes flew wide and the girl covered her mouth with a gloved hand.

'You are the one—' then she squealed softly with delight, and mimicked him, 'just as soon as you say please!'

Storm Courtney had not looked round, and she was paying exaggerated attention to her father, but Mark watched her small perfect ears turn pink, and she tossed her head again, but this time with an aggressive, angry motion.

'I think we might forget that,' Mark murmured.

'Forget it?' chirruped Irene. 'I'll never forget it. It was absolutely classic.' She leaned over and placed a bold hand on Mark's forearm. At that moment Storm could contain herself no longer; she swivelled in the saddle and was about to speak to Irene, when she saw the hand on Mark's arm.

For a moment Storm's expression was ferocious, and the dark blue eyes snapped with electric sparkle. Irene held her gaze undaunted, making her own paler blue eyes wide and artless, and deliberately, challengingly, she let her hand linger, squeezing lightly on Mark's sleeve.

The understanding between the two girls was instantaneous. They had played the game before, but this time intuitively Irene realized that she had never been in a stronger position to inflict punishment. She had never seen such a swift and utterly malevolent reaction from Storm – and they knew each other intimately. This time she had Missy Storm in a vice, and she was going to squeeze and squeeze.

She edged her mare in until her knee touched Mark's, and she turned away from Storm, deliberately looking up at the rider beside her.

'I hadn't realized you were so tall,' she murmured. 'How tall are you?'

'Six foot two.' Mark only dimly realized that something mysterious, which promised him many awkward moments, was afoot.

'Oh, I do think height gives a man presence.'

Storm was now laughing gaily with her father, and trying to listen to the conversation behind her at the same time. Anger clawed her cruelly and she clutched the riding-crop until her fingers ached. She was not quite sure what had affected her this way, but she would have delighted in lashing the crop across Irene's silly simpering face.

It was certainly not that she felt anything for Mark Anders. He was, after all, merely a hired servant at Emoyeni. He could make an idiot of himself over Irene Leuchars and she would not even glance aside at any other time or place. It was just that there were some things that were not done, the dignity of her position, of her father, and family – yes, that was it, she realized. It was an insult that Irene Leuchars, as a guest in the Courtney home, should make herself free, should flaunt herself, should make it so blatant that she would like to lead Mark Anders along the well-travelled pathway to her steamy – she could not continue the thought, for the vivid mental image of that pale, deceptively fragile-looking body of Irene's spread out, languid and naked, and Mark about to – another wave of anger made her sway in the saddle, and she dropped the riding crop she carried and turned quickly.

'Oh Mark, I've dropped my crop. Won't you be a dear and fetch it for me?'

Mark was taken aback, not only by the endearment, but also by the stunning smile and warmth of Storm's voice. He almost fell from the saddle in his haste, and when he came alongside Storm to hand the crop back to her, she detained him with a smile of thanks, and a question.

'Mark, won't you help me label my cases? It's only a few days and we'll all be leaving for Cape Town.'

'I'm so looking forward to it,' Irene agreed as she pushed her mare up on Mark's other side, and Storm smiled sweetly at her.

'It should be fun,' she agreed. 'I love Cape Town.'

'Grand fun,' Irene laughed gaily, and Storm regretted bitterly the invitation that would make her a guest for four months in the Courtneys' Cape Town home. Before Storm could find a cutting rejoinder, Irene leaned across to Mark.

'Come on, then,' she said, and turned her mare aside.

'Where are you going?' Storm demanded.

'Mark is taking me down to the river to show me the monument where Dick King crossed on his way to fetch the English troops from Grahamstown.'

'Oh, Irene darling,' Storm dabbed at her eye with the

tail of her scarf. 'I seem to have something in my eye. Won't you see to it? No, don't wait for us, Mark. Go on ahead with the General. I know he needs you still.'

And she turned her small perfect head to Irene for her ministrations.

With patent relief, Mark spurred ahead to catch up with the General, and Irene told Storm in honeyed tones, 'There's nothing in your eye, darling, except a touch of green.'

'You bitch,' hissed Storm.

'Darling, I don't know what you mean.'

The *Dunottar Castle* trembled under the thrust of her engines and ran southwards over a starlit sea that seemed to be sculpted from wet black obsidian, each crest marched with such weighty dignity as to seem solid and unmoving. It was only when the ship put her sharp prow into them that they burst into creaming white, and hissed back along the speeding hull.

The General paused and looked at the southern sky, to where the great cross burned among its myriad cohorts, and Orion the hunter brandished his sword.

'That's the way the sky should be,' he nodded his approval. 'I could never get used to the northern skies. It was as though the universe had disintegrated, and the grand designs of nature had been plunged into anarchy.'

They went to the rail and paused there to watch the moon rise out of the dark sea, and as it pushed its golden dome clear of the horizon, the General pulled out the gold hunter watch from his waistcoat pocket and grunted. 'Twenty-one minutes past midnight, the moon is punctual this morning.' Mark smiled at the little joke. Yet he knew that it was part of the General's daily ritual to consult his almanac for sunrise and moonrise, and the moon phases. The man's energy was formidable.

They had worked until just a few minutes previously and had been at it since mid-morning. Mark felt muzzy and woolly headed with mental effort and the pungent incense of the General's cigars which had filled the suite.

'I think we overdid it a little today, my boy,' Sean Courtney admitted, as though he had read the thought. 'But I did want to be up to date before we dock in Table Bay. Thank you, Mark. Now why don't you go down and join the dancing?'

From the boat deck, Mark looked down on to the swirling orderly confusion of dancing couples in the break of the promenade deck. The ship's band was belting out a Strauss waltz and the dancers spun wildly, the women's skirts flaring open like the petals of exotic blooms and their laughing cries a sweet and musical counterpoint to the stirring strains of the waltz.

Mark picked Storm Courtney out of the press, her particular grace making it easy to distinguish her; she lay back in the circle of her partner's arms and spun dizzily, the light catching the dark sparkle of her hair and glowing on the waxy golden perfection of her bare shoulders.

Mark lit a cigarette, and leaned on the rail, watching her. It was strange that he had seldom felt lonely in the great silences and space of the wilderness, and here, surrounded by music and gaiety and the laughter of young people, he knew deep loneliness.

The General's suggestion that he go down and join the dancing had been unwittingly cruel. He would have been out of place there among the rich young clique who had known each other since childhood, a close-knit élite that jealousy closed ranks against any intruder, especially one that did not possess the necessary qualifications of wealth and social standing.

He imagined going down and asking Storm Courtney for a waltz, her humiliation at being accosted by her father's secretary, the nudging and the snide exchanges, the patronizing questions. 'Do you actually type letters, old boy?' And he felt himself flushing angrily at the mere thought of it.

Yet he lingered by the rail for another half hour, delighting in each glimpse of Storm, and hating each of her partners with a stony implacable hatred; and when at last he went down to his cabin, he could not sleep. He wrote a letter to Marion Littlejohn, and found himself as warmly disposed towards her as he had been in months. Her gentleness and sincerity, and the genuineness of her affection for him were suddenly very precious assets. On the pages he recalled the visit she had made to Durban just before his departure. The General had been understanding and they had had many hours together during the two days. She had been awed by his new position, and impressed by his surroundings. However, their one further attempt at physical intimacy, even though it had been made in the security and privacy of Mark's cottage, had been, if anything, less successful than the first. There had been no opportunity, nor had Mark had the heart, to break off their engagement, and in the end Mark had put her on the train to Ladyburg with relief, but now loneliness and distance had enhanced her memory. He wrote with real affection and sincerity, but when he had sealed the envelope, he found that he still had no desire for sleep.

He had found a copy of *Jock of the Bushveld* in the ship's library and was rereading the adventures of man and dog, and the nostalgic and vivid descriptions of African bush and animals with such pleasure, that his loneliness was forgotten. There was a light tap on the door of his cabin.

'Oh Mark, do let me hide in here for a moment.' Irene Leuchars pushed quickly past him before he could protest, and she ordered, 'Quickly, lock the door.' Her tone made him obey immediately, but when he turned back to her he had immediate misgivings.

She had been drinking. The flush of her cheeks was not all rouge, the glitter in her eyes was feverish, and when she laughed it was unnaturally high.

'What's the trouble?' he asked.

'Oh God, darling, I have had the most dreadful time. That Charlie Eastman is absolutely hounding me. I swear I'm terrified to go back to my cabin.'

'I'll talk to him,' Mark offered, but she stopped him quickly.

'Oh, don't make a scene. He's not worth it.' She flicked the tail of the ostrich feather boa over her shoulder. 'I'll just sit here for a while, if you don't mind.'

Her dress was made of layers of filmy material that floated in a cloud about her as she moved, and her shoulders were bare, the bodice cut so low that her breasts bulged out, very round and smooth and white and deeply divided.

'Do you mind?' she demanded, very aware of the direction of his eyes, and he lifted them quickly to her face. She made a moue of impatience as she waited for his reply. Her lipstick was startling crimson and glossy, so her lips had a full ripe look.

He knew he must get her out of his cabin. He knew that he was in danger. He knew how vulnerable he was, how powerful her family, and he guessed how shallow and callous she could be. But he was lonely, achingly grindingly lonely.

'You can stay, of course,' he told her, and she drooped her eyelids and ran a sharp pink tongue across the painted lips.

'Have you got a drink, darling?'

'No, I'm sorry.'

'Don't be, don't ever be sorry.' She swayed against him and he could smell the liquor on her breath, but it was not offensive and, with her perfume, blended into a spicy fragrance.

'Look,' she told him, holding up the silver evening bag she carried. 'The "It" girl with every home comfort,' and she took a small silver jewelled flask from the bag. 'Every comfort known to man,' she repeated, and parted her lips in a lewd but intensely provocative pout.

'Come and I'll give you a little sample.' Her voice dropped to a husky whisper, and then she laughed and swirled away in a waltzing turn, humming a bar of the Blue Danube and the gossamer of her skirts floated about her thighs. Clad in silk, her limbs gleamed in the soft light and when she dropped carelessly on to Mark's bunk, her skirts ballooned and then settled so high that he could see that the black elastic suspender-belt that held her stocking tops was decorated with embroidered butterflies. The butterflies were spangled with brilliant colour and in exotic contrast to the pale soft skin of her inner thighs.

'Come, Markie, come and have a little itsy bitsy drinkie.' She patted the bunk beside her and then wriggled her bottom across to make room for him. The skirts rucked up higher and exposed the wedge of her panties between her thighs. The material was so sheer that he could see the pale red-gold curls trapped and flattened by the silk.

Mark felt something crack inside him. For another moment, he tried to reckon consequence, to force himself back on to the course that was both moral and safe, but he knew that in reality the decision had been made when he had allowed her to stay.

'Come, Mark.' She held the flask like bait, and the light reflected off it in silver splinters that she played into his eyes. The crack opened, and like a bursting dam, all restraint was swept aside. She recognized the moment and her eyes flared with triumph and she welcomed him to the bed with a little animal squeal, and with slim pale arms that wrapped about his neck with startling strength.

She was small and strong, quick and demanding, and as skilled as Helena MacDonald – but she was different, so very different.

Her youth gave her flesh a sweetness and freshness, her skin an unblemished lustre, a luscious plasticity that was made more startling by her pale pigmentation.

When she slipped the strap off one shoulder and popped one of her glossy breasts out of the top of her bodice, offering it to Mark with a sound in her throat which was like the purr of a cat, he gasped aloud. It was white as porcelain and had the same sheen, too large for the slim fragile body but hard and firm and springy to his touch. The nipple was tiny, set like a small jewel in the perfect coin of its aureole, so pale and delicate pink when he remembered Helena, dark and puckered and sprinkled with sparse black hair.

'Wait, Mark. Wait,' she chuckled breathlessly, and stood quickly to drop the boa and dress to the cabin floor in one quick movement, and then to slip the sheer underwear to her ankles and kick it carelessly aside. She lifted her hands above her head and twirled slowly in front of him.

'Yes?' she asked.

'Yes,' he agreed. 'Oh very much yes.'

Her body was hairless and smooth except for that pale red mist that hazed the fat mound at the base of her belly, and her breasts rode high and arrogant.

She came back to him, kneeling over him.

'There,' she whispered. 'There's a good boy,' she crooned, but her hands were busy, unbuckling, unbuttoning, questing, finding – and then it was her turn to gasp.

'Oh, Mark, you clever boy – all by yourself too!'

'No,' he laughed. 'I had a little help.'

'And you are going to get a lot more,' she promised, and dropped her soft, fluffy golden head over him. He thought that her mouth was as red and voracious as one of those low-tide rock-pool anemones that he had fed with such delight as a child, watching it softly enfold each tidbit, sucking it in deeply.

'Oh God,' he croaked, for her mouth was hot – hotter and deeper than any sea animal could ever be.

Irene Leuchars carried her shoes in one hand and the feather boa hung over her other arm and trailed on the floor behind her. Her hair stood out in a soft pale halo around her head, and her eyes were underlined by dark blue smudges of sleeplessness, while the outline of her mouth was smudged and blurred, her lips puffed and inflamed.

'God,' she whispered, 'I'm still tiddly,' and she giggled, and lurched unsteadily to the roll of the ship. Then she pulled up the strap which had slipped from her shoulder.

Behind her in the long passageway, there was a clatter of china and she glanced back, startled. One of the white-jacketed stewards was pushing a trolley of cups and pots towards her. The morning ritual of tea and biscuits was beginning and she had not realized the hour.

Irene hurried away, turning the corner from the steward's sly and knowing grin, and she reached the door of Storm Courtney's cabin without another encounter.

She hammered on the door with the heel of one shoe, but it was a full five minutes before the door swung open and Storm looked out at her, a gown wrapped around her shoulders and her big dark eyes owlish from sleep.

'Irene, are you crazy?' she asked. 'It's still night!' Then she saw Irene's attire and smelled the rich perfume of her breath. 'Where on earth have you been?'

Irene pushed the door open and almost tripped over the threshold.

'You're drunk!' accused Storm resignedly, closing the door behind her.

'No.' Irene shook her head. 'It isn't liquor – it's ecstasy.'

'Where have you been?' Storm asked again. 'I thought you were in bed hours ago.'

'I have flown to the moon,' intoned Irene dramatically. 'I have run barefooted through the stars, I have soared on eagles' wings above the mountain peaks.'

Storm laughed, coming fully awake now, as beautiful even in *déshabillé* as Irene would never be, so graceful and lovely that Irene hated her again. She savoured the moment, drawing out the pleasure of anticipation.

'Where have you been, you mad bad woman?' Storm started to catch the spirit of the moment. 'Tell all!'

'Through the gates of paradise, to the land of never-never on the continent of always—' Irene's smile became sharp, spiteful and venomous, 'in short, darling, Mark Anders has been bouncing me like a rubber ball!'

And the expression on Storm Courtney's face gave her the most intense satisfaction she had known in her life.

'On the third day of January, the Chamber of Mines deliberately tore up the Agreement that it had come to with your Union to maintain the status quo. It tore that agreement to a thousand pieces and flung them in the faces of the workers.' Fergus MacDonald spoke with a controlled icy fury that carried to every corner of the great hall, and it stilled even the rowdies in the back seats who had brought their bottles in brown paper packets. Now they listened with intensity. Big Harry Fisher, sitting beside him on the dais, turned his head slowly to assess the man, peering at him under beetling eyebrows and with the bulldog folds of his face hanging mournfully. He marvelled again at how Fergus MacDonald changed when he stood to speak.

Usually he cut a nondescript figure with the small bulge of a paunch beginning to distort the spare frame, the cheap and ill-fitting suit shiny at the elbows and seat with wear, the collar of the frayed shirt darned, and grease spots on the drab necktie. His hair was thinning, starting up in wispy spikes around the neck, pushing back from the brow and with a pink bare patch in the crown. His face had that grey tone from the embedded filth of the machine shops, but when he stood under the red flag and the emblem of the Amalgamated Mineworkers Union on the raised dais facing the packed hall, he grew in stature, a physical phenomenon that was quite extraordinary. He seemed younger and there was a fierce and smouldering passion which stripped away his shoddy dress and armoured him with presence.

'Brothers!' He raised his voice now. 'When the mines reopened after the Christmas recess, two thousand of our members were discharged, thrown out into the street, discarded like worn-out pairs of old boots—'

The hall hummed, the warning sound of a beehive on a hot summer's day, but the stillness of thousands of bodies pressed closely together was more menacing than any movement.

'Brothers!' Fergus moved his hands in a slow hypnotic movement. 'Brothers! Beginning at the end of this month, and for every month after that, another six hundred men will be,' he paused again and then spat the official word at them, 'retrenched.'

They seemed to reel with the word, the whole concourse stunned as though by a physical blow, and the silence drew out – until a voice at the back yelled wildly, 'No, brothers. No!'

They roared then, a sound like the surf on a stormy day when it breaks upon a rocky shore.

Fergus let them roar, and he hooked his thumbs into his rumpled waistcoat and watched them, gloating in the feeling of exultation, the euphoria of power. He judged the strength of their reaction, and the moment it began to falter he raised both hands, and almost immediately the silence fell upon the hall again.

'Brothers! Do you know that the wages of a black man are two shillings and two pence a day? Only a black man can live on that wage!' He let it sink in a moment, but not too long before he went on, asking a reasonable question, 'Who will take the place of two thousand of our brothers who are now out of work? Who will replace the six hundred that will join them at the end of this month, and the next – and the next? Who will take *your* job,' he was picking out individuals, pointing at them with an accuser's finger, 'and *yours*, and *yours*? Who will take the food from your children's mouths?' He waited theatrically for an answer, cocking his head, smiling at them while his eyes smouldered.

'Brothers! I tell you who it will be. Two and tuppenny black kaffirs – that's who it will be!'

They came upon their feet, a bench here and there crashing over backwards and their voices were a blood-roar of anger, clenched fists thrust out in fury.

'No, brothers. No!' Their booted feet stamped in unison and they chanted, their fists punching into empty air.

Fergus MacDonald sat down abruptly and Harry Fisher congratulated him silently, squeezing his shoulder in a bear's paw before lumbering to his feet.

'Your executive has recommended that all members of our Union come out on general strike. I put it to you now, brothers, all those in favour—' he bellowed, and his voice was drowned in a thousand others.

'Out, brothers! We're out! Out! Out!'

Fergus leaned forward in his seat and looked down the length of the trestle table.

Helena's dark head was bowed over the minute book, but she sensed his gaze and looked up. Her expression glowed with a fanatic's ecstasy, and there was open adoration in her eyes that he saw only at moments like this.

Harry Fisher had told him once, "For all women, power is the ultimate aphrodisiac. No matter how puny in body, no matter what he looks like – power makes a man irresistible.'

In the thunder of thousands of voices, the pounding feet and the heady roar of power, Fergus was on his feet again.

'The mine-owner, the bosses have challenged us, they have scorned your executive, they have stated publicly that we are too faint-hearted to rally the workers and come out on general strike! Well, brothers, we are going to show them.' The lion's voice of the crowd rose again and he silenced it only after another minute. 'First, we are going to drive on the scabs, there are going to be no strikebreakers.' When the sound subsided he went on, 'Slim Jannie Smuts has talked of force to beat a strike, he has an army, but we are going to have one also. I think the bosses have forgotten that we fought their bloody war for them in France and East Africa, at Tabora and Delville Wood.' The names sobered them and they were listening again. 'Last time we fought for them, but this time we are fighting for ourselves. Each one of you will report to his area commander – you will be formed into fighting commandos, each man will know his job, and each man will know what is at stake. We will beat them, brothers, the bloody bosses and their greedy grasping minions. We will fight them and beat them!'

'They are organized into military-style commandos,' said the Prime Minister softly, breaking the crisp brown roll of bread with fingers that were surprisingly small, neat and capable as a woman's. 'Of course, we know that George Mason wanted to form labour commandos in 1914. It was the main reason I had him deported.' The other guests at the luncheon table were silent. The deportation of Mason was not an episode that reflected credit on Jannie Smuts. 'But this is a different animal we are dealing with now. Nearly all the younger members of the unions are trained veterans. Five hundred of them paraded outside the Trade Union Hall in Fordsburg last Saturday.' He turned and smiled that impish, irresistible smile at his hostess. 'My dear Ruth, you must forgive my bad manners. This talk detracts from the delicious meal you have provided.'

The table was set under the oak trees on lawns so vivid green that Ruth always thought of them as 'English green'. The house itself had the solid imposing bulk of Georgian England, so different from the frivolous fairy castle at Emoyeni; the illusion of old England was spoiled only by the soaring cliffs of grey rock that rose as a backdrop to the scene. The sheer slopes of Table Mountain were softened by the pine trees that clung precariously for footholds on each ledge and in each tiny pocket of soil.

Ruth smiled at him. 'In this house, General, you may do as you wish.'

'Thank you, my dear.' The smile flickered off his face and the merry twinkle of the pale blue eyes changed to the glint of swords, as he turned back to his listeners. 'They are seeking confrontation, gentlemen, it's a blatant test of our power and resolution.'

Ruth caught Mark's eye at the foot of the table and he rose to refill the glasses with cold pale wine tinged with a touch of green, dry and crisp and refreshing, but as he moved down the board, pausing beside each guest – three Cabinet ministers, a visiting British Earl, the Secretary of the Chamber of Mines – he was listening avidly.

'We can only hope you put it too highly, Prime Minister,' Sean Courtney intervened gruffly. 'They have only broomsticks with which to drill, and bicycles on which to ride into battle . . .'

And while they laughed, Mark paused behind Sean's chair with the bottle forgotten in his hand. He was remembering the cellars below the Trade Union Hall in

Fordsburg, the racks of modern rifles, the gleaming P.14 reserved for him and the sinister squatting Vickers machine-gun. When he returned to the present, the conversation had moved on.

Sean Courtney was assuring the company that militant action by the unions was unlikely, and that in the worst circumstances, the army was geared to immediate call-up.

Mark had a small office adjoining the General's study. It had previously been a linen room, but was just large enough to accommodate a desk and several shelves of files. The General had ordered a large window knocked through one wall to give it air and light, and now, with his ankles crossed and propped on the desk-top, Mark was staring thoughtfully out of the window. The view across lawns and through oaks encompassed a sweep of Rhodes Avenue, named after that asthmatic old adventurer who had seized an empire in land and diamonds, and ended up Prime Minister of the first Cape Parliament, before suffocating from his weak lungs and heavy conscience. The Cape home of the Courtneys was named Somerset Lodge after Lord Charles, the nineteenth-century governor, and the great houses on the opposite side of Rhodes Avenue perpetuated the colonial tradition, Newlands House and Hiddingh House, gracious edifices in spacious grounds.

Looking out at them through the new window, Mark was comparing them with the miners' cottages in Fordsburg Dip. He had not thought of Fergus and Helena in many months, but the conversation at lunch had brought them back forcibly, and he felt himself torn by sharply contradictory loyalties.

He had lived in both worlds now, and seen how each opposed the other. He was trying to think without emotion, but always a single image intruded, the cruel shape of weapons in orderly racks, deep in a dark cellar, and the slick smell of gun oil in his throat.

He lit another cigarette, delaying the decision. Through

the solid teak door, the sound of voices from the General's study was muted, the higher clearer tones of the Prime Minister, bird-like almost, set against the rumbling of Sean's replies.

The Prime Minister had stayed on after the other luncheon guests had left, as he often did, but Mark wished that he would leave now, thus deferring the decision with which he was wrestling.

He had been trusted by a comrade, somebody who had shared mortal danger with him, and then had unstintingly shared the hospitality of his home, had trusted him like a brother, had not hesitated to give him access to the direst knowledge, had not hesitated to leave him alone with his wife. Mark had betrayed half of that trust – and he stirred restlessly in his seat as he remembered those wicked stolen days and nights with Helena. Now must he betray the rest of the trust that Fergus MacDonald had placed in him?

Once more the image of racked weapons passed before his eyes; they faded only slowly to be replaced with a vivid shocking picture of a face.

It was the face of a marble angel, smooth and white and strangely beautiful, with blue eyes in pale blue sockets, a burst of pale golden curls escaping from under the rim of the steel helmet on to the smooth pale forehead –

Mark dropped his feet from the desk with a crash, fighting away the memory of the young German sniper, forcing it from his mind, and coming to his feet abruptly.

He found that his hands were shaking and he crushed out the cigarette and turned to the door. His knock was over-loud and demanding, and the voice from beyond was gruff with irritation.

'Come in.' He stepped through. 'What do you want, Mark, you know I don't—' Sean Courtney cut himself short and the tone of his voice changed to concern as he saw Mark's face. 'What is it, my boy?'

'I have to tell you something, sir,' he blurted.

They listened with complete attention as he described his involvement with the executive of the Communist Party, and then broke off to steel himself for the final betrayal.

'These men were my friends, sir, they treated me as a comrade. You must understand why I am telling you this, please.'

'Go on, Mark,' Sean Courtney nodded, and the Prime Minister had drawn back in his chair – still and quiet and unobtrusive, sensing the struggle of conscience in which the young man was involved.

'I came to believe that much of what they were striving for was good and just – opportunity and a share of life for every man, but I could not accept the methods they had chosen to bring these about.'

'What do you mean, Mark?'

'They are planning war, a class war, sir.'

'You have proof of that?' Sean's voice did not rise, and he asked the question carefully.

'Yes. I have.' Mark drew a deep breath before he went on. 'I have seen the rifles and machine guns they have ready for the day.'

The Prime Minister shifted in his chair and then was still again, but now he was leaning forward to listen.

'Go on,' Sean nodded, and Mark told them in detail, stating the unadorned facts, reporting exactly what he had seen and where, accurately estimating the numbers and types of every weapon, and finally ending, 'MacDonald led me to believe that this was only one arsenal, and that there were others, many others, on the Witwatersrand.'

Nobody spoke for many seconds, and then the Prime Minister stood up and went to the telephone on Sean's desk. He wound the crank handle, and the whirr-whirr was loud and obtrusive in the silent room.

'This is the Prime Minister, General Smuts, speaking. I want a maximum priority connection with Commissioner Truter, the Chief of the South African Police in Johannesburg,' he said, and then listened, his expression bleak and his eyes sparkling angrily. 'Get me the Exchange Supervisor,' he snapped and then turned to Sean, still holding the earpiece. 'The line is down. Floods in the Karroo,' he explained, 'indefinite delay.' Then he turned his attention back to the telephone and spoke quietly for many minutes with the Supervisor, before cradling the earpiece. 'They will make the connection as soon as possible.'

He returned to his seat by the window and spoke across the room. 'You have done the right thing, young man.'

'I hope so,' Mark answered quietly, and the doubts were obvious, shadows in his eyes and the strains of misery in his voice.

'I'm proud of you, Mark,' Sean Courtney agreed. 'Once again you have done your duty.'

'Will you excuse me now, please gentlemen?' Mark asked, and without waiting for a reply, crossed to the door of his own office.

The two men stared at the closed teak door long after it had closed, and it was the Prime Minister who spoke first.

'A remarkable young man,' he mused aloud. 'Compassion and a sense of duty.'

'He has qualities that could carry him to great heights, qualities for which one day we may be grateful,' Sean nodded. 'I sensed them at our first meeting, so strongly that I sought him out.'

'We will need him – and others like him in the years ahead, old Sean,' Jannie Smuts stated and then switched his attention. 'Truter will have a search warrant issued immediately, and with God's help we will crush the head of the snake before it has a chance to strike. We know about this man MacDonald, and of course we have been watching Fisher for years.'

M ark had walked for hours, escaping from the tiny box of his office. He had been driven by his conscience and his fears, striding out under the oaks, following narrow lanes, crossing the little stone bridge over the Liesbeeck stream, torturing himself with thoughts of Judas.

'They hang traitors in Pretoria,' he thought suddenly, and he imagined Fergus MacDonald standing on the trap in the barn-like room while the hangman pinioned his arms and ankles. He shuddered miserably and stopped walking, with his hands thrust deeply into his pockets and shoulders hunched, and he looked up to find himself standing outside the Post Office.

Afterwards he realized that it had probably been his destination all along, but now it seemed an omen. He did not hesitate a moment, but hurried into the office and found a pile of telegram forms on the desk. The nib of the pen was faulty and it spluttered the pale watery ink, and stained his fingers.

'MACDONALD 55 LOVERS WALK FORDSBURG.
THEY KNOW WHAT YOU HAVE GOT IN THE CELLAR
GET RID OF IT.'

He did not sign it.

The Post Office clerk assured him that if he paid the sevenpence for urgent rating, the message would have priority as soon as the northern lines were reinstated.

Mark wandered back into the street, feeling sick and depleted by the crisis of conscience, not certain that he had done the right thing in either circumstance, and he wondered just how futile was his hope that he might have forced Fergus MacDonald to throw that deadly cargo down some disused mine shaft before death and revolution was turned loose upon the land.

I t was almost dark as Fergus MacDonald wheeled his bicycle into the shed and paused in the small backyard to slip the clips off the cuffs of his trousers, before going on to the kitchen door.

The smell of cooking cabbage filled the small room with a steamy moist cloud that made him pause and blink.

Helena was sitting at the kitchen table and she hardly glanced up as he entered. A cigarette dangled from her lips with an inch of grey ash clinging hopelessly to the end of it.

She still wore the grubby dressing-gown she had worn at breakfast, and it was clear that she had neither bathed nor changed since then. Her hair had grown longer and now dangled in oily black snakes to her cheeks. She had grown heavier in the last months, the line of her jaw blurring with a padding of fat and the hair on her upper lip darker and denser, breasts bulging and drooping heavily in the open front of the gown.

'Hello then, love.' Fergus shrugged out of his jacket and dropped it across the back of a kitchen chair. She turned the page of the pamphlet she was reading, squinting at the curl of blue smoke that drifted across her eyes.

Fergus opened a black bottle of porter and the gas hissed fiercely. 'Anything happened today?'

'Something for you,' she nodded at the kitchen dresser, and the cigarette ash dropped down the front of her gown, settling in fine grey flakes.

Carrying the bottle, Fergus crossed to the dresser and fingered the buff envelope.

'One of your popsies,' Helena chuckled at the unlikeliness of her sally, and Fergus frowned and tore open the envelope.

He stared at the message for long uncomprehending seconds before he swore bitterly. 'Jesus Christ!' He slammed the bottle down on the kitchen table with a crash.

Even this late in the evening, there were small groups on each street corner. They had that disconsolate and bored air of men with too little to fill their days, even the commando drilling and the nightly meetings were beginning to pall. As Fergus MacDonald pedalled furiously through the darkening streets, his first alarm and fright turned to fierce exultation.

The time was right, they were as ready as they would ever be, if time drifted on without decisive action from either side, the long boring days of strike inactivity would erode their determination. What had seemed like disaster merely minutes before, he now saw was a heaven-sent opportunity. *Let them come, we will be ready for them*, he thought, and braked alongside a group of four loungers on the pavement outside the public bar of the Grand Fordsburg Hotel.

'Get a message to all area commanders, they are to assemble at the Trade Hall immediately. It's an emergency. Brothers, hurry.'

They scattered quickly, and he pedalled on up the rising ground of the dip, calling out his warning as he went.

In the Trade Union offices, there were still a dozen or so members; most of them were eating sandwiches and drinking Thermos tea, while a few worked on the issue of strike relief coupons to Union families, but the relaxed atmosphere changed as Fergus burst in.

'All right, comrades, it's beginning. The ZARPS* are on their way.'

* Zuid Afrikaanse Republiek Polisie, used as a derogatory term.

It was classic police tactics. They came in the first light of dawn. The advance guard rode down into the dip of land between Fordsburg and the railway crossing, where the Johannesburg road ran down between sleazy cottages and overgrown plots of open ground, thick with weeds and mounds of rotting refuse.

There was a heavy ground-mist in the dip, and the nine troopers on police chargers waded through it, as though fording the sluggish waters of a river crossing.

They had muted harness and muffled accoutrements, so that it was in ghostly silence that they breasted the softly swirling mists. The light was not yet strong enough to pick out their badges and burnished buttons, it was only the dark silhouette of their helmets that identified them.

Fifty yards behind the leading troopers followed the two police carriages. High four-wheelers with barred windows to hold prisoners, and beside each one of them marched ten constables. They carried their rifles at the slope, and were stepping out sharply to keep up with the carriages. As they entered the dip, the mist engulfed them, chest-high, so that their disembodied trunks bobbed in the white soft surface. They looked like strange dark sea-animals, and the mist muted the tramp of their boots.

Fergus MacDonald's scouts had picked them up before they reached the railway crossing and for three miles had been pacing them, slipping back unseen ahead of the advance, runners reporting every few minutes to the cottage where Fergus had established his advance headquarters.

'All right,' Fergus snapped, as another of the dark figures ducked through the hedge of the sanitary lane behind the cottage and mumbled his report through the open window. 'They are all coming in on the main road. Pull the other pickets out and get them here right away.'

The man grunted an acknowledgement and was gone. Fergus had his pickets on every possible approach to the town centre. The police might have split into a number of columns, but it seemed his precautions were unnecessary. Secure in the certainty of complete surprise and in overwhelming force, they were not bothering with diversion or flanking manoeuvres.

Twenty-nine troopers, Fergus calculated, together with the four drivers, was indeed a formidable force. More than sufficient, if it had not been for the warning from some unknown ally.

Fergus hurried through into the front parlour of the cottage. The family had been moved out before midnight, all the cottages along the road had been cleared. The grumpy squalling children in pyjamas carried on the shoulders of their fathers, the women with white frightened faces in the lamplight, bundling a few precious possessions with them as they hurried away.

Now the cottages seemed deserted, no lights showed, and the only sound was the mournful howling of a mongrel dog down in the dip. Yet in each cottage, at the windows that faced on to the road, silent men waited.

Fergus spoke to one of them in a whisper and he pointed down into the misty hollow, then spat and worked a round into the breech of the Lee-Enfield rifle which was propped on the windowsill.

The rifle bolt made a small metallic clash that lit a sparkle of memory and made the hair rise on Fergus' neck. It was all so familiar, the silence, the mist and the night fraught with the menace of coming violence.

'Only on my order,' Fergus warned him softly. 'Easy now, lads. Let them come right in the front door before we slam it on their heads.'

He could see the leading horsemen now, half a mile away but coming on fast in the strengthening light. It wasn't shooting light yet, but the sky beyond the dark hills of the mine dumps was turning to that pale gull's-egg blue that promised shooting light within minutes.

Fergus looked back at the road. The mist was an added bonus. He had not counted on that, but often when you did not call for fortune, she came a-knocking. The mist would persist until the first rays of the morning sun warmed and dispersed it – another half hour at least.

'You all know your orders.' Fergus raised his voice and they glanced at him, distracted for only a moment from their weapons and the oncoming enemy.

They were all good men, veterans, blooded, as the sanguine generals of France would have it. It flashed through Fergus' mind once again how ironical it was that men who had been trained to fight by the bosses were now about to tear down the structure which the bosses had trained them to defend.

'We will tear down and rebuild,' he thought, with exultation tingling in his blood. 'We will destroy them with their own weapons, strangle them with their own dirty loot—' he stopped himself, and pulled the dark grey cloth down over his eyes and turned up the collar of his coat.

'Good luck to all of us, brothers,' he called softly, and slipped out through the front door.

'That old bugger has got guts,' acknowledged one of the soldiers at the window.

'You're right, he ain't afraid of nothing,' agreed another, as they watched him dodge under the cover of the hedge and run forward until he reached the ditch beside the road, and jumped down into it.

There were a dozen men lying there below the lip, and as he dropped beside them, one of them handed him a pick-handle.

'You strung that wire good and tight?' Fergus asked, and the man grunted.

'Tighter than a monkey's arsehole,' the man grinned wolfishly at him, his teeth glinting in the first soft light of morning. 'And I checked the pegs meself – they'll hold against a charging elephant.'

'Right, brothers,' Fergus told them. 'With me when I give the word.'

And he lifted himself until he could see over the low blanket of mist. The troopers' helmets bobbed in the mist as they came on up the slope, and now he could make out the sparkle of brass cap badges and see the dark stick-like barrels of their carbines rising above each right shoulder.

Fergus had paced out the ranges himself and marked them with pieces of rag tied to the telephone posts on the verge.

As they came up to the one-fifty-yard mark Fergus stood up from the ditch, and stepped into the middle of the road. He held his pick-handle above his head and shouted, 'Halt! Stay where you are!'

His men rose out of the mist behind him and moved swiftly into position like a well-drilled team; dark, ominous figures standing shoulder to shoulder, blocking the road from verge to verge, holding their pick-handles ready across their hips, faces hidden by caps and collars.

The officer in the centre of the squadron of horsemen raised a hand to halt them and they bunched up and sat stolidly while the officer rose in his stirrups.

'Who are you?'

'Strikers' Council,' Fergus shouted back, 'and we'll have no scabs, black-legs or strike-breakers on this property!'

'I am under orders from the Commissioner of Police, empowered by a warrant of the Supreme Court.' The officer was a heavily built man, with a proud erect seat on his horse, and a dark waxed moustache with points that stuck out on each side of his face.

'You're strike-breakers!' Fergus yelled. 'And you'll not set a foot on this property.'

'Stand aside!' warned the officer. The light was good enough now for Fergus to see that he wore the insignia of a Captain, and that his face was ruddy from sun and beer; his eyebrows thick and dark and beetling under the brim of his helmet. 'You are obstructing the police. We will charge if we have to.'

'Charge and be damned, puppets of imperialism, running dogs of capitalism—'

'Troop, extend order,' called the Captain, and the ranks opened for the second file to come up into a solid line. They sat on the restless horses, knee to knee.

'Strike-breakers!' yelled Fergus. 'Your hands will be stained with the blood of innocent workers this day!'

'Batons!' called the Captain sternly, and the troopers drew the long oaken clubs from the scabbards at their knees and held them in the right hand, like cavalry sabres.

'History will remember this atrocity,' screamed Fergus, 'the blood of the lamb—'

'Walk, march! Forward!' The line of dark horsemen waded forward through the mist as it swirled about their booted legs.

'Gallop, charge!' sang out the Captain, and the riders swung forward in their saddles, the batons extended along the horses' necks, and they plunged forward; now the hooves drummed low thunder as they came down upon the line of standing figures.

The Captain was leading by a length in the centre of the line, and he went on to the wires first.

Fergus' men had driven the steel jumper bars deep into the verge, pounding them in with nine-pound hammers, until only two feet of their six-foot length protruded, and they had strung the barbed wire across the road, treble strands pulled up rigid with the fencing strainers.

It cut the forelegs out from under the leading charger; the bone broke with a brittle snap, startlingly loud in the dawn, and the horse dropped, going over on to its shoulder still at full gallop.

An instant later the following wave of horsemen went on to the wire, and were cut down as though by a scythe, only three of them managing to wheel away in time. The cries of the men, and the screaming of the horses, mingled with the exultant yells of Fergus' band as they ran forward, swinging their pick-handles.

One of the horses was up, riderless, its stirrups flapping, but it was pinned on its haunches, the broken forelegs flapping and spinning as it pawed in anguish at the air, its squeals high and pitiful above the cries of fallen men.

Fergus pulled the revolver out of the waist-band of his trousers, dodged around the crazed screaming animals and pulled the police Captain to his knees.

He had hit the ground with his shoulder and the side of his face. The shoulder was smashed, sagging down at a grotesque angle and the arm hanging twisted and lifeless. The flesh had been shaved from his face, ripped off by stone and gravel, so that the bone of his jaw was exposed in the mangled flesh.

'Get up, you bastard,' snarled Fergus, thrusting the pistol into the officer's face, grinding the muzzle into the lacerated wound. 'Get up you bloody black-leg. We'll learn you a lesson.'

The three troopers who had escaped the wire had their mounts under control, and had circled to pick up their downed comrades, calling to them by name.

'Grab a stirrup, Heintjie!'

'Come on, Paul. Get up!'

Horses and men, milling and shouting and screaming in the mist, a savage confused conflict, above which Fergus raised his voice.

'Stop them, don't let the bastards get away,' and his men swung the pick-handles, dodging forward under the police batons to thrust and hack at the horsemen, but they were not quick enough.

With men hanging from each stirrup leather, the horsemen reared and wheeled away, leaving only the badly hurt officer and another inert body lying among the wires and the terribly mutilated animals, while the police escort was doubling forward up the road in two columns.

Fergus saw them and fumed impatiently, trying to force his captive to his feet, but the man was hardly capable of sitting unaided.

The twenty constables stopped at fifty yards and one rank knelt, while the others fell in behind them, rifles at the ready. The command carried clearly.

'One round. Warning fire!'

The volley of musketry crashed out. Aimed purposely high, it hissed and cracked over the heads of the strikers, and they scattered into the ditch.

For one moment, Fergus hesitated and then he pointed the pistol into the air and fired three shots in rapid succession. It was the agreed signal, and instantly a storm of rifle fire crashed from the silent cottages along the road, the muzzle flashes of the hidden rifles dull angry red in the dawn. The fire swept the road.

Fergus hesitated a second only and then he lowered the pistol. It was a Webley .455, a British officer's sidearm. The police Captain saw his intention in his eyes, the merciless glare of the stooping eagle, and he mumbled a plea through his mangled lips, trying to lift hands to protect his face.

The pistol shot was lost in the storm of rifle fire from the cottages, and the answering police fire as they fell back in confusion into the dip.

The heavy lead bullet smashed into the Captain's open pleading mouth, knocking the two front teeth out of his upper jaw, and then it plunged on into his throat and exited through the back of his skull in a scarlet burst of blood and bone chips, clubbing him down into the dirt of the roadway – while Fergus turned and darted away under the cover of the hedge.

Only at Fordsburg were the police raids repelled, for at the other centres there had been no warning, and the strikers had not taken even the most elementary precautions of placing sentries.

At the Trades Hall in Johannesburg, almost the entire leadership of the strike was assembled, meeting with the other unions who had not yet come out, but were considering sympathetic action. There were representatives of the Boilermakers' Society, the Building and Allied Trades, the Typographical Union and half a dozen others – together with the most dynamic and forceful of the strikers. Harry Fisher was there, Andrews and Ben Caddy, and all the others.

The police were into the building while they were deep in dialectic, debating the strategy of the class struggle, and the first warning they had was the thunderous charge of booted feet on the wooden staircase.

Harry Fisher was at the head of the conference table, slumped down in his chair with his tangled wiry hair hanging on to his forehead and his thumbs hooked in his braces, his sleeves rolled up around the thick hairy arms.

He was the only one to move. He leaned across the table and grabbed the rubber stamp of the High Council of Action and thrust it into his pocket.

As the rifle butts smashed in the lock of the Council Chamber, he leapt to his feet and thrust his shoulder into the shuttered casement. It burst open and, with surprising nimbleness for such a big man, he slipped through it.

The façade of the Trades Hall was heavily encrusted with fancy cast-iron grille work, and it gave him handholds. Like a bull gorilla, he swarmed up on to the third-floor ledge and worked his way to the corner.

Below him he heard the crash of overturning furniture, the loud challenges of the arresting officers and the outraged cries of the labour leaders.

With his back pressed to the wall and his hands spread

out to balance himself, Harry Fisher peered around the corner into the main street. It swarmed with uniformed police, and more squads were marching up briskly. An officer was directing men to the side alleys to surround the building, and Harry Fisher drew back quickly and looked around him for escape.

It was senseless to re-enter another window, for the whole building was noisy with the tramp of feet and shouted orders.

Fifteen feet below him was the roof of a bottle store and general dealer's shop, but the alleyway between was ten feet wide and the roof of galvanized corrugated iron.

If he jumped, the noise he would make on landing would bring police running from all directions – yet he could not stay where he was. Within minutes the building would be surrounded.

He inched sideways to the nearest downpipe and began to climb. He reached the overhang of the roof and had to lean out to get a grip on the rim of the guttering, then he kicked his feet clear and hung from his arms. The drop of fifty feet below him sucked at his heels, and the guttering creaked and sagged perceptively under his weight – but he drew himself up on his arms, wheezing and straining until he could hook one elbow over the gutter and wriggle the rest of his body up and over the edge.

Still panting from the effort, he crawled slowly round the steeply gabled roof and peered down into the main street, just as the police began hustling the strike leaders out of the front doors.

Fifty helmeted constables with sloped rifles had formed a hollow square in the road, and the strikers were pushed into it; some of them bare-headed and in their shirt-sleeves.

Already a crowd was forming on the sidewalks, and every minute it swelled, as the news was shouted from door to door and the curious hurried from every alleyway.

Harry Fisher counted the prisoners as they were brought

out and the total was twenty before the mood of the crowd began changing.

'That's it, comrades,' Harry Fisher grunted, and wished he could have been down there to lead them. They surged angrily up to the police lines, calling to the prisoners and hissing and booing the officer who ordered them, through a speaking trumpet, to disperse.

Mounted police wheeled into line, pushing the crowd back and as the last prisoner was led out, the escort stepped out, maintaining its rigid box-formation which enclosed the dejected huddle of strikers.

Somebody began to sing the 'Red Flag', but the voices that joined in were thin and tuneless, and the escort moved off towards the fort, carrying away not only most of the strike leadership but all of its moderate faction, those who had so far counselled against violence, against criminal activity and bloody revolution.

Harry Fisher watched them go with a rising sense of triumph. In one stroke he had been given a band of martyrs for the cause and had all serious opposition to his extreme views swept away. He had also in his hip pocket the seal of the Action Committee. He smiled a thin, humourless grin and settled down on the canted roof-top to wait for nightfall.

M ark Anders carried the General's heavy crocodile-skin brief case down the steps to the Rolls and placed it on the seat beside the chauffeur while he gave him his instructions.

'To Groote Schuur first, and then to the City Club for lunch.' He stood back as the General came out of the house and paused on the top step to kiss his wife as though he were about to leave on a crusade to far places. He smothered her in a vast bear-hug and when he released her, he whispered something in her ear that made her bridle and slap his shoulder.

'Off with you, sir,' she told him primly, and Sean Courtney came down the steps looking mightily pleased with himself, and grinned at Mark.

'The Prime Minister is making a statement to the House today, Mark. I'll want to see you directly afterwards.'

'Very well, sir,' Mark returned the grin.

'I'll look for you in the visitors' gallery as soon as he's finished, and give you the nod. Then we'll meet in the lobby and I'll see you up to my office.'

Mark helped him into the back seat of the Rolls while he was speaking. He was always clumsy and awkward when moving sideways on to the bad leg, nevertheless he resented the helping hand fiercely, hating any weakness in himself even more than he disliked it in others, and he shrugged Mark's hand away the moment he was comfortably seated.

Mark ignored the gesture and went on levelly, 'Your notes for the Cabinet meeting are in the first folder,' he indicated the crocodile bag on the front seat beside the chauffeur, 'and you are lunching at the Club with Sir Herbert. The House sits at 2.15 and you have three questions from Opposition members, even Hertzog himself has one for you.' Sean growled like an old lion bated by the pack.

'That bastard!'

'I have your replies clipped to your Order Paper. I checked with Erasmus and then I added a few little touches of my own, so please have a look at them before you stand up – you may not approve.'

'I hope you stuck it to them hard!'

'Of course,' Mark smiled again. 'With both barrels.'

'Good boy,' Sean nodded. 'Tell him to drive on.'

Mark watched the Rolls go down the driveway, check at the gates and then swing out into Rhodes Avenue, before he turned back into the house.

Instead of going down the passageway to his own office, Mark paused in the hall and glanced guiltily about him. Ruth Courtney had gone back into the domestic depths of the kitchen area and there were no servants in sight.

Mark took the stairs three at a time, swung through the gallery and down to the solid teak door at the end.

He did not knock but turned the handle and went in, closing the door behind him quietly.

The stench of turpentine was a solid shock that made his eyes water for a few seconds until they adjusted.

Mark knew that he was quite safe. Storm Courtney never emerged before mid-morning from that sacrosanct area beyond the double doors that were painted with gold cherubim and flying doves. Since arriving in Cape Town, Storm Courtney had kept such hours that even her father had grumbled and huffed.

Mark found himself lying awake at night, just as he was sure the General did, listening for the crunch of wheels on the gravel drive, straining his ears for the faint sounds of gay voices and mentally judging the length and passion of each farewell, troubled by feelings to which he could not place a name.

His relations with Storm had retrogressed drastically. In Natal there had been the beginnings of a relaxed acceptance and undertones of warmth. It had begun with a smile and a friendly word from Storm, then he had escorted her on the daily ride, driven with her to South Beach to swim in the warm surf and sat in the sun arguing religion with her instead. Storm was going through a fashionable period of spiritualism and Mark had felt it his duty to dissuade her.

From religion, the next step had been when Storm had announced, 'I need a partner to practise a new dance with.'

Mark had wound the gramophone, changed the needles and danced to Storm's instruction.

'You really are quite good, you know,' she had told him

magnanimously, smiling up at him, light and graceful in his arms as they spun around the empty ballroom of Emoyeni.

'You would make a crippled blacksmith look good.'

'Oh la!' she laughed. 'You are the gallant, Mr Anders!'

This had all changed abruptly. Since they had arrived in Cape Town she had neither smiled nor spoken directly to him, and Irene Leuchars, who was to have been a house guest of Storm's for four months, stayed only one night, and then caught the next mailship home.

Her name had not been mentioned again, and Storm's hostility to Mark had been so intense that she could hardly bear to be in the same room with him.

Now Mark felt like a thief in her studio, but he had not been able to resist the temptation to steal a glimpse of the progress she had made on her latest canvas.

Full-length windows had been put into the north wall for the light, and they looked out on the mountain. Storm's easel stood in the centre of the bare uncarpeted floor – and the only other items of furniture were the artist's stool, a carpenter's table cluttered with paint pots and a chair on the raised model's dais.

Framed canvases in all sizes and shapes were stacked against the walls, most of them still blank. At one stage, during the period of friendliness, she had even asked Mark to help with the timber framework. He felt a pang when he remembered; she was a ruthless supervisor, checking every joint and tack with a perfectionist's meticulous care.

The canvas was almost completed, and he wondered when she had found time to do so much work in the last few days, and realized that he had misjudged her. She had been working in the mornings when he had believed she was lying abed, but now he became absorbed by the picture.

He stood before it with his hands thrust into his pockets and felt a glow of pleasure spread slowly through his body.

It was a picture of trees, a forest glade with sunlight

playing on earth and rock and two figures – a woman in a white dress, stooping to gather wild flowers, while a man sat aside, sprawled against a tree trunk and watching her.

Mark was aware that it was a great advance on anything she had painted before, for although it was a simple picture, it evoked in him an emotion so strong that he felt it choke in his throat. He was awed by the peculiar talent which could have produced this work.

He marvelled at how she had taken reality and refined it, captured its essence and made of it an important occasion.

Mark thought how it was possible for an untrained eye to pick out special talent in any field, just as a person who had never watched *épée* used before would recognize a great swordsman after the first exchange; now Mark, who knew nothing of painting, was moved by the discovery of real beauty.

The latch clicked behind him, and he spun to face it. She was well into the studio before she saw him. She stopped abruptly and her expression changed. Her whole body stiffened and her breathing sounded stifled.

'What are you doing here?'

He had no answer for her, but the mood of the picture was still on him. 'I think that you will be a great artist one day.'

She faltered, taken completely off balance by the compliment and its obvious sincerity, and her eyes slipped away to the picture. All the antagonism, all the haughtiness drained from her.

Suddenly she was just a very young girl in a baggy smock, smeared and daubed with oil paint, and with a wash of pleased and modest colour spreading over her cheeks.

He had never seen her like this, so artless – so open and vulnerable. It was as though for a moment she had unveiled the secret compartments of her soul to allow him to see where she kept her real treasures.

'Thank you, Mark,' she said softly, and she was no longer the glittering butterfly, the spoiled flighty little rich girl, but a creature of substance and warmth.

The rush of his own feelings must have been as obvious – he had almost succumbed to the desire he felt to take her in his arms and hold her hard – for she stepped back a pace, looking flustered and uncertain of herself, as though she had read his intention.

'And yet you won't slide out of it that easily.' The curtains were drawn hastily across the secret places, and the old familiar ring was in her voice. 'This is my private place, even my father wouldn't dare come in here – without my permission first obtained.'

The change was extraordinary. It was like a superb actress slipping into a familiar role, she even stamped her foot, a gesture that he found suddenly insupportable.

'It won't happen again,' he assured her brusquely, and he stepped to the doorway, passing her closely. He was so angry he felt himself trembling.

'Mark!' She stopped him imperiously, but it was with an effort he forced himself to turn back; his whole body felt rigid, and his lips were numb and stiff with anger.

'My father asks permission to come in here,' she told him, and then she smiled, a slightly tremulous but utterly enchanting thing. 'Couldn't you just do the same?'

She had him off balance, his anger not fully aroused before she assuaged it with that smile, he felt the rigidity melting out of his body, but she had turned to the bench and was clattering her pots busily and she spoke without looking up.

'Close the door as you leave,' she instructed, a princess tossing an order to a serf. His anger, not yet fully assuaged, flared again brightly and he strode to the door with his heels clashing on the bare boards and he was about to slam it with all of his strength, and hope that it smashed off its hinges, when she stopped him again.

'Mark!'

He stopped, but could not bring himself to answer.

'I will be coming down to Parliament with you this afternoon. We will leave directly after lunch – I want to hear General Smuts' speech, my father says it will be important.'

He thought that if he tried to answer her, his lips might tear, they felt as stiff and brittle as parchment.

'Oh dear,' she murmured. 'I had completely forgotten – when addressing Mark Anders Esquire, one must always say please!'

She crossed her hands demurely in front of her, hung her head in a caricature of contrition and made those dark blue eyes huge and soulful.

'Please may I ride to Parliament with you today?' I would be ever so grateful, I really would. And now you can slam the door.'

'You should be on the stage – you're wasted as a painter,' he told her, but he closed the door with studied deliberation and she waited to hear the latch click before she dropped into the model's chair, and began to shake with laughter, hugging herself delightedly.

Gradually the laughter dried up, but she was still smiling as she selected a blank canvas from the stock and placed it on the easel.

Working with charcoal, she blocked in the shape of his head, and it was right at the first attempt.

'The eyes,' she whispered, 'his eyes are the key.' And she smiled again as they appeared miraculously out of the blank canvas, surprised that she had them fixed perfectly in her mind. She began to hum softly as she worked, completely absorbed.

The Assembly Chamber of Parliament House was a high square hall, tiered with the galleries for Press and visitors. It was panelled in dark carved indigenous wood, and the canopy above the Speaker's chair was ornately worked in the same wood.

Softly muted green carpeting set off the richer green leather of the members' benches, and every seat was filled, the galleries crowded, but the silence that gripped that concourse was of extraordinary intensity, a cathedral hush into which the high piping voice of the Prime Minister carried clearly. He made a slight but graceful figure as he stood in his seat below the Speaker's dais.

'The entire Witwatersrand complex is passing slowly into the hands of the red commandos—' He used his hands expressively, and Mark leaned forward to obtain a better view. The movement brought his outer leg against Storm Courtney's, and he was aware of the warmth of her thigh against his during the rest of the speech. 'Three members of the police have been killed in a brutal attack at Fordsburg, and two others have been critically injured in clashes with strikers' commandos. These groups are armed with modern pattern military firearms, and they are marching freely through the streets in quasi-military formations, committing acts of outrage on innocent members of the public, on public officers going about their duties, on all who cross their paths. They have interfered with public services, transport, power and communication, and have attacked and occupied police stations.'

Sean Courtney, who had been slumped in his front bench seat with one hand covering his eyes, lifted his head and said 'Shame!' in a sonorous voice; it was his third-whisky voice, and Mark could not help but grin as he guessed that the club lunch had fortified him for the session.

'Shame indeed,' Smuts agreed. 'Now the strikers have gathered about them all the feckless and dissolute elements in the community, their mood has become ugly and threatening. Legitimate strike action has given way to a reign of terror and criminal violence. Yet the most disturbing aspect of this terrible business is that the management of this labour dispute – or should I say, the stage-managing of the strike – has passed into the hands of the most reckless and lawless men, and these men seek nothing less than the overthrow of civilized government, and a rule of Bolshevik anarchy.'

'Never!' boomed Sean, and the cry was taken up across the assembly.

'This house, and the whole nation, is faced by the prospect of bloodshed and violence on a scale which none of us expected or believed possible.'

The silence was unbroken now as Smuts went on carefully.

'If any blame attaches to this Government, it is that we have been too patient and shown too much forbearance for the miners' grievances, we have allowed them too much latitude, too much expression of their demands. This was because we have always been aware of the temper of the nation, and the rights of individuals and groups to free expression.'

'Quite right too,' Sean agreed, and, 'Hear! Hear!' answered, 'Hoor! Hoor!' across the floor.

'Now, however, we have been forced to reckon the cost of further forbearance – and we have found it unacceptable.' He paused and bowed his head for a moment, and when he lifted it again, his expression was bleak and cold. 'Therefore a state of martial law now exists throughout the Union of South Africa.'

The silence persisted for many seconds, and then a roar of comment and question and interjection filled the house. Even the galleries buzzed with confusion and speculation, and the Press reporters jostled and fought each other at the exit doors in the race to reach a telephone.

Martial law was the weapon of last resort, and had only

been used once before, during the 1916 rebellion, when De Wet had raised his commandos again and ridden against Botha and Smuts. Now there were cries of protest and anger from the Opposition benches, Hertzog shaking his fist and his pince-nez glinting, while the government members were also on their feet voicing their support. The Speaker's vain cries of 'Order! Order!' were almost drowned in the uproar.

Sean Courtney was signalling to Mark in the gallery, and he acknowledged and helped Storm to her feet, shielding her through the excited press of bodies as they left the gallery and went down the passage to the staircase.

The General was waiting for them at the visitors' entrance. He was scowling and dark-faced with concern; a measure of his agitation was the perfunctory kiss he dropped on Storm's uplifted face before turning to Mark.

'A pretty business, my boy.' He seized his elbow. 'Come on, let's go where we can talk,' and he led them to the members' entrance, and up the stairs under the portraits of stern-faced Chief Justices to his own office.

Immediately the door was closed, he waved Storm away to one of the chairs, and told Mark, 'The regiment was called out at ten o'clock this morning. I managed to get Scott on the telephone at his home – and he's got it in hand. He's a good man. They will be fully mobilized by now, and there is a special train being made up. They will entrain and leave for the Witwatersrand at eleven o'clock tonight, in full battle order.'

'What about us?' Mark demanded. Suddenly he was a soldier again and he dropped neatly into the role. His place was with the regiment.

'We'll join there. We leave tonight. We are going up in convoy with the Prime Minister, and we'll travel all night – you will drive one of the cars.' Sean was at his desk now, beginning to pack his briefcase. 'How long will it take us?'

'It's a thousand miles, sir,' Mark pointed out.

'I know that, damn it,' snapped Sean. 'How long?' Sean had never liked nor understood the internal combustion engine, and his dislike showed in his ignorance of their speed and capability whereas he could finely judge a journey by wagon or horseback.

'We won't be there before tomorrow evening – it's a hell of a road.'

'Bloody motorcars,' Sean growled. 'The regiment will be there before us by rail.'

'They've only three hundred miles to go.' Mark felt obliged to come to the defence of the car, and Sean grunted.

'I want you to get on home now. Have my wife pack my campaign bag and get your duffle together. We'll leave immediately I get home.' He turned to Storm. 'Go along with Mark, now, Missy. I'm going to be busy here for a while.'

Mark strapped up his bag, and reflected how his worldly possessions had multiplied since he had joined the Courtney household. There had been a time when he could carry everything he owned in his pockets – the thought was broken by a knock on the door.

'Come in,' he called, expecting a servant. Only Ruth Courtney ever came down this end of the house on her weekly inspection, a determined crusade against dust and cockroaches.

'Please take it down to the car,' he said in Zulu, adjusting his uniform cap in the mirror above the wash-basin.

'All on my own?' Storm asked sweetly in the same language, and he turned startled.

'You shouldn't be here.'

'Why not – am I in danger of violation and ravishment?'

She had closed the door and leaned against it, her hands behind her back, but her eyes bold and teasing.

'It would be safer, I should imagine, to attempt to ravish a swarm of hornets.'

'That was merely boorish, coarse and insulting,' she said. 'You really are improving immensely.' And she looked at the strapped case on the bed.

'I was going to offer to help you pack – most men are hopeless at that. But I see you've managed. Is there anything else I can do for you?'

'I am sure I could think of something,' he said with a solemn expression, but something in the tone of his voice made her smile and caution him.

'Not too much improvement in one day, please.' She crossed to the bed and bounced on it experimentally. 'God! Who filled it with bricks? No wonder Irene Leuchars went home! The poor darling must have sprained her back!' Her expression was innocent, but her gaze raked him and Mark felt himself blushing furiously. Suddenly, much that had puzzled him was clear, and as he turned back to the mirror, he wondered how she had found out about Irene. For something to do, he tipped the brim of his cap.

'Beautiful,' she agreed. 'Are you going up there to brutalize those poor strikers – or to bounce on their wives also?' And before he could give expression to the shock he felt she went on, 'Funnily enough, I didn't really come down here to fight with you. I once had another old tomcat and I was really very fond of him, but he got run over by a car. Have you got a cigarette, Mark?'

'You don't smoke.' He had found it difficult to keep up with the conversation.

'I know – but I have decided to learn. It's so suave, don't you think?' Suave was the fashionable word at that moment.

She held the cigarette with an exaggerated vampish pose after he had lit it.

'How do I look?'

'Bloody awful,' he said, and she batted her eyes and took a tentative draw, held it for a moment and then started to cough.

'Here, give it to me.' He took it away from her, and it tasted of her mouth. He felt the ache in his body, the terrible wanting, mingled now with a strange tenderness he had never felt before. She seemed, for once, so tender and young.

'Will it be dangerous?' she asked, suddenly serious.

'I don't think so – we'll be just like policemen.'

'They are killing policemen.' She stood up and walked to the window. 'The view is dreadful, unless you like dustbins. I'd complain, if I were you.' She turned back to face him.

'I've never seen a man off to war before. What should I say?'

'I don't know. Nobody ever saw me off before.'

'What did your mother say?'

'I never knew my mother.'

'Oh Mark. I'm sorry. I didn't mean to—' Her voice trailed off, and he was shocked to see that her eyes were brimming with tears.

'It doesn't matter,' he assured her quickly, and she turned back to the window.

'Actually, you can just see the top of Devil's Peak, if you twist your head.' Her voice was thick and nasal, and it was many seconds before she turned back.

'Well, we're both new to this, so we'll just have to help each other.'

'I suppose you should say, "Come back soon."'

'Yes, I suppose I should – and then what do I do?'

'You kiss me.' It was out before he had thought about it, and he was stunned by his own audacity.

She stood very still, rooted by the words, and when she began to move, it was with the slow deliberation of a sleepwalker, and her eyes were huge and unblinking. She came across the room.

She stopped in front of him, and, as she lifted her arms, she came up on her toes.

The air about her was filled with her fragrance, and her arms were slim and strong about his neck, but it was the softness and the warmth of her lips that amazed him.

Her body swayed against him, and seemed to melt with his own, and the long artistic fingers slowly caressed the nape of his neck.

He passed an arm around her waist, and was again amazed at how narrow and slim it was; but the muscles of her back were firm and pliant as she arched it, pushing forward with her hips.

He heard her gasp as she felt him, and a slow voluptuous shudder shook her. For long moments she lingered, her hips pressed to his and her breasts flattened against his tunic.

He stooped over her, his hands beginning to move up the hard resilient little back, his mouth forcing hers open so the soft lips parted like the fleshy red petals of an exotic blooming orchid.

She shuddered again, but then the sound in her throat turned into a panicky moan of protest and she twisted out of his arms, though he tried desperately to hold her. But she was strong and supple and determined.

At the door, she stopped to stare at him. She was trembling, her eyes were wide and dark, as though she had truly only seen him for the first time. 'Oh la! Who was talking about swarms of hornets!' she mocked, but her voice was gusty and unsteady.

She twisted the door open, and tried to smile, but it was a poor lopsided thing, and she did not yet have control of her breathing. 'I'm not so sure of that "Come back soon" any more.' She held the door open to give herself courage, and her next smile was more convincing. 'Don't get run over, you old tomcat,' and she slipped out into the passageway.

Her receding footsteps were light and dancing in the silence of the big house, and Mark's own legs were suddenly so weak that he sat down heavily on his bed.

M ark drove fast, concentrating all his attention on the twisting treacherous road through the mountains, driving the big heavily laden Rolls down the path of its own glaring brass-bound headlights, up Baines Kloof where the mountain fell away on his left hand sheer into the valley, past Worcester with its orderly vineyards standing in dark lines in the moonlight, before the final ascent up the Hex River Mountains to the rim of the flat compacted shield of the African interior.

They came out over the top, and the vast land stretched away ahead of them, the dry treeless karroo, where the flat-topped kopjes made strangely symmetrical shapes against the cold starry sky.

Now at last, Mark could relax in the studded leather driver's seat, driving instinctively, the road pouring endlessly towards him, pale and straight out of the darkness, and he could tune his ears to the voice of the two men in the rear seat.

'What they don't understand, old Sean, is that if we do not employ every black man who offers himself for work – no, more than that, if we don't actively recruit all the native labour we can get hold of – it will result not only in fewer jobs for white men, but, in the long run, it will mean, finally, no jobs at all for the white men of Africa.'

A jackal, small and furry as a puppy, lolloped into the path of the headlights with its ears erect, and Mark steered carefully to miss it, his own ears cocked for Sean's reply.

'They think only of today.' His voice was deep and grave. 'We must plan for ten years from now – for thirty, fifty years ahead, for a nation firm and undivided. We cannot afford once again to have Afrikander against Briton, or worse, we dare not have white against black. It is not enough that we are forced to live together, we must learn to work together.'

'Slowly, slowly – old Sean,' the Prime Minister chuckled. 'Don't let dreams run away with reality.'

'I don't deal in dreams, Jannie. You should know that. If we don't want to be torn to pieces by our own people, we must give all of them, black, white and brown, a place and a share.'

They ran on hard into the endless land, and the light of a lonely farm house on a dark ridge emphasized how vast and empty it was.

'Those who clamour so loudly for less work and more pay may find that what benefit they get now will have to be paid for at a thousand per cent interest some day in the future. A payment in misery and hunger and suffering,' Sean Courtney was speaking again. 'If we are to steer off the reef of national disaster, then men will have to learn to work again, and to take seriously once more the demands of a disciplined and orderly society.'

'Have you ever wondered, Sean, at how many people these days depend for their livelihood on nothing else but finding areas of dispute between the employers and the employed, between labour and management?'

Sean nodded, taking it up where Smuts left off. 'As though the two were not shackled to each other with bonds that nothing can break. They travel the same road, to the same goal, bound together irretrievably by destiny. When one stumbles, he brings the other down on bloody knees, when one falls the other comes down with him.'

Slowly, as the stars made their circuit of grandeur across the heavens, the talk in the back seat of the Rolls dwindled into silence.

Mark glanced in the mirror and saw that Sean Courtney was asleep, a travelling rug about his shoulders and his black beard on his chest.

His snores were low and regular and deep, and Mark felt a rush of feeling for the big man. It was a fine mixture of respect and awe, of pride and affection. 'I suppose that is what you would feel, if you had a father,' he thought, and then, embarrassed by the strength and presumption of his feeling, he once again concentrated all his attention on the road.

The night wind had sifted the sky with fine dust, and the dawn was a thing of unbelievable splendour. From horizon to horizon, and right across the vaulted domes of the heavens, vibrant colour throbbed and glowed and flamed, until at last the sun thrust clear of the horizon.

'We won't stop in Bloemfontein or any of the big towns, Mark. We don't want anybody to see the Prime Minister.' Sean leaned across the back of the seat.

'We'll need petrol, General.'

'Pick one of the roadside pumps,' Sean instructed. 'Try and find one with no telephone lines.'

It was a tiny iron-roofed general dealer's store set back from the road under two scraggy eucalyptus blue gum trees. There was no other building in sight, and the open empty veld stretched dry and sun-seared to the circle of the horizon. The plaster walls of the store were cracked and in need of whitewash, plastered with advertisement boards for Bovril and Joko tea. The windows were shuttered and the door locked, but there were no telephone lines running from the solitary building to join those that followed the road, and a single red-painted petrol pump stood at rigid attention in the dusty yard below the stoep.

Mark blew a long continuous blast on the Rolls' horn, and while he was doing so, the Prime Minister's black Cadillac that was following turned off the main road and parked behind them. The driver and the three members of the ministerial staff climbed out and stretched their stiff muscles.

When the proprietor of the store emerged at last, unshaven, red-eyed, but cheerfully doing up his breeches, he spoke no English. Mark asked in Afrikaans, 'Can you fill up both cars?'

While the storekeeper swung the handle of the pump back and forth, and the fuel rose alternately into the two one-gallon glass bowls on the top of the pump, his wife came out from the store with a tray of steaming coffee mugs and a platter of crisp golden freshly baked rusks. They ate and drank gratefully, and were ready to go on again within twenty minutes.

The storekeeper stood in the yard, scratching the stubble of his beard and watched the twin columns of red dust billowing into the northern sky. His wife came out on to the stoep and he turned to squint up at her.

'Do you know who that was?' he asked, and she shook her head.

'That was Clever Jannie – and his English gunmen. Didn't you see the uniform the young one wore?' He spat into the red dirt, and his phlegm balled and rolled. 'Khaki! Damned khaki!' He ripped the word out bitterly, and went around the side of the building to the little lean-to stable.

He was clinching the girth on the old sway-backed grey mare, when she followed him into the stall.

'It's none of our business, Hendrick. Let it stand.'

'None of our business?' he demanded indignantly. 'Didn't I fight khaki in the English war, didn't I fight it again in 1916 when we rode with old De Wet – isn't my brother a rock-breaker on the Simmer and Jack mine, and isn't that where Clever Jannie is going with his hangmen?'

He swung up on the mare and put his heels to her. She jumped away, and he pointed her at the ridge. It was eight miles to the railway siding, and there was a telegraph in the ganger's cottage; the ganger was a cousin of his. The

Railway Workers' Union was out in sympathy with the miners now. The Action Committee would have the news in Johannesburg by lunch time that Clever Jannie was on his way.

While Mark Anders drank coffee at the wayside store, Fergus MacDonald lay under the hedge at the bottom of a garden ablaze with crimson cannas in orderly beds, and peered through a pair of binoculars down the slope at the Newlands Police Station. They had sand-bagged the windows and doors.

The lady of the house had sat on her veranda the previous evening, drinking coffee and counting forty-seven police constables arriving by motor lorry to reinforce the station. Her son was a shift boss on the Simmer and Jack. Whoever commanded the police at Newlands was no soldier, Fergus decided, and grinned that wolfish wicked grin.

He had seen the dead ground instantly, any soldier would have picked it up at a glance.

'Pass the word for the Mills bombs,' he muttered to the striker beside him, and the man crawled away.

Fergus swung the glasses up along the road where it started to climb the kopjes, and grunted with satisfaction. The telephone wires had been cut, along with the power lines. He could see the loose ends dangling from the poles.

The police station was isolated.

The striker crawled back to Fergus' side, dragging a heavy rucksack. He had a tooth missing from his upper jaw, and he grinned gap-toothed at Fergus.

'Give them hell, comrade.'

Fergus' face was blackened with soot and his eyelashes were singed away. They had burned the Fordsburg Police Station a little before midnight.

'I want covering fire – on my whistle.'

'You'll get it – never fear.'

Fergus opened the rucksack and glanced at the steel globes, with their deeply segmented squares for fragmentation, then he slung the strap over his shoulder and adjusted the burden to hang comfortably on his flank.

'Look after it well.' He handed his Lee-Enfield rifle to the gap-toothed striker. 'We'll need it again today.' He crawled away down the shallow drainage ditch that led to a concrete culvert which crossed under the road.

The culvert was lined with circular tubes of rusty corrugated iron, and Fergus wriggled through it carefully, emerging on the far side of the road.

Lying on his side, he raised himself slightly to peer over the edge of the drainage ditch. The police station was a hundred and fifty yards away. The blue light over the front door, with the white lettered 'POLICE', was dead, and the flag hung limply on its pole in the still windless morning.

It was fifty yards to the slope of dead ground under the eastern windows of the brick building, and Fergus could see the rifle barrels of the defenders poked through the gaps in the sand-bags.

He pulled the silver whistle from his back pocket by its lanyard, and came up on his knees like a sprinter on the blocks.

He drew a deep breath and blew a long shrill ringing blast on the whistle. Immediately a storm of rifle fire crashed out from the hedges and ditches that surrounded the station.

The blue lamp shattered into flying fragments, and red brick dust popped off the walls like dyed cotton pods.

Fergus came out of the ditch at a run. A bullet kicked dust and stone chips stung his ankles, and another jerked like an impatient hand at the tail of his coat, then he was into the dead ground and out of their field of fire.

He still ran doubled over, however, until he reached the

police station. Then he flattened himself against the wall between two of the sand-bagged windows while he struggled with his breathing.

A rifle barrel protruded from the left-hand window as it blazed away up the slope of the kopje. Fergus opened the rucksack and took out a grenade with his left hand. He pulled the pin with his teeth, while he groped for the Webley .455 revolver stuck into the belt of his trousers.

He locked one arm over the barrel of the police rifle, dragging it harmlessly aside, then he stepped into the window, and, still holding the rifle, looked through the narrow hole in the sand-bags.

A young, beardless face stared back at him, the eyes wide with amazement, the mouth hanging open slightly and the police helmet pulled down low over his eyes.

Fergus shot him in the bridge of the nose, between the startled staring eyes, and the head was smashed backwards out of view.

Fergus hurled the grenade through the gap and ducked down. The explosion in the confined space was vicious and ear-numbing. Fergus bobbed up and tossed in another grenade.

Glass and smoke blew from the windows, and from within there were the screams and cries of the trapped police constables, the groans and gasping wails of the wounded.

Fergus threw in a third grenade, and screamed, 'Chew on that, you bloody strike-breakers.' The bomb exploded, shattering out a panel from the front door, and smoke billowed from all windows.

Inside a single voice started screaming. 'Stop it! Oh God, stop it! We surrender!'

'Come out with your hands in the air, you bastards!'

A police sergeant staggered out of the shattered doorway. He held one hand above his head, the other hung at his side in a torn and blood-soaked sleeve.

The last call that went out from Newlands Police Station before the strikers cut the lines was a call for help. The relieving column coming over the ridge from Johannesburg in a convoy of three trucks got as far as the Hotel in Main Street where it was halted by rifle fire, and the moment it stopped, strikers ran out into the roadway behind it and set all the trucks ablaze with petrol bombs.

The police abandoned their vehicles and raced for cover in a cottage beside the road. It was a strong defensive position and they looked set to hold out against even the most determined attacks, but they left three dead constables lying in the road beside the burning trucks, and another two of their number lying near them, so badly wounded they could only cry out for succour.

A white flag waved from across the road, and the police commander stepped out on to the veranda of the cottage.

'What do you want?' he called across.

Fergus MacDonald walked out into the road, still waving the flag, a slight unwarlike figure in shabby suit and cloth cap.

'You can't leave these men out here,' he shouted back, pointing at the bodies.

The commander came out with twenty unarmed police into the road to carry away the dead and wounded, and while they worked, strikers under Fergus' orders slipped in through the back of the cottages.

Suddenly Fergus whipped the Webley out from under his coat and pressed it to the commander's head.

'Tell your men to put their hands up – or I'll blow your bloody brains all over the road.'

In the cottage, Fergus' men knocked the weapons out of the hands of the police, and in the roadway armed strikers were among them.

'You were under a flag of truce,' protested the commander bitterly.

'We aren't playing games, you bloody black-leg,' snarled Fergus. 'We're fighting for a new world.' The commander opened his mouth to protest again and Fergus swung the revolver sideways, slashing the barrel into his face, snapping out the front teeth from his upper jaw, and crushing the lip into a red wet smear. The man dropped to his knees, and Fergus strode among his men.

'We'll siege the Brixton ridge now – and after that Johannesburg. By tonight, we'll have the red flag flying on every public building in town. Onward, comrades, nothing will stop us now.'

The Transvaal Scottish detrained at Dunswart Station that same morning to march in and seize the mining town of Benoni, which was under full control of the Action Committee's commandos, but the strikers were waiting for them.

The advancing troops were caught in flank and rear by the cross-fire from hundreds of prepared positions, and fought hard all that day to extricate themselves, but it was late afternoon when, still under sniping fire, they were able to retrain at Dunswart.

They carried with them three dead officers and nine dead other rankers. Another thirty were suffering from gunshot wounds, from which many would later die.

From one end to the other of the Witwatersrand, the strikers were on the rampage. The Action Committee controlled that great complex of mining towns and mining properties that follows the sweep of the gold-bearing reef across the bleak African veld, sixty miles from Krugersdorp to Ventersdorp, with the city of Johannesburg at its centre.

It is the richest gold-bearing formation yet discovered by man, a glittering treasure house, the foundation stone of the prosperity of a nation – and now the strikers carried the red flag across it at will, and at every point the force of law and order reeled back.

Every police commander was loath to initiate fire, and every constable loath to act upon the order when it did come. They were firing upon friends, countrymen, brothers.

I n the cellars of the Fordsburg Trade Union Hall they were holding a kangaroo court; a traitor was on trial for his life.

Harry Fisher's huge bulk was clad now in a military style bushjacket, with buttoned patch-pockets, over which he wore a bandolier of ammunition. On his right arm was a plain band of red cloth, but his unkempt black hair was uncovered, and his eyes were fierce.

His desk was a packing case, and Helena MacDonald stood behind his stool. She had cropped her hair as short as a man's, and she wore breeches tucked into her boots, and the red armband on her tunic. Her face was pale and gaunt, her eyes in deep plum-coloured sockets were invisible in the bad light, but her body was tensed with the nervous energy of a leashed greyhound with the smell of the hare in its nostrils.

The accused was a storekeeper of the town, with pale watery eyes behind the steel-rimmed spectacles which he blinked rapidly as he watched his accuser.

'He asked to be connected with police headquarters in Marshall Square.'

'Just a minute,' Helena interrupted. 'You are on the local telephone exchange, is that right?'

'Yes, that's right. I am Exchange Supervisor.' The woman looked like a schoolteacher, iron-haired, neatly dressed, unsmiling.

'Go on.'

'I thought I'd better listen in, you know, see what he was up to.'

The storekeeper was wringing white bony hands, and chewing nervously on his lower lip. He looked at least sixty years old with the pale silver fluff of hair standing up comically from his bald pink pate.

'Well, when he started giving them the details of what was happening here, I broke the connection.'

'What exactly did he say?' Fisher demanded.

'He said that there was a machine gun here.'

'He said that?' Fisher's expression was thunderous. He transferred his glare to the storekeeper, and the man quailed.

'My boy is in the police – he's my only boy,' he whispered, and then blinked back the tears from the pale eyes.

'That's as good as a confession,' said Helena coldly, and Fisher glanced over his shoulder at her and nodded.

'Take him out and shoot him,' he said.

The light delivery van bumped along the overgrown track and stopped beside the old abandoned No. 1 shaft on the Crown Mine's property. It had not been used for twelve years, and concrete machinery slabs and the collar of the shaft were thick with rank grass that grew out of the cracks in the concrete and covered the rusted machinery.

Two men dragged the storekeeper to the dilapidated barbed-wire fence that protected the dark black hole of the shaft. No. 1 shaft was fifteen hundred feet deep, but had flooded back to the five-hundred-foot level. The warning notices on the barbed-wire fence were embellished with the skull and cross-bones device.

Helena MacDonald stayed at the wheel of the delivery van. She lit a cigarette and stared ahead, waiting without visible emotion for the executioner's shot.

The minutes passed, while the cigarette burned down between her fingers, and she snapped impatiently when one of the armed strikers came to the side window of the van.

'What's keeping you?'

'Begging your pardon, missus, neither of us can do it.'

'What do you mean?' Helena demanded.

'Well,' the man dropped his eyes. 'Old Cohen's been selling me my groceries for ten years now. He always gives the kids a candy bar when they go in –'

With an impatient exclamation, Helena opened the van door and stepped out.

'Give me your revolver,' she said, and as she strode to where the second striker guarded the old storekeeper she checked the load and spun the chamber of the pistol.

Cohen started to smile, a mild ingratiating smile as he peered at her face myopically, then he saw her expression and the pistol in her hand.

He dropped to his knees, and he began to urinate in terrified spurts down the front of his baggy grey flannel trousers.

When Helena parked the van in the street behind the market buildings, she was aware immediately of a new charge of excitement in the air. The men at the sandbagged windows called out to her, 'Your old man's back, missus. He's down in the cellar with the boss!'

Fergus looked up from the large-scale map of the East Rand over which he and Harry Fisher were poring. She hardly recognized him.

He was sooty and grimed as a chimney sweep, and his

eyelashes had been burned away, giving him a bland startled look. His eyes were bloodshot and there were little wet beads of dirty mucus in the corners.

'Hello, luv,' he grinned wearily at her.

'What are you doing here, comrade?' she demanded. 'You are supposed to be at Brixton ridge.'

Harry Fisher intervened, 'Fergus has taken the ridge. He's done fine work, really fine work. But now we have been granted a stroke of really good fortune.'

'What is it?' Helena demanded.

'Slim Jannie Smuts is on his way from Cape Town.'

'That's bad news,' Helena contradicted coolly.

'He's coming by road – and he's got no escort with him,' Harry Fisher explained.

'Like a lover – right into our arms,' grinned Fergus, and spread his own arms wide. There were dark splotches of dried blood on his sleeves.


The Prime Minister's aide-de-camp had spelled Mark at the wheel of the Rolls on the long stretch northwards from Bloemfontein. Mark had been able to sleep, hunched up on the front seat, oblivious of the lurching and shaking over the bad stretches of road, so that he woke refreshed when Sean Courtney stopped the little convoy on a deserted hilltop fifteen miles south of the built-up complex of mines and towns of the Witwatersrand.

It was late afternoon and the lowering sun turned the banks of low false cloud in the north to a sombre purple hue. It was not cloud but the discharge from the hundreds of chimneys of the power stations and refineries, of the coal-burning locomotives and the open fires of tens of thousands of African labourers in their locations, and of burning buildings and vehicles.

Mark wrinkled his nose as he smelled the acrid taint of the city fouling the clean dry air of the highveld.

The entire party took the opportunity to stretch cramped muscles and to relieve other physical needs. Mark noted wryly that nice social distinctions were observed when those members of the party who had general officer's rank and Cabinet Minister's status used the screened side of the parked cars, while the lesser members stood out in the open road.

While they went about their business, there was an argument in progress. Sean was advocating caution and a roundabout approach through the suburbs and outlying areas of Johannesburg.

'We should cut across to Standerton and come in on the Natal road – the rebels are holding all the southern suburbs.'

'They'll not be expecting us, old Sean. We'll go through fast and be at Marshall Square before they know what's happened,' Jannie Smuts decided. 'I can't afford the extra two hours it will take us to circle around.'

And Sean growled at him, 'You always were too damned hot-headed, Jannie. Good God, you were the one who rode into the Cape with a hundred and fifty men in your commando to capture Cape Town from the whole British army.'

'Gave them the fright of their lives,' the Prime Minister chuckled as he came around the back of the Rolls, buttoning his trousers, and Sean, following him, went on with relish, 'That's right, but when you tried the same tricks on Lettow von Vorbeck in German East Africa, you were the one who got the fright. He roasted your arse for you.'

Mark winced at Sean's choice of words, and the Prime Minister's party looked to heaven and earth, anywhere except at their master's suddenly unsmiling countenance.

'We are going into Johannesburg on the Booysens Road,' said Jannie Smuts coldly.

'You'll be no damned good to us dead,' grumbled Sean.

'That's enough, old Sean. We'll do it my way.'

'All right,' Sean agreed lugubriously. 'But you'll ride in the second car. The Cadillac will lead with your pennant flying.' He turned to the Prime Minister's driver, 'Flat out, you understand, stop for nothing.'

'Yes, sir.'

'Have you gentlemen got your music with you?' he demanded, and all of them showed him the sidearms they carried.

'Mark,' Sean turned to him. 'Get the Mannlicher off the roof.' Mark unstrapped the leather case from the luggage rack and assembled the 9.3 mm sporting rifle, the only effective weapon they had been able to find at short notice in Somerset House before leaving. He loaded the magazine and handed the weapon to Sean, then slipped two yellow packets of Eley Kynoch ammunition into his own pockets.

'Good boy,' Sean grunted, and peered at him closely. 'How are you feeling? Did you get some sleep?'

'I'm fine, sir.'

'Take the wheel.'

Darkness fell swiftly, smearing the silhouettes of the blue gum trees along the low crests of the rolling open ground, crowding in the circle of their vision.

There were the flickering pinpoints of open cooking fires from a few of the native shacks among the hills, but these were the only signs of life. The road was deserted, and even when they began to speed past the first brick-built buildings, there were no lights, and the stillness was unnatural and disquieting.

'The main power station has shut down. The coalminers were limiting supply to fifty tons a day for essential services, but now they've stopped even that,' the Prime Minister mused aloud, and neither of them answered him. Mark followed the twinkling red rear lights of the Cadillac, and the darkness pressed closer. He switched on the main beams of his headlights, and suddenly they were into the narrow streets of Booysens, the southernmost suburb of Johannesburg.

The miners' cottages crowded the road like living and menacing presences. On the left, against the last faint glimmer of the day, Mark could make out the skeletal shape of the steel headgear at Crown Mines' main haulage, and ahead, the low table-like hillocks of the mine dumps gave him a nostalgic twinge.

He thought suddenly of Fergus MacDonald, and Helena, and glanced once again to his left, lifting his eyes from the road for a moment.

Just beyond the Crown Deep headgear, not more than a mile away, was the cottage on Lover's Walk where she had taught him he was a man.

The memory was too wrapped around with pain and guilt, and he thrust it aside and turned his full attention back to the road just as the first rifle shots sparkled from the darkened cottage windows on the right side of the road ahead.

Instantly, he was judging the angle and field of the enemy fire, noticing how they had chosen the curve of the road where the vehicles must slow. 'Good,' he thought dispassionately, applauding the choice, and he hit the gear lever of the Rolls, double declutching into a lower gear to build up revolutions for the turn.

'Get down!' he shouted at his illustrious passengers.

Ahead the Cadillac swerved wildly at the volley and then recovered, and went roaring into the turn.

'Six or seven rifles,' Mark estimated, and then saw the high hedge and the open pavement below the cottage windows. He would give them a changing closing target, he decided, and used the power and rush of the Rolls to broadside up on to the pavement, under the cover of the hedge.

Foliage brushed with a light rushing whisper against the side of the roaring vehicle and behind him a service revolver banged lustily as Sean Courtney fired through the open window.

Mark hit the brakes and fanned the back of the Rolls through the turn, bounded off the pavement and let her sway out across the road, to further confuse the riflemen in the cottages. Then he tramped down hard on the accelerator, gunned her through the turn and went howling down into the dark deserted commercial area of Booysens, leaving the stupefied riflemen staring into the deserted bend, and listening to the receding note of the Rolls-Royce engine.

Only two miles and they would be through the danger area, over the ridge and into Johannesburg proper.

Ahead of him, the Cadillac was running through the area of shops and warehouses and small factories, its headlights blazing harshly on the buildings that lined the road, carving a tunnel of light down their avenue to safety.

In the back seat of the Rolls, the two Generals had not taken Mark's advice to seek cover, and were both sitting bolt upright, discussing the situation objectively in cool measured tones.

'That was quick thinking,' Smuts said. 'They weren't expecting that turn.'

'He's a good lad,' Sean agreed.

'But you are wasting your time with that pistol.'

'Gives me something to do,' Sean explained, as he reloaded the chambers of his revolver.

'You should have ridden with my commando, old Sean, I would have taught you to save ammunition.' Smuts sought revenge for Sean's earlier remarks.

The headlights of the Cadillac tipped slightly upwards as it charged through the dip and reached the first rising ground. They all saw the road-block at the same moment.

It was flung up crudely across the road, oil drums, baulks

of timber, iron bedsteads, sand-bags and household furniture obviously dragged from the cottages.

Sean swore loudly and with ferocity.

'I can turn now,' Mark shouted. 'But they'll get us when we slow down – and we'll have to go back through the ambush.'

'Watch the Cadillac,' Sean shouted back.

The heavy black machine had not hesitated, and it roared up the slope at the barricade, picking the spot which seemed weakest.

'He's going to open a breach! Follow him, Mark.'

The Cadillac smashed into the road-block, and tables and chairs flew high into the night. Even above the roar of wind and engine, Mark could hear the tearing crashing impact, and then the Cadillac was through and going on up the ridge, but its speed was bleeding away and a white cloud of steam plumed from the torn radiator.

However, they had forged a breach in the barricade and Mark steered for it, bumping over a mangled mass of timber and then accelerating away up the slope, gaining rapidly on the leading vehicle.

The Cadillac was losing speed, clearly suffering a mortal injury.

'Shall I stop for them?' Mark demanded.

'No,' said Sean. 'We have to get the Prime Minister—'

'Yes,' said Smuts. 'We can't leave them.'

'Make up your bloody minds,' yelled Mark, and there was a stunned disbelieving silence in the back, and Mark began to brake for the pick up.

The machine gun opened from the scrubby bush at the base of the nearest mine dump. The tracer flailed the night, brilliant white fire sweeping down the road in a blinding storm; the high ripping tearing sound was unmistakable and Mark and Sean exclaimed together in appalled disbelief.

'Vickers!'

The Prime Minister's green and golden pennant on the bonnet of the Cadillac drew the deadly sheet of fire, and in the horrified micro-seconds that Mark watched, he saw the car begin to break up. The windshield and side windows blew away in a sparkling cloud of glass fragments, the figures of the three occupants plucked to pieces like chickens caught in the blades of a threshing-machine.

The Cadillac slewed off the road and crashed headlong into the blank wall of a timber warehouse on the edge of the road, and still the relentless stream of Vickers fire tore into the carcass, punching neat black holes into the metalwork, holes that were rimmed with bare metal that sparkled in the headlights of the Rolls like newly minted silver dollars.

It would only be seconds before the gunner swivelled his Vickers on to the Rolls, Mark realized, and he searched the road ahead for a bolthole.

Between the timber warehouse and the next building was a narrow alleyway, barely wide enough to admit the Rolls. Mark swung out to make a hay-cart turn for the alley, and the gunner guessed his intention, but was stiff and low on his traverse as he swung the Vickers on to the Rolls.

The sheet of bullets ripped the surface of the road, a boiling teeming play of dust and tarmac that ran down under the side of the car.

Before the gunner could correct his aim, the petrol tank of the ruined Cadillac exploded in a woofing clap of sound and a vivid rolling cloud of scarlet flame and dense black smoke.

Under its cover Mark steered for the alleyway, and slammed the Rolls into it although she was suddenly heavy on the steering, and thumping brutally in her front end.

Fifty feet down, the alley was blocked with a heavy haulage trailer, piled high with newly sawn timber baulks – and Mark skidded to a halt, and jumped out.

He saw that for the moment they were covered by the corner of the warehouse from the Vickers, but the timber trailer cut off their escape down the alley and it would be only minutes before the strikers realized their predicament and moved the Vickers to enfilade the alleyway and shoot them to pieces. One glance showed him that machine-gun fire had shredded the off-side leading wheel. Mark jerked open the rear door and snatched the Mannlicher from Sean, and paused only a moment to snap at the two Generals.

'Get the wheel changed. I'll try and hold them off.' Then he was sprinting back down the alleyway.

'I shall have to insist that in future, when he gives me an order, he calls me sir,' Sean said with thin humour, and turned to Smuts. 'Have you ever changed a wheel, Jannie?'

'Don't be stupid, old Sean. I'm a horse soldier, and your superior officer,' Smuts smiled back at him, with his golden beard looking like a refined Viking in the reflected headlights.

'Bloody hell!' grunted Sean. 'You can work the jack.'

Mark reached the corner of the warehouse and crouched against it, checking the load of the Mannlicher before glancing around.

The Cadillac burned like a huge pyre, and the stink of burning rubber and oil and human flesh was choking. The body of the driver still sat at the wheel, but the smoky red flames rushed and drummed about him so that his head was blackening and charring, and his body twisted and writhed in a slow macabre ballet of death.

There was a wind that Mark had not noticed before, a fitful inconstant wind that gusted and puffed down the ridge, rolling thick clouds of the stinking black smoke across the road and then changing strength and direction so that for a few seconds the smoke pall once again poured straight upwards into the night sky.

Over all blazed the flickering orange wash of the flames,

uncertain light which magnified shadow and offered false perspective.

Mark realized that he had to get across the road into the scrub and eroded ground below the mine dump before he could get a chance at the Vickers gunner. He had to cross fifty open yards before he reached the ground where he could turn the clumsiness and relative immobility of the Vickers to his own account. He waited for the wind.

He saw it coming, rustling the grass tops in the firelight and rolling a dirty ball of newspaper down the road, then it picked up the smoke and wafted it in a stinking black pall across the open roadway.

Mark launched himself from the corner of the warehouse and had run twenty paces before he realized that the wind had tricked him. It was merely a gust, passing in seconds and leaving the night still and silent when it had gone, silent except for the snapping, crackling flames of the burning Cadillac.

He was halfway across as the smoke opened again, and the cold weight of dread in his belly seemed to spread down into his legs and slow them as he ran like a man in shackles; but the battle clock in his head was running clearly, tolling off the seconds, judging finely the instant that the Vickers gunner up on the dump spotted his shadowy running figure, judging the time it took for him to swing and resight the heavy weapon.

'Now!' he thought, and rolled forward from the waist without checking his speed, going on to his shoulder and somersaulting, ducking under the solid blast of machine-gun fire that came at the exact second he had expected it.

The momentum of his fall carried him up on to his feet again, and he knew he had seconds before the unsighted gunner picked him up again. He plunged onwards and lances of pain shot through the old bullet wounds in his back, wounds which he had not felt in over a year; the pain was in anticipation, as well as from the wrench of his fall.

The bank of red earth on the far side of the road seemed to loom far off while instinct warned him that the Vickers was on to him again. He launched himself feet first, like a baseball player sliding for the plate, and at the same instant the stream of Vickers' bullets tore a leaping sheet of dust off the lip of the bank, and the ricochets screamed like frustrated banshees and wailed away into the night.

Mark lay under the bank for many seconds with his face cradled in the crook of his arm, sobbing for breath while the pain in his old wounds receded and his heart picked up its normal rhythm. When he lifted his head again, his expression was bleak and his anger was cold and bright and functional.

Fergus MacDonald swore softly with both hands on the firing handles of the Vickers, his forefingers still holding the automatic safety-catch open and his thumbs poised over the firing button. He kept the weapon swinging in short rhythmic traverses back and forth as he peered down the slope, but he was swearing, monotonous profanity in a low tight whisper.

The man beside him was kneeling, ready to feed the belt to the gun, and now he whispered hoarsely, 'I think you got him.'

'The hell I did,' hissed Fergus, and jerked the gun across as something in shadow caught his eye down on the road. He fired a short holding burst, and then muttered, 'Right, let's pull out.'

'Damn it, comrade, we've got them—' protested the loader.

'You bloody fool, didn't you see him?' Fergus asked. 'Didn't you see the way he crossed the road, don't you realize we've got a real ripe one on our hands? Whoever he is, he's a killer.'

'Are we going to let one bastard chase us—'

'You're so right,' snapped Fergus. 'When it's that bucko down there, I'm not going to risk this gun. It's worth a hundred trained men,' he patted the square steel breech block. 'We came here to kill Clever Jannie, and he's down there, cooking in his fancy motorcar. Now, let's get the hell out of here—' and he started the complicated process of unloading the Vickers, cranking it once to clear the chamber of its live round and then cranking again to clear the round in the feed block. 'Tell the boys to cover us when we pull back,' he grunted, as he extracted the ammunition belt from the breech pawls, and then started uncoupling the Vickers from its tripod.

'Come on, work quickly,' he snapped at his loader. 'That bastard is on his way, I can feel him breathing down my neck already.'

There were eight strikers on the slope of the dump, Fergus and two for the Vickers, with five riflemen spread out around the gun to support and cover.

'Right, let's go.' Fergus carried the thick-jacketed barrel over one shoulder and a heavy case of ammunition in his left hand; his number two wrestled with the ungainly fifty-pounds weight of metal tripod and the number three carried the five-gallon can of cooling water and the second case of ammunition.

'We are pulling out,' Fergus called to his riflemen, 'look lively, that's a dangerous bastard coming after us!'

They ran in a group, bowed under their burdens, feet slipping in the loose white cyanided sand of the dump.

The shot was from the left, Fergus had not expected that, and it was impossibly high on the dump. The bastard must have grown wings and flown to get there, Fergus thought.

The report was a heavy booming clap, some sort of sporting rifle, and behind him the number three made a strange grunting sound as though his lungs had been forcibly emptied by a heavy blow. Fergus glanced back and saw him down, a dark untidy shape on the white sand.

'Good Christ,' gasped Fergus. It had to be flukey shooting at that range, and in this impossible light, just the early stars and the ruddy glow of the burning Cadillac.

The rifle boom boomed again, and he heard one of his riflemen scream and then thrash about wildly in the undergrowth. Fergus knew he had judged his adversary fairly, he was a killer. They were all running now, shouting and firing wildly as they scattered back under the lee of the dump, and Fergus ran with them, only one thought in his mind – he must get his precious Vickers safely away.

The sweat had soaked through his jacket between the shoulders, and had run down from under his cap so that he was blinded, and unable to speak when at last he tumbled into the cover of a deep donga and sat against the earth of the bank, with the machine gun cradled in his arms like an infant.

One after another his riflemen reached the donga and fell thankfully into cover.

'How many were there?' gasped one of them.

'I don't know,' panted another, 'must have been a dozen ZARPS, at least. They got Alfie.'

'And they got Henry also, I saw five of them.'

Fergus had recovered his breath enough to speak now. 'There was one, only one – but a good 'un.'

'Did we get Slim Jannie?'

'Yes,' said Fergus grimly. 'We got him all right. He was in the first car – I saw his flag and I saw him cooking. We can go home now.'

It was a little before eleven o'clock when the solitary Rolls-Royce was halted at the gates of police head-quarters on Marshall Square by the suspicious sentries, but when the occupants were recognized, half a dozen high-ranking police and military officers hurried down the steps to welcome them.

The Prime Minister went directly to the large visitors' drawing-room on the first floor which had been transformed into the headquarters of the military administration, empowered and entrusted by the declaration of martial law with the Government of the nation. The relief on the faces of the assembled officers was undisguised. The situation was a mess, but Smuts was here at last and now they could expect order and direction and sanity to emerge from the chaos.

He listened to their reports quietly, tugging at his little goatee beard, his expression becoming more grim as the full extent of the situation was explained.

He was silent a little longer, brooding over the map, and then he looked up at General van Deventer, an old comrade-in-arms during two wars, a man who had ridden with him on that historic commando into the Cape in 1901 and who had fought beside him against the wily old German, Lettow von Vorbeck, in German East Africa.

'Jacobus,' he said, 'you command the East Rand.' Van Deventer whispered an acknowledgement, his vocal cords damaged by a British bullet in '01.

'Sean, you have the west. I want the Brixton ridge under our control by noon tomorrow.' Then, as an afterthought, 'Have your lads arrived from Natal yet?'

'I hope so,' said Sean Courtney.

'So do I,' Smuts smiled thinly. 'You will have a merry time taking the ridge single-handed.' The smile flickered off his face. 'I want your battle plans presented by breakfast time, gentlemen. I don't have to remind you that, as always, the watchword is speed? We have to cauterize this ulcer and bind it up swiftly.'

In early autumn, the highveld sun has a peculiar brilliance, pouring down through an atmosphere thinned by altitude out of a sky of purest gayest blue.

It was weather for picnicking and for lovers in quiet gardens, but on 14th March 1922 it was not calm, but a stillness of a menacing and ominous intensity which hung over the city of Johannesburg and its satellite towns.

In just two days van Deventer had swept through the East Rand, stunning the strikers with his Boer Commando tactics, rolling up all resistance in Benoni and Dunswart, recapturing Brakpan and the mine, while the Brits column under his command drove through the Modder and Geduld mines and linked with van Deventer at Springs. In two days, they had crushed the revolt on the East Rand, and thousands of strikers came in under the white flag to be marched away to captivity and eventual trial.

But Fordsburg was the heart and the Brixton ridge which commanded it was the key to the revolt.

Now at last, Sean Courtney had the ridge, but it had been two days of hard and bitter fighting. With artillery and air support, they had swept the rocky kopjes, the school buildings, brickfields, the cemetery, the public buildings and the cottages, each of which the strikers had turned into a strongpoint; and in the night they had carried in the dead of both sides, and buried them in the Milner Park cemetery, each with his own comrades, soldier with soldier and striker with striker.

Now Sean was ready for the thrust to the heart, and below them the iron roofs of Fordsburg blinked in the fine clear sunlight.

'Here he comes now,' said Mark Anders, and they all lifted their binoculars and searched for the tiny fleck of black in the immense tall sky.

The DH.9 sailed in sedately, banking slowly in from the south and levelling for the run over the cowering cottages of Fordsburg.

Through the lens of his glasses, Mark could make out the head and shoulders of the navigator in the forward cockpit as he hoisted each stack of pamphlets on to the edge of the cockpit, cut the strings and then pushed them over the side. They flurried out in a white storm behind the slow-moving machine, caught in the slipstream, spreading and spinning and drifting like flocks of white doves.

A push of the breeze spread some of the papers towards the ridge, and Mark caught one out of the air and glanced at the crude printing on cheap thick paper.

*MARTIAL LAW*
*NOTICE*

Women and children and all persons well disposed towards the Government are advised to leave before 11 a.m. today that part of Fordsburg and vicinity where the authority of the Government is defied and where military operations are about to take place. No immunity from punishment or arrest is guaranteed to any person coming in under this notice who has broken the law.

SEAN COURTNEY
CONTROL OFFICER

It was clumsy syntax. Mark wondered who had composed it as he crumpled the notice and dropped it into the grass at his feet.

'What if the pickets won't let them come out, sir?' he asked quietly.

'I don't pay you to be my conscience, young man,' Sean growled warningly, and they stood on in silence for a minute. Then Sean sighed and took the cigars from his breast pocket and offered one to Mark as a conciliatory gesture.

'What can I do, Mark? Must I send my lads into those streets without artillery support?' He bit the tip off his cigar and spat it into the grass. 'Whose lives are more important – the strikers and their families or men who trust me and honour me with their loyalty?'

'It's much easier to fight people you hate,' Mark said softly, and Sean glanced at him sharply.

'Where did you read that?' he demanded, and Mark shook his head.

'At least there are no blacks caught up in this,' he said. Mark had personally been in charge of sending disguised black policemen through the lines to warn all tribesmen to evacuate the area.

'Poor blighters,' Sean agreed. 'I wonder what they make of this white men's madness.' Mark strode to the edge of the shallow cliff, ignoring the danger of sniping fire from the buildings below, and glassed the town carefully. Suddenly he exclaimed with relief, 'They're coming out!'

Far below where they stood, the first tiny figures straggled out of the entrance of the Vrededorp subway. The women carried infants and dragged reluctant children at arm's length. Some were burdened with their personal treasures, others brought their pets, canaries in wire cages, dogs on leashes. The first small groups and individuals became a trickle and then a sorry, toiling stream, pushing laden bicycles and hand carts, or simply carrying all the possessions they could lift.

'Send a platoon down to guide them, and give them a hand,' Sean ordered quietly, and brooded heavily with his beard on his chest. 'I'm glad to see the women out of it,' he growled. 'But I'm sad for what it means.'

'The men are going to fight,' Mark said.

'Yes,' Sean nodded. 'They're going to fight. I had hoped we had had enough slaughter – but they are going to make a bitter ending to a tragic tale.' He crushed the stub of his cigar under his heel. 'All right, Mark. Go down and tell Molyneux that it's on. Eleven hundred hours we'll open the barrage. Good luck, son.'

Mark saluted, and Sean Courtney left him and limped back from the crest to join General Smuts and his staff who had come out to watch the final sweep of the battle.

The first shrapnel bursts clanged across the sky, and burst in bright gleaming cotton pods of smoke above the roofs of Fordsburg, cracking the sky and the waiting silence, with startling violence.

They were fired by the horse artillery batteries on the ridge, and immediately the other batteries on Sauer Street joined in.

For twenty minutes, the din was appalling and the brilliant air was sullied by the rising mist of smoke and dust. Mark stood in the hastily dug trench and peered over the parapet. There was something so dreadfully familiar in this moment. He had lived it fifty times before, but now he felt his nerves screwing down too tightly and the heavy indigestible lump of fear in his guts nauseated him.

He wanted to duck down below the parapet, cover his head to protect his ears from the great metallic hammer-blows of sound, and stay there.

It required an immense effort of will to stand where he was and to keep his expression calm and disinterested – but the men of 'A' Company lined the trench on each side of him and, to distract himself, he began to plan his route through the outskirts of the town.

There would be road-blocks at every corner, and every cottage would be held. The artillery barrage would not have affected the strikers under cover, for it was limited to shrapnel bursts. Sean Courtney was concerned with the safety of over a hundred police and military personnel who had been captured by the strikers and were being held somewhere in the town.

'No high explosive,' was the order, and Mark knew his company would be cut to ribbons on the open streets.

He was going to take them through the kitchen yards and down the sanitary lanes to their final objective, the Trades Hall on Commercial and Central Streets.

He checked his watch again, and there were four minutes to go.

'All right, Sergeant,' he said quietly.

The order passed quickly down the trench and the men came to their feet, crouching below the parapet.

'Like old times, sir,' the Sergeant said affably; and Mark glanced at him. He seemed actually to be enjoying this moment – and Mark found himself hating the man for it.

'Let's go,' he said abruptly, as the minute hand of his watch touched the black hair-line division, and the Sergeant blew his whistle shrilly.

Mark put one hand on the parapet and leapt nimbly over the top.

He started to run forward, and from the cottages ahead of him came the harsh crackling of musketry. Suddenly, he realized he was no longer afraid.

H e was little more than a youth, with smooth pink cheeks and the lightest golden fluff of a moustache on his upper lip.

They shoved him down the last few steps into the cellars, and he lost his footing and fell.

'Another yellow belly,' called the escort, a strapping bearded fellow with a rifle slung on his shoulder and the red band around his upper arm. 'Caught him trying to sneak out of the subway.'

The boy scrambled to his feet. He had skinned his knees

in his fall and he was close to tears as Harry Fisher towered above him. He carried a long black sjambok in his right hand, a vicious tapered whip of cured hippo-hide.

'A traitor,' bellowed Fisher. In the last days of continuous planning and fighting, the strain had started to show. His eyes had taken on a wild fanatical glare, his movements were jerky and exaggerated, and his voice ragged and overloud.

'No, comrade, I swear I'm no traitor,' the youth bleated pitifully.

'A coward, then,' shouted Fisher, and caught the front of the boy's shirt in one big hairy fist and ripped it open to the waist.

'I didn't have a rifle,' protested the boy.

'There'll be rifles for all later – when the first comrades die.'

The lash of the sjambok split the smooth white skin of the boy's back like a razor stroke, and the blood rose in a vivid bright line as he fell to his knees.

Harry Fisher stood over him and swung the sjambok until there were no more screams or groans, and the only sound in the cellar was the hiss and splat of the lash – then he stood back panting and sweating.

'Take him out so the comrades can see what happens to traitors and cowards.'

A striker took each of the boy's arms and as they dragged him up the steps, the flesh of his back hung in ribbons and tatters and the blood ran down over his belt and soaked into the gaberdine of his breeches.

Mark dropped cat-footed over the back wall into the tiny paved yard. Cases of empty beer bottles were piled high along the side walls, and the smell of stale liquor was fruity and heady in the noon heat.

He had reached the bottle store in Mint Road less than an hour after the starting time of the drive, and the route he had led his men, through the backyards and over the roof-tops, had been more successful than he had dared hope.

They had avoided the road-blocks and twice had out-flanked groups of strikers dug into strong positions, surprising them completely, and scattering them with a single volley.

Mark ran across the yard and kicked in the back door of the bottle store, and in the same movement flattened himself against the wall, clear of the gaping doorway and any striker fire from the interior of the building.

The Sergeant and a dozen men followed him over the wall, and spread out to cover the doorway and barred windows. He nodded at Mark, and Mark dived through the doorway sideways with the rifle on his hip, and his eyes screwed up against the gloom after the bright sunlight outside.

The store was deserted, the shutters bolted down over the front windows and the shelves of bottles untouched by looters, in testimony of the strikers' discipline. The tiers of bottles stood neatly in their gaily coloured labels, glinting in the dusky light.

The last time Mark had been in here was to buy a dozen bottles of porter for Helena MacDonald, but he pushed the thought aside and went to the shuttered windows just as the Sergeant and his squad burst in through the back door.

The shutters had been pierced by random shrapnel and rifle fire, and Mark used one aperture as a peephole.

Fifty yards across the road was the Trades Hall, and the

complex of trenches and defences that the strikers had thrown up around the square.

Even the public lavatories had been turned into a blockhouse, but all the defenders' attention was directed into the streets across the square.

They lined the parapets and were firing frantically at the kilted running figures of the Transvaal Scottish racing towards the Square from the station side.

The strikers were dressed in a strange assortment of garb, from greasy working overalls and quasi-military safari jackets, caps and slouch hats and beavers, to Sunday suits, waistcoats and ties. But all of them wore bandoliers of ammunition draped from their shoulders, and their backs were exposed to Mark's attack.

A volley through the bottle-store windows would have done terrible execution among them, and already the Sergeant was directing his men to each of the windows in a fierce and gleeful croak of anticipation.

'I could order up a machine gun,' Mark thought, and something in him shied away from the mental image of a Vickers firing into that exposed and unsuspecting group. 'If only I hated them.'

As he watched, first one and then others of the strikers at the barricades crouched down hopelessly from the withering fire the Highlanders were now pouring on to them.

'Fix bayonets,' Mark called to the men, and the steel scraped from the metal scabbards in the sombre gloom of the store. A stray bullet splintered the shutter above Mark's head and burst a bottle of Scotch whisky on the shelves behind him. The smell of the spirit was sharp and unpleasant, and Mark called again, 'On my order, break open the windows and doors, and we'll show them steel.'

The shutters crashed back, the main doors flew open, and Mark led his company in a howling racing line across the road. Before they reached the first line of sand-bags, the strikers began throwing down their rifles and jumping up with their hands lifted above their heads.

Across the square, the Highlanders poured into the street cheering and shouting and raced for the barricades; Mark felt a surge of relief that he had taken the risk of going with the bayonet, rather than ordering his men to shoot down the exposed strikers.

As his men ran into the square, knocking the weapons out of their hands and pushing the strikers into sullen groups, Mark was racing up the front steps of the Trades Hall.

He paused on the top step, shouted, 'Stand back inside' and fired three rifle bullets into the brass lock.

Harry Fisher leaned against the wall and peered out of the sand-bagged window into the milling yelling chaos of the square.

The madness of unbearable despair shook the huge frame, and he breathed like a wounded bull when it stands to take the matador's final thrust. He watched his men throw down their arms, saw them herded like cattle, with their hands held high, stumbling on weary careless feet, their faces grey with fatigue and sullen in defeat.

He groaned, a low hollow sound of emotional agony stretched to its furthest limits, and the thick shoulders sagged. He seemed to be shrinking in size. The great unkempt head lowered, the blazing vision dimmed in his eyes as he watched the young lieutenant in barathea battledress race up the stairs below him, and heard the rifle shots shatter the lock.

He shambled across to his desk and slumped down into the chair facing the closed door, and his hand was shaking as he drew the service revolver from his belt and cocked the hammer. He laid the weapon carefully on the desk in front of him.

He cocked his head and listened to the shouted orders and the trampling confusion in the square below for a minute, then he heard the rush of booted feet up the wooden staircase beyond the door.

He lifted the revolver from the desk, and leaned both elbows on the desk-top to steady himself.

Mark burst in through the main doors of the hall and stopped in surprise and confusion. The floor was covered with prostrate bodies, it seemed there must be hundreds of them.

As he stared, a Captain of Highlanders and half a dozen men burst in behind him. They stopped also.

'Good God,' panted the Captain, and then suddenly Mark realized that the bodies were all uniformed, police khaki, hunting green kilts, barathea.

'They have slaughtered their prisoners,' Mark thought with nightmare horror, staring at the mass of bodies, then suddenly a head lifted cautiously and another.

'Oh thank God,' breathed the Captain beside Mark, as the prisoners began scrambling to their feet, their faces shining with relief, a single voice immediately becoming a hubbub of nervous gaiety.

They surged for the door, some to embrace their liber-ators and others merely to run out into the sunlight.

Mark avoided a big police Sergeant with rumpled uni-form and three days' growth of beard, ducked under his arms and ran for the staircase.

He took the stairs three at a time, and paused on the landing. The doors to five offices on this floor were standing open, the sixth was closed. He moved swiftly down the corridor, checking each of the rooms.

Cupboards and desks had been ransacked, and the floors were ankle-deep in paper, chairs overturned, drawers pulled from desks and dumped into the litter of paper.

The sixth door at the end of the passage was the only one closed. It was the office of the local Union chairman, Mark knew, Fergus MacDonald's office. The man for whom he was searching, driven by some lingering loyalty, by the dictates of shared comradeship and friendship to find him now – and to give him what help and protection he could.

Mark slipped the safety-catch on the rifle as he approached the door. He reached for the handle, and once again that sense of danger warned him. For a moment he stood with his fingers almost touching the brass lock, then he stepped quietly out of the line of the doorway; reaching sideways he rattled the handle softly and then turned it.

The door was unlocked, and the latch snicked and he pushed the door open. Nothing happened, and Mark grunted with relief and stepped through the doorway.

Harry Fisher sat at the desk facing him, a huge menacing figure, crouching over the desk with the big tousled head lowered on massive shapeless shoulders and the revolver held in both hands, pointing directly at Mark's chest.

Mark knew that to move was death. He could see the rounded leaden noses of the bullets in the loaded chambers of the cylinder and the hammer fully cocked, and he stood frozen.

'It is not defeat,' Harry Fisher spoke with a strangled hoarse voice that Mark did not recognize. 'We are the dragon's teeth. Wherever you bury one of us, a thousand warriors will spring up.'

'It's over, Harry,' Mark spoke carefully, trying to distract him, for he knew he could not lift the rifle and fire in the time Harry Fisher could pull the trigger.

'No.' Fisher shook the coarse tangled locks of his head. 'It is only just beginning.'

Mark did not realize what he was doing, until Harry Fisher had reversed the pistol and thrust the muzzle into his own mouth. The explosion was muffled, and Harry Fisher's head was stretched out of shape, as though it were a rubber ball struck by a bat.

The back of his skull erupted, and a loose mass of bright scarlet and custard yellow splattered the wall behind him.

The impact of the bullet hurled his body backwards and his chair toppled and crashed over.

The stench of burned powder hung in the room on filmy wisps of gunsmoke, and Harry Fisher's booted heels kicked and tapped a jerky, uneven little dance on the bare wooden floor.

'Where is Fergus MacDonald?' Mark asked the question a hundred times of the files of captured strikers. They stared back at him, angry, bitter, some of them still truculent and defiant, but not one of them even deigned to answer.

Mark took three of his men, under the pretext of a mopping-up patrol, down to Lover's Walk as far as the cottage.

The front door was unlocked, and the beds in the front room were unmade. Mark felt a strange repugnance of mind, balanced by a plucking of lust at his loins, when he saw Helena's *crêpe de Chine* dressing-gown thrown across the chair, and a crumpled pair of cotton panties dropped carelessly on the floor beside it.

He turned away quickly, and went through the rest of the house. The dirty dishes in the kitchen had already grown a green fuzz of mould, and the air was stale and disused. Nobody had been in these rooms for days.

A scrap of paper lay on the floor beside the coal-black stove. Mark picked it up and saw the familiar hammer and sickle device on the pamphlet. He screwed it up and hurled it against the wall. His men were waiting for him on the stoep.

The strikers had dynamited the railway lines at Braamfontein station, and at the Church Street level-crossing, so the regiment could not entrain at Fordsburg. Most of the roads were blocked with rubble and the detritus of the final struggle, but most dangerous was the possibility of stubborn strikers still hiding out in the buildings that lined the road through the dip to Johannesburg.

Sean Courtney decided to move his men out up the slope to the open ground of the Crown Deep property.

They marched out of Fordsburg in the darkness, before good shooting light. It had been a long uncomfortable night, and nobody had slept much. Weariness made their packs leaden to carry and shackled their legs. There was less than a mile to go, however.

The motor transport was drawn up in the open ground near the headgear of Crown Mine's main haulage, a towering structure, shaped like the Eiffel Tower, steel girders riveted and herring-boned for strength, rising a hundred feet to the huge wheels of the winching equipment. When the shift was in, these wheels spun back and forth, back and forth, lowering the cages filled with men and equipment, hundreds of feet into the living earth, and raising the millions of tons of gold-bearing rock out of the depths.

Now the great wheels stood motionless; they had been dead for three months now, and the buildings clustered about the tower were gloomy and deserted.

The transport was an assortment of trucks and commercial vans, commandeered under martial law – gravel lorries from the quarries, mining vehicles, even a bakery van, but it was clear that there was not enough to take out six hundred men.

As Mark came up, marching on the flank of 'A' Company, there were half a dozen officers in discussion at the head of the convoy. Mark recognized the familiar bearded figure of General Courtney standing head and shoulders above the others, and his voice was raised in an angry growl.

'I want all these men moved before noon. They've done fine work, they deserve hot food and a place—'

At that moment he saw Mark, and frowned heavily, waving him over and beginning to speak before he had arrived.

'Where the hell have you been?'

'With the company—'

'I sent you to take a message, and expected you back. You know damned well I didn't mean you to get into the fighting. You are on my staff, sir!'

Mark was tired and irritable, still emotionally disturbed by all that he had seen and done that day, and he was in no mood for one of the General's tantrums.

His rebellious expression was unmistakable. 'Sir,' he began, and Sean shouted at him, 'And don't take that tone to me, young man!'

An uncaring, completely irresponsible dark rage descended on Mark. He didn't give a damn for the consequences and he leaned forward, pale with fury, and opened his mouth.

The regiment was bunched up now, halted in the open roadway, neat symmetrical blocks of khaki, six hundred men in ranks three deep.

The shouted orders of the N.C.O.s halted each section, one after the other, and stood them at the easy position.

From the top of the steel headgear, they made an unforgettable sight in the rich yellow light of early morning.

'Ready, luv,' whispered Fergus MacDonald, and Helena nodded silently. Reality had long faded and been replaced by this floating dreamlike state. Her shoulders were raw where the carrying straps of the heavy ammunition boxes had bitten into the flesh, but there was no pain, just a blunting numbness of body. Her hands seemed bloated, and

374

clumsy, the nails broken off raggedly and rinded with black half-moons of dirt, and the harsh canvas of the ammunition belts between her fingers felt smooth as silk, the brass cartridge cases cool, so that she felt like pressing them to her dried cracked lips.

Why was Fergus staring at her that way, she wondered with a prickle of irritation that did not last, once again the dreamy floating sensation.

'You can go down now,' Fergus said quietly. 'You don't have to stay.' He looked like a very old man, his face shrivelled and falling in upon itself. The stubble of beard on his lined and haggard cheeks was silvery as diamond chips, but the skin was stained by smoke and dirt and sweat.

Only the eyes below the peak of the cloth cap still burned with the dark fanatic flames.

Helena shook her head. She wanted him to stop talking, the sound intruded, and she turned her head away.

The men below stood shoulder to shoulder in their orderly ranks. The low sun threw long narrow shadows from their feet across the red dust of the roadway.

A second longer Fergus stared at her. She was a pale, wasted stranger, the bones pushing through the smooth drawn flesh of her face, the scarf wound like a gypsy around her head, covering the black cropped hair.

'All right then,' he murmured, and tapped the breech of the Vickers, once, twice, training it slightly left.

There was a group of officers near the head of the column. One of them was a big powerful man with a dark beard. The sunlight sparkled on his shoulder-tabs. Fergus lowered his head and looked through the rear sight of the Vickers.

There was a younger slimmer officer with the other, and Fergus blinked twice rapidly, as something stirred deep in his memory.

He hooked his fingers into the automatic safety-bar and

375

lifted it, priming the gun, and he brought his thumbs on to the firing button.

He blinked again. The face of the young officer moved something in him, he felt a softening and blurring of his determination and he rejected it violently and thrust down on the button with both thumbs.

The weapon juddered on its tripod, and the long belt was sucked greedily into the breech, Helena's small pale hands guiding it carefully, and the empty brass cases spewed out from under the gun, tinkling and ringing and bouncing off the steel girders of the headgear.

The sound was a deafening tearing roar that seemed to fill Helena's head and beat against her eyes, like the frantic wings of a trapped bird.

Even the most skilled marksman must guard against the tendency to ride up on a downhill shot. The angle from the top of the headgear was acute and the soft yellowish early light further confused Fergus' aim. His first burst carried high – shoulder-high instead of belly-high, which is the killing line for machine-gun fire.

The first bullets struck before Mark heard the gun. One of them hit Sean Courtney high up in the big bulky body. It flung him forward, chest to chest with Mark, and both of them went down, sprawling in the roadway.

Fergus tapped the breech block, dropping his aim a fraction on to the belly line, and traversed in a long unhurried sweep along the ranks of standing soldiers, cutting them with the scythe of the Vickers in the eternal seconds that they still stood in stunned paralysis.

The stream of tracer hosed them, and washed them into crazy heaps, piled them on each other, dead and wounded together, their screams high and thin in the rushing hurricane of Vickers fire.

Sean rolled half off Mark, and his face was contorted, angry and outraged, as he tried to struggle on to his knees, but his one arm was dangling. His blood splattered them both and he flopped helplessly.

Mark wriggled out from under him, and looked up at the headgear. He saw the tracer flickering like fire-flies and darting into the crowded roadway on the triumphant fluttering roar of the gun. Even in his own confusion and despair, he saw that the gunner had picked a good stance. He would be hard to come at.

Then he looked down the road and a cold fist clenched on his guts as he saw the bloody execution. The ranks had broken, men running and stumbling for what little cover the vehicles and ditches offered, but the road was still filled.

They lay in windrows and piles, they crawled and cried and twisted in the dust which their blood was turning to chocolate-red mud – and the gun swivelled and came back, flickering tracer into the carnage, chopping up the road surface into a spray of dust and leaping gravel, running viciously over the piles of wounded, coming back to where they lay.

Mark twisted up into a crouch, and slipped an arm under the General's chest. The weight of the man was enormous, but Mark found strength that he had not known before, goaded on by the fluttering rushing roar of the Vickers. Sean Courtney heaved himself up like a bull caught in quick sand, and Mark got him on to his feet.

Bearing half his weight, Mark steadied him and kept him from falling. He weaved drunkenly, hunched over, bleeding badly, breathing noisily through his mouth, and Mark forced him into an ungainly crouching run.

The gun swept their heels, kicking and smashing into the back of a young lieutenant who was creeping towards the ditch, dragging both useless legs behind him. He dropped face down and lay still.

They reached the drainage ditch and tumbled into it. It was less than eighteen inches deep, not enough to cover the General fully, even when he lay flat on his belly, and the Vickers was still hunting.

After that first long slicing traverse, it was firing short accurate bursts at selected targets, more deadly than random fire, keeping the gun from overheating and preventing a stoppage, conserving ammunition. Mark, weighing it all, realized that there was an old soldier up there in the tower.

'Where are you hit?' he demanded, but Sean struck his hands away irritably, twisting his head to peer up into the tall steel headgear.

'Can you get him, Mark?' he grunted, and pressed his fingers into his shoulder, where the blood welled up thick and dark as molasses.

'Not from here,' Mark answered quickly. It had taken him seconds to assess the shoot. 'He's holed up tight.'

'Merciful Jesus! My poor boys.'

'He's built himself a nest.' Mark studied the steelwork. The platform below the winch wheels was covered with heavy timber, fitted loosely into the framework of steel.

The gunner had pulled these up and built himself four walls of wood, perhaps two feet thick. Mark could see the light glimmering through the open gaps in the floor boards, and make out the shape and size of the fortified nest.

'He can hold us here all day!' Sean looked down at the piles of khaki bodies in the roadway, and they both knew many of the wounded would bleed to death in that time. Nobody dared go out to them.

The gun came back, ripping a flail across the earth near their heads and they ducked their faces to the ground, pressing their bodies into the shallow ditch.

The ground sloped down very gradually towards the steel tower; only when you lay at ground level like this was the gradient apparent.

'Somebody will have to get under him, or behind him,' Mark spoke quickly, thinking it out.

'It's open ground all the way,' Sean grunted.

On the opposite side of the road fifty yards away, a narrow-gauge railway ran down the short open grassy slope to the foot of the tower. It was used to truck the waste material from the shaft-head to the rock dump, half a mile away.

Almost opposite where they lay, half a dozen of the steel cocoa pans had been abandoned at the beginning of the strike. They were small four-wheeled tip-trucks, coupled to each other in a line, each of them heaped high with big chunks of blue rock.

Mark realized he was still wearing his pack and he shrugged out of the straps as he planned his stalk, judging angles and range as he groped for the field-dressing and handed it to Sean.

'Use this.'

Sean tore open the package and wadded the cotton dressing into the front of his tunic. His fingers were sticky with his own blood.

Mark's P.14 rifle lay in the road where he had dropped it, but there were five clips of ammunition in the pouches on his webbing belt.

'Try and give me some covering fire when I start to go up,' he said, and watched the tower for the next burst of tracer.

'You'll never get there,' said Sean. 'We'll bring up a thirteen-pounder and shoot the bastard out of there.'

'That will take until noon, it will be too late for them.' He glanced at the wounded in the road, and at that moment a stream of brilliant white tracer flew from the tower, aimed at the far end of the column, and Mark was up and running hard, stooping to gather the rifle at full run, crossing the road in a dozen flying strides, stumbling in the rough ground beyond, catching his balance and sprinting on.

That stumble had cost him a tenth of a second, the margin of life and death perhaps, while the gunner high up in the tower spotted him, swivelled the gun and lined up. The steel cocoa pans were just ahead, fifteen paces, but he wasn't going to make it – the warning flared in his brain, and he dropped into the short grass and rolled sideways, just as the storm of Vickers fire filled the air about him with the lash of a hundred bullwhips.

Mark kept rolling, like a log, and the gun gouged a furrow out of the dry stony earth inches from his shoulder.

He came up against the wheels of the cocoa pan with a force that bruised his hip and made him cry out involuntarily. Vickers bullets hammered and clanged against the steel body of the truck and howled off in ricochet, but Mark was under cover now.

'Mark, are you all right?' the General's bull-bellow carried across the road.

'Give me covering fire.'

'You heard him, lads,' shouted the General, and one or two rifles began firing spasmodically from the ditches, and from behind the stranded motor lorries.

Mark dragged himself on to his knees, and quickly checked the rifle, brushing the sights with his thumb to make certain they were cleaned of dirt and undamaged in the fall.

Then he worked his way to the coupling of the cocoa pan and threw the release toggle. The brake wheel was stiff and required both his hands to unwind it. The brake chocks squeaked softly as they disengaged, but the slope of the ground was so gentle that the truck did not move until Mark put his shoulder to it.

He strained with all his weight before the steel wheels made a single reluctant revolution, then gravity took her and the cocoa pan began to roll.

'Give the bastard hell!' Sean Courtney yelled, as he realized suddenly what Mark was going to do, and Mark grinned without mirth at that characteristic exhortation, and he trotted along, doubled up behind the heavily-laden steel truck.

A terrible tearing, hammering storm of Vickers broke over the slowly rolling truck, and instinctively Mark ducked lower and steadied himself against the metal side.

He realized that as he came closer to the tower, so the gunner's angle would change until he was shooting almost directly down on top of Mark – then the side of the truck would give him no cover, but he was committed. Nothing would stop the slowly accelerating rush of the cocoa pan down the slope, it had the weight of ten tons of rock behind it and its speed was gathering. Soon he would not be able to keep up with it, already he was running – and the Vickers roared again, the bullets screeching and wailing furiously off the steel body.

Twisting as he ran, he slung the rifle on one shoulder and reached up to hook both hands over the side of the truck. He was pulled instantly off his feet, and they dangled without foothold, in danger of being caught up in the spinning steel wheels. He drew his knees up under his chin, hanging all his weight on his arms and taking the intolerable strain in his belly muscles as the truck flew down into the stretching octopus shadow of the headgear.

Still hanging on his arms, Mark flung his head back and looked up. The tower was foreshortened by perspective, and it crouched over him like some menacing monster, stark against the mellow morning sky, crude black steel and timber baulks pyramiding into the heavens. At its zenith, Mark could see the pale mirror-like face of the gunner, and the thick water-jacketed barrel of the Vickers trained down at its maximum depression.

The gun flamed, and bullets rang the steel near his head like a great bell. They churned into the blue rock, disintegrating into chips of buzzing metal and shattering the rock into vicious splinters and pellets that cut at his hands so that he screwed his eyes shut and clung helplessly.

Such was the speed of the truck now that he was under fire for only seconds, and the gunner's aim could not follow it, as it raced down on to the concrete loading bank, and slammed into the buffers. The force of the impact was brutal and Mark was hurled from his perch, the rifle-strap snapped and the weapon sailed away, and Mark turned in the air and hit the sloping concrete ramp on his side with a crash that jarred his teeth in his head. The rough concrete ripped away the thick barathea cloth from his hip and leg and shoulder, and seared the flesh beneath with gravel burn.

He came up at least against a stack of yellow-painted oil-drums, and his first concern was to roll on to his back and stare upwards.

He was under the headgear now, protected from the gunner by the legs and intricate steel girders of the tower itself, and he pulled himself to his feet, dreading the give and crippling drag of broken bone. But though his body felt crushed and bruised, he could still move, and he hobbled to where his rifle lay.

The strap was broken, and the butt was cracked and splintered, and as he lifted it, it snapped into two pieces. He could not fire from the shoulder.

The foresight had been knocked off, and the broken metal had a sugary grey crystalline look. He could not aim the weapon. He would have to get close, very close.

There was a deep bright scar in the steel of the breech. He muttered a prayer, 'Please God!' as he tried to work the bolt open. It was jammed solid and he struggled with it fruitlessly for precious seconds.

'All right,' he thought grimly. 'No butt to hold to the shoulder, no foresight with which to aim, and only the one cartridge in the breech – it's going to be interesting.' He looked around him quickly.

Beneath the steel tower, the two square openings to the main shaft were set into the concrete collar, protected by screens of steel mesh. The one cage stood at the surface station, doors open, ready for the next shift. The other was at the bottom station, a thousand feet below ground level.

They had stood that way for months now. On the far side was the small service elevator which would take maintenance teams the hundred feet to the summit of the tower in half a minute. However, there was no power on the shaft head, and the elevator was useless.

The only other way up was the emergency ladder. This was an open steel stairway that spiralled up around the central shaft, protected only by a low handrail of inch piping.

High above Mark's head the Vickers fired again, and Mark heard a scream of agony out there on the roadway. It hastened him, and he limped to the stairway.

The steel-mesh gate was open, the padlock shattered, and Mark knew by what route the sniper had reached his roost.

He stepped on to the stairway and began to climb, following the coils up the casing round and round, and up and up.

Always at his right hand, the open black mouth of the shaft gaped, an obscene dark orifice in the earth's surface, dropping straight and sheer into the very bowels, a thousand dark terrifying feet.

Mark tried to ignore it, dragging his bruised and aching body up by the handrail, carrying the broken weapon in his other hand, and strained his neck backwards for the first glimpse of the gunner above.

The Vickers fired again, and Mark glanced sideways. He was high enough now to see into the road.

One of the trucks was burning, a tall dragon's breath of smoke and sullen flame pouring into the sky – and the drab khaki bodies were still strewn in the open, death's discarded toys.

Even as he watched, the Vickers fire thrashed over them,

mangling already dead flesh, and Mark's anger became cold and bright as a dagger's blade.

'Keep firing, luv,' Fergus croaked in that husky stranger's voice. 'Short bursts. Count to twenty slowly, and then a touch on the button. I want him to think that I am still up here.' He pulled the Webley from his belt, and crawled on his belly towards the head of the steep staircase.

'Don't leave me, Fergus.'

'It'll be all right,' he tried to grin, but his face was grey and crumpled. 'Just you keep firing. I'm going down to meet him halfway. He'll not expect that.'

'I don't want to die alone,' she breathed. 'Stay with me.'

'I'll be back, luv. Don't fuss yourself,' and he slid on his belly into the opening of the staircase.

She felt like a child again, in one of those terrible dark nightmares, trapped and enmeshed in her own fate, and she wanted to cry out. The sound reached her lips but died there as a low blubbering moan.

A rifle bullet chunked into the barricade of timber beside her. They were shooting from down below. She could not pick them out, for they were hidden in the ditches and the irregularities of the ground, screened by long purple shadows, and her eyes were blurred with tears and with exhaustion; yet she found the last few grains of her strength and crawled to the gun.

She squatted behind it and her hands were almost too small to reach the firing button. She pressed the barrel downwards, and forced her blearing vision to focus, marvelling at the little toy figures in the field of the sight. The gun juddered in her hands like a living creature.

'A short burst,' she whispered to herself, repeating Fergus' instructions, and lifted her thumbs from the firing button. 'One-two-three,' she began to count to the next burst.

Mark paused at the next burst of firing and stood for a moment staring up. He was over halfway to the top, and now he could make out the floor of the service platform below the winch wheels, the platform on which the Vickers was sited.

There were narrow cracks in the woodwork through which bright lines of open sky showed clearly, and as he watched he saw one of the lines of light interrupted by a dark movement beyond. It was that flicker of movement that caught his attention, and he realized that he was looking at the body of the person who served the gun. He must be squatting directly over one of the narrow joints in the floor of the platform, and his movements blocked out part of that bright line of light.

A bullet through the gap would cripple and pin him, but he glanced at the broken weapon in his hand and knew that he would have to get closer, much closer.

He began to run upwards and though he tried to keep his weight lightly on the balls of his feet, the hobnails in his boots rang on the steel stairs.

Fergus MacDonald heard them and checked his own run, shrinking into the protective lee of one of the steel girders.

'One man only,' he muttered. 'But coming up fast.' He dropped on one knee and peered down through the gaps between the stairs, hoping for sight of the man who he was hunting. The steps overlapped each other like fanned playing-cards, and the lateral supports of the tower formed an impenetrable steel forest below him.

The only way he could hope for a glimpse was to hang out over the handrail and look down the central shaft-well.

The idea of that thousand-foot black hole repelled him, and he had formed an estimate of his opponent high enough to guess that the reward for putting his head over the side would be a bullet between the eyes.

He edged into a better position where he could cover the next spiral of staircase below him.

'I'll let him come up to me,' he decided, and braced his

arm against the girder at the level of his chin, and laid the Webley over the crook of his elbow to give the heavy pistol support. He knew that over ten paces it was wildly inaccurate, but the dead rest would give him at least one fair shot.

He cocked his head slightly to listen to the clatter of booted feet on steel, and he judged that the man was very close. One more spiral of the stair would bring him into shot. Carefully, he thumbed back the hammer of the Webley and looked down over the slotted rear-sight.

Above them, the Vickers fired again, and Mark paused to catch his breath and check the situation of the gunner, and to his dismay he realized that he had climbed too high in the tower.

He had changed the angle of sight, and could no longer see through the cracks in the timber platform. He had to retreat carefully down the staircase before once again the bright lines of light opened in the dark underbelly of timber.

A vague blur of movement reassured him that the gunner had not changed his position. He was still squatting over the joint, but the shot was almost impossible.

He was shooting directly upwards, awkward even in the best conditions, but now he had no butt to steady the rifle and no foresight, he was shooting into a single dark mass of timber and had to guess the position of the crack because the gunner's body obscured the light from the far side. The crack itself was only two inches wide, and if he missed by a smallest fraction the bullet would bury itself harmlessly in the thick timber.

He tried not to think that there would be only one shot, the jammed breech made that certain.

He put his hip to the guardrail and leaned out over the open shaft, squinting upwards trying to set the target in his mind as he lifted the broken rifle in an easy natural movement. He knew that he had to make the shot entirely by instinct. He had no chance if he hesitated or tried to hold his aim steadily on the target.

He swept up the shattered weapon and at the moment the long barrel aligned, he pressed the trigger.

In the flash and thunder of the shot a tiny white splinter of wood jumped from the edge of the crack. The bullet had touched wood and Mark felt an instant of utter dismay.

Then the body that had obscured the light was jerked abruptly aside, and the crack was a single uninterrupted line again – and on the platform somebody screamed.

Helena MacDonald had just reached the count of twenty again, and was aiming at a gathering of men she could see grouping beyond one of the lorries. She squatted low over the gun and was on the point of jamming her thumbs down on the firing button, when the bullet came up through the floor timbers.

It had touched one of the hard mahogany baulks, just enough to split the casing of the bullet and alter its shape, mushrooming it slightly, so that it did not enter her body through a neat round puncture.

It tore a ragged entry into the soft flesh at the juncture of her slightly spread thighs and plunged upwards through her lower abdomen, striking and shattering the thick bony girdle of her pelvis, glancing off the bone with still enough impetus to bruise and weaken the lower branch of the descending aorta, the great artery that runs down from the heart, before going on to embed itself in the muscles high in the left side of her back.

It lifted Helena into the air, and hurled her across the platform on to her face.

'Oh God, oh God, help me! Fergus! Fergus! I don't want to die alone,' she screamed, and the sound carried clearly to the two men in the steel tower below her.

Mark recognized the voice instantly. It did not need the name to confirm it.

His mind shied at the enormity of what he had done. The broken rifle almost slipped from his hands, but he saved it and caught at the handrail for support.

Helena cried again, a sound without words – it was exactly that strange wild cry that she had uttered at the zenith of one of their wildest flights of passion together, and for an instant Mark remembered her face shining and triumphant, the dark eyes burning and the open red mouth and the soft pink petal of her tongue aflutter.

Mark started to run, hurling himself upwards.

The screams caught Fergus like a flight of arrows in the heart. A piercing, physical agony, he dropped the pistol to his side and stood irresolute, staring upwards, not knowing what had happened, except that Helena was dying. He had heard the death scream too often to have any doubt about that. What he was listening to was mortal agony, and he could not force his body to begin the climb upwards, to the horror he knew waited him there.

While he hesitated, Mark came around the angle of the staircase and Fergus was not ready for him. The pistol was at his side, and he fell back and tried to bring it up, to fire at point-blank range into the chest of the uniformed figure.

Mark was as off balance as he was. He had not expected to run into another enemy, but he saw the pistol and swung the broken rifle at Fergus' head.

Fergus ducked, and the Webley fired wide, the bullet flew inches past Mark's temple and the report slammed against his eardrum and made him flinch his head. The rifle struck the girder behind Fergus and was jerked from Mark's grip, then they came together chest to chest. Mark seized the wrist of his pistol hand and held with all his strength.

Neither of them had recognized the other. Fergus had aged into a grey caricature of himself and his eyes were shaded by the cloth cap. Mark was in unfamiliar uniform, dusty and bloodied, and he had changed also, youth had become man.

Mark was taller, but they were matched in weight and Fergus was endowed with the terrible fighting rage of the berserker which gave him superhuman strength.

He drove Mark back against the guardrail, and bowed his back out over the open shaft, but Mark still had his pistol wrist, and the weapon was pointed up over his head.

Fergus was sobbing wildly, driving with all the wiry uncanny strength of a body tempered by hard physical work, and fired now by the strength of anger and sorrow and despair.

Mark felt his feet slip, the hob-nails of his boots skidding on the steel steps and he went over further, feeling the mesmeric suck of a thousand feet of open space plucking at his back.

Above them, Helena screamed again, and the sound drove like a needle into the base of Fergus' brain; he shuddered, and his body convulsed in one great rigid spasm that Mark could not hope to hold. He went backwards over the guardrail, but still he had his grip on Fergus's gun hand and his other arm he had wound about his shoulders.

They slid into the void, locked together in a horrible parody of a lovers' embrace, but as they started to fall, Mark hooked both legs over the rail, like a trapeze artiste, and jerked to a halt, hanging upside down into the shaft.

Fergus was somersaulted over him by the force of his own thrust; as he turned in the air, the cloth cap flew from his head and he was torn from the arm that Mark had around his shoulder.

He came up with a jerk that almost tore Mark's shoulder from its socket, for some animal instinct had kept Mark's grip locked on the pistol hand, and he dangled from that precarious hold.

The two of them pendulumed out over the black emptiness of the shaft, Mark's legs hooked over the rail, hanging at full stretch, with Fergus' body the next link in the chain.

Fergus' head was thrown back, staring up at Mark, and with the cap gone, his lank sandy hair fell back from his face and Mark felt fresh shock loosen his grip.

'Fergus!' he croaked, but the madman's eyes that stared back at him were devoid of recognition.

'Try and get a grip,' Mark pleaded, swinging Fergus towards the staircase. 'Grab the rail.'

He knew he could not hold many seconds longer, the fall had wrenched and weakened his arm, and the blood was rushing to his head in this inverted position, he could feel his face swelling and suffusing and the pounding ache in his temples – while the black and hungry mouth of the shaft sickened him; with his other hand he groped and got a second hold on Fergus' wrist.

Fergus twisted in his grip, but instead of going for the rail he reached upwards and took the pistol from his own hand, transferring it to his free hand.

'No,' Mark shouted at him. 'Fergus, it's me! It's me, Mark!'

But Fergus was far past all reason, as he juggled with the Webley, getting a firing grip on the hilt with his left hand.

'Kill them,' he muttered. 'Kill all the scabs.'

He lifted the barrel to aim upwards at Mark, dangling over the drop, twisting slowly in that double retaining grip.

'No, Fergus!' screamed Mark, and the muzzle of the revolver pointed into his face. At that range, it would tear half his head away, and he saw Fergus' forefinger tighten on the trigger, the knuckle whitening under pressure.

He opened his hands and Fergus' wrist slipped from his fingers.

He spun away, falling swiftly, and the revolver never fired but Fergus began to scream a high thin wail.

Still hanging upside down Mark watched Fergus' body, limbs spread and turning like the spokes of a wheel, as it dropped away, shrinking rapidly in size, and the despairing wailing cry receding with it, dwindling away to a small pale speck, like a dust mote which was swallowed abruptly into the dark mouth of the shaft far below and the wailing cry with it.

In the silence afterwards, Mark hung batlike, blinking the sweat out of his eyes and for many seconds unable to find strength to move. Then from the platform above him came a long shuddering moan and it roused him.

Forcing his bruised body to respond, he managed to get a grip on the guardrail and drag himself up, until he tumbled on to the staircase, and started up it on rubbery legs.

Helena had dragged herself to the pile of timber, leaving a dark wet smear across the platform. The khaki breeches she wore were sodden with blood and it oozed from her still to form a spreading puddle in which she sat.

She lay back against the timber next to the tripoded Vickers in an attitude of utter weariness, and her eyes were closed.

'Helena,' Mark called her, and she opened her eyes.

'Mark,' she whispered, but she did not seem surprised. It was almost as though she expected him. Her face was completely drained of all colour, the lips seemed rimed with frost, and her skin had an icy sheen to it. 'Why did you leave me?' she asked.

Hesitantly, he crossed to her. He knelt beside her, looked down at her lower body and felt the scalding flood of vomit rise into his throat.

'I truly loved you,' her voice was so light, breathing soft as the dawn wind in the desert, 'and you went away.'

He put out his hand to touch her legs, to spread them and examine the wound, but he could not bring himself to do it.

'You won't go away again, Mark?' she asked, and he

could hardly catch the words. 'I knew you'd come back to me.'

'I won't go away again,' he promised, not recognizing his own voice, and the smile flickered on her icy lips.

'Hold me, please Mark. I don't want to die alone.'

Awkwardly, he put an arm around her shoulders and her head lolled sideways against him.

'Did you ever love me, Mark, even a little bit?'

'Yes, I loved you,' he told her, and the lie came easily. Suddenly there was a hissing spurt of brighter redder blood from between her thighs as the damaged artery erupted. She stiffened, her eyes flew wide open, and then her body seemed to melt against him and her head dropped back.

Her eyes were still wide open and dark as a midnight sky. As he stared at it, slowly her face changed. It seemed to melt like white candle wax held too close to the flame, it ran and wavered and reformed – and now it was the face of a marble angel, smooth and white and strangely beautiful, the face of a dead boy in a land far away – and the fabric of Mark's mind pulled and tore.

He began to scream, but no sound came from his throat – the scream was deep down in his soul, and his face was without expression, his eyes dry of tears.

They found him like that an hour later. When the first soldiers climbed cautiously up the iron staircase to the top of the steel tower, he was sitting quietly, holding the woman's dead body in his arms.

'Well,' said Sean Courtney, 'they've hanged Taffy Long!' He folded the newspaper with an angry gesture and dropped it on to the paving beside his chair.

In the dark shiny foliage of the loquat tree that spread

above them, the little white-eyes pinkled and twittered as they probed the blossoms with sharp busy beaks and their wings fluttered like moths about the candle.

Nobody at the breakfast table spoke. All of them knew how Sean had fought for leniency for those strikers on whom the death sentence had been passed. He had used all his influence and power, but it had not availed against the vindictive and vengeful who wanted full measure of retribution for all the horrors of the revolt. Sean brooded now at the head of the table, hunched in his chair with his beard on his chest, staring out over the Ladyburg valley. His arm was still supported by the linen sling; it had not healed cleanly and the bullet wound was still open and draining. The doctors were anxious about it, but Sean had told them, 'Leopard, and bullet and shrapnel and knife – I've had them all before. Don't twist a gut for me. Old meat heals slowly, but it heals hard.'

Ruth Courtney watching him now was not worried about the wounds of the flesh. It was the wounds of the mind that concerned her.

Both the men of her household had come back deeply marked by the lash of guilt and sorrow. She was not sure what had happened during those dark days, for neither man had spoken about it, but the horror of it still stalked even here at Lion Kop, even in the bright soft days, on these lovely dreaming hills where she had brought them to heal and rest.

This was the special place, the centre and fortress of their lives, where Sean had brought her as his bride. They owned other great houses, but this was home, and she had brought Sean here now after the strife and the turmoil. But the guilt and the horror had come with them.

'Madness,' muttered Sean. 'Utter raving madness. How they cannot see it, I do not know.' He shook his head, and was silent a moment. Then he sighed. 'We hang them now

– and make them live for ever. They'll haunt and hound us all our days.'

'You tried, dear,' said Ruth softly.

'Trying isn't enough,' he growled. 'In the long run, all that counts is succeeding.'

'Oh Pater, they killed hundreds of people,' Storm burst out, shaking her shining head at him, with angry colour in her cheeks. 'They even tried to kill you!'

Mark had not spoken since the meal began, but now he lifted his head and looked at Storm across the table. She checked the other words that sprang to her lips as she saw his expression.

He had changed so much since he had come home. It was as though he had aged a hundred years. Though there was no new line or mark on his face, yet he seemed to have shed all his youth and taken upon himself the full burden of knowledge and earthly experience.

When he looked at her like that, she felt like a child. It was not a feeling she relished. She wanted to pierce this new armour of remoteness that invested him.

'They're just common murderers,' she said, addressing the words not to her father.

'We are all murderers,' Mark answered quietly, and though his face was still remote, the knife clattered against his plate as he put it down.

'Will you excuse me, please, Mrs Courtney—' he turned to Ruth, and she frowned quickly.

'Oh Mark, you've not touched your food.'

'I'm riding into the village this morning.'

'You ate no dinner last night.'

'I want the mail to catch the noon train.' He folded his napkin, rose quickly and strode away across the lawn – and Ruth watched the tall, graceful figure go with a helpless shrug before turning to Sean.

'He's wound up so tight – like a watch spring about to snap,' she said. 'What's happening to him, Sean?'

Sean shook his head. 'It's something that nobody under-stands,' he explained. 'We had so much of it in the trenches. It's as though a man can stand just so much pressure, and then something breaks inside him. We called it shell-shock, for want of a better name, but it's not just the shelling,' he paused. 'I have never told you about Mark before, about why I picked him, about how and when I first met him—' and he told it to them. Sitting in the cool green shade of the loquat tree, he told them of the mud and the fear and the horror of France. 'It's not just for a single time, or a day or a week – but it goes on for what becomes an eternity. But it is worse for a man who has special talents. We, the Generals, have to use them ruthlessly. Mark was one of those—' And he told them how they had used Mark like a hunting dog, and his two women listened intently, all of them bound up in the life of the young man who had gradually come to mean so much to each of them. 'A man gathers horror and fear like a ship gathers weed. It's below the waterline, you cannot see it, but it is there. Mark carries that burden, and at Fordsburg something happened that brought him close to the breaking-point. He is on the very edge of it now.'

'What can we do for him?' asked Ruth softly, watching his face, happy for him that he had a son at last – for she had long known that was what Sean saw in Mark. She loved her husband enough not to resent that it was not her own womb that had given him what he so desperately wanted, glad only that he had it at last, and that she could share it with him.

Sean shook his head. 'I don't know.' And Storm made an angry hissing sound. They both looked at her.

Sean felt that soft warmth spreading through his chest, a feeling of awe that this lovely child could be part of him. Storm looked so smooth and fragile, yet he knew she had the strength of braided whipcord. He knew also that though she had the innocence of a newly opened bloom, yet she could sting like a serpent; she had the brightness and beauty that dazzled, and yet below that were depths that mystified and awed him; and when her moods changed so swiftly, like this unaccountable spurt of anger, he was enchanted by her, under her fairy spell.

He frowned heavily now to hide his feelings.

'Yes, Missy, what is it now?' he grumped at her.

'He's going away,' she said, and Sean blinked at her, swaying back in his chair.

'What are you talking about?' he demanded.

'Mark. He's going away.'

'How do you know that?' Something deep inside of Sean cringed at the prospect of losing another son.

'I know, I just know,' she said, and came to her feet with a flash of long sleek limbs, like a gazelle rising in alarm from its grassy bed. She stood over him.

'You didn't think he would be your lap dog for ever?' she asked, a biting scorn in her tone that at another time would have brought from him a sharp retort. Now he stared at her speechless.

Then suddenly she was gone, crossing the lawn in the sunlight that gilded her loose dark hair with stark white light and struck through the flimsy stuff of her dress, revealing her long slim body in a stark dark silhouette, surrounding her with a shimmering halo of light, that made her seem like some lovely unearthly vision.

'Don't you see that it's better you cry a little now – than cry for the rest of your life?' Mark asked gently, trying not to let her see how the tears had eroded his resolve.

'Won't you ever come back?' Marion Littlejohn was not one of those women who cried well. Her little round face seemed to smear and lose its shape like unfired clay, and her eyes swelled and puffed pinkly.

'Marion, I don't even know where I am going. How can I know if I'm coming back?'

'I don't understand, Mark, I truly don't understand.' She twisted the damp linen handkerchief in her hands, and she sniffed wetly. 'We were so happy. I did everything I knew to make you happy – even that.'

'It's not you, Marion,' Mark assured her hurriedly. He did not want to be reminded of that which Marion always referred to as 'that'. It was as though she had loaned him a treasure which had to be returned with interest at usurious rates.

'Didn't I make you happy, Mark? I tried so hard.'

'Marion, I keep trying to tell you. You are a fine, pretty girl – you're kind and good and the nicest person I know.'

'Then why don't you want to marry me?' Her voice rose into a wail, and Mark glanced with alarm down the length of the porch. He knew that sisters and brothers-in-law were probably straining their hearing for snatches of the conversation.

'It's that I don't want to marry anybody.'

She made a low moaning sound and then blew her nose loudly on the inadequate scrap of sodden linen. Mark took his own handkerchief from his inside pocket, and she accepted it gratefully.

'I don't want to marry anybody, not yet,' he repeated.

'Not yet,' she seized the words. 'But some day?'

'Some day,' he agreed. 'When I have discovered what it is I want out of my life and how I am going to get it.'

'I will wait for you.' She tried to smile, a brave watery pink smile. 'I'll wait for you, Mark.'

'No!' Mark felt alarm flare through every nerve of his body. It had taken all his courage to tell her, and now it seemed that he had achieved nothing. 'God knows how long it will be, Marion. There will be dozens of other men – you're a kind sweet loving person—'

'I'll wait for you,' she repeated firmly, her features regaining their usual pleasant shape, and her shoulders losing their dejected droop.

'Please, Marion. It's not fair on you,' Mark tried desperately to dissuade her, realizing that he had failed dismally. But she gave one last hearty sniff and swallowed what was left of her misery, as though it were a jagged piece of stone. Then she smiled at him, blinking the last tears from her eyes.

'Oh, it doesn't matter. I am a very patient person. You'll see,' she told him comfortably.

'You don't understand,' Mark shrugged with helpless frustration.

'Oh, I do understand, Mark,' she smiled again, but now it was the indulgent smile of a mother for a naughty child. 'When you are ready, you come back here to me.' She stood up and smoothed down the sensible skirts. 'Now come along, they are waiting lunch for us.'

S torm had taken great care choosing her position. She had wanted to catch the play of afternoon light and the run of the clouds across the escarpment, and yet to be able to see into the gorge, for the white plume of falling spray to be the focus of the painting.

She wanted also to be able to see down along the Ladyburg road, and yet not be overlooked by a casual observer.

She placed her easel on the lip of a small saucer of folded ground near the eastern boundary peg of Lion Kop, positioning both easel and herself with an artist's eye for aesthetic detail. But when she posed on the lip of the saucer, with the palette cradled in the crook of her left arm and the brush in the other, she lifted her chin and looked up at the powerful sweep of land and forest and sky, at the way the light was working and at the golden-tinged turquoise of the sky – and immediately she was intrigued.

The pose was no longer theatrical, and she began to work, tilting her head to appraise a colour mix, moving about the canvas in a slow ritual, like a temple maid making the sacrifice, so completely absorbed that when she heard the faint putter of Mark's motorcycle, it did not penetrate into the silken cocoon of concentration she had woven about herself.

Although her original intention in coming to this place had been to waylay him, now he was almost past before she was aware of him, and she paused with the brush held high in one hand, caught in the soft golden light of late afternoon, a much more striking picture than she could have composed with studied care.

The dusty strip of road snaked five hundred feet below where she stood, making its first big loop on to the slope of the escarpment, and, as he came into the bend, Mark's eyes were drawn naturally to the small delicate figure on the slope.

There were clouds along the summit of the escarpment, and the late sun burned through the gaps, cutting long shimmering beams across the valley, and one of these fell full on Storm.

She stood completely still, staring down the slope at him, making no gesture of recognition or welcome.

He pulled the big machine into the side of the road, and sat astraddle, pushing the goggles on to his forehead.

Still she did not move, and they stared at each other. Mark made a move at last as though to restart the machine, and Storm felt a shock of deprivation, although it did not show either on her face nor in the stillness of her body.

She exerted all her will, trying consciously to reach him with mind, and he paused and looked up at her again.

'Come!' she willed him, and with an impatient, almost defiant gesture, he pulled the goggles off his head and stripped the gloves off his hands.

Serenely, she turned back to the painting, a small secret smile playing like light across her softly parted lips and she did not watch him climbing up through the yellow knee-high grass.

She heard his breathing behind her, and she smelled him. He had a special smell that she had learned to know, a floury smell a little like a suckling puppy or freshly polished leather. It made her skin feel hot and sensitized, and put a painful little catch in her breathing.

'That's beautiful,' he said, and his voice felt like the touch of fingers along the nape of her neck. She felt the fine soft hair there rise, and the flush of blood spread warmly down her chest and turn her nipples into hard little pebbles. They ached with something which was not pain – something more obsessive. She wanted him to touch her there, and at the thought she felt her legs tremble under her and the muscles cramped deeply in the wedge of her thighs.

'It's truly beautiful,' he said again, and he was so close she could feel his breath stir the fine hair of her neck, and another thrill ran down her spine, this time it was like a claw cutting through her flesh and she clenched her buttocks to ride the shock of it as though she was astride a mettlesome horse.

She stared at the painting, and she saw that he was right. It was beautiful, even though it was half-finished. She could see the rest of it in her mind – and it was beautiful and right, but she wanted the touch of his hands now.

It was as though the painting had heightened her emotional response, opened some last forbidden door and now she wanted his touch with a terribly deep physical ache.

She turned to him, and he was so close and tall that she felt her breathing catch again, and she looked up into his face.

'Touch me,' she willed him. 'Touch me,' she commanded silently, but his hands hung at his side and she could not fathom his eyes.

She could not stand still a moment longer, and she stirred her hips in a slow voluptuous gesture; something was melting and burning deep in her lower body.

'Touch me,' she tried to force him silently to her will. 'Touch me there where it hurts so fiercely.'

But he did not heed her, would not respond to all her silent pleas, and suddenly she was angry.

She wanted to lash out at him, to strike him across that solemn handsome face, she had a mental image of ripping his shirt away and sinking her nails deep into the smoothly muscled chest. She stared now at the vee of his open shirt, at the coils of dark hair, and his skin had an oiled gloss gilded by the sun to warm golden brown.

Her anger flared and focused. He had aroused these surging emotions which she could neither understand nor control, these heady terrifying waves of physical arousal, and she wanted to punish him for it, to make him suffer, to have him mauled by his desires as she was; at the same instant in time, she wanted to take that splendid proud head of his and hold it to her bosom like a mother holds her child, she wanted to cherish, and gentle and love him, and claw and ravage and hurt him, and she was confused and giddy and angry and puzzled – but most of all she was racing high on a wave of physical excitement that turned her birdlike and quick and vital.

'I suppose you've been bouncing about on that fat little trollop of yours,' she almost snarled it at him. Immediately the hurt and shock showed in his eyes, and she was pleased and savagely triumphant, but also aching with contrition, wanting to fall at his feet and plead for forgiveness, or to lash out with her nails and raise deep bleeding lines across that smooth brown dearly beloved face.

'Wouldn't it have been wonderful if the providence that gave you your beauty and your talent had thought to make you a nice person at the same time,' he said quietly, almost sadly. 'Instead of a vicious spoiled little brat.'

She gasped with the delicious profane shock of it, the insult gave her cause to discard the last vestige of control. Now she could loose the rein and use lash and spur without restraint.

'Oh you swine!' she flew at him, going for his eyes, knowing he was too quick and strong for her, but forcing violent physical contact on him, forcing him to seize her, and when he held her powerless by both arms, she flung her body against his, driving him back a pace, and she saw the surprise on his face. He had not expected such strength. She turned against him, her body fined and tuned and hardened by physical exercise on the courts and in the saddle, forcing him off balance, and, as he shifted his weight from foot to foot, she hooked one ankle with hers and threw her weight in the opposite direction.

They fell together, tumbling backwards into the grassy saucer of ground, and he released her wrists, using both hands to break their fall and cushion her shock as she landed on her back.

Instantly she was at him with both hands, and her nails stung his neck. He grunted and she saw the first flare of real anger in his eyes. It delighted her, and when he seized her wrist, she twisted and bit him in the hard sinewy muscle of his forearm. Hard enough to break the skin, and leave a double crescent of small neat teeth-marks.

He gasped and his anger mounted as he rolled over her, pinning her lower body with one leg as he fought to hold her flying flailing hands.

She bucked under him, her skirts pulled up to her waist, one slim smooth thigh thrusting up, natural, untutored, cunning, into his groin, not hard enough to injure him, but enough to make him suddenly conscious of his own arousal.

As he realized what was happening, his grip of her arms slackened and he tried desperately to disengage, but one of her arms slid around his neck and the silken warmth of her cheek was pressed to his.

His hands acted without command, running down the deep groove in the centre of her arched back, following the small hard knuckles of her spine to the rounded divide of her buttocks, felt through the glossy slipperiness of silken underwear.

Her breathing rasped hoarsely as sandpaper, and she shifted her head and her mouth joined his, arching her back and lifting her lower body to let her silk underwear come away freely in his hands.

The waxen fork of her body rose out of the bright disordered petals of her skirts like the stamen of some wondrously exotic orchid; its flowing perfection interrupted only by the deep finely sculptured pit in the centre of the perfect plain of her belly, and below that the shockingly abrupt explosion of dark smoky curls, a fat deep wedge that changed shape as she relaxed in a slow voluptuous movement.

'Oh Mark,' she breathed. 'Oh Mark, I can't stand it.' Her anger had all evaporated, she was soft and breathless, slowly entwining, warm and gentle and loving, but the sound of her voice woke him suddenly to reality. He realized the betrayal of the trust placed in him by Sean Courtney, the abuse of a privileged position, and he pulled away from her, appalled at his own treachery.

'I must be mad,' he gasped with horror, and tried to roll away from her. Her response was instantaneous, the instinctive reaction of a deprived lioness, that uncanny ability to go from soft purring repose to dangerous blazing anger in the smallest part of a second.

Her open hand cracked across his face, in an explosion of brilliant Catherine wheels of colour that starred his vision, and she screamed at him.

'What kind of a man are you?'

She tried to strike him again, but he was ready for her and they rolled together chest to chest in the grass.

'You're a nothing, and you'll stay like that because you haven't the guts and the strength to be anything else,' she hissed at him, and the words hurt a thousand times worse than the blow. His own anger flared to match hers and he came up over her.

'Damn you. How dare you say that!'

She shouted back at him. 'At least I dare, you wouldn't dare—' But she broke off then as she felt it happen, then she cried out again but in a different voice.

'Oh God!' Her whole body racked as she locked him to her, enfolding and holding him while she purred and murmured with a voice gone low and husky and victorious.

'Oh Mark, oh darling, darling Mark.'

Sean Courtney sat his horse with the slumping comfortable seat of the African horseman. Long stirrups and legs thrust forward, sitting well back on his mount, sjambok trailing from his left hand and reins held low on the pommel of the saddle.

In the shade of the leadwood tree, his stallion stood with the patience of a trained gun horse, its weight braced on three legs and the fourth cocked at rest, neck stretched against the reins as it reached to crop the fine sweet grass that covered the upper slopes of the escarpment, its teeth making a harsh tearing sound with each mouthful.

Sean looked out across the spreading forests and grassland below him, and realized how much it had all changed since he had run across it barefooted with his hunting dogs and throwing sticks, a small boisterous child.

Four or five miles away, nestled against the protective wall of the escarpment, was the homestead of Theunis Kraal, where he had been born in the old brass bedstead in the front room, both he and Garrick, his twin brother, in the course of a single sweltering summer morning, a double birthing that had killed the mother he had never known. Garrick lived there still, and at last he had found peace and pride among his books and his papers. Sean smiled with affection and sympathy, tinged with ancient guilt – what might his brother have been if one leg had not been shattered by the careless shotgun that Sean had fired? He thrust the thought aside, and instead turned in the saddle to survey his own domain.

The thousands upon thousands of acres that he had planted to timber, and which had given him the foundation of his fortune. From where he sat he could see the sawmills and timber yards adjoining the railway yards down in the town, and once again he felt the warm contentment of a life not thrown to waste, the glow of achievement and endeavour rewarded. He smiled and lit one of the long dark cheroots, striking the match off his boot, adjusting easily to the shifting balance of the horse under him.

A moment longer he indulged this rare moment of self-gratification, almost as though to avoid thinking of the most pressing of his problems.

Then he let his eyes drift away across the spreading rooftops of Ladyburg to that new ungainly structure of steel and galvanized sheet iron that rose tall enough to dwarf any other structure in the valley, even the massive four-storey block of the new Ladyburg Farmers Bank.

The sugar refinery was like some heathen idol, ugly and voracious, crouching at the edge of the neat blocks of planted sugar which stretched away beyond the limit of the eye, carpeting the low rolling hills with waving, moving green that roiled in the wind like the waves of the ocean, planted to feed that eternally hungry structure.

The frown puckered the skin between Sean's eyes at the bridge of his big beaky nose. Where he counted his land in thousands of acres, the man who had once been his son counted his in tens of thousands.

The horse sensed his change of mood and gathered itself, nodding its head extravagantly and skittering a little in the shade, ready to run.

'Easy, boy,' Sean growled at him, and gentled him with a hand on his shoulder.

He waited now for that man, having come early to the rendezvous as was always his way. He liked to be there first and let the other man come to him. It was an old trick, to let the other seem the interloper in established territory, while the waiting man had time to consider and arrange his thoughts, and to study the other as he approached.

He had chosen the place and the time with care. He had not been able to sanction the thought of Dirk Courtney riding on to his land again, and entering his home. The aura of evil that hung around the man was contagious, and he did not want that evil to sully the inner sanctum of his life which was the homestead of Lion Kop. He did not even want him on his land, so he had chosen the one small section of boundary where his land actually bordered on that of Dirk Courtney. It was the only half-mile of any land of Sean's along which he had strung barbed wire.

As a cattleman and horseman, he had an aversion to barbed wire, but still he had strung it between his land and that of Dirk Courtney, and when Dirk had written asking him for this meeting, he had chosen this place where there would be a fence between them.

He had chosen the late afternoon with intent also. The low sun would be behind him and shining into the other man's eyes as he came up the slope of the escarpment.

Now Sean drew the watch from his waistcoat and saw it was one minute before four, the appointed time. He looked down into the valley, and scowled. The slope below him was deserted, and he could follow the full length of the road into town beyond that. Since he had seen young Mark puttering past on his motorcycle half an hour before, the road also had been deserted.

He looked beyond the town to the flash of the white walls of the grand mansion that Dirk Courtney had built when first he returned to the valley. Great Longwood, a pretentious name for a pretentious building.

Sean did not like to look at it. To him it seemed that the same aura of evil shimmered about it, even in the daylight an almost palpable thing, and he had heard the stories – they had been repeated to him with glee by the gossipmongers – about what happened up there under the cover of night.

He believed those stories, or he knew with the deep instinct which had once been love, the man who had once been his son.

He looked again at the watch in his hand, and scowled at it. It was four o'clock. He shook the watch and held it to his ear. It ticked stolidly, and he slipped it back into his pocket and gathered the reins. He wasn't coming, and Sean felt a sneaking coward's relief, because he found any meeting with Dirk Courtney draining and exhausting.

'Good afternoon, Father.' The voice startled him, so that he gripped the horse with his knees and jerked the reins. The stallion pranced and circled, tossing his head.

Dirk sat easily on a golden red bay. He had come down out of the nearest edge of the forest, walking his mount carefully and silently over the thick mattress of fallen leaves.

'You're late,' growled Sean. 'I was just leaving.' Dirk must have circled out, climbing the escarpment below the falls on to Lion Kop, avoiding the fence and riding up through the plantations to come to the rendezvous from the opposite direction. Probably he had been sitting among the trees watching Sean for the last half hour.

'What did you want to speak to me about?' He must never again underestimate this man. Sean had done so many times before, each time at terrible cost.

'I think you know,' Dirk smiled at him, and Sean was reminded of some beautiful glossy and deadly dangerous animal. He sat his horse with a casual grace, at rest but in complete control – and he was dressed in a hunting-jacket of finely woven thorn-proof tweed, with a yellow silk cravat at the throat; his long powerful legs were encased in polished chocolate leather.

'Remind me,' invited Sean, consciously hardening himself against the fatal mesmeric charm that the man could project at will.

'Oh come now, I know you have been busy thrashing the sweating unwashed hordes back into their places. I read with pride of your efforts, Father. Your butcher's bill at Fordsburg was almost as fearsome as when you put down Bombata's rebellion back in 1906. Magnificent stuff—'

'Get on with it.' Sean found himself hating again. Dirk Courtney had a high skill at finding weakness or guilt, and exploiting it mercilessly. When he spoke like this of the manner in which Sean had been forced to discharge his duty, it shamed him more painfully than ever.

'Of course it was necessary to get the mines operating again. You do sell most of your timber to the gold mines, I have the exact sales figures somewhere.' Dirk laughed lightly. His teeth were perfect and white, and the sunlight played in the shining curls of his big handsome head, backlighting him and making his looks more theatrically magnificent. 'Good on you, dear Papa. You always had a keen eye for the main chance. No future in letting a bunch of wild-eyed reds put us all out of business. Even I am utterly dependent on the gold mines in the long run.'

Sean could not bring himself to answer, his anger was choking him. He felt dirtied and ashamed.

'It's one of the many things for which I'm indebted to you,' Dirk went on, watching him carefully, smiling and urbane and deadly. 'I am your heir, I have inherited from you the ability to recognize opportunity and to seize it. Do you recall teaching me how to take a snake, how to pin it and hold it with thumb and forefinger at the back of the neck?'

Sean remembered the incident suddenly and vividly. The fearlessness of the child had frightened him even then.

'I see you do remember.' The smile faded from Dirk's face, the lightness of his manner was gone with it. 'So much, so many little things – do you remember when we were lost after the lions stampeded the horses in the night?'

Sean had forgotten that also. Hunting in Mopani country, the child's first overnight away from the security and safety of the wagons. A little adventure that had turned into nightmare, one horse killed by the lions and the other gone, and a fifty-mile walk back through dry sandveld and thick trackless bush.

'You showed me how to find water. The puddle in the hollow tree – I can still taste the stink of it. The bushmen wells in the sand, sucking it up with a hollow straw.'

It all came back, though Sean tried to shut his mind against it. They had gone wrong on the third day, mistaking one small dry stony river bed for another and wandering away into the wilderness to a lingering death.

'I remember you made a sling from your cartridge belt, and carried me on your hip.'

When the child's strength had gone, Sean had carried him, mile after mile, day after day in the thick dragging sand. When finally his own great strength had been expended also, he had crouched down over the child, shielding him from the sun with his shadow, and had worked his swollen tongue painfully for each drop of saliva to inject into Dirk's cracked and blackening mouth, keeping him alive just long enough.

'When Mbejane came at last, you wept.'

The stampeded horse had reached the wagons with the lion's claw-marks slashed deeply across its rump. The old Zulu gunbearer, himself sick with malaria, had saddled the grey and taken a pack horse on the lead rein. He had backtracked the loose horse to the lion camp, and then picked up the spoor of man and child, following them for four days along a cold wind-spoiled spoor.

When he reached them, they were huddled together in the sand, under the sun – waiting for death.

'It was the only time in my life I ever saw you cry,' Dirk said softly. 'But did you ever think how often you made me weep?'

Sean did not want to listen longer. He did not want to be further reminded of that lovely, headstrong, wild and beloved child who he had reared as mother and father together, yet Dirk's quiet insidious voice held him captive in a web of memory from which he could not escape.

'Will you ever know how I worshipped you? How my whole life was based on you, how I mimicked every action, how I tried to become you?'

Sean shook his head, trying to deny it, to reject it.

'Yes, I tried to become you. Perhaps I succeeded—'

'No.' Sean's voice was strangled and thick.

'Perhaps that's why you rejected me,' Dirk told him. 'You saw in me the mirror-image of yourself, and you could not bring yourself to accept that. So you turned me away, and left me to weep.'

'No. God, no – that's not true. It was not that way at all.'

Dirk swung his horse in until his leg touched Sean's.

'Father, we are the same person, we are one – won't you admit that I am you, just as surely as I fell from your loins, just as surely as you trained and moulded me?'

'Dirk,' Sean started, but there were no words now, his whole existence had been touched and shaken at its very core.

'Don't you realize that every thing I have ever done was for you? Not only as a child, but as a youth and a man. Did you never think why I came back here to Ladyburg, when I could have gone to any other place in the world – London, Paris, New York – it was all open to me. Yet I came back here. Why, Father, why did I do that?'

Sean shook his head, unable to answer, staring at this beautiful stranger, with his vital strength and his compelling disturbing presence.

'I came back because you were here.'

They were both silent then, holding each other's eyes in a struggle of wills and a turmoil of conflicting emotions. Sean felt his resolve weakening, felt himself sliding slowly under the spell that Dirk was weaving about him. He heeled his horse, forcing it to wheel and break the physical contact of their legs, but Dirk went on remorselessly.

'As a sign of my love, of this love that has been strong enough to stand against all your abuse, against the denials you have made, against every blow you have dealt it – as a sign of that, I come to you now – and I hold out my hand to you. Be my father again, and let me be your son. Let us put our fortunes together and build an empire. There is a land here, a whole land, ripe and ready for us to take.'

Dirk reached out across the space between the horses with his right hand, palm upwards, fingers outstretched.

'Take my hand on it, Father,' he urged. 'Nothing will stop us. Together we will sweep the world from our path, together we will become gods.'

'Dirk,' Sean found his voice, as he fought himself out of the coils in which he had been trapped. 'I have known many men, and not one of them was all good nor completely evil. They were all combinations of those two elements, good and evil – that is, until I came to know you.

You are the only man who was totally evil, evil unrelieved by the slightest shading of good. When at last I was forced to face that fact, then I turned my back on you.'

'Father.'

'Don't call me that. You are not mine, and you never will be again.'

'There is a great fortune, one of the great fortunes of the world.'

'No,' Sean shook his head. 'It is not there for either you or me. It belongs to a people, to many peoples – Zulu, and Englishman and Afrikander – not to me, but especially not to you.'

'When I came to see you last, you gave me cause to believe,' Dirk began to protest.

'I gave you no cause, I made no promise.'

'I told you everything, all my plans.'

'Yes,' said Sean. 'I wanted to hear it, I wanted to know every detail, not so that I could help you – but so that I could stand in your way.'

Sean paused for emphasis, and then leaned across so his face was close to Dirk's and he could look into his eyes.

'You will never get the land beyond the Bubezi River. I swear that to you.' He said it quietly, but with a force that made every word ring like a cathedral bell.

Dirk recoiled, and the high colour drained away from his face.

'I rejected you because you are evil. I will fight you with all my strength, with my life itself.'

Dirk's features changed, the line of the mouth and the set of the jaw altered, the slant and tilt of the eyes became wolfish.

'You deceive yourself, Father. You and I are one. If I am evil, then you are the source and fountain and father of that evil. Don't spout noble words to me, don't strike postures. I know you, remember. I know you perfectly – as I know myself.' He laughed again, but not the bright easy laughter of before. It was a cruel thin sound and the shape of the mouth did not lose its hard line. 'You rejected me for that Jewish whore of yours, and the bastard slut you spawned on her soft white belly.'

Sean bellowed, a low dull roar of anger, and the stallion reared under him, coming up high on his hindquarters and cutting at the air, and the bay mare swung away in alarm, milling and trampling as Dirk sawed at its mouth with the curb.

'You say you will fight me with your life,' Dirk shouted at his father. 'It may just come to that! I warn you.'

He brought the horse under control, barging in on the stallion so he could shout again.

'No man stands in my way. I will destroy you – as I have destroyed the others who have tried it. I will destroy you and your Jewish whore.'

Sean swung back-handed with the sjambok, a polo cut, using the wrist so the thin black lash of hippo-hide fluted like the wing of a flighting goose. He aimed at the face, at the snarling vicious wolf's head of the man who once had been his son.

Dirk threw up his arm and caught the stroke; it split the woven tweed of his sleeve like a sword cut and bright blood sprang to stain the luxurious cloth, as he kneed the bay away in a wide prancing circle.

He held the wound, pressing the lips of the cut together while he glared at Sean, his face contorted with utter malevolence.

'I'll kill you for that,' he said softly, and then he swung the bay away and put her into a dead gallop, straight at the five-stranded, barbed fence.

The bay went up and stretched at the jump, flying free of earth and then landing again on the far side, neatly gathered and fully in hand, reached out again into a run, a superb piece of horsemanship.

Sean walked the stallion, fighting the temptation to lash

him into a gallop, following the path over the high ground, a path now almost indiscernible, long overgrown. Only a man who knew it well, who had been along it often before, would know it as a path.

There was nothing left of the huts of Mbejane's kraal, except the outline of building stones, white circles in the grass. They had burned the huts, of course, as is the Zulu custom when a chief is dead.

The wall of the cattle kraal was still intact, the stone carefully and lovingly selected, each piece fitted into the shoulder-high structure.

Sean dismounted and tethered the stallion at the gateway. He saw that his hands were still shaking, as though in high fever, and he felt sick to the gut, the aftermath of that wild storm of emotion.

He found his seat on the stone wall, the same flat rock that seemed moulded to his buttocks, and he lit a cheroot. The fragrant smoke calmed the flutter of his heart, and soothed the tremble in his hands.

He looked down at the floor of the kraal. A Zulu chief is buried in the centre of his cattle kraal, sitting upright facing the rising sun, with his induna's ring still on his head, wrapped in the wet skin of a freshly killed ox, the symbol of his wealth, and with his food pot and his beer pot and his snuff box, his shield and his spears at his side, in readiness for the journey.

'Hello, old friend,' said Sean softly. 'We reared him, you and I. Yet he killed you. I do not know how, nor can I prove it, but I know he killed you – and now he's vowed to kill me also.' And his voice quivered.

'Well,' smiled Sean. 'If you have to make an appointment to speak with me, it must be some business of dire consequence.'

Through the merry twinkle of his eye, he was examining Mark with a shrewd assessing gaze. Storm had been right, of course. The lad had been gathering himself to make the break. To go off somewhere on his own, like a wounded animal perhaps, or a cub lion leaving the pride at full growth? Which was it, Sean wondered, and how great a wrench would the parting make on the youngster?

'Yes, sir, you could say that,' Mark agreed, but he could not meet Sean's eyes for once. The usually bright and candid eyes slid past Sean's and went to the books on the shelves, went on to the windows and the sweeping sunlit view across the tops of the plantations and the valley below. He examined it as though he had never seen it before.

'Come on in then.' Sean swivelled his chair away from the desk, and took the steel-rimmed spectacles off his nose and waved with them at the armchair below the window.

'Thank you, sir.'

While he crossed to the chair, Sean rose and went to the stinkwood cabinet.

'If it's something that important, we'd best take a dram to steel ourselves – like going over the top.' He smiled again.

'It's not yet noon,' Mark pointed out. 'That's a rule you taught me yourself.'

'The man who makes the rules is allowed to change them,' said Sean, pouring two huge measures of golden brown spirit, and spurting soda from the siphon. 'That's a rule I've just this moment made,' and he laughed, a fat contented chuckle, before he went on, 'Well, my boy, as it so happens, you have chosen a good day for it.' He carried one glass to Mark, and returned to his desk. 'I also have dire and important business to discuss.'

He took a swallow from his glass, smacked his lips in evident relish, and then wiped his moustaches on the back of his hand.

'As the elder, will it be in order if we discuss my business first?'

'Of course, sir.' Mark looked relieved and sipped cautiously at his glass, while Sean beamed at him with ill-concealed self-satisfaction.

Sean had conceived of a scheme so devious and tailored so fittingly to his need, that he was a little in awe of the divine inspiration which had fostered it. He did not want to lose this young man, and yet he knew that the surest way of doing so was trying to hold him too close.

'While we were in Cape Town I had two long discussions with the Prime Minister,' he began, 'and since then we have exchanged lengthy correspondence. The upshot of all this is that General Smuts has formed a separate portfolio, and placed it under my ministry. It is simply the portfolio of National Parks. There is still legislation to see through Parliament, of course, we will need money and new powers – but I am going ahead right away with a survey and assessment of all proclaimed areas, and we will act on that to develop and protect—' He went on talking for almost fifteen minutes, reading from the Prime Minister's letters and memoranda explaining and expanding, going over the discussions, detailing the planning, while Mark sat forward in his chair, the glass at his side forgotten, listening with a rising sense of destiny at work, hardly daring to breathe as he drank in the great concept that was unfolded for him.

Sean was excited by his own vision, and he sprang up from the desk and paced the yellow wood floor, gesturing, using hands and arms to drive home each point, then stopping suddenly in full flight and turning to stand over Mark.

'General Smuts was impressed with you – that night at Booysens, and before that.' He stopped again, and Mark was so engrossed that he did not see the cunning expression on Sean's face. 'I had no trouble persuading him that you were the man for the job.'

'What job?' Mark demanded eagerly.

'The first area I am concentrating on is Chaka's Gate and the Bubezi valley. Somebody has to go in there and do a survey, so that when we go to Parliament, we know what we are talking about. You know the area well—'

The great silences and peace of the wilderness rushed back to Mark, and he felt himself craving them like a drunkard.

'Of course, once the Bill is through Parliament, I will need a warden to implement the act.'

Mark sank slowly back in his chair. Suddenly the search was over. Like a tall ship that has made its offing, he felt himself come about and settle on true course with the wind standing fair for a fine passage.

'Now, what was it you wanted to talk to me about?' Sean asked genially.

'Nothing,' said Mark softly. 'Nothing at all.' And his face was shining like that of a religious convert at the moment of revelation.


M ark Anders had been a stranger to happiness, true happiness, since his childhood. He was like an innocent discovering strong liquor for the first time, and he was almost entirely unequipped to deal with it.

It induced in him a state of euphoria, a giddy elation that transported him to levels of human experience whose existence he had not previously guessed at.

Sean Courtney had engaged a new secretary to take over Mark's duties from him. He was a prematurely bald, unsmiling little man, who affected a shiny black alpaca jacket, an old-fashioned celluloid butterfly collar, a green eye-shade and cuff-protectors. He was silent, intense and totally efficient, and nobody at Lion Kop dreamed of calling him anything but 'Mr Smathers'.

Mark was to stay on for a further month to instruct Mr Smathers in his new duties, and at the same time Mark was to set his own affairs in order and make the preparations for his move to Chaka's Gate.

Mr Smathers' inhuman efficiency was such that within a week Mark found himself relieved almost completely of his previous duties, and with time to gloat over his new happiness.

Only now that it had been given to him did he realize how those tall stone portals of Chaka's Gate had thrown their shadows across his life, how they had become for him the central towers of his existence, and he longed to be there already, in the silence and the beauty and the peace, building something that would last for ever.

He realized how the recent whirlpool of emotion and action had driven from his mind the duty he had set himself – to find the grave of old Grandfather Anders, and fathom the mystery of his death. It was all now before him, and his life had purpose and direction.

But, this was only the foundation and base of his happiness, from which he could launch himself into the towering heady heights of his love.

True enchantment had sprung from that incredible moment in the grassy saucer on the slopes of the Ladyburg escarpment.

His love, which he had borne secretly, a burden cold and heavy as a stone, had in a single magical instant burst open, flowering like a seed into a growth of such vigour and colour and beauty and excitement, that he could not yet grasp it all.

He and Storm cherished it so dearly that no other must even guess at its existence. They made elaborate plans and pacts, weaved marvellously involved subterfuges about themselves to protect this wondrous treasure of theirs.

They neither spoke to each other, nor even looked at the other in the presence of a third party and the restraint taxed each of them so that the moment they were alone together they fell ravenously each upon the other.

When they were not alone together, they spent most of their time planning and scheming how to be so.

They wrote each other flaming notes which were passed under the table in the presence of Sean and Ruth and should have seared the fingers that touched them. They developed codes and signs, they found secret places, and they took hideous chances. Danger spiced their already piquant banquet of love and delight, and they were both insatiable.

At first, they rode to hidden places in the forest along separate and convoluted pathways and galloped the last mile, arriving breathless and laughing, embracing, still in the saddle while the horses stamped and snorted. The first time they were still locked together when they tumbled from the saddles to the forest bed of dead leaves and ferns, and they left their horses loose. It had been a long walk home, especially as they clung to each other like drunkards, laughing and giggling all the way. Luckily their horses had found a field of lucerne before they reached the homestead, and their riderless return had not alerted the grooms. Their secret remained intact, and after that they wasted a few seconds of their precious time together while Mark hobbled the horses.

Soon it was not enough to have only a stolen hour in the day and they met in Storm's studio. Mark climbed the banyan tree, crawling out along the branch, while Storm held the window open and squealed softly with horror when his foot slipped, or hissed a warning when a servant passed, then clapped her hands and flung her arms around his neck as he came in over the sill.

The studio was furnished with a single wooden chair, the floor was bare and hard, and the danger of sudden intrusion too great for even them to ignore. However, they were undaunted and inventive, and they found almost immediately that Mark was strong enough and she was light enough and that all things are possible.

Once Mark became unsteady at the scorching noonday of their loving and backed her into one of her own unfinished masterpieces. Afterwards, she knelt on the wooden chair holding her skirts to her waist and elevated her perfect little round stern while Mark removed the smudges of burnt umber and prussian blue with a rag moistened with turpentine. Storm was shaking so violently with suppressed laughter that Mark's task was much complicated. She was also blushing so furiously that even her bottom glowed a divine ethereal pink, and for ever afterwards, the smell of turpentine acted on Mark as a powerful aphrodisiac.

On another terrifying occasion, there was the heavy tramp, and the unmistakable limping drag in the passageway beyond the studio door, and they were frozen and ashen-faced, unable to breathe as they listened to its approach.

The peremptory knock on the door almost panicked her and she stared into Mark's face with huge terrified eyes. He took control instantly, realizing just how terrible was the danger. Sean Courtney, faced with the sight of somebody actually tupping his ewe lamb, was fully capable of destroying both them and himself.

The knock came again, impatient, demanding, and Mark whispered quickly as they adjusted their clothing with frantic hands. She responded bravely, though her voice caught and quavered.

'One moment, Daddy.'

Mark seized her paint-stained smock and slipped it over

her head, grabbed a brush from the pot and put it in her right hand, squeezed her shoulders to brace her, and then pushed her gently towards the door.

There was just enough space between the wall and a canvas for him to crawl in and crouch, trying to still his breathing, while he listened to Storm shoot the door-bolt and greet her father.

'Locking the door now, Missy?' Sean growled at her, throwing a suspicious glance around the bare studio. 'Intruding, am I?'

'Never, Pater, not you!'

And they were into the room, Storm following meekly, while Sean gave critical judgement of her work.

'There isn't a tree on Wagon Hill.'

'I'm not taking photographs, Daddy. There should be a tree there. It balances the composition. Don't you see?' She had recovered like a champion and Mark loved her to the point of pain.

Mark was emboldened enough to take a cautious glance around the edge of the canvas, and the first thing he saw was a five-guinea pair of cami-knickers in sheer oyster silk, the wide legs cuffed with ivory cambrai lace, lying crumpled and abandoned on the studio floor where Storm had dropped them earlier.

He felt a cold sheen of sweat break out afresh across his brow; on the bare floor, the lovely silk was as conspicuous as a battle ensign. He tried to reach that blatantly sinful little pile, but it was beyond his finger-tips.

Storm was hanging on to her father's arm, probably because her legs were too weak to support her, and she saw what Mark's desperate arm and groping hand protruding from behind the canvas was trying to reach. Her panic flooded back again at high spring tide.

She gabbled meaningless replies to her father's questions and tried to lead him towards the door, but it was like trying to divert a bull elephant from his set purpose. Inexorably Sean bore down upon the discarded knickers and the canvas where Mark cowered.

At his next step, the silk wrapped itself around the toe of his boot. The material was so filmy and light that he did not notice it, and he limped on happily, one foot draped in an exotic piece of feminine underwear, while two young people watched in abject terror the knickers' slow circuit of the room.

At the door, Storm flung her arms around his neck and kissed him, managing to anchor the knickers with the toe of her shoe, and then propelling her father into the passage with indecent despatch and slamming the door behind him.

Weak with terror and laughter, they clung together in the middle of the studio, and Mark was so chastened that, when he regained his voice, he told her sternly, 'We are not going to take any more chances, do you understand?'

'Yes, master,' she agreed demurely, but with a wicked sparkle in her eye. Mark was awakened a few minutes after midnight with a wet pointed tongue probing deeply into his ear and he would have let out a great shout but a strong little hand was pressed firmly across his mouth.

'Are you mad?' he whispered, as he saw her bending over him in the moonlight from the open window, and realized that she had made the journey across the full length of the house, down cavernous passageways and creaking staircases, in pitch darkness and clad only in a gossamer pair of pyjamas.

'Yes,' she laughed at him. 'I'm mad, completely wonderfully insane, a magnificent noble rage of the mind.'

He was only half awake or he would not have asked the next question. 'What are you doing here?'

'I have come to ravish you,' she said, as she slipped into the bed beside him.

'My feet are cold,' she announced regally. 'Warm them for me.'

'For God's sake, don't make so much noise,' he pleaded, which was a ridiculous request in the circumstances, for only minutes later they were both raising such a chorus of cries that should have woken the entire household.

Long afterwards, she murmured in that special purry feline voice of hers that he had come to know so well.

'You really are an amazingly talented man, Mr Anders. Where ever did you learn to be so utterly depraved?' And then she chuckled sleepily, 'If you tell me, I shall probably claw your eyes out of your head.'

'You mustn't come here again.'

'Why not? It's so much better in bed.'

'What will your father do if he finds out?'

'He'll murder you,' she said comfortably. 'But what on earth has that got to do with it?'

One of the ancillary benefits which accrued to Storm from this relationship was that she had at last a fine male figure model for her work, something which she had always needed but had never found the courage even to ask her father to give her. She knew exactly what his reaction would be.

Mark was not gushing with enthusiasm for the idea either, and it took all her wheedling and cooing to have him disrobe in cold blood. She had picked one of their secret places in the forest for her figure studio, and Mark perched self-consciously on a fallen log.

'Relax,' she pleaded. 'Think beautiful thoughts.'

'I feel such an ass,' he protested, wearing only a pair of striped cotton underpants, at which he had drawn the line, despite her entreaties.

'Anyway, there's nothing under there you could paint on canvas,' he pointed out.

'But that's not the point, you're supposed to be an ancient Greek, and who ever saw an Olympic athlete—'

'No,' Mark cut her short. 'They stay on. That's final.' She sighed at the intransigence of men, and applied herself to her paints and canvas. Slowly he did relax, and even began to enjoy the freedom and the feel of the sunlight and the air on his skin.

He enjoyed watching her work also, the little frown of total concentration, the half-closed eyes, the porcelain white teeth nibbling thoughtfully at her lower lip, the almost dancing ritual of movement she performed around the canvas, and while he watched her he fantasized a future in which they walked hand in hand through the garden wilderness beyond Chaka's Gate. A future bright with happiness, and radiant with shared labour and achievement, and he began to tell her about it, letting his thoughts find expression in words, that Storm did not hear. Her ears were closed, her whole existence transferred into eyes and hands, seeing only colour and form, sensitive only to mood.

She saw the awkwardness and rigidity of his body flowing into a pose of natural grace such as she could never have composed; she saw the rapture dawning on his features, and she nodded and murmured agreement softly, not wanting to spoil it or break the mood; her fingers racing to capture the moment, all her mind and art concentrated on that single task; her own rapture rising to complement and buoy his even higher, seemingly bound close and fast by the silken traces of love and common purpose, but in reality as far from each other as earth is from moon.

'I'll be studying the ground for the exact place to site the homestead,' he told her, 'and it will take a full year to see it all in every season. Good water in the dry, but safe from flood in the rains. The cool sea breeze in summer and protected from the cold weather in winter.'

'Oh yes,' she murmured, 'that's marvellous.' But she was looking at his eyes.

'If only I can capture that fleck of light that makes them shine so,' she thought, and dabbed a touch of blue to the white to mix the shade.

'Two rooms to start. One to sleep and one to live. Of course a wide veranda looking out across the valley.'

'That's wonderful,' she exulted softly, as she touched the eye with the tip of the brush and it came instantly alive, gazing back at her from the canvas with an expression that squeezed her heart.

'I'll quarry the stone from the cliff, but away from the river so there'll be no scar to spoil it, and we'll cut the thatch from the edge of the swamp, and the roof poles from the forest.'

The sun had swung to the west and it filtered down through the forest roof with a cool greenish light that touched the smooth hard muscles of his arm and the sculptured marble of his back, and she saw that he was beautiful.

'We can build on slowly, as we need new rooms. I'll design it that way. When the children come, we can change the living room to a nursery and add a new wing.'

He could almost smell the aromatic shavings of the witels poles, and the sweet perfume of new cut thatch, and in his mind he saw the bright new roof mellowing and darkening in the weather, felt the cool of the high deep rooms at midday, and heard the crackle of the fiercely burning mimosa thorn in the stone fireplace on the cold and starry nights.

'We'll be happy, Storm, I promise you that.' They were the only words she heard – and she lifted her head and looked at him.

'Oh yes. We'll be happy,' she echoed, and they smiled at each other in total misunderstanding.

When Sean had told Ruth Courtney that Mark was leaving, her dismay had alarmed him. Sean had not realized that he had taken such a place in her affections also.

'Oh, no, Sean,' she had protested.

'It's not as bad as it might have been,' he assured her quickly. 'We'll not lose him altogether, it's just that he'll be on a longer rein, that's all. He'll still be working for me, but now only in my official capacity.' And he explained it all to her. She was silent for a long time when he had finished, considering it from every angle before she gave her opinion.

'He'll be good at that, I think,' she nodded at last. 'But I had rather got used to having him around us. I'll miss him.'

Sean grunted what could have been agreement, not able to make such a sentimental admission outright.

'Well,' Ruth went on immediately, her whole attitude becoming businesslike, 'I'll have to get on with it,' which meant that Mark Anders was to be fitted out for his move to Chaka's Gate by one of the world's leading experts. She had sent her man on campaign or on safari so often, that she knew exactly what was necessary, the absolute bare necessity for survival and comfort in the African bush. She knew that anything more than that would not be used, bundles of luxuries would come home untouched, or be abandoned along the way. Yet everything she selected was of the finest quality, for she raided Sean's campaign bag blatantly, justifying each theft with the firm utterance, 'Sean won't be using that again.'

The sleeping roll needed darning, and she made the repair a little work of art. Then she applied herself to the one luxury the pack would contain, books. This choice she and Mark discussed at length, for weight and space made it essential that each book must be able to withstand numerous rereadings. They had a wide selection from which to make their choice, hundreds of battered old volumes, stained by rain and mud, spilled tea and, in more than one case, by splotches of dried blood, and faded by sunlight and age, all of them having been carried great distances in Sean's old canvas book-bag.

Macaulay and Gibbon, Kipling and Tennyson, Shakespeare and even a small leather-bound Bible were given place, after being carefully screened by the selection committee, and Mark, whose previous camping equipment had been limited to a blanket, a pot and a spoon, felt as though he had been given a permanent suite at the Dorchester.

Sean provided the other essentials for the expedition. The 9.3 Mannlicher in its leather case and two mules. They were big rangy animals, both hard workers and of equitable temper, both salted by having been deliberately exposed to the bite of the tsetse fly and surviving the onslaught of the disease that resulted. They had cost Sean dearly for this immunity, but then the nagana had an almost ninety per cent mortality rate. Salted animals were essential. It would have been less trouble and had the same end result to shoot them between the eyes, rather than take unsalted animals into the fly belt beyond Chaka's Gate.

Each day, Sean set aside an hour or so to discuss with Mark the objects and the priorities of the expedition. They drew up a list, which was added to daily and, as it grew, so did Sean Courtney's enthusiasm. More than once he broke off to shake his head and grumble. 'You lucky blighter, what I wouldn't give to be your age again – and to be going back into the bush.'

'You could come and visit me,' Mark smiled.

'I might just do that,' Sean agreed, and then resettled his spectacles on his nose to bring up the next point for discussion.

The first of Mark's tasks was to compile an estimate of what species of wild animal still existed in the proclaimed area, and how many of each there were. Clearly this was of the utmost importance to any attempt at protection and conservation. All would depend on there being sufficient wild-life surviving to make their efforts worthwhile.

'It may already be too late in the afternoon,' Sean pointed out.

'No.' Mark would not even listen to the suggestion. 'There is game there. Just enough to give us a chance. I'm sure of it.'

Next important was for him to contact the people living in the area of Chaka's Gate, the Zulus grazing cattle along the edge of the tsetse fly belt, the native hunters and gatherers living within the belt, each wandering group, each village, each headman, each chief, and hold discussions with them; gauging the attitude of the Zulu peoples to the stricter administration of the proclaimed area, and warning them that what for many years they and their ancestors had looked upon as commonage and tribal hunting-ground was under new control. Men were no longer free to cut timber and thatch, to gather and hunt at will. Mark's intimate knowledge of the Zulu language would serve him well here.

He was to build temporary accommodation for himself, and conduct a survey to choose the final site for a permanent warden's post. There were fifty other tasks less important, but no less demanding.

It was a programme to excite and intrigue Mark, and make him want to begin, and as the day drew nearer, only one cloud lay dark and heavy on the splendid horizon ahead of him. He would be parting from Storm, but he consoled himself with the sure knowledge that it would not be for long. He was going ahead into Eden to prepare a place for his Eve.

As Storm watched him sleep flat on his back, spread like a crucifix on the forest floor, without even the cotton underpants between him and nature, the possessive smile of a mother watching over the child at her breast warmed and softened Storm's lips.

She was naked also, her clothing scattered around them like the petals of an overblown rose, thrown there by the storm winds of passions which were now spent and quiescent. She sat over him cross-legged on the corner of the plaid rug, and she studied his face, wondering at how young he looked in sleep, feeling a choking of tenderness in her throat, and the soft melting after-glow of loving deep in her body where he had been.

She leaned over him, and her breasts swung forward with a new weightiness, the tips darker and wrinkled like small pinky brown raisins. She dipped her shoulders and let the nipples brush lightly across his face, and smiled again as he screwed up his nose and pursed his lips in his sleep, snorting as if to blow away a bothersome fly.

He came awake suddenly and as he reached for her, she squealed softly and plucked her breasts away from him, slapping at his hands.

'Unhand me, sir, this instant!' she commanded, and he caught her and pulled her down on to his chest, so that she could hear his heart beating under her ear.

She snuggled down, making throaty little sounds of comfort. He sighed deeply, and his chest swelled and expanded under her cheek and she heard the air rush into his lungs.

'Mark?' she said.

'I'm here.'

'You're not going. You know that, don't you?'

The air in his lungs stayed there as he held his breath, and the hand that was stroking lightly up from the small of her back to the nape of her neck stilled. She could feel the tension in his fingers.

They stayed like that for many seconds and then he let the air out of his lungs with an explosive grunt.

'What do you mean?' he asked. 'Where am I not going?'

'This place up there in the bush,' she said.

'Chaka's Gate?'

'Yes. You're not going.'

'Why not?'

'Because I forbid it.'

He sat up abruptly, joggling her roughly off his chest.

They sat facing each other, and he was staring at her with such an expression that she ran her fingers through her hair and then folded her arms across her breasts, covering them protectively.

'Storm, what on earth are you talking about?' he demanded.

'I don't want you to waste any more time,' she told him. 'You must start making your way now, if you're ever going to amount to anything.'

'This is my way – our way,' he said, bewildered. 'We agreed on it. I will go up there to Chaka's Gate and build our home.'

'Home!' She was truly appalled. 'Up there in the bush – me in a grass hut? Mark, are you out of your mind!'

'I thought—'

'What you're going to do is start making some money,' she told him fiercely, and, picking up her blouse, she pulled it over her head, and as her tousled head emerged she went on, 'and forget about little boys' games.'

'I'll be making money.' His expression was stiff, and becoming hostile.

'What money?' she asked, just as frostily.

'I'll have a salary.'

'A salary!' She flung back her head and gave a high peal of scornful laughter. 'A salary, forsooth! How much?'

'I don't know,' he admitted. 'It isn't really all that important.'

'You're a child, Mark. Do you know that? A salary,

twenty pounds a week? Can you really and truly imagine me living on your salary?' She gave the word a world of contempt. 'Do you know who earns salaries? Mr Smathers earns a salary,' she was on her feet now, hopping furiously on one leg as she drew on her knickers. 'Daddy's foremen at the saw-mills earn salaries. The servants that wait on the table, the stable-grooms earn salaries.'

She was pulling up her riding breeches, and with them all her dignity.

'Real men don't earn salaries, Mark.' Her voice was high and shrill. 'You know what real men do, don't you?'

He was buttoning the fly of his breeches also, forced to follow her example, and he shook his head silently.

'Real men pay salaries – not take them,' she said. 'Do you know that when my father was your age he was already a millionaire!'

Mark was never able to fathom what it was that triggered him, perhaps the mention of Sean at that particular moment, but suddenly he lost his temper. He felt it like a hot red fog behind his eyes.

'I'm not your bloody father,' he shouted.

'Don't you swear at my father,' she shouted back. 'He's five times the man you'll ever be.'

They were both panting and flushed, clothing rumpled, half-clad, with wild hair and wilder eyes glaring at each other like animals, speechless with hurt and anger.

Storm made the effort. She swallowed painfully, and held out her hands palms upwards.

'Listen, Mark. I've got it all planned. If you went into timber, selling to the mines, Daddy would give you the agency and we could live in Johannesburg.'

But Mark's anger was still on him, and his voice was rough and scaly with it.

'Thank you,' he said. 'Then I could spend my life grubbing money for you to buy those ridiculous clothes and—'

'Don't you insult me, Mark Anders,' she blazed.

'I'm me,' Mark told her. 'And that's what I'm going to be the rest of my life. If you loved me, you'd respect that.'

'And if you loved me, you wouldn't want me to live in a grass hut.'

'I love you,' he shouted her down. 'But you'll be my wife and you'll do what I decide.'

'Don't challenge me, Mark Anders. I warn you. Don't ever do that!'

'I'll be your husband,' he began, but she snatched up her boots and ran to her horse, stooping to loose the hobble and then flinging herself on to its back bare-footed, and looked down at him. She was breathless with anger, but she struggled to make her voice icy and cutting.

'Don't take any bets on that!' And she dragged the horse's head around and kicked him into a run.

'Where is Missy?' Sean demanded as he unfolded his napkin and tucked the corner into his waistcoat, glancing at Storm's empty place at the table.

'She's not feeling very well, dear,' Ruth told him, as she began serving the soup, ladling it out of the fat-bellied tureen in a cloud of fragrant steam. 'I allowed her to have her dinner sent up to her room.'

'What's wrong with her?' Sean looked up with concern creasing his forehead.

'It's nothing serious,' said Ruth firmly, closing the door on further discussion. Sean stared at her for a moment, and then understanding dawned.

'Oh!' he said. The functions of the female body had always been shrouded for Sean Courtney in deepest mystery, and awakened in him an abiding awe.

'Oh!' he said again, and leaned forward to blow noisily on a spoonful of soup to cover his embarrassment, and the niggling resentment that his beloved child was a child no longer.

Across the table, Mark applied himself to his spoon with equal determination, but with an empty aching feeling below his ribs.

'Where is Missy tonight?' Sean asked, with what was for him a certain diffidence. 'Still not well?'

'She telephoned Irene Leuchars this morning. Apparently the Leuchars are having a huge party tonight and she wanted to go. She left after lunch. She's driving herself back to Durban in the Cadillac.'

'Where will she stay?' Sean demanded.

'With the Leuchars, naturally.'

'She should have asked me,' Sean frowned.

'You were down at the saw-mills all day, dear. The decision had to be made immediately, or she would have missed the party. I knew you wouldn't mind.'

Sean minded everything that took his daughter away from him, but he could not say so now. 'I thought she hated Irene Leuchars,' he complained.

'That was last month,' said Ruth.

'I thought she was sick,' Sean persisted.

'That was last night.'

'When is she coming home?'

'She may stay in town for the race-meeting at Greyville on Saturday.'

Mark Anders listened with the empty space in his chest turning to a great bottomless void. Storm had gone back to join that close group of rich, indolent and privileged young people, to their endless games and their eternal round of extravagant partying, and on Saturday Mark was leaving with two mules for the wilderness beyond Chaka's Gate.

M ark would never fathom how Dirk Courtney knew. To him it seemed further evidence of the man's power, the tentacles of his influence that reached into every corner and crevice.

'I understand you are to make the survey for the Government, to decide whether it's worth developing the proclaimed area beyond Chaka's Gate?' he asked Mark.

Mark could still hardly believe the fact that he stood unarmed and completely unprotected here at Great Long-wood. His skin tingled with warning of deadly danger, his nerves were drawn like bow-strings, and he walked with exaggerated care, one hand clenched in the hip-pocket of his breeches.

Beside him, Dirk Courtney was tall and courteous and affable. When he turned to make that statement, he smiled, a warm spread of the wide and handsome mouth – and he laid a hand on Mark's upper arm. A light but friendly touch, which shocked Mark as though a mamba had kissed him with its little flickering black tongue.

'How does he know it?' Mark stared at him, his feet slowing, so that he pulled gently away from Dirk's touch.

If Dirk noticed the withdrawal, it did not show in his smile, and he let his hand fall naturally to his side and took the flat silver cigarette-case from his jacket pocket.

'Try one,' he murmured. 'They are made especially for me.'

Mark tasted the incense of the sweetish Turkish tobacco, using the act of lighting the cigarette to cover his uncertainty and surprise. Only Sean Courtney and his close family knew, and of course the Prime Minister's office – the

Prime Minister's office, if that was it, as it seemed it must be, then Dirk Courtney's tentacles stretched far indeed.

'Your silence I must take as confirmation,' Dirk told him, as they came down the paved alleyway between two lines of whitewashed loose boxes. From over the half-doors, the horses stretched out their necks to Dirk and he paused now and then to caress a velvety muzzle with surprisingly gentle fingers, and to murmur an endearment.

'You are a very silent young man.' Dirk smiled that warm endearing smile again. 'I like a man who can keep his own counsel, and respect the privacy of others.' He turned to confront Mark, forcing him to meet his eyes.

Dirk reminded Mark of some glossy cat, one of the big predators, not the tabby domestic variety. The leopard, golden and beautiful and cruel. He wondered at his own courage, or foolhardiness, in coming here right into the leopard's lair. A year ago it might have been suicidal to put himself in this man's hands. Even now, without Sean Courtney's protection, he would never have dared. Yet although it was logical to believe that nobody, not even Dirk Courtney, would dare touch him, now that he was Sean Courtney's protégé with all that that implied, yet prickles of apprehension nettled his spine as he looked into those leopard's eyes.

Dirk took his elbow, not giving him opportunity to avoid the touch, and led him through a gateway to the stud pens.

The two pens were enclosed with ten-foot high pole fences, carefully padded to prevent damage to the expensive animals that would be confined here. The earth within the rectangular enclosures was ankle-deep with fresh saw-dust, and though one was empty, there was a group of four grooms busy in the nearest pen.

Two of them had the mare on a double lead rein. She was a young animal, a deep red bay in colour, and she had the beautiful balanced head of the Arab, wide nostrils which promised great heart and stamina, and strong but delicate bones.

Dirk Courtney placed a booted foot on the bottom rail of the pen, and leaned forward to look at her with a gloating pride.

'She cost me a thousand guineas,' he said, 'and it was a bargain.'

The two other grooms had the stallion in check. An old, heavily built animal, with grey dappling his muzzle. He wore a girdle, strapped under his belly, and up between the hindlegs, a cage like an old-fashioned chastity belt of woven light chain that was called the teaser. It would prevent him effectively covering the mare.

The grooms gave him rein to approach the mare, but the instant she felt his gentle nuzzling touch under her tail, she put her head down and lashed out with both back legs, a murderous hissing cut of hooves that flew within inches of the stallion's head.

He snorted and backed away. Then, undeterred, he closed with her once more, reaching out to touch her flank, running his nose with a gentle lover's touch across the glossy hide, but the mare made her skin shudder wildly, as though she were beset by bees, and she let out a screaming whinny of outrage at the importunate touch on her maidenly virtue. One of the grooms was dragged down on his knees as she flashed at the stallion with terrible yellow teeth, catching him in the neck and ripping open his old dappled hide in a shallow bloody cut before they pulled her off.

'Poor old beggar,' murmured Mark, although the injury was superficial; it was the indignity of the whole business that aroused Mark's sympathy. The old stallion must endure the kicks and bites, until at last the temperamental filly was wooed and willing. Then he would be led away, his work done.

'Never waste sympathy for the losers in this world,' Dirk advised him. 'There are too many of them.'

In the sawdust-covered arena, the filly lifted her tail, the long glossy hairs forming a soft waving plume, and she urinated a sharp spurt that was evidence of her arousal.

The stallion circled her, rolling back his upper lip, exposing his teeth, and his shoulder muscles spasmed violently as he nodded his head vigorously and reached out to her again.

She stood quietly now, with her tail still raised, and trembled at the soft loving touch of his muzzle, ready at last to accept him.

'All right,' Dirk shouted. 'Take him out.' But it required the strength of both grooms to drag his head around and lead him out of the tall gate that Dirk swung open.

'Strangely enough, I don't believe that you are one of this life's losers,' Dirk told Mark easily, as they waited by the gate. 'That is why you are here at this moment. I only trouble myself with a certain type of man. Men with either talent, or strength or vision – or all of those virtues. I believe you may be of that type.'

Mark knew then that all this had been carefully arranged, the meeting with Peter Botes, Marion Littlejohn's brother-in-law, outside the post office in Ladyburg, the urgent summons to Dirk Courtney's estate he had delivered, so there was no opportunity to report to Sean Courtney and discuss the invitation, and now this erotic show of mating horses – all of it planned to confuse and unsettle Mark, to keep him unbalanced.

'I think you are more like this,' Dirk went on, as the grooms led in the stud stallion, an animal too valued to risk damaging by putting to an unwilling female, a tall horse, black as a rook's wing, high-stepping and proud, kicking the soft sawdust with polished hooves, and then coming up hard and trembling on stiff legs as he smelt the waiting mare, and the great black root grew out of his belly, long as a man's arm and as thick, arrogant, and with a flaring head that pulsed with a life of its own and beat impatiently against the stallion's chest.

'The losers toil, and the winners take the spoil,' said Dirk, as the huge beast reared up over the mare. One of the grooms darted forward to guide him, and the mare hunched her back to receive the long gliding penetration.

'The winners and the losers,' he repeated, watching the stallion work with glistening bulging quarters, and Dirk's handsome face was flushed with high colour, and his hands gripped the poles of the fence until the knuckles blanched like marble.

When at last the stallion dropped back off the mare on to four legs, Dirk sighed, took Mark's elbow again and led him away.

'You were present when I spoke with my father of my dream.'

'I was there,' Mark agreed.

'Oh good,' Dirk laughed genially. 'You have a voice – I was beginning to doubt it. But my information is that you have a good brain also.'

Mark glanced at him sharply and Dirk assured him, 'Naturally, I have made it my business to find out all about you. You know certain details of my plans. I must be in a position to protect myself.'

They skirted the ornamental pond, below the homestead, the surface covered with flat lily pads and the smell of their blooms light and sugary in the afternoon heat, and they went on through the formal rose garden, neither of them speaking again until they had entered the high-ceilinged and overfurnished study; Dirk had closed the wooden shutters against the heat, making the room cool and gloomy, and somehow forbidding.

He waved Mark to a chair across from the fireplace and

went to the table on which stood a silver tray of bottles and crystal.

'Drink?' he asked, and Mark shook his head and watched Dirk pour from a black bottle.

'You know my dream,' Dirk spoke, still concentrating on his task. 'What did you think of it?'

'It's a large concept,' Mark said cautiously.

'Large?' Dirk laughed. 'It's not the word I would have chosen.' He saluted Mark with the glass and sipped at it, watching him over the rim.

'Strange how the fates work,' Dirk thought, watching the slim graceful figure. 'Twice I tried to be rid of the nuisance he could have caused me. If I had succeeded, I would not be able to use him now.'

He hitched one leg over the corner of his desk and set the glass aside carefully to leave both hands free, and he gesticulated as he talked.

'We are talking of opening a whole new frontier, a huge step forward for our nation, work for tens of thousands of people, new towns, new harbours, railways – progress.' He spread his hands, a gesture of growth and limitless opportunity. 'That one wonderful word that describes it all – progress! And anybody who tries to stop that is worse than a fool, he's a criminal, a traitor to his country, and should be treated as one. He should be brushed mercilessly aside, by any means that comes to hand.'

He paused now and glowered at Mark. The threat was barely concealed, and Mark stirred restlessly in his chair.

'On the other hand,' Dirk smiled suddenly, like a flooding beam of sunlight bursting through the grey overcast of a storm sky. 'Every man who works towards the fulfilment of this huge concept will be fully entitled to a share of the rewards.'

'What do you want from me?' Mark asked, and the abrupt question caught Dirk with his hands poised and the next flight of oratory on his lips. He let the hands drop to his sides, and watched Mark's face expectantly, as though there was something still to come. 'And what are the rewards you speak of?' Mark went on, and Dirk laughed delightedly, those were the words for which he had been waiting – each man has a coin for which he will work.

'You know what I want from you,' he said.

'Yes, I think I do,' Mark agreed.

'Tell me what I want,' Dirk laughed again.

'You want a report that recommends that the development of the Chaka's Gate proclaimed area as a National Park is not practical.'

'You said it, not me.' Dirk picked up his glass again and lifted it to Mark. 'But, none the less, I'll drink to it.'

'And the rewards?' Mark went on.

'The satisfaction of knowing that you are doing your patriotic duty for the peoples of this nation,' Dirk told him solemnly.

'I had all the satisfaction I need for a lifetime in France,' Mark said softly. 'But I found out you can't eat or drink it,' and Dirk laughed delightedly.

'That really is choice, I must remember it. Are you certain you won't have a drink?'

Mark smiled for the first time. 'Yes, I'll change my mind.'

'Whisky?'

'Please.'

Dirk stood up and went to the silver tray, and he realized that he felt a sneaking relief. If it had proved that this man had no price, as he had started to believe possible, it would have destroyed one of the headstones on which he had based his whole philosophy of life. But it was all right again now. The man had a price, and he felt a sudden contempt and scorn – it would be money, and a paltry sum at that. There was nothing different about this fellow.

He turned back to Mark.

'Here is something you can drink.' He gave him the crystal glass. 'Now let's discuss something you can eat.'

He went back to the desk, slid open one of the drawers, and took out of it a brown manilla envelope, sealed with red wax.

He laid it on the desk-top, and picked up his own glass. 'That contains an earnest of my good will,' he said.

'How earnest?'

'One thousand pounds,' Dirk said. 'Enough to buy a mountain of bread.'

'One of your companies bought a farm from my grandfather,' Mark spoke carefully. 'He had promised that farm to me, and he died without leaving any of the money.'

Dirk's expression had closed suddenly and his eyes were wary and watchful. For a moment he played with the idea of feigning ignorance, but already he had admitted he had investigated Mark thoroughly.

'Yes,' he nodded. 'I know about that. The old man wasted it all away.'

'The price of that farm was three thousand pounds,' Mark went on. 'I feel that I am still owed that money.'

Dirk dropped his hand into the drawer again, and brought out two identical sealed envelopes. He laid them carefully on top of the first envelope.

'By a strange coincidence,' he said. 'I just happen to have that exact amount with me.'

A paltry sum indeed, he smiled his contempt. What had made him suspect that there was something unusual about this man, he wondered. In the desk drawer were seven other identical manilla envelopes, each containing one hundred ten pound notes. He had been prepared to go that high for the report – no, he corrected himself, I would have been prepared to go further, much further.

'Come,' he smiled. 'Here it is.' And he watched Mark Anders rise from the chair and cross the room, pick up the envelopes and slip them into his pocket.

S ean Courtney's beard bristled like the quills on the back of an angry porcupine, and his face turned slowly to the colour of a badly fired brick.

'Good God!' he growled, as he stared at the three envelopes on his desk top. The seals had been carefully split and the contents arranged in three purple blue fans of crisp treasury bills. 'You took his money?'

'Yes, sir,' Mark agreed, standing in front of the desk like a wayward pupil before the head pedagogue.

'Then you have the brass to come to me with it?' Sean made a gesture as though to sweep the piles of bills on to the floor. 'Take the filthy stuff away from me.'

'Your first lesson, General. The money is always important,' Mark said quietly.

'Yes, but what must I do with this?'

'As patron of the Society for the Protection of African Wildlife, your duty would be to send the donor a letter of acceptance and thanks for his generous donation—'

'What on earth are you talking about?' Sean stared at him. 'What society is this?'

'I have just formed it, sir, and elected you patron. I am sure we will be able to draw up a suitable memorandum of objects and rules of membership, but what it boils down to is a campaign to make people aware of what we are going to do, to gather public support—' Mark spoke rapidly, pouring it all out, and Sean listened with the brick colour of his face slowly returning to normal, and a slow but delighted grin pulling his beard out of shape. 'We'll use this money for advertisements in the press to make people aware of their heritage,' Mark raced on, ideas tumbling out of him, and immediately spawning new ideas, while Sean listened, his grin becoming a spasmodic chuckle that shook his shoulders, and then finally a great peal of laughter, that went on for many minutes.

'Enough!' at last he bellowed delightedly. 'Sit down, Mark, that's enough for now.' And he groped for a handkerchief to mop his eyes and blow the great hooked beak of a nose like a trumpet, while he recovered his self-control. 'It's indecent,' he chortled. 'Positively sacrilegious! You have no respect for money at all. It's unnatural.'

'Oh, yes, I have – but money is only a means, not an end, sir,' Mark laughed also, for the General's mirth was contagious.

'My God, Mark. You are a prize, you really are. Where ever did I find you?' He gave one last chuckle, and then grew serious. He drew a clean sheet of paper from the sidedrawer and began to make notes. 'As though I haven't enough work already,' he growled. 'Now let's draw up a list of objects for this bloody society of yours.'

They worked for nearly three hours, and Ruth Courtney had to come and call them to the dinner table.

'In a minute, dear,' Sean told her, and placed a paper-weight on the thick pile of notes he had made; he was about to rise when he frowned at Mark.

'You have chosen a dangerous enemy for yourself, young man,' he warned him.

'Yes, I know,' Mark nodded soberly.

'You say that with feeling.' He stared at Mark question-ingly. Mark hesitated a moment and then he began.

'You know my grandfather, John Anders, you spoke of him once before.' Sean nodded, and sank back into the padded leather chair. 'He had land, eight thousand acres, he called it Andersland—'

Sean nodded again, and Mark went on carefully, telling it all without embellishment, stating the facts, and when he had to guess or make conjecture, stating that it was so. Again Ruth came to call them to dinner, just when Mark was describing the night on the escarpment when the gunmen had come to his camp. She was about to insist they come before the meal spoiled, but then she saw their faces and came silently to stand behind Sean's chair and listen, her face becoming paler and more set.

He told them about Chaka's Gate, how he had searched for his grandfather's grave and the men who had come to hunt him, and when he had finished the story they were all silent, until at last Sean roused himself, sighed – a gusty, sorrowful sound – before he spoke.

'Why didn't you report this?'

'Report what? Who would have believed me?'

'You could have gone to the police.'

'I have not a shred of evidence that points to Dirk Courtney, except my own absolute certainty.' And he dropped his eyes. 'It's such a wild, unlikely story that I was afraid to tell even you, until this moment.'

'Yes,' Sean nodded. 'I can see that. Even now I don't want to believe it is true.'

'I'm sorry,' said Mark simply.

'I know it's true – but I don't want to believe it.' Sean shook his head, and lowered his chin on to his chest. Ruth, standing behind him, placed a comforting hand on his shoulder. 'Oh God, how much more must I suffer for him?' he whispered, then lifted his head again.

'You will be in even greater danger now, Mark.'

'I don't think so, General. I am under your protection, and he knows it.'

'God grant that is enough,' Sean muttered, 'but what can we do against him? How can we stop this – ' Sean paused, seeking the word, and then hissed it savagely, 'this monster?'

'There is no evidence,' Mark said. 'Nothing to use against him. He has been too clever for that by far.'

'There is evidence,' said Sean with complete certainty. 'If all this is true, then there is evidence – somewhere.'

Trojan the mule's broad back felt like a barrel under Mark, and the sun beat through his shirt so that his sweat rose in dark damp patches between his shoulder blades and at his armpits, as he jogged down the bank of the Bubezi with Spartan, the second heavily burdened mule, following him on a lead rein.

In the river bed on one of the sugary white sandbanks, he let the mules wade in knee-deep and begin to drink, sucking up the clear water noisily so that he could feel the animal's belly swelling between his knees.

He pushed his hat on to the back of his head and wiped away the drops from his brow with one thumb as he looked up at the portals of Chaka's Gate. They seemed to fall out of the sky like cascades of stone, sheer and eternal, so vast and solid that they dwarfed the land and the river at their feet.

The double pannier on the back of the lead mule was the less onerous of the burdens that he had brought with him from the teeming reaches of civilization. He had brought also a load of guilt and remorse, the sorrow of a lost love, and the galling of duty left unperformed. But now, beneath the cliffs of Chaka's Gate, he felt his burden lightening, and his shoulders gathering strength.

Something indefinable seemed to reach out to him from across the Bubezi River, a feeling of destiny running its appointed course, or more a sense of home-coming. Yes, he thought, with sudden joy, I am coming home at last.

Abruptly Mark was in a hurry. He pulled up Trojan's reluctant head, with water still pouring from his loose rubbery lips, and kicked him forward into the swirling green eddy of the river, slipping from the saddle to swim beside him when he lost his footing.

As the big soup-plate hooves touched bottom, he threw his leg back across the saddle and rode up the far bank, his breeches clinging to his thighs and his sodden shirt streaming water.

Suddenly, for the first time in a week, and for no good reason, he laughed, a light unstrained burst of laughter that hung about him like a shimmering halo long afterwards.

T he sound was so low, and the hooves of Trojan the grey mule were plugging into the soft earth along the river with a rhythmic chuffing sound, so that Mark was not sure of what he had heard.

He reined Trojan to a stop and listened. The silence was so complete that it seemed to hiss like static, and when a wood dove gave its melodious and melancholy whistle a mile along the river, it seemed close enough to touch.

Mark shook his head, and flicked the reins. At the first hoof fall, the sound came again – and this time there was no mistaking it. The hair down the nape of Mark's neck prickled, and he straightened quickly out of his comfortable saddle slouch. He had heard that sound only once before, but in circumstances that made certain he would never forget it.

It was close, very close, coming from the patch of thick green riverine bush between him and the river, a tangled thicket of wild loquat and hanging lianas, typical cover for the animal that had called.

It was a weird unearthly sound, a fluid sound, almost like liquor poured from the neck of a stone jug – and only one who had heard it before would recognize the distress and warning call of a fully grown leopard.

Mark swung the mule away, and set him lumbering up the rising ground until he reached the spreading shade of a leadwood, where he tethered him and loosened his girth. Then he slipped the Mannlicher out of its scabbard, and quickly checked the loaded magazine; the fat brass cartridges with their copper-jacketed noses were still bright and slick with wax, and he snapped the bolt closed.

He carried the rifle casually in his left hand, for he had no intention at all of using it. Instead he was aware of a pleasurable glow of excitement and anticipation. In the two months of hard riding and walking since his return to Chaka's Gate, this was the first chance he had been given of sighting a leopard.

There were many leopard along the Bubezi, he had seen their sign almost daily, and heard them sawing and coughing in the night. Always the leopard and the kudu are the last to give way before man and his civilization. Their superior cunning and natural stealth protect them long after the other species have succumbed.

Now he had a chance at a sighting. The patch of riverine bush, though dense, was small, and he longed for a sighting, even if just a flash of yellow in deep shade, something concrete, a firm entry in his logbook, another species to add to the growing list of his head count. He circled out cautiously, his eyes flickering from the thick green wall of bush to soft ground at his feet, checking for spoor as well as for actual sight of the yellow cat.

Just above the steep river bank he stopped abruptly, and stared down before going on to one knee to touch the earth.

They weren't leopard tracks, but others he had grown to know and recognize. There was no special distinguishing characteristic, no missing toes, no scarring or deformity, but Mark's trained eye recognized the shape and size, the slight splaying toe-in way the man walked, the length of his stride and a toe-heavy impression, that of a quick alert tread. The distress call of the animal in the thicket made sense now. 'Pungushe,' said Mark quietly. 'The jackal at work again.' The tracks were doubled, entering the thicket and returning. The inward tracks seemed deeper, less extended, as though the man carried a burden, but the outward tracks were lighter, the man walked freely.

Slowly, Mark edged in towards the thicket, following

the man's prints. Pausing for long minutes to examine the undergrowth carefully every few paces, or squatting down to give himself better vision along the ground under the hanging lianas and branches.

Now that he knew what he was going to find, the pleasurable glow of excitement had given way to the chill of anger and the cold knowledge of mortal danger.

Something white caught his eye in the gloomy depths of the thicket. He stared at it moments before he saw the white, bleeding pith of a tree trunk, where it had been ripped by the claws of an anguished beast, long raking marks deep through the dark woody bark. His anger slid in his belly like an uncoiling serpent.

He moved sideways and slowly forward, the rifle held ready now, low across his hips, three paces before he stopped again. On the edge of the thicket there was an area of flattened grass and scrub; the soft black leaf-mould earth had been churned and disturbed, something heavy had been dragged back and forth, and there was a fleck of wet red lit by a single beam of falling sunlight that might have been the petal of a wild flower – or a drop of blood.

He heard another sound then, the clink of metal on metal, link on link, steel chain moved stealthily in the dark depths of the thicket and it sighted him. He knew where the animal was lying now, and he moved out sideways, crabbing step after step, slipping the safety-catch of the rifle, and holding it at high port across his chest.

White again, unnatural white, a round blob of it against dark foliage and he froze staring at it. Long seconds passed before he realized that it was the raw wood of a cut log, a short fork-shaped log as thick as a young girl's waist, so freshly cut that the gum was still bleeding from it in sticky wine-coloured drops. He saw also the twist of stolen fencing wire that held the chain to the log. The log was the anchor, a sliding drag weight which would hold the trapped animal without giving it a solid pull against which to pit itself and tear itself free.

The chain clinked again.

The leopard was within twenty paces of him. He knew exactly where it was but he could not see it, and as he stared, his mind was racing, remembering everything he had heard about the animal, the old man's stories.

'You won't see him until he comes, and even then he will only be a yellow flash of light, like a sunbeam. He won't warn you with a grunt, not like a lion. He comes absolutely silently, and he won't chew your arm or grab you in the shoulder. He'll go for your head. He knows all about two-legged animals, he feeds mostly on baboon, so he knows where your head is. He'll take the top off your skull quicker than you open your breakfast egg, and for good measure his back legs will be busy on your belly. You've seen a cat lie on his back and hook with his back legs when you scratch his belly. He'll cat you the same way, but he'll strip your guts out of you just like a chicken, and he'll do it so quickly that if there are four of you in the hunting-party he'll kill three of them before the fourth man gets his gun to his shoulder.'

Mark stood absolutely still and waited. He could not see the animal, but he could feel it, could feel its eyes, they stung his skin like the feet of poisonous crawling insects, and he remembered the shiny marble white scar tissue that Sean Courtney had shown him once in one of those mellow moments after the fourth whisky, pulling up his shirt and flexing muscle, so the cicatrice bulged with the gloss of satin.

'Leopard,' he had said. 'Devil cat – the worst bastard in all the bush.'

He felt his feet pulling back slowly, and the dead leaves rustled. He could walk away and leave it, come back when the vultures told him the animal was dead or too weak to

449

be a danger. Then he imagined the terror and anguish of the animal – and suddenly it was not the animal, but his animal, his charge, his sacred charge, and he stepped forward.

The chain clinked again and the leopard came. It came with a terrible silent rush, and in the blurring streaming charge, only the eyes blazed, they blazed yellow with hatred and fear and agony. The chain flailed out behind it, spinning and snapping, and as Mark brought the rifle up the last six inches to his shoulder he saw the trap hanging on its fore-leg like a sinister grey metallic crab. The heavy steel trap slowed the charge just that fraction.

Time seemed to pass with a dreamlike slowness, each microsecond falling heavily as drops of thick oil, so that he saw that the leopard's foreleg above the grip of the steel jaws was eaten through. He felt his stomach turn over as he realized that the frenzied animal had gnawed through its own bone and flesh and sinew in its desperate try for freedom. The leg was held by only a thread of bloody ragged skin, and that last thread snapped at the heavy jerk of the steel trap.

The leopard was free, mad with pain and fear, as it launched itself at Mark's head.

The muzzle of the Mannlicher almost touched the broad flat forehead; he was so close that he could see the long white whiskers bristling from the puckered snarling lips like grass stalks stiff with the morning frost, and the yellow fangs behind wet black lips, the furry pink tongue arched across the open throat, and the eyes. The terrible hating yellow eyes.

Mark fired and the bullet clubbed the skull open, the yellow eyes blinked tightly at the jarring shock, and the head was wrenched backwards, twisted on the snakelike neck, while the lithe body lost its grace and lightness and turned heavy and shapeless in mid-air.

It fell like a sack at Mark's feet, and tiny droplets of

brilliant red blood spattered the scuffed toe cap of Mark's boot, and glittered there like cut rubies.

Mark touched the open staring eye, but the fierce yellow light was fading and there was no blinking reflex of the eyelids with their long beautiful fans of dark lashes. The leopard was dead, and Mark sat down heavily in the leaf-mould beside the carcass and groped for his cigarette tin. The hand that held the match shook so violently that the flame fluttered like a moth's wing. He shook out the flame, threw the match away, and then stroked his open palm across the soft thick fur, the amber gold dabbed with the distinctive rosettes of black, as though touched by the five bunched fingertips of an angel's right hand.

'Pungushe – you bastard!' he whispered again. The animal had died for that golden dappled hide, for the few silver shillings that it would bring when sold in the village market, at a country railway halt, or on the side of a dusty road. A death in unspeakable agony and terror to make a rug, or a coat for a lady. Mark stroked the glowing fur again, and felt his own fear give way to anger for the man who had saved his life once, and who he had hunted these two months.

He stood up and went to the steel trap, lying at the end of its chain. The severed leg was still held between the relentless jaws, and Mark squatted to examine it. The trap was the type they call a 'Slag Yster', a killing iron, and the spikes of the jaws had been carefully filed to bite but not sever. It weighed at least thirty pounds and it would take a thick branch to lever those jaws open, and reset the mechanism.

The steel was dark and sooty where the poacher had scorched it with a torch of dry grass to kill the man-smell on the metal. Lying at the edge of the thicket was the half decomposed carcass of a baboon, the odoriferous bait which had been irresistible to the big yellow cat.

Mark reloaded the Mannlicher, and his anger was so

intense that he would have shot down the man who had done this thing, if he had come across him in that moment, despite the fact that he owed him his life.

He walked back up the slope and unsaddled Trojan, hobbled him with the leather straps, and hung his saddle-bags in the branches of the leadwood out of the way of a questing hyena or badger.

Then he went back and picked up the poacher's spoor at the edge of the thicket. He knew it would be useless to follow on the mule. The poacher would be alerted at a mile range by that big clumsy animal, but he had a chance on foot.

The spoor was fresh and the poacher's camp would be close, he would not stray far from such a valuable asset as his steel trap. Mark had a very good chance.

He would be cagey, of course, sly and cunning, for he would know that it was now forbidden to hunt in the valley. Mark had visited each village, spoken with each tribal headman and drank his beer while he explained to him the new order.

The poacher knew that he was outside the law. Mark had followed his spoor so often, and the precautions Pungushe took, the elaborate ruses to throw any pursuit, made it clear that he was in guilt, but now Mark had a good chance at him.

The spoor crossed the river half a mile downstream, and then started to zig-zag back and forth among the scrub and forest and brush as the poacher visited his trap line.

The leopard trap was clearly the centre of his line, but he was noosing for small game, using light galvanized baling wire, probably purchased for a few shillings at a country general dealer's store. He was also using copper telegraph wire, probably obtained by blatantly scaling a telegraph pole in some lonely place.

He was trapping for jackal, baiting with offal, and he

was trapping indiscriminately at salt licks and mud wallows, any place that might attract small game.

Following the trap line diligently, Mark sprang every wire noose and ripped it out. He closed rapidly with his quarry, but it was three hours before he found the poacher's camp.

It was under the swollen, bloated reptilian grey branches of a baobab tree. The tree was old and rotten, its huge trunk cleaved by a deep hollow, a cave that the poacher had used to shield his small smokeless cooking fire. The fire was dead now, carefully smothered with sand – but the smell of dead smoke led Mark to it. The ashes were cold.

Tucked away in the deepest recess of the hollow tree were two bundles tied with plaited bark string. One bundle held a greasy grey blanket, a carved wooden head-rest, a small black three-legged pot and a pouch of impala skin which contained two or three pounds of yellow maize and strips of dried meat. The poacher travelled light, and moved fast.

The other bundle contained fifteen jackal skins, sundried and crackling stiff, beautiful furs of silver and black and red, and two leopard skins, a big dark golden tom and a smaller half-grown female.

Mark relit the fire and threw the blanket, the head-rest and the bag upon it, deriving a thin vindictive satisfaction as they smouldered and blackened. He smashed the iron pot with a rock and then he slung the roll of dried skins on his shoulder and started back.

It was almost dark when he got back to the leopard thicket beside the river.

He dropped the heavy bundle of dried skin, which by this time felt like a hundredweight sack of coal on his shoulder, and he stared uncomprehendingly at the leopard's carcass.

It swarmed with big green metallic shiny flies. They were

laying their eggs on the dead flesh, like bunches of white boiled rice, but what astonished Mark was that the carcass was naked. It had been expertly stripped of its golden fur, and now it was a raw pink, laced with yellow fat and the white tracery of muscle ligaments. The head was bare, the mask stripped away so that dull startled eyes started out of the skull like marbles, and tufts of black hair sprang from the open ear holes, the fangs were exposed in a fixed yellow grin.

Quickly Mark ran to the anchor log. The chain and trap were gone.

It was fully a minute before the next logical step occurred to him. He ran up the slope to the leadwood tree. Trojan was gone. The hobbling straps had been cut with a razor-sharp blade and laid out neatly under the leadwood tree.

Trojan, unexpectedly relieved of his hobble, had reacted gratefully in a fully predictable manner. He had set off, arrow-straight through the forest, back home to his rude stable, his nightly ration of grain, and the congenial company of his old buddy Spartan.

It was a fifteen-mile walk back to main camp, and it would be dark in fifteen minutes.

The saddle-bags had been taken down from the tree, and the contents meticulously picked over. What Pungushe had rejected, he had folded and stacked neatly on a flat rock. He clearly did not think much of William Shakespeare, his tragedies had been put aside, and he had left Mark his chamois hunting-jacket, a last minute gift from Ruth Courtney.

He had taken the gentleman's sleeping bag, which had once belonged to General Courtney, with its built-in ground sheet and genuine eider filling, twenty-five guineas' worth from Harrods of London, good exchange for a threadbare greasy blanket and wooden head-rest.

He had taken the cooking pot, pannikin and cutlery,

the salt and flour and bully beef, but had left a single tin of beans.

He had taken the clean shirt and khaki trousers, but had left the spare woollen socks and rubber-soled boots. Perhaps it was chance that the boots pointed down-stream to Mark's camp – or was it mockery? A can of beans and boots to carry Mark home.

Through the red mists of his humiliation and mounting rage, Mark glimpsed suddenly a whimsical sense of humour at work. The man had been watching him. Mark was sure of that now, his selection from the saddle-bags echoed too faithfully what Mark had burned of his.

In his imagination, Mark heard the deep bell of Zulu laughter, and he snatched up the Mannlicher and picked up Pungushe's outgoing spoor.

He followed it for only a hundred yards and then stopped. Pungushe was heavily laden with trap, wet skin, and booty, but he had hit the Zulu's stride '*Minza umhlabathi*,' and he was eating ground to the north at a pace which Mark knew was pointless to try and imitate.

He walked back to the leadwood tree and sank down beside the trunk. His rage turned to acute discomfort at the thought of the fifteen-mile walk home, carrying the saddle-bags, and the roll of dried skins, for honour dictated he did not abandon his meagre spoils.

Suddenly he began to laugh, a helpless, hopeless shaking of his shoulders, and he laughed until tears ran down his cheeks and his belly ached.

'Pungushe, I'll get even for this,' he promised weakly, through his laughter.

It rained after midnight, a quick hard downpour, just enough to soak Mark and to bow the grass with clinging drops.

Then a small chill wind came nagging like an old wife, and the wet grass soaked his boots until they squelched and chafed with each step, and his cigarettes had disintegrated into a yellow porridge of mangled tobacco and limp rice paper, and the roll of skin and the saddle and the bags cut into his shoulders, and he did not laugh again that night.

In the pre-dawn, the cliffs of Chaka's Gate were purple and milky smooth, flaming suddenly with the sun's ardent kiss in vivid rose and bronze, but Mark plodded on under his burden, tired beyond any appreciation of beauty, beyond feeling or even caring, until he came out of the forest on the bank of the Bubezi River and stopped in mid-stride.

He sniffed in total disbelief, and was immediately assailed by the demands of his body, the quick flood of saliva from under his tongue and the cramping of his empty belly. It was the most beautiful odour he had ever smelled, bacon frying and eggs in the pan, slowly gelling and firming in the sizzling fat. He knew it was only a figment of his exhaustion, for he had eaten his last bacon six weeks before.

Then his ears played tricks also, he heard the ring of an axe-blade on wood and the faint melody of Zulu voices, and he lifted his head and stared ahead through the forest into his old camp below the wild figs.

There was a cone of pristine white canvas, an officer's bell tent, recently pitched beside his own rudely thatched lean-to shelter. The camp fire had been built up, Hlubi, the old Zulu cook, was busy with his pans over it, while, beyond the flames, in a collapsible canvas camp chair, sitting comfortably, was the burly figure of General Courtney, watching his breakfast cook with a critical eye.

He looked up and saw Mark, bedraggled and dirty as an

urchin at the edge of the camp, and his grin was wide and boyish.

'Hlubi,' he said in Zulu. 'Another four eggs and a pound of bacon.'

Sean Courtney's vast energy and enthusiasm were the beacon flames that made the next week one of the memorable interludes in Mark's life. He would always remember him as he was in those days, belly-laughing at Mark's tale of woe and frustration with Pungushe, and then still chuckling, calling to his servants and repeating the story to them, with his own comments and embellishments, until they rocked and reeled with mirth and old fat Hlubi overturned a pan of eggs, his great paunch bouncing like a ball and his cannon-ball of a head, with its hoar-frosting of pure white wool, rolling uncontrollably from side to side.

Mark, half-starved on a diet of bully and beans, gorged himself on the miraculous food that flowed from Hlubi's spade-sized, pink palmed hands. He was amazed at the style in which Sean Courtney braved the hardships of the African bush, from his full sized hip-bath to the portable kerosene-burning ice-box that delivered endless streams of frothing cold beer against the stunning heat of midday.

'Why travel in steerage, when you can go first class?' Sean asked, and winked at Mark as he spread a large-scale map of northern Zululand on the camp table. 'Now, what have you got to tell me?'

Their discussions lasted late into each night, with a Petromax hissing in the tree overhead and the jackals yipping and piping along the river, and in the days they rode the ground. Sean Courtney up on Spartan, so clearly enjoying every moment of it, with the vitality of a man half his age, keeping going without a check even in the numbing heat of noon, inspecting the site that Mark had chosen for the main camp, arguing as to where the Bubezi bridge should be built, following the road through the forest where

Mark had blazed the trees, exulting at the sight of a big black nyala ram with his heavy mane and ghostly stripes, as it raced away panic-stricken by the approach of man, sitting in his hip-bath under the fig trees, up to his waist in creaming white suds, with a cigar in his mouth and a long glass of beer in his hand, bellowing for Hlubi to top up with boiling water from the big kettle when his bath cooled. Big and scarred and hairy – and Mark realized then what a wide space this man had filled in his life.

As the day drew closer when he must leave again, Sean's mood changed, and in the evenings he brooded over the list of animals that Mark had compiled.

'Fifty zebra,' he read Mark's estimate, and poured the last few inches of whisky from the pinch-bottle into his glass. 'On the Sabi River in '95 a single herd crossed in front of my wagons. It took forty minutes at the gallop to go by, and the leaders were over the horizon when the tail passed us. There were thirty thousand animals in that one herd.'

'No elephant?' he asked, looking up from the list, and when Mark shook his head, he went on softly, 'We thought it would last for ever. In '99 when I rode into Pretoria from the north, I had ten tons of ivory on board. Ten tons, twenty thousand pounds of ivory.'

'No lions there?' and again Mark shook his head.

'I don't think so, General. I've seen no sign of them, nor heard them in the night, but when I was a boy I shot one near here. I was with my grandfather.'

'Yes,' Sean nodded. 'When you were a boy – but, what about your son, Mark? Will he ever see a lion in the wild?'

Mark did not answer, and Sean grunted.

'No lions on the Bubezi River, God! What have we done to this land?' He stared into the fire. 'I wonder if it was mere chance that you and I met, Mark. You have opened my eyes and conscience. It was I, and men like me, that did this—'

He shook that great shaggy head and groped in the side-pocket of his baggy hunting-jacket, and produced a leather-bound pocket-size book, a thick little volume, well-thumbed and shiny with the grease of grubby hands.

Mark did not recognize it for a moment, but when he did, he was startled.

'I did not know you read the Book,' he exclaimed, and Sean glanced up at him from under beetling brows.

'I read it,' he said gruffly. 'The older I get, the more I read it. There is a lot of solace here.'

'But, sir,' Mark persisted, 'you never go to church.'

This time Sean frowned as though he resented the prying questions. 'I live my religion,' he said. 'I don't go singing about it on Sunday, and drop it for the rest of the week, like some I know.' His tone was final, forbidding further discussion, and he turned his attention to the battered volume.

He had marked his place with a pressed wild flower, and the Bible fell open at the right page.

'I found it last night,' he told Mark, as he propped the steel-rimmed spectacles on his nose. 'It seemed like an omen, and I marked it to read to you. Matthew x.' He cleared his throat and read slowly:

'Are not two sparrows sold for a farthing?

And one of them shall not fall on the ground without your Father.'

When he had finished, he tucked the Bible away in his pocket, and they were both silent, thinking about it and watching the shapes in the ashes of the fire.

'Then perhaps he will help us to save the sparrow from its fall, here at Chaka's Gate,' said Sean, and he leaned forward to take a burning twig from the fire. He lit a fresh cigar with it and puffed deeply, savouring the taste of wood smoke and tobacco before speaking again.

'It is just unfortunate that it all comes at a time like this. It will be the end of the next year before we can make an official move to have the proclamation ratified and budget for full development here.'

Mark was instantly alert, and his voice sharp as he demanded, 'Next year?'

'I'm afraid so.'

'But why so long?'

'The grim reality of politics, son,' Sean growled. 'We have just received a shattering blow, and all else must wait while we play the game of power.'

'What has happened?' Mark asked with real concern now. 'I haven't read a newspaper in two months.'

'I wish I were that lucky.' Sean smiled without humour. 'There was a by-election in a little place up in the Transvaal. It's a seat that has always been ours, a good safe seat, in the hands of a respected backbencher of great loyalty and little intellect. He had a heart attack in the dining-room of the House, expiring between the soup and the fish. We went to our safe little constituency to elect a new member,' here Sean paused, and his expression went bleak, 'and we got the trouncing of our lives. A fifteen per cent swing to the Hertzog Party. They fought us on our handling of the strike last year – and it was a disaster.'

'I didn't know. I'm sorry.'

'If that swing, fifteen per cent, carries for the whole country, then we will be in opposition after the next election. Everything else is of no significance. General Smuts has decided to go to the country next year in March, and we will be fighting for our existence. Until then, we cannot introduce this type of legislation, or ask for funds.'

Mark felt cold despair spread out to numb his very fingertips. 'What happens here?' he asked. 'In the meantime must we stop what I am doing? Do we just leave it? Another year of poaching and hunting, another year without protection or development?'

Sean shook his head. 'I've had my people studying the

460

existing proclamation. We have powers there that we can enforce, but no money to do it.'

'You can't do anything without money,' said Mark miserably.

'Ah, so at last a little respect for the power of money.' Sean shot him a thin smile across the fire, and then went on seriously. 'I've decided to finance the development and running of the proclaimed area until I get a budget allocation for it. I'll foot the bill from my own pocket. Perhaps I'll get reimbursed from the budget later, but if I don't,' he shrugged, 'I reckon I owe that much at least. I've had a pretty good run.'

'It won't need much,' Mark rushed in eagerly but Sean quieted him irritably.

'You'll get the same salary as before, and we'll make a start on the main camp. I'm going to give four men to do the work,' he went on, speaking quietly. 'We'll have to make do without a bridge across the river, and only a wagon track for our first road, but it'll be a start – and let's just hope like hell we win our election.'

O n the last day at breakfast, Sean laid a folder in front of Mark.

'I talked Caldwell, the man who did the drawings for *Jock of the Bushveld*, into designing the layout,' he smiled, as Mark opened the folder. 'I wanted you to get the best for your three thousand pounds.'

In the folder was a mock-up of the full-page Press announcement which would launch the 'Friends of African Wildlife'.

The margin contained magnificent line-drawings of wild animals, and under the heavy typed announcement were set out the objects of the Society, and an eloquent plea for support and membership.

'I had my lawyers draft the articles and draw up the wording. We'll run it in every newspaper in the country. The Society's address is the Head Office of Courtney Holdings and I have taken on a full-time clerk to handle all the paper work. I've also got a young journalist to edit the Society's newspaper. He's full of ideas and caught up in the whole thing. With luck, we'll get huge public support behind us.'

'It's going to cost more than three thousand pounds.' Mark was torn between delight, and concern for the size to which his simple idea had grown.

'Yes,' Sean laughed. 'It's going to cost more than three thousand pounds, which reminds me. I sent Dirk Courtney a receipt for his money – and a life membership of the Society!' The joke carried them over the awkwardness of the last moments before departure.

Sean's bearers disappeared among the trees, carrying headloads of equipment to where the motor lorry had been left on the nearest road twenty miles beyond the cliffs of Chaka's Gate, and Sean lingered regretfully.

'I'm sad to go,' he admitted. 'It's been a good time, but I feel stronger now – ready to face whatever the bastards have got to throw at me.' He looked about him, taking farewell of river and mountain and wilderness. 'There is magic here.' He nodded. 'Look after it well, son,' and he held out his hand.

It was Mark's last opportunity to ask the question which he had tried to ask a dozen times already, but each time Sean had turned it aside, or simply ignored it. But now he had to have an answer, and he took Sean's big gnarled bony fist in a grip that would not be denied.

'You haven't told me how Storm is, sir. How is she? Is she well? How is her painting?' he blurted.

It seemed even then that Sean would not be drawn. He stiffened angrily, made as if to pull his hand away, and then the anger faded before it reached his eyes. For a moment there showed in the deep-set eyes a dark unfathomable grief, and his grip tightened on Mark's hand like a steel trap.

'Storm was married a month ago. But I have not seen her since you left Lion Kop,' he said, and he dropped Mark's hand. Without another word, he turned and walked away. For the first time he went slowly and heavily, swaying against the drag of his bad leg, shuffling like an old man – a very tired old man.

Mark wanted to run after him, but his own heart was breaking and his legs would not carry him.

He stood forlornly and watched Sean Courtney limp away into the trees.

The Natal Number Two came in along the line, his pony's hooves kicking up little spurts of white marking-lime like a machine-gun traversing, and he caught the ball two feet before it dribbled out of play.

He leaned low out of the saddle and took it backhanded under his pony's neck, a full-blooded stroke that finished with the mallet high above his head, and the ball rose in a floating arc, a white blur against the stark blue of summer sky.

From the club house veranda, and the deck-chairs beneath the coloured umbrellas, applause splattered above the drum of hooves, and then rose into a swelling hum as they saw that Derek Hunt had anticipated.

He was coming down in a hard canter with Saladin not yet asked to extend. Saladin was a big pony, with a mean and ugly head that he cocked to watch the flight of the white ball, his over-large nostrils flaring so the shiny red mucous membrane flashed like a flag. The eye that watched the ball rolled in the gaunt skull, giving the horse a wild and half-crazed air. He was of that raggedy roan and grey that no amount of currying would ever brighten into a gloss, and his hooves like those of a cart-horse. He had to lift them high in the ungainly action that was quickly carrying him ahead of the hard-running Argentinian pony at his shoulder.

Derek sat him as though he were an armchair, idly penduluming his stick from his wrist, his pith helmet hard down over his ears and strapped up tightly under the chin. His belly bulged out over the belt of his breeches, his arms were long and thick as those of a chimpanzee, covered in a thick fuzz of ginger hair. The skin was heavily freckled and had a raw red look between the freckles, as though it had been scalded with boiling water. His face was the same raw painful looking red, tinged by the purplish glaze of the very heavy drinker, and he was sweating.

The sweat glistened like early dew on his face and dripped from his chin. His short-sleeved cotton singlet looked as though he had been caught in a tropical downpour. It clung to the thick bearlike shoulders, and was stretched so tightly over his bulging paunch and so transparent with wetness, that you could see the deep dark pit of his belly button from the sidelines.

At each jar, as Saladin's hooves struck the hard-baked earth, Derek Hunt's great backside in the tight-fitting white breeches quivered like a jelly in the saddle.

Two Argentinian ponies were cutting across field to cover, their handsome riders olive-skinned and dashing as cavalry officers, riding with huge verge and excited Spanish cries, and Derek grinned under his bristling ginger moustache, as the ball started its long plummeting curve back to earth.

'Christ,' drawled one of the members on the club house steps. 'The ugliest horse in Christendom.' And he raised his pink gin to salute Saladin.

'And the ugliest four-goal handicapper in the entire

world on his back,' agreed the masher beside him. 'Poor bloody dagoes should turn to stone just looking at them.'

Saladin and the Argentinian Number One arrived at the drop of the ball at exactly the same moment. The Argentinian rose in the saddle to trap the fall, his white teeth sparkling under the trim black pencil-line of his moustache, the smooth darkly tanned muscles of his arm bulging as he prepared to go on to the forehand drive, his sleekly beautiful pony wheeling into line for the shot, nimble and quick as a ferret.

Then an extraordinary thing happened. Derek Hunt sat fat-gutted and heavy in the saddle and nobody could see the touch of rein and heel that made Saladin switch his quarters. The Argentinian pony cannoned off him as though she had hit a granite kopje, and the rider went over her head, going in an instant from balanced perfection to sprawling windmilling confusion, falling heavily in a cloud of red dust, and rolling to his knees to scream hysterical protest to the umpire and the skies.

Derek leaned slightly and there was the tap of mallet against bamboo root, a gentle almost self-effacing little tap, and the ball dropped meekly ahead of Saladin's slugging, hammering head.

It bounced once, twice, and then came up obediently for the next light tap that kept it hopping down the field. The Argentinian Number Four swept in from the right, with all the smooth-running grace of a charging lioness – and the roar of the crowd carried across the open field, spurring him on to make the challenge. He shouted a wild Spanish oath, his eyes flashing with excitement.

Smoothly, Derek changed the mallet from his right hand to his left, and tapped the bouncing white ball on to his off-side, forcing the Argentinian to increase the angle of his interception.

The instant he was drawn, Derek cropped hard,

lofting the ball in an easy lob high over the Argentinian's head.

He said, 'Ha!' but not loudly, and touched Saladin with his heels. The big ugly roan stretched out his neck and extended, with Derek moving now to help him push.

They ran past the Argentinian as though he had indeed turned to stone, they left him floundering in their wake and picked up the ball beyond him. Tap! Tap! And tap again, he ran it down through the exact centre of the stubby goal-posts and then turned and trotted back to the pony lines.

Chuckling so that his belly bounced, Derek swung one leg forward over Saladin's neck and slid down to the ground, letting him go free to the grooms.

'I'll take Satan for the next chukka,' he shouted in that beery throaty voice.

Storm Courtney saw him coming, and knew what was going to happen. She tried to rise, but she was slow and clumsy, the child in her womb anchored her like a stone.

'One for the poor, what!' shouted Derek, and caught her with one long, ginger-fuzzed, boiled red arm.

The sweat on his face was icy cold and smeared down her own cheek, and he smelled of sour beer and horse. He kissed her with an open mouth, in front of Irene Leuchars and the four other girls, and their husbands, and all the grinning grooms, and the members on the veranda.

She thought desperately that she was going to be ill. The acid vomit rose into her throat, and she thought she was going to throw up in front of them all.

'Derek, my condition!' she whispered desperately, but he held her under his one arm as he took the bottle of beer that one of the white-jacketed club servants brought on a silver tray, and, scorning the glass, he drank straight from the bottle.

She struggled to be free, but he held her easily with

466

immense and careless strength – and he belched, a ripping explosion of gas. 'One for the poor,' he shouted again, and they all laughed – like courtiers at the king's jest. Good old Derek. Law unto himself, old Derek.

He dropped the empty bottle. 'Keep it until I get back, wifey!' he laughed, and took one of her swollen breasts in his huge raw-knuckled, red-boiled hand and squeezed it painfully. She felt cold and trembly and weak with humiliation and hatred.

She had missed a month many times before, so Storm did not begin to worry until the second blank came up on her pocket diary. She had been about to tell Mark then, but that had been the time they had parted. Still, she had expected it all to resolve itself, but as the weeks passed, the enormity of it all began to reach her in her gold and ivory castle. This sort of thing happened to other girls, common working girls, ordinary girls – it did not happen to Storm Courtney. There were special rules for young ladies like Storm.

When it was certain, beyond all doubt, the first person she thought of was Mark Anders. As the panic caught at her heart with fiery little barbs, she wanted to rush to him and throw her arms about his neck. Then that stubborn and completely uncontrollable pride of the Courtneys smothered the impulse. He must come to her. She had decided, he must come on her terms – and she could not bring herself to change the rules she had laid down. Though still, even in her distress, her chest felt tight and her legs shaky and weak, whenever she thought of Mark.

She had wept, silently in the night, when she had first left Mark – and now she wept again. She longed for him even more now, with his child growing in the secret depths of her body. But that perverse and distorted pride would not release its bulldog hold on her, would not allow her even to let him know of her predicament.

'Don't challenge me, Mark Anders,' she had warned him, and he had done it. She hated him, and loved him for that. But now she could not bend.

The next person she thought of was her mother. She and Ruth Courtney had always been close, she had always been able to rely on her mother's loyalty and shrewdly practical hard sense. Then she was stopped dead by the knowledge that if Ruth were told, then her father would know within hours. Ruth Courtney kept nothing from Sean, or he from her.

Storm's soul quailed at the thought of what would happen once her father knew that she carried a bastard. The immense indulgent love he had for her would make his anger and retribution more terrible.

She knew also Mark would be destroyed by it. Her father was too strong, too persistent and single-minded for her to believe she would be able to keep Mark's name from him. He would squeeze it out of her.

She knew of her father's affection for Mark Anders, it had been apparent for anyone to see, but that affection would not have been sufficient to save either of them.

Sean Courtney's attitude to his daughter was bound by iron laws of conduct, the old-fashioned view of the father that left no latitude for manoeuvre. Mark Anders had contravened those iron laws and Sean would destroy him, despite the fact he had come to love him, and in doing so, he would destroy a part of himself. He would reject and drive out his own daughter, even though it left him ruined and broken with grief.

So, for her father's sake and for Mark Anders' sake, she could not go for comfort and help to her mother.

She went instead to Irene Leuchars, who listened to Storm's hesitant explanations with rising glee and anticipation.

'But you silly darling, didn't you take precautions?'

Storm shook her head glumly, not quite certain what Irene meant by precautions, but certain only that she hadn't taken them.

'Who was it, darling?' was the next question, and Storm shook her head again, this time fiercely.

'Oh dear,' Irene rolled her eyes. 'That many candidates for the daddy? You are a dark horse, Storm darling.'

'Can't one – well, can't one actually do something?' Storm asked miserably.

'You mean an abortion, darling?' Irene asked brutally, and smiled a sly spiteful smile when Storm nodded.

He was a tall pale man, very grey and stooped, with a reedy voice and hands so white as to be almost transparent. Storm could see the blue veins and the fragile ivory bones through the skin. She tried not to think of those pale transparent hands as they pried and probed, but they were cold and cruelly painful.

Afterwards, he had washed those pale hands at the kitchen sink of his small grey apartment with such exaggerated care that Storm had felt her pain and embarrassment enhanced by a sense of affront. The cleansing seemed to be a personal insult.

'I imagine you indulge in a great deal of physical activity – horse-riding, tennis?' he asked primly, and when Storm nodded he made a little sucking and glucking sound of disapproval. 'The female body was not designed for such endeavour. You are very narrow, and your musculature is highly developed. Furthermore, you are at least ten weeks pregnant.' At last he had finished washing, and now he began to dry his hands on a threadbare, but clinically white towel.

'Can you help me?' Storm demanded irritably, and he shook his pale grey head slowly from side to side.

'If you had come a little earlier—' and he spread the white transparent hands in a helpless gesture.

They had drawn up a list of names, she and Irene, and each of the men on the list had two things in common. They were in love, or had professed to be in love with Storm, and they were all men of fortune.

There were six names on the list, and Storm had written cards to two of them and received vague replies, polite good wishes, and no definite suggestion for a meeting.

The third man on the list she had contrived to meet at the Umgeni Country Club. She could still wear tennis clothes, and the pregnancy had given her skin a new bloom and lustre, her breasts a fuller ripeness.

She had chatted lightly, flirtatiously, with him, confident and poised, giving him encouragement he had never received from her before. She had not noticed the sly, gloating look in his eyes, until he leaned close to her and asked confidentially, 'Should you be playing tennis – now?'

She had only been able to keep herself from breaking down until she reached the Cadillac parked in the lot behind the courts. She was weeping when she drove out through the gates, and she had to park in the dunes above the ocean.

After the first storm of humiliation had passed, she could think clearly.

It had been Irene Leuchars, of course. She must have been blind and stupid not to realize it sooner. Everybody, every single person, would know by now, Irene would have seen to that.

Loneliness and desolation overwhelmed her.

Derek Hunt had not been on the list of six, not because he was not rich, not because he had never shown interest in Storm.

Derek Hunt had shown interest in most pretty girls. He had even married two of them, and both of them had divorced him in separate blazes of notoriety, not before they had, between them, presented him with seven off-spring.

Derek Hunt's reputation was every bit as vast and flamboyant as his fortune.

'Look, old girl,' he had told Storm reasonably. 'You and I have both got a problem. I want you, have always wanted you. Can't sleep at night, strewth!' and his ginger whiskers twitched lasciviously. 'And you need me. The word's out about you, old girl. Mark of the beast, condemnation of society, and all that rot, I'm afraid.

'Your loss, my gain. I've never given a stuff for the condemnation of society. I've got seven little bastards already. Another one won't make any difference. What about it, then? One for the poor, what?'

They had driven up to Swaziland, and Derek had been able to get a special licence, lying about her age.

There had been nobody she knew at the ceremony, only five of Derek's cronies – and she had not told her father, nor her mother, nor Mark Anders.

She heard him coming home, like a Le Mans Grand Prix winner, a long cortege of motor cars roaring up the driveway, then the squeal of brakes, the cannonade of slamming doors, the loud comradely shouts and the snatches of wild song.

Derek's voice, louder and hoarser than the rest. 'Caramba, me hearties! Whipped your pants off on the field, going to drink you blind now. This way, the pride of the Argentine—' the stamping and shouting, as they trooped up the front staircase.

Storm lay flat on her back and stared at the plaster cupids on the ceiling. She wanted to run, this senseless panicky urge to get up and run. But there was no place to run to.

She had spoken to her mother three times since the wedding, and each time had been agony for both of them.

'If only you had told us. Daddy might have been able to understand, to forgive—'

'Oh darling, if you only knew the plans he used to make for your wedding. He was so proud of you – and then not to be at your wedding. Not even invited—'

'Give him time, please, Storm. I am trying for you. Believe me darling, I think it might have been better, if it was anybody in the world but Derek Hunt. You know what Daddy thinks of him.'

There was nowhere to run, and she lay quietly, dreading, until at last the heavy unsteady boots came clumping up the staircase, and the door was thrown open.

He had not changed, and he still wore riding-boots. The backside of his breeches was brown with dubbin from the saddle, and the crotch drooped almost to his knees, like a baby's soiled napkin; the sweat had dried in salty white circles on the cotton singlet.

'Wake up, old girl. Time for every good man and true to perform his duty.' He let his clothing lie where it fell.

His bulging belly was fish white, and fuzzed with ginger curls. The heavy shoulders were pitted and scarred purple with the old cicatrices of myriad carbuncles and small boils, and he was massively virile, thick and hard and callous as the branch of a pine tree.

'One for the poor, what?' he chuckled hoarsely, as he came to the bed.

Suddenly and clearly, she had an image of Mark Anders' slim and graceful body, with the clean shape of young muscle, as he sat in the dappled sunlight of the glade.

She remembered with a terrible pang of loss the lovely head with the fine strong lines of mouth and brow, and the serene poet's eyes.

As the bed dipped beneath the solid weight of her

husband, she wanted to scream with despair and the knowledge of coming pain.

For breakfast, Derek Hunt liked a little Black Velvet, mixing the Guinness stout and champagne in a special crystal punch bowl. He always used a Bollinger Vintage 1911 and drank it out of a pewter tankard.

He believed in a substantial breakfast, and this morning it was scrambled eggs, Scotch kippers, devilled kidneys, mushrooms and a large well-done fillet steak – all of it on the same plate.

Although his eyes were watery and pink-rimmed with the previous night's revelry, and his face blazed crimson as the rising sun, he was cheerful and loudly friendly, guffawing at his own jokes, and leaning across the table to prod her with a thick red thumb like a boiled langouste to emphasize a point.

She waited until he had picked up the bowl and tilted the last of the Black Velvet into his tankard, and then she said quietly, 'Derek, I want a divorce.'

The grin did not leave his face, and he watched the last drops fall into the tankard.

'Damn stuff evaporates – or the dish has got a hole in it,' he wheezed, and then chuckled merrily. 'Get it? A hole in it! Good, what?'

'Did you hear what I said? Aren't you going to answer?'

'Needs no answer, old girl. Bargain is a bargain, you've got a name for your bastard – I've still got my share coming.'

'You've had that, as many times as you could wish,' Storm answered quietly, with a whole world of resignation in her voice. 'Won't you let me go now?'

'Good God!' Derek stared at her over the rim of his

tankard, his moustache bristling and the pink eyes wide with genuine amazement. 'You don't think I was really interested in the crumpet, do you? Can get that anywhere, all of it looks the same in the dark.' He snorted with real laughter now. 'Good God, old girl – you didn't really think I fancied your lily-white titties that much?'

'Why?' she asked.

'Ten million good reasons, old girl.' He gulped a mouthful of scrambled eggs and kidney, 'and every single one of them in General Sean Courtney's bank account.'

She stared at him. 'Daddy's money?'

'Right first time,' he grinned. 'Up you go to the head of the class.'

'But – but—' she made fluttery little gestures of incomprehension with both hands. 'I don't understand. You are so rich yourself.'

'Was, old girl, used to be – past tense.' And he let out another delighted guffaw. 'Two loving wives, two unsympathetic divorce judges, seven brats, forty polo ponies, friends with big right hands, rocks that shouldn't have been where the road was going, a mine with no diamonds, a building that fell down, a dam that burst, a reef that pinched out, cattle that got sick and myopic lawyers who don't read the small print, that's the way the money goes, pop goes the weasel!'

'I don't believe it.' She was aghast.

'Would never joke about that,' he grinned. 'Never joke about money, one of my principles. Probably my only principle.' And he prodded her. 'My only principle – get it? Skunked, absolutely flatters, I assure you. Daddy is the last resort, old girl – you'll have to speak to him, I'm afraid. Last resort, what? One for the poor, don't you know?'

There was no answer to the front door and Mark almost turned away and went back into the village, feeling a touch of relief and a lightening of heart that he recognized as cowardice. So instead, he jumped down off the veranda and went around the side of the house.

The stiff collar and tie chafed his throat and the jacket felt unnatural and constricting, so that he shrugged his shoulders and ran a finger around inside his collar as he came into the kitchen yard of the cottage. It was five months since last he had worn clothes or trodden on a paved sidewalk – even the sound of women's voices was unfamiliar. He paused and listened to them.

Marion Littlejohn was in the kitchen with her sister, and their merry prattle had a lilt and cadence to which he listened with new ears and fresh pleasure.

The chatter ceased abruptly at his knock, and Marion came to the door.

She wore a gaily striped apron, and her bare arms were floury to the elbows. She had her hair up in a ribbon but tendrils of it had come down in little wisps on to her neck and forehead.

The kitchen was filled with the smell of baking bread, and her cheeks were rosy from the heat of the oven.

'Mark,' she said calmly. 'How nice,' and tried to push the curl of hair off her forehead, leaving a smudge of white flour on the bridge of her nose. It was a strangely appealing gesture, and Mark felt his heart swell.

'Come in.' She stood aside, and held the door open for him.

Her sister greeted Mark frostily, much more aware of the jilting than Marion herself.

'Doesn't he look well?' Marion asked, and they both looked Mark over carefully, as he stood in the centre of the kitchen floor.

'He's too thin,' her sister judged him waspishly, and began untying her apron-strings.

'Perhaps,' Marion agreed comfortably, 'he just needs the proper food.' And she smiled and nodded as she saw how brown and lean he was, but she recognized also, with eyes as fond as a mother's, the growing weight of maturity in his features. She saw also the sorrow and the loneliness, and she wanted to take him in her arms and hold his head against her bosom.

'There is some lovely butter-milk,' she said instead. 'Sit down, here where I can see you.'

While she poured from the jug, her sister hung the apron behind the door and without looking at Mark said primly, 'We need more eggs. I'll go into the village.'

When they were alone, Marion picked up the roller, and stood over the table, leaning and dipping as the pastry spread and rolled out paper thin.

'Tell me what you have been doing,' she invited, and he began, hesitantly at first, but with blossoming sureness and enthusiasm, to tell her about Chaka's Gate, about the work and the life he had found there.

'That's nice.' She punctuated his glowing account every few minutes, her mind running busily ahead, already making lists and planning supplies, adapting pragmatically to the contingencies of a life lived far from the comforts of civilization, where even the small comforts become luxuries – a glass of fresh milk, a light in the night – all of it has to be planned for and carefully arranged.

Characteristically she felt neither excitement nor dismay at the prospect. She was of pioneer stock. Where a man goes, the woman follows. It was merely work that must be done.

'The site for the homestead is up in the first fold of the hills, but you can see right down the valley, and the cliffs of Chaka's Gate are right above it. It's beautiful, especially in the evenings.'

'I'm sure it is.'

'I have designed the house so it can be added on to, a

room at a time. To begin with there will only be two rooms—'

'Two rooms will be enough to begin with,' she agreed, frowning thoughtfully. 'But we'll need a separate room for the children.'

He broke off and stared at her, not quite certain that he had heard correctly. She paused with the rolling-pin held in both hands and smiled at him.

'Well, that's why you came here today, isn't it?' she asked sweetly.

He dropped his eyes from hers and nodded. 'Yes.' He sounded bemused. 'I suppose it is.'

She lost her aplomb only briefly during the ceremony, and that was when she saw General Sean Courtney sitting in the front pew with his wife beside him, Sean in morning suit and with a diamond pin in his cravat, Ruth cool and elegant in a huge wagon-wheel sized hat, the brim thick with white roses.

'He came!' Marion whispered ecstatically, and could not restrain the triumphant glance she threw to her own friends and relatives, like a lady tossing a coin to a beggar. Her social standing had rocketed to dizzying heights.

Afterwards the General had kissed her tenderly on each cheek, before turning to Mark. 'You've picked the prettiest girl in the village, my boy.' And she had glowed with pleasure, pink and happy and truly as lovely as she had ever been in her life.

With the help of the four Zulu labourers Sean had given him, Mark had opened a rough track in as far as the Bubezi River. He brought his bride to Chaka's Gate on the pillion of the motorcycle, with the side-car piled high with part of her dowry.

Far behind them, the Zulus led Trojan and Spartan under heavy packs, the rest of Marion's baggage.

In the early morning the mist lay dense along the river, still and flat as the surface of a lake, touched to shades of delicate pink and mauve by the fresh new light of coming day.

The great headlands of Chaka's Gate rose sheer out of the mist, dark and mysterious, each wreathed in laurels of golden cloud.

Mark had chosen the hour of return so that she might have the best of it for her first glimpse of her new home. He pulled the cycle and side-car off the narrow, stony track and switched off the motor.

In the silence they sat and watched the sun strike upon the crests of the cliffs, burning like the beacons that the mariner looks for in the watery deserts of the ocean, the lights that beckon him on to his landfall and the quiet anchorage.

'It's very nice, dear,' she murmured. 'Now show me where the house will be.'

She worked with the Zulus, muddy to the elbows as they puddled the clay for the unburned Kimberley bricks, joshing them in their own language and bullying them cheerfully to effort beyond the usual pace of Africa.

She worked behind the mules, handling the traces, dragging up the logs from the valley, her sleeves rolled high on brown smooth arms and a scarf knotted around her head.

She worked over the clay oven, bringing out the fat golden brown loaves on the blade of a long handled spade, and watched with deep contentment as Mark wiped up the last of the stew with the crust.

'Was that good, then, dear?'

In the evenings she sat close to the lantern, with her head bowed over the sewing in her lap, and nodded brightly as he told her of the day's adventures, each little triumph and disappointment.

'What a shame, dear.' Or, 'How nice for you, dear.'

He took her, one bright, cloudless day, up the ancient pathway to the crest of Chaka's Gate. Holding her hand as

478

he led her over the narrow places, where the river flowed six hundred sheer feet below their feet. She tucked her skirts into her bloomers, took a firm hold on the basket she carried and never faltered once on the long climb.

On the summit, he showed her the tumbled stone walls and overgrown caves of the old tribesmen who had defied Chaka, and he told her the story of the old king's climb, pointing out the fearsome path up which he had led his warriors – and finally he described the massacre and pictured for her the rain of human bodies hurled down into the river below.

'How interesting, dear,' she murmured, as she spread a cloth from the basket she had carried. 'I brought scones and some of that apricot jam you like so much.'

Something caught Mark's eye, unusual movement far down in the valley below, and he reached for his binoculars. In the golden grass at the edge of the tall reed beds they looked like a line of fat black bugs on a clean sheet. He knew what they were immediately, and with a surging uplift of excitement he counted them.

'Eighteen!' he shouted aloud. 'It's a new herd.'

'What is it, dear?' She looked up from the scone she was spreading with jam.

'It's a new herd of buffalo,' he exulted. 'They must have come in from the north. It's beginning to work already.'

In the field of the binoculars he saw one of the great bovine animals emerge into a clearing in the long grass. He could see not only its wide black back, but the heavy head and spreading ears beneath the mournfully drooping horns. The sunlight caught the bosses of the polished black horns so that they glittered like gunmetal.

He felt an enormous proprietary pride. They were his own. The first to come into the sanctuary he was building for them.

'Look.' He offered her the binoculars, and she wiped her

hands carefully and pointed the glasses over the cliff. 'There on the edge of the swamp.' He pointed, with the pride and joy shining on his face.

'I can see them,' she agreed smiling happily for him. 'How nice, dear.'

Then she swung the binoculars in a wide sweep across the river to where the roof of the homestead showed above the trees.

'Doesn't it look so nice with its new thatch?' she said proudly. 'I just can't wait to move in.'

The following day they moved up from the shack of crude thatch and canvas at the old camp under the sycamore fig trees, and a pair of swallows moved in with them. The swiftly darting birds began to build their neat nest with little shiny globs of mud under the eaves of the new yellow thatch against the crisply whitewashed wall of Kimberley brick.

'That's the best of all possible luck,' Mark laughed.

'They make such a mess,' said Marion doubtfully, but that night, for the first time ever, she initiated their love-making; rolling comfortably on to her back in the double-bed, drawing up her nightdress to her waist, and spreading her warm womanly thighs.

'It's all right, if you want to, dear.' And because she was kind and loved him so, he was as quick and as considerate as he could be.

'Was that good, then, dear?'

'It was wonderful,' he told her, and he had a sudden vivid image of a lovely vital woman, with a body that was lithe and swift and – and his guilt was brutal like a fist below the heart. He tried to thrust the image away, but it ran ahead of him through his dreams, laughing and dancing and teasing, so that in the morning there were dark blue smears beneath his eyes and he felt fretful and restless.

'I'm going up the valley on patrol.' He did not look up from his coffee.

'You only came back last Friday.' She was surprised.

'I want to look for those buffalo again,' he said.

'Very well, dear. I'll pack your bag – how long will you be gone – I'll put in your sweater and the jacket, it's cool in the evenings – it's a good thing I baked yesterday—' she prattled on cheerfully, and he had a sudden terrible urge to shout at her to be silent. 'It will give me a chance to plant out the garden. It will be nice to have fresh vegetables again, and I haven't written a letter for ages. They'll be wondering about us at home.' He rose from the table and went out to saddle Trojan.

The flogging explosion of heavy wings roused Mark from his reverie and he straightened in the saddle just as a dozen of the big birds rose from the edge of the reed-beds.

They were those dirty buff-coloured vultures, powering upwards as they were disturbed by Mark's approach, and undergoing that almost magical transformation from gross ugliness into beautiful planing flight.

Mark tethered Trojan and slipped the Mannlicher from its scabbard as a precaution. He felt a tickle of excitement, hopes high that he had come upon a kill by one of the big predatory cats. Perhaps even a lion, one of the animals for which he still searched the valley in vain.

The buffalo lay at the edge of the damp soft ground, half hidden by the reeds, and it was so freshly dead that the vultures had not yet managed to penetrate the thick black hide, nor spoil the sign which was deeply trodden and torn into the damp earth. They had only gouged out the uppermost eye and, with their beaks, scratched the softer skin around the bull's anus, for that was always their access point to a big thick-skinned carcass.

The buffalo was a big mature bull, the great boss of his horns grown solidly together across the crown of his skull, a huge head of horn, forty-eight inches from tip to tip. He was big in the body also, bigger than a prize Hereford stud bull, and he was bald across the shoulders, the scarred grey hide scabbed with dried mud and bunches of bush ticks.

Mark thrust his hand into the crease of skin between the back legs and felt the residual body warmth.

'He's been dead less than three hours,' he decided, and squatted down beside the huge body to determine the cause of death. The bull seemed unmarked until Mark managed to roll him over, exerting all his strength and using the stiffly out-thrust limbs to move the ton and a half of dead weight.

He saw immediately the death wounds, one was behind the shoulder, through the ribs, and Mark's hunter's eye saw instantly that it was a heart-stroke, a wide-lipped wound, driven home deeply; the clotted heart blood that poured from it had jellied on the damp earth.

If there was any doubt at all as to the cause of that injury, it was dispelled instantly when he looked to the second wound. This was a frontal stroke, at the base of the neck, angled in skilfully between bone, to reach the heart again, and the weapon had not been withdrawn, it was still plunged in to the hilt and the shaft was snapped short where the bull had fallen upon it.

Mark grasped the broken shaft, placed one booted foot against the bull's shoulder and grunted with the effort it required to withdraw the blade against the reluctant suck of clinging flesh.

He examined it with interest. It was one of those broad bladed stabbing spears, the assegai which had been designed by the old king Chaka himself. Mark remembered Sean

Courtney reminiscing about the Zulu wars, Isandhlwana, and Morma Gorge.

'They can put one of those assegais into a man's chest and send the point two feet out between his shoulder blades, and when they clear the blade, the withdrawal seems to suck a man as white as though he had his life blood pumped out of him by a machine.' Sean had paused for a moment to stare into the camp fire. 'As they clear, they shout "*Ngidhla!*" – I have eaten! Once you have heard it, you'll not forget it. Forty years later, the memory still makes the hair come up on the back of my neck.'

Now still holding the short heavy assegai, Mark remembered that Chaka himself had hunted the buffalo with a similar weapon. A casual diversion between campaigns – and as Mark glanced from the blade to the great black beast, he felt his anger tempered with reluctant admiration. His anger was for the wanton destruction of one of his precious animals, and his admiration was for the special type of courage that had done the deed.

Thinking of the man, Mark realized that there must have been special circumstances for that man to abandon such a valuable, skilfully and lovingly wrought weapon together with the prize he had risked his life to hunt.

Mark began to back-track the sign in the soft black earth and he found where the bull had come up one of the tunnel-like pathways through the reeds after drinking. He found where the huntsman had waited in thick cover beside the path, and his bare footprints were unmistakable.

'Pungushe!' exclaimed Mark.

Pungushe had lain upwind and, as the bull passed, he had put the steel behind his shoulder, deeply into the heart.

The bull had leapt forward, crashing into a ponderous gallop as Pungushe cleared his point, and the blood had sprayed from the wide wound as though the standing reeds had been hosed by a careless gardener.

The buffalo is one of the few wild animals which will turn and actively hunt its tormentor. Although the bull was dead on his feet, spurting blood with every lunging stride, he had swung wide into the wind to take Pungushe's scent and when he had it, he had steadied into that terrible crabbing, nose up, wide-horned, relentless charge that only death itself will stop.

Pungushe had stood to meet him as he came thundering down through the reeds, and he had picked the point at the base of the neck for his second stroke and put the steel in cleanly to the heart, but the bull had hit him also, before blundering on a dozen paces and falling to his knees with that characteristic death bellow.

Mark found where Pungushe had fallen, his body marks etched clearly in the soft clay.

Mark followed where he had dragged himself out of the edge of the reed beds and shakily regained his feet.

Slowly Pungushe had turned northwards, but his stride was cramped, he was heeling heavily, not up on his toes, not extended into his normal gait.

He stopped once where he had left his steel-jawed spring trap, and he hid it in an ant bear hole and kicked sand over it, obviously too sick and weak to carry it or to cache the valuable trap more securely. Mark retrieved the trap and, as he tied it on to Trojan's saddle, he wondered briefly to how many of his animals it had dealt hideous death.

A mile further on, Pungushe paused to gather leaves from one of the little turpentine bushes, a medicinal shrub, and then he had gone on slowly, not using the rocky ridges, not covering or back-tracking as he usually did.

At the sandy crossing of one of the steep narrow dry water courses, Pungushe had dropped on one knee, and had used both hands to push himself upright.

Mark stared at the sign for there was blood now for the first time, black droplets that had formed little pellets of loose sand, and in his anger and jubilation, Mark felt a prick of real concern.

The man was hard hit, and he had once saved Mark's life. Mark could still remember the blessed taste of the bitter medicine in the black baked pot cutting through the terrible thirsts of malaria.

He had been leading Trojan up to this point, to keep down, to show a low silhouette, so as not to telegraph heavy hoof-beats ahead to his quarry.

Now he swung up into the saddle, and kicked the mule into a plunging sway-backed canter.

Pungushe was down. He had gone down heavily at last, dropping to the sandy earth. He had crawled off the game path, under a low bush out of the sun, and he had pulled the light kaross of monkey-skins over his head, the way a man settles down to sleep – or to die.

He lay so still that Mark thought he was indeed dead. He slipped down off Trojan's back and went up cautiously to the prostrate body. The flies were buzzing and swarming gleefully over the bloody bundle of green turpentine leaves that were bound with strips of bark around the man's flank and across the small of his back.

Mark imagined clearly how he had received that wound, Pungushe standing to meet the charging buffalo, going for the neck with the short heavy-bladed assegai, putting the steel in cleanly and then jumping clear, but the bull pivoting hard on his stubby front legs and hooking with the massive bossed and wickedly curved horns.

Pungushe had taken the hook low in the side, far back behind the hip-bone of the pelvis. The shock would have hurled him clear, giving him time to crawl away while the bull staggered on, fighting the deep steel in his chest, until at last he had gone down on his fore-legs with that last defiant death bellow.

Mark shuddered in the harsh sunlight at the wound that bundle of leaves covered, and went down on one knee to brush the flies away.

Now for the first time, he became aware of the man's physique. The kaross covered his head and shoulders only, the great chest was exposed. A loin-cloth of softly tanned leather embroidered with blue beads was drawn up between his legs, leaving free the solid bulge of his buttocks, and the sinewy thews of his thighs and the flat hard plain of the belly.

Each separate muscle was clearly defined, and the ropey veins below the surface of the skin were like bunches of serpents, testimony to the man's tremendous physical development and fitness. The skin itself was lighter than that of the average Zulu. It had the smooth dark buttery colour and lustre of a woman's skin, but tight dark curls covered the chest.

'I baited for a jackal,' Mark thought wonderingly, 'and I caught myself a lion, a big old black-maned lion.' And now he felt real concern that Pungushe was dead. For such a splendid animal, death was a shabby bargain.

Then he saw the gentle, almost imperceptible rise and fall of the deep muscled chest, and he reached out and touched the shoulder through the kaross.

The man stirred, and then painfully lifted himself on one elbow, letting the kaross fall back, and he looked at Mark.

He was a man in the full noon of his strength and pride and dignity, perhaps forty years of age, with just the first frosts of wisdom touching the short cap of dark wool at his temples.

The agony did not show in his face, the broad forehead was smooth as polished amber, the mouth was in repose, and the eyes were dark and fierce and proud. It was the handsome moon face of the high-bred Zulu.

'Sakubona, Pungushe,' said Mark. 'I see you, O Jackal.'

The man looked at him for a moment, thinking about the name and the style of greeting, the language and the accent in which it was spoken. The calm expression did not change, no smile nor snarl on the thick sculptured lips, only a new light in the dark eyes.

'Sakubona, Jamela. I see you, O Seeker.' His voice was deep and low, yet it rang on the still air with the timbre of a bronze gong, and then he went on immediately, 'Sakubona, Ngaga.'

Mark blinked. It had never occurred to him that the jackal might think of him by a name every bit as derogatory. Ngaga is the pangolin, the scaly ant-eater, a small creature that resembles an armadillo, a nocturnal creature, which if caught out in daylight, scurries around like a bent and wizened old man pausing to peer shortsightedly at any small object in its path, then hurrying on again.

The two names 'Jamela' and 'Ngaga' used together described with embarrassing clarity somebody who ran in small circles, peering at everything and yet blindly seeing nothing.

Suddenly Mark saw himself through the eyes of a hidden observer, riding a seemingly pointless patrol through the valley, dismounting to peer at anything that caught his interest, then riding on again – just like an ngaga. It was not a flattering thought.

He felt with sudden discomfort that despite Pungushe's wounds, and Mark's position of superiority, so far he had had the worst of the exchange.

'It seems that ngaga has at last found what he seeks,' he pointed out grimly, and went to the mule for his blanket roll.

Under the bloody bunch of leaves there was a deep dark

hole where the point of the buffalo horn had driven in. It might have gone in as far as the kidneys, in which case the man was as good as dead. Mark thrust the thought aside, and swabbed out the wound as gently as he could with a solution of acriflavine.

His spare shirt was snowy white and still crisp from Marion's meticulous laundering and ironing. He ripped off the sleeves, folded the body into a wad and placed it over the gaping hole, binding it up with the torn sleeves.

Pungushe said nothing as he worked, made no protest nor showed any distress as Mark lifted him into a sitting position to work more easily. But when Mark ripped the shirt he murmured regretfully.

'It is a good shirt.'

'There was once a young and handsome ngaga who might have died from the fever,' Mark reminded him, 'but a scavenging old jackal carried him to a safe place and gave him drink and food.'

'Ah,' Pungushe nodded. 'But he was not such a stupid jackal as to tear a good shirt.'

'The ngaga is much concerned that the jackal is in good health, so that he will be able to labour mightily at the breaking of rocks and other manly tasks when he is an honoured guest at the kraal of King Georgey.' Mark ended that subject, and repacked his blanket roll. 'Can you make water, O Jackal? It is necessary to see how deep the buffalo has speared you.'

The urine was tinged pinky brown, but there were no strings of bright blood. It seemed that the kidneys may merely have been badly bruised, and that the thick pad of iron muscle across the Zulu's back had absorbed much of the brutal driving thrust. Mark found himself praying silently that it was so, although he could not imagine why he was so concerned.

Working quickly, he cut two long straight saplings, and plaited a drag litter from strips of wet bark. Then he padded the litter with his own blankets and Pungushe's kaross, before hitching it up to Trojan.

He helped the big Zulu into the litter, surprised to find how tall he was, and how hard was the arm he placed around Mark's shoulder to support himself.

With Pungushe flat in the litter, he led the mule back along the game trail, and the ends of two saplings left a long snaking drag mark in the soft earth.

It was almost dark when they passed the scene of the buffalo hunt. Looking across the reed banks, Mark could make out the obscene black shapes of the vultures in the trees, waiting their turn at the carcass.

'Why did you kill my buffalo?' he asked, not certain that Pungushe was still conscious. 'All men know the new laws. I have travelled to every village, I have spoken with every induna, every chief – all men have heard. All men know the penalty for hunting in this valley.'

'If he was your buffalo, why did he not carry the mark of your iron? Surely it is the custom of the *Abelungu* – the white men – to burn their mark upon their cattle?' Pungushe asked from the litter, without a smile nor with any trace of mockery, yet mockery Mark knew it was. He felt his anger stir.

'This place was declared sacred, even by the old king, Chaka.'

'No,' said Pungushe. 'It was declared a royal hunt, and,' his voice took a sterner ring, 'I am Zulu, of the royal blood. I hunt here by my birthright – it is a man's thing to do.'

'No man has the right to hunt here.'

'Then what of the white men who have come here with their *isibamu* – their rifles – these past hundred seasons?' asked Pungushe.

'They are evil-doers, even as you are.'

'Then why were they not taken to be guests at the kraal of King Georgey, as I am so honoured?'

'They will be in future,' Mark assured him.

'Ho!' said Pungushe, and this time his voice was thick with contempt and mockery.

'When I catch them, they will go also,' Mark repeated doggedly, but the Zulu made a weary gesture of dismissal with one expressive pink-palmed hand, a hand that said clearly that there were many laws – some for rich, some for poor, some for white and some for black. They were silent again until after dark when Mark had camped for the night, and put Trojan to graze on a head-rope.

As he squatted over the fire, cooking the evening meal for both of them, Pungushe spoke again from his litter in the darkness beyond the firelight.

'For whom do you keep the *silwane* – the wild animals of the valley? Will King George come here to hunt?'

'Nobody will ever hunt here again, no king nor common man.'

'Then why do you keep the *silwane?*'

'Because if we do not, then the day will dawn when there will be no more left in this land. No buffalo, no lion, no kudu, nothing. A great emptiness.'

Pungushe was silent for the time it took Mark to spoon a slop of maize porridge and bully beef into the lid of the pannikin and take it to the Zulu.

'Eat,' he commanded, and sat crosslegged opposite him with his own plate in his lap.

'What you say is true,' Pungushe spoke thoughtfully. 'When I was a child – of your age,' Mark noted the barb but let it pass, 'there were elephant in this valley, great bulls with teeth as long as a throwing-spear, and there were many lions, herds of buffalo like the great king's cattle,' he broke off. 'They have gone, soon what is left will go also.'

'Is that a good thing?' Mark asked.

'It is neither a good thing nor a bad thing.' Pungushe shrugged and began to eat. 'It is merely the way of the world – and there is little profit in pondering it.'

They finished eating in silence and Mark cleared the plates and brought coffee, which Pungushe waved away.

'Drink it,' snapped Mark. 'You must have it to cleanse the blood from your water.'

He gave Pungushe one of his cigarettes, and the Zulu carefully broke off the brown cork tip before putting it between his lips. He wrinkled his broad flat nose at the insipid taste, for he was accustomed to the ropey black native tobacco, but he would not belittle a man's hospitality by making comment.

'When it is all gone, when the great emptiness comes here to this valley, what will become of you, O Jackal?' Mark asked.

'I do not understand your question.'

'You are a man of the *silwane*. You are a great hunter. Your life is yoked to the *silwane*, as the herdsman is yoked to his cattle. What will become of you, O mighty hunter, when all your cattle are gone?'

Mark realized that he had reached the Zulu. He saw his nostrils flare, and something burn up brightly within him, but he waited while Pungushe considered the proposition at great length and in every detail.

'I will go to *Igoldi*,' said Pungushe at last. 'I will go to the gold mines, and become rich.'

'They will put you to work deep in the earth, where you cannot see the sun nor feel the wind, and you will break rocks, just as you go now to do at the kraal of King Georgey.'

Mark saw the repugnance flit across the Zulu's face.

'I will go to *Tekweni*,' Pungushe changed his mind. 'I will go to Durban and become a man of much consequence.'

'In *Tekweni* you will breathe the smoke of the cane mills into your lungs, and when the fat babu overseer speaks to you, you will reply, *yehbo*, Nkosi – yes, master!'

This time the repugnance on the Zulu's face was deeper

still and he smoked his cigarette down to a tiny sliver of paper and ash which he pinched out between thumb and forefinger.

'Jamela,' he said sternly. 'You speak words that trouble a man.'

Mark knew well that the big Zulu's injury was more serious than his stoic acceptance of it would indicate. It was womanly to show pain.

It would be a long time before he was ready to make the journey by side-car over the rough tracks and rutted dusty roads to the police station and magistrate's court at Ladyburg.

Mark put him into the small lean-to tool-shed that he had built on the far wall of the mule stables. It was dry and cool, and had a sturdy door with a Yale padlock. He used blankets from Marion's chest and the mattress she had been saving for the children's room, despite her protests. 'But he's a native, dear!'

Every evening, he took the prisoner's meal down to him in the pannikin, inspected the wound and dressed it afresh.

Then while he waited for Pungushe to eat, he sat on the top step in the doorway to the shed and they smoked a cigarette while they talked.

'If the valley belongs now to King Georgey, how is it that you build your house here, plant your gardens and graze your mules?'

'I am the king's man,' Mark explained.

'You are an induna?' Pungushe paused with a spoon of food halfway to his mouth, and stared at Mark incredulously. 'You are one of the king's counsellors?'

'I am the keeper of the royal hunt.' Mark used the old Zulu title, and Pungushe shook his head sadly.

'My father's father was once the keeper of the royal hunt

– but he was a man of great consequence, with two dozen wives, a man who had fought in a dozen wars and killed so many enemies that his shield was as thick with oxtails as there is grass on the hills in springtime.' The oxtail was the decoration which the king grants a warrior to adorn his shield when he has distinguished himself in battle. Pungushe finished his meal and added simply, 'King Chaka knew better than to send a child to do man's work.'

The next evening Mark saw that the wound was healing cleanly and swiftly. The man's tremendous fitness and strength were responsible for that. He was able to sit cross-legged now, and there was a new jauntiness in the way he held his head. It would be sooner than Mark had thought that Pungushe would be fit enough to make the journey to Ladyburg, and Mark felt an odd sinking feeling of regret.

'King Georgey is doubtlessly a great, wise and all-seeing king,' Pungushe opened the evening's debate. 'Why then does he wait until sundown to begin work that should have been started at dawn? If he wanted to avoid the great emptiness in this valley, his father should have begun the work.'

'The king's affairs are many, in far countries. He must rely on indunas to advise him who are not as wise or allseeing,' Mark explained.

'The *Abelungu* – the white men – are like greedy children, grabbing up handfuls of food they cannot eat. Instead they smear it over their faces.'

'There are greedy and ignorant black men also,' Mark pointed out. 'Some who even kill leopards with steel traps for their fur.'

'To sell to the greedy white men, to dress their ignorant women,' Pungushe agreed, and that makes the score deuce, Mark thought as he gathered up the empty pannikins.

The next evening Pungushe seemed sad, as at the time of leave-taking.

'You have given me much on which I must think heavily,' he said.

'You will have much time to do so,' Mark agreed. 'In between the breaking of rocks.' And Pungushe ignored the reference.

'There is weight in your words, for one who is still young enough to be herding the cattle,' he qualified the compliment.

'Out of the mouths of babes and sucklings,' Mark translated into Zulu and Pungushe nodded solemnly, and in the morning he was gone.

He had opened the thatch at the back of the roof, and wriggled through the small hole. He had taken his kaross and left Marion's blankets neatly folded on the mattress. He had tried for the steel spring-trap, but Mark had locked it in the kitchen, so he had left it and gone northwards in the night.

Mark was furious for so misjudging his prisoner's recovery, and he muttered darkly as he plunged along after him on Trojan.

'This time I'm going to shoot the bastard on sight,' he promised, and realized at that moment that Pungushe had backtracked on him. He had to dismount and laboriously unravel the confused trail.

Half an hour later, Pungushe led him into the river, and it was well after noon when he at last found where the Zulu had left the water, stepping lightly on a fallen log.

He finally lost the cold spoor in the rocky ground on the far rim of the valley, and it was almost midnight when he rode wearily back to the thatched cottage. Marion had his dinner ready and ten gallons of hot bath water bubbling on the fire.

Six weeks later, Pungushe returned to the valley. Mark sat astounded on the stoep of the cottage, and watched him come.

He walked with the long gliding stride that showed he was fully recovered from his wound. He wore the beaded loin-cloth and the jackal-skin cloak over his shoulders. He carried two of the short-shafted stabbing assegai, with the broad steel blades, and his wives followed at a respectable distance behind him.

There were three of them. They were bare-breasted, with the tall clay headdress of the Zulu matron. The senior was of the same age as her husband, but her dugs were flat and empty as leather pouches and she had lost her front teeth. The youngest wife was a child still in her teens, a pretty plump little thing with jolly melon breasts, and a fat brown infant on her hip.

Every wife carried an enormous bundle on her head, balancing it easily without use of hands, and they were followed by a gaggle of naked and half-naked children. Like their mothers, the little girls each carried a headload, the size of it directly proportional to the age and stature of the bearer. The smallest, perhaps four years of age, carried a beer gourd the size of a grapefruit, echoing faithfully the straight erect carriage and swaying buttocks of her seniors.

Mark counted seven sons and six daughters.

'I see you, Jamela.' Pungushe paused below the stoep.

'I see you also, Pungushe,' Mark acknowledged cautiously, and the Zulu squatted down comfortably on the lowest step. His wives settled down at the edge of Marion's garden – politely out of earshot. The youngest wife gave one of her fat breasts to the infant and he suckled lustily.

'It will rain tomorrow,' said Pungushe. 'Unless the wind goes into the north. In which case it will not rain again until the full moon.'

'That is so,' Mark agreed.

'Rain now would be good for the grazing. It will bring

the *silwane* down from the Portuguese territory beyond the Pongola.'

Mark's astonishment had now given way to lively curiosity.

'There is talk in the villages, common word among all the people that has only recently come to my ears,' Pungushe went on airily. 'It is said that Jamela, the new keeper of the royal hunt of King Georgey, is a mighty warrior who has slain great multitudes of the king's enemies in the war beyond the sea.' The Jackal paused and then went on, 'Albeit, he is still unbearded and green as the first flush of the spring-time grass.'

'Is that the word?' Mark inquired politely.

'It is said that King Georgey has granted Jamela a black oxtail to wear on his shield.' A black oxtail is the highest honour, and might loosely be considered the equivalent of a M.M.

'I am also a warrior,' Pungushe pointed out. 'I fought with Bombata at the gorge, and afterwards the soldiers came and took away my cattle. This is how I became a man of *silwane*, and a mighty hunter.'

'We are brothers of the spear,' Mark conceded. 'But now I will make ready my *isi-du-du-du*, my motorcycle, so that we may ride to Ladyburg and speak with the magistrate there of matters of great interest to all of us.'

'Jamela!' The Zulu shook his head grievingly, like a father with an obtuse son. 'You aspire to be a man of the *silwane*, you aspire to fill the great emptiness – and yet who will there be to teach you, who will open your eyes to see and your ears to hear, if I am in the kraal of King Georgey breaking his rocks?'

'You have come to help me?' Mark asked. 'You and your beautiful fat wives, your brave sons and nubile daughters?'

'It is even so.'

'This is a noble thought,' Mark conceded.

'I am Zulu of royal blood,' Pungushe agreed. 'Also my

fine steel trap was stolen from me, even as my cattle were stolen, thus making me a poor man once more.'

'I see,' Mark nodded. 'It remains only for me to put out of my mind the business of leopard skins and dead buffalo?'

'It is even so.'

'Doubtless I will also find it in my heart, to pay you for this help and advice.'

'That also is so.'

'What size is the coin in which you will be paid?'

Pungushe shrugged with disinterest. 'I am royal Zulu, not a Hindu trader, haggling in the market-place. The coin will be just and fair,' he paused delicately, 'always bearing in mind the multitude of my beautiful wives, my many brave sons and the host of nubile daughters. All of whom have unbelievable appetites.'

Mark had to remain silent, not trusting himself to speak until he controlled the violent urge to burst out laughing. He spoke again, solemnly, but with laughter rippling his belly muscles.

'In what style will you address me, Pungushe? When I speak, will you answer "*Yehbo*, Nkosi – Yes, Master"?'

Pungushe stirred restlessly, and an expression flitted across the broad smooth features like a fastidious eater who has just discovered a large fat worm on his plate. 'I will call you Jamela,' he said. 'And when you speak as you have just spoken, I will answer "Jamela, that is a great stupidity."'

'In what style will I address you?' Mark inquired politely, fighting his mirth.

'You will call me Pungushe. For the jackal is the cleverest and most cunning of all the *silwane*, and it is necessary for you to be reminded of this from time to time.'

Then something happened that Mark had not seen before. Pungushe smiled. It was like the break-through of the sun on a grey overcast day. His teeth were big and perfect and white, and the smile stretched so wide that it seemed his face might tear.

Mark could no longer contain it. He laughed out loud, beginning with a strangled chuckle. Hearing it, Pungushe laughed also, a great ringing bell of laughter.

The two of them laughed so long and hard, that the wives fell silent and watched in amazement, and Marion came out on to the stoep.

'What is it, dear?'

He could not answer her, and she went away shaking her head at the craziness of men.

At last they both fell silent, exhausted with mirth, and Mark gave Pungushe a cigarette from which he carefully broke the corked tip. They smoked in silence for nearly a minute, then suddenly without warning Mark let out another uncontrolled guffaw, and it started them off again.

The cords of sinew stood out on Pungushe's neck, like columns of carved ebony, and his mouth was a deep pink cavern lined with perfect white teeth. He laughed until the tears ran down his face and dripped from his chin, and when he lost his breath, he let out a great whistling snort like a bull hippo breaking surface, and he wiped the tears away with his thumb and said, 'Ee – hee!' and slapped his thigh like a pistol shot, between each fresh paroxysm of laughter.

Mark ended it by reaching out his shaking right hand, and Pungushe took it in a reverse grip, panting and heaving still.

'Pungushe, I am your man,' Mark sobbed.

'And I, Jamela, am yours.'

There were four men sitting in a semi-circle around the wall of the hotel suite. They were all dressed in such fashion that it seemed a uniform. The dark high-buttoned suits, the glazed celluloid collars and sober neckties. Although their ages were spread over thirty years, although one of them was bald with grey wisps around his ears and another had a fiery red bush of hair, although one wore a prim gold pince-nez pinched on to a thin aquiline nose while another had the open far-seeing gaze of the farmer, yet all of them had those solid hewn calvinistic faces, indomitable, unrelenting and strong as granite.

Dirk Courtney spoke to them in the young language which had only recently received recognition as a separate entity from its parent Dutch, and had been given the name of Afrikaans.

He spoke it with an elegance and precision that softened the reserve in their expressions, and eased the set of jaw and the stiffness in their backs.

'It's a Jingo area,' Dirk told them. 'There is a Union Jack flying on every roof-top. It's a rich constituency, land-owners, professional men – your party has no appeal there.' He was talking of the parliamentary constituency of Lady-burg. 'In the last elections you did not even present a candidate, nobody fool enough to lose his deposit, and the Smuts party returned General Courtney unopposed.'

The eldest of his listeners nodded over his gold pince-nez, inviting him to continue.

'If you are to fight the Ladyburg seat, you will need a candidate with a different approach, an English speaker, a man of property, somebody with whom the voters can identify—'

It was a beautiful performance. Dirk Courtney, hand-some, debonair, articulate in either language, striding back and forth across the carpeted lounge, holding all their attention, stopping dramatically to make a point with a graceful gesture of strong brown hands, then striding on again. He talked for half an hour, and he was watching his audience, noting the reaction of each, judging their weaknesses, their strengths.

At the end of that half hour, he had decided that all four of them were dedicated, completely committed to their political faith. They stirred only at appeals to patriotism, to national interest, at reference to the aspirations of their people.

'So,' Dirk Courtney thought comfortably. 'It's cheaper to buy honest men. Rogues cost good bright gold – while honest men can be had with a few fine words and noble sentiments. Give me an honest man every time.'

One of the older men leaned forward and asked quietly, 'General Courtney has had the seat since 1910. He is a member of the Smuts Cabinet, a war hero, and a man of huge popular appeal. He is also your father. Do you think the voters will take the young dog when they can have the sire?'

Dirk answered: 'I am prepared not only to risk my deposit if I achieve the National Party nomination, but I am confident enough of my eventual success to make a substantial earnest of my serious intentions to the campaign funds of the party.' He named a sum of money that made them exchange quick glances of surprise.

'In exchange for all this?' the elder politician asked.

'Nothing that is not in the best interest of the nation, and of my constituency,' Dirk told them soberly, and he pulled down the map that hung on the far wall facing them.

Again he began to speak, but now with the contagious fervour of the zealot. In burning words, he built up a vision of ploughed fields stretching to the horizon, and sweet clean water running deep in endless irrigation furrows. The listeners were all men who had farmed and ploughed the rich but hostile soil of Africa, and all of them had searched blue and cloudless skies with hopeless eyes for the rain clouds that never came. The image of deeply turned furrows and slaking water was irresistible.

'Of course, we will have to repeal the proclamation on the Bubezi Valley,' Dirk said it glibly, and not one of them showed shock or concern at the statement. Already they could see the inland sea of sweet limpid water ruffling in the breeze.

'If we win at this election,' the eldest politician began.

'No, Menheer,' Dirk interrupted gently, '*when* we win.'

The man smiled for the first time. 'When we win,' he agreed.


D irk Courtney stood high on the platform, with thumbs hooked into his waistcoat. When he smiled and tilted that noble lion head with the shining mane of curls, the women in the audience that packed the church hall rustled like flowers in the breeze.

'The Butcher,' said Dirk Courtney, and his voice rang with a depth and resonance that thrilled them all, man and woman, young and old. 'The Butcher of Fordsburg, his hands red with blood of our countrymen.'

The applause began with the men that Dirk Courtney had in the audience, but it spread quickly.

'I rode with Sean Courtney against Bombata—' one man was on his feet, near the back of the hall. 'I went to France with him,' he was shouting to be heard above the applause. 'And where were you, Mr Dirk Courtney, when the drums were beating?'

The smile never left Dirk's face, but two little spots of hectic colour rose in his cheeks.

'Ah!' He faced the man across the craning heads of the audience. 'One of the gallant General's gunmen. How many women did you shoot down at Fordsburg?'

'That doesn't answer my question,' the man shouted back, and Dirk caught the eye of one of the two big men who had risen and were closing in quietly on the questioner.

'Four thousand casualties,' said Dirk. 'The Government would like to hide that fact from you, but four thousand men, women and children—'

The two big men had closed in on their quarry, and Dirk Courtney drew all eyes with a broad theatrical gesture.

'A Government that has that contempt for the life, property and freedom of its people.'

There was a brief scuffle, a yelp of pain and the man was hustled out of the side door into the night.

The newspapers started picking it up almost immediately, the same editorials which had ranted against the 'Red Cabal' and the 'Bolshevik threat', which had praised Smuts' 'direct and timely action', were now remembering 'a highhanded and brutal solution'.

Across the nation, begun by Dirk Courtney and picked up by all the Hertzogites, the balance of public feeling was swinging back, like a pendulum, or the curved blade of the executioner's axe.

Dirk Courtney spoke in the Town Hall of Durban, to three thousand, in the Church Hall of Ladyburg to three hundred. He spoke at every country church in the constituency, at little crossroad general-dealer shops where a dozen voters assembled for an evening's entertainment, but always the Press was represented.

Dirk Courtney worked slowly northwards, during the day visiting all his land holdings, each of his new cane mills, and each evening he spoke to the little assemblies of voters. Always he was vibrant and compelling, handsome and articulate, and he painted a picture for them of a land crossed with railways and fine roads, of prosperous towns, and busy markets. They listened avidly.

'There are two,' said Pungushe. 'One is an old lion. I know him well. He stayed last year in Portuguese territory along the north bank of the Usutu River. He was alone then, but now he has found a mate.'

'Where did they cross?' Mark asked.

'They crossed below Ndumu, and came south between the swamp and the river.'

The lion was five years old, and very cunning, a lean tom, tall at the shoulder and with a short ruff of reddish mane. There was an ugly bald scar across his forehead, and he favoured his right foreleg where a piece of hammered pot-leg fired from a Tower musket two years previously had lodged against the shoulder joint. He had been hunted by man almost without remission since he was a cub, and he was getting old now, and tired.

He crossed the river in the dark, swimming his lioness ahead of him, going south from the hunters who had assembled to drive the bush along the river the next morning. He could hear the drums still beating, and smell the smoke of their fires. He could hear also the yapping clamour of the dog packs. They had assembled, two or three hundred tribesmen with their hunting dogs and a dozen Portuguese half-breeds with breech-loading rifles, for the lions had killed two trek oxen on the outskirts of one of the river villages. In the morning the hunt would begin, and the lion took his mate south.

She was also a big animal, and though she was still very young and not as experienced, yet she was quick and strong, and she learned from him each day. Her hide was still clean and unscarred by claw or thorn. Across the back she was a sleek olive tan shading down to a lovely buttery yellow at the throat and fluffy cream on the belly.

She still had traces of her kitten spots dappling her quarters, but the night they swam the Usutu, she came into season for the first time.

On the south bank, they shook the water from their

503

bodies, with fierce shuddering spasms, and then the lion snuffed at her, drumming softly in his throat and then lifting his snout to the bright white stars, his back arching reflexively at the tantalizing musk of her pale blood-tinged oestrous discharge.

She led him half a mile up one of the thickly wooded tributary valleys, and then she crept into the heart of the thicket of tangled bush, a stronghold guarded by the fierce two-inch, wickedly hooked thorns, tipped in red as though they had already drawn blood.

Here in the dawn, he covered her for the first time. She crouched low against the earth, hissing and crackling with angry snarls, while he came over her, biting at her ears and neck, forcing her to submit. Afterwards, she lay close against him, licking at his ears, nuzzling his throat and belly, turning half away from him and nudging him flirtatiously with her hind quarters, until he rose and she crouched down submissively and snarled at him while he mounted her briefly once again.

They mated twenty-three times that day, and in the night they left the thorn thicket and wandered southwards again.

A half hour before the set of the moon, they reached the edge of the ploughed land, and the lion stopped and growled softly at the smell of man and cattle.

Tentatively he reached out one paw and tested the freshly turned earth, then he drew his leg back and made a little troubled mewing sound of indecision. The lioness brushed herself lovingly against him, but he turned aside and led her along the edge of the ploughed land.

'Will they reach the valley, Pungushe?' Mark asked, leaning out of the saddle to speak to the Zulu as he trotted at Trojan's shoulder.

Pungushe spoke easily, despite the fact he had run without rest for nearly three hours. 'They must cross almost half a day's march of land where men are working, where the ploughs of the new sugar-growers are busy. Besides, Jamela, they know nothing of your valley, and the mad Ngaga who would welcome them.' Mark straightened in the saddle and rode on grimly. He knew that this pair, this matting pair, would be his last chance to have lions in his valley. Yet there was twenty miles of danger to cross such as these animals, coming out of the wilderness of Portuguese Mozambique, would never have experienced before, ploughlands, declared cattle area, where lions were vermin. An area devoid of wild prey, but heavily populated with domestic animals. An area where the cry of 'Lion' would send fifty men running eagerly for a rifle, fifty white men competing fiercely for the trophy, hating the big predatory cats with a blind unthinking hatrèd, welcoming what was probably their only chance at one of them, safe in the knowledge that they were fair game, unprotected by law in the cattle areas.

The lions came to the camp downwind, and they lay flat in the short grass in the darkness at the edge of the camp.

They listened to the drowsy voices of the men at the fire, and smelled the myriad strange smells, of tobacco smoke, of cooking maize meal and the sour tang of Zulu beer, and they lay very flat and tense against the earth, only their round black-tipped ears cocked and their nostrils flaring and sucking the air.

The oxen were kraaled with a low circular enclosure of felled thorn trees, arranged with their trunks inward and the bushy thorny tangle outwards. The smell of the cattle was strong and tempting.

There were seventy-two oxen in the kraal, two full spans. They belonged to Ladyburg Sugar Company and they were ploughing the new lands east of Chaka's Gate, after the labour teams had stumped out the standing timber and burned it in long windows.

The lion waited, patient, but alert and tensed and silent, while the silver moon went down below the trees and the men's voices dwindled into silence. He waited while the fires died down into puddles of dull ruddy ash. Then he rose silently.

The lioness did not move, except that the great muscles in her chest and limbs swelled, rigid with tension, and her ears cocked fractionally forward.

The lion circled cautiously upwind of the camp. There was a soft cool wash of breeze coming steadily out of the east and he used it skilfully.

The oxen caught the whiff of lion as he moved into the wind, and he heard them coming up, rising in that awkward plunging leap from where they had settled.

Horns clashed together as they swung into a tight group facing upwind, and one of them let out a soft mournful lowing. Immediately it was taken up, and their low bellows woke the men at the fires. Somebody shouted, and threw a log on the fire. A torrent of sparks rose into the dark branches of the mimosa and the log caught, lighting the camp with a yellow leaping dancing light. The ploughmen and the lead boys were gathered fearfully around the fire, still with skin karosses draped around their shoulders, owl-eyed with sleep and alarm.

The lion slipped like a shadow, dark and flat against the earth towards the kraal, and the cattle bunched and bellowed wildly at the sharp rank cat smell.

Against the thorny windward side of the kraal, the lion crouched, arched his back and ejected a stream of urine.

The pungent, biting ammoniac stink was too much for the mass of cattle. In a single solid bunch, they swung away downwind and charged the thorny wall of the temporary kraal, crashing through it without check, and they thundered free, quickly spreading, losing the solid formation and scattering away into the night.

The lioness was ready for them, and she streaked in across the flank of the panicking plunging formation, selecting a single victim, a heavy young beast. She drove him onwards, chivvying him like a sheep dog, crossing and recrossing his frantic driving quarters, running him far from the fires and the ploughmen before coming snaking up alongside and hooking expertly at one of his powerfully driving forelegs, and the curved yellow claws bitting in just above the hock until they grated against the bone. Then she went back on her own bunched quarters and dragged the leg to cross the other.

The ox dropped as though he had been shot through the brain, and he somersaulted haunch over head, and slid against the earth on his back, all four legs kicking to the starry sky.

In a rubbery flash of supple speed, the cat closed, judging finely the massive hooves that could have crushed her skull and the wide straight horns which could have impaled her rib to rib.

She bit in hard at the base of the skull, driving the long ivory yellow eye teeth into the first and second vertebrae, so they crunched sharply like a walnut in the jaws of the cracker.

When the lion came padding hurriedly out of the night, she had already opened the belly cavity of the ox and her whole head was red and toffee sticky with blood as she went for liver and spleen and kidneys.

She flattened her ears against her bloody skull and snarled murderously at him, but he put his shoulder to her flank and pushed her aside; she snarled again and he cuffed her with a lordly paw and began to feed in the hole she had made.

She glared at him for a second, then her ears came erect and she began to lick his shoulder with long pink voluptuous strokes, purring with a deep soft rattle in her throat, pressing her long sleek body against him. The lion tried to ignore her and fed with snuffling grunts and wet tearing ripping sounds.

But she became bolder, the eternal female taking

advantage of her new highly attractive condition, liberties which before would have brought swift and stern disciplinary action.

Desperately the lion tried to restrain her by placing a huge paw on her head, claws carefully retracted, and gulped furiously, trying to eat the entire ox before she could join in, but she wriggled out from under the paw and licked his ear. He growled half-heartedly, flickered the ear. She inched forward and licked his eyes, so he had to close them tightly, furrowing his brow and trying to feed blind, but finally he surrendered to the inevitable and allowed her to force her head into the bloody crater.

Side by side, purring and growling softly, they fed.

There were eighteen of them, gathered on the wide mosquito-screened veranda of the foreman's cottage under the hissing Petromax lamps. The brandy bottle had been out since sundown, and most of the men were red-faced and bright-eyed as they listened to Dirk Courtney.

'There will be schools and hospitals within a twenty mile ride of everybody,' he promised, and the women looked up from their knitting. They knew what it was like to raise a young family out here. 'This is the beginning only,' he promised the men. 'And those of you who were first in will be the first to profit. Once I am in Parliament, you'll have a strong voice speaking up for you. You'll see improvement here you couldn't imagine possible – and quickly.'

'You're a rich man, Mr Courtney,' one of them said. He was a small trader, not directly employed by Ladyburg Sugar, but sufficiently reliant on it to phrase his question with respect. 'One of the bosses. How come you speak out for the working man?'

'I'm rich because I worked hard, but I know that without you men, I won't be rich much longer. We are linked together like a team.'

They nodded and murmured and Dirk went on quickly. 'One thing I promise you. When I can hire a white man at a decent wage, I won't push in coolie or nigger labour!'

They cheered him then, and filled their glasses to toast him.

'Your present Government, the Smuts men, tried that on the gold mines. Two and tuppence a day for black men, and white men out on the street. When the workers protested, they sent the bloody Butcher of Fordsburg, a man who I am ashamed to call my father—'

There was an urgent hammering on the kitchen door, and the foreman excused himself quietly and hurried out. He was back within a minute and whispered to Dirk Courtney. Dirk grinned and nodded, and turned back to his audience.

'Well, gentlemen, a fine bit of sport in the offing – a lion has killed one of my oxen, down on the new Buli block. The plough boy has just come in to report it. It happened only an hour ago, so we will have an excellent sporting chance at him. May I move closure of this meeting, and we'll meet here again at,' he glanced at his watch, 'at five o'clock tomorrow morning, every man with a horse and rifle!'

Mark and Pungushe slept, each under a single blanket, on the sunbaked earth, with Trojan cropping the scraggy dry yellow grass nearby. There was a cold little breeze out of the east, and they woke in the total dark of not-yet dawn and sat over the fire drinking coffee and smoking silently until Pungushe could take the spoor again.

From the back of Trojan it was still too dark to see the ground, but Pungushe ran confidently ahead, forcing the mule into a reluctant lumbering trot to keep pace.

At the edge of the ploughed land, he had to cast, but he cut the lion spoor on its new track almost immediately. They went off again, with the sunrise outlining the upper branches of the trees, turning them black and spiky against the ruddy gold.

The soft amber rays were without warmth, and threw long distorted shadows of mule and men on the hard red earth.

Mark marvelled once again that the Zulu could run a spoor in this light over such ground, where he could see no mark or sign of the lion's passing.

There was a single gun shot, so faint that Mark thought he might have imagined it, but Pungushe stopped instantly and signalled him to rein in the mule.

They stood and listened intently, and suddenly there was a distant popping fusillade, ten, eleven rifle-shots and then silence again.

Pungushe turned and looked at Mark expressionlessly. The silence was complete, even the morning bird chorus was stilled by the gunfire for a moment. Then as the silence persisted, a troop of little brown francolin started chirruping again on the edge of the ploughed lands.

'Go on!' Mark nodded to Pungushe, trying to keep his face as expressionless, but his voice shook with outrage. They were too late. The last lions south of the Usutu were dead. He felt sick with helpless anger.

They did not notice Mark until he was right up to them. They were too excited, too intent on their work.

There were eight white men, all heavily armed and dressed in rough hunting clothes, with two Zulu grooms holding the horses.

In a trampled opening among the mimosa trees lay the half-eaten carcass of a red and white ox. However, this was not what was engaging their attention. They were grouped in a tight circle beyond the ox, and their voices were raucous, raised in rough jest and cheerful oath.

Mark dismounted and handed the reins to Pungushe. He walked slowly towards the group, dreading what he would find, but he stopped again as one of the men looked up and saw him. He recognized Mark instantly.

'Ah, warden!' Dirk Courtney laughed, tossing that splendid head of glossy curls. 'We are doing your job for you.' The laughter was sly and spiteful, the malice so apparent that Mark knew he was thinking of the bribe that Mark had accepted and then turned against him.

'Here is one that you can cross off your report,' Dirk chuckled again, and gestured for his men to stand aside. The circle opened and Mark stepped into the opening. The men around him were still red-faced and garrulous, and he could smell the stale liquor on them.

'Gentlemen, may I present the newly appointed warden of Chaka's Gate proclaimed area.' Dirk stood opposite him, across the circle, with one hand thrust carelessly into the pocket of his chamois-leather jacket, a hand-made double barrelled .450 elephant rifle by Gibbs of London tucked into the crook of his elbow.

The lion lay on its side with all four legs extended. He was an old, scarred tom, so lean and rangy that each rib showed clearly through the short tan hair. There were four bullet-holes in the body; the one behind the shoulder would have raked both lungs, but another heavy bullet had shattered the skull. The mouth hung open slackly and a little blood-stained saliva still oozed out on to the lolling pink tongue.

'Congratulations, gentlemen,' Mark nodded, and only Dirk Courtney caught the irony in his voice.

'Yes,' he agreed. 'The sooner we clear this area and make it safe for settlement – the better for all.'

There was a hearty chorus of agreement and one of them

produced a brown bottle from his back pocket, and passed it from hand to hand, each in turn pointing its base briefly heavenwards, then exclaiming appreciatively and smacking their lips.

'What about the lioness?' Mark asked quietly, refusing his turn at the bottle.

'Don't worry about her,' one of them assured him. 'She's down already. I hit her clean in the shoulder. We are just giving her a chance to stiffen up, before we go after her to finish her off.' And he drew his sheath knife and began to skin out the carcass of the lion, while his comrades passed loud comment and advice.

Mark walked back to Pungushe who squatted patiently at Trojan's head.

'The lioness is wounded, but has run.'

'I have seen the spoor,' Pungushe nodded, and pointed it out with his eyes, not moving his head.

'How bad is she hit?'

'I do not know yet. I must see how she settles to run before judging.'

'Take the spoor,' said Mark. 'Let us go quietly, without alerting these mighty hunters.'

They drifted away from the clearing, leading the mule casually, Mark following a dozen paces behind the Zulu.

Five hundred yards further on, Pungushe stopped and spoke quietly.

'She is hit in the right shoulder or leg, but I do not think the bone has gone, for she touches with every second pace. She goes well on three legs, and at first there was a little blood, but it dries quickly.'

'Perhaps she bleeds inside?' Mark asked.

'If that is so, we will find her within a short while – dead,' Pungushe shrugged.

'All right.' Mark swung up into the saddle. 'Let us go swiftly, that we may outrun these others, none of them will be able to follow across such hard ground.'

He was too late.

'Anders!' Dirk Courtney shouted, riding up at the head of his band. 'What the hell do you think you are doing?'

'My job,' Mark answered. 'I'm following a wounded beast.'

'We are coming with you.'

Mark glanced at Pungushe, and a silent accord flashed between them, then he turned back to the group.

'You all realize the danger involved? These animals have probably been hunted before, and my tracker thinks the lioness is only lightly hit.'

There was a little sobering and hesitation, but all eight of them rode on after Pungushe. He went hard, loping away, *minza umhlabathi*, stretching the horses into an easy canter and after the first hour Dirk Courtney swore bad-temperedly.

'I don't see any blood.'

'The blood has dried,' Mark told him. 'The wound has closed.'

The contents of the brown bottle were long ago exhausted. Red faces were sweating heavily in the rising heat, eyes were bloodshot and high good humour turning to headaches and woolly tongues; none of them had remembered to bring a water bottle.

Two of them turned back.

An hour later Dirk Courtney snarled suspiciously, 'This bloody nigger is giving us a bum run. Tell him I'll take the horse-whip to him.'

'The lioness is going strongly—'

'I don't believe it. I can't see any spoor.'

Pungushe stopped abruptly, motioned them to stay and went forward cautiously into a low thicket of waterbessie scrub.

'I've had a guts full of this,' muttered one of the hunters miserably.

'Me too.'

'I've got work to do.'

Three more of them turned back, and those that remained sat their restless horses until Pungushe emerged from the thicket and beckoned them forward.

In the heart of the thicket, impressed deeply into the soft mound of a mole heap, he showed them the unmistakable pad of a lioness. It headed relentlessly southward.

'All right,' Dirk Courtney acknowledged. 'He's still on the spoor. Tell him to keep going.'

An hour after noon, the lioness led them on to a low unbroken cap of solid grey granite, and Pungushe sat down wearily. His muscles shone in the sunlight with sweat, as though they had been oiled. He looked up at Mark on the mule and shrugged with an expressive gesture of helplessness.

'Dead spoor,' said Mark. 'Gone away.'

Dirk Courtney pulled up his horse's head with a cruel jerk of the curb, and snapped at Mark.

'Anders. I want to speak to you.' He trotted away out of earshot of the group, and Mark followed him.

They stopped and faced each other, and Dirk's mouth was twisted into a pinched and bitter line.

'This is the second time you have been clever at my expense,' he started grimly. 'You could have had me as an ally – but instead you had my father send me a receipt for my gift. Now you and your savage have pulled another trick. I don't know how you did it, but it's the last time it will happen.'

He stared at Mark, and the slant of the eyes altered, once again that mad malevolent light burned in their depths.

'A powerful friend I would have been – but a much more powerful enemy I am now. So far only my father's protection has saved you. That will change. No man stands in my way, I swear that to you.'

He wheeled his horse, put spurs to it and galloped away. The other two disconsolate hunters trailed away after him.

Mark rode back to Pungushe, and they drank from the water-bottle and smoked a little before Mark asked, 'Where is the lioness?'

'We left her spoor two hours back.'

Mark glanced sharply at him, and Pungushe stood up and walked to another mole heap at the edge of the granite. He squatted beside it, and with a roll of his open palm outlined the fleshy pad of a lion paw, then he bunched his knuckles and rolled them for the toe marks.

Miraculously, the spoor of a full-grown lion appeared in the soft earth, and Pungushe looked up at Mark's startled unbelieving expression and let out one of those whistling hippo-snorts of laughter, rocking back on his heels delightedly. 'For two hours we followed the Tokoloshe,'* he hooted.

'I cannot see her,' said Mark, carefully glassing the shallow wooded valley below them.

'Oh! Jamela, who cannot see.'

'Where is she, Pungushe?'

'Do you see the forked tree, beyond the three round rocks—' A step at a time he directed Mark's gaze, until suddenly he made out just the two dark round blobs of her ears above the short yellow grass, about six hundred yards from where they sat. She was lying close in under the spread of a thorn thicket, and even as he watched, she lowered her head and the ears vanished.

'Now that she is alone, she wishes to return to the place she knows well, beyond the Usutu. That is why she moves always that way, when the pain of the wound allows.'

* A Tokoloshe is a mythical creature from Zulu magical legend.

Before they had come up with her, they had found three places where she had lain to rest, and at one such place there had been a smear of blood and a dozen yellow hairs glued into the clot. Pungushe had inspected the hairs, minutely; by colour and texture he could tell from which part of the lioness' body they had come.

'High in the right shoulder – and if she was bleeding inside she would be down already. But she is in great pain, for she walks short. The wound has stiffened. She cannot go far.'

Now Mark swung the glasses towards the west, and longingly stared through them at the blue misty loom of the cliffs of Chaka's Gate, half a dozen miles away.

'So close,' he murmured, 'so close.' But the exhausted cat was dragging herself painfully away from sanctuary, back towards the ploughed lands, towards cattle and men and the dog packs.

Instinctively he turned in that direction now, swinging the binoculars in a long slow traverse across the north and east.

From the low ridge he had a good field of sight, across miles of light forest to the open chocolate expanse of ploughed land.

Something moved in the field of the binoculars and he blinked his eyes and refocused carefully. Three horsemen were coming slowly in their direction, and even at this range Mark could see the dogs running ahead of them.

Quickly he looked back at the leading rider. There was no mistaking that arrogantly erect figure. Dirk Courtney had not given up the hunt. He had merely returned to assemble a hunting-pack, and now the dogs were coming down fast on the smell of the wounded cat.

Mark laid a hand on the hard muscle of Pungushe's shoulder, and with his free hand he pointed. The Zulu stood up and stared for a full minute at the oncoming horsemen, then he began to speak quickly.

'Jamela, I will try to call the lioness, and lead her—'

Mark started to ask a question, but Pungushe stopped him harshly. 'Can you pull the dogs away, or stop them?'

Mark thought for a moment, then nodded. 'Give me your snuff, Pungushe.'

He took the snuff horn that hung on a thong around his neck and handed it to Mark without question.

'Go,' said Mark. 'Call my lioness for me.'

Pungushe slipped away down the ridge and left Mark to hurry to Trojan.

There were three sticks of black dried meat left in Mark's food bag. He found two flat stones and pounded the dry meat into a fine powder between them, glancing up every few seconds to see the huntsmen coming on rapidly.

Once the meat was powdered he scooped it into his pannikin and added an ounce of native snuff from the horn, mixing the two powders with his fingers as he ran back down the ridge to intersect the lioness trail at the point they had left it.

When he reached the shoulder of the ridge where the wounded cat had skirted a rocky outcrop, he knelt and made three neat piles of the mixed powder directly in the path of the oncoming dogs.

The dried meat would be irresistible when they reached it, the dogs would sniff at it greedily.

He could hear them already, baying excitedly, coming on swiftly, leading the hunters at a canter. As he ran back up the ridge to where Trojan stood, Mark smiled bleakly. A hound with a good suck of fiery native snuff up his nose wasn't going to smell anything else for at least twelve hours.

The lioness lay on her side, with her mouth open. She panted for air, and her chest pumped like a blacksmith's bellows, and her eyes were tightly closed.

The bullet had been fired from her right quarter. It was a soft lead slug from a .455 Martini Hendry and it had taken her high in the shoulder, but far forward, cutting in through the heavy muscle and grazing the big joint of the shoulder, lacerating sinew and shattering that extraordinary small floating bone, found only in the shoulder of a lion, the lucky bone so prized as a hunter's talisman.

The bullet had missed the artery as it plunged into the neck and lodged there beneath the skin, a lump the size of the top joint of a man's thumb.

The flies swarmed joyously into the mouth of the wound, and she lifted her head and snapped at them, and then mewing softly at the agony that movement had caused, she began to lick the bullet hole carefully, the long tongue rasping roughly against her hide, curling pink and dextrous as it cleansed the fresh little trickle of watery blood that had sprung from it. Then she sank back wearily and closed her eyes again.

Pungushe was aware of the wind in the same way as the helmsman of a tall ship is, for it was as important to him as it is to a mariner. He knew exactly at each moment of the day its force and direction, anticipated any change before it occurred and he did not have to carry an ash bag nor wet a finger, the knowledge was instinctive.

Now he moved carefully into a downwind position from the wounded animal. It did not occur to him to thank any providence for the constant easterly breeze that put him fairly between the cat and the near boundary of Chaka's Gate.

Silent as the cloud shadow moves across the earth, he moved in on the cat, judging the extreme limit of her acute hearing before kneeling facing where she lay three hundred yards away.

He filled and deflated his lungs rapidly a dozen times, the great muscled chest swelling and subsiding as he built up reserves of oxygen in his blood. Then he caught a full breath and stretched out his neck at a peculiar angle, cupping his hands to his gaping mouth to act as a sounding board.

From the depths of the straining chest issued a low drumming rattle, that rose and sank to a natural rhythm and ended with an abrupt little cough.

The lioness' head came up in a single flash of movement, her ears erect, her eyes alight with yellow lights, for in her pain and fear and confusion she had heard the old tom calling to her, that low, far-carrying assembly call with which he had directed her hunting so often, and which he had used to bring her to him when separated in thick bush.

The pain of rising was almost too much for her, the wound had stiffened and her neck and shoulder and chest were crushed under a granite boulder of agony, but at that moment she heard for the first time the distant yelping chorus of the dog pack. She and the old tom had been hunted by dogs before, and the sound gave her strength.

She came up and stood for a moment on three legs, favouring the right fore, panting heavily and then she went forward, whining softly at the pain, carrying the bad leg high, lunging for balance at each stride.

Mark watched from the ridge, saw the yellow cat start to move again, hobbling slowly westwards at last. Far ahead of her, keeping out of sight, the big Zulu trotted, pausing whenever she faltered to kneel and repeat the assembly call of a dominant male lion, and each time the lioness answered him with eager little mewling grunts and hobbled after him, westward towards the dreaming blue hills that guarded the Bubezi Valley.

Mark had heard the old hunters' stories before; old man Anders had always claimed that his gunbearer, who had been killed by an elephant on the Sabi River in '84, could call lions. However, Mark had never seen it done, and secretly had put the story into the category of the picturesque but apocryphal.

Now he saw it happening, and still wanted to doubt it. He watched fascinated from his grandstand upon the ridge, and only a change in the clamour of the dog pack made him swing his binoculars back towards the east.

At the rocky shoulder of the ridge, where he had set his bait of powdered biltong and snuff, the pack milled confusedly. There were eight or nine dogs, a mongrel pack of terriers and boer hounds and ridgebacks.

The determined hunting chorus had disintegrated into a cacophony of whines and yelps, while Dirk Courtney over rode them, standing in his stirrups to lay about them furiously with the horse-whip.

Mark took Trojan's reins and led him down off the ridge, using what little cover there was, but confident that the huntsmen were too involved with their own problems to look ahead and see him.

When he reached the place beside the thorn thicket where the lioness had last lain, he cut a branch with his clasp knife, and used it like a broom to brush away any sign the cat had left.

He followed slowly westwards towards Chaka's Gate, pausing every few minutes to listen for the drumming lion call, watching the ground as he moved, and using the branch to brush away all lion sign, covering for his lioness, until in the dusk they climbed a low saddle through the hills and in slow, drawn-out procession, went down to the Bubezi River.

Pungushe made his last call in darkness, and then ran out in a wide circle, leaving the lioness within a hundred yards of the river, knowing how she would be burned up by the heat of the wound and crazed for water.

He found Mark by the glow of his cigarette.

'Get up,' said Mark, and gave him an arm. Pungushe did not argue. He had run almost without a pause since before dawn, and he swung up behind Mark.

They rode home, two up on Trojan's broad sway back, and neither of them spoke until they saw the lantern light in the cottage window.

'Jamela,' said Pungushe. 'I feel the way I did the day my first son was born.' And there was a tone of wonder in his voice. 'I did not believe a man could feel thus for a devil that kills cattle and men.'

Lying in the darkness, with Marion beside him in the double bed, Mark told her about it. Trying to convey the wonder and the sense of achievement. He told her what Pungushe had said, and stumbled for words to describe his own feelings, to come haltingly at last into silence.

'That's very nice, dear. When are you going into town again? I want to buy some curtains for the kitchen. I though a checked gingham would look pretty, what do you think, dear?'

The lioness gave birth to her cubs in the thick jessie bushes that choked one of the narrow tributary valleys which came down off the escarpment.

There were six cubs, but they were almost three weeks old when Mark first saw them. He and Pungushe lay belly down on the edge of the cliff that overlooked the valley when she led them back from the river in the dawn. The cubs followed her in an untidy straggle spread over a hundred yards. The sinew in her right fore had healed crooked and slightly shorter, which gave her a heaviness in her gait, a roll like a sailor's as she came up the draw. One of the cubs, more persistent than the rest, was trying to suckle from her pendulous, heavy, multiple dugs as she walked. He kept making clumsy flying leaps at them as they swung above his head; mostly he fell on his head and got trodden on by his mother's back feet, but once he succeeded and hung like a fat brown tick on one nipple. The lioness whirled about and cuffed him left and right, then began to lick him with a tongue that wrapped around his head entirely and knocked him on his back again.

One of the other cubs was stalking his siblings, crouching in ambush behind a single blade of grass, with flattened ears and viciously slitted eyes. When he leapt out on his brothers and sisters and they totally ignored his warlike manoeuvres, he covered his embarrassment by turning back and sniffing the grass blade with such attention that it seemed this had been his original intention.

Three of the others were hunting butterflies. There had been a new hatching of colotis ione. On white and purple wings they fluttered close to the earth and the cubs reared on their hind legs and boxed at them with more gusto than skill, over-balancing at the end of each attack and collapsing in a fluffy tangle of outsized paws.

The sixth cub was hunting the tails of the butterfly-hunters. Every time they slashed their little tufted tails in the feverish excitement of the chase, he pounced upon them with savage growls and they were forced to turn and defend themselves against the sting of his needle-sharp baby teeth.

The progress of the family from river to jessie thicket was a long drawn out series of unseemly brawls, which the lioness finally broke up. She turned back and gave that drumming cough which promised imminent retribution if not obeyed instantly. The cubs abandoned their play, formed an Indian file and trotted after the lioness into the shelter of the jessie.

'I would like to know how many females there are in the litter,' Mark whispered, grinning fondly like a new father as he watched them go.

'If you wish, Jamela, I will go down and look under their tails,' Pungushe offered solemnly. 'And you will treat my widows generously.'

Mark chuckled and led the way back down the side of the hill.

They had almost reached the tree where Mark had left Trojan, when something caught his eyes. He turned aside and kicked hopefully at the little heap of stones, before he realized that they had not been erected by human hands, but had been pushed up by the surface roots of a siringa tree.

He gave a grunt of disappointment and turned away. Pungushe watched him speculatively, but made no comment. He had seen Mark perform that strange little ritual a hundred times before, whenever an unusual rock or pile caught his attention.

It had become a custom that every few evenings Mark would wander across from the thatched cottage at main camp, half a mile to where Pungushe's wives had erected the cluster of huts that was the family home.

Each hut was shaped in the perfect cone of a beehive, long whippy saplings bent in to form the framework and the thatch bound in place by the plaited string of bark stripped from the saplings.

The earth between the huts was smoothed and brushed, and Pungushe's carved wooden stool set before the low doorway of his personal sleeping hut. After Mark's fourth visit another, newly carved stool appeared beside it. Though it was never spoken of, it was immediately apparent that this had been reserved exclusively for Mark's visits.

Once Mark was seated, one of the wives would bring him a bowl to wash his hands. The water had been carried laboriously all the way from the river, and Mark merely damped his fingertips so that it would not be wasted.

Then the youngest wife knelt in front of him, smiling shyly, and offered with both hands a pot of the delicious sour utshwala, the Zulu millet beer, thick as gruel and mildly alcoholic.

Only when Mark had swallowed the first mouthful would Pungushe look up and greet him.

'I see you, Jamela.'

Then they could talk in the relaxed desultory fashion of men totally at ease in each other's company.

'Today, when we came down off the hill after watching the lions, you turned off the path and kicked at some stones. It was for this strange custom I named you, this endless seeking, this looking and never finding.'

Pungushe would never ask the direct question, it would have been the grossest bad manners to ask outright what Mark was looking for; only a child or an umlungu, a white man, would be so callow. It had taken him many months to ask the question, and now he framed it in the form of a statement.

Mark took another pull at his beer pot and offered Pungushe his cigarette case. The Zulu declined with an open hand, and instead began to roll his own smoke, coarse tarry black tobacco in a thick roll of brown paper, the size of a Havana cigar. Watching his hands Mark replied:

'My father and my mother died of the white sore throat, diphtheria, when I was a child, and an old man became both father and mother to me.' He started to answer the question in as devious a manner as it had been asked, and Pungushe listened, nodding and smoking quietly.

'So this man, my grandfather whom I loved, is buried somewhere in this valley. It is his grave I seek,' he ended simply, and realized suddenly that Pungushe was staring at him with a peculiar sombre expression.

'What is it?' Mark asked.

'When did this happen?'

'Six seasons ago.'

'Would this old man have camped beneath the wild figs?' Pungushe pointed down the valley. 'Where first you camped?'

'Yes,' Mark agreed. 'He always camped there.' He felt the surge of something in his chest, foreknowledge of something momentous about to happen.

'There was a man,' said Pungushe, 'who wore a hat, a hat under which an impi could have camped—' and he made a circle of his arms, exaggerating only a little the size of a double terai brim, 'and who had a beard, shaped thus like the wings of a white egret—' An image of the old man's forked beard, snowy and stained only around the mouth with tobacco juice, leapt in Mark's mind. 'An old man who walked like the secretary bird when it hunts for locusts in the grass.' The long thin legs, the stooped arthritic shoulders, the measured stride, the description was perfect.

'Pungushe!' Mark exploded with excitement. 'You know him!'

'Nothing moves in this valley, no bird flies, no baboon barks, but the jackal hears and sees.'

Mark stared at him, appalled at his own oversight. Of course Pungushe knew everything. Pungushe the silent watcher, why in God's name had he not thought to ask him before?


'He followed this path!' Pungushe walked ahead of Mark, and with the natural skill of the born actor he mimicked John Anders, the halting gait, and stooped shoulders of an old man. If Mark half closed his eyes, he could see his grandfather as he had seen him so many times before.

'Here he turned off the path,' Pungushe left the game trail and started up one of the narrow dried-out water-courses. Their feet crunched in the sugary sand. Half a mile further, Pungushe stopped and pointed at one of the shiny water-polished black boulders.

'Here he sat and set his rifle aside. He lit his pipe and smoked.'

Pungushe turned and scrambled up the steep bank of the water-course.

'While the old man smoked, the fourth man came up the valley. He came as a hunter, silently, following the easy spoor of the old man.' He used the Zulu word of respect for an elder, *ixhegu*.

'Wait, Pungushe,' Mark frowned. 'You say the fourth man? I am confused. Count the men for me.'

They squatted down on the bank and Pungushe took a little snuff, offered the horn to Mark who refused, then sniffed the red powder out of his palm, closing one nostril at a time with his thumb. He screwed his eyes closed and sneezed deliciously before going on.

'There was the old man, your grandfather, *ixhegu*.'

'That is one.'

'Then there was another old man. Without hair on his head nor on his chin.'

'That is two,' Mark agreed.

'Then there was a young man with very black hair, a man who laughed all the time and walked with the noise of a buffalo herd.'

'Yes. That is three.'

'These three came together to the valley. They hunted together and camped together below the wild figs.'

Pungushe must be describing the Greylings, the father and son who had made the sworn deposition to the Ladyburg magistrate. That was as he had expected, but now he asked, 'What of the fourth man, Pungushe?'

'The fourth man followed them secretly and *ixhegu*, your

grandfather, did not know of him. He had always the manner of the hunter of men, watching from cover and moving silently. But once when your grandfather, *ixhegu*, had left camp to hunt alone for birds along the river, this secret man came to the camp below the wild figs and all three of them spoke together, quietly but with closed faces and wary eyes of men who discuss affairs of deadly moment. Then the silent man left them again and went to hide in the bush before *ixhegu* returned.'

'You saw all this, Pungushe?' Mark asked.

'What I did not see, I read in the spoor.'

'Now I understand about the fourth man. Tell me what happened that day.'

'*Ixhegu* was sitting there, smoking his pipe,' Pungushe pointed down into the water-course. 'And the silent one came and stood here, even where we now sit, and he looked down at your grandfather without speaking, holding his *isibamu*, his rifle, thus.'

'What did *ixhegu* do then?' Mark asked. He felt nauseous with the horror of it.

'He looked up and asked a question in a loud voice, as a man does when he is afraid, but the silent one did not reply.'

'Then?'

'I am sorry, Jamela, knowing that *ixhegu* was of your blood, the telling of it gives me pain.'

'Go on,' said Mark.

'Then the silent one fired once with his rifle, and *ixhegu* fell face down in the sand.'

'He was dead?' Mark asked, and Pungushe was silent a moment.

'He was not dead. He was shot here, in the belly. He moved, he cried out.'

'The silent one fired again?' Mark felt the acid bite of vomit in the back of his throat.

Pungushe shook his head.

'What did he do?'

'He sat down on the bank, here where we sit, and he smoked silently, watching the old man *ixhegu* lying down there in the sand, until he died.'

'How long did he take to die?' Mark asked in a choked, angry voice.

Pungushe swept a segment of the sky to indicate two hours of the sun's course. 'At the end *ixhegu* was calling out in Zulu as well as his own language.'

'What did he say, Pungushe?'

'He asked for water, and he called to God and to a woman who might have been his mother or his wife. Then he died.'

Mark thought about it with surges of nausea alternating with flashes of bitter hating anger, and racking grief. He tried to imagine why the killer had let his victim die so slowly, and it was many minutes before he remembered that the story must have already been arranged that the old man was to die in a hunting accident. No man accidentally shoots himself twice. The body was to have only one gunshot wound. But the stomach was always the most agonizing wound. Mark remembered how the gut-wounded screamed in the trenches as they were being carried back by the stretcher-bearers.

'I grieve with you, Jamela.'

Mark roused himself at Pungushe's words.

'What happened after *ixhegu* died?'

'The other two men, the old bald one and the young loud one, came from the camp. All three of them talked here, beside the body. They talked for a long time, with shouting and red angry faces, and they waved their hands thus, and thus.' Pungushe imitated men in heated argument. 'One pointed here, another pointed there, but in the end the silent one spoke and the other two listened.'

'Where did they take him?'

'First they opened his pockets, and took from them some papers and a pouch. They argued again, and the silent one took the papers and put them back in the dead man's pockets—' Mark realized the wisdom of this. An honest man does not rob the corpse of an accident victim. 'Then they carried him up the bank, and this way—' Pungushe stood and led Mark four hundred yards into the forest, below the first steep gradient of the escarpment. 'Here they found a deep ant-bear hole, and they pushed the old man's body down into it.'

'Here?' Mark asked. There was short rank grass and no sign of a cairn nor a mound. 'I see nothing.'

'They collected rocks from the cliff there and placed them in the hole on top of the body, so that the hyena would not dig it out. Then they covered the rocks with earth, and they smoothed it with a tree branch.'

Mark went down on one knee and inspected the ground.

'Yes,' he exclaimed. There was a very shallow depression in the earth, as though it had subsided a little over an excavation.

Mark drew his sheath-knife and blazed four of the nearest trees, making it easier to return to this place, and he built a small pyramid of rocks on the depressed saucer of earth.

When he had finished, he asked Pungushe, 'Why did you not tell anybody of this before? Why did you not go to the police in Ladyburg?'

'Jamela, the madness of white men does not concern me. Also it is a very long journey to Ladyburg, to the policeman who would say, 'Ho, kaffir, and what were you doing in the Bubezi Valley to see such strange events?' Pungushe shook his head. 'No, Jamela, sometimes it better for a man to be blind and deaf.'

'Tell me truly, Pungushe. If you saw these men again, would you remember them?'

'All white men have faces like boiled yams, red, lumpy and without shape.' Then Pungushe remembered his manners. 'Except you, Jamela, who are not so ugly as all that.'

'Thank you, Pungushe. So you would not know them again?'

'The old bald one and the young loud one I might know.' Pungushe furrowed his brow in thought.

'And the silent one?' Mark asked.

'Ho.' Pungushe's brow cleared. 'Does one forget what a leopard looks like? Does one forget the killer of men? The silent one I would remember at any time and in any place.'

'Good!' Mark nodded. 'Go back home now, Pungushe.'

He waited until the big Zulu was out of sight among the trees, then Mark went down on his knees and removed his hat.

'Well, Pops,' he said, 'I'm not very good at this. But I know you'd have liked to have the words said.' His voice was so hoarse and low that he had to clear his throat loudly before he went on.


The house on Lion Kop was shuttered, and the furniture all under white dust sheets, but the head servant met Mark in the kitchen yard.

'Nkosi has gone to *Tekweni*. He left two weeks ago.'

He gave Mark a breakfast of grilled bacon and fried eggs. Then Mark went out and mounted his motorcycle again. It was a long hard run down to the coast, and Mark had plenty of time to think as the dusty miles spun away under the wheels of the Ariel Square Four.

He had left Chaka's Gate within hours of finding the old man's grave, going instinctively to one man for advice and guidance.

He had wanted Marion to come with him, at least as far as Ladyburg where she could have stayed with her sister.

However, Marion had refused to leave her home or her garden, and Mark had felt secure in the knowledge that Pungushe would be sleeping in the toolshed behind the stables to guard the homestead in Mark's absence.

Mark had waded the river and trudged up the slope below to the beginning of the track where he kept the motorcycle in its thatched shelter.

It had been a slow, bumpy journey in the dark, and he had reached Lion Kop in the dawn to find Sean Courtney had moved his household to Durban.

Mark rode through the gates of Emoyeni in the late afternoon, and it was like coming home again.

Ruth Courtney was in the rose garden, but she dropped the basket of cut flowers and lifted her skirts to her knees as she ran to meet him, the wide-brimmed straw hat flying from her head and hanging by its ribbon around her throat and her delighted spontaneous laughter ringing like a young girl's.

'Oh Mark – we've missed you so.' She took him in a motherly embrace, kissing both his cheeks. 'How brown and hard you look, and you've filled out beautifully.' She held him at arm's length and felt his biceps in mock admiration before embracing him again. 'The General will be delighted to see you.' She took Mark's arm and led him towards the house. 'He hasn't been well, Mark, but seeing you again will be a tonic to him.'

Mark stopped involuntarily in the doorway and felt the shock dry the saliva under his tongue.

General Sean Courtney was an old man. He sat at the bay windows of the bedroom suite. He wore a plaid dressing-gown and a mohair rug was tucked around his legs. On the table beside him was a pile of files and reports, Parliamentary White Papers and a sheaf of letters, all the documentation of his life that Mark remembered so well, but the General had fallen asleep, and the metal-rimmed spectacles had slid down on to the tip of his nose. He snored softly, his lips fluttering at each breath. His face seemed to have wasted so that the bones of cheek and brow stood out gauntly. His eyes receded into deep plum purple cavities, and his skin had a greyish lifeless tinge to it.

But the truly shocking thing was the colour of his beard and the once thick bush of his hair. On Sean Courtney the late snows were falling. His beard had turned into a silver cascade, and his hair was as white and as thin as the fine sun-bleached grasses of the Kalahari desert.

Ruth crossed to his chair and lifted the spectacles off his nose, then gently, with a loving wife's concern, she touched his shoulder.

'Sean, darling. There is somebody here to see you.'

He woke the way an old man wakes, blinking and mumbling, with small inconclusive movements of his hands. Then he saw Mark and his expression firmed, suddenly there was a little of the old sparkle in the dark eyes and the warmth in his smile.

'My boy!' he said, lifting his hands, and Mark stepped forward quite naturally. Then for the first time they embraced like father and son, and afterwards Sean beamed at him fondly.

'I was beginning to believe we had lost you for ever to the ways of the wild.' Then he looked up at Ruth beside his chair. 'In celebration I think we can advance the hour a little, my dear. Won't you have Joseph bring up the tray?'

'Sean, you know what the doctor said yesterday.' But Sean snorted with disgust.

'For fifty years, man and boy, my stomach has got used to its evening dash of John Haig pinch bottle. Lack of it will kill me more swiftly and surely than Doctor Henderson and all his pills and potions and blatant quackeries.' He placed one arm about her waist and squeezed her winningly. 'There's a bonnie girl!'

When Ruth had gone, smiling and shaking her head

disapprovingly, Sean waved Mark to the chair opposite him.

'What does the doctor say is wrong with you, sir?'

'Doctor!' Sean blew through his lips. 'The older I get, the less faith I have in the whole sorry bunch.' He reached for the cigar box. 'They even wanted me to stop these. What on earth is the use of living, if you have to give up all the processes of life – I ask you.' He lit the cigar with a flourish and drew on it with relish.

'I'll tell you what's wrong with me, son. Too many years of running hard, of fighting and riding and working. That's all it is. Now I'm having a nice little rest, and in a week or so I'll be chipper and fly as I ever was.'

Ruth brought the silver tray and they sat until it was dark, talking and laughing. Mark told them of the life at Chaka's Gate, about each little triumph, describing the cottage and the work done on the roads; he told them of the buffalo and the lioness and the cubs, and Sean told him of the progress made by their Wildlife Society.

'It's disappointing, Mark, nothing like I had hoped for. It's extraordinary just how little people care about things that don't affect their daily lives directly.'

'I never expected instant success. How can people care about something they have never seen? Once we have made the wilderness accessible, once people can have the experience, like seeing these cubs, it will begin then.'

'Yes,' Sean agreed thoughtfully. 'That's what the true object of the Society is. To educate them.'

They talked on while darkness fell and Ruth closed the shutters and drew the curtains. Mark waited for an opportunity to speak of the true reason for his coming to Emoyeni, but he was uncertain of how it might affect a man who was already sick.

At last he could wait no longer. He drew a deep breath, hoped for grace, and told it quickly and without trimmings, repeating Pungushe's story exactly and describing what he had seen himself.

When he finished, Sean was silent for a long time, staring into his glass. At last he roused himself and began asking questions, shrewd cutting questions that showed his mind was as quick and crisp as it had been before.

'Have you opened the grave?' and Mark shook his head.

'Good,' said Sean and went on. 'This Zulu, Pungushe, was the only witness. How reliable is he?'

They discussed it for another half hour, before Sean asked the one question he had obviously been avoiding.

'You think Dirk Courtney is responsible for this?'

'Yes,' Mark nodded.

'What proof is there?'

'He is the only one who could have profited by my grandfather's murder, and the style is his.'

'I asked what proof there is, Mark.'

'There is none,' he admitted, and Sean was silent again while he weighed it all.

'Mark, I understand just how you feel – and I think you know how I feel. However, there is nothing we can do now that will have any effect, beyond alerting the murderer, whoever he is.' He leaned forward in his chair and stretched out a hand to grip Mark's forearm in a gesture of comfort. 'All we have now is the unsupported testimony of a Zulu poacher who speaks no English. A good lawyer would eat him without spitting out the bones, and Dirk Courtney would have the best lawyer, even if we could trace this mysterious "Silent One" to him and get him into court. We need more than this, Mark.'

'I know,' Mark nodded. 'But I thought we might be able to trace the Greyling father and son. They went to Rhodesia, I believe. The foreman at Ladyburg railway station told me that.'

'Yes, I'll get somebody on to that. My lawyers will know

a good investigator.' He made a note on the pad at his side. 'But in the meantime, we can only wait.'

They talked on, but it was clear that the discussion had tired Sean Courtney, and grey and blue shadows etched the lines and wrinkles on his face. He settled down a little deeper in his chair, his beard lowered on to his chest, and suddenly he had fallen asleep again. He sagged slowly sideways, the crystal glass fell from his hand to the carpet with a soft thud and splattered a few drops of whisky, and he snored a soft single snort.

Ruth picked up the glass, arranged the rug carefully around his shoulders and signalled Mark to follow her.

In the passage she chatted brightly. 'I have told Joseph to make up your bed in the blue room, and there is a good hot bath waiting. There will be only the two of us for dinner, Mark. The General will have a tray in his room.'

They had reached the door of the library and Mark could be silent no longer. He caught Ruth's arm.

'Mrs Courtney,' he pleaded. 'What is it? What is wrong with him?'

The bright smile faded slowly, and she swayed slightly on her feet. Now for the first time he noticed how the few strands of white had turned to deep iron grey wings at her temples. He saw also the little lines and creases around her eyes, and the deeper furrows of worry across her brow.

'His heart is broken,' she said simply, and then she was weeping. No hysterical sobs or wild cries of grief, but a slow deep welling up of tears that was more harrowing, more poignant than any theatrical display.

'They have broken his heart,' she repeated, and swayed again, so that Mark caught and steadied her.

She clung to him, her face pressed to his shoulder.

'First the estrangement from Dirk and then Michael's death,' she whispered. 'He never let it show, but they destroyed some part of him. Now the whole world has turned against him. The people to whom he has devoted his life in peace and war. The newspapers call him the Butcher of Fordsburg, Dirk Courtney has whipped them upon him like a pack of wild dogs.'

He led her into the library and made her sit on the low buttoned sofa while he knelt beside her and found a crumpled handkerchief in his jacket pocket.

'On top of it all, there is Storm. The way she ran off and married that man. He was a horrible man, Mark. He even came here asking for money, and there was a terrible scene. That's when Sean had his first attack, that night. Then finally there was further shame, further heartbreak when Storm was divorced. It was all too much, even for a man like Sean.'

Mark stared at her. 'Storm is divorced?' he asked softly.

'Yes,' Ruth nodded, and then her expression lightened. 'Oh Mark, I know you and Storm were becoming such good friends. I am sure she is fond of you. Can't you go to her? It might be the cure for which we all pray.'

Umhlanga Rocks was one of those little seaside villages that were scattered along the sandy coast line on each side of the main port of Durban. Mark crossed the low bridge over the Umgeni River, and headed north.

The road cut through the thick jungly coastal bush, dense as an equatorial forest, and hung with ropes of lianas from which the little blue vervet monkeys swung and chattered.

The road ran parallel with the white beaches, but at the twelfth milestone Mark reached the turn-off and went directly down to the coast.

The village was clustered around the iron-roofed Oyster Box Hotel where Mark and Dicky Lancome had danced and dined with Marion and that other nameless girl so long ago.

The only other buildings were twenty or thirty cottages set in large gardens, over-run by the rampant jungle, and overlooking the sea with its rowdy frothing surf and rocky points jutting out from the smooth white beaches.

Ruth had given him accurate directions and Mark parked the motorcycle on the narrow dusty lane and followed the pathway that wound without apparent direction through a wild garden of purple bougainvillaea and brilliant poinsettia.

The cottage was small, and the bougainvillaea had climbed up the pillars of the veranda and spread in brilliant, almost blinding display across the thatched roof.

Mark knew at once that he had the right place, for Storm's Cadillac was parked in the open under the trees. It looked neglected and in careless disrepair. The tread was worn from the tyres, there was a long deep scratch down one side. A side window was cracked, and the paintwork was dull with dust and splattered with the dung of the fruit bats hanging in the tree above.

Mark stopped and stared at the Cadillac for a full minute. The Storm he had known would have stamped her foot and screamed for her father if anybody had tried to make her ride in that.

Mark climbed the veranda steps, and paused to look about him. It was a peaceful and lovely spot, such as an artist might choose, but in its remoteness and its neglected and untrimmed profusion hardly suitable for one of the elegant young ornaments of society.

Mark knocked on the front door, and heard somebody moving about inside for some minutes before the door was opened.

Storm was more beautiful by far than he had remembered. Her hair was long and bleached at the ends by salt water and sun. Her feet were bare, her arms and legs were tanned and slim and supple as ever, but it was her face that had changed.

Although she wore no cosmetics, the skin had the shine of vibrant youth like the lustre inside a sea shell, and her eyes were clear and bright with health, yet there were new depths to them, the petulant set of her mouth had softened, her arrogance had become dignity.

In that moment as they stared at each other he knew that she had indeed grown from girl to woman in the time since he had last seen her. And he sensed that the process had been agonizing, but that from it all was emerging a new value, a new strength, and the love which had been in him all this time spread out to fill his soul.

'Storm,' he said, and her eyes opened wide as she stared at him.

'You!' Her voice was a little cry of pain, and she tried to drag the door closed.

Mark jumped forward and held it.

'Storm, I must speak with you.'

She tugged desperately at the door handle.

'Go away, Mark. Please go away.' All the new dignity and poise seemed to crumble and she looked at him with the wide frightened eyes of a child waking from nightmare. At last she knew that she could not force the door against his strength, and she turned away and walked slowly back into the house.

'You shouldn't have come,' she said miserably, and the child seemed to sense the changed air. It squalled.

'Oh hush, baby,' Storm called softly, but her voice goaded it into a fresh outburst, and she crossed the room on bare feet with the long veil of hair hanging down her back.

The room was starkly furnished, the cement floor bare and cool, no rugs to soften them, but along the walls were stacked her canvases, many of them blank, but others half-finished, or completed, and the familiar evocative smell of turpentine was heavy and pungent.

The child lay belly down on a kaross of monkey skins laid out on the cement floor. Legs and arms were spread in that froglike baby attitude, and except for a towelling napkin around the hips, it was naked and sun-tanned. The head was thrown back angrily, and the face flushed with the force of its yells.

Mark stepped into the room, and stared with sickly fascination at the child. He knew nothing of babies, but he could see that this was a sturdy and aggressively healthy small animal. The limbs were strong, kicking and working with a violent swimming motion, and the back was broad and robust.

'Hush now, darling,' cooed Storm, she knelt beside him, and lifted him under the armpits. The napkin slid down to the child's knees and there was no doubting that he was a boy. His tiny penis stuck out at half mast, like a white finger with its little floppy chef's cap of loose wrinkled skin.

Mark found himself hating this other man's child, with a sudden frightening hatred. Yet he went forward involuntarily to where Storm knelt with the baby in her lap.

Mother's touch had quelled the shouts of anger, and now the boy was smacking his lips and making little anticipatory hunger grunts and pawing demandingly at Storm's bosom.

The child had a fine golden cap of hair, through which Mark could see the perfect round of his skull and the little blue veins under the almost translucent skin. Now that the furious crimson tide of anger had receded from his face, Mark saw how beautiful was the child, as beautiful as the mother – and he hated it, he hated it with a bitter sickening feeling in his stomach, and a corrosive taste in his mouth.

He moved closer, watching Storm wipe a dribble of

saliva from the child's chin and hoist up his napkin to his waist.

The child became aware of a stranger. He started and lifted his head to stare at Mark, and there was something hauntingly familiar in that face. The eyes that looked at him had looked at him before, he knew them so well.

'You should not have come,' said Storm, busy with her baby, not able to lift her eyes to him. 'Oh God, Mark, why did you come?'

Mark went down on one knee and stared into the child's face, and it reached out towards him with a pair of plump hands, dimpled and pink and damp with spit.

'What is his name?' Mark asked. Where had he seen those eyes? Involuntarily, he extended his forefinger and the child grabbed it with a fat little chuckle and tried to stuff it into his mouth.

'John,' Storm answered, still not looking at him.

'John was my grandfather's name,' Mark said huskily.

'Yes,' whispered Storm. 'You told me.'

The words meant nothing for a moment, all he was aware of was that the hatred he felt for this little scrap of humanity slowly faded. In its place there grew something else.

Then suddenly he knew where he had seen those eyes.

'Storm?' he asked.

Now she lifted her head, and stared into his face. When she replied she was half proud and half defiant.

'Yes!' she said, and nodded once.

He reached for her clumsily. They knelt facing each other on the monkey-skin kaross, and they embraced fiercely, the child held awkwardly between them, gurgling and hiccuping and drooling merrily as it chewed Mark's finger with greedy toothless gums.

'Oh God, Mark, what have I done to us?' whispered Storm brokenly.

B aby John woke them in the silvery slippery-grey light of before dawn. Mark was grateful to him, for he did not want to miss a minute of that coming day. He watched Storm light the candle and then work over the cradle.

She made small soothing sounds as she changed the baby, and the candlelight glowed on the sweet clean lines of her naked back. Dark silky hair hung over her shoulders, and he saw that childbirth had not thickened her waist, it still had the flared graceful line, like the neck of a wine bottle above the tight round double bulge of her buttocks.

At last she turned and carried the baby to the bed, smiling at Mark as he lifted the blankets for her.

'Breakfast time,' she explained. 'Will you excuse us, please?' She sat cross-legged in the bed, and she took one of her nipples between thumb and forefinger and directed it into the open questing mouth.

Mark drew as close as he could and placed one arm around Storm's shoulders. He watched with total fascination. Her breasts were big now, and heavy, jutting out into rounded cones. There was a pale blue dappling of active veins deep below the skin, and the nipples were the colour of almost ripe mulberries, with the same rough shiny texture. The child's tugging induced a sympathetic blue-white drop of milk to well from the tip of her other breast. It glistened there like a pearl in the candlelight.

John fed with tightly closed eyes and piglet grunts and snuffles. The milk ran from the corners of his mouth, and after the first pangs of his hunger were appeased, Storm had to prod him to keep him from falling asleep again.

At each prod, his jaw worked busily for a minute or so, and then the level of activity slowly declined until the next prod.

Storm changed him from one breast to the other and laid her own cheek gratefully against the hard lean muscle of Mark's chest.

'I think I am happy,' she murmured. 'But I've been unhappy for so long that I am not quite sure.'

J ohn lay in a puddle of sea water two inches deep. He was stark naked and brown all over to prove this was no unusual state. He slapped at the water with both hands, and it splashed into his face so that he gasped and blinked his eyes and licked his lips, uncertain whether to be angry or to cry. Instead he repeated the experiment with exactly the same consequences, and he spluttered sand and sea water.

'Poor little devil,' Storm watched him. 'He has inherited the Courtney pride and stubbornness. He won't give up until he drowns himself.'

She lifted him from the puddle and there was instantly such a howl of protest that she had to return him hurriedly.

'I am sure if you went to the General – with John,' Mark preserved.

'You don't really understand us Courtneys.' Storm sat back and began to plait her hair over one shoulder. 'We don't forget or forgive that easily.'

'Storm, won't you try it? Please go to him.'

'I know exactly how he is, Mark. Better than you, better than Daddy knows himself. I know him so well as I do myself, because we are one person. I am he, and he is me. If I go to him now, having done what I did – having insulted him, having destroyed all the dreams he wove about me – if I go now, when I am destitute of pride and honour, if I go as a beggar, he will despise me for ever.'

'No, Storm, you are wrong.'

'On this I am never wrong, Mark darling. He would not want to despise me, just as he does not want to hate me now, but he would not be able to help himself. He is Sean

Courtney, and he is trapped in the steel jaws of his own honour.'

'He is a sick man – you must give him the chance.'

'No, Mark. It would kill him. I know that – and it would destroy me. For both our sakes, I dare not go to him now.'

'You don't know how much he cares for you.'

'Oh I do, Mark. I also know how much I care for him – and one day, when I am proud again, I will go to him. I promise you that. When I know he can be proud of me, I will take him that as a gift—'

'Oh damn you and your stiff cruel pride, you nearly destroyed us with it also.'

'Come, Mark,' she stood up. 'Take John's other hand.'

They walked the child between them along the firm wet sand at the edge of the surf. He hung on their hands, leaning forward to watch his own feet appear and disappear magically below him, and he let out great shouts of triumph at his accomplishment.

The day was bright and clean, and the gulls caught the wind and rode above them on smoky white wings, answering the child's shouts with their own harsh cries.

'Oh, I had so many fine clothes and fancy friends.' Storm watched the gulls. 'I sold the clothes and lost the friends, and found how little any of it really meant to me. Look at the gulls!' she said, head thrown back. 'See the sunlight through the spread feathers. I was so busy that I never had time to see clearly before. I never saw myself, nor those around me. But now I am learning to look.'

'I saw that in your painting,' Mark said, and lifted John to his chest, delighting in the hot restless little body. 'You are painting different subjects.'

'I want to be a great artist.'

'I think you will be. That Courtney stubbornness again.'

'We don't always get what we want,' she told him, and the spent surf came sliding up the beach and creamed around their ankles.

The child slept face down on the monkey-skin kaross, exhausted with sun and sea and play, his belly bulging with food.

Storm worked at the easel under the window with narrowed eyes and cocked head.

'You are my favourite model,' she said.

'That's just because I'm so cheap.' And she laughed lightly.

'With what I pay you, I could be rich,' she pointed out.

'You know what they call ladies who do it for money?' Mark asked lazily and relapsed into silence, giving himself up to the full pleasure of watching her and they were silent for nearly an hour – silent but close and spiritually in tune.

Mark spoke at last. 'I know what you mean by seeing more clearly now. That one,' he pointed at one of the larger canvases against the wall, 'that's probably the best thing you've ever done.'

'I hated to sell it – the man who bought it is coming tomorrow.'

'You've sold some of your paintings?' He was startled.

'How do you think John and I live?'

'I don't know.' He hadn't thought about that. 'I supposed your husband.'

Her expression changed, darkening swiftly. 'I want nothing from him.' And she tossed her head so that the braid of hair flicked like the tail of an angry lioness. 'I want nothing from him, and his friends, and my loving friends, all those nice loyal people who stay away from me in droves now that I am the scarlet divorcée. I've learned a lot since last I saw you, and especially I have learned about that kind of person.'

'They are rich,' Mark pointed out. 'You once told me how important that is.'

The dark anger went out of her, and she drooped a little, the brush falling to her side.

'Oh Mark, please don't be bitter with me. I don't think I could stand that.'

He felt something tear in his chest, and he rose swiftly and went to her, picked her up with a swing of his shoulders and carried her high, through the curtained doorway into the small cool dark bedroom.

It was strange, but their love-making was never the same, always there were new wonders, new accords of desire, the discovery of some little things that excited them both beyond all relation to its apparent significance.

Repetition could not weary nor dull the appetite they had for each other, and even as that appetite was totally satiated, so the endless well of their mutual desire began to fill again.

It would start again immediately with the lazy touch of fingers as they lay curled together like sleepy puppies, the sweat of their loving cooling on their skin, raising little goose bumps around the dark rosy aureoles of her nipples.

A finger drawn lightly down his cheek, rasping on the sandpaper of his beard, and then pushing lightly between his lips, making him turn his head for another gentle kiss, a mere touch of lips and the mingling of their breath so that he could smell that peculiar perfume of passion from her mouth, a smell like newly dug truffles, a mushroomy exciting smell.

She saw the new spark of interest in his eyes and drew softly away to chuckle at him, a throaty sensuous sound, and she drew one sharp finger-nail swiftly down his spine so that little sparks of fire flew along his nerves and his back arched.

'I am going to claw you because you deserve it, you randy old tomcat.' She made a growly sound in her throat and curled her nails into a lion's claw, drawing it lightly across his shoulder, and then hard down his belly, so that her nails left red lines against the skin.

She studied the red lines, with her lips parted and the tip of her pink tongue touching her small white teeth. The nipples of her breast swelled as she watched, growing like new buds, as though they were about to burst. She saw the direction of his eyes, and she put her hand behind his head, drawing him down gently, pulling back her shoulder so that the heavy rounded bosom was offered like a sacrifice.

Mark took some of the big scaly crayfish from the lowtide pools, and they smelled of kelp and iodine, thumping their tails furiously in his grip, snapping their legs and bubbling at the small mouths with their multiple mandibles.

Mark rose, streaming salt water, from the depths of the pool and handed them up to Storm, who squealed with excitement on the rocky edge of the pool and took them gingerly, using her straw hat as a glove against the spiky carapace and waving legs.

Mark built a fire in a scooped fireplace in the sand, while Storm held John on her lap and fed him through a discreetly unbuttoned blouse, offering advice and ribald comment as he worked.

Mark threw wet seaweed over the coals, put the crayfish on top of that and covered them with another layer of seaweed, topping it off with a final layer of sand, and while they waited for the crayfish to cook and John to finish his noisy guzzling, they drank wine and watched the setting sun turn the sea clouds into a brilliant display.

'God, Nature's an old ham. If I painted like that, they'd say I had no sense of colour, and I could go work for a chocolate company painting boxes.'

Afterwards, Storm laid John in the apple basket that served as a portable cradle and they ate crayfish, pulling the long luscious sticks of white meat from the horny legs and washing it down with the tart white Cape wine.

In the darkness the stars were stark pricks of brilliant white, and the surf boomed in long soft phosphorescent lines.

'It's so wonderfully romantic.' Storm watched it, sitting hugging her knees, and then turned her head and smiled wickedly. 'And you can take that as a hint, if you want to.'

On the rug together she said, 'Do you know what some people do?'

'No, what do some people do?' Mark seemed more interested in what he was doing than the actions of the nameless somebodies.

'You don't expect me just to say it out like that.'

'Why not?'

'It's rude.'

'All right, so whisper it.'

So she whispered it, but she was giggling so much that he was not sure he had heard right.

She repeated it, and he had heard right. He was truly stunned, so that he found himself blushing in the dark.

'That's terrible,' he answered huskily. 'You would never do that!' However, he was over the first shock, and the idea intrigued him.

'Of course not,' she whispered, and then after a silence, 'Unless of course you want to.'

There was another long silence during which Storm made some investigations. 'If I'm any judge, and I should be by now, you want to,' she stated flatly.

Long afterwards, naked in the dark, they swam together out beyond the first line of breakers. The water was warm as fresh milk and they trod water to kiss with wet salty lips.

On the beach Mark built up the fire and they sat close to it, cuddled together in the yellow light of the flames, and they drank the rest of the wine.

'Mark,' she said at last, and there was a sadness in her voice that he had never heard before. 'You have been with us two days now, which is two days too much. Tomorrow I want you to go. Go early before John and I are awake, so we don't have to watch you.'

Her words struck like a lash so that he writhed at the sting. He turned to her with a stricken face in the firelight.

'What are you saying? You and John are mine. We belong together the three of us, always.'

'You didn't understand a word of what I was saying, did you?' she asked softly. 'You didn't understand when I said I must rebuild my pride, refashion my honour?'

'I love you, Storm. I have always loved you.'

'You are married to somebody else, Mark.'

'That doesn't mean anything,' he pleaded.

'Oh yes, it does.' She shook her head. 'And you know it does.'

'I will leave Marion.'

'Divorce, Mark?'

'Yes.' He was desperate. 'I'll ask her for a divorce.'

'That way we can both be truly proud. That will be a fine way for me to go to my father. Think how proud we will make him. His daughter, and the son he never had, for that's the way he thinks of you, both of them divorced. Think of baby John. How high he will hold his head. Think of us – what a noble life we can build on the misery of the girl who was your wife.' Looking into her eyes in the firelight, he saw that her pride was iron and her stubbornness was steel.

Mark dressed quietly in the dark, and when he was ready he groped his way to the cradle and kissed his son. The child made a little whimpering sound in his sleep, and he smelt warm and milky, like a new-born kitten.

He thought that Storm was sleeping also as he stooped over her, but then he realized that she was lying rigidly with her face pressed into the pillow to stifle the harsh silent sobs that convulsed her.

She did not lift her face to him and he kissed her hair and her neck, then he straightened up and walked out into the dark. The motorcycle started at the first kick and he wheeled it out into the lane.

Storm lay in the dark and listened to the sound of the engine die away into the night, and afterwards there was only the lonely mournful sound of the surf and the clink of the tree frogs outside the window.

Mark sat on the carved wooden stool in the sunset, in front of Pungushe's hut, and he asked for the first time something that had been in his mind since their first meeting.

'Pungushe, tell me of the time when the Jackal pulled the Ngaga from the flooding river.'

And the Zulu shrugged. 'What is there to tell? I found you caught in the branches of a flooded tree on the edge of the river – and if I had sense, I would have walked away, for you were clearly a very dead Ngaga and the brown water was washing over your head.'

'Did you see how it was that I fell into the river?'

There was a pause, while Pungushe steeled himself to admit ignorance. 'It seemed to me that you had been blinded with fever and fallen into the river.'

'You did not see the man I killed, nor the man that fired at me with a rifle?'

Pungushe covered his amazement nobly, but shook his head. 'A little time before I found you in the river I heard the sound of guns, four, perhaps five shots, from up the valley. This must have been you and the one who hunted you, but I saw no man and the rain washed away all sign, before the next morning. The flood waters would have washed the dead man away and the crocodiles eaten him.'

They were silent again while the beer pot passed between them.

'Did you see the man who fired at you?' Pungushe asked.

'Yes,' said Mark. 'But my eyes were weak with fever, and as you say, it was raining. I did not see him clearly.'

Hobday stood within the hall, against the wall, out of the crush of excited bodies. He stood like a rock, solid and immovable, his head lowered on the thick wrestler's neck. His eyes were hooded, as though he were able like a great bird of prey to draw an opaque nictitating membrane across them. Only his jaw made an almost imperceptible chewing motion, grinding the big flat teeth together so that the muscle in the points of his jaw bulged slightly.

He was watching Dirk Courtney across the crowded hall, the way a faithful mastiff watches its master.

Tall and urbane, Dirk Courtney had a warm double handshake for each of those who crowded forward to assure him of support and to wish him luck. His gaze was straight and calm, but it kept flicking back to the long counting tables.

They were trestle tables that had done duty at a thousand church socials, and as many weddings.

Now the scrutineers sat along them, and the last ballot boxes from the outlying areas were carried in through the front doors of the Ladyburg Church Hall.

The sprawling shape of the constituency of Ladyburg meant that some of the boxes had come in sixty miles, and although the voting had closed the previous evening, it was now an hour before noon and no result had yet been announced.

Mark crossed slowly towards where General Sean Courtney sat, pushing his way gently through the throng that lined the roped-off area around the counting tables.

Mark and Marion had come in from Chaka's Gate three days before, especially to assist at the elections. There were never enough helpers, and Marion had been completely at home, cutting sandwiches and dispensing coffee, working with twenty other women under Ruth Courtney's supervision in the kitchens behind the hall.

Mark had scoured the village district with other party organizers. Like a press gang, they had hunted down missing or recalcitrant voters and brought them into the ballot stations.

It had been hard work, and then none of them had slept much the previous night. The dancing and barbecue had lasted until four in the morning – and after that the anticipation of the announcement of the result had kept most of them from sleep.

For Mark it all had a special significance. He knew now with complete certainty that if Dirk Courtney was returned as the member of Parliament for Ladyburg, then his dreams for Chaka's Gate were doomed.

As the voters had come in during the day, their hopes had see-sawed up and down. Often it seemed that the end of the hall where Dirk Courtney's organizers sat under huge posters of their candidate was as crowded as Sean Courtney's end of the hall was deserted.

When this happened, Marion's brother-in-law, Peter Botes, removed his pipe from his mouth and smirked comfortably at Mark across the length of the hall. He had become an enthusiastic supporter of Dirk Courtney's, and his circumstances had altered remarkably in the last six months. He had opened offices of his own on the first floor of the Ladyburg Farmers Bank. He drove a new Packard and had moved from the cottage to a fine rambling house in three acres of garden and orchard, where he had insisted that Marion and Mark dine with him the previous night.

'The evening star sets, the morning star rises, my dear Mark. The wise man recognizes that,' he had sermonized as he carved the roast.

'General Courtney's star has not set yet,' said Mark stubbornly.

'Not yet,' agreed Peter. 'But when it does, you will need new friends. Powerful friends.'

'You can always rely on us,' said Marion's sister kindly. 'You don't always have to live out there in the bush.'

'You don't understand,' Mark interrupted quietly. 'My life's work is out there – in the bush.'

'Oh, I wouldn't bank on that.' Peter heaped slices of roast beef on to Mark's plate. 'There are going to be changes in the Ladyburg district when Mr Dirk Courtney takes over. Big changes!'

'Besides, it isn't fair on poor Marion. No woman wants to live out there—'

'Oh, I am quite happy wherever Mark wants to go,' Marion murmured.

'Don't worry,' Peter assured them. 'We'll look after you.' And he patted Mark's shoulder in a brotherly fashion.

'Mr Dirk Courtney thinks the world of Peter,' said his wife proudly.

Now as Mark crossed the hall towards General Sean Courtney, he felt the heavy doughy feeling of dread in his guts. He did not want to bear the tidings he had for the General, yet he knew it was better that they came gently from a friend, rather than in gloating triumph from an enemy.

He paused to watch Sean Courtney from a distance, feeling both pity and anger. Sean had rallied strongly since those low days at Emoyeni. His shoulders had regained some of that wide rakish set, and his face had filled out. Some of the gaunt shadows had smoothed away, and he had been in the sun again. The skin was tanned brown against the silver of his beard and his hair.

Yet he was seated now. The strain of the last few days had taxed him sorely. He sat erect on a hard-backed chair, both hands resting on the silver head of his cane. With him were many of his old friends who had gathered to give him support, and he listened seriously to his brother Garrick who sat in the chair beside him, nodding his agreement.

Mark did not want to go to him, he wanted to delay the moment, but then there was a stir across the hall. Mark saw Peter Botes scurrying across to where Dirk Courtney stood, and his face was bright scarlet with excitement. He spoke rapidly, gesticulating widely, and Dirk Courtney leaned forward to listen eagerly.

Mark could not delay a moment longer. He hurried forward and Sean saw him coming.

'Well, my boy, come and sit a while. They tell me the voting is extremely close so far, but we'll have the result before noon.' Then he saw Mark's face. 'What is it?' he demanded harshly.

Mark stooped over him, his mouth almost touching the General's ear, and his voice croaked in his own ears.

'It's just come in on the telegraph, General. We have lost Johannesburg Central, Doornfontein and Jeppe—' They were all solid safe Smuts seats, they had been South Africa Party since Union in 1910, and now they were gone. It was a disaster, a stunning catastrophe. Sean gripped Mark's forearm as if to take strength from him, and his hand shook in a gentle palsy.

Across the hall they heard the wild gloating cheers start ringing out, and Mark had to hurry.

'That's not all, sir. General Smuts himself has lost his seat.' The nation had rejected them, the coalition of the Labour and the National Party under Hertzog were sweeping into power.

'My God,' muttered Sean. 'It's come. I didn't believe it possible.'

Still gripping Mark's arm, he pulled himself to his feet. 'Help me out to the car, my boy. I don't think I can bring myself to congratulate the new member for Ladyburg.'

But they were too late. The announcement came before they reached the door. It was shouted in a stentorian voice, by the chief scrutineer from the platform at the end of the hall.

'Mr Dirk Courtney, National Labour Party: 2683 votes. General Sean Courtney, South Africa Party: 2441 votes. I give you the new member for Ladyburg—'. And Dirk Courtney leapt lightly on to the platform, clasping both hands above his head like a prize-fighter.

'Well.' There was a twisted grin on Sean's face, the skin had that greyish tone again and his shoulders had slumped. 'So, exit the Butcher of Fordsburg—' and Mark took him out to where the Rolls waited in the street.



The champagne was a Dom Perignon of that superb 1904 vintage, and Sean poured it with his own hands, limping from guest to guest.

'I had hoped to toast victory with it,' he smiled. 'But it will do as well to drown our sorrows.'

There was only a small gathering in the drawing-room of Lion Kop homestead, and the few attempts at joviality were lost in the huge room. The guests left early. Only the family sat down to dinner, with Marion in Storm's old seat and Mark between her and Ruth Courtney.

'Well, my boy, what are your plans now?' Sean abruptly asked in one of the silences, and Mark looked up with genuine astonishment.

'We'll be going back to Chaka's Gate, of course.'

'Of course.' Sean smiled with the first spontaneous

warmth of that dark day. 'How foolish of me to think otherwise. But you do realize what this,' Sean made a gesture with one hand, unable to say the word defeat, 'what this could mean for you?'

'Yes, sir. But you still have enormous influence. There is our Wildlife Society – we can fight. We have to fight to keep Chaka's Gate.'

'Yes,' Sean nodded, and there was a little sparkle in his eyes again. 'We'll fight, but my guess is it will be a hard, dirty fight.'

A t first there was no sign of the gathering clouds to darken the tall blue sky above Chaka's Gate. The only change was that Mark was submitting his monthly report, not to Sean Courtney, but to the new Minister of Lands, Peter Grobler, a staunch Hertzog man. His reports were acknowledged formally, but although his salary was still paid regularly by the Department, in a short official letter Mark was informed that the whole question of the proclaimed areas was now under consideration at Cabinet level, and that new legislation would be promulgated at the next session of Parliament. His appointment as game warden was to be considered a temporary post, without pension benefits, and subject to monthly notice.

Mark worked on doggedly, but many nights he sat late in the lantern light writing to General Courtney. The two of them were planning at long distance their campaign to awaken public interest in Chaka's Gate, but when Marion had gone off to bed in the next room, he would take a fresh page and cover it with the small cramped lines to Storm, pouring out to her all his thoughts and dreams and love.

Storm never replied to his letters, he was not even certain that she was still in that thatched cottage above the beach, but he imagined her there, thinking of her at odd hours of the day and the night, seeing her working at her easel, or walking the beach with baby John tottering at her side. One particular night he lay awake and imagined her in the tiny shuttered bedroom with the child at her breast, and the image was too vivid, too painful to allow him sleep.

He rose quietly, left a note for Marion as she slept heavily, and, with Pungushe trotting at Trojan's head, set off up the valley.

Marion woke an hour after he had gone, and her first waking thought was that if there was still no show on this morning then it was certain. She had waited all these weeks for that absolute certainty, before telling Mark. Somehow she had been afraid that if she had spoken of it too soon, it would have been bad luck.

She slipped from the bed and crossed the still dark room to the bathroom. When she returned minutes later she was hugging herself with suppressed joy, and she lit the candle by her bedside, eager to see Mark's face when she woke him to tell him.

Her disappointment when she saw the empty rumpled bed and the note propped on the pillow was intense, but lasted only a short while before her usual gentle placid nature reasserted itself.

'It will give me more time to enjoy it by myself,' she said aloud, and then she spoke again. 'Harold – Harold Anders? No, that's too common. I will have to think of a really fine-sounding name.'

She hummed happily to herself as she dressed, and then went out into the kitchen yard.

It was a cool still morning with a milky pink sky. A baboon called from the cliffs of Chaka's Gate, the short explosive bark ringing across the valley, a salute to the sunrise that was turning the heights to brazen splendour.

It was good to be alive and to have a child growing on such a day, Marion thought, and she wanted to do something to celebrate it. Mark's note had told her that he would be home by nightfall.

'I'll bake a new batch of bread, and—' She wanted something very special for this day. Then she remembered that it had rained five days previously. There might be wild mushrooms coming up from the rains, those rounded buds with sticky brown tops; the rich meaty flesh was a favourite of Mark's and he had taught her when and where to find them.

She ate her breakfast absentmindedly with Mark's copy of *The Home Doctor* propped against the jam jar, re-reading the section on 'The Expectant Mother'. Then she began on her housework, taking a comfortable pride in the slippery glaze of the cement floors and the burnish which she had worked on to the wood of the simple furniture, in the neatness and order, the smell of polish, the wild flowers in their vases. She sang as she worked and once laughed out loud for no reason.

It was mid-morning before she tied her sun bonnet under her chin, put a bottle of 'Chamberlain's Superior Diarrhoea Remedy' into her basket, and set off up the valley.

She stopped at Pungushe's kraal and the youngest wife brought the baby to her. Marion was relieved to see that he was much improved, and Pungushe's wife assured her that she had given him much liquid to drink. Marion took him in her lap and fed him a spoonful of the diluted remedy, despite his violent protests, and afterwards the five women sat in the sun and talked of children and men and childbirth, of sickness and food and clothing, and all the things that absorb a woman's life.

It was almost an hour later that she left the four Zulu women and went down towards the river.

The downpour of rain had disquieted the lioness. Some deep instinct warned her that it was but the harbinger of the great storms to come.

The jessie thickets in the valley were a suitable retreat for her litter no longer. Heavy rain on the escarpment would soon turn the steep narrow valley into a cascading torrent.

Twice already she had tried to lead the cubs away, but they were older now and had developed a stubbornness and tenacity. They clung to the haven of the thick thorny jessie, and her efforts had failed. Within half a mile, one or two of the faint-hearts would turn and scurry back to what they considered home. Immediately the lioness turned back to seize the deserter; it precipitated an undignified rush by the others in the same direction, and within five minutes they were all back in the jessie.

The lioness was distracted. This was her first litter, but she was governed by instinct. She knew that it was time to wean her cubs, to take them out of the trap of the narrow valley, to begin their hunting lessons, but she was frustrated by the size of her litter, six-cub litters were a rarity in the wilderness and so far there had been no casualties among the cubs; her family was becoming too ungainly for her to handle.

However, instinct drove her and in the middle of a cool bright morning in which she could smell the rain coming, she tried again. The cubs gambolled along behind her, falling over each other and sparring amicably, as far as the river. This was familiar ground and they went along happily.

When the lioness started out across the open white sand-banks towards the far side, there was immediately the usual crisis in confidence. Three cubs followed her willingly, two stood undecidedly on the high bank and whined and mewled with concern, while the sixth turned and bolted straight back up the valley for the ebony.

The lioness went after him at a gallop and bowled him on his back. Then she took the scruff of his neck and lifted him. The cubs were big now, and although she lifted him to the full stretch of her neck, his backside still bumped on every irregularity of the ground. He curled up his legs, wrapped his tail tightly up under his quarters and closed his eyes, hanging from her mouth as she carried him down into the bed of the Bubezi River.

The river was five hundred yards wide at this point, and almost completely empty at the end of the dry season. There were still deep green pools of water between the snowy-white sand-banks, and the pools were connected by a slow trickle of warm clear water only a few inches deep. While five cubs watched in an agony of indecision from the near bank, the lioness carried the cub through the shallows, soaking his dragging backside so he hissed and wriggled indignantly, then she trotted up the far bank and found a clump of dense wit-els where she placed him.

She turned back to fetch another cub, and he followed her with a panicky rush. She had to stop and box him about the ears, snarling until he squealed and fell on his back. She grabbed him by the neck and dragged him back into the wit-els. She started back across the river to find the cub stumbling along on her heels again. This time she nipped hard enough to really hurt, and bundled him back into the thicket. She nipped again at his hindquarters until he cowered flat on the earth, so subdued and chastened that he could not gather the courage to follow again. He lay under the bush and made distraught little sounds of anguish.

M arion had never been this far from the cottage alone, but it was such a lovely warm clear morning, peaceful and still, that she wandered on in a mood of enchantment and happiness such as she had seldom known before.

She knew that if she followed the river bank, she could not lose herself, and Mark had taught her that the African bush is a safer place in which to wander abroad than the streets of a city – as long as one followed a few simple rules of the road.

At the branch of the two rivers she stopped for a few minutes to watch a pair of fish eagles on top of their shaggy nest in the main fork of a tall leadwood tree. The white heads of the two birds shone like beacons in contrast to the dark russet plumage, and she thought she could just make out the chirruping sound of the chicks in the cup of the hay-stack nest.

The sound of the young heightened the awareness of the life in her own belly, and she laughed and went on down the branch of the Red Bubezi.

Once a heavy body crashed in the undergrowth nearby, and there was a clatter of hooves on stony earth. She froze with a fleeting chill of fear, and then when the silence returned she regained her courage and laughed a little breathlessly and went on.

There was a perfume on the warm still air, sweet as full-blooming roses, and she followed it, twice going wrong but at last coming on a spreading creeper hanging over a gaunt dead tree. The leaves were dark shiny green and the dense bunches of flowers were pale butter yellow. She had never seen the plant before, nor the swarm of sunbirds that fluttered about it. They were tiny restless darting birds, with bright, metallic, shiny plumage like the little humming-birds of America, and they dipped into the perfumed flowers with long slim curved beaks. Their colours were unbeliev-able in the sunlight, emerald greens and sapphire blue, black like wet anthracite and reds like the blood of kings. They thrust their beaks deep into the open throats of the yellow blooms to sip out the thick clear drops of nectar through their hollow tubular tongues.

Watching them, Marion felt a deep pervading delight, and it was a long time before she moved on again.

She found the first batch of mushrooms a little further on, and she knelt to snap the stems off at the level of the earth and then hold the umbrella-shaped fleshy plant to her face and inhale the delicious musty odour, before laying it carefully, cap uppermost, in the basket so that grit and dirt would not lodge in the delicately fluted gills. She took two dozen mushrooms from this one patch, but she knew they would cook down to a fraction of their bulk.

She went on, following the lip of the steep bank.

Something hissed close by and her heart skipped again. Her first thought was of a snake, one of those thick bloated reptiles, with the chocolate and yellow markings and flat scaly heads, which blew so loudly that they were called puff-adders.

She began moving backwards carefully staring into the clump of first growth wit-els from which the sound had come. She saw small movement, but it was some seconds before she realized what she was seeing.

The lion cub was flat on its belly in the dappled shadow of the thicket, and its own dappled baby spots blended beautifully against the bed of dried leaves and leaf mould on which it lay.

The cub had learned already the first lesson of conceal-ment, absolute stillness; except for his two round fluffy ears. The ears flicked back and forth, signalling clearly every emotion and intention. He stared at Marion with wide round eyes that had not yet turned the ferocious yellow of full growth, but were still hazed with the bluish glaze of kittenhood. His whiskers bristled stiffly, and his ears sig-nalled wildly conflicting messages.

Flattening against the skull: 'One step nearer and I'll tear you to pieces.'

Shooting out sideways: 'One step nearer and I'll die of fright.'

Coming up and cupping forward: 'What the hell are you anyway?'

'Oh,' exclaimed Marion. 'You darling little thing.' She set down the basket, and squatted. She extended one hand and made soft cooing noises.

'There's a darling. Are you all alone then, poor baby?'

She moved forward slowly, still talking and cooing.

'Nobody's going to hurt you, baby.'

The cub was uncertain, its ears rising into an attitude of curiosity and indecision as it stared at her.

'Are you all alone then? You'll make a lovely pet for my own baby, won't you?'

Closer and closer she edged, and the cub warned her with a half-hearted apologetic hiss.

'What a cheeky darling we are,' Marion smiled and squatted three feet from the cub.

'How are we going to take you home?' Marion asked. 'Will you fit in the basket?'

In the river bed, the lioness carried the second cub through the shallows, and was followed by one of the heroes of the litter, struggling along gamely through the thick white sand. However, when he reached the edge of the shallow stream and tested it with one paw, his newfound courage deserted him at the cold wet touch, and he sat down and wept bitterly.

The lioness, by this time almost wild with distraction and frustration, turned back, and dropped her burden which immediately set off in clumsy gallop for the jessie thicket again, then she seized the weeping hero instead and trotted back through the stream and set off determinedly for the far bank.

Her huge round pads made no sound in the soft earth as she came up the bank, carrying the cub.

Marion heard the crackling spluttering explosion of sound behind her, and she whirled to her feet in one movement.

The lioness crouched on the lip of the bank fifty yards away. It warned her again with that terrible sound.

All that Marion saw were the eyes. They were a blazing yellow, a ferocious terrifying yellow – and she screamed, a wild high ringing, rising sound.

The sound launched the lioness into her charge, and it came with an unbelievably fluid flowing speed that turned into a yellow rushing blur. She snaked in low, and the sand spurted beneath her paws, all claws fully extended, the lips drawn back in a fixed silent snarl, the teeth exposed, long and white and pointed.

Marion turned to run, and had gone five paces when the lioness took her. She pulled her down with a swipe of a forepaw across the small of her back and five curved yellow claws cut deeply – four inches through skin and muscle, opening the abdominal cavity like a sabre cut, crushing the vertebrae and bursting both kidneys instantaneously.

It was a blow that would have killed even a full-grown ox, and it hurled Marion twenty feet forward, but as she fell on her back, the lioness was on her again.

The jaws were wide open, the long white fangs framed the deep wet pink cavern of tongue and throat. In an instant of incredibly heightened perception, Marion saw the smooth ridges of firm pink flesh that covered the arched roof of the lioness' mouth in regular patterns, and she smelt the meaty stink of her breath.

Marion lay twisted under the great yellow cat; she was

still screaming and her lower body lay at an odd angle from the shattered spine, but she lifted both arms to protect her face.

The lioness bit into the forearms, just below the elbows and the bone crunched sharply, shattering into slivers and splinters in the mangled flesh; both arms were severed almost through.

Then the lioness seized Marion's shoulder, and worried it until the long eye teeth meshed through broken bone and fat and tissue – and Marion kept screaming, twisting and writhing under the cat.

The lioness took a long time to kill her, confused by her own anger and the unfamiliar taste and shape of the victim. She tore and bit and ripped for almost a minute before she found the throat.

When the lioness stood up at last, her head and neck were a gory mask, her fur sticky and sodden with blood.

Her tail still lashed from side to side in residual anger, but she licked her face with a long dextrous tongue and her lip curled at the sweet unfamiliar flavour. She wiped her face carefully with her paws before trotting back to her cub, and licking him also with long pink protective strokes.

Marion's broken torn body lay where she left it, until Pungushe's wives came, a little before sundown.

Mark and Pungushe crossed the river in darkness with the moonlight turning the sand-banks to ghostly grey, and the round white moon itself reflected perfectly in the still mirror-surface of the pool below the main camp. The turbulence of their fording shattered the image into a thousand points of light, like a crystal glass flung on to a stone floor.

As they rode up the bank, they heard the death wail in the night, that terrible keening, the mourning of Zulu women. The men halted involuntarily, the sound striking dread into both of them.

'Come!' shouted Mark and kicked one foot from the stirrup. Pungushe grabbed the leather and swung off his feet as Mark lashed Trojan into a gallop and they tore up the hill.

The fire that the women had lit threw a grotesque yellow wavering glow, and weird dancing shadows.

The four women sat in a group around the long, kaross-wrapped bundle.

None of them looked up as the men ran forward into the firelight.

'Who is it?' Mark demanded. 'What has happened?'

Pungushe seized his eldest wife by the shoulders, and shook her, trying to interrupt the hysteria of mourning, but Mark strode forward impatiently and lifted one end of the kaross.

He stared for a moment, not understanding, not recognizing, then suddenly all colour fled from his face and he turned and ran into the darkness. There he fell to his knees and leaned forward to retch up the bitter bile of horror.

Mark took Marion into Ladyburg, wrapped in a canvas buck-sheet, and strapped into the side-car of the Ariel.

He stayed for the funeral and for the grief and recriminations of her family.

'If only you hadn't taken her out there into the bush—'

'If only you had stayed with her—'

'If only—'

On the third day he went back to Chaka's Gate. Pungushe was waiting for him at the ford of the river.

They sat together in the sunlight under the cliffs, and when Mark gave Pungushe a cigarette, he broke off the cork tip carefully and they smoked in silence until Mark asked,

'Have you read the sign, Pungushe?'

'I have, Jamela.'

'Tell me what happened.'

'The lioness was moving her little ones, taking them one at a time across the river from the jessie bush.' Slowly, accurately, Pungushe reconstructed the tragedy from the marks left in the earth which he had studied in Mark's absence, and when he was finished speaking, they were silent again.

'Where is she now?' Mark asked quietly.

'She has taken the little ones north, but slowly, and three days ago, the day after,' Pungushe hesitated, 'the day after the thing was done, she killed an impala ram, and the cubs ate a little with her. She begins now to wean them.'

Mark stood up and they forded the river, climbing together slowly up through the forest to the cottage.

While Pungushe waited on the front stoep, Mark went into the small deserted home. The wild flowers had died and wilted in their vases, giving the room a sad and dejected feeling. Mark began to gather up all Marion's personal possessions, her clothing, her cheap but treasured jewellery, her combs and brushes, and the few hoarded pots of cosmetics. He packed them carefully into her largest suitcase to take to her sister, and when he was finished he carried the case out and locked it in the tool shed. It was too painful a reminder to keep in the house with him.

Then he went back and changed out of his town clothes. He took the Mannlicher down from the rack and loaded it with brass cartridges from a fresh package. The casings of the cartridges were glistening yellow under their film of wax, the bullets soft-nosed for maximum shock at impact.

When he went out on to the stoep carrying the rifle, Pungushe was still waiting.

'Pungushe,' he said. 'We have work to do now.'

The Zulu stood up slowly, and for a moment they stared at each other. Then Pungushe dropped his eyes and nodded.

'Take the spoor,' Mark commanded softly.

They found where the lioness had killed the impala, but the scavengers of the bush had cleaned the area effectively. There were a few splinters of bone that had fallen out of the crushing jaws of the hyena, a little hair, pulled out in tufts, a shred of dried skin, and part of the skull with the twisted black horns still intact. But the spoor was cold. Wind and the trampling feet of the scavengers, the jackals, and hyena, the vultures and marabou storks, had wiped the sign.

'She will keep going north,' said Pungushe, and Mark did not ask how he knew that, for the Zulu could not have answered. He simply knew.

They went slowly on up the valley, Pungushe scouting ahead of the mule, making wide tracks back and forth, casting carefully for the sign, and on the second day he cut the spoor.

'She has turned now.' Pungushe squatted over the pug marks, the big saucer-sized pads and the smaller myriad prints of the cubs.

'I think she was going back towards the Usutu.' He nodded over the spoor, touching it with the thin reed wand he carried as a tracking stick. 'She was taking the little ones back, but now she has changed her mind. She has turned southwards, she must have passed close to where we camped last night. She is staying in the valley. It is her valley now, and she will not leave it.'

'No,' Mark nodded grimly. 'She will not leave the valley again. Follow, Pungushe.'

The lioness was moving slowly and the spoor ran hotter every hour. They found where she had hunted without success. Pungushe pointed out where she had stalked, and then the deep driving back claws had raked the earth as she leapt to the back of a full-grown zebra. Twenty paces further, she had fallen heavily, dislodged by the stallion's wild plunging. She had struck shoulder first, Pungushe said, and the zebra had run free but bleeding from the long slash of her claws. The lioness had limped away, and lain under a thorn tree for a long time before rising and going back slowly to where she had left her cubs. Probably she had torn muscle and sinew in that fall.

'When will we come up with her?' Mark asked, his face a stony mask of vengeance.

'Perhaps before sunset.' But they lost two hours on a rocky ridge, and Pungushe had to cast widely and work with all his skill to cut the spoor again at the point where it doubled sharply and turned west towards the escarpment.

Pungushe and Mark camped on her spoor with only a tiny fire for comfort and they lay directly on the earth. Mark did not sleep. He lay and watched the waning moon come up over the tree tops, but it was only when Pungushe spoke quietly that he realized that the Zulu also was sleepless.

'The cubs are not weaned,' he said. 'But they will take a long time to die.'

'No,' Mark replied. 'I will shoot them also.'

Pungushe roused himself and took a little snuff, leaning on one elbow and staring into the coals of the fire.

'She has tasted human blood,' Mark said at last. Even in his grief and anger, he sensed Pungushe's quiet disapproval and wanted to justify what he was about to do.

'She did not feed,' Pungushe stated. Mark felt his gorge rise and the bitter taste of it again as he remembered the terrible mutilation, but Pungushe was right, the lioness had not eaten any of that poor torn flesh.

'Pungushe, she was my wife.'.

'Yes,' Pungushe nodded. 'That is so. Also it was her cub.'

Mark considered the words, and felt for the first time a confusion of his own objects. The lioness had acted out of one of the oldest instincts of life, the urge to protect her young – but what were his motives?

'I have to kill her, Pungushe,' he said flatly, and there was some slimy obscene thing in his belly; it moved there for the first time, and he tried to deny its existence.

Marion was dead. Sweet, loyal, dutiful Marion, who had been all that a man could ask for in a wife. She had died an unspeakable death – and now Mark was alone, or did the word 'free' come too readily to his tongue?

Suddenly he had an image of a slim, dark lovely girl and a lusty naked little boy walking in the sunset at the edge of the sea.

Guilt, that slimy thing, uncoiled in his belly and began to ripple and undulate like a serpent, and he could not crush it down.

'She has to die,' Mark repeated, and perhaps his own guilt could die in that same purging.

'Very well,' Pungushe agreed. 'We will find her before noon tomorrow.' He lay back and pulled his kaross over his head and his voice was muffled, the words almost lost. 'Let us hurry now towards the great emptiness.'

They found the lioness early the next morning. She had moved in close under the hills of the escarpment, and when the first heat of the day made the cubs flag and begin to trail disconsolately along behind her, she had selected an umbrella thorn with a flat-topped mass of foliage spreading from the straight trunk and she had lain in the shade on her side, exposing the soft creamy fur of her belly and the double row of flat black nipples.

Now the cubs were almost satiated, only two of the greediest still suckled valiantly, their bellies bulging and the effort of swallowing almost too much.

The indefatigable hunter of tails was now concentrating all his prowess on his mother's long whip-lash with its fine black tuft of hair which she jerked out from under his nose at the very instant of each attack.

The other three were fighting off sleep, with violent outbursts of undirected energy, succumbing slowly to drooping eyelids and strained bellies, until at last they lay in an untidy heap of fluff and fur.

Mark was one hundred and twenty yards downwind. He lay belly down behind a small ant-heap, and it had taken almost an hour to work in this close. The umbrella thorn was set in an area of short open grassland, and he had been forced to stalk flat, tortoising forward on his elbows with the rifle held across the crook.

'Can we get closer?' Mark asked, his whisper merely a soft breath. The short stiff yellow grass was just high enough to screen the cat when she lay flat on her side.

'Jamela, I could get close enough to touch her.' He put the emphasis on the word 'I' and left the rest of it unstated.

So they waited in the sun, another twenty minutes until at last the lioness lifted her head.

Perhaps some deep sense of survival had warned her of the presence of the hunters. Her head came up in a flash of yellow movement, the extraordinary swiftness so characteristic of all the big cats, and she stared fixedly downwind, the sector of maximum danger.

For long seconds she watched, and the wide yellow eyes were steady and unblinking. Sensing her concern, two of the cubs sat up sleepily and waited with her.

Mark felt the lioness was looking directly at him, but he obeyed the law of absolute stillness. The first movement of lifting the Mannlicher would send her away in a blur of speed. So Mark waited while the seconds spun out. Then suddenly the lioness dropped her head and stretched out flat once again.

'She is restless,' warned Pungushe. 'We can get no closer.'

'I cannot shoot from here.'

'We will wait,' said Pungushe.

All the cubs slept now, and the lioness dozed, but always all her senses were working, nostrils tasting carefully each breath of the wind for the taint of danger, the big round ears never still, flicking to the slightest sound of wind or branch, bird or animal.

Mark lay in the direct sunlight, and the sweat rose to stain his shirt. A tsetse fly settled behind his ear and bit into the softness of his neck, but he did not make the movement of brushing it away. It was an hour before his chance came.

The lioness rose suddenly to her full height, and swung her tail from side to side. She was too restless to stay here under the thorn tree any longer. The cubs sat up groggily, and looked to her with puzzled furrowed faces.

The lioness was standing broadside to where Mark lay. She held her head low, and her jaws were a little open as she panted softly in the heat. Mark was close enough to see the dark specks of the tsetse fly sitting on her flanks.

She was still in shadow but now she was backlit by the pale yellow grass beyond her. It was a perfect shot – the point of the elbow the hunter's aiming mark; the span of a hand back from there, and the bullet would rake both lungs, the span of a hand lower would take the heart cleanly.

The lungs were certain, but the heart was swift. Mark chose the heart and lifted the rifle to his shoulder. The safety-catch had long before been set at the firing position.

Mark took up the slack in the trigger and felt the final resistance before the mechanism tripped.

The bullet was 230 grains in weight, and the bronze jacket of the slug was tipped with a grey blob of lead so that it would mushroom on impact and open massive damage through the lioness's chest cavity.

The lioness called her cubs with a soft moaning grunt, and they scrambled obediently to their feet, still a little unsteady from sleep.

She walked out into the sunlight, with that loose feline gait, her head swinging from side to side at each pace, the long back slightly swayed and the heavy droop of her full dugs thickening the graceful line of her body.

'No,' thought Mark. 'I will take the lungs.' He lifted his aim a fraction, holding steady and true four inches behind the point of the elbow, swinging the rifle to follow her as she went into a short restless trot.

The cubs tumbled along behind her in disorder.

Mark held his aim until she reached the edge of the bush, and then she was gone with the insubstantial blurred movement of a wisp of brown smoke on the wind.

When she was gone, he lowered the rifle and stared after her.

Pungushe saw the thing break in him at last. The cold stillness of hatred and guilt and horror broke, and Mark began to cry, hacking tearing sobs that scoured and purged.

It is a difficult thing for a man to watch another weep, especially if that man is your friend.

Pungushe stood up quietly and walked back to where they had tethered the mule. He sat alone in the sun and took a little snuff and waited for Mark.

### GOVERNMENT MINISTER SPEAKS ON DUTY TO HUMANITY

The newly appointed Deputy Minister of Lands, Mr. Dirk Courtney, expressed concern today at the mauling of a young woman in the proclaimed area of Northern Zululand.

The woman, Mrs. Marion Anders, was the wife of the Government Ranger in the area. She was mauled to death by a lioness last Friday.

This unfortunate incident underlines the grave danger of allowing wild animals to exist in proximity to settled areas of human habitation.

Residents in these areas will be in constant danger of animal attack, of crop depredation and game-borne diseases of domestic animals as long as this position is allowed to continue.

Mr. Dirk Courtney said that the rinderpest epidemic at the turn of the century had accounted for a loss of domestic cattle estimated to exceed two million head. Rinderpest was a game-borne disease. The minister pointed out, 'We cannot risk a repetition of such a calamity.'

The proclaimed area of Northern Zululand encompasses both highly valuable arable land, and a major watershed vital to proper conservation of our natural resources. If the full potential of our national assets is to be exploited, these areas must be turned over to properly controlled development. The minister went on, 'Your Government has placed priority on this issue, and we will be placing legislation before Parliament at the next sitting.'

Mark read the article through carefully. It was placed prominently on the leader page of the *Natal Witness*.

'There are more,' General Sean Courtney thumbed open a slim folder with half a dozen other cuttings, 'take them with you. You'll see it's all the same general purport. Dirk Courtney is beating the drum with a very big stick, I'm afraid.'

'He's in such a position of power now. I never dreamed he would be a Deputy Minister.'

'Yes,' Sean nodded. 'He has rushed to power, but on the other hand we still have a voice. One of our members in a solid seat has stood down for Jannie Smuts, even I have been offered a seat in a safer constituency.'

'Will you take it, sir?'

Sean shook his silver beard slowly. 'I've had a long time in public life, my boy – and anything you do too long becomes a bore.' He nodded as he thought about his words. 'Of course, that's not strictly true. I am tired, let the younger ones with more energy pick up the reins now. Jannie Smuts will keep in close touch, he knows he can call on me, but I feel like an old Zulu chief. I just want to sit in the sun, drink beer, grow fat and count my cattle.'

'What about Chaka's Gate, sir?' Mark pleaded.

'I have spoken to Jannie Smuts and some of the others, on both sides of the house. We have a lot of support in the new Government as well. I don't want to make it a party issue, I'd like to see it as an issue of each man's own conscience.'

They went on talking until Ruth intervened reluctantly. 'It's after midnight, dear. You can finish your talk in the morning. When are you leaving, Mark?'

'I should be back at Chaka's Gate tomorrow night.' Mark felt a prick of guilt as he lied. He knew damned well he was not going home just yet a while.

'But you'll stay for lunch tomorrow?'

'Yes, I'd like that. Thank you.'

As Mark rose he picked up the file of newspaper clippings from Sean's desk. 'I'll let you have them back tomorrow, sir.'

However, the moment Mark was alone in his room, he dropped into an easy chair and turned avidly to the reverse side of the newspaper cutting he had brought with him. He had not dared to turn over the cutting and read the words that had caught his eye in the General's presence, but now he lingered over them, re-reading and savouring. Part of the article was missing, scissored away when the Deputy Minister's speech had been trimmed, but there was enough.

## EXCEPTIONAL EXHIBITION BY YOUNG ARTIST

Presently showing at the sample rooms of the Marine Hotel on the Marine Parade is an exhibition of thirty paintings by a young lady artist.

For Miss Storm Courtney, it is her first public exhibition and even a much older and more established artist could have been justly gratified with such a reception by the art-lovers of our fair city. After the first five days, twenty-one of her paintings had found enthusiastic purchasers at prices as high as fifty guineas each. Miss Courtney has a classical conception of form, combined with both a sure sense of colour and a mature and confident execution rare in an artist of such tender years.

Worthy of special mention is Number 16, 'Greek athlete at rest'. This painting, property of the artist and not for sale, is a lyrical composition that would perhaps raise the eyebrows of the more old-fashioned. It is an unashamedly sensual ode to –

Here the scissors had cut through, leaving Mark with a disturbing unfinished feeling. He read it once more, inordinately pleased that Storm had reverted to her maiden name with which to sign her work. Then carefully he folded the cutting into his wallet, and he sat in the chair staring at the wall, until he fell asleep, still fully dressed.

A young Zulu lass, no more than sixteen years of age, opened the door of the cottage. She was dressed in the traditional white cotton dustcoat of the nanny and she carried baby John on her hip.

Both nanny and child regarded Mark with huge solemn eyes, but the nanny's relief was patent when Mark addressed her in fluent Zulu.

At the sound of Mark's voice John let out an excited squawk that could have been recognition, but was probably merely a friendly greeting. He began to leap up and down on the nanny's hip with such force that she had to grab to prevent him taking off like a sky rocket.

He reached out both hands towards Mark, burbling and laughing and shouting, and Mark took him, all warm and wriggling and baby-smelling, from the maid. John immediately seized a handful of Mark's hair and tried to remove it by the roots.

Half an hour later when Mark handed him back to the little moon-faced maid, and went down the steep pathway to the beach, John's indignant howls of protest followed him, only fading with distance.

Mark kicked off his shoes and left them and his shirt above the high-tide mark, then he turned northwards and followed the white sweep of sand, his bare feet leaving wet prints on the smooth firm edge of the seashore.

He had walked a mile, and there was no sign of any other person. The beach sand was rippled by static wind-blown wavelets, and dappled with the webbed prints of seabirds.

On his right hand, the surf rose in long glassy lines, curling green and then dropping over in a crash of white water that shook the sand beneath his feet. On his left hand, the dense, dark green bush rose above the white beach, and again beyond that, the far blue hills and taller bluer sky.

He was alone – until he saw, perhaps a mile ahead,

another solitary figure, also following the edge of the sea, a far small and lonely figure, coming towards him, still too distant to tell whether it was man or woman, friend or stranger.

Mark lengthened his stride, and the figure drew nearer, clearer.

Mark began to run, and the figure ahead of him stopped suddenly, and stood with that stillness poised on the edge of flight.

Then suddenly the stillness exploded, and the figure was racing to him.

It was a woman, a woman with dark silky hair streaming in the wind, a woman with outstretched arms and flying bare brown feet, and white teeth and blue, very blue eyes.

They were alone in the bedroom. Baby John's cot had been removed to the small dining-room next door, since he had begun to show an interest in everything that looked like a good romp, hanging on the edge of his cot with shouts of applause and approbation, and then trying his utmost to scale the wooden railings and join the play.

Now they were enjoying those contented minutes between love and sleep, talking softly in the candlelight under a single sheet, lying on their sides facing each other, holding close, with their lips almost touching as they murmured together.

'But darling Mark, it is still a thatched hut, and it is still wild bush.'

'It's a big thatched hut,' he pointed out.

'I don't know. I just don't know if I have changed that much.'

'There is only one way to find out. Come with me.'

'But what will people say?'

'The same as they'd say if they could see us now.'

She chuckled easily, and snuggled a little closer. 'That was a silly question. The old Storm speaking. People have said all there is to say about me, and none of it really mattered a damn.'

'There aren't a lot of people out there to sit in judgment. Only Pungushe, and he's a very broad-minded gentleman.'

She laughed again sleepily. 'Only one person I care about – Daddy mustn't know. I've hurt him enough already.'

So Storm came at last to Chaka's Gate. She came in the beaten and neglected Cadillac, with John on the seat beside her, her worldly possessions crammed into the cab or strapped on the roof and Mark riding his motorcycle escort ahead of her over the rude and bumpy track.

Where the track ended above the Bubezi River, she climbed out and looked around her.

'Well,' she decided after a long thoughtful survey of the towering cliffs, and the river in its bed of green water and white banks, framed by the tall nodding strands of fluffy-headed reeds and great spreading sycamore figs, 'at least it's picturesque.'

Mark put John on his shoulder. 'Pungushe and I will come back with the mules for the rest of your gear.' And he led her down the footpath to the river.

Pungushe was waiting for them under the trees on the far bank, tall and black and imposing in his beaded loin cloth.

'Pungushe, this is my lady and her name is Vungu Vungu – the Storm.'

'I see you, Vungu Vungu, I see also that you are mis-named,' said Pungushe quietly, 'for a storm is an ugly thing which kills and destroys. And you are a lady of beauty.'

'Thank you, Pungushe.' Storm smiled at him. 'But you are also misnamed, for a jackal is a small mean creature.'

'But clever,' said Mark solemnly, and John let out a

shout of greeting and bounced on Mark's shoulder, reaching out with both hands for Pungushe.

'And this is my son.'

Pungushe looked at John. There are two things a Zulu loves dearly, cattle and children. Of the two, he prefers children, preferably boy-children. Of all boy-children, he likes best those that are robust, and bold and aggressive.

'Jamela, I should like to hold your son,' he said, and Mark gave John to him.

'I see you Phimbo,' Pungushe greeted the child. 'I see you little man with a great voice.' And then Pungushe smiled that great beaming radiant smile, and John shouted again with joy and thrust his hand in Pungushe's mouth to grab those white shining teeth, but Pungushe swung him up on to his shoulder and laughed with a great hippo-snort and carried him up the hill.

So they came to Chaka's Gate, and there was never any doubt, right from that first day.

Within an hour, there was a polite tap on the screen-door of the kitchen and when Mark opened it there stood in a row on the covered stoep all of Pungushe's daughters, from the eldest who was fourteen to the youngest of four.

'We have come,' announced the eldest, 'to greet Phimbo.'

Mark looked at Storm inquiringly, and she nodded. The eldest daughter swung John up on to her back with a practised action, and strapped him there with a strip of cotton limbo. She had played nurse-maid to all her brothers and sisters, probably knew more about small children than both Storm and Mark combined, and John took to the froglike position on her back as though he had been born Zulu. Then the little girl bobbed a curtsey to Storm and trotted away, with all her sisters in procession, bearing John off to a wonderland peopled entirely with playmates of endless variety and fascination.

On the third day, Storm began sketching, and by the

end of the first week she had taken over the household management on a system that Mark referred to as comfortable chaos, alternating with brief periods of pandemonium.

Comfortable chaos was when everybody ate what they wanted, perhaps chocolate biscuits and coffee for dinner one night and a feast of barbecued meat the next. They ate it where they felt like it, perhaps sitting up in bed or lying on a rug on the sand-bank of the river. They ate when they wanted, breakfast at noon or dinner at midnight, if talking and laughing delayed it that long.

Comfortable chaos was when the dusting of furniture or polishing of floors were forgotten in the excitement of living, when clothes that needed mending were tossed into the bottom of the cupboard, when Mark's hair was allowed to grow in points over the back of his collar. Comfortable chaos ended unpredictably and abruptly to be replaced by pandemonium.

Pandemonium began when Storm suddenly got a steely look in her eye and announced, 'This place is a pig sty!' followed by the snipping of scissors, buckets of steaming water, clouds of flying dust, banging pots, and flashing needles. Mark was shorn and clad in refurbished clothing, the cottage gleamed and sparkled, and Storm's housekeeping instincts were exhausted for another indefinite period. And the next day she would be up on Spartan's back, John strapped Zulu-fashion behind her, following Mark on patrol up the valley.

The first time John had been taken on patrol, Mark had asked anxiously, 'Do you think it's wise to take him, he's still very small?'

And Storm had replied, 'I am older and more important than Master John. He fits into my life, not me into his.'

So John rode patrol on muleback, slept in his apple basket under the stars at night, and took his daily bath in the cool green pools of the Bubezi River, quickly developed an immunity to the occasional tsetse bite, and flourished.

They climbed the steep pathway to the summit of Chaka's Gate, sat with their feet dangling over that fearful drop, and they looked across the whole valley, the far blue hills and the plains and swamps and the wide winding rivers.

'When I first met you, you were poor,' Storm said quietly, leaning against Mark's shoulder with her eyes filled with the peace and wonder of it, 'but now you are the richest man in the world, for you are the owner of paradise.'

He took her up the river to the lonely grave below the escarpment. Storm helped him to build a pile of rocks, and to set the cross that Mark had made over it. He told her Pungushe's story of how the old man had been killed, and she cried openly and unashamedly, holding John on her lap, sitting on the gravestone, listening and living every word.

'I have looked – but never truly seen before,' she said, as he showed her the nest of a sunbird, cunningly woven of lichen and spider web, turning it carefully so she could peer into the funnel entrance and see the tiny speckled eggs.

'I never knew what true peace was until I came to this place,' she said, as they sat on the bank of the Bubezi in the yellow light of fading day, and watched a kudu bull with long spiral corkscrew horns and chalk-striped shoulders lead his big-eared cows down to the water.

'I did not know what happiness was before,' she whispered, when they had woken together a little after midnight for no reason and reached for each other in the darkness.

Then one morning she sat up in the rumpled bed,

over which John was rampaging unchecked and sowing crumbles of lightly chewed biscuit, and she looked at Mark seriously.

'You once asked me to marry you,' she said. 'Would you like to repeat that question, sir?'

And it was later that same day they heard the axeman at work up the valley.

The blade of a two-handed axe, swung against the bole of a standing hardwood tree, rings like a gunshot, and the sound of it bounced against the cliffs of Chaka's Gate and was flung back to break in dying echoes down the valley, each stroke still lingering on the air while the next cracked off the grey cliffs. There was more than one axeman at work, so that the din was continuous, like the sounds of battle.

Storm had never before seen such a passion of anger on Mark's face. His skin was drained of blood so that the tan of the sun was fever-yellow and his lips seemed frost-bitten and pinched by the force of it. Yet his eyes blazed, and she had to run to match his angry stride as they went up the scree slope from the river beneath the cliffs, and the sound of the axes broke over them, each separate stroke as brutal and shocking as the ones that preceded it.

Ahead of them, one of the lofty leadwoods quivered as though in agony and moved against the sky. Mark stopped in mid-stride to watch it, with his head thrown back and the same agony twisting his own lips. It was a tree of extraordinary symmetry, the silvery trunk rising with such grace as to seem as slim as a young girl's waist. It had taken two hundred years to reach its towering height. Seventy feet above the ground, it spread into a dark green dome of foliage.

As they watched, the tree shuddered again and the axes

fell silent. Slowly, majestically, the leadwood swung into a downward arc, gathering ponderous momentum, and the partially severed trunk groaned and popped as the fibres tore; faster and faster still she fell, crashing through the tops of the lesser vegetation below her, the twisting tearing wood shrieking like a living thing until she struck solid earth with a jarring impact they could feel in their guts.

The silence lasted many seconds, and then there was the sound of men's voices, awed voices, as though intimidated by the magnitude of the destruction they had wrought. Then almost immediately after that, the axes started again, fragmenting the great silences of the valley – and Mark began to run. Storm could not keep pace with him.

He came out in an area of devastation, a growing swathe of fallen trees where fifty black men worked like ants, half-naked and burnished with their own sweat, as they stripped the branches and piled them in windrows for burning. The wood chips shone white as bone in the sunlight and the sap that oozed from the axe cuts had the sweetish smell of newly spilled blood.

At the head of the long narrow clearing, a single white man crouched to the eyepiece of a theodolite set on its squat tripod. He was aiming the instrument down the clearing and directing with hand signals the setting of brightly painted markers.

He straightened from the instrument to face Mark – a young man with a mild friendly face, thick spectacles in silver wire frames, lank sandy hair flopping on to his forehead.

'Oh, hello there,' he smiled, and then the smile froze as Mark hissed at him.

'Are you in charge here?'

'Well, yes, I suppose I am,' the young surveyor stuttered.

'You are under arrest.'

'I don't understand.'

'It's quite simple,' Mark blazed at him. 'You are cutting standing timber in a proclaimed area. I am the Government Ranger, and I am placing you under arrest.'

'Now look here,' the surveyor began placatingly, spreading his open hands in a demonstration of his friendly intentions. 'I'm just doing my job.'

In his blind wholesale rage, Mark had not noticed the approach of another man, a heavy broad-shouldered man who moved silently out of the uncut brush along the edge of the clearing. However, the thick north-country accent was instantly familiar, and struck sparks along the surface of Mark's skin. He remembered Hobday from that day when first he had returned to Andersland to find his world turned upside down.

'That's all right, chummy. I'll talk to Mister Anders.' Hobday touched the young surveyor's shoulder placatingly and smiled at Mark, a smile that exposed the short evenly ground teeth, but was completely lacking in any warmth or humour.

'There is nothing you can tell me,' Mark started, and Hobday lifted one hand to stop him.

'I am here in my official capacity as a Provincial Inspector for the Ministry of Lands, Anders. You'd better listen.'

The angry words died and Mark stared at him, while Hobday calmly unfolded a letter from his wallet and proffered it to Mark. It was typewritten on Government paper and signed by the Deputy Minister of Lands. The signature was bold and black – Dirk Courtney. Mark read through the letter slowly, with a plunging sense of despair, and when he finished, he handed it back to Hobday. It gave him unlimited powers in the valley, powers backed by all the authority and weight of Government.

'You are going up in the world,' he said, 'but still working for the same master.' And the man nodded complacently, and then his eyes switched away from Mark's face as Storm came up. The expression on his face changed, as he looked at her.

Storm had her hair in thick twin braids, dangling forward on to each breast. The sun had turned her skin to a rich reddish brown, against which her eyes were startlingly blue and clear. Except for the eyes, she looked like a Sioux princess from some romantic novel.

Hobday dropped his eyes slowly over her body, with such intimate lingering insolence that she reached instinctively for Mark's arm and drew closer to him, as though to bring herself under his direct protection.

'What is it, Mark?' She was still breathless from her climb up the slope, and high colour lit her cheeks. 'What are they doing here?'

'They're Government men,' said Mark heavily. 'From the Ministry of Lands.'

'But they can't cut our trees,' she protested, her voice rising. 'You've got to stop them, Mark.'

'They're cutting survey lines,' Mark explained. 'They are surveying the valley.'

'But those trees—'

'It don't really matter, ma'am,' Hobday told her. His voice was lower now with a thick gloating tone, and his eyes were still busy on her body, like insects crawling greedily to the scent of honey, moving over the thin sun-bleached cotton that covered her breasts. 'It don't matter a damn,' he repeated. 'They are all going to be under water anyway, cut or standing – it's all going under.' He turned away from her at last, and swept one hand down the rude clearing. 'From that side to this,' he said, indicating the gap between the towering grey cliffs of Chaka's Gate, 'right across it, we're going to build the biggest bloody dam in the whole world.'

They sat together in darkness, close together as though for comfort, and Mark had not lit the lantern. The reflected glow of stars was thrown in under the thatched veranda of the cottage, giving them just enough light to make out each other's faces.

'We knew it was coming,' whispered Storm. 'And yet somehow I did not believe it. Just as though wishing could make it stop.'

'I'm going through early tomorrow to see your father,' Mark told her. 'He has to know.'

She nodded. 'Yes, we must be ready to confront them.'

'What will you do? I can't leave you here with John.'

'And you can't take me with you. Not to my father,' she agreed. 'It's all right, Mark, I'll take John back to the cottage. We'll wait for you.'

'I'll come for you there, and next time we return here, you'll be my wife.'

She leaned against him. 'If there is anything to return to,' she whispered. 'Oh Mark, Mark – they can't do it! They can't drown all this – this—' The words eluded her and she fell silent, clinging to him.

They did not speak again, until minutes later a low polite cough roused them, and Mark straightened to see the dark familiar bulk of Pungushe standing below the veranda in the starlight.

'Pungushe,' he said. 'I see you.'

'Jamela,' the Zulu replied, and there was a tone and tightness in his voice that Mark had never heard before. 'I have been to the camp of the strangers. The cutters of wood, the men with painted poles, and bright axes.'

He turned his head to look down the valley, and they followed his gaze. The ruddy glow of many camp fires flickered against the lower slopes of the cliffs and on the still night air, the sounds of laughter and men's voices carried faintly.

'Yes?' Mark asked.

'There are two white men there. One of them is young and blind and of no importance – while the other is a square thick man, who stands solid on his feet like a bull buffalo, and yet moves silently, and speaks little and quietly.'

'Yes?' Mark asked again.

'I have seen this man before in the valley,' Pungushe paused. 'He is the silent one of whom we have spoken. He is the one who shot *ixhegu*, your grandfather – and smoked as he watched him die.'

Hobday moved quietly, solidly, along the edge of the slash line of the trees. The axes were silent, now, but the end of the noon break would be enforced to the minute. At the stroke of the hour they would be back at work. He was driving them hard, he always worked his gangs hard, took a pride in his ability to extract from each man effort beyond his wage. It was one of the qualities that Dirk Courtney valued in him – that and his loyalty, a fierce unswerving loyalty that baulked at no demand upon it. There was no squeamishness, no hesitating. When Dirk Courtney ordered it, there was no question asked. Hobday's reward was every day more apparent, already he was a man of substance, and when the new land was apportioned, that red sweet well-watered soil, rich as newly butchered beef, then his reward would be complete.

He paused at the spot where the slope increased sharply, angling into its plunge to the river bed below, and he looked out across the land. Involuntarily he licked his lips, like a glutton smelling rich food.

They had worked so long for this, each of them in his own way, led and inspired by Dirk Courtney, and although Hobday's personal share of the spoil would be a minute

587

fraction of a single per cent, yet it was riches such as most other men only dream of.

He licked his lips again, standing very still and silent in the shadows and he looked to the sky. The clouds were piled to the very heavens, mountains of silver, blinding in the sunlight, and as he watched they moved ponderously down on the light wind. He could feel the closeness, and he stirred impatiently. Rain would delay them seriously, and rain was coming, the big torrential summer rains.

Then he was distracted again. Something moved on the far side of the slash line, and his eye darted to the movement. It was a flash of bright colour like the flick of sunbird's wing, and his veiled eyes jumped to it instantly, his body without moving became charged with tension.

The girl came out of the brush line, and paused thirty paces away. She had not seen him, and she stood poised, listening, head cocked like a forest animal.

She stood lightly, gracefully, and her limbs were slim and brown, the flesh so firm and young and sweet that he felt the quick bright rush of lust again as he had when, the previous day, he had seen her for the first time.

She wore a loose, wide peasant skirt of gay colour, and a thin cotton bodice pulled low at the front and drawn loosely with a string that left the bulge of bosom pushing free, the fine skin shading from dark ruddy brown to pale cream. She was dressed like a girl going to meet a lover, and there was a deliciously fearful tenseness in the way she took a step forward and stopped again uncertainly. He felt the lust fuelled in his groin, and he was suddenly aware of his own hoarse breathing.

The girl turned her head and looked directly at him, and as she saw him, she started visibly, dropping back a pace with one hand flying to her mouth. She stared at him for fully five seconds, and then slowly a transformation came over her.

The fingers dropped away from her face and she put

both hands behind her back, a movement that thrust the pert breasts against the cotton of her bodice so he could see the rosy dark buttons of her nipples through the material. She thrust out one hip at a saucy angle, and lifted her chin boldly. Deliberately she let her eyes slide down his body, let them linger on his groin, and then rise again to his face. It was an invitation as clear as the spoken word, and Hobday heard the blood roaring in his ears.

She tossed her head, flicking the thick braid of hair over her shoulder, and she turned away, walking deliberately back to the tree-line, exaggerating the roll of tight round buttocks under the skirt.

She looked back over her shoulder, and as he started forward to follow, she let out a tingling flirt of laughter and ran lightly on sandalled feet, turning at an angle down the slope and Hobday began to run.

Within fifty yards Storm had lost sight of him in the heavy underbrush, and she stopped to listen, fearful that he might have given up the pursuit. Then there was movement above her, at the crest of the slope, and she realized with the first pang of real alarm that he had moved more swiftly than she had anticipated, and he had not followed her down, but had stayed above her in a position of command.

She went off again, running, and almost immediately she realized that he was ahead of her, moving fast along the crest. From up there, he could trap her by a swift turn directly down the slope.

She felt panic spur her, and started to run in earnest. Immediately the loose scree betrayed her and slipped away under her feet. She fell and rolled, flailing her arms for support and coming up on to her knees the moment her fall was broken.

She let out a little sob of fear. The man had seen her fall and had come down the slope. He was so close that she could see the square white teeth in the brown smooth face. He was grinning, a keen excited grimace, and he was steady and quick, moving down directly into the path along which she must run to safety, cutting her off squarely from where Mark waited.

'She jumped to her feet and swirled away, doubling the slope, instinctively turning directly away from her pursuer – and from all help. Suddenly, she was completely alone, fleeing on frantic feet into the lonely spaces of the bush, beyond earshot of succour. Mark had been right, she realized, he had not wanted her to act as the bait. He had known just how dangerous a game she had set out to play, but in her stubborn arrogant way she had insisted, laughing at his protests, belittling his fears, until he had reluctantly agreed. Now she was running, terrified, the terror making her heart pound and squeezing her lungs so that her legs felt weak and rubbery under her.

Once she tried to turn back, but like an old and wily hound coursing a hare, he had anticipated and was there to block her, again she ran and suddenly the river was in front of her. The up-country rains had spated the course of the Bubezi and it rolled past in wide green majesty. She had to turn again along the bank, and was immediately into the area of thick jessie bush. The heavy thorn crowded her closely, leaving only narrow passages, a labyrinth of dark and secret twists and turns in which almost immediately she lost direction. She stopped and stood, trying to listen over the rush of her own breathing, trying to see through the wavering mist of her tears, tears of fear and of helplessness.

Her hair had come down in little wisps over her forehead, her cheeks blazed with high colour, and the tears made her eyes glitter with a feverish sheen.

She heard nothing, and the brown thorn encircled her. She turned slowly, almost like a blind woman, and now she was sobbing softly in her terror; she chose one of the narrow passages for escape and dived into it.

He was waiting for her. She came round the first twist of the pathway and ran almost directly into his chest.

Only at the very last instant she saw the outstretched arms, thick and brown and smooth, with the fingers of both hands hooked to seize her.

She screamed, high and shrill, and spun away, back along the path she had come, but his fingers caught in the thin cotton of her blouse. It tore like paper, and as she ran, the smooth creamy flesh of her back shone through the rent, flashing with a pearly promise that spurred his lust even higher, and when he laughed, it was a hoarse breathless blurt of sound that launched Storm into a fresh paroxysm of terror.

He hunted her through the jessie, and twice when he could have taken her, he deliberately let her slip through his fingers, drawing out the excruciating pleasure of it, cat with mouse, delighting at the way she shrieked at his touch, and at the fresh outburst of frantic terror with which she tried to escape him.

But at last she was finished, and she backed up into a corner of solid impenetrable thorn wall, and crouched there, clutching the shreds of her torn blouse about her, trembling with the wild uncontrollable shudders of a patient in high fever, her face smeared with tears and her sweat, staring at him with huge dark blue eyes.

He came slowly to her. He stooped and she was unresisting as he placed his big square brown hands on her shoulders.

He was still chuckling, but his own breath was unsteady, and his lips were drawn back from the square white teeth in a grimace of lust and excitement.

He pressed his mouth down over hers, and it was like one of those nightmares in which she could not move nor scream. His teeth crushed painfully against her lips, and she tasted her own blood, a slick metallic salt on her tongue and she felt herself suffocating, his hands were hard and rough as granite on the soft silk of her breasts and she came to life again, tugging unavailingly at his wrists, trying to drag them away.

'Yes,' he grunted, in the soft thick choked voice. 'Fight. Keep fighting me. Yes. Yes. That's right – struggle – don't stop.'

His voice roused her from the hypnotic spell of terror, and she screamed again.

'Yes,' he said. 'Do that. Scream again.' And he turned her across his body, forcing her down until his knee caught her in the small of the back, and her body bent backwards like a drawn bow, her hair sweeping the ground and the curve of her throat was soft and white and vulnerable; he placed his open mouth on her throat.

She was pinned helplessly as with one hand he swept the wide peasant skirt up above her waist.

'Scream!' he whispered gutturally. 'Scream again.' And with complete and horrified disbelief she felt those thick brown fingers, calloused and deliberately cruel, begin to prise open her body. They seemed to tear her tenderest, most secret flesh, like the talons of an eagle – and she screamed and screamed.

Mark had lost them in the labyrinthine maze of the jessie bush, and there had been silence now for many minutes.

He stood bareheaded and panting, listening with every fibre of his being in the aching silence of the jessie thorn; his eyes were wild, and he hated himself with bitter venom for letting himself be persuaded by Storm.

He had known how dangerous this man was, he was a killer, a coldly competent killer, and he had sent a girl, a young and tender girl, to bait him.

Then Storm screamed, close by in the jessie, and with a violent lift of savage relief, Mark began to run again.

At the last moment Hobday heard him coming, and he

dropped Storm's slim abused body and turned with unbelievable speed, dropping into the crouch of a heavyweight prize fighter, solid and low behind lifted arms and hunched shoulders, thick and rubbery with muscle.

Mark swung the weapon he had made the night before, a long sausage of raw-hide, the seams double sewn, and then filled with lead buckshot. It weighed two pounds, and it made a sound through the air like the wings of a wild duck and he swung full-armed, the blow given power and weight by his terrible anger and hatred.

Hobday threw up his right arm to catch the blow. The bones of his forearm broke cleanly, with a sharp crackle, but still the force of the blow was not fully expended and the leaded bag flew on, directly into Hobday's face.

Had he not caught the full weight of it on his arm, the blow would have killed him. As it was, his face seemed to collapse and his head snapped backwards to the full stretch of his neck.

Hobday crashed backwards into the wall of jessie and the curved, red-tipped thorns caught in his clothing and flesh and held him there, sprawling like a boneless doll, arms outspread, legs dangling, his face hanging forward on his chest and the thick dark droplets of blood beginning to fall on to his shirt and roll softly downwards across his belly, leaving wet crimson lines down the khaki drill.

The rain began as they carried Hobday up the track to where the two vehicles were kept under the lee of the cliffs of Chaka's Gate, on the south bank of the Bubezi. It came with the first splattering of fat warm drops, that stung exposed skin with their weight and momentum. It fell heavily and still more heavily, turning the surface of the track to a glaze like melting chocolate, so they slipped under their burden.

Hobday was chained at his ankles with the manacles that Mark used for holding arrested poachers. His good arm was cuffed to the leather belt at his waist, the other arm was crudely splinted and strapped down to the same belt.

Mark had tried to force him to walk, but either he was shamming or he was really too weak. His face was grotesquely distorted, the nose was swollen and pushed to one side, both eyes almost closed and leaden blue with bruises, his lips also were swollen and thickly scabbed with black dried blood where they had been mashed against his teeth, and through the mangled flesh were the dark gaps where five of the big square teeth had been torn out or snapped off level with the gum by the murderous force of Mark's blow.

Pungushe and Mark carried him between them, laboriously up the steep path in the teeming, stinging rain, and behind them trailed Storm with baby John on her hip, her hair melting in long black shiny smears down her face in the rain. She was shivering violently, in sudden uncontrollable spasms, either from the cold or from lingering shock. The child on her hip squalled petulantly, and she covered him with a fold of oilskin and tried to hush him distractedly.

They reached the two vehicles under the crude thatched shelter Pungushe had built to protect them from the elements. They put Hobday into the sidecar of the Ariel, and Mark buttoned the canvas screen over him to protect him from the rain and to hold him secure. He lay like a corpse.

Then Mark crossed to where Storm sat, shivering, and sodden and miserable, behind the wheel of the battered old Cadillac.

'I'm sending Pungushe with you,' he said, as he took her in his arms and held her briefly. She did not have the strength or will to argue, and she leaned heavily against Mark's chest for comfort.

'Go to the cottage – and stay there,' he instructed. 'Don't move out of it until I come for you.'

'Yes, Mark,' she whispered, and shuddered again.

'Are you strong enough to drive?' he asked with sudden gentleness, and she roused herself and nodded gamely.

'I love you,' he said. 'More than anything or anybody in this world.'

Mark led on the motorcycle over the slippery, muddy track, and it was almost dark when they reached the main road, itself hardly better than a track with deeply churned double ruts in the glutinous mud, and all the time the rain fell.

At the crossroads, Mark pulled the motorcycle off the road, and hurried back to talk to Storm through the open window of the Cadillac.

'It's six hours from here to Umhlanga Rocks in this mud, don't try and push it,' he told her, and reached through the window. They embraced awkwardly but fiercely, and then she rolled up the window and the Cadillac pulled away, the rear end sliding and skidding in the mud.

Mark watched it over a rise in the land, and when the rear lights winked out over the ridge, he went back to the motorcycle and kicked the engine to life.

In the sidecar the man stirred, and his voice was mushy and distorted through the mangled lips.

'I'm going to kill you for this,' he said.

'Like you killed my grandfather?' Mark asked softly, and wheeled the cycle into the road. He took the fork to Ladyburg, thirty miles away through the darkness and the mud and the rain, and his hatred and anger warmed him all the way like a bonfire in his belly, and he marvelled at his own restraint in resisting the temptation to kill Hobday with the bludgeon when he had the chance.

The man who had tortured and murdered the old man, and who had abused and desecrated Storm, was in his power – and still the temptation to avenge himself was fierce. Mark pushed it aside and drove on grimly into the night.

The motorcycle slipped and slid from one verge of the road to the other as he took it up the steep ascent of the Ladyburg escarpment, and below him the lights of the town were blanketed by the falling white fog of rain.

Mark was uncertain as to whether or not the General was in residence at Lion Kop, but as he gunned the machine into the walled kitchen yard he saw lights in the windows, and a clamorous pack of the General's hunting dogs rushed out into the night followed by three Zulu servants with lanterns. Mark shouted at them.

'Is the Nkosi here?'

Their answers were superfluous, for as Mark dismounted, he looked up and saw the bulky familiar beloved shape step into the lighted window of the study, head held low on broad shoulders, as Sean Courtney peered down at him.

Mark ran into the house, stripping off his streaming oilskins, and he burst into the General's study.

'My boy.' Sean Courtney hurried to meet him across the huge room. 'What is it?' Mark's whole being was charged with a fierce and triumphant purpose.

'I have the man who killed my grandfather,' he exulted, and halfway across the study Sean stopped dead and stared at him.

'Is it—' he stopped, and the dread was plain on his face, 'is it Dirk Courtney, is it my son?'

The servants carried Hobday's heavy inert body into the study and laid him on the buttoned leather sofa in front of the fire.

'Who put those chains on him?' growled Sean, studying the man, and then without waiting for a reply, 'Take them off him. My God, what happened to his face?'

Ruth Courtney came then, awakened by the uproar and excitement, dressed in a long dressing-gown with her night cap still knotted under her chin.

'Good Lord,' she stared at Hobday. 'His arm is broken, and perhaps his jaw also.'

'How did it happen?' Sean demanded.

'I hit him,' Mark explained, and Sean was silent for a long moment staring at him, before he spoke again.

'I think you had better tell me the whole story,' he said. 'From the beginning.'

While Ruth Courtney worked quietly over Hobday's broken face, Mark began his explanation to the General.

'His name is Hobday, he works for Dirk Courtney – has done so for years. One of his right-hand men.'

'Of course,' Sean nodded. 'I should have recognized him. It was the swollen face. I've seen him before.'

Quietly, quickly, Mark told everything he knew about the man, starting from his first meeting with Hobday at the deserted homestead on Andersland.

'He told you he was working for Dirk Courtney then?' Sean demanded.

'For Ladyburg Sugar,' Mark qualified, and Sean nodded his white beard on to his chest.

'Go on.'

Mark repeated Pungushe's story of the old man's death, how the three men had come with him to the valley, and how 'the silent one' had shot him and waited for him to die, and how they had buried him in an unmarked grave.

However, Sean shook his head, frowning, and Hobday on the couch stirred and tried to sit up. His swollen, distorted jaw worked and the words were blurred.

'It's a bloody nigger lie,' he said. 'First time I've ever been to Chaka's Gate was three days ago.'

Sean Courtney's worry showed clearly on his gaunt features as he turned back to Mark.

'You say you hit this man, that you are responsible for his injuries. How did it happen?'

'When he came to the valley, Pungushe recognized him as the man who killed John Anders. I lured him out of his camp, and Pungushe and I captured him and brought him here.'

'After half killing him?' Sean asked, heavily, and did not wait for Mark's reply. 'My boy, I think you've put yourself into a very serious position. I cannot see a shred of evidence to support all this, evidence that would convict a man in a court of law – while on the other hand you have assaulted somebody, grievous bodily harm and abduction at the least—'

'Oh, I do have proof,' Mark cut in quickly.

'What is it?' Sean asked gruffly.

The man on the couch turned his battered face to Sean, and his voice rose confidently.

'He's a bloody liar. It's all lies—'

'Quiet!' Sean waved him to silence, and looked to Mark again. 'Proof?' he asked.

'My proof will be in the fact that Dirk Courtney kills this man, or has him killed, the moment we turn him free.'

They all stared at Mark in stunned silence, and Mark went on seriously.

'We all know how Dirk Courtney works. He destroys anything that stands in his way, or that is a danger to him.'

Hobday was watching him, and for once the eyes were no longer veiled and cold. His mangled lips quivered and gaped slightly, showing the black gaps where the teeth were missing from his jaw.

'It isn't necessary for this man to confess anything to us. The fact that he has been here, in this house, with the General and myself, in the camp of Dirk Courtney's enemies, the fact that his face bears the marks of heavy persuasion – that will be enough for Dirk Courtney. Then one phone call is all it would take. Something like this.' Mark paused, then went on. '"Hobday was with us, he is ready to make a sworn statement – about the killing of John Anders." Then we take Hobday down to the village and leave him there. Dirk Courtney kills him, but this time we are ready. For once we can trace the murder directly to him.'

'God damn you,' snarled Hobday, struggling into a sitting position. 'It's a lie. I haven't confessed anything.'

'You can tell that to Dirk Courtney. He might believe you,' Mark told him quietly. 'On the other hand, if you turned king's evidence and did confess, you'd have the protection of the General and the law, all the force of the law – and we would not turn you loose.'

Hobday looked around him wildly, as though some avenue of escape might open miraculously for him, but Mark went on remorselessly.

'You know Dirk Courtney better than any of us, don't you, Hobday? You know how his mind works. Do you think he will take the chance that you didn't confess? Just how useful are you going to be to him in the future? Can you trust his loyalty, now that the shadow of doubt is on you? You know what he is going to do, don't you? If you think about it, you'll realize that your only chance of survival will be to have Dirk Courtney locked up safely, or dancing at the end of a rope.'

Hobday glared at him. 'You bastard,' he hissed through his broken lips, and it was as though a cork had been drawn; a steady stream of obscenity poured from him, vicious filth, the ugly meaningless words repeated over and over again, while his naked eyes glittered with helpless hatred.

Mark stood up and cranked the handset of the telephone on Sean's desk.

'Exchange,' he said into the mouthpiece. 'Please connect me with the residence of Mr Dirk Courtney.'

'No!' choked Hobday. 'Don't do that!' and now terror had replaced hatred, and his face seemed to collapse around the ruined nose and mouth.

Mark made no effort to obey, and clearly everybody in the room heard the click of a connection being made, and then the squawk of a voice distorted by the wires and distance.

'This is the residence of the Honourable Deputy Minister for Lands, Mr Dirk Courtney—'

Hobday lumbered off the couch, and staggered to the desk, he snatched the earpiece from Mark's hand and slammed it back on to its bracket of the telephone.

'No,' he panted, with pain and fear. 'Please don't do that.' He hung on to the corner of the desk, hunched up with the pain, clutching his broken arm to his chest, his mashed features working convulsively. They waited quietly, Mark and Ruth and Sean, waiting for him to reach his decision.

Hobday turned and staggered heavily back to the sofa. He collapsed upon it with his head hanging forward, almost touching his knees, and his breathing hissed and sobbed in the silence.

'All right,' he whispered hoarsely. 'What do you want to know?'

General Sean Courtney shook himself as though awaking from a nightmare, but his voice was decisive and brisk.

'Mark, take the Rolls. Go down into town and get me a lawyer. I want this statement drawn up in proper form – I'm still a Justice of the Peace and Commissioner of Oaths. I will witness the document.'

M ark parked the Rolls in Peter Botes' gravel driveway of the big new house on the outskirts of town.

The house was dark and silent, but to Mark's heavy knocking on the carved teak front door, a dog began to bark in the house somewhere, and at last a light bloomed in an upstairs window and the sash slid up with a squeal.

'Who is it? What do you want?' Peter's voice was querulous and fuddled with sleep.

'It's Mark,' he shouted up at the window. 'You've got to come with me, now!'

'My God, Mark, it's after eleven o'clock. Can't it wait until morning?'

'General Courtney wants you, now.'

The name had its effect. There was a mumble of voices within the bedroom, Marion's sister protesting sleepily, and then Peter called down again.

'All right, give me a minute to dress, Mark.'

As he waited in the driver's seat of the Rolls with the rain slashing down on the roof, and rippling in wavering lines down across the windshield, Mark pondered briefly why he had chosen Peter Botes. It was not only that he knew exactly where to find him so late at night. He realized that he wanted Peter to be there when they tore down his idol, he wanted to rub his nose in it when they proved Dirk Courtney a thief and a murderer. He wanted that satisfaction, and he smiled bleakly without humour in the darkened Rolls.

'I deserve at least that,' he whispered to himself, and the front door of the house opened. Peter hurried out, ducking his head against the slanting rain.

'What is it?' he demanded, through the window of the Rolls. 'It had better be important – getting me out at this time of night.'

'It's important enough,' Mark told him, and started the engine. 'Get in!'

'I'll follow you in my Packard,' Peter told him and ran to the garage.

Peter Botes sat at General Courtney's big desk. Hurriedly dressed, he was without a necktie and his small prosperous paunch bulged the white shirt, pulling it free of his trousers' waistband. His sandy hair was thinning and ruffled, so that pink scalp showed through as he bowed over the foolscap sheet of paper.

He wrote swiftly, a neat regular script, his features betraying each new shock at the words he was transcribing, his cheeks pale and his mouth set and thin.

Every few minutes he would pause incredulously and stare at Hobday across the room, breathing heavily at some new and terrible admission.

'Have you got that?' the General demanded, and Peter nodded jerkily and began to write again.

The others listened intently. The General slumped in his chair by the fire. His eyes were closed, as though he slept, but the questions he rapped out every few minutes were bright and penetrating as a rapier blade.

Mark stood behind his chair, quiet and intent, his face expressionless, although his anger and his hatred cramped in his guts.

Hobday sat forward on the sofa and his voice was a muffled drone in his thick north-country accent, muted in contrast to the terrible words he spoke.

It was not only the killing of John Anders. There was more, much more. Forgery of State documents, bribery of high officials, direct abuse of public office, and Mark started and leaned forward with shock as Hobday recounted how he had tried on two occasions, following Dirk Courtney's orders, to kill him.

Mark had not realized nor recognized him, but now Hobday's stocky shape tied in his memory with the shadowy faceless hunter in the night on the escarpment – and with the other figure seen through the rain and the fever mists. Hobday did not look up as he told it, and Mark had no questions to ask. It was as though once Hobday had started, he must purge himself of all this filth, as though he were now deriving some perverse satisfaction from the horror his words struck into his audience.

They listened, appalled by the magnitude of it all. Every few minutes, Ruth exclaimed involuntarily, and Sean would open his eyes briefly to stare at her, before closing them again and covering them with one hand.

At last Hobday came to the murder of John Anders, and each detail was exactly as Pungushe had described it. Mark felt sickened and wretched as he listened, but he asked only one question.

'Why did you let him die so slowly – why didn't you finish him?'

'It had to look like an accident.' Hobday did not look up. 'One bullet only. A man does not shoot himself twice by accident. I had to let him die in his own time.'

There was no breadth nor horizon to Mark's anger, and this time Ruth Courtney caught her breath with a sound like a sob. Again Sean Courtney opened his eyes. 'Are you all right, my dear?'

She nodded silently, and Sean turned back to Hobday. 'Go on,' he said.

At the end, Peter Botes read the statement back, his voice quivering and fading at the more horrendous passages, so that Sean had to gruff at him fiercely.

'Speak up, man.' He had made two fair copies, and Hobday signed each page with an illiterate scrawl, and then each of them signed below him, and Sean pressed his wax seal of office on to the final page of each copy.

'All right,' he said, as he carried the top document to the iron safe built into the wall behind his desk. 'I want you to keep and file the other copy,' he said to Peter. 'Thank you for your help, Mr Botes.' He locked the safe and turned back into the room. 'Mark, will you telephone

Doctor Acheson now, please? We've got to take care of our witness, I suppose. Though, for my money, I'd just as soon see him suffer.'

When Doctor Acheson arrived at Lion Kop, it was almost two in the morning, and Ruth Courtney took him up to the guest room where Hobday lay.

Neither Sean Courtney nor Mark went up; they stayed in the study, sitting quietly together across the fire which a servant had built. Against the windows, the wind bumped and the rain spattered. Sean was drinking whisky, and Mark had filled his glass twice for him in the last hour. He was slumped down in his favourite chair now, tired and old and bowed with grief, holding the glass with both hands.

'If I had the courage, I would take the rifle to him myself – like a rabid dog. But he is still my son, no matter how often I deny it, he is still of my blood, of my loins.'

Mark was silent, and Ruth came into the room.

'Doctor Acheson is setting that man's arm,' she said. 'He will be another hour, but I think you should come up to bed now, my dear.' She crossed to Sean's chair and laid a gentle hand on his shoulder. 'We have all had more than enough for one day.'

The telephone rang on the desk, a tinny irritant sound that startled them all. They stared at it for a full five seconds, until it rang again demandingly and Ruth crossed to it and lifted the earpiece.

'Mrs Ruth Courtney,' she said softly, almost fearfully.

'Mrs Courtney, are you the mother of Mrs Storm Hunt?'

'Yes, this is correct.'

'I am afraid we have very bad news. This is the Superintendent of Addington Hospital in Durban. Your daughter has been involved in a motor accident. The rain and the mud, I am afraid. Her son, your grandchild, has been killed outright. Thankfully he suffered no pain, but your daughter is in a critical condition. Can you come to her, as soon as you possibly can? We don't know if she will last the night, I'm afraid.'

The telephone dropped from Ruth's hand, and she swayed on her feet, the colour flying from her face, leaving it frosted with icy white.

'Oh God!' she whispered, and she started to fall, her legs collapsed and she crumpled forward. Mark caught her before she hit the floor and lowered her on to the sofa.

Sean crossed to the dangling earpiece and lifted it. 'This is General Courtney,' he barked angrily. 'What is it?'

Mark took the big Rolls down the long slanting right hand turn towards the bridge very fast. The woman he loved, the mother of his dead child, was dying – and Mark's heart was breaking. The road was deep with chocolate mud, and other vehicles had rutted it deeply, churning the mud to a thick ugly porridge. The Rolls flared and kicked in the ruts, but Mark fought the wheel grimly.

The bridge over the Baboon Stroom was five hundred yards ahead of them, still invisible in the endless driving rain. The headlights faded fifty feet ahead, overwhelmed by the flights of white raindrops, thick as javelins.

In the rear seat, Ruth Courtney sat quietly, staring ahead with eyes that did not see. The collar of her fur coat was pulled up around her ears, so she looked small and frail as a child.

General Sean Courtney sat beside Mark, and he was talking quietly, as though to himself.

'I've left it too late. I've been a stubborn old fool. I wanted too much from her – I wanted her to be better than human, and I was too harsh on her when she did not meet the standards I set for her. I should have gone to her long ago, and now perhaps it's too late.'

'It's not too late,' Mark denied. 'She will live, she must live.'

'It's too late for my grandson,' whispered Sean. 'I never saw him – and only now I realize how much I wanted to—'

At the mention of baby John, Mark felt the sickening jolt of despair in his stomach again and he wanted to shout,

'He was my son. My first born!' But beside him, Sean was talking again.

'I've been a spiteful and unforgiving old man. God have mercy on me, but I even cut my own daughter out of my will. I disowned her, and now I hate myself for that. If only we can reach her, if only I can talk to her once more. Please, God, grant me that.'

Ahead of them the steel guard railings of the bridge loomed out of the torrential darkness, and lightning bounced off the belly of the clouds. For an instant Mark saw the spidery steel tracery of the railway bridge spanning the chasm two hundred yards downstream. Under it, the rocky sides of the gorge dropped almost sheer a hundred and fifty feet to the swollen racing brown flood waters of the Baboon Stroom.

Mark touched the brakes, and then double-declutched the gears, bringing the Rolls under tighter control as he lined up for the entrance to the road bridge.

Suddenly, dazzling light flared from the darkness on the right hand side of the road, and Mark threw up one hand to protect his eyes.

Out of the darkness rushed a great dark shape, with two blazing headlights glaring like malevolent eyes as it came.

With sudden clarity of mind, Mark realized that the Rolls was trapped helplessly on the approach ramp to the bridge, and that on his left hand, only a frail railing of iron pipes screened them from the drop and that the monstrous vehicle racing down from the right would come into a collision which would hurl the Rolls through the railing as though it were a child's toy.

'Hold on!' he screamed, and swung the wheel to meet the roaring towering monster of steel, and the blinding white light cut into his eyes.

Peter Botes pulled off the road into the pine trees and switched off the engine of the Packard. In the silence he could hear the pine branches thrashing restlessly on the wind, and the dislodged rain-drops tapped on the roof.

Peter lit a cigarette and the match danced in his cupped hands. He inhaled deeply, waiting for the calming effect of the tobacco smoke, and he stared ahead up the straight roadway that led to Great Longwood, the homestead of Dirk Courtney.

He sensed that the decision he must make now was the most vital of his entire life. Whichever way he decided, his life was already changed for ever.

When Dirk Courtney fell, he would bring down all those close to him, even the innocent, as he was innocent. The scandal and the guilt would sully him, and he had worked so hard for it. The prestige, the blooming career and all the sweets that he was just now staring to enjoy. All of it would be gone, and he would have to begin again, perhaps in another town, another land, to begin again right at the very bottom. The thought appalled him, he had become used to being a man of substance and importance. He did not know if he could face a new beginning.

On the other hand, if Dirk Courtney did not come down, if he were saved from death and disaster – just how grateful would he be to the man who worked his salvation? He knew the extent of Dirk Courtney's present fortune and power, and it was conceivable that some of that, perhaps a large slice of that might come to him, to Peter Botes, the man who had saved Dirk Courtney and yet still retained the instrument of his destruction.

It was one of those moments of destiny, Peter realized, that come only occasionally to a chosen few. On one hand dishonour and obscurity – on the other, power and riches, tens of thousands, perhaps even millions.

He started the engine of the Packard and the rear wheels spun in the slimy mud, and then he swerved back on to the driveway, and put the big machine to the hill.

Dirk Courtney sat on the corner of his desk, one foot swinging idly. He wore a dressing-gown of patterned silk, and the lustrous material caught the lamplight as he moved. There was a white silk scarf at his throat, and his eyes were clear and alert in the handsome tanned face, as though he had not just risen from deep sleep.

He spun the duelling pistol on his forefinger as he listened intently.

Peter Botes sat nervously on the edge of the chair, and though there was a fire in the grate that Dirk had poked and fed to a fierce blaze, still he shivered every few moments and rubbed his hands together. The cold was in his soul, he realized, and his voice rose a little as he gabbled on.

Dirk Courtney did not speak, made no comment nor exclamation, asked no question until he was done. He spun the pistol, two turns and the butt snapped into the palm of his hand. Two turns, and snap.

When Peter Botes finished, Dirk cocked the hammer of the pistol and the click of the mechanism was unreasonably loud in the silent room.

'Hobday, my father, his wife, young Anders – and yourself. The only others that know.'

'And the Zulu.'

'And the Zulu,' Dirk agreed, and dry-fired the pistol. The hammer cracked against the pan.

'How many copies of the statement?'

'One,' lied Peter. 'In the iron safe of the General's study.'

Dirk nodded and re-cocked the pistol. 'All right. If there is another copy, you have it,' he said. 'But we don't lie to each other, do we, Peter?'

It was the first time he had used his given name, there was a familiarity and a threat in it, and Peter could only nod with a dryness in his throat.

Again Dirk dry-fired the pistol, and smiled. It was that warm and charming smile, that frank and friendly smile that Peter knew so well.

'We love each other too much for that, don't we?' He kept smiling. 'That's why you came to tell me this, isn't it? Because we love each other?'

Peter said nothing, and Dirk went on, still smiling, 'And of course you are going to be a rich man, Peter – if you do as I ask. A very rich man. You will do as I ask, won't you, Peter?'

And Peter nodded again. 'Yes, of course,' he blurted.

'I want you to make a phone call,' said Dirk. 'If you speak through a handkerchief, it will sound as though it's long distance, and it will muffle your voice. Nobody will recognize it. Will you do that?'

'Of course,' Peter nodded.

'You will phone my father's house, speak either to him or his wife. I want you to pretend that you are the Superintendent of Addington Hospital, and here is what you will tell them—'

D irk Courtney sat in the darkened cab of the truck, and listened to the rain as he reviewed his plans and preparations carefully.

He did not like having to move in a hurry, without time for careful planning. It was too easy to overlook some vital detail.

He did not like having to do this type of work himself. It was best to send another. He did not take personal risks, not any more, not unless there was no other way.

Regrets and misgivings were vain and wasted the moments which still remained before action. He turned all his attention back to his planning.

They would use the Rolls, and there would be three of them, the General and his Jewish whore, and that arrogant scheming puppy Anders.

Dirk had picked the spot with care, and the farmyard truck was loaded with fifty sacks of horse-feed. Three tons of dead weight. It would give it irresistible momentum.

Afterwards he must do two things, firstly he must make sure of them. He had a length of lead piping wrapped in hessian packing. It would crack a skull without breaking skin. Then he must take the General's keys. The key of the safe was on the bunch, and it was on his watch chain. The thought of plundering his father's dead body did not cause him even a tremor. His only concern was that the keys were retrievable, that there was no fire and that the Rolls was not submerged in the roaring torrent of the Baboon Stroom.

If that did happen, he must rely then on the General not having changed his habits of twenty years before. The spare key had been kept in the wine cellar then, on the rack above the champagne bottles. Dirk had discovered it there when he had used the cellar in a boyhood game, and he had taken the key twice for his own ends, and returned it secretly. The General was an old dog, a creature of habit. It would still be there. Dirk was certain.

All right, then, the safe. Two keys. If neither was available, then it was an old safe, but he did not want to use force on it. He must hope for the keys. Anyway, he was content that he could open it one way or another.

The statement was his, to be carefully burned, and that left Hobday. Probably in one of the guest rooms, sedated, helpless. The lead pipe again, and then an overturned parafin lamp. It was a big house of old dry wooden beams and thick thatch. It would burn as a pyre, with Hobday lying in it like a Viking chieftain.

That left only Peter Botes, Dirk glanced sideways at him. The situation was containable, it was no worse than fifty others he had survived. It needed only swift, direct action. He spoke encouragingly to Peter.

'Don't worry,' he said. 'After tonight, a new life awaits you. I'm going to take you with me along the paths of wealth and power, Peter. You'll never regret this night, I swear it to you.'

He squeezed Peter's upper arm, a comradely gesture in the darkness. Of course, he had a copy of the statement, Dirk thought, but afterwards there would be time – plenty of time to find it and to be rid of the pompous little prig. In a year or so, when the excitement had died down, another little accident, and it would all be over.

'Have you got the pistol?' he asked, and Peter gulped nervously, clutching the bulky military model Smith Wesson with both hands between his knees.

'You are not to use it,' Dirk warned again. 'Except as the very last resort. We don't want bullet holes to explain. You do understand?'

'Yes, I understand.'

'You are insurance, that's all. Final insurance.' And out in the darkness, through the slanting arrows of rain a light glowed and faded and grew again higher up the slope.

'Here they come,' said Dirk, and started the engine of the truck.

Mark spun the wheel hard right, and thrust the accelerator pedal flat against the floor-boards, trying to ride off the collision and beat the great roaring vehicle to the threshold of the bridge.

Behind him Ruth Courtney screamed shrilly, but Mark thought he had made it, he thought for an instant that the sudden acceleration had forged the Rolls ahead, but the truck slewed hard, swinging viciously, and he felt the crack of impact in every bone of his body.

It struck at the level of the rear wheels of the Rolls, and the big heavy car snapped sideways, tearing his hands from the steering-wheel and hurling Mark against the door. He felt bones break in his chest like dry twigs, and then the world turned end over end as the Rolls cartwheeled. A shower of bright white sparks flamed like the tail of a meteor in the darkness as steel brushed murderously against steel. There was another jerk as the Rolls crashed through the guardrail of the bridge and then they were dropping free, plunging silently into black space.

In the rear seat, Ruth Courtney was still screaming, and the Rolls struck, a glancing shuddering blow, bounding off the rock wall of the gorge, and leaping out into space once more.

Mark was pressed against the side door, held there by the accelerating dropping force of the plunging Rolls, but at the next impact the door was burst open, and Mark was hurled like a stone from a slingshot, out into resounding swirling darkness.

He saw the burning headlights of the Rolls, spinning in a great vortex of blinding white, below him, and the gorge rang with the iron echoes of steel on rock, and the crazy bellowing roar of the Rolls-Royce engine jammed at full power.

He seemed to fall for ever, through darkness, and then suddenly he struck with a force that drove the air from his lungs. The hard, unyielding impact convinced him for a moment that his body was crushed to boneless pulp on the rocky floor of the gorge, but then the cold, tumultuous torrent of racing water overwhelmed him. He had been thrown far enough to fall into the river itself.

Clinging to his last shreds of consciousness, he fought for breath, fought to keep his head above the surface, as the torrent swept him away. Glistening black boulders leapt like predators out of the dark, clawing at his legs, pummelling his injured chest, barging into him with numbing bruising power in the flood, and icy water gushed down his straining throat – burning his lungs, and making him choke and retch for each breath.

He slid down a racing spill of white rapids, feeling skin stripped from his hip and shoulder at the contact of harsh rock and then, at the bottom, he struck again, jammed solid between two monumental rocks. In the darkness, they stood over him like gravestones.

He was held in their jaws, and the water tore furiously at him, as though denied of its prey, trying to pluck him away.

There was light, just enough to make out shapes and distances, and Mark marvelled at that with a brain jellied by pounding and starved of oxygen. Then he looked up, and through streaming eyes saw that the truck was parked on the threshold of the bridge high above the gorge, its headlights struck the ironwork and the light was broken up and diffused by the rain. It cast a vague uncertain glow into the gorge.

Added to this was a closer, more powerful light source. The smashed carapace of the Rolls-Royce lay at the foot of the cliff, half in the water, half upon the rocky ledge. It lay on its back, with all four wheels spiralling idly, but both headlights still burned fiercely, striking the uneven rock walls, providing a dramatic stage lighting.

Mark looked around him, and saw that the current had swept him in under the cliff, and that a ledge of glistening black rock extended out over his head. He reached up with his right hand, and then cried out as his fingers touched the ledge, and bright agony flared in his wrist.

Something was broken there, he realized, as he clung desperately to the slippery boulders, and tried to force the fingers of his right hand to open or close.

The torrent was too strong to resist much longer, and he felt himself starting to slide, dragging over the boulders, on the point of being swept away once more. He knew that less than a hundred yards downstream, the first waterfall plunged, frothing and thundering, down the sheer side of the escarpment.

He released his grip with the left hand, and threw himself upwards with all his strength. His fingers caught on the sharp lip of the ledge above his head, and his body swung like a pendulum, the hungry waters slashing at his knees, testing the strength of his grip, trying to drag him away, trying to break the hooked fingers, tearing the fingernails loose so that droplets of blood squeezed out from under them.

Slowly, achingly, Mark bent the arm at the elbow, lifting his knees, drawing his feet clear of the water and its murderous drag.

He hung another moment, gathering what was left of his strength and resolve, and then, with one last convulsive heave, he threw his right arm upwards and hooked his elbow over the ledge, and followed it immediately with his left elbow.

Another moment of rest, and then he wriggled painfully out on the ledge and lay face down. He thought he was blind now, or that the lights had been doused, but the darkness was in his head only.

Slowly the darkness cleared, and he lifted his head. The thunder of the river drowned out all other sound, he could not hear the scrabble of loose stone and the slide of booted feet as Dirk Courtney came down the almost vertical pathway below the bridge. It did not surprise Mark that it was him — it seemed only natural that Dirk Courtney should be here, at the scene of disaster. He was dressed in hunting breeches and calf-length boots, a thick navy pea jacket and a woollen cap pulled low over his face.

He slid down the last ten feet of the cliff, keeping his balance, light as a dancer on his feet, and he paused on the ledge beside the shattered Rolls. Carefully he looked about him, flashing a lantern into the shadows and crevices.

Mark flattened himself down on the rock, but he was beyond the range of the lantern beam.

Dirk turned the beam on to the Rolls, and Mark groaned with the shock of it.

General Sean Courtney had been thrown halfway through the windscreen, and then the full weight of the machine had rolled on to his upper torso. His head was almost severed, and the thick white beard was sodden with bright blood, that shone like rubies in the lantern light.

Dirk Courtney stooped over him, and felt for the carotid pulse in the throat. Despite the fearful mutilation, he must have detected some flutter of stubborn life there. Dirk rolled the head sideways, and the eyes were open and startled. Dirk lifted the short thick club he carried in his right hand. It was wrapped in coarse brown hessian, but its weight and heft were obvious, by the way he handled it.

Mark tried to cry out, but his hoarse croak was lost in the roar of waters. Dirk struck his father across the temple, above the right ear, where the wet grey curls were plastered against the skull, and Mark seemed to feel the thud of the blow in his own soul.

Then with one exploring forefinger, Dirk pressed the temple and felt the give of mortal damage, the grating of the rough edges of shattered bone shard deep in his father's head.

Dirk's features were expressionless, cold and remote, but then he did something which seemed to Mark more dreadful, more shocking than the killing blow. With a tender touch of his fingertips, he closed the eyelids over Sean Courtney's dead staring eyes. Then he went down on one knee and kissed his father's bloodied lips lightly, without a change of expression. It was the act of an unhinged mind. It was only at that moment that Mark realized that Dirk Courtney was insane.

Almost immediately, Dirk's manner changed and his hands lost the gentle touch, becoming once again businesslike and precise. He rolled the body, unbuttoned the camel-hair overcoat and searched swiftly through Sean's clothing. Then he drew out a gold watch chain with the keys and gold hunter attached.

He examined the keys briefly and then pushed them into his pocket. He stood and went to the rear door of the Rolls and struggled with the handle. The door burst open at last, and Ruth Courtney's body spilled out sideways and lay at his feet. He took a handful of her thick dark hair and drew her head back. Again he swung the short thick club against her temple, and again he felt the skull like a doctor making his diagnosis, prodding to feel the soft spot of crushed bone.

Satisfied, he lifted Ruth Courtney's limp, childlike body in his arms and carried her to the edge of the water. He dropped her over the side, and she was gone instantly, dashed away on the dark current, down to where the plunging waterfalls would tumble her body into the Lady-burg valley, and the cruel rocks would leave no doubt in a coroner's mind as to how she had died.

Helpless with his injuries and exhaustion, his body battered and strained beyond its natural limits, Mark could not move, could hardly breathe as he watched Dirk Court-ney stoop and grasp his father's ankles. He dragged the General's heavy body to the edge of the torrent, straining backwards, against the dead weight.

Mark droped his face into his hands and found that he

was weeping, great racking dry sobs that probed the injuries deep in his chest.

When he looked up again, Sean Courtney's body was gone, and Dirk Courtney was coming towards where he lay, cautiously following the narrow ledge, searching the darkness with the lantern beam, sweeping the dark tumbling waters, examining each foot of the ledge, looking for him – looking for Mark, knowing he had been in the Rolls. The headlights of the truck had struck full into Mark's face in that fatal instant of collision. Dirk Courtney knew he was here – somewhere.

Mark rolled on to his side and tried to unfasten the buttons of his coat but in his haste he had tried with the right hand, and he whimpered with the pain. With his left hand now, he ripped the buttons away and struggled out of the garment, its wet folds resisting each movement so that when he at last was free of it, Dirk Courtney was only fifty feet away, coming steadily, carefully along the ledge, the lantern in one hand, the short heavy club dangling in the other.

Lying on the edge of the river, Mark flipped the jacket sideways, trying to make it fall on to the rocks in the torrent below, but he had no time to see if he had succeeded. Dirk Courtney was too close.

Mark rolled in towards the foot of the cliff, stifling the cry of pain as his damaged ribs and broken wrist came in rude contact with the rock.

In the lee of the cliff there was a dark shallow chimney, screened from the light of the headlights and lantern. Mark came to his feet. Dirk Courtney was out of sight beyond the angle of the cliff, but the beam of his lantern jumped and swept and swung, bobbing with each pace as he came on.

Mark turned his face to the cliff, gathered himself, and found that some of his dissipated strength was returning, and his anger was still alive, like small warm flame in his

617

chest. He did not know if it was enough strength, or anger, to carry him through, but he began to climb, slowly, clumsily, like a maimed insect he clung to the cold wet rock and dragged himself upwards.

He was twenty feet up when Dirk Courtney stopped on the ledge directly below him. Mark froze into stillness, the last defence of the helpless animal, but he knew that the instant Dirk lifted the beam, he was discovered. He waited for it, with the numbed resignation of the beast waiting in the abattoir chute.

Dirk made another careful search, swinging the lantern in a full slow traverse of both sides of the river, and he was on the point of lifting the beam to play it on to the cliff where Mark hung, when something caught his attention.

He took two hurried paces to the edge of the rocky ledge and shone the lantern downwards.

Mark's jacket was caught on one of the boulders, and Dirk went down on one knee to try and reach it with one outstretched arm.

It was the respite that Mark needed. Dirk's full attention was on the stranded jacket and the rush and roar of water covered the noise of Mark's scrabbling feet and hands on the cliff.

He did not look down again until he had dragged himself fifty feet higher, and then he saw that the jacket had succeeded as a decoy. Dirk Courtney was a hundred feet downstream, standing on the lip of the first steep waterfall, on the very edge of the escarpment. He had the sodden jacket in his hands and he was peering over the fearsome drop. In the lantern light, the water was black and smooth as oil, as it streamed into the abyss, turning slowly to thick white spume as it fell.

Dirk Courtney threw the jacket out into black space and stood back from the drop. He settled down comfortably on his haunches, sheltered by the cliff from rain and wind, and quite calmly he selected a cigar, like a workman taking a break after performing satisfactorily a difficult task.

That casual little act, the flare of a sulphur match, and the contented puff of blue tobacco smoke in the lantern light, probably saved Mark's life. It stoked his anger to the point when it could overcome his agony and bodily exhaustion. It provided him with the will to go on, and he began to climb again.

Sometimes during the climb, reality faded away from Mark. Once a sense of warmth and well-being began to suffuse his whole body, a wonderful feeling, floating as though on the very frontiers of sleep, but he caught himself before he fell, and deliberately punched his right hand against the rock face. He screamed with the pain of it, but with the pain came new resolve.

But resolve faded slowly in the cold and the pain, and fantasy grew again. He believed that he was one of King Chaka's chosen, following the old king up that terrible cliff to the summit of Chaka's Gate, and he found himself talking gibberish in broken Zulu, and in his head he heard the deep resonant voice of the old king calling him on, giving him encouragement, and he knew if he climbed faster he might catch a glimpse of the king's face. He lost his grip in his impatience, and slid away, gathering momentum down the incline, until he crashed into one of the stunted dwarf trees that grew from the cliff face. It broke his fall, but he screamed again at the pain of broken ribs.

He climbed on, and then he heard Storm's voice. It was so clear and close that he stopped, and turned his face up into the rain and darkness. She was there, floating above his head, so beautiful and pale and graceful.

'Come, Mark,' she said, and her voice echoed and rang like a silver bell in his head. 'Come, my darling.'

He knew then that she was alive, that she was not dying

in a cold hospital bed, that she was here, come to him in his pain and exhaustion.

'Storm,' he cried, and threw himself upwards, falling forward, and lying face down in the short wet grass at the top of the cliff.

He just wanted to lie there, for ever. He was not even sure that he had reached the top, was not sure if this was not yet another fantasy, perhaps he was dead already and this was all there was to it.

Then slowly he was aware of the rain drops on his cheek, and the sound of the little tree frogs clinking in the rain, and the cold breath of the wind, and he realized with regret that he was still alive.

The pain began returning then. It started in his wrist first, and began to spread, and he did not think he had the strength left to ride it.

Then suddenly he had the image, clearly formed in his mind, of Dirk Courtney stooped over his father's body, with the club raised in his hand to strike – and Mark's anger came to save him again.

Mark pushed himself to his knees and looked about him. A hundred yards away, the truck was parked on the threshold of the iron bridge, and in its headlights, he could make out the shape of a man.

With one more huge, draining effort, Mark came to his feet, and stood swaying, gathering himself for his next lumbering step.

Peter Botes stood in the rain, holding the heavy pistol hanging in his right hand. The rain had soaked his fine sandy hair, and it ran down his cheeks and forehead, so he kept wiping it away with his left hand.

The rain had soaked through the shoulders of his overcoat also, and he shivered spasmodically, as much from fear as from cold.

He was caught up in the great swirl of events over which

he had no control, an encircling web from which he could see no escape, even though his lawyer's mind twisted and turned.

'Accessory to murder – before and after the fact.' He did not want to know what was going on down there at the foot of the cliff, and yet he felt the sick fascination and dread of it.

This was not what he had imagined when he had made the decision to go to Dirk Courtney. He had thought it would be a few words, and he could walk away, pretending it had not happened, crawling back into his wife's warm bed and pulling the blankets over his head.

He had not been prepared for this horror and violence, for a gun in his hand, and this ugly bloody business in the gorge.

'The penalty is death,' he thought, and shivered again. He wanted to run, but there was no place to run now.

'Oh God, why did I do it?' he whispered aloud. 'I wish, oh God, I wish—' the age-old cry of the weakling, but he did not finish the wish. There was a sound behind him and he began to turn, lifting the pistol and beginning to point it with both arms at full stretch in front of him.

A figure came towards him out of the darkness, and Peter opened his mouth to cry out.

The figure was an apparition of blood and mud, with a distorted pale face, and it came so swiftly that the cry never reached his lips.

Peter Botes was a man of words and ideas, a soft little man of desks and rich foods, and the man who came out of the darkness was a soldier.

Mark knelt over him in the mud, panting and holding his ribs, waiting for the pain of movement to recede, and for his starred vision to clear.

He looked down at the man under him. His face was pressed into the mud, and Mark took a handful of his hair and rolled the head on its narrow shoulders to prevent the man drowning; it was only then that Mark recognized him.

'Peter!' he whispered hoarsely, and felt his senses reel again, uncertain if this was another fantasy.

He touched the unconscious man's lips, and they were warm and soft as a girl's.

'Peter!' he repeated stupidly, and suddenly he knew it all. It did not have to be thought out a step at a time. He understood how Dirk Courtney had known where to set his ambush. He knew that Peter was the traitor, and he knew that the decoy had been Storm and baby John, he knew it was all a lie then. He knew that Storm and her child were safe and sleeping in the tiny bedroom above the beach – and the knowledge buoyed him.

He picked the Smith Wesson revolver out of the mud with his left hand and wiped it carefully on his shirt.

Dirk Courtney paused at the head of the pathway. He was only slightly breathless from the climb, but his boots were thick with mud and raindrops dewed his shoulders, glittering in the burning headlights of the truck.

The headlights dazzled him, and there was an area of unfathomable darkness behind them.

'Peter?' he called, and lifted one arm to shield his eyes. He saw the shadowy figure of the waiting man leaning against the cab of the truck, and he walked forward.

'It's done,' he said. 'You have nothing to worry about now. I have the key to the safe, it's just the cleaning up left to do.'

He stopped abruptly, and peered again at the waiting figure. The man had not moved.

'Peter,' his voice cracked. 'Come on, man! Pull yourself together. There is still work to do.'

And he started forward again, stepping out of the beam of the headlights.

'What time is it?' he asked. 'It must be getting late.'

'Yes.' Mark's voice was thick and slurred. 'For you, it's very late.' And Dirk stopped again, staring at him. The silence seemed to last for all of eternity, but it was only the instant that it took Dirk to see the revolver and the pale mud-smeared face. He knew that the bullet would come now, and he sought to delay it, just long enough.

'Listen to me,' said Dirk urgently. 'Wait just one second.'

He changed his grip on the lantern in his right hand, and his voice was compelling, the tone quick and persuasive, just enough to hold Mark's finger on the trigger.

'There is something you must know.' Dirk made a disarming gesture, swinging the lantern back, and then hurling it forward in a wide arc of his long powerful arm, and, at the same instant, hurling himself forward.

The lantern struck Mark on the shoulder, a glancing blow, just enough to deflect his gun hand as he fired.

But he heard the bullet strike, that muffled thumping sound of soft lead expanding into living flesh, and he heard the grunt of air driven forcibly from Dirk Courtney's lungs by the strike.

The the man's big hard body crashed into Mark, and as they reeled sideways, supported by the chassis of the truck, he felt one arm lock around his chest and hard fingers close over his gun hand.

In that first moment of direct encounter, Mark knew instantly that Dirk Courtney's strength and weight were far greater than his own. Even if he had been uninjured, it would have been no contest, he was so out-matched that he felt as though he had been caught up in the cogs of a powerful piece of machinery. Dirk Courtney's body seemed not to be made of flesh and bone, but of brutal iron.

Mark's broken ribs moved in the vast encircling grip, and he cried out as the sharp edges of splintered bone lanced into his flesh. He felt his gun hand being forced back, the muzzle of the pistol training up into his own face, and Dirk Courtney swung him off his feet, both of them spinning into a turn like a pair of waltzing dancers, so that only the wildest effort and a lucky trick of balance allowed Mark to come down on his feet again. But now he no longer had the support of the truck chassis and the next effort would throw him headlong into the mud.

He felt Dirk Courtney gather himself for the next effort, the hard athlete's muscles moving him into perfect balance. Mark tried desperately to meet it, but it came with a smooth surge of power as irresistible as a huge comber rushing towards the beach. Then miraculously, at the moment when he was going, Mark felt the big body hit with a tremor, heard the sobbing outrush of Dirk Courtney's breath, and almost instantly Mark's stomach was drenched with a copious rush of warm liquid as it poured from his adversary.

The strength melted out of Dirk Courtney's body, Mark could feel his balance go, the grip on his pistol hand relaxed slightly – and Mark realized that his bullet had done damage, and that that last effort had torn something open in Dirk's chest. His life blood was expelled from the wound in thick hissing jets by the powerful pump of his heart, and Mark found he was able, by a supreme effort, to reverse the direction of the pistol barrel, swinging it in a slow arc back, back until pointed into Dirk Courtney's face.

Mark did not believe that he had the strength left to pull the trigger. The weapon seemed to fire of its own accord, and the muzzle flash almost blinded him.

Dirk Courtney's head snapped back as though he had been hit in the mouth with the full swing of a baseball bat. He was hurled backwards, out of the beam of the headlights into the darkness, and Mark heard his body sliding and tumbling down the steep side of the gorge.

The pistol dropped from Mark's hand, and he fell, first on to his knees, and then slowly toppled forward on to his face in the mud.

*This is the last will and Testament of SEAN COURT-NEY, married out of community of property to RUTH COURTNEY, (formerly FRIEDMAN, born COHEN), and presently residing at Lion Kop Ranch in the district of Ladyburg.*

*......................... I give and bequeath my entire estate and effects, movable or immovable, whether in possession, reversion, expectancy or contingency, wherever situate and of whatever description nothing excepted, to my wife the said RUTH COURTNEY.*

At first light the next morning, Mark led the search party down the steep river banks. His right arm was in a sling, his ribs were strapped tightly under his shirt, and he hobbled painfully with his injuries.

They found Sean Courtney half a mile below the last cataract, where the Baboon Stroom debouched into the valley.

He lay on his back, and there was no blood, the waters had cleansed every drop of it, and even his wounds were clean and washed pale blue. Except for the dent in his temple, his features were almost unmarked, and the white bush of his beard had dried in the early morning sun. It curled proudly on his chest. He looked like a carved stone effigy of a medieval knight laid out with his armour and sword on a sarcophagus in the dim depths of an ancient cathedral.

*In the event of my wife predeceasing me, or dying simultaneously, or within six months of each other –*

The river had been kind and carried her down to the same sand-bank. She was lying face down, half buried in the soft white sand. One slim naked arm was outflung, and on the third finger was the simple band of bright gold. The fingers almost, but not quite, touched her husband's arm.

They buried them together, side by side, in the same deep excavation on the slope of the escarpment, a little way beyond the big house of Lion Kop.

......................... *I direct that the following shall apply in regard to the rest and residue of my estate.*

There followed almost five hundred separate bequests which covered fifty pages, and totalled almost five millions of sterling. Sean Courtney had forgotten nobody. Beginning with the humblest grooms and domestic servants – enough for a piece of ground, a small herd, the equivalent of a life pension.

To those with a lifetime of service and loyalty, the gift was greater, in proportion.

To those who had laboured to build up the various prosperous companies and enterprises, there was a share of those companies, a large share.

He had not forgotten a single friend nor relative – not one of them.

*I acknowledge that I have one legitimate man-child, though I hesitate to employ the word son – one DIRK COURTNEY, presently residing at Great Longwood in the district of Ladyburg. However, God or the devil has already provided for him so abundantly, that anything I could add would be superfluous. Therefore I leave him nothing – not even my blessing.*

They buried Dirk Courtney in the pine forest, below the dog ring. No priest could be found to recite the office of burial, and the undertaker closed the grave under the curious eyes of a few members of the Press and a throng of sensation-seekers. Though there were many to stare, there was nobody to weep.

*To my daughter STORM HUNT (born COURT-NEY), who took lightly her filial duties, I, in turn, discharge my paternal duties with the bequest of a single guinea.*

'He did not mean it,' Mark whispered to her. 'He was talking about you that night – as it happened, he was remembering you.'

'I had his love,' she said softly. 'Even though – at the end – he tried to deny it, I will have it always. That is riches enough. I don't need his money as well.'

*To MARK ANDERS, for whom I have conceived the affection a man usually accords only to his natural son, I leave no money, as I am well aware of the contempt he holds for that commodity. I bequeath to him, in lieu of cash, all my books, paintings, guns, pistols and rifles, personal jewellery, and all my domestic animals, including dogs, horses and cattle.*

The paintings in themselves made up a considerable fortune, and many of the books were unique in rarity and condition.

Mark sold only the cattle and horses, for they were many and there was no place for them all in the tsetse-infested valley of the Bubezi.

*The rest and residue of my Estate I bequeath to the said MARK ANDERS in his capacity as the Trustee of the Wild Life Protection Society. The bequest to be used to further the aims of the Society, particularly to the development and extension of the proclaimed lands presently known as Chaka's Gate, into a Wild Life Reservation.*

'No one in Government will want to touch a Bill that was drawn up and piloted by the former Deputy Minister of

Lands,' General Jannie Smuts prophesied to Mark, as they stood talking quietly together after the funeral. 'The man's name will leave a pungent stink on anything he ever touched. Political reputations are too fragile to risk like that – I foresee a stampede by the new Government to dissociate themselves from his memory. We can confidently expect a new Bill being introduced, confirming and upgrading the status of the proclaimed lands of Chaka's Gate, and I can assure you, my boy, that the Bill will have the full support of my party.'

As General Smuts had foreseen, the Bill passed through the House at the following Session, becoming law on 31st May 1926, as Act No. 56 of 1926 of the Parliament of the Union of South Africa. Five days later, the telegram from the Minister of Lands arrived at Ladyburg confirming Mark's appointment as first Warden of Chaka's Gate National Park.

There was no trial at which Hobday could turn king's evidence and claim immunity from the crime of murder; so at Hobday's own trial, the Public Prosecutor asked for the death sentence. In his summing up, the Chief Justice mentioned the evidence given by Sithole Zama, alias Pungushe. 'He made an excellent impression on this Court. His answers were clear and precise. At no time did the defence shake his transparent honesty and powers of total recall.'

On Christmas Eve in the whitewashed room at Pretoria Central Gaol, with his arms and legs pinioned by leather straps, and his head covered by a black cotton bag, Hobday dropped to eternity through the crashing wooden trap.

P eter Botes, cleared of any implication in the crimes of murder and attempted murder by the testimony of Mark Anders, was not placed on trial.

'His crimes were weakness and greed,' Mark tried to explain to Storm. 'If there were punishment for those, then there would be a gallows waiting for each of us. Besides, there has been enough vengeance and death already.'

Peter Botes left Ladyburg immediately after the hearings, and Mark never learned where he went or what became of him.

N ow, when you cross the Bubezi River by the low concrete bridge, where Dirk Courtney's dam wall and hydro-electric station might have stood, you will come to the barrier on the far bank.

A Zulu ranger in smart suntans and a slouch hat will salute you, and give you a smile that sparkles like the Parks Board badge on his hat brim.

When you leave your vehicle and go into the office building of hewn stone and neat thatch to sign the register, look then to the left wall beyond the reception desk. In a glass case there is a permanent display of photographs and memorabilia from the park's early days. The centre-piece of this collection is a large photograph of a sprightly old gentleman, lean and tanned and tough as a strip of rawhide, with a shock of pure white hair and a marvellous pair of spiky moustaches.

His cotton jacket is a little rumpled and fits him as though it was made for his elder brother, the knot of his tie has slipped down an inch and one tab of his shirt collar is slightly awry. Although his smile is impish, his jaw is firm and determined. However, it is the eyes that arrest attention. They are serene and direct, the eyes of a visionary or a prophet.

Under the photograph is the legend: 'Colonel Mark Anders, First Warden of Chaka's Gate National Park.' And below that again in smaller letters, 'Because of this man's energy and farsightedness, Chaka's Gate National Park has come down to posterity. Colonel Anders served on the Board of the National Parks Trust from its inception in 1926. In 1935, he was elected Chairman. He fought with distinction in two world wars, was severely wounded in one, and commanded his battalion in North Africa and Italy in the second. He is the author of many books on wildlife, including *Sanctuary* and *Vanishing Africa*. He has travelled the world to lecture and to gain support for the work of conservation. He has been honoured by monarchs and governments and universities.'

In the photograph, a tall slim woman stands beside the Colonel. Her hair is streaked with grey and drawn back severely from her face, and although there are crow's-feet at the corners of her eyes and deep lines around her mouth, yet they are the lines of laughter and the planes and angles of her face still show traces of what must once have been great beauty. She leans half protectively, half possessively against the Colonel's right arm and below the photograph the legend continues:

'His wife and life-long companion in his work was the internationally celebrated artist, who painted her memorable African landscapes and wildlife studies under her maiden name of Storm Courtney.

'In 1973, Colonel Anders retired from his position of Chairman of the Parks Board, and went with his lady to live in a cottage overlooking the sea at Umhlanga Rocks on the Natal Coast.'

When you have read the legend you may go back to your motorcar. The Zulu ranger will salute you again and raise the barrier. Then you too can go, for a short time, into Eden.

# THE DIAMOND HUNTERS

This book is for my wife and the jewel
of my life, Mokhiniso, with all my love
and gratitude for the enchanted years
that I have been married to her

His flight had been delayed for three hours at Nairobi, and despite four large whiskies he slept only fitfully until the intercontinental Boeing touched down at Heathrow. Johnny Lance felt as though someone had thrown a handful of grit in each eye, and his mood was ugly as he came through the indignity of Customs and Immigration into the main hall of the international terminus.

The Van Der Byl Diamond Company's London agent was there to meet him.

'Pleasant trip, Johnny?'

'Like the one to Hell,' Johnny grunted.

'Good practice for you.' The agent grinned. The two of them had seen some riotous times together.

Reluctantly Johnny grinned back at him.

'You got me a room and a car?'

'Dorchester – and Jag.' The agent handed over the car keys. 'And I've got two first-class seats reserved on tomorrow's nine o'clock flight back to Cape Town. Tickets at the hotel reception desk.'

'Good boy.' Johnny dropped the keys into the pocket of his cashmere overcoat and they started for the exit. 'Now where is Tracey van der Byl?'

The agent shrugged. 'Since I wrote to you she has dropped out of sight. I don't know where you can start looking.'

'Great, just great!' said Johnny bitterly as they came out into the car park. 'I'll start with Benedict.'

'Does the Old Man know about Tracey?'

Johnny shook his head. 'He's a sick man. I didn't tell him.'

1

'Here's your car.' The agent stopped by the pearl-grey Jaguar. 'Any chance of a drink together?'

'Not this trip, sorry.' Johnny slipped in behind the wheel. 'Next time.'

'I'll hold you to that,' said the agent and walked away.

It was almost dark by the time Johnny crossed the Hammersmith flyover in the moist smoky grey of the evening, and he lost himself twice in the maze of Belgravia before he found the narrow mews behind Belgrave Square and parked the Jaguar.

The exterior of the flat had been lavishly redecorated since his last visit, and Johnny's mouth twisted. He might not be so hot at earning the stuff – but our boy Benedict certainly was a dab hand at spending it.

There were lights burning and Johnny hit the door knocker half a dozen lusty cracks. It echoed hollowly about the mews, and in the silence that followed Johnny heard the whisper of voices from behind the curtains, and a shadow passed quickly across the window.

Johnny waited three minutes in the cold, then he stepped back into the middle of the mews.

'Benedict van der Byl,' he bellowed. 'I'll give you a count of ten to get this door open. Then I'll kick the bloody thing down.'

He drew breath, and bellowed again.

'This is Johnny Lance – and you know I mean it.'

The door opened almost immediately. Johnny pushed his way through it, not glancing at the man who held it, and started for the lounge.

'Dammit, Lance. You can't go in there.' Benedict van der Byl started after him.

'Why not?' Johnny glanced back at him. 'It is a Company flat – and I'm the General Manager.'

Before Benedict could reply, Johnny was through the door.

One of the girls picked up her clothing from the floor

2

and ran naked into the bedroom passage. The other pulled a full-length caftan over her head and glared at Johnny sulkily. Her hair was in wild disorder, fluffed out into a grotesque halo of stiff curls.

'Nice party,' said Johnny. He glanced at the movie projector on the side table, and then at the screen across the room. 'Films and all.'

'Are you the Fuzz?' demanded the girl.

'You've got an infernal cheek, Lance.' Benedict van der Byl was beside him, tying the belt of his silk dressing-gown.

'Is he Fuzz?' the girl demanded again.

'No,' Benedict assured her. 'He works for my father.' With the statement he seemed to gather self-assurance, drawing himself up to his full height and smoothing his long dark hair with one hand. His voice regained its polish and lazy inflection. 'Actually, he is Daddy's messenger boy.'

Johnny turned to him, but he addressed the girl without looking at her.

'Beat it, girlie. Follow your friend.'

She hesitated.

'Beat it!' Johnny's voice crackled like a bush fire, and she went.

The two men stood facing each other. They were the same age, in their early thirties – both tall, both dark-haired – but different in every other way.

Johnny was big in the shoulder and lean across the hips and belly, his skin polished and browned by the desert sun. The line of his heavy jawbone stood out clearly, and his eyes seemed still to seek far horizons. His voice clipped and twanged with the accents of the other land.

'Where is Tracey?' he asked.

Benedict lifted one eyebrow in a pantomine of arrogant surprise. His skin was pale olive, unstained by sunlight for it was months since he had last visited Africa. His lips were very red, as though they had been painted, the classical

3

lines of his features were blurred by flesh. There were soft little pouches under his eyes, and a plumpness beneath the silk dressing-gown that suggested he ate and drank often and exercised infrequently.

'My dear chap, what on earth makes you think I know where my sister is? I haven't seen her for weeks.'

Johnny turned away and crossed to one of the paintings on the far wall. The room was hung with good original South African artists – Alexis Preller, Irma Stern and Tretchikof – an unusual mixture of techniques and styles, but someone had convinced the Old Man they were sound investments.

Johnny turned back to face Benedict van der Byl. He studied him as he had the paintings, comparing him with the clean young athlete he had been a few years before. A clear mental image in his mind pictured Benedict moving with leopard grace across the green field of play under the packed grandstands, turning smoothly beneath the high floating arc of the ball to gather it neatly, head high, and break back infield to open the line for the return kick.

'You're getting fat, Laddy Buck,' he said softly, and Benedict's anger stained his cheeks dull red.

'Get out of here,' he snapped.

'In a minute – tell me about Tracey first.'

'I've told you – I don't know where she is. Whoring it up around Chelsea, I expect.'

Johnny felt his own anger surge fiercely, but his voice remained level.

'Where is she getting the money, Benedict?'

'I don't know – the Old Man—'

Johnny cut him short. 'The Old Man is keeping her on an allowance of ten pounds a week. From what I hear she's throwing more than that around.'

'Christ, Johnny,' Benedict's tone became conciliatory, 'I don't know. It's not my business. Perhaps Kenny Hartford is—'

Again Johnny interrupted impatiently. 'Kenny Hartford is giving her nothing. That was part of the divorce agreement when they split up. Now I want to know who is subsidizing her trip to oblivion. How about it, big brother?'

'Me?' Benedict was indignant. 'You know there is no love wasted between us.'

'Must I spell it out?' Johnny asked. 'All right, then. The Old Man is dying – without losing his horror of all weakness and sin. If Tracey turns into a drug-soaked little tramp – then there's a good chance that our boy Benedict will come back into full favour. It would be a good gamble on your part to lay out a few thousand now, to send Tracey to Hell. Cut her off completely from her father – and all those nice fat millions.'

'Who said anything about drugs?' Benedict blustered.

'I did.' Johnny stepped up to him. 'You and I have a little unfinished business. It would give me intense pleasure to take you to pieces and see what makes you work.'

He held Benedict's eyes for long seconds, then Benedict looked down and fiddled with the cord of his dressing-gown.

'Where is she, Benedict?'

'I don't know, damn you!'

Johnny moved softly across to the movie projector and picked up a reel of film from the table beside it. He peeled off a few feet of celluloid from the reel and held it up to the light.

'Pretty!' he said, but the line of his mouth tightened with disgust.

'Put that down,' snapped Benedict.

'You know what the Old Man thinks about this sort of thing, don't you, Benedict?'

Suddenly Benedict went pale.

'He wouldn't believe you.'

'Yes, he would.' Johnny tossed the reel on the table and turned back to Benedict. 'He believes me because I've never lied to him.'

Benedict hesitated, wiped his lips nervously with the back of his hand.

'I haven't seen her for two weeks. She was renting a place in Chelsea. Stark Street. No. 23. She came to see me.'

'What for?'

'I lent her a couple of pounds,' Benedict muttered sulkily.

'A couple of pounds?' Johnny asked.

'All right, a couple of hundred. After all, she is my sister.'

'Damn decent of you,' Johnny lauded him. 'Write down the address.'

Benedict crossed to the leather-topped writing desk and scribbled on a card. He came back and handed the card to Johnny.

'You like to think you're big and dangerous, Lance.' His voice was pitched low but it shook with fury. 'Well, I'm dangerous too – in a different sort of way. The Old Man can't live for ever, Lance. When he's gone I'm coming after you.'

'You frighten the hell out of me.' Johnny grinned at him, and went down to the car.

The traffic was solid in Sloane Square as Johnny eased the Jaguar slowly down towards Chelsea. There was plenty of time to think; to remember how close they had been – the three of them. He and Tracey and Benedict.

Running together as wild young things with the endless beaches and mountains and sun-washed plains of Namaqualand as their playground. That was before the Old Man made the big strike on the Slang River, before there was money for shoes. When Tracey wore dresses made from flour sacks sewn together, and they rode to school each day, all three of them bare-back on a single pony like a row of bedraggled little brown sparrows on a fence.

He remembered how the long sun-drenched weeks while the Old Man was away were spent in laughter and secret games. How they climbed the *kopje* behind the mud-walled shack each evening and looked towards the north across

6

the limitless land, flesh-coloured and purple in the sunset, searching for the wisp of dust in the distance that would mean the Old Man was coming home.

Then the almost painful excitement when the dusty, rackety Ford truck with its mudguards tied on with wire was suddenly there in the yard, and the Old Man was climbing down from the cab, a sweat-stained hat on the back of his head and the dust thick in the stubble of his beard, swinging Tracey squealing above his head. Then turning to Benedict, and lastly to Johnny. Always in that order – Tracey, Benedict, Johnny.

Johnny had never wondered why sometimes he was not first. It was always that way. Tracey, Benedict, Johnny. The same way as he had never wondered why his name was Lance and not van der Byl. Then it had come to an end suddenly, the whole brightly sunlit dream of childhood was gone and lost.

'Johnny, I'm not your real father. Your father and mother died when you were very young.' And Johnny had stared at the Old Man in disbelief.

'Do you understand, Johnny?'

'Yes, Pa.'

Tracey's hand groped for his beneath the table top like a little warm animal. He jerked his own hand away from it.

'I think you'd better not call me that any more, Johnny.' He could remember the exact tone of the Old Man's voice, neutral, matter of fact, as it splintered the fragile crystal of his childhood to fragments. The loneliness had begun.

Johnny accelerated the Jaguar forward and swung into the King's Road. He was surprised that the memory hurt so intensely – time should have mellowed and softened it.

His life from then on had become a ceaseless contest to win the Old Man's approval – he dare not hope for his love.

Soon there were other changes, for a week later the old Ford had come roaring unexpectedly out of the desert in the night, and the barking of the dogs and the Old Man's

7

shouted laughter had brought them, sleepy-eyed, tumbling from their bunks.

The Old Man had lit the Petromax lamp and sat them on the kitchen chairs about the scrubbed deal table. Then with the air of a conjuror he had lain something that looked like a big lump of broken glass on the table.

The three sleepy children had stared at it solemnly, not understanding. The harsh glare of the Petromax was captured within the crystal, captured, repeated, magnified and thrown back at them in fire and blue lightning.

'Twelve carats – ' gloated the Old Man, 'blue-white and perfect, and there is a cartload more where that came from.'

After that there were new clothes and motor cars, the move to Cape Town, the new school and the big house on Wynberg Hill – but always the contest. The contest that did not earn the Old Man's approval as it was designed to do, but earned instead Benedict van der Byl's jealousy and hatred. Without his drive and purpose, Benedict could not hope to match Johnny's achievements in the classroom and on the sports field. He fell far behind the pace that Johnny set – and hated him for it.

The Old Man did not notice for he was seldom with them now. They lived alone in the big house with the thin silent woman who was their housekeeper, and the Old Man came infrequently and for short periods. Always he seemed tired and distracted. Sometimes he brought presents for them from London and Amsterdam and Kimberley, but the presents meant very little to them. They would have liked it better had it stayed the way it was in the desert.

In the void left by the Old Man the hostility and rivalry between Johnny and Benedict flourished to such proportions that Tracey was forced to choose between them. She chose Johnny.

In their loneliness they clung to each other.

The grave little girl and the big gangling boy built

8

together a castle against the loneliness. It was a bright secure place where the sadness could not reach them – and Benedict was excluded from it.

Johnny swung the Jaguar out of the line of traffic into Old Church Street, down towards the river in Chelsea. He drove automatically and the memories came crowding back.

He tried to recapture and hold the castle of warmth and love that he and Tracey had built so long ago, but instantly his mind leapt to the night on which it had collapsed.

One night in the old house on Wynberg Hill Johnny had come awake to the sound of distant weeping. He had gone barefooted in his pyjamas, following that heart-rending whisper of grief. He was afraid, fourteen years old and afraid in the dark house.

Tracey was weeping into her pillow and he had stooped over her.

'Tracey. What is it? Why are you crying?'

She had jumped up, kneeling on the bed, and flung both arms about his neck.

'Oh, Johnny. I had a dream, a terrible dream. Hold me, please. Don't go away, don't leave me.' Her whisper was still thick and muffled with tears. He had gone into her bed and held her until at last she slept.

Every night after that he had gone to her room. It was innocent and completely childlike, the twelve-year-old girl and the boy who was her brother, in fact if not in name. They held each other in the bed, and whispered and laughed secretly until sleep carried them both away.

Then suddenly the castle was blasted by the bright electric glare of the overhead light. The Old Man was standing in the door of the bedroom, and Benedict was behind him in his pyjamas dancing with excitement and chanting triumphantly.

'I told you, Pa! I told you so!'

The Old Man was shaking with rage, the bush of grey

hair standing erect like the mane of a wounded lion. He had dragged Johnny from the bed, and struck away Tracey's clinging hands.

'You little whore,' he bellowed, holding the terrified boy easily with one hand and leaning forward to strike his daughter in the face with his open hand. Leaving her sobbing, face down on the bed, he dragged Johnny down the passages to the study on the ground floor. He threw him into the room with a violence that sent him staggering against the desk.

The Old Man had gone to the rack and taken out a light Malacca cane. He came to Johnny and, taking a handful of his hair, threw him face down over the desk.

The Old Man had beaten him before, but never like this. Mad with rage the Old Man's blows had been unaimed, some fell across Johnny's back.

Yet in the agony it was deadly important to the boy that he should not cry out. He bit through his lip so the taste of blood was salt and copper in his mouth. He must not hear me cry! And he choked back the moans feeling his pyjama trousers hanging heavy and sodden with blood.

His silence served only as a goad to the Old Man's fury. Flinging the cane aside, he pulled the boy upright and attacked him with his hands. Slamming Johnny's head from side to side with full, open-handed blows that burst in Johnny's skull with blinding flashes of light.

Still Johnny kept on his feet, clinging to the edge of the desk. His lips broken and swollen and his face bloated and darkening with bruises, until at last the Old Man was driven far beyond the borders of sanity. He bunched his fist and drove it into Johnny's face – and with a wonderful sense of relief Johnny felt the pain go out in a warm flood of darkness.

Johnny heard voices first. A strange voice:

'– As though he's been savaged by a wild beast. I'll have to inform the police.'

Then a voice he recognized. It took him a little time to place it. He tried to open his eyes but they seemed locked tight, his face felt enormous, swollen and hot. He forced the fat lids of his eyes back and recognized Michael Shapiro, the Old Man's secretary. He was talking quietly to the other man.

There was the smell of antiseptic and the doctor's bag lay open on the table beside the bed.

'Listen, Doctor. I know it looks bad – but hadn't you better talk to the boy before you stir up the police?'

They both looked towards the bed.

'He's conscious.' The doctor came to him quickly. 'What happened to you, Johnny? Tell us what happened. Whoever did this to you will be punished – I promise you.'

The words were wrong. Nobody must ever punish the Old Man.

Johnny tried to speak but his lips were stiff and swollen. He tried again.

'I fell,' he said. 'I fell. Nobody! Nobody! I fell down.'

When the doctor had gone Mike Shapiro came and stood over him. His Jewish eyes were dark with pity, and something else – anger perhaps, or admiration. 'I'm taking you to my house, Johnny. You will be all right now.'

He stayed two weeks under the care of Michael Shapiro's wife, Helen. The scabs came away, the bruises faded to a dirty yellow, but his nose stayed crooked with a lump at the bridge. He studied his new nose in the mirror, and liked it. It made him look like a boxer, he thought, or a pirate, but it was many months before the tenderness passed and he could finger it freely.

'Listen, Johnny, you are going to a new school. A fine boarding-school in Grahamstown.' Michael Shapiro tried to sound enthusiastic. Grahamstown was five hundred miles

away. 'In the holidays you'll be going to work in Namaqualand – learning all about diamonds and how to mine them.
You'll enjoy that, won't you?'

Johnny had thought about it for a minute, watching
Michael's face and reading in it his shame.

'I won't be going home again then?' By home he meant
the house on Wynberg Hill. Michael shook his head.

'When will I see—' Johnny hesitated as he tried to find
the right words, ' – when will I see them again?'

'I don't know, Johnny,' Michael answered him honestly.

As Michael had promised it was a fine school.

On his first Sunday after the church service, he had
followed the other boys back to their classroom for the
session of compulsory letter-writing. The others had
immediately begun dashing off hasty scribbles to their
parents. Johnny sat miserably until the master in charge
stopped at his desk.

'Aren't you going to write home, Lance?' he asked kindly.
'I'm sure they'll all want to hear how you are.'

Johnny picked up his pen obediently, and puzzled over
the blank writing-pad.

He wrote at last:

Dear Sir,
    I hope you will be pleased to hear that I am now at
school. The food is good, but the beds are very hard.
    We go to church every day and play rugby football.
                        Yours faithfully,
                            Johnny.

From then until he left school and went up to University
three years later, he wrote every week to the Old Man.
Every letter began with the same salutation and went on, 'I
hope you will be pleased to hear—' There was never a reply
to any of these letters.

Once each term he received a typewritten letter from

Michael Shapiro setting out the arrangements that had been made for the school holidays. Usually these involved a train journey hundreds of miles across the Karroo to some remote village in the vast dry wasteland, where a light aircraft belonging to Van Der Byl Diamonds was waiting to fly him still deeper into the desert to one of the Company's concession areas. Again, as Michael Shapiro had promised, he learned about diamonds and how to mine them.

When the time to move on to University arrived, it was completely natural that he chose to take a degree in Geology.

During all that time he was an outcast from the van der Byl family. He had seen none of them – not the Old Man, nor Tracey, nor even Benedict.

Then, in one long eventful afternoon, he saw all three of them. It was his final year at University. His degree was a certainty. He had headed the lists at every examination from his first year onwards. He had been elected the senior student of Stellenbosch University, but now there was a further honour almost within his grasp.

In ten days' time the National Selectors would announce the rugby team to meet the New Zealand All Black touring team – and Johnny's place at flank forward was as certain as his degree in Geology.

The sporting press had nicknamed Johnny 'Jag Hond' after that ferocious predator of the African wilds, the Cape hunting dog; an animal of incredible stamina and determination that savages its prey on the run. The nickname had stuck fast, and Johnny was a favourite of the crowds.

In the line-up of the team from Cape Town University was another crowd-pleaser whose place in the National Side to meet the All Blacks seemed equally assured. From his position at full back Benedict van der Byl dominated the field of play with a grace and artistry that were almost god-like. He had grown tall and wide-shouldered, with long powerful legs and dark brooding good looks.

Johnny led the visiting team out on to the smooth green velvet field, and while he jogged and flexed his back and shoulders he looked up at the packed stands seeking assurance that the high priests of rugby football were all there. He saw Doctor Danie Craven sitting with the other selectors in their privileged position below the Press enclosure. While in front of the Doctor, leaning back to exchange a few words with him, sat the Prime Minister.

This meeting between the two universities was one of the high spots of the rugby season, and the *aficionados* travelled thousands of miles to watch it.

The Prime Minister smiled and nodded, then leaned forward to touch the shoulder of the big white-headed figure that sat in the row below him.

Johnny felt an electric tingle run up his spine as the white head lifted and looked directly at him. It was the first time he had seen the Old Man in the seven years since that terrible night.

Johnny lifted an arm in salute, and the Old Man stared at him for long seconds before he turned away to speak with the Prime Minister.

Now the drum majorettes came out in ranks on to the field. White-booted, dressed in Cape Town University colours with short swinging skirts and tall hats, they high-stepped and paraded, lovely young girls flushed with excitement and exertion.

The roar of the crowd drummed with the blood in Johnny's ears, for Tracey van der Byl was leading the first rank. He knew her instantly, despite the passage of years in which she had grown to young womanhood. Her legs and arms were sun-bronzed and her dark hair hung glossily to her shoulders. She cavorted and kicked and stamped shouting the traditional cheers, jiggling her firm young bottom with innocent abandon while the crowds screamed and writhed, beginning already to work themselves into an hysterical frenzy. Johnny watched Tracey. He stood completely still in the thunderous uproar. She was the most beautiful woman he had ever seen.

Then the show was over, the drum majorettes retreating back through the stadium entrance, and the home team trotted on to the field.

The presence of the Old Man and Tracey added intensity to the glare of hatred that Johnny turned on the tall white-clad figure that fell back to take control of the Cape Town back field.

Benedict van der Byl reached his position and turned. From inside his calf-length sock he took a comb and ran it through his dark hair. The crowd bellowed and whistled, loving this little theatrical gesture. Benedict returned the comb to his sock and posed with one hand on his hip, his chin lifted arrogantly as he surveyed the opposition.

Suddenly he intercepted Johnny's glare, and the pose altered as he dropped his eyes and shuffled his feet a little.

The whistle fluted, and play began. It was everything the crowds had hoped for, a match that would long be remembered and gloated over. Massive Panzer offensives by the forwards, long probing raids by the backs with the oval ball flickering from hand to hand, until a bone-jarring tackle smashed the carrier to the turf. Hard and fast and clean play swung from side to side, a hundred times the crowd came up on its feet as one, eyes and mouths wide in screaming unbearable tension, to sink back with a groan as the ball was held by a desperate defence within inches of the try line.

No score and three minutes of play left, Cape Town attacking from a set scrummage, driving through a gap in the defence and then putting the ball in the air with a long raking pass, taken cleanly by the Cape Town wing without a break in his stride. His feet twinkled across the green turf, and again the crowd came up with a gasp.

Johnny hit him low, just above the knee, with his shoulder. The two of them rolled together out of the field of play lifting a puff of white lime from the line and the crowd groaned and sank back.

While they waited to receive the throw, Johnny whispered hoarse orders. His gold and maroon jersey was soaked with sweat, and blood from a grazed hip stained his white shorts.

'Get it back fast. Don't run with it. Give it to Dawie. Kick high and deep, Dawie.'

Johnny leapt high to the flight of the thrown ball, with a bunched fist he punched it back accurately into Dawie's hands, at the same moment twisting his body to block the attackers.

Dawie fell back two paces and kicked. The power of the kick swung his right foot above his head, and the impetus flung him forward to put his forwards 'on side'.

The ball climbed slowly, flying like a dart with no wobble or roll in the air, reaching the zenith of its trajectory high over mid-field, then floating back to earth.

Twenty thousand heads followed its flight, a hush had fallen over the field – and in the unnatural silence Benedict van der Byl was drifting back deep into his own territory, anticipating the drop of the ball with deceptively unhurried strides, yet timing it with the precision of the gifted athlete.

The ball slotted neatly into his arms, and he began moving lazily infield to open his angle for the return kick. Still a tense throbbing mesmeric hush hung over the field, Benedict van der Byl was at the focus of attention.

'Jag Hond!' A single voice in the crowd alerted them, and twenty thousand heads swung downfield.

'Jag Hond!' A roar now. Johnny was well clear of the pack, arms pumping and legs churning as he bore down on Benedict. It was a futile effort, he could not hope to intercept a player of Benedict's calibre from such long range, yet Johnny was burning the last of his physical reserves in that charge. His face was a sweat-shining mask

16

of determination, and clods of torn grass flew from under his savagely driving boots.

Then something happened which was unaccountable, almost past belief. Benedict van der Byl glanced round and saw Johnny. He broke his stride, two clumsy shuffling paces, and tried to pivot away deeper into his own ground. All the assurance had gone from his body, all the skill and grace. He tripped and stumbled, almost fell and the ball popped out of his hands, bouncing awkwardly.

Benedict scrambled after it, groping blindly, looking back over his shoulder. Now on his face was an expression of naked terror. Johnny was very close. Grunting at each stride like a gut-shot lion, massive shoulders already bunching for the strike, his lips drawn back into a murderous parody of a grin.

Benedict van der Byl dropped to his knees and covered his head with both arms, cringing down on to the green turf.

Johnny swept past him without a check, stooping easily in his run to gather the bouncing ball.

When Benedict uncovered his head and, still kneeling, looked up, Johnny stood ten yards away between the goal posts watching him. Then, deliberately, Johnny placed the ball between his feet to complete the formality of the touch-down.

Now, as if by agreement, both Johnny and Benedict looked towards the main grandstand. They saw the Old Man rise from his seat and make his way slowly through the ecstatic crowds towards the exit.

The day after the match, Johnny went back into the desert.

17

He was down in the bottom of a fifteen-foot prospect trench that had been dug across the grain of the country rock. It was oppressively hot in the confines of the trench and Johnny was stripped to a skimpy pair of khaki shorts, his sun-browned muscles oily with sweat, but he worked steadily at his sampling. He was establishing the contours and profile of an ancient marine terrace that the ages had buried beneath the sand. It was here on the bedrock that he expected to find the thin layer of diamond-bearing gravel.

He heard the Jeep pull up at ground level above him, and the crunch of footsteps. Johnny straightened up and held his aching back muscles.

The Old Man stood at the edge of the trench and looked down at him. He held a folded newspaper in his hand. This was the first time Johnny had seen him at close range in all the years, and he was shocked at the change. The mass of bushy hair was so white, and his features were folded and creased like those of a mastiff, leaving the big hooked nose standing like a hillock from his face. But there was no wasting or deterioration in his body, and his eyes were still that chilling enigmatic blue.

He dropped the newspaper into the trench and Johnny caught it, still staring up at the Old Man.

'Read it!' said the Old Man. The paper was folded to the sports page, and the headline was thick and bold.

JAG HOND IN. VAN DER BYL OUT.

The shock was as delicious as the plunge into a mountain stream. He was in – he would carry the gold and green, and wear the leaping Springbok on his blazer pocket.

He looked up, proud and happy, standing bare-headed in the sun waiting for the Old Man to speak.

'Make up your mind,' said the Old Man softly. 'Do you want to play ball – or work for Van Der Byl Diamonds? You can't do both.' And he walked back to the Jeep and drove away.

Johnny cabled his withdrawal from the team to the Doctor personally. The storm of outraged protest and abuse in the national press, and the hundreds of viperous letters Johnny received accusing him of cowardice and treachery and worse made him thankful for the sanctuary of the desert.

Neither Johnny nor Benedict had ever played the game again. Thinking about it, even at this remove of time, Johnny felt the sting of disappointment. He had wanted that green and gold badge of honour so very deeply. Brusquely he pulled the Jaguar off the road and scanned the street map of London and found Stark Street tucked away off the King's Road. He drove on remembering how it had been after the Old Man had taken it from him. The agony of mind had been scarcely endurable.

His companions in the desert were Ovambo tribesmen from the north, and a few of those taciturn white men that the desert produces, as hardy and uncompromising as her vegetation or her mountain ranges.

The deserts of the Namib and the Kalahari are amongst the loneliest places on earth, and the desert nights are long. Not even the day's unremitting physical labour could tire Johnny sufficiently to drug his dreams of a lovely girl in a short white skirt and high boots – or an old white-headed man with a face like a granite cliff.

Out of those long days and longer nights came solid achievements to stand like milestones marking the road of his career. He brought in a new diamond field, small but rich, in country which no one else had believed would yield diamonds. He pegged a uranium lode which Van Der Byl

Diamonds sold for two and a half millions, and there were other fruits from his efforts as valuable if not as spectacular.

At twenty-five, Johnny Lance's name was whispered in the closed and forbidding halls of the diamond industry as one of the bright young comers.

There were approaches – a junior partnership in a firm of consulting geologists, field manager for one of the struggling little companies working marginal ground in the Murderers' Karroo. Johnny turned them down. They were good offers, but he stayed on with the Old Man.

Then the big Company noticed him. A century ago the first payable pipe of 'blue ground' in Southern Africa was discovered on a hard scrabble farm owned by a Boer named De Beer. Old De Beer sold his farm for £6,000, never dreaming that a treasure worth £300,000,000 lay beneath the bleak dry earth. The strike was named De Beers New Rush, and a horde of miners, small businessmen, drifters, chancers, rogues and scoundrels moved in to purchase and work minute claims, each the size of a large room.

From this pretty company of fortune's soldiers two men rose high above the others, until between them they owned most of the claims in De Beers New Rush. When these two, Cecil John Rhodes and Barney Barnato, at last combined their resources, a formidable financial enterprise was born. From such humble beginnings the Company has grown to awesome respectability and dignity. Its wealth is fabled, its influence immeasurable, its income is astronomical. It controls the diamond supply to the world. It controls also mineral concessions over areas of Central and Southern Africa which total hundreds of thousands of square miles, and its reserves of unmined precious and base minerals cannot be calculated. Small diamond companies are allowed to co-exist with the giant until they reach a certain size – then suddenly they become part of it, gobbled up as a tiger shark might swallow any of its pilot fish who become too large and daring. The big Company can afford to buy the best prospects, equipment – and men. It reached out one of its myriad tentacles to draw in Johnny Lance. The price they set on him was twice his present salary, and three times his future prospects.

Johnny turned it down flat. Perhaps the Old Man did not notice, perhaps it was mere coincidence that a week later Johnny was promoted Field Manager of Beach Operation. The nickname that went with the job was 'King Canute'.

Van Der Byl Diamonds had thirty-seven miles of beach concession. The tiny ribbon of shoreline, one hundred and twenty feet above high-water mark, and one hundred and twenty feet below low-water mark. Inland the concession belonged to the big Company. It had purchased the land, a dozen vast ranches, simply to obtain the mineral rights. The sea concessions, territorial up to waters twelve miles off shore, belonged to them also. Granted to them by Government charter twenty years before. But Van Der Byl Diamonds had the Admiralty strip – and it was 'King Canute's' job to work it.

The sea-mist came smoking in like ground pearl dust off the cold waters of the Benguela current. From out of the mist bank the high unhurried swells marched in towards the bright yellow sands and the tall wave-cut cliffs of Namaqualand.

The swells peaked up sharply as they felt the land. Their crests trembled and turned luminous green, began to dissolve in plumes of wind-blown spray, arched over and slid down upon themselves in the roar and rumble of white water.

Johnny stood on the driver's seat of the open Land-Rover. He wore a sheepskin jacket against the chill of the dawn mist, but his head was bare and his dark hair fluttered nervously against his forehead in the wind.

His heavy jaw was thrust forward, and his hands in the pockets of the sheepskin jacket were balled into fists. He scowled aggressively as he measured the height and push of the surf. With his crooked nose he looked like a boxer waiting for the gong.

Suddenly with an awkward angry movement he jerked his left hand from his pocket and looked down at the dial of his wrist watch. Two hours and three minutes to low tide. He pushed his fist back into his pocket, and swivelled quickly to look at his bulldozers.

There were eleven of them, big bright yellow D.8 Caterpillars, lined up along the high-water mark. The operators sat goggled and tense in their high stern seats. They were all watching him anxiously.

Beyond them, standing well back, were the earthloaders. They were ungainly, pregnant-looking machines with swollen bellies, and heavily lugged tyres that stood taller than a man. When the time came they would rush in at thirty miles an hour, drop a steel blade beneath their bellies and scrape up a fifteen-ton load of sand or gravel, race back inland and drop their load, turn and rush back for another gargantuan bite out of the earth.

Johnny was steeling himself, judging the exact moment in which to hurl a quarter of a million pounds' worth of machinery into the Atlantic Ocean, in the hope of recovering a handful of bright pebbles.

The moment came, and Johnny spent half a minute of precious time in scrutinizing his preparations before committing himself to action.

Then 'GO!' he shouted into his loudhailer and windmilled his right arm in the unmistakable command to advance.

'Go!' he shouted again, but his voice was lost. Even the sound of the wild surf was lost in the bull bellow of the diesels. Lowering their massive steel blades, a chorus line of steel monsters, they crawled forward.

Now the golden sand curled before the scooped blades, like butter from the knife. It built up before the monstrous machines, becoming a pile and then a high wall. Thrusting, pulling back, butting, worrying, the bulldozers swept the wall of sand forward. The arms of the operators pumping the handles of the controls like mad barmen drawing a thousand pints of beer, the diesels roaring and muttering and roaring again.

The wall of sand met the first low push of sea water up the beach and smothered it. In seeming astonishment and uncertainty the sea pulled back, swirling and creaming before the advancing dyke of sand.

The bulldozers were performing a complicated but smoothly practised ballet now. Weaving and crossing, blades lifting and falling, backing and advancing, all under the supervision of the master choreographer, Johnny Lance.

The Land-Rover darted back and forward along the edge of the huge pit that was forming, with Johnny roaring orders and instructions through the electric loudhailer.

Gradually a sickle-shaped dyke of sand was thrown out into the sea, while behind it the bulldozer blades cut down, six, ten, fifteen feet through the loose yellow sand.

Then suddenly they hit the oyster line, that thin layer of fossilized oyster shell that so often covers the diamond gravels of South West Africa.

Johnny saw the change in the character of his pit, saw the shell curling from the blades of the bulldozers.

With half a dozen orders and hand signals he had his 'dozers flatten a ramp at each end of his pit, to give the earthloaders access. Then he ordered them away to hold the dyke against the sea.

He glanced at his watch. 'One hour thirteen minutes,' he muttered. 'We're running tight!'

Quickly he checked his pit. Two hundred yards long, fifteen feet deep, the overburden of sand stripped away, the oyster line showing clean and white in the sun, the bulldozers clear of the pit bottom – fighting back the sea.

'Right,' he grunted. 'Let's see what we've got.'

He turned to face the two earthmovers waiting expectantly above the high-water mark.

'Go in and get it!' he shouted, and gave the windmill arm signal.

Nose to tail the earthloaders roared forward, swinging wide at the head of the pit, then swooping down the ramp and dashing along the bottom. They scooped up a load of shell and gravel without checking their speed and went bellowing up the far ramp, swinging again to race up and deposit their load below the cliff, but above the high-water mark.

Round they went, and round again, chasing their tails, while the bulldozers held back the sea which was now becoming angry – sending its cohorts to skirmish along the dyke, seeking a weak place to attack.

Johnny glanced at his watch again.

'Three minutes to low water,' he spoke aloud, and grinned. 'We're going to make it – I think!'

He lit a cigarette, relaxing a little now. He dropped into the driving seat and swung the Land-Rover up the beach, parking it beyond the mountain of gravel that the earthloaders were building.

He climbed out and took up a handful of the gravel.

'Lovely!' he whispered. 'Oh sweet! Sweet!'

It was right. All the signs were good. In the single handful he identified a small garnet, and a larger lump of agate.

He scooped another handful.

'Jasper,' he gloated. 'And banded ironstone!'

All these stones were the team-mates of the diamond, you found them together.

The shape was right also, the stones polished round and shiny as marbles, not flattened like coins which would mean they had washed in only one direction. Round stones meant a wave action zone – a diamond trap!

'We've hit a jewel box – I'll take Lysol on that!'

From thirty-seven miles of beach Johnny had picked a two-hundred-yard stretch, and hit it right on the nose. A choice not by luck, but by careful study of the configuration of the coastline, aerial photographs of the wave patterns and bottom contours of the sea, an analysis of the beach sands, and finally by that indefinable 'feel' for ground that a good diamond man has.

Johnny Lance was mightily delighted with himself as he climbed back into the Land-Rover. The earthloaders had scraped the gravel down to bedrock. Their job was finished, and they pulled out of the pit and stood with panting exhausts beside the enormous pile of gravel they had recovered.

'Bottom boys!' roared Johnny, and the patient army of Ovambo tribesmen who had been squatting above the beach came swarming down into the pit. Their job was to sweep and clean the pit bottom, for a high proportion of the diamonds would have worked their way down through the gravel into the crevices and irregularities of the bedrock.

The sea changed its mood, furious at the brutal rape of its beaches it came hissing and tearing at the sand dyke. The tide was making now, and the bulldozers had to redouble their efforts to keep it out.

In the pit the Ovambos worked in a frenzy of activity, sparing only an occasional apprehensive glance for the wall of sand that held the Atlantic at bay.

Now Johnny was tensing up again. If he pulled them out early he would be leaving diamonds down there, if he left them in too late he might drown machinery – and men.

He cut it fine, just a fraction too fine. He pulled the bottom boys out with the sea beginning to break over the dyke, and to seep through under it.

Then he began to pull out his bulldozers, ten of them out – one still coming infinitely slowly, waddling across the wide bottom of the empty pit.

The sea broke through, it broke simultaneously in two places and came boiling into the pit in a waist-high wave.

The bulldozer operator saw it, hesitated one second, then his spirit failed him and he jumped down from his machine; abandoning it to the sea he sprinted ahead of the wave, making for the steep nearest side of the pit.

'Bastard!' swore Johnny as he watched the operator scramble to safety. 'He could have made it.' But his anger was against himself also. His decision to withdraw had been too long delayed, that was £20,000 worth of machinery he had sacrificed to the sea.

He slammed the Land-Rover into gear, and put her to the pit. She went off the edge like a ski jump, falling fifteen feet before she hit the bottom, but her fall was cushioned by the slope of sand and she sprang forward bravely to meet the rush of sea water.

It broke over the bonnet, slewing the vehicle viciously, but Johnny fought her head round and kept her going towards the stranded bulldozer.

The engine of the Land-Rover had been sealed and water-proofed against just such an emergency, and now she ploughed forward throwing a sheet of water to each side. But her forward rush faltered as the green water poured over her.

Now suddenly the entire sand dyke collapsed under the white surf and the Atlantic took control. The tall wave of green water that raced across the pit hit the Land-Rover, upending her, throwing Johnny into the jubilant frothing water, while the Land-Rover rolled over on her back, pointing all four wheels to the sky in surrender.

Johnny went under but came up immediately. Half swimming, half wading, battered by the boisterous sea he struggled on towards the yellow island of steel.

The sea struck him down, and he went under again. Found his feet for a moment, then had them cut from under him once more.

Then suddenly he had reached the bulldozer and was dragging himself up over the tracks to the driver's seat. He was coughing and vomiting sea water, as he reached the controls.

The bulldozer sat immovable, held down by her own twenty-six tons of dead weight on to the hard bedrock of the pit. Although the sea burst over her, and swirled through her tracks, it could not move her.

Through eyes blurred and swimming with salt water and his own tears, Johnny briefly checked the gauges on the instrument panels. She had oil pressure and engine revs, and high above his head the exhaust pipe chugged blue smoke.

Johnny coughed again. Vomit and sea water shot up his throat in a scalding jet, but he pushed the throttle wide and threw in both clutch levers.

Ponderously the great machine ground forward, almost contemptuously shouldering the sea aside, her tracks solidly gripping the bedrock.

Johnny looked about him quickly. The sand ramps at each end of the pit were washed away. The sides were sheer now, and behind him the sea was rushing unimpeded into the pit.

A wave broke over his head, and Johnny shook the water from his hair like a spaniel and looked around with mounting desperation for an avenue of escape.

With a shock of surprise he saw the Old Man. He had thought him to be four hundred miles away in Cape Town, but here he was on the edge of the pit. The white hair shone like a beacon.

Instinctively Johnny swung the bulldozer in his direction, crawling through the turbulent waters towards him.

The Old Man was directing two of the other bulldozers, reversing them as close as he dared to the lip of the bank of sand, while from the service truck parked below the cliff a line of Ovambos came staggering down the beach with the heavy tractor tow chain over their shoulders. They shuffled bow-legged under the tremendous weight of the chain, sinking ankle deep into the sand with each step.

The Old Man roared at them, urging them on, but the words were lost in the thunder of diesel engines and the ranting of the wind and the sea. Now he turned back to Johnny.

'Get her in close,' the Old Man yelled through cupped hands. 'I'll bring the end of the chain down to you!'

Johnny waved an acknowledgement, then grabbed at the controls as the force of the next wave pushed even the giant tractor off its line, and Johnny felt the diesel falter for the first time – the water had found its way in through the seals at last.

Then he was under the high bank of yellow sand that towered twenty feet above him and he scrambled forward over the engine bonnet to meet the Old Man.

The Old Man was poised on the lip of the pit with the end of the chain draped in a loop over both shoulders. He was stooped beneath its weight, and when he stepped forward the sand crumpled away beneath him and he came sliding and slipping down the steep incline, buried waist deep, the great chain snaking after him.

Judging the rush of the sea Johnny jumped down to help him. Together, battered by the sea, they dragged the chain to the bulldozer.

'Fix it on to the blade arm,' grunted the Old Man, and they got a double turn of chain around the thick steel arm.

'Shackle!' Johnny snapped at him, and while the Old Man untied the length of rope which secured the steel shackle around his waist, Johnny looked up at the cliff of sand that hung over them.

'Christ!' he said softly, the sea was attacking it – and now it was soft and trembling above them, ready to collapse and smother them.

The Old Man passed him the huge shackle, and Johnny

began with numbed hands to secure the end of the chain. He must pass the thick case-hardened pin through two links and then screw it closed. It was a Herculean task under these conditions, with the surf bursting over his head, the drag of the sea on the chain, and the cliff of sand threatening to fall on them at any moment. From twenty feet above them Johnny's foreman was watching anxiously, ready to pass the word to the two waiting bulldozers to throw their combined weights on the chain.

The thread of the pin caught, half a dozen turns would secure it, he would have finished the job by the time the word was passed to the 'dozer operators.

'Okay,' he nodded and gasped at the Old Man. 'Pull!'

The Old Man lifted his head and bellowed up the bank, 'Pull!'

The foreman acknowledged with a wave.

'Okay.' And his head disappeared behind the bank as he ran back to the bulldozers, and at that moment the surf swung the chain. A movement of a few inches, but enough to catch Johnny's left index finger between two of the links.

The Old Man saw his face, saw him struggling to free himself.

'What is it?'

Then the water sucked back for a moment, and he saw what had happened. He waded forward to help – but from above them came the throaty roar of the diesels and the chain began running away, snaking and twisting up the bank like a python.

The Old Man reached Johnny and caught him about the shoulders to steady him. They braced themselves in horror, staring at the captive hand.

The chain jerked taut, severing the finger cleanly in a bright burst of scarlet, and Johnny reeled back into the Old Man's arms. The great yellow bulk of the bulldozer was dragged relentlessly down on top of them, threatening to crush them both, but using the next break and push of the sea the Old Man dragged Johnny clear – and they were carried sideways along the bank, tumbled helplessly by the strength of the water out of the bulldozer's path.

Johnny clutched his injured hand to his chest, but it hosed a bright stream of blood that discoloured the water about them. His head went under and salt water shot down his throat into his lungs. He felt himself drowning, the strength oozing out of him.

He surfaced again, and through bleary eyes saw the glistening wet bulldozer half-way up the sand bank. He felt the Old Man's arms about his chest and he went under again relaxing as the darkness closed over his eyes and brain.

When the darkness cleared from his eyes, he was lying on the dry sand of the beach and the first thing he saw was the Old Man's face above him, furrowed and pouched, his silver white hair plastered across his forehead.

'Did we get her out?' Johnny asked thickly.

'Ja,' the Old Man answered. 'We got her out.' And he stood up, walked to the Jeep, and drove away, leaving the foreman to tend to Johnny.

Johnny grinned at the memory, and lifting his left hand off the driving-wheel of the Jaguar he licked the shiny stump of his index finger.

'It was worth a finger,' he murmured aloud, and still searching for road signs he drove on slowly.

He smiled again comfortably, shaking his head with amusement as he remembered his hurt and disappointment when the Old Man had walked away and left him lying on the beach. He had not expected the Old Man to fall on his shoulders sobbing his gratitude and begging forgiveness for all the years of misery and loneliness – but he had expected something more than that.

After a two-hundred-mile round Jeep-journey through the desert night to the nearest hospital where they had trimmed and bound the stump, Johnny was back at the workings the next day in time to watch the first run of gravel from the beach.

In his absence, the gravel had been screened to sieve off all the over-size rock and stone, then it had been puddled through a tank of silicon mud to float off all the material with a specific gravity less than 2.5, then finally what was left had been run through a ball mill – a long steel cylinder containing steel balls the size of baseballs. The cylinder revolved continually and the steel balls crushed to powder all substance softer than 4 on Mohs hardness scale.

Now there was a residue, a thousandth part of the gravel they had won from the sea. In this remainder would be the diamonds – if diamonds there were.

When Johnny arrived back at the shed of galvanized iron and wood on the cliff above the beach that housed his separation plant, he was still half groggy from the anaesthetic and lack of sleep.

His hand throbbed with the persistence of a lighthouse, his eyes were reddened and a thick black stubble covered his jaws.

He went to stand beside the grease table that filled half the shed. He was swaying a little on his feet, as he looked around at the preparations. The massive bin at the head of the table was filled with the concentrated diamond gravels, the plates greased down, and his crew was standing ready.

'Let's go!' Johnny nodded at his foreman, who immediately threw in the lever that set the table shaking like an old man with palsy.

The table was a series of steel plates, each slightly inclined and thickly coated with dirty yellow grease. From the bin at the head of the shuddering table a mixture of gravel and water began to dribble, its consistency and rate of flow carefully regulated by the foreman. It spread over the greased table like spilled treacle, dropping from one plate to the next, and finally into the waste bin at the end of the table.

A diamond is unwettable, immerse it in water, scrub it, – but it comes out dry. A coat of grease on a steel plate is also unwettable, so wet gravel and sea shell will slide over it and keep moving across the agitating, sloping table.

But a diamond when it hits grease sticks like a half-sucked toffee to a woollen blanket.

In the excitement and anxiety of the moment Johnny felt his weariness recede, even the pain in his stump was muted by it. His eyes and whole attention were fastened on that glistening yellow sheet of grease.

The little stuff under a carat in weight, or the industrial black diamond and boart would not be visible on the table; the agitation was too rapid – blurring with speed, and the flow of loose material would disguise them.

So complete was his absorption that it was some seconds before he was aware of a presence beside him. He glanced up quickly.

The Old Man was there, standing with the wide stance and tension-charged attitude that was his own special way.

Johnny was acutely conscious of the Old Man's bulk beside him – and he felt the first flicker of alarm. What if this was a barren run? He needed diamonds now – as he had never needed anything in his life. He scanned the blurring plates of yellow grease, seeking the purchase price that could buy back the Old Man's esteem. The speckled gravel flowed imperturbably across the plates, and Johnny felt a flutter of panic.

Then from across the table the foreman let out a whoop, and pointed.

'Thar she blows!'

Johnny's eyes darted to the head of the table. There beneath the outlet from the bin, half buried in the thick grease by its own weight, anchored solidly while the worthless gravel washed past it, was a diamond.

A big fat five-carat thing, that glowed sulky and yellow, like a wild animal resenting its captivity.

Johnny sighed softly and darted a sideways glance at the Old Man. The Old Man was watching the table without expression, and though he must have been conscious of Johnny's scrutiny, he did not look up. Johnny's eyes were dragged irresistibly back to the table.

By some freakish chance, the next diamond fell from the bin directly on to the one already anchored in the grease.

When diamond strikes diamond it bounces like a golf ball off a tarmac road.

The second diamond, a white beauty the size of a peach pip, clicked loudly as it struck the other then spun head high in the air.

Both Johnny and the foreman laughed involuntarily with delight at the beauty of that twinkling drop of solid sunlight.

Johnny reached across the table with his good hand, and snatched it out of the air. He rubbed it between his fingers – revelling in the soapy feel of it, then turned and offered it to the Old Man.

The Old Man looked at the diamond, nodded in acknowledgement. Then he pulled back the cuff of his coat and checked his wrist watch.

'It's late. I must get back to Cape Town.'

'Won't you stay for the rest of the run, sir?' Johnny realized his tone was too eager. 'We could have a drink together afterwards.' He remembered after he had spoken, that the Old Man abhorred alcohol.

'No.' The Old Man shook his head. 'I have to get back by this evening.' Now he looked steadily into Johnny's eyes. 'You see, Tracey is getting married tomorrow afternoon and I must be there.'

Then he smiled, watching Johnny's face, but nobody could ever guess the meaning of a smile on the Old Man's lips – for it never showed in his eyes.

'Didn't you know?' he asked, still smiling. 'I thought you had received an invitation.' And he went out of the shed to where his Jeep stood in the bright sunshine waiting to take him out to the aircraft landing-strip among the sand dunes.

The pain in his injured hand, and the Old Man's words denied Johnny the sleep he so desperately needed, but it was two o'clock in the morning before he threw back his blankets and lit the lamp beside his camp bed.

'He said I had been invited – and, by God, I'll be there.'

He drove through the night, and the next morning. The first two hundred miles were on desert tracks of sand and stone, then he reached the metalled highway in the dawn and turned south across the great plains and over the mountains. It was noon before he saw the squat blue silhouette of Table Mountain on the skyline dwarfing the city that huddled beneath it.

He checked in at the Vineyard Hotel, and hurried to his room to bath and shave and change into a suit.

The grounds of the old house were crowded with expensive automobiles, and the overflow was parked along both sides of the street outside, but he found a space for the dusty Land-Rover. He walked up through the white gates and across the green lawns.

There was a band playing in the house, and a hubbub of voices and laughter drifted out through the windows of the ballroom.

He went in through the side door. The passages were thronged with guests, and he made his way amongst them seeking a familiar face in the groups of loud-voiced gesticulating men and giggling women. At last he found one.

'Michael.' And Michael Shapiro looked round, recognizing him and letting the conflicting emotions of pleasure, surprise and alarm show clearly on his face.

'Johnny. It's good to see you.'

'Is the ceremony over?'

'Yes, and the speeches also – thank God.' He took Johnny's arm and led him aside. 'Let me get you a glass of champagne.' Michael hailed a waiter and put a crystal glass into Johnny's hand.

'Here's to the bride,' Johnny murmured and drank.

'Does the Old Man know you are here?' Michael came out with the question that was burning his mouth, and when Johnny shook his head, Michael's expression became thoughtful.

'What's he like, Michael, Tracey's husband?'

'Kenny Hartford?' Michael considered the question. 'He's all right, I suppose. Nice-looking boy, plenty of money.'

'What's he do for a crust of bread?'

'His daddy left him the whole loaf – but to fill in the time he does fashion photography.' And Johnny pulled down the corners of his mouth.

Michael frowned. 'He's all right, Johnny. The Old Man picked him carefully.'

'The Old Man?' Johnny's jaw thrust out.

'Of course, you know him – he wouldn't leave an important decision like that to anybody else.'

Johnny finished his champagne in silence, and Michael watched his face anxiously.

'Where is she? Have they left yet?'

'No.' Michael shook his head. 'They're still in the ballroom.'

'I think I'll go and wish luck to the bride.'

'Johnny.' Michael caught hold of his elbow. 'Don't do anything stupid – will you?'

Johnny stood at the head of the marble staircase that led down into the ballroom. The floor was crowded with dancing couples and the music was loud and merry. The bridal party sat at a raised table across the floor.

Benedict van der Byl saw Johnny first. His face flushed and he leaned quickly to whisper to the Old Man, then began to rise from his seat. The Old Man placed a restraining hand on Benedict's shoulder, and smiled across the room at Johnny.

Johnny went down the stairs and made his way through the dancers. Tracey had not seen him. She was talking to the silky-faced young man who sat beside her. He had wavy blond hair.

'Hello, Tracey.' She looked up at Johnny and caught her breath. She was more beautiful than he remembered.

'Hello, Johnny.' Her voice was almost a whisper.

'May I dance with you?' She was pale now, and her eyes went to the Old Man, not to her new husband. The gleaming white bush of hair nodded slightly, and Tracey stood up.

They made one circuit of the dance floor before the band stopped playing. Johnny had planned a hundred different things to say to her, but he was dumb until the music ended and the opportunity was passing. Hurriedly now in the few seconds that were left Johnny told her: 'I hope you will be happy, Tracey. But if you ever need help – ever – I will come, I promise you that.'

'Thank you.' Her voice was husky, and for a moment she looked like the little girl who had cried in the night. Then he took her back to her husband.

The promise had been made five years ago, and now he had come to London to honour it.

Number 23 Stark Street was a neat double-storeyed cottage with a narrow front. He parked outside it. It was dark now and lights burned on both floors. He sat in the parked Jaguar, suddenly reluctant to go further. Somehow he knew that Tracey was here, and he knew it would not be pretty. For a moment he recaptured the image of her as a lovely young woman in a wedding dress of white satin, then he climbed out of the Jaguar and went up the steps to the front door. He reached for the bell before he noticed with surprise that the door was ajar. He pushed it open and walked into a small sitting-room furnished with feminine taste.

The room had been hastily ransacked, one of the curtains was spread on the floor and on it were piled books and ornaments. Pictures had been taken down from the walls and stacked ready for removal.

Johnny picked up one of the books, and opened the cover. On the fly leaf was a handwritten name. 'Tracey van der Byl.' He dropped it back on the pile as he heard footsteps on the stairs from the floor above.

A man came down the stairs. He was dressed in soiled green velvet trousers, sheepskin boots, and shabby frock coat of military cut frogged with tarnished gold braid. He was carrying an armful of women's dresses.

He saw Johnny and stopped nervously, his pink lips opened in vacant surprise but his eyes were beady and bright under the thatch of lank blond hair.

'Hello,' Johnny smiled pleasantly. 'Are you moving out?' And he drifted quietly closer to the man on the stairs and stood looking up at him.

Suddenly from the floor above a low wail echoed down the stairs. It was an eerie sound, without passion or pain, as though steam were escaping from a jet, only just recognizable as human. Johnny went rigid at the sound, and the man on the stairs glanced nervously over his shoulder.

'What have you done to her?' Johnny asked softly, without menace.

'No. Nothing! She's on a trip. A bad trip.' The man's denial was frantic. 'It's her first time on acid.'

'So you're cleaning the place out, are you?' Johnny asked mildly.

'She owes me plenty. She can't pay. She promised – and she can't pay.'

'Oh,' said Johnny. 'That's different. I thought you were hitting the place.' He reached into his overcoat and brought out his wallet, riffling the wad of banknotes. 'I'm a friend of hers. How much does she owe you?'

'Fifty nicker.' The man's eyes sparkled when he saw the wallet. 'I gave her credit.'

Johnny counted off ten fivers, and held them out. The

man dropped the bundle of clothing over the banisters and came eagerly down the last few stairs.

'Did you sell her the stuff – the acid?' Johnny asked, and the man stopped a pace from him, his expression stiffening with suspicion.

'Oh, for God's sake.' Johnny grinned. 'We are not children – I know the score.' He offered the banknotes. 'Did you get the stuff for her?'

The man grinned back at him weakly, and nodded as he reached for the money. Johnny's free hand snapped closed on the thin wrist and he swung him off his feet, forcing his wrist up between his shoulder-blades.

Johnny stuffed the money into his pocket, and marched him up the stairs.

'Let's go and have a look, shall we?'

There was a mattress on the iron bedstead covered with a grey army blanket. Tracey sat cross-legged on the blanket. She wore only a thin cotton slip and her hair hung lank and lustreless to her waist. Her arms crossed over her chest were thin and white as sticks of chalk. Her face also was pale, the skin translucent in the light of the electric bulb. She was rocking gently back and forth and wailing softly, her breath steaming in the icy cold room.

It was her eyes that shocked Johnny the most. They seemed to have expanded to an enormous size, and beneath each was a dark bruised-looking smear. The pupils of the eyes were distended and glittery with the same adamant sheen as uncut diamonds.

The big glittery green eyes fastened on Johnny and the man in the doorway, and the wail rose abruptly to a shriek. The shriek died away, and she bowed forward and buried her face in her hands, covering her eyes.

'Tracey,' said Johnny softly. 'Oh God, Tracey!'

'She'll be all right,' the man whimpered and twisted in his grip. 'It's the first time – she'll be all right.'

'Come.' Johnny dragged him out of the room, and pushed

the door closed with his foot. He held him against the wall, and his face was set and pale, his eyes merciless – but he spoke quietly, patiently as though he was explaining to a child.

'I'm going to hurt you now. I'm going to hurt you very badly. Just as badly as I can without killing you. Not because I enjoy it, but because that girl is a very special person to me. In the future when you think about giving poison to another girl – I want you to remember what I did to you tonight.'

Johnny held him with his left hand against the wall and he used his right hand, punching up under the ribs at an angle to tear the stomach muscles. With three or four blows he was too high, and he felt ribs crack and snap under his fist.

When he stepped back the man sagged slowly face forward, and Johnny caught him cleanly in the mouth snapping his teeth off at the gums, splitting his lips open like the petals of a rose. The man had made a lot of noise. Johnny looked into Tracey's room to make sure she had not been disturbed, but she was still bowed forward, rocking rhythmically on her haunches.

He found the bathroom and dampened his handkerchief to wipe the blood off his hands and the front of his overcoat. He came out into the passage again and stooped over the unconscious body to check the pulse. It was strong and regular, and he felt a lift of relief as he dragged the man's face out of the puddle of his own vomit and blood to prevent him drowning.

He went through to Tracey and, despite her frantic struggles, wrapped her in the greasy army blanket and carried her down to the Jaguar.

She quietened down and lay like a sleeping child in the back seat while he tucked the blanket round her, then he went back into the house and phoned 999, giving the address and hanging up immediately.

He left Tracey in the car outside the Dorchester, while he went in to speak to the reception clerk. Within minutes Tracey was in a wheelchair on her way up to the two-bedroom suite on the second floor. The doctor was there fifteen minutes later.

After the doctor had gone Johnny bathed, and carrying a tumbler of Chivas Regal in one hand he went into Tracey's room and stood by her bed. Whatever the doctor had given her had put her out cleanly. She lay gaunt and pale – yet with a strangely fragile beauty that seemed enhanced by the bruised discoloration of her eye sockets.

He stooped to brush the hair from her cheek, and her breath was light and warm on his hand. He felt such an infinity of tenderness for her then as he had never known for any other person, he was amazed by the strength of it.

He stooped over her and gently brushed her lips with his own. Her lips were dry and flaky white, and their touch was harsh as sandpaper.

Johnny straightened up and went to the armchair across the room. He sank into it wearily, and sipped the whisky, feeling its warmth spread from his belly and untie the knots in his muscles. He watched the pale ruined face on the pillows.

'We are in a hell of a mess, you and I,' he spoke aloud, and felt anger again. For long minutes it was undirected, but slowly it gelled and found an object to focus on.

For the first time in his life he was angry with the Old Man.

'He has brought you to this,' he said to the girl on the bed. 'And me—'

The reaction was swift, his loyalty was a thing grown part of his existence. Always he had trained himself to believe that the Old Man's machinations were just and wise – even if at times the justice and wisdom were hidden from him. Mortal man does not doubt the omnipotence of his gods.

Sickened by his own treachery, he began to examine the Old Man's motives and actions under the bright light of reason.

Why had the Old Man sent Michael Shapiro to fetch him out of the desert?

'He wants you in Cape Town, Johnny. Benedict didn't measure up. The Old Man has given him the London Office, it's a form of exile. He's picked you to take over the Company,' Michael explained. 'Tracey is out of the way. She and her husband are in London also. I guess the Old Man thinks it's safe to have you back in Cape Town now.'

Michael watched Johnny's undisguised joy and went on slowly.

'I'm speaking out of turn, perhaps. Mr van der Byl is a strange man. He's not like other people. I know how you feel about him, I've watched it all, you know – but listen, Johnny, you can go anywhere on your own now. There are a lot of other companies that want you—' But he had seen the expression on Johnny's face, and stopped ' – okay, Johnny. Forget I ever said it. I only spoke because I like you.'

Thinking on it now, there had been substance in Michael's warning. Certainly he was General Manager of Van Der Byl Diamonds, but he was no nearer to the Old Man than he had ever been. He lived under the mountain but the mountain was remote and he had not been able to scale the lowest slopes.

He had found the city as lonely as the desert, and he was ripe for the first attractive woman who set her snares for him.

Ruby Grange was tall and slim with hair the colour they call 'Second Cape' in a diamond, like sunlight through a crystal glass of champagne.

He wondered now at his own naïvety. That he should be so easily misled, and should have rushed so headlong into her web. After the wedding she had revealed herself, exposing the deeply calculating greed, the driving hunger for flattery and material possessions which was her mainspring, and her complete absorption with herself – Johnny had not been able to believe it. For months he fought off the growing certainty until it could be denied no longer, and he looked with chilled dismay on the shallow selfish little creature he had married.

He had withdrawn from her and flung all his energies into the Company.

This, then, was his life and he saw that it was an empty thing, hollowed out by the Old Man's hand.

For the first time his mind skirted the idea that it was a carefully calculated and sadistic revenge for the innocent action of a half-grown boy.

As though it were an escape from thoughts too dreadful to be borne, he fell asleep in the chair and the glass fell from his hand.


Jacobus Isaac van der Byl sat in a leather chair before the X-ray viewer. Fear had blasted the granite of his features, leaving them cracked and sagging, recognizable but subtly alerted below the gleaming white mane.

Fear was in his eyes also, moving below the surface like slimy water creatures in the pale blue pools. With the fear chilling and numbing his limbs he watched the cloudy and swirling images on the screen.

The specialist was talking softly, impersonally, as though he were lecturing one of his classes.

' – enveloping the thymus here, and extending beyond the trachea.'

The point of his gold pencil followed the ghostly outline on the screen. The Old Man swallowed with an effort. It seemed to be swelling in his throat as he listened, and his voice was hoarse and blurred to his own ears.

'You will operate?' he asked, and the specialist paused in his explanation. He glanced at the surgeon across the desk. The exchange was as guilty as that of conspirators.

The Old Man swivelled his chair and faced the surgeon.

'Well?' he demanded harshly.

'No.' The surgeon shook his head apologetically. 'It's too late. If only you had—'

'How long?' The Old Man overrode his explanation.

'Six months, not more.'

'You are certain?'

'Yes.'

The Old Man's chin sank on to his chest and he closed his eyes. There was complete silence in the room, they watched him with professional pity and interest as he reached his own personal acceptance of death.

At last the Old Man opened his eyes and stood up slowly. He tried to smile but his lips would not hold the shape.

'Thank you, gentlemen,' he croaked in this new rough voice. 'Will you excuse me, please. There are many things to arrange now.'

He went down to where the Rolls waited at the entrance. He walked slowly, shuffling his feet and the chauffeur came to him quickly, but the Old Man shrugged away his helping hands and climbed into the back seat of the car.

Michael Shapiro was waiting for him in the study of the big house. He saw the change in him immediately and jumped up from his chair. The Old Man stood in the doorway, his body seemed to have shrunk.

'Six months,' he said. 'They give me six months.' He said it as though he had expected to buy off death, and they had tricked him. He closed his eyes again, and when he opened them there was a glint of cunning in them, even his face had a pinched foxy look to it.

'Where is he? Is he back yet?'

'Yes, the Boeing got in at nine this morning. He's at the

office now.' Michael was shocked, it was the first time he had seen the Old Man without the mask.

'And the girl?' He had not called her 'daughter' since the divorce.

'Johnny has her in a private nursing home.'

'Worthless slut,' said the Old Man softly, and Michael stilled the protest before it reached his lips. 'Get your pad. I want you to take something down.' The Old Man chuckled hoarsely. 'We'll see!' he said, making it sound like a threat. 'We'll see!'


J ohnny's doctor was waiting at Cape Town airport.

'Take her, Robin. Dry her out, and fatten her up. She's up to her gills with drugs and she probably hasn't eaten for a month.'

Tracey showed her first spark of spirit.

'Where do you think—'

'Into a nursing home.' Johnny anticipated her questions. 'For as long as is necessary.'

'I'm not—'

'Oh, yes, you bloody well are.' He took her arm, and Robin grabbed the other. They walked her, still protesting weakly to the car park.

'Thanks, Robin Old Soldier, give her the full workout.'

'I'll send her back to you like new,' Robin promised and drove away. Johnny took a few moments to look at the massive square silhouette of the mountain – his own private home-coming ceremony. Then he fetched the Mercedes from the airport garage, and hesitated between home or the office, decided he was not up to an interrogation from Ruby and chose the office. He kept a clean shirt and shaving tackle in his private bathroom there.

They descended on him like a tribe of man-eating Amazons as he came in through the glass doors into the lusciously furnished and carpeted reception area of Van Der Byl Diamonds head office.

The two pretty little receptionists began yipping joyously in chorus.

'Oh, Mr Lance, I have a whole sheaf of messages—'

'Oh, Mr Lance, your wife—'

Trying not to run he made it to within ten feet of his own door, when the Old Man's secretary popped out of ambush from behind her frosted-glass panel.

'Mr Lance, where on earth have you been? Mr van der Byl has been asking—'

Which alerted Lettie Pienaar, his own secretary.

'Mr Lance, thank goodness you're back.'

Johnny stopped and held up his hands in an attitude of surrender.

'One at a time, ladies. There is enough to go round – don't panic.'

Which broke the reception team into a quivering jelly of giggles, and sent the Old Man's watchdog back behind her panel sniffing disgustedly.

'Which is the most important, Lettie?' he asked as he went to his desk and flipped through his mail, shrugged out of his coat and began stripping tie and shirt as he headed for his bathroom.

They shouted at each other through the open door of the bathroom, as Johnny shaved quickly and showered, Lettie bringing him up to date on every aspect of Company and domestic business.

'Mrs Lance has phoned regularly. She called me a liar when I told her you were at Cartridge Bay.' Lettie was silent a moment, then as Johnny came out of the bathroom she asked, 'By the way, where have you been?'

'Don't you start that.' Johnny stood over the desk, and began flipping through the accumulated papers. 'Get my wife on the phone, please – no, hold it. Tell her I'll be home at seven.'

Lettie saw she had lost his attention, and she stood and went out. Johnny settled down behind his desk.

Van Der Byl Diamonds was a sick company. Despite Johnny's protests the Old Man had been drawing off its reserves and feeding them into his other ventures – the property-developing company, the clothing factory, Van Der Byl fisheries, the big irrigation scheme on the Orange River – and now the cupboard was almost bare.

The beach concessions were reaching the end of a short but glorious life. They were starting to work break-even ground. The Old Man had sold the Huib Hoch concession to the big Company for a quick profit – but the profit had been just as quickly transferred out of Johnny's control.

There was only one really fat goose left in his pen, and it wasn't laying eggs yet.

Eighteen months earlier Johnny had purchased two offshore diamond grounds from a company which had died in attempting to work them. It had been strangled by its own inefficiency.

Taking diamonds from the sea is about eight times more expensive than working them from a dry opencast. One must dredge the gravel from the wild and unpredictable waters of the Skeleton Coast, load it into dumb barges, tow the barges to a safe base, off-load it and then begin the recovery process – or rather, that was the method the defunct company had attempted.

Johnny had dreamed up, and then ordered a vessel which was completely self-contained. It could lie out at sea, suck up the gravel and process it, spilling the waste gravel back into the sea as rapidly as it was sucked aboard. It was fitted with a sophisticated recovery plant that was completely computerized and contained within the ocean-going hull. It needed only a small crew, and it could work in all weather conditions short of a full tornado.

The *Kingfisher* was lying at Portsmouth dockyards rapidly

nearing completion. Her trials were scheduled for early August.

Financing the building of this vessel had been a nightmare for Johnny. The Old Man had been unhelpful, when he wasn't being downright obstructive. He never discussed the venture without that little smile twitching at his lips. He had restricted Van Der Byl Diamonds' monetary involvement in the project so severely that Johnny had been forced to raise two millions outside the company.

He had found the money, and the Old Man had smiled again.

*Kingfisher* should have been lying on the grounds three months ago, sucking up diamonds. The whole financial structure of the scheme was based on her completion on schedule, but *Kingfisher* was running six months behind and now the foundations were shivering.

Sitting at his desk Johnny was working out how to shore up the whole edifice and keep it from collapsing before he could get *Kingfisher* working. The creditors were rumbling and creaking, and Johnny had only his own enthusiasm and reputation left to keep them quiet.

Now he must ask them to defer their interest payments for another three months. He picked up the telephone.

'Get me Mr Larsen at Credit Finance,' he said, steeling himself as he did so, jutting out his jaw and thrusting one bunched fist into his jacket pocket.

At five o'clock he stood up from his desk and went to the cabinet. He poured three fingers of whisky and went back to lower himself wearily into his swivel chair. He felt no elation at having won another reprieve, he was too tired.

The unlisted telephone on his desk rang and he picked it up.

'Lance,' he said.

'How was London?' he recognized the voice instantly, feeling no surprise that the Old Man knew about his

47

journey. The Old Man knew everything. Before he could answer the hoarse croak came again, 'Come up to the house – now!' And the receiver clicked dead.

Johnny looked at the whisky in his hand regretfully and set it down untouched. The Old Man would smell it and smile.

Cloud was blowing over the mountain, and the setting sun turned it to the colour of tangerine and peaches. The Old Man stood at the window and watched the cloud cascade down into the valley, dispersing as it fell.

He turned from the window as Johnny entered the study and instantly Johnny was aware that something momentous had taken place in his absence.

He glanced quickly at Michael Shapiro for a cue, but Michael's grey-streaked head was bowed over the papers he held on his lap.

'Good evening.' Johnny addressed the Old Man.

'Sit there.' The Old Man indicated the Spanish leather chair opposite his desk.

'Read it,' the Old Man ordered Michael, and Michael cleared his throat and patted the papers into a neat square before he began.

The Old Man sat with his eyes on Johnny's face. It was a candid, intimate scrutiny, but Johnny felt no discomfort under it. It was almost as though the Old Man's eyes were caressing him.

Mike Shapiro read intelligently, bringing out the meaning of the involved and convoluted legal phrases. The document was the Old Man's Last Will and Testament, and it took twenty minutes for Mike to complete the reading of it. When he had finished there was silence in the room, and the Old Man broke it at last.

'Do you understand?' he asked. There was a gentleness about him that there had never been before. He seemed to have shrunk, the flesh withering on his bones and leaving them dry and light – like the sun-dried bones of a long dead seabird.

'Yes, I understand.' Johnny nodded.

'Explain it to us simply, not in your lawyer's gobbledygook, just to be certain,' the Old Man insisted, and Mike began to speak.

'Mr van der Byl's private estate, with the exception of his shares in Van Der Byl Diamond Co. Ltd, after taxes and expenses, is placed in Trust for his two children, Tracey—'

The Old Man interrupted impatiently, swatting Mike's words out of the air as though they were flies.

'Not that. The Company. Tell him about the shares in the Company.'

'Mr van der Byl's shares in the Company are to be divided equally between you and the two van der Byl children, Tracey—'

Again the Old Man interrupted.

'He knows their names, dammit.'

It was the first time ever that either of them had heard him swear. Mike grinned ruefully at Johnny, as though asking for his sympathy, but Johnny was intent on the Old Man, studying his face, feeling the deep satisfying thrill swelling within his chest.

A third share in Van Der Byl Diamonds was no great fortune – nobody knew that better than Johnny.

However, by placing Johnny's name on the list with Tracey and Benedict – he had made him his own. This was what he had worked for all these years. The declaration was public, an acknowledgement to the world.

Johnny Lance had a father at last. He wanted to reach out and touch the Old Man. His chest felt swollen, tight with emotion. Behind his eyelids was a slow soft burning. Johnny blinked.

'This is—' His voice was ragged, and he coughed. 'I just don't know how to tell you—'

The Old Man interrupted him impatiently, silencing him with an imperious gesture, and he croaked at Mike.

'Now read him the codicil to the Will. No, don't read it. Explain it to him.'

Michael's expression changed; he looked down at his papers as he spoke, as though reluctant to meet Johnny's eyes. He cleared his throat unnecessarily and shifted in his seat.

'"By the codicil to the Will, dated the same date, and duly signed by Mr van der Byl the bequest of shares in Van Der Byl Diamond Co. Ltd to JOHN RIGBY LANCE, is made conditional on the issue by the said JOHN RIGBY LANCE of a personal guarantee for the debts of the company, including the present loan account and amounts outstanding to tributary companies for royalties and options."'

'Christ,' said Johnny, stiffening in his chair and turning to stare incredulously at the Old Man. The tightness in his chest was gone. 'What are you trying to do to me?'

The Old Man dismissed Mike Shapiro quietly, without even looking at him. 'I'll call you when I want you.' And when he had gone he repeated Johnny's question.

'What am I trying to do to you?' he asked. 'I am trying to make you responsible for debts totalling about two and a half million Rand.'

'No creditor would come to me for half a million, I would be hard pressed to raise ten thousand on my personal account.' Johnny shook his head irritably, the whole thing was nonsensical.

'There is one creditor who could come to you, and subject you to the full process of law. Not to receive payment in cash – but in personal satisfaction. He would smash you – and delight in doing so.'

Johnny's eyes narrowed disbelievingly. 'Benedict?'

The Old Man nodded. 'For once Benedict will hold the top cards. He won't be able to dislodge you from the management of the company, because Tracey will support you as she always has done – but he will be able to watch every move you make from his seat on the Board of Directors. He will be able to hound you, bring you and the Company down without suffering financial loss himself. And when you fall – you know better than to expect mercy from him. You will be devoured by the ogre you have created.'

'Created?' Johnny's voice was shocked. 'What do you mean?'

'You turned him into what he is now. You broke his heart, made him weak and useless—'

'You are crazy.' Johnny came to his feet. 'I have never done anything to Benedict. It was he who—'

But the Old Man's husky croak brushed aside Johnny's protests. 'He tried to run with you – but could not. He gave up, became small and vicious. Oh, I know about the way he is – how you made him.'

'Please, listen to me. I did not—'

But the Old Man went on remorselessly. 'Tracey also, you have ruined her life. You enslaved her, in your sin—'

'That night!' Johnny shouted at him. 'You never let me explain. We never—'

Now the Old Man's voice was a whiplash.

'Silence!' And Johnny could not defy him, the habit was too deeply engrained. The Old Man was trembling, his eyes glittering with passion. 'Both my children! You have plagued me and my family. My son is a weak-willed drifter, trying to hide his hurt in a hunt for pleasure. I have given him the instruments to destroy you, and when he does so perhaps he will become a man.'

The Old Man's voice was strained now, rusty and pain-racked. He swallowed with an effort, his throat convulsing – but there was no softening of the glitter in his eyes.

'My daughter also, tortturned by her lust. A lust which you awakened – she also seeks an escape from her guilty passion. Your destruction will be her release.'

'You're wrong,' Johnny cried out, half in protest, half in entreaty. 'Please, let me explain—'

'This is how it will work. I have made you vulnerable, linking you to a crippled and foundering enterprise. This time we will be rid of you.' He stopped to pant quickly, like a running dog. His breathing was strangled, harsh-sounding. 'Benedict will cut you down, and Tracey will have to watch you go. She cannot help you, her inheritance is carefully tied up, she has no control of the capital. Your only hope is the *Kingfisher*. The *Kingfisher* will turn into a vampire and suck your life blood! You asked why I was systematically transferring the assets of Van Der Byl Diamonds to my other companies? Well, now you know the answer.'

Johnny's lips moved. He was very pale. His voice came out small and whispery.

'I could refuse to sign the guarantee.'

The Old Man smiled bleakly, a drawing back of the lips that was without warmth or humour.

'You will sign it.' His voice was wheezy. 'Your pride and conceit will not let you do otherwise. You see, I know you. I've studied you all these years. But if you refuse to sign the guarantee, I will still have smashed you. Your shares will go to Benedict. You will be out. Out! Gone! We will be finished with you at last.' Then his voice dropped, 'But you will sign. I know it.'

Involuntarily Johnny lifted his hands towards the Old Man, a gesture of supplication. 'In all this time. When I stayed with you, when I—' His voice went husky and dried up. 'Did you never feel anything for me – anything at all?'

The Old Man sat up in his chair. He seemed to regain his bulk and he began to smile. He spoke quietly now, he did not have to shout.

'Get out of my nest, Cuckoo. Get out and fly!' he said.

Slowly Johnny's expression changed, the line of his jaw hardened, thrusting out aggressively. His shoulders went back. He pushed his hands into his pockets, balling his fists into bony hammers.

He nodded once in understanding.

'I see.' He nodded again, and then he started to grin. It was an unconvincing grin, that twisted his mouth out of shape and left his eyes dark and haunted.

'All right, you mean old bastard, I'll show you.'

He turned and walked from the room without looking back.

The Old Man's expression lit in deep satisfaction. He chuckled, then his breath caught. He began to cough, and the pain ripped his throat with a violence that left him clinging weakly to the edge of his desk.

He felt the crab of death move within his flesh, sinking its claws more deeply into his throat and lungs – and he was afraid.

He called out in his pain and fear, but there was nobody in the old house to hear him.

*K*ingfisher was launched in August and ran her trials in the North Sea. Benedict was aboard, by the Old Man's express command. With a vessel of such complexity, and of such revolutionary design, it would have been a miracle had she functioned perfectly. August that year was not the month for miracles. At the end of the trials Johnny had compiled a list of twenty-three modifications that were necessary.

'How long?' he asked the representative of the shipyard.

'A month.' The reply was hesitant.

'You mean two,' said Benedict and laughed out loud. Johnny looked at him thoughtfully, he guessed that the Old Man had spoken to him.

'I'll tell you something, Johnny.' Benedict was still laughing. 'I'm glad this cow isn't my dream of paradise.'

Johnny froze. Those words were the Old Man's, repeated parrot fashion. It was all the confirmation that he needed.

Johnny flew back to Cape Town to find his creditors on the verge of mutiny. They wanted to sell out, and take the loss.

Johnny spent two whole precious days on Larsen's wine farm at Stellenbosch calming his fears. When Fifi Larsen, twenty years younger than her husband, squeezed Johnny's thigh under the lunch table he knew it would be all right – for another two months.

During the next hectic, strength-sapping week of argument and negotiation, Johnny made time to see Tracey.

She had been out of the nursing-home for a month now, staying with friends on a small farm near Somerset West.

When Johnny climbed out of the Mercedes, and Tracey came down from the stoop to greet him, he had his first real lift of pleasure in a long time.

'God,' he said. 'You look great.'

She was dressed in a cotton summer dress with open sandals on her feet. Her friends were away for the day, so they walked through the orchards. He studied her openly, noticing how her cheeks and arms had filled out and the colour had come back into them. Her hair was bright and springing with lights in the sun, but there were still the dark smears under her eyes, and she smiled only once when he picked a sprig of peach blossoms for her. She seemed to be afraid of him, and unsure of herself.

At last he faced her and placed his hands on her shoulders. 'All right. What's eating you?'

It came out in a quick staccato rush of words.

'I want to thank you for coming to find me. I want to explain why I was – like that. In that state. I don't want you to believe – well, bad things about me.'

'Tracey, you don't have to explain to me.'

'I want to. I must.' And she told him, not looking at his face, twisting and tearing the blossoms in her hands.

'You see, I didn't understand, I thought all men were like that. Not wanting, I mean not doing it—' She broke off, and started again. 'He was kind, you understand. And there were lots of parties and friends around all the time, every night. Then he wanted to go to London – for his career. There was not enough scope here. Even then I didn't know. Well, I knew he had lots of men friends and that some of them were different – but . . . Then I went to his studio and found them, and they laughed, Kenny and the boy twined together like snakes. "But you must have known," he said. Something just snapped in my head, I felt spoiled, dirty and horrible and I wanted to die. There was nobody to go to and I didn't want anybody – I just wanted to die.' She stopped and stood waiting for him to speak.

'Do you still want to die?' he asked gently, and she looked up startled and shook her shining hair.

'I don't want you to die either.' And suddenly they were both laughing. After that it was good between them and they talked with all the strangeness gone until it was almost dark.

'I must go,' Johnny said.

'Your wife?' she asked, the laughter fading.

'Yes. My wife.'

It was dark when Johnny went in through the front door of the new split-level ranch type in Bishopscourt which was his house but not his home; the telephone was ringing. He picked up the receiver.

'Johnny?'

'Hello Michael.' He recognized the voice.

'Johnny, get up here to the old house right away.'

Michael Shapiro's voice was strained.

'Is it the Old Man?' Johnny asked anxiously.

'No talk – just come, quickly!'

The curtains were drawn, and a log fire roared on the stone hearth. But the Old Man was cold. The coldness was deep inside him where the flames could not warm it. His hands shook as he picked sheets of paper from the open document box, glanced at them and then dropped them into the fire. They exploded into orange flame, then curled and blackened to ash. At last the box was empty but for a thick wad of multi-coloured envelopes bound together with a ribbon. He loosened the knot, picked out the first envelope, and slipped from it a single sheet of writing-paper.

'Dear Sir,
I hope you will be pleased to hear that I am now at school. The food is good but the beds are very hard—'

He dropped both envelope and letter on the fire and selected another. One at a time he read and then burned them.

'—that I have been selected to play for the first fifteen—'

Sometimes he smiled, once he chuckled.

'—I was top in all subjects except history and religious teaching. I hope to do better next—'

When there was one envelope left he held it a long time in his blue-veined bony hands. Then with an impatient flick of his wrist he threw it on to the fire and reached up to the mantelpiece to pull himself to his feet. As he stood he looked into the gilt-framed mirror above the fireplace.

He stared at his reflection, mildly surprised by the change that the last few weeks had wrought in his appearance. His eyes had lost the sparkle of life, fading to a pale dirty brownish blue – the colour of putrefaction. They bulged from the sockets, in the glassy startled stare which is peculiar to the later stages of terminal cancer.

The watery feeling of limb, and the coldness were not the result of the pain-killing drugs, he knew. Nor was the shuffling feet-dragging gait with which he crossed the thick Bokhara carpet to the stinkwood desk.

He looked down at the oblong leather case with its brass-bound corners, and he coughed, a single flesh-tearing bark. He caught at the desk to steady himself, waiting for the pain to pass before he sprang the catch on the case and laid the lid back.

His hands were quite steady as he took the barrel and butt section of the Purdy Royal twelve-bore shotgun from the case and fitted them together.

He died the way he had lived – alone.

'God, how I hate black.' Ruby Lance stood in the centre of the bedroom floor, staring at the clothing laid out on the double bed. 'It makes me look so washed out.'

She swung her head from side to side, setting the champagne-coloured cascade of her hair swinging. She turned and moved lazily across the room to the tall mirrors. She smiled at herself, a languid slanting of the eyes, and then she spoke over the shoulder of her own image.

'You say that Benedict van der Byl has arrived from England?'

'Yes,' Johnny nodded. He sat slumped in the chair beside his dressing-room door, pressing his fingers into his eyes.

Ruby came up on her toes, pulling in her stomach and pushing forward her small hard breasts.

'Who else will be there?' she asked, cupping her hands under her breasts and squeezing out the nipples between thumb and forefinger, inspecting them critically. Johnny took his hand from his eyes.

'Did you hear me?' Ruby's voice took on a sharp admonishing note. 'I'm not talking to myself, you know.'

She turned away from the mirror to face him. Standing long and slim and golden as a leopard, even her eyes had the yellow intentness of a leopard's stare. She gave the impression that at any moment she would draw her lips back in a snarl.

'It's a funeral,' he said quietly. 'Not a cocktail party.'

'Well, you can't expect me to die of sorrow. I couldn't stand him.' She crossed to the bed and picked up the pair of peach-coloured panties and rubbed the glossy material against her cheek. Then she stepped into them with two long-legged strides.

'At least I can wear something pretty under the weeds.' She snapped the elastic against her sun-gilt belly, and the almost colourless blonde curls were flattened beneath the sheer silk.

Johnny stood up slowly, and went into his dressing-room. Scornfully she called after him. 'Oh for God's sake, Johnny Lance, stop dragging that long face around as though it's the end of the world. Nobody owes that old devil a thing – he collected all his debts long before they fell due.'

T hey were a few minutes early, and they stood together beneath the pine-trees outside the entrance to the chapel.

When the pearl-grey Rolls drew up at the gate and brother and sister stepped down and came up the paved path, Ruby could not contain her interest.

'Is that Benedict van der Byl?'

Johnny nodded.

'He's very good-looking.'

But Johnny was looking at Tracey. The change in her appearance since he had last seen her was startling. She walked like a desert girl again, straight and proud. She came directly to Johnny and stopped in front of him. She removed her dark glasses, and he could see she had been weeping, for her eyes were slightly puffy. She wore no make-up, and with the dark scarf framing her face she looked like a nun. The marks that sorrow had left gave her face maturity.

'I did not think this day would ever come,' she said softly.

'No,' Johnny agreed. 'It was as though he would live for ever.'

Tracey moved a step closer to him, she reached out as if to touch Johnny's arm but her fingers stopped within inches of his sleeve. Johnny understood the gesture, it was a sharing of sorrow, an understanding of mutual loss, and an unstated offer of comfort.

'I don't think we have met.' Ruby used her sugar and arsenic tone. 'It is Miss van der Byl, isn't it?'

Tracey turned her head and her expression went flat and neutral. She replaced the dark glasses, masking her eyes.

'Mrs Hartford,' she said. 'How do you do.'

Mike Shapiro stood beside Johnny in the pew. He spoke without moving his lips, just loud enough for Johnny to catch the words.

'Benedict knows the conditions of the Will. You can expect his first move immediately.'

'Thanks, Mike.'

Johnny kept his eyes on the massive black coffin. The candlelight glinted and sparkled on the elaborate silver handles.

As yet he could find no interest for the conflict that lay

ahead. That would come. Now he was too deeply involved in the passing of an era, his life had reached another point of major departure. He knew it would change, had already changed.

He looked across the aisle suddenly, his gaze drawn intuitively.

Benedict van der Byl was watching him, and at that moment the priest asked for the pallbearers.

They went to stand beside the coffin, Benedict and Johnny on opposite sides of the polished black casket among the massed display of arum lilies. They watched each other warily. It seemed to Johnny that the whole scene was significant. The two of them standing over the Old Man's corpse, facing each other, with Tracey looking on anxiously.

Johnny glanced back into the body of the church, looking for Tracey. Instead he found Ruby. She was watching them both, and Johnny knew suddenly that the board had changed more than he realized. A new piece had been added to the game.

He felt Mike Shapiro nudge him, and he stooped forward and grasped the silver handle. Between them they carried the Old Man out into the sunshine.

The handle had cut into his palm with the weight of the coffin. He went on massaging it, even after the coffin had gone down into the pit. The crude mounds of fresh earth were covered with blankets of bright green artificial grass. The mourners began to drift away, but Johnny went on standing there bare-headed. Until Ruby came to touch his arm.

'Come on.' Her voice pitched low, but stinging. 'You're making a fool of yourself.'

Benedict and Tracey were waiting under the pine-trees by the churchyard gate, shaking hands and talking quietly to the departing mourners.

'You are Ruby, of course.' Benedict took her hand, smiling a little, urbane and charming. 'The flattering reports I've had of you hardly do you justice.' And Ruby glowed, seeming like a butterfly to spread her wings to the sun.

'Johnny.' Benedict turned to him, and Johnny was taken off balance by the friendly warmth of his smile and the grip of his hand. 'Michael Shapiro tells me that you have accepted my father's legacy and the conditions attached to it – you have signed the guarantee. It's wonderful news. I don't know what we would have done without you in Van Der Byl Diamonds. You are the only one that can pull the Company though this difficult period. I want you to know I am behind you all the way, Johnny. I intend becoming much more involved with the Company now, giving you all the help you need.'

'I knew I could depend on you, Benedict.' Johnny accepted the challenge as smoothly as it was thrown down. 'I think everything is going to turn out all right.'

'We have a meeting on Monday, then I must return to London on Thursday – but I hope you can have dinner with me before then – you and your lovely wife, of course.'

'Thank you.' Ruby seeing the refusal on Johnny's lips, interrupted quickly. 'We'd enjoy that.'

'You were going to refuse, weren't you?' She sat with her legs curled up sideways under her, watching him from the passenger seat of the Mercedes with the slanting eyes of a Persian cat.

'You're damn right.' Johnny nodded grimly.

'Why?'

'Benedict van der Byl is poison.'

'You say so.'

'Yes, I say so.'

'Could be you're jealous of him.' Ruby lit one of her gold-tipped cigarettes, putting the smoke through her lips.

'Good God!' Johnny gave one harsh snort of laughter, then they were silent awhile, both staring ahead.

'I think he's pretty dreamy.'

'You can have him.' Johnny's tone was disinterested, but her retort was shrill.

'I could too – if I wanted to. Anyway you and that Tracey creature mooning—'

'Cut it out, Ruby.'

'Oh my, I've said the wrong thing. The precious Mrs Hartford—'

'Cut it out, I said.' Johnny's tone was sharp.

'Little Miss Fancy Pants – God! She almost had them down for you in the bloody graveyard—'

'Shut up, damn you.'

'Don't you swear at me.' And she lashed out at him flat-handed, leaning forward across the seat to strike him in the mouth. His lower lip smeared against his teeth, and the taste of blood seeped into his mouth. He took the handker-chief from his breast pocket and held it to his mouth, steering the Mercedes with one hand.

Ruby sat curled in her corner of the seat, puffing quickly at the cigarette. Neither of them spoke again until he drew up in front of the double garage. Then Ruby slipped out of the Mercedes and ran across the lawns to the front door. She slammed it behind her, with a force that rattled the full-length glass panel.

Johnny parked the Mercedes, closed the garage door and followed her slowly into the house. She had kicked off her shoes on the wall-to-wall carpet in the lounge, and run through on to the patio beside the swimming pool. She stood barefooted staring down into the clear water, hugging herself about the shoulders.

'Ruby.' He came up behind her, forcing the anger out of

his voice with an effort, trying to keep it conciliatory. 'Listen to me—'

She spun around to face him, eyes blazing like a cornered leopard.

'Don't try and gentle talk me, you bastard. What do you think I am – your damned servant. When did I last get to do anything I wanted?'

With Ruby he had long ago realized that placation was the short cut to peace, so he was roused by the implication.

'I've never stopped you from—'

'Good! That's just fine! Then you won't stop me going away.'

'What do you mean?' He was caught between shock and a sneaking sense of hope. 'Are you talking about divorce—'

'Divorce? Are you out of your little mind! I know all about the big bagful of goodies the Old Man left you in his will. Well, little Ruby is getting her pinkies into that bag – starting right now.'

'What do you want exactly?' His voice was cold and flat.

'A new wardrobe, and a quick whip around all those nice places you go to all the time – London, Paris and the rest. That will do for a start.'

He thought a moment, assessing how far he could stretch his overdraft; since his marriage his bank statement had seldom been typed in black. It was worth it, he decided. He could afford no distraction over the next few months. He could move faster and think quicker without having Ruby Lance sitting between his shoulder-blades – much better she should go.

'All right,' he nodded. 'If that's what you want.'

Her eyes narrowed slightly and her mouth pinched in as she studied his face.

'That was too easy,' she said. 'You want to get rid of me? Don't get any ideas, Johnny boy, you put one finger – or anything else – out of line and I'll chop it off.'

'There is a Mrs Hartford to see you, sir.' Lettie Pienaar's voice whispered through on the intercom, then just audibly she added, 'Lucky you!'

Johnny grinned. 'You're fired for insolence – but send her in before you go.'

He stood up as Tracey came in, and went around his desk to meet her. She wore a no-nonsense grey suit, with her hair scraped back from her face. She should have looked like a school marm – but she didn't.

'You've got your times mixed up, Tracey. The Directors' meeting is at two this afternoon.'

'That's a sweet greeting.' She sat down in an egg-shaped swivel chair, crossing long legs which Johnny dragged his eyes off with an effort. 'I've come looking for a job.'

'A job?' He stared at her blankly.

'Yes, a job. You know – work? Employment?'

'What on earth for?'

'Well, now that you've dragged me back from the bright lights with all the finesse of a caveman – you don't expect me to sit around until I drop dead of boredom. Besides, your tame doctor feels that good healthy employment is essential to the completion of my – ah – cure.'

'I see.' He sank back into his own chair. 'Well – what can you do?'

'Mr Lance.' Tracey widened her eyes suggestively, but made her voice prim. ' – Really!'

'All right,' Johnny chuckled. 'What are your qualifications?'

'You may or may not know that I have a law degree from the University of Cape Town.'

'I didn't.'

'Also, it occurred to me that during the next few months you might need someone around whom you can trust.' She was serious now, and Johnny's smile faded also. 'Like the old days.' She added quietly. They were silent for a few seconds.

'It just so happens that we are looking for a personal assistant in our legal department,' Johnny murmured, and then softly, 'Thanks, Tracey.'

T he Board Room of Van Der Byl Diamonds was furnished in soft forest colours, browns and greens. A long luxurious room that reflected the opulence of the days when the Company had been glutted with capital. But now the air was charged with a tension that crackled in the air like static electricity.

The subject of debate was the diamond recovery vessel, *Kingfisher*. The Company's last hope. Her only substantial asset, and Johnny's personal cross.

'This vessel should have been in operation nine months ago. All the estimates were based on that assumption – yet, she is still lying awaiting completion on the slips at Portsmouth.' Benedict was speaking with unconcealed relish. 'In consequence, the interest charges that are accruing put us in a position—'

'The shipyard was out on strike for a total of four months during construction – in addition they were working to rule for—' Johnny's jaw was thrust out, he was ready to fight.

'Ah! I don't think we are particularly interested in the unpredictability of the British workman – the contract should have gone to the Japanese company. Their tender was lower—'

'It would have,' grated Johnny, 'if your father had not insisted—'

'Please, let us not attempt to lay the blame at the door of a dead man.' Benedict's tone was sanctimonious. 'Let us rather try and rectify a grievous situation. When will *Kingfisher* be ready for sea?'

'On the thirteenth of September.'

'It had better be.' Benedict dropped his eyes to his notes.

'Now, this man whom you have engaged to captain the vessel – Sergio Caporetti – let us hear a little about him, please.'

'Fifteen years' experience on offshore oil-drilling vessels in the Red Sea. Three years as Captain of Atlantis Diamonds' offshore dredger operating off the West Coast. He's one of the best, no doubt about it.'

'All right.' Almost reluctantly Benedict accepted this, and consulted his notes. 'Now, we have two sea-concession areas. No. 1 area off Cartridge Bay; No. 2 some twenty miles north of that. Judging by your prospecting results you will elect to work No. 1 area first.'

Johnny nodded, waiting for the next attack to develop. Benedict sat back in his chair.

'Atlantis Diamonds Ltd went broke working our No. 1 area – what makes you think you can succeed where they failed?'

'We've been over this before,' Johnny snapped.

'I wasn't there, remember? Humour me, please. Go over it again.'

Quickly Johnny explained that Atlantis Diamonds' costs had been inflated by their method of operation. Their dredgers were not self-propelled but had to be towed by tugs. The gravel they recovered had been stored, taken into Cartridge Bay in bulk, transhipped ashore to be processed at a land-based plant. *Kingfisher* was a self-propelled and self-contained vessel. She would suck up the gravel, process it through the most sophisticated system of cyclone and X-ray equipment and dump the waste overboard.

'Our costs will be one quarter those of Atlantis Diamonds,' he finished.

'And our loan account is a mere two millions,' Benedict murmured dryly. Then he looked towards Mike Shapiro at the bottom of the table. 'Mr Secretary, please note the following motion – "That this Company proceed to sell the vessel *Kingfisher* presently building at Portsmouth. That it then sells all diamond concessions at the most advantageous terms negotiable, and goes into voluntary liquidation forthwith." Have you got that?'

It was a direct frontal attack. Clearly if the motion succeeded the Company was worthless. They could not recover the price of the *Kingfisher* on a forced sale. There would be a shortfall – and Johnny had signed the guarantee. It was a straight test that Benedict was making. A setting of the lines of battle. Tracey held the balance between Johnny and Benedict. He was forcing her to declare herself.

Benedict watched her while the motion was put to the vote. He leaned forward in the padded leather chair, a slightly amused smile on the full red lips. Beautifully groomed and tailored, with the grace that wealth and position give to a man and which cannot be counterfeited. But the clean athletic lines of his body were fractionally blurred by indulgence, and there was a little too much flesh along the line of his jaw that gave him the petulant look of a spoilt child.

Tracey voted with Johnny Lance, not hesitating a second before lifting her hand. Returning Benedict's smile levelly, and watching her brother's smile alter subtly – become wolfish, for Benedict did not like to lose.

'Very well, my darling sister. Now we know how we stand at least.' He turned easily to Johnny. 'I presume you wish me to continue with my duties in London.'

For years now Benedict had handled the London sales of the Company's stones. It was an unexacting task, which the Old Man had judged within his capabilities.

'Thank you, Benedict,' Johnny nodded. 'Now, I have a proposal to put to the meeting – "That the Directors of this Company, as a gesture of solidarity, agree to waive their rights to Directors' fees until such time as the Company's financial position is on a more sound footing."'

It was a puny counter-attack, but the best he could mount at the moment.

Take-off was in the first light from Youngsfield, and Johnny swung the twin-engined Beechcraft on to a northerly heading, leaving the blue massif of Table Mountain on the left hand.

Tracey wore an anorak over her rose-coloured shirt, and the bottoms of her denim pants were tucked into soft leather boots, her dark hair caught at the nape of her neck with a leather thong.

She sat very still, looking ahead through the aircraft's windshield at the dawn-touched contours of the land ahead. At the bleak lilac and purple mountains and the great lion-coloured plains spreading down to meet the mists that hung over the cold Atlantic.

In her stillness Johnny sensed her excitement and found it infectious.

The sun exploded over the horizon, washing golden and bright over the plains, and tipping the mountains with flame.

'Namaqualand.' Johnny pointed ahead.

She laughed with excitement, like a child at Christmas, turning in the seat to face him.

'Do you remember—' She began, then stopped in confusion.

'Yes,' said Johnny. 'I remember.'

They landed before noon on a rough airstrip bulldozed out of the wilderness. There was a Land-Rover waiting to take them down to the beach to inspect the progress of the workings.

There was little remaining along the thirty-seven-mile Admiralty strip worth working. It was a clean-up and shut-down operation.

When the reigning 'King Canute' handed over the parcel of diamonds that made up the month's recovery, he was apologetic.

'You took out all the plums, Johnny. It's not like the old days.'

Johnny prodded the pathetic pile of small, low-grade stones with his forefinger.

'No, it's not,' he agreed. 'But every little bit helps.'

They climbed back into the Beechcraft and flew on northwards.

Now they passed over areas where the desert had been scratched and torn over wide areas.

The tractors had left centipede tracks in the soft earth.

'Ours?' asked Tracey.

'I wish they were. We'd have no worries then. No, all this belongs to the big Company.'

Johnny checked his watch, automatically comparing the progress of the flight to his estimates. Then he lifted the microphone from the R/T set.

'Alexandra Bay Control. This is Zulu Sugar Peter Tango Baker.'

He knew that they had him on the radar plot, and were watching him – not because they were worried about his safety, but because he was now over the Proclaimed Diamond Area of South West Africa – that vast jealously guarded tract of nothingness.

The radio crackled back at him instantly, demanding his permit number, his flight plan, querying his intentions and his destination.

Having convinced Control of his innocence, and received their permission to continue his flight, he switched off his R/T set, and grimaced at Tracey.

He felt ruffled by this small brush with Olympus. He knew that most of it was professional jealousy. He smarted under the knowledge that he was working ground that the big Company would despise as not sufficiently lucrative to bother about.

Sometimes Johnny dreamed about discovering a fault in a land title, or an error in a survey that had been casually performed seventy years previously before the value of this parched denuded earth had been realized. He imagined himself being able to claim the mineral rights to a few square miles plumb in the middle of the big Company's richest field. He shivered voluptuously at the thought, and Tracey looked at him enquiringly.

He shook his head, then his line of thought took him on to a further destination.

He banked the aircraft, crossing the coastline with its creamy lines of surf running in on the freezing white sands of the beach.

'What?' She was expectant, receptive to the new tone in his voice.

'Thunderbolt and Suicide,' he said, and she made a small grimace of incomprehension.

'There.' He pointed ahead, and through the light smoke of the sea mist she saw them show bare – white and shiny, like a pair of albino whales.

'Islands?' she asked. 'What's so special about them?'

'Their shape,' he answered. 'See how they lie like the mouth of a funnel, with a small opening between them.'

She nodded. The two islands were almost identical twins, two narrow wedges of smooth granite, each about three miles long, lying in a chevron pattern to each other – but not quite meeting at the peak. The mighty Atlantic swells bore up from the south and ran into the mouth of the funnel. Finding themselves trapped in this granite corral, the swells reared up wildly and hurled themselves on the cliffs in massive bomb-bursts of spray before streaming out in white foam through the narrow opening between the two islands.

'I can see how Thunderbolt gets its name.' Tracey eyed the wild booming surf with awe. 'But how about Suicide?'

'The old guano collectors must have called it that, after they tried landing on it.'

'Guano,' Tracey nodded. 'That accounts for the colour.'

Johnny put the Beechcraft into a shallow dive, hurtling in low over the green water. Ahead of them the seabirds rose in alarm, streaming in a long black smear into the sky, the cormorants and gannets whose excreta through the ages had painted the rocks that glaring white.

As they flashed through the gap below the level of the cliffs, Tracey exclaimed, 'There's some sort of tower there – look! In the back of the island.'

'Yes,' Johnny agreed. 'It's an old wooden gantry they used for loading the guano into the longboats.'

He pulled the Beechcraft up in a climbing turn, gaining height to look down on the two islands.

'Do you see where the surf comes through the gap? Now look beneath the surface, can you see the reefs under the water?'

They lay like long dark shadows through the green water, at right angles to the drift of white foam.

'Well, you are looking at the most beautifully designed natural diamond trap in the world.'

'Explain,' Tracey invited.

'Down there,' he pointed south, 'are the big rivers. Some of them dried up a million years ago, but not before they had spat the diamonds they carried into the sea. The tide and the wind has been working them up towards the north for all these ages. Throwing some of them back on the beach but carrying others up this way.'

He levelled the Beechcraft out and resumed their interrupted flight northwards.

'Then suddenly they run up against Thunderbolt and Suicide. They are concentrated and squeezed through the gap, then they are confronted by a series of sharp reefs across their path. They cannot cross them – they just settle down in the gullies and wait for someone to come and suck them out.'

He sighed like a man crossed in love.

'My God, Tracey. The smell of those diamonds reeks in my nostrils. I can almost see the shine of them through a hundred and sixty feet of water.'

He shook himself as though waking from a dream.

'I've been in the game all my life, Tracey. I've got the "feel", the same as a water-diviner has. I tell you with absolute certainty there are millions of carats of diamonds lying in the crotch of Thunderbolt and Suicide.'

'What's the snag?' Tracey asked.

'The concession was granted twenty years ago to the big Company.'

'By whom?'

'The Government of South West Africa.'

'Why aren't they mining it?'

'They will – sometime in the next twenty years. They aren't in any hurry.'

They lapsed into silence, staring ahead, though once Johnny clucked his tongue irritably and shook his head – still thinking about Thunderbolt and Suicide.

To distract him Tracey asked, 'Where do they come from in the first place – the diamonds?'

'Volcanic pipes,' Johnny answered. 'There are more than a hundred known pipes in Southern Africa. Not all yield stones, but then some do. New Rush – Finsch – Dutoitspan – Bulfontein – Premier – Mwadui. Great oval-shaped treasure chests, filled with the legendary "Blue Ground" – the mother lode of the diamond.'

'There are no pipes here – surely?' Tracey turned towards him in his seat.

'No,' Johnny agreed. 'We are after the alluvial stones. Some of those ancient pipes exploded with the force of a hydrogen bomb, spraying diamonds over hundreds of square miles. Others were sub-marine pipes that discharged their treasure into the restless sea. Others of the more passive volcanic pipes were simply eroded away by wind and water and the diamonds were exposed.'

'Then they were washed down to the sea?' she guessed.

Johnny nodded. 'That's right. Over millions of years they

were moved infinitely slowly by landslides, floods, rivers and rainwater. Where all the other pebbles and stones were abraded and worn away to nothingness – the diamonds, four hundred times harder than any other natural substance on earth, were unmarked. So at last they reached the sea and mingled with the others from the sub-marine pipes, to be laid down by wave action on the beaches, or finally to come up against a place like Thunderbolt and Suicide.'

Tracey opened her mouth to ask another question, but Johnny interrupted.

'Here we are. There is Cartridge Bay.' And he pushed the nose of the aircraft down slightly. It was more a lagoon than a bay. Separated from the sea by a narrow sandspit, it spread away into the treeless waste, an enormous extent of quiet shallow water in tranquil contrast to the unchecked surf that burst on the sandspit. There was a deep water entrance through the sandspit, and a channel meandered across the lagoon to where a cluster of lonely whitewashed buildings sprang up on the edge of the desert.

Johnny banked steeply towards the buildings, and below them flocks of black and white pelicans and pink flamingoes rose in panic from the shallows.

Johnny landed and taxied across to the waiting Land-Rover with the white lightning insignia of Van Der Byl Diamonds painted on its side.

Lugging the cool box that contained their lunch, Johnny led Tracey to the vehicle and introduced her to his foreman. Then they climbed in and went bumping down to the buildings on the lagoon. Johnny received from his foreman a report on progress of the work. The buildings had been abandoned by the defunct Atlantis Diamond Company. Johnny was renovating them to serve as a base for the *Kingfisher*; a rest and recreation centre for the crew, a radio centre, a refuelling depot and a workshop to handle running maintenance and repairs. In addition he was putting a jetty out into the lagoon for the converted seventy-foot pilchard trawler that would be *Kingfisher*'s service boat – acting as tender and ferry.

They ran an extensive inspection of the base. Johnny was pleased with the interest Tracey showed, and he enjoyed answering her questions for his own enthusiasm was high. It was nearly two o'clock before they had finished.

'How are the watchtowers coming?' Johnny asked.

'All up, ready and waiting.'

And suddenly Johnny had a two-edged inspiration.

'Might as well go and have a look.' He made it casual.

'Okay, I'll fetch the Land-Rover,' the foreman agreed.

'I know the way.' Johnny put him off. 'You go and get your lunch.'

'It's no trouble—' the foreman began, caught Johnny's frown, cut himself short, then glanced at Tracey. 'Yeah! Sure! Fine! Okay – here are the keys.' He handed Johnny the Land-Rover keys, and disappeared into his own quarters.

Johnny checked the grub box, and they climbed into the open Land-Rover.

'Where are we going?' Tracey asked.

'Inspect the watchtowers along the sandspit.'

'Watchtowers?'

'We've put up a line of fifty-foot wooden towers along the beach. From them we will take continual bearings on *Kingfisher* when she is working offshore. By radio we will be able at any time to give her the exact position over the bottom to within a few feet, as a check to the computer.'

'My, you are clever.' Tracey fluttered her eyelashes at him in mock admiration.

'Silly wench,' said Johnny, and let out the clutch. He swung down past the radio shack on to the hard wet sand at the edge of the lagoon; accelerating he hit second then third and they went away around the curve of the lagoon, headed towards the great yellow wind-carved dunes that lined the coast.

Tracey stood up on her seat, clutching the edge of the windscreen, and the wind snatched at her hair. She pulled the retaining thong from it, and shook it out into a shiny black flag that snapped and snaked behind her.

'Look! Look!' she cried as the flocks of startled flamingoes lurched into flight, streaming white and pink and black over the glossy silver water.

Johnny laughed with her, and swung the Land-Rover towards the dunes.

'Hold on!' he shouted, and she clung to the windscreen, shrieking in delicious terror as they flew up the steep side of a dune, spinning a cloud of sand from the rear wheels and then dropped over the crest in a stomach-churning swoop. They crossed the sandspit and hit the beach, racing along it, playing tag with the waves that shot up the sand.

Five miles up the beach Johnny parked above the high-water mark and they ate cold chicken and drank a bottle of chilled white wine sitting side by side in the sand, leaning against the seat cushions from the Land-Rover. Then they went down to the edge of the sea to wash the chicken grease from their fingers.

'Yipes! It's cold.' Tracey scooped a double handful of sea water. Then she looked at Johnny and her expression became devilish.

He backed away, but not quickly enough. The icy water hit him in the chest, and he gasped.

'War!' It was their childhood cry.

Tracey whirled and went off long-legged along the beach, with Johnny pounding after her. She sensed him gaining on her, and shouted.

'It was a mistake! I didn't mean it! I'm sorry!'

At the last moment as he reached out to grip her shoulder, she jinked and ran knee-deep into the sea. Turning at bay to face him, she kicked a spray of water at him, shouting defiance and laughter.

'All right, come on then!'

Braving the flying spray, he reached her and picked her up kicking and struggling and waded out waist deep.

'No, no – please. Johnny. I give in – I'll do anything.'

At that moment a freak wave, bigger and stronger than the others, knocked Johnny's legs out from under him. They went under, and were rolled up the beach, to stagger out, completely soaked, clinging together, helpless with laughter.

They stood beside the Land-Rover trying to wring the water out of their clothing.

'Oh, you beast!' sobbed Tracey through her laughter. Her hair was a sodden mass, and drops of sea water clung in her eyelashes like dew.

Johnny took her in his arms and kissed her, and they stopped laughing.

She went loose against his chest, her eyes tightly closed and her lips, salty with sea water, opened against his.

The radio telephone in the Land-Rover beside them began to bleat fretfully, flashing its little red warning light.

They drew apart slowly, reluctantly, and stared at each other with dazed, bemused eyes.

Johnny reached the Land-Rover, unhooked the microphone and lifted it to his lips.

'Yes?' his voice cracked. He cleared his throat and repeated. 'Yes?'

The foreman's voice was distorted and scratchy through the speaker.

'Mr Lance, I'm sorry to have—' he was clearly about to finish ' – interrupted you.' But he stopped abruptly, and began again. 'It's just that I think you should know we've had a gale warning. Northerly gale building up quickly. If you want to get back to Cape Town you had better get airborne before it hits us – otherwise you could be shut in for days.'

'Thanks. We'll be back right away.' He hung up, and

Tracey smiled shakily. Her voice was also husky and unnatural-sounding.

'And a damn good thing too!'

Tracey's hair was still damp, and the borrowed polo-neck jersey swamped her. The grey trousers were also borrowed, rolled up to show her bare feet.

She sat very quietly and thoughtfully in the passenger seat of the Beechcraft. Far below them a small fishing vessel lay with a white cloud of seabirds hovering over it, and she watched it with exaggerated attention. There was a heavy feeling of restraint between them now, they could no longer meet each other's eyes.

'Pilchard trawler.' Johnny noticed her gaze.

'Yes,' said Tracey, and they were silent again.

'Nothing happened.' Johnny spoke again gruffly.

'No,' she agreed. 'Nothing happened.' Then shyly she reached out and took his hand. Lightly she rubbed the stump of his missing finger.

'Still friends?' she asked.

'Still friends.' He grinned at her with relief, and they flew on towards Cape Town.

Hugo Kramer watched the aircraft through his binoculars, balancing easily against the roll and pitch of the bridge.

'Police patrol?' asked the man at the helm beside him.

'No,' Hugo replied without lowering the glasses. 'Red and white twin Beechcraft. Registration ZS – PTB. Private aircraft, probably one of the diamond companies.'

He lowered the glasses, and crossed to the wing of the bridge. 'Anyway, we are well outside territorial waters.'

The drone of the aircraft engine faded away, and Hugo transferred his attention to the frantic activity on the deck below him.

The trawler, *Wild Goose*, lay heeled over under the weight of fish that filled her purse seine-net; at least a hundred tons of seething silver pilchards bulging the net out alongside the trawler into a round bag fifty feet across. While above it a shrieking canopy of seabirds swirled and wheeled and dived, frantic with greed.

Three of the crew on a scoop-net which hung from the overhead derrick were dipping the fish out of the net, swinging a ton of fish at each scoop over the side, and dropping them like a silver cloudburst into the trawler's hold. The donkey engine on the winch clattered harshly in time to their movements.

Hugo watched with satisfaction. He had a good crew, and although the fishing was only a cover for the *Wild Goose* – yet Hugo took pride in his teutonic thoroughness which dictated that the cover should be as solid as possible. In any case, all profits from fishing were for his personal account. It was part of the agreement with the Ring.

He packed the binoculars carefully into their leather case, and hung them behind the chartroom door. Then he clambered swiftly down the steel ladder to deck level, moving with catlike grace despite the heavy rubber hip boots he wore.

'I'll take her here for a while,' he told the man at the winch controls. He spoke in Afrikaans, but his accent was shaded with the German of South West Africa.

Wide-shouldered under the blue fisherman's jersey, he worked with smooth economic movements. His hands on the winch control were rough and reddened by wind and sun, for his skin was too fair to weather. The skin of his face was also red, and half-boiled, peeling so there were pinky raw places on his cheeks and black scabs on his lips.

The hair that hung out under his cap was white as

bleached sisal, and his eyelashes were thick and colourless, giving him a mild near-sighted look. His eyes were the palest of cornflower blue, yet without being weak and watery as those of most albinos; they were slitted now, as he judged the roll and dip of the boat – engaging the clutch to meet the movement, or pulling on the drum brake.

'Skipper!' A shout from the bridge above him.

'Ja.' Hugo did not allow his attention to waver as he replied, 'What is it?'

'Gale warning! There is a northerly buster building up.'

And Hugo grinned, pulled on the brake and shut the throttle.

'All right, clean up. Cut the purse rope, let the fish go free.'

He turned and swarmed up the ladder to the bridge, and went to his chart table.

'It will take us three hours to get in position,' he muttered aloud, leaning over the chart, then he barged out on to the wing of the bridge again to chase up his crew.

They had cut the purse rope on the net, allowing the net to fall open like a woman's skirt, and the fish were pouring out, a dark spreading stain through the gap. Two men had the pressure hose on, washing loose fish from the deck into the sea, others were slamming the hatch-covers closed.

Within forty minutes *Wild Goose* was running south under full throttle to take up her waiting station.

The diamond coast of South West Africa lies in the belt of the Trades. The prevailing wind is the south-easter, but periodically the wind system is completely reversed and a gale comes out of the north, off the land.

It is a Scirocco-type wind like the 'Khamsin' of the Libyan desert, or the 'Simoom' of Tripoli.

It was the same searing dry wind out of the desert, filling the sky with brooding dust and sand clouds, smothering everything beneath a hellish pall like the smoke from a great battlefield.

The dust clouds were part of the design, the Ring had taken account of them when they planned the system – for the north wind lifted into the sky such a quantity of mica dust that the radar screens of the diamond security police were cluttered and confused, throwing up phantom echoes and making it impossible to pick up the presence of a small airborne object.

Turn Back Point was three miles inland, and sixty miles north of the Orange River. The name was given by the first travellers, and expressed their views on continuing a journey northwards. Those old travellers had not known that they stood in the centre of an elevated marine terrace, an ancient beach now lifted above the level of the sea, and that it was the richest prospect of an area so diamond-rich that it was to be ring-fenced, patrolled by Jeep and dog and aircraft, guarded by gun and radar, a laager so secure that a man leaving it would have to submit to X-ray, and take nothing out with him but the clothes he wore.

At Turn Back Point was one of the four big separation plants where all the gravel from the big Company's workings from miles around was processed. The settlement was comparatively large, with plant, workshops and stores, and accommodation for five hundred men and their families. Yet not all the Company's efforts to make it attractive and liveable could alter the fact that Turn Back Point was a hell-hole in a savage and forbidding desert.

Now with the north wind blowing, what had been unpleasant before was almost unbearable. The buildings were tightly sealed, even the joints around the windows and doors were plugged with cloth or paper – and yet the red dust seeped in to powder the furniture, the desks, the bed linen, even the interior of the refrigerators, with a thin gritty film. It settled in the hair, was sugary between the teeth, clogged the nostrils – and with it came that searing heat that seemed to dry the moisture from the eyeballs.

Outside the dust was a red glittering fog which reduced visibility to a dozen yards. Men who were forced out into that choking dry soup wore dust goggles to protect their eyes, and the mica dust covered their clothing with a shiny coating that glittered even in that dun light.

Beyond the settlement a man moved now through the fog, carrying a small cylindrical object. He leaned forward into the wind, moving slowly away into the desert. He reached a shallow depression and went down into it. Setting his burden on the sand, he rested a moment. Then he knelt over the cylinder. He appeared monstrous under his leather jacket and cap, his face covered by goggles and a scarf.

The fibre-glass cylinder was painted with yellow fluorescent paint. At one end was a transparent plastic bubble which housed an electric globe, at the other end was a folded envelope of rubberized nylon material attached to the cylinder by a stainless steel coupling, and linked to the coupling was a small steel bottle of hydrogen gas. The whole assembly was eighteen inches long, and three inches in diameter. It weighed a few ounces more than fifteen pounds.

Within the cylinder were two separate compartments. The larger contained a highly sophisticated piece of transistorized electronic equipment which would transmit a homing signal, light or extinguish its lamp on long-distance radio signal command, and also at command it would control the inflow of hydrogen gas into the nylon balloon through the connecting coupling.

The smaller compartment held simply a sealed plastic container into which were packed twenty-seven diamonds. The smallest of these stones weighed fourteen carats, the largest a formidable fifty-six carats. Each of these stones had been selected by experts for colour, brilliance, and perfection. These were all first-water diamonds, and once they were cut they would fetch in the open market between seven hundred thousand and a million pounds – depending on the skill of the cutting.

There were four members of the Ring at Turn Back Point. Two of them were long service and trusted diamond sorters employed behind the guarded walls of the processing plant. They worked together, to check each other, for the Company operated a system of employee double check – which was completely useless when there was collusion. These men selected the finest stones and got them out of the plant.

The third member of the Ring was a diesel mechanic in the Company workshops. It was his job to receive and assemble the equipment which arrived concealed in a marked drum of tractor grease. He also packed the stones into the cylinder and passed it on to the man who was now kneeling out in the desert, preparing to launch the cylinder into the swirling dust fog.

His final check completed, the man stood up and went to the lip of the depression and peered out into the dust storm. At last he seemed satisfied, and hurried back to the yellow cylinder. With an incisive twist of the bevelled release ring he opened the valve on the bottle of hydrogen gas. There was a snakelike hiss, and the nylon balloon began to inflate. The folds of material crackled as they filled. The balloon lifted, eager to be gone, but the man restrained it with difficulty until the balloon was smooth and tight. He let go, and the balloon with its dangling cylinder leapt into the sky, and almost instantly was gone into the dust clouds.

The man stood with his face lifted to the dark furnace-red sky. His goggles glinted blindly, but his attitude was one of triumph, and when he turned away he walked lightly with the step of a man freshly released from danger.

'One more package,' he promised himself. 'Just one more,

and I'll pull out. Buy that farm on the Olifants River, do a bit of fishing, take a shooting trip every year—'

He was still dreaming when he reached the parked Land-Rover and climbed into the driver's seat. He started the engine, switched on the headlights, and drove slowly down the track towards the settlement.

The sign on the rear of the departing Land-Rover was in white paint so that it showed clearly through the haze of red dust.

'SECURITY PATROL,' it read.


*W*ild *Goose* lay on station, with her diesels throbbing softly, ticking over to hold her head into the wind. Even twenty miles out at sea the wind was searing hot and the occasional splatter of spray on Hugo's face was refreshing.

He stood in the corner of the bridge where he could watch the sea and the helmsman, but he was anxious. *Wild Goose* had been lying on station for fifteen hours now, during ten of which the norther had howled dismally through her rigging.

He was always anxious at the beginning of a pick-up. There was so much that could have gone wrong, anything from a police sweep to a tiny electrical fault in the equipment.

'What time is it, Hansie?' he shouted and the helmsman glanced up at the chronometer above his head.

'Three minutes after six, skipper.'

'Dark in half an hour,' Hugo grunted disgustedly, slitted those pale-lashed eyes into the wind once more, then shrugged and ambled back into the bridge house.

He stopped at the console beside his chart table. Even to an experienced eye the machine was an ordinary 'Fish-Finder', an adaptation of the old wartime anti-submarine device, the ASDIC, to the more prosaic business of plotting the depth and position of the pilchard shoals beneath the surface.

However, this model had undergone a costly and specialized conversion. The Ring had flown an expert out from Japan to do the work.

Now that the set hummed softly, its control panel lit soft green by the internal light, but the sound was neutral, and the circular glass screen was blank.

'You want some coffee, Hansie?' Hugo asked the old coloured man at the wheel. His crew were handpicked, loyal and trusted. They had to be – one loud mouth could blow a multi-million pound business.

'*Ja dankie*, skipper.' The old man creased his weather-battered face in appreciation, and Hugo shouted down the companionway to the galley.

'Cooky, how's it for a pot of coffee?'

But the reply was lost, for at that moment the console came to life dramatically. A row of lights blinked on above the control panel, the muted hum changed to a rapid beep-beep signal, and the screen glowed ghostly green.

'She's up!' Hugo shouted his relief, and ran to the set. His first mate rushed through from his cabin behind the bridge, tucking his shirt into unbuttoned trousers, his face puckered with sleep.

'About bloody time,' he blurted, groggily.

'Take over from Hansie,' Hugo told him, and he settled into the padded seat in front of the ASDIC set.

'Right, bring her round two points to port and open her up.'

The *Wild Goose* swung her head into the sea, and her motion changed from easy swoop and glide to a crabbing butting lunge, and the spray burst over the glass of the bridge.

Sitting before the console Hugo was tracking the flight of the balloon and keeping *Wild Goose* on an interception course.

Driven by the forty-knot norther the balloon crossed the coastline, climbing swiftly to three thousand feet. Hugo manipulated the knob on the console which sent the balloon a command to release gas and maintain altitude. Her response was recorded immediately on the screen.

'Good,' Hugo whispered. 'Good girl.' Then louder. 'Bring her round a bit, Oscar – the balloon is drifting to the south.'

For twenty minutes more they butted through the swells.

'Okay,' Hugo broke the silence. 'I'm going to ditch her.' He twisted the knob clockwise slowly, expelling all the gas from the nylon balloon.

'Ja. That's it. She's down.' He looked out of the window above the set. The dust-laden clouds had brought the night on prematurely. It was dark outside, with a low black ceiling through which no star showed.

Hugo turned his attention back to the set.

'That's it, Oscar. You're right on course. Hold her there.'

Then he glanced across at old Hansie and another younger crewman. They were sitting patiently on the bench against the far bulkhead. Both of them were clad in full oilskins, shiny yellow plastic from head to ankle, with gumboots below that.

'Okay, Hansie,' Hugo nodded. 'You can get up in the bows. We are only a mile or so away now.'

They climbed down on to the wave-swept deck, and Hugo watched them scuttling forward between each green burst of water and crouching in the bows. Both of them ducking each time another swell poured over the top of them, their yellow plastic suits showing clearly in the murky deck lights.

'I'm going to switch her on now,' Hugo warned the helm. 'We should have her on visual.'

'Right.' Oscar peered ahead, and Hugo flicked a switch on the panel, commanding the balloon to turn on her guide light.

Almost immediately there was a shout from Oscar.

'There she is. Dead ahead!'

Hugo jumped up and ran forward. It took a few seconds for his eyes to adjust, then he made out the tiny red firefly of light ahead of them in the vast blackness of sea and sky. It showed for a second then was gone in the trough of the next wave.

'I'll take her.' Hugo replaced Oscar at the wheel. 'You get on the spotlight.'

The beam of the spotlight was a solid white shaft through the darkness. The fluorescent yellow paint of the cylinder glowed in the circle of the spot.

Hugo lay *Wild Goose* upwind of the cylinder, and then allowed her to drift down gently on it. Hansie and his assistant were ready with the twenty-foot boat-hook.

Delicately Hugo manoeuvred down over the bobbing yellow cylinder, and grunted with satisfaction as the boat-hook slipped through the recovery ring and the cylinder was hauled in over the bows.

He watched while the two dripping oilskin-clad figures clambered back up the ladder into the wheelhouse, and laid the cylinder on the chart table.

'Good! Good!' Hugo slapped their backs heartily. 'Now, go and get dry – both of you!' They climbed down the companionway, and Hugo handed the wheel over to Oscar.

'Home!' he instructed him. 'As quick as you like.' And he carried the cylinder through into his cabin.

Sitting at the fold-down table in his cabin, Hugo unscrewed the lower section of the cylinder and took out the plastic container. He opened it and spilled the contents out on the table top.

He whistled softly, and picked up the biggest stone. Although he was no expert he knew instinctively that it was a brilliant of exceptional quality. Even the roughness of its exterior could not mask the fire in its depths.

To him it was worthless, there was nowhere he could market a stone like that. There was no temptation to take it out of the Ring – all it would mean for him was fifteen years at hard labour.

The Ring was based on this mutual reliance, no one part of it could function without all the others – yet each part was self-contained and watertight. Only one man knew all its parts, and nobody knew who that one man was.

From the drawer beside him Hugo took out his tools and set them on the table. He lit the spirit stove and set the pot of paraffin wax in the gimbal above it to heat.

Then he poured the diamonds into a shiny metal can. It was the type of ordinary commercial can used for packing and preserving foodstuffs.

Balancing against the ship's motion, he lifted the pot from the stove, and poured the steaming liquid wax over the diamonds, filling the can to rim level.

The wax cooled and solidified quickly, turning opaque and white. The stones were now incorporated in a cake of wax that would prevent them rattling, and would give the sealed can authentic weight.

Hugo lit a cigarette and crossed the cabin to look out into the wheelhouse. The helmsman winked at him and Hugo smiled.

He went back to the table, the can was cool enough to handle. He placed the circular lid over it, and moved to the portable Jenny bolted to a chest of drawers. Carefully he clinched the lid into place, his eyes squinting at the smoke from the cigarette that dangled from his lips.

Satisfied at last he set the sealed can on the table, while he went to where his jacket hung on the door. From the inside pocket he pulled out a manilla envelope, then from the envelope he drew a printed, colour-screened label. He came back to the bench and meticulously pasted the label around the can. On the label was a highly glamorized artist's conception of a leaping pilchard, making it look like a Scottish salmon.

'Pilchards in Tomato Sauce.' Hugo read the label aloud,

as he leaned back to admire his work. 'A product of South West Africa.' He smiled with satisfaction and began packing his equipment away.

'How much?' The foreman of the fish pump called across the narrowing gap between *Wild Goose* and the jetty.

'About fifty tons,' Hugo shouted back. 'Then the norther chased us home.'

'*Ja*. None of the boats stayed out.' The foreman watched his gang secure the mooring ropes, and swing the hose of the vacuum pump over *Wild Goose*'s hold to begin pumping out her pilchards.

'Take over, Oscar.' Hugo picked up his jacket and cap. 'I'll be back tomorrow.' He jumped down on to the jetty and strode down towards the canning factory with its awesome stink of pilchard oil. His jacket was slung over his shoulder, one finger hooked through the tag.

He went down an alley between the boiler rooms and the fish-drying plant, across a wide yard where the bags of fish meal were piled to the height of a double-storey building. He turned in through the double doors of the cavernous warehouse filled to roof height with cardboard cartons, each stencilled with the words:

1 gross cans.      Pilchards in tomato sauce.
Consign to:       Vee Dee Bee Agencies Ltd.
                  32, Bermondsey Street,
                  London, S.E.1.

He went into the cubicle that served the warehouse storeman as an office.

'Hello, Hugo. Good trip?' The storeman was Hugo's brother-in-law.

'Fifty ton.' Hugo hung his coat casually on the hook behind the door. 'I've got to take a leak,' he said, and went to the latrine across the floor of the warehouse.

He came back, and drank a cup of tea with his brother-in-law. Then he stood and said, 'Jeannie will be waiting.'

'Give her my love.'

'She don't need yours. She's going to get plenty of mine!' Hugo winked, and took his coat from the hook. It was lighter now, the can was gone from the pocket.

He went through the main gates of the harbour, exchanging a casual greeting with the customs officer, and went to the battered early model convertible in the car park.

He kissed the girl at the driving-wheel, threw his coat on the back seat and climbed in over the door.

'You drive,' he told her, grinning. 'I want both hands free.'

She squeaked and pulled his hand out of her skirts.

'Can't you wait till we get home?'

'I've been at sea for five days and I'm hungry as hell.'

'You're a caution, you are.' She laughed at him and started the car.

T his was Sergio Caporetti, the man Johnny had chosen to captain *Kingfisher*. He was a round man, the same shape as a snowman. He filled the doorway of Johnny's office, and his great belly bulging into the room ahead of him. His face was round also, like a baby's – but the beautiful dark Italian eyes fringed with thick lashes like a girl's.

'Come in, Sergio,' Johnny greeted him. 'Nice to see you.'

The Italian crossed the room deceptively quickly, and Johnny's hand was completely engulfed by the enormous hairy paw.

'So, at last we are ready,' Sergio grunted. 'Three months

I sit on bum – do nothing. Look at me – ' He slapped his belly with a sound like a pistol shot. ' – fat! No good.'

'Well, not quite ready.' Johnny qualified the statement. He was flying Sergio and his crew over to England well ahead of time. He wanted the big Italian to have plenty of opportunity to study and get to know the revolutionary new equipment with which *Kingfisher* was fitted. Then when the vessel was ready for sea, Sergio would sail her out to Africa.

'Sit down, Sergio. Let's go over the crew list—'

When Sergio left an hour later, Johnny went as far as the lift with him.

'If you have any problems phone me, Sergio.'

'*Si.*' Sergio shook hands. 'Don't worry – Caporetti is in charge. All is well.'

On his way back Johnny stopped at the reception desk.

'Is Mrs Hartford in today?' he asked one of the little receptionists, and both of them replied in chorus like Tweedledum and Tweedledee.

'No, Mr Lance.'

'Has she phoned to say where she is?'

'No, Mr Lance.'

Tracey had disappeared. Five days now there had been no sign of her, her new office was deserted and unused. Johnny was worried and angry. He was worried that she had gone on another binge, and he was angry because he missed her.

He was scowling ferociously as he went back into his office.

'Goodness me.' Lettie Pienaar stood beside his desk with a batch of mail in her hand. 'We do look happy. Here's something to cheer you.'

She handed him a postcard with a colour picture of the Eiffel Tower. It was the first word from Ruby since she had left. Johnny read it quickly.

'Paris – ' he said, ' – is fun, it seems.' He tossed the card on to the desk and plunged back into the day's work.

He worked late, stopped at a steakhouse to eat, then drove back to the silent house in Bishopscourt.

The crunch of tyres on the gravel drive and head-lights flashing across the bedroom wall woke him. He sat up in bed as the front-doorbell began a series of urgent peals and he switched on the bedside light. Two o'clock – Christ!

He pulled a dressing-gown over his nudity and tottered down the passage, switching on lights as he went. The doorbell kept ringing.

He turned the front door key. The door flew open and Tracey came in like a strong wind, clutching a briefcase to her chest.

'Where the hell have you been?' Johnny was suddenly fully awake, angry and relieved.

'Johnny! Johnny!' She was dancing with excitement, incoherent, her cheeks flaming and eyes shining. 'I've got them – at least, it, both of them.'

'Where have you been?' Johnny was not to be so easily sidetracked, and with an obvious effort Tracey brought her excitement under control, but she was still smiling and gave the impression of humming like an electric motor.

'Come.' She took his hand and dragged him into the lounge. 'Get yourself a large whisky and sit down,' she ordered, imperious as a queen.

'I don't want a whisky, and I don't—'

'You'll need one,' she interrupted, and went to the open liquor cabinet, poured a massive whisky into a crystal glass, squirted soda into it, and brought it back to Johnny.

'Tracey, what the hell is going on?'

'Please, Johnny. It's so wonderful, don't spoil it for me. Just sit there, please!'

Johnny sank reluctantly into the chair, and Tracey

slipped the catch on her briefcase and drew out a sheaf of documents. She stood in the centre of the floor, and took up the pose of a Victorian actress.

'This – ' she explained, ' – is a translation from the original German of a proclamation by Governor in Council dated 3rd May 1899 and issued at Windhoek. I will leave out the preamble and go straight to the meat.'

She cleared her throat and began reading:

'In consideration of the sum of 10,000 marks which is hereby paid and received, the rights to mine, win, recover, collect or carry away all metals, whether base or precious, stones whether base, semi-precious or precious, minerals, guano, vegetation and other substances organic or inorganic for a period of Nine Hundred and Ninety-Nine years is granted to Messrs Farben, Hendryck and Mosenthal S.A., Guano Merchants of 14 Bergenstrasse, Windhoek, in respect of a circular area ten kilometres in radius whose centre shall be a point situated at the highest elevation of the island lying on latitude 23° 15' South and longitude 15° 12' East.'

Tracey paused and looked at Johnny. He was frozen, stony-faced, staring at her with all his attention. She went on quickly, gabbling it out.

'All the old German mineral concessions and rights were ratified by the Union Parliament when the Union of South Africa took over the mandate after the Great War.'

He nodded, unable to speak. Tracey's smile kept breaking out.

'That concession still has all the force of law behind it. The grant of any subsequent rights is invalid, and although the original grant was mainly for the recovery of guano – yet it covers precious stones also.'

Again Johnny nodded, and Tracey put the document at the bottom of the sheaf of papers in her hand.

'The concession Company, Farben, Hendryck and

Mosenthal S.A., is still in existence. The Company's only remaining asset, apart from any long-forgotten concessions, is an old building at 14 Bergenstrasse, Windhoek.'

Tracey seemed to change the subject suddenly.

'You asked me where I have been, Johnny. Well I've been to Windhoek, and over most of the worst roads in South West Africa.

'The Farben, Hendryck and Mosenthal Company is owned by the brothers Hendryck, a couple of Karakul fur farmers. They are a pair of horrible old men, and when I saw them slitting the throats of those poor little Persian lambs just to prevent the fur uncurling, well—' Tracey paused, and gulped. 'Well, I didn't explain to them about the concession. I just offered to buy the Company, and they asked twenty thousand and I said "sign", and they signed and I left them chuckling with glee. They thought they'd been terribly clever. There! It's all yours!'

Tracey handed the Agreement to Johnny and while he read it she went on.

'I made the Agreement in the name of Van Der Byl Diamonds, I signed it as a Director – I hope you don't mind.'

'Christ!' Johnny took a long deep swallow of whisky, then set the glass down and stood up.

'Mind?' he repeated. 'You bring me the concession to Thunderbolt and Suicide – and ask me if I mind.'

He reached for her and eagerly she went to him.

'Tracey, you're wonderful.' They hugged each other ecstatically, and Johnny swung her off her feet. Without either of them planning it they were suddenly lying, still in each other's arms, on the couch. Then they were kissing, and the laughter dwindled into small murmurs and incoherent sounds.

Tracey pulled away from him at last, and slipped off the couch. She stood in the centre of the floor. Her breathing was ragged. Her hair was a dark tangle.

'Whoa! That's enough.'

'Tracey.' He started up from the couch, wild for her, but she held him at the full stretch of her arms, her hands flat on his chest, backing away in front of him.

'No, Johnny, no!' She shook her head urgently. 'Listen to me.'

He stopped. The wild look faded from his eyes.

'Look, Johnny, God knows I'm no saint, but – well, I don't want us to – well, not on a couch in some other woman's house. That's not how I want it to be.'

B enedict eased the big honey-coloured Bentley out of the traffic stream that clogged Bermondsey Street and turned into the gates of the warehouse. He parked beside the loading bay and climbed out.

As he pulled off his gloves, he glanced along the bank. Mountains of goods were stacked ready for distribution. Cases of Cape wine and spirits, canned fruit in brown cartons, canned fish, forty-gallon drums of fish oil, bundles of raw hides stiff as boards, and cases of indefinable goods – all of it the produce of Southern Africa.

Vee Dee Bee Agencies had grown out of all recognition in the ten years since Benedict had launched it.

Benedict climbed the steps to the bank three at a time, and strode down between the towering stacks of goods that reached up into the murk of the high ceiling. He walked with the assurance of a man on his own ground, the skirts of his overcoat swirling about his knees, broad-shouldered and tall. The storemen and porters greeted him deferentially as he passed, and when he entered the main office there was a stirring and whispering among the ranks of typists as though a wind had blown through a forest.

The Managing Director hurried out of his office to greet Benedict and usher him in.

'How are you, Mr van der Byl? There's tea coming now.'
And he stood behind Benedict to take his coat.

The meeting lasted half an hour, Benedict reading through the weekly sales and cost reports, querying an item here, remarking on a figure with pleasure or displeasure as it deserved. Many people watching him work would have been startled. This was not the indolent playboy they thought they knew, this was a hard-eyed businessman coldly and unemotionally milking the maximum profit from his enterprise.

There would have been others who wondered where Benedict had found the capital to finance a business of this magnitude, especially if they had known that he owned the premises, and that Vee Dee Bee Agencies was by no means his only stake in the world of business. He had not received money from his father – the Old Man had not believed Benedict capable of successfully negotiating the purchase of a pound of butter.

The meeting ended, and Benedict stood up and shrugged on his overcoat, while his Managing Director went to the grey steel safe in the corner, tumbled the combination and swung the heavy door open.

'The shipment arrived yesterday,' he explained as he reached into the safe and brought out the can. 'On the SS *Loch Elsinore* from Walvis Bay.'

He handed the can to Benedict, who examined it briefly, smiling a little at the painting of the leaping fish and the lettering 'Pilchards in Tomato Sauce'.

'Thank you.' He slipped the can into his briefcase, and the Managing Director walked with him back to the Bentley.

B enedict left the Bentley in a garage in Broadwick Street, and walked through the jostle of Soho until he reached the grimy brick building behind the square. He pressed the bell opposite the card that read Aaron Cohen, Manufacturing Jeweller, and when the door opened he climbed the stairs to the top and fourth floor. Again he rang, and after a while an eye peeped at him through the peephole – but the door opened almost immediately.

'Hello, Mr van der Byl. Come in! Come in!' The young doorman welcomed him in and locked the door behind him. 'Papa is expecting you!' he went on as they both looked up at the eye of the closed-circuit TV camera above the wrought-iron grille that barred the passage.

Whoever was viewing the screen was satisfied, for there was an electrical buzz and the grille swung open. The doorman led Benedict down the passage.

'You know the way. Papa is in his office.'

Benedict was in a shabby little reception room, with a threadbare carpet and a pair of chairs that looked like Ministry of Works rejects. He turned to the right-hand door and went through it into a long room that clearly occupied most of the top floor of the building.

Along one side of the room ran a narrow bench, to which were bolted twenty small lathes. Each machine ran off a belt from a central drive below the bench. The man tending the machines wore a white dust jacket, and he grinned at Benedict. 'Hello, Mr van der Byl, Papa is expecting you.' But Benedict delayed a moment to watch the operation of the saws. In the jaws of each lathe was set a diamond, and spinning against the diamond was a circular blade of phosphor bronze. As Benedict watched, the man turned back to the task of spreading a fine paste of olive oil and diamond dust on to the cutting edge of each blade – for it was not the bronze that cut. Only a diamond will cut a diamond.

'Some nice stones, Larry,' Benedict remarked, and Larry Cohen nodded.

'All of them between four and five carats.'

Benedict leaned close and examined one of the diamonds. The line of the cut was marked with Indian ink on the stone. Benedict knew what heart-searching and discussion, what examination and drawing upon the rich storehouses of experience had preceded the positioning of that ink line. It might take two days to saw through each diamond, so Benedict left the bench and moved on.

In a row down the other side of the room sat the other Cohen brothers. Eight of them. Old Aaron was a great breeder of boys. They ranged in age from nearly forty to nineteen years and there were a couple who were still in school and hadn't yet come into the business.

'How do you like this one, Mr van der Byl?' Michael Cohen looked up as Benedict approached. Michael was shaping a fine diamond, cutting it into a round using a lesser stone as a blade. A small tray beneath the lathe caught the dust from the two stones. This dust would be used later for sawing and polishing.

'A beauty,' said Benedict. These men were of the brotherhood, working with diamonds all their lives and loving them as other men loved women or horses and fine paintings.

He moved on down the room, greeting each of the brothers, stopping to watch for a minute the loving care with which the elder boys, master craftsmen each of them, were cutting the precisely angled facets that make up the perfect round brilliant. The fifty-eight facets – table, stars, pavilions and the others which endow a cut stone with its mystic 'life' and 'fire'.

Leaving them crouched over their wheels, so similar to those of a potter, he went through the door at the end of the room.

'Benedict, my friend.' Aaron Cohen came from his desk

to embrace him. He was a tall thin man in his late sixties with a thick silver-grey mane of hair, round-shouldered from years of crouching over a diamond wheel. 'I did not know you were in London, they told me you were in Cape Town. Yesterday was Ruby's birthday. If we had known—'

Benedict took the envelope from his pocket and shook twenty-seven diamonds on to the blotter of the desk.

'What do you think of those, Papa?'

'*Shu! Shu!*' Papa patted his own cheeks with delight, and he reached instinctively for the biggest stone.

'I should live to see such a stone!' He screwed a jeweller's *loupe* into his eye, turning to catch the natural light from the high windows, and scrutinized the diamond through the eyepiece.

'Ah, yes. There is a feather*, but small. V.V.S.I.† But we will cut through it. Yes, we will take two gems from this stone. Two perfect diamonds of ten or twelve carats each, and perhaps five smaller ones.' More than half a diamond's bulk is lost in the cutting.

'Yes! Yes! From this stone we will sell a hundred thousand pounds' worth of polished diamonds!'

Aaron crossed to the door. 'Boys! Come see! I will show you a prince among diamonds.' And his sons crowded into the office. Michael took it first and gave his opinion. 'A good stone, yes. But not of the same water as the stone we had in the last batch. You remember that octahedron crystal—'

'What you talking!' his father interrupted. 'You wouldn't know a diamond from a piece of gorgonzola cheese already!'

'He is right, Papa.' Larry joined in the discussion. 'The other stone was better.'

'So the Big Lover argues with his father! Little shiksas with skirts up around their tochis you know all about.

* Semi-transparent veinlike flaw.
† Very very slight imperfection.

Dancing the Watsui and the Cha-Cha. Yes! But diamonds you know from nothing.' This declaration precipitated a full-scale, family argument in which each of the brothers joined with gusto.

'Shuddup! Shuddup! Back to work all of you! Out! Out!' Aaron broke up the meeting, driving his sons from the office and slamming the door behind them.

'*Shu!*' He looked to heaven. 'What a business! Now we can weigh the stones.'

When they had weighed and tallied the stones, and Aaron had locked them into the safe, Benedict told him:

'I am thinking of breaking up the Ring.'

Aaron froze and looked across the desk at Benedict. Between them there was always the pretence that their relationship was legitimate. They never spoke about the Ring, or where the unregistered stones came from, or how the finished gems were sent to Switzerland.

'Why?' Aaron asked carefully.

'I am a rich man now. With my father's money, and what I have made from the Ring and invested. A very rich man. I no longer need to take the risks.'

'Such problems I wish I had. But perhaps you are wise – I would not think to argue with you.'

'There will be one or two more packages. Then it will be finished.'

Aaron nodded. 'I understand,' he said. 'Like all good things it must end.'

It was a little after noon when Benedict parked the Bentley outside the mews flat off Belgrave Square. He went to shower immediately he was home. In all the years he had lived here he had never grown accustomed to London's grime-laden atmosphere, and he bathed or showered at least three times a day.

He sang in the shower, and then enveloped in a huge bath towel he left a string of damp footprints through to the lounge where he mixed a Martini, and screwed up his eyes at the first stinging taste of the drink.

The phone rang.

'Van der Byl,' he said into the mouthpiece, and then his expression changed as he listened. Quickly he put down the glass and used both hands to hold the telephone receiver.

'What on earth are you doing here?' His tone of astonishment was not faked.

'What a wonderful surprise. When can I see you? How about right now – for lunch? That's great! No, nothing I can't put off – this is a pretty special occasion, you know. Where are you staying? The Lancaster. Fine. Look, give me forty-five minutes, and I'll meet you in the Looking-Glass Room on the top floor. Yes, ten past one. God, what a delightful – I've said that already. See you in three-quarters of an hour.'

He replaced the receiver, swallowed the remains of his Martini and headed for his bedroom suite. This would make a good day into a truly remarkable one, he thought, as he quickly selected a silk shirt. He looked at his reflection in the mirror and grinned.

'The ball has really started bouncing your way, Benedict,' he whispered.

She was not at the bar, nor in the Looking-Glass Room. Benedict crossed to the tall picture windows for a glimpse of one of London's finest views across Hyde Park and the Serpentine. It was a smoky blue day, and the pale sun added bronze to the autumn shades of gold and red in the park.

He turned from the windows, and she was crossing the room towards him. His stomach swooped with delight for she also was pale gold with the coppery sheen of sun on her long legs and bare arms. The grace of her carriage was as he remembered it, the precise lifting and laying down of narrow feet on the thick pile of the carpet.

He stood quite still, letting her come to him. Heads turned all across the room, for she was a splendid golden creature. Benedict knew suddenly and clearly that he wanted this woman for himself.

'Hello, Benedict,' she said, and he stepped forward to take her hand in both of his.

'Ruby Lance!' He squeezed her long fingers gently. 'It's so good to see you again.'

The use of her surname was the clue to the strength of his reaction. She belonged to the one man in the world that Benedict most envied and hated. For this reason she was infinitely desirable.

'Let us celebrate with a little drink. I think the occasion deserves at the very least a champagne cocktail.'

She sat with those long slim legs neatly crossed, leaning back in her chair, holding the stemmed glass with tapering fingers. Her hair hung straight to her shoulders, like some rare silken tapestry in white gold, and her eyes watched him with a catlike candour, a calm feline intentness that seemed to look into his soul.

'I should not have bothered you,' she said. 'But I know so few people here.'

'How long can you stay?' He brushed aside the disclaimer. 'I must cancel my other arrangements.'

'A week.' She made it sound like an offer that was subject to negotiation.

'Oh, no!' His voice was mock distressed. 'You can do better than that – we won't be able to do half what I had planned in so short a time. You can stay longer, surely?'

'Perhaps,' she agreed, and lifted the glass an inch. 'It's good to see you.'

'And you.' Benedict agreed with emphasis. They sipped the sparkling wine watching each other's eyes.

Where others must wait weeks and months Benedict went in immediately as though it were his right. A smile and a murmured word, and theatre tickets were his or the doors of fashionable restaurants opened magically.

That first night he took her to the National Theatre, then for dinner at Le Coeur de France where a very famous movie actor stopped at their table.

'Hello, Benedict. We are all going on to the yacht later for a bit of a party. Join us, won't you?' And those legendary eyes turned to Ruby. 'And bring your beautiful friend with you.'

They ate breakfast under the awning on the after-deck of the yacht, eggs and bacon and Veuve Clicquot champagne, and watched the hubbub of dawn traffic on the wondrously smelly old Thames. Ruby was the only girl in the party without a fur to cheat the chill of the river dawn. Benedict made a mental note of the fact.

On the way home she sat with those long legs curled under her in the seat of the Bentley, still sleek and golden despite the night's exertions, but with the lightest touch of blue beneath her eyes.

'I can't remember having enjoyed an evening so much, Benedict.' She patted a tiny pink-lipped yawn. 'You're a wonderful companion.'

'Tonight again?' he asked.

'Yes, please,' she murmured.

She sensed an urgency in him, when she came down into the lobby of the Lancaster that evening. He came quickly to meet her as she stepped out of the lift, and the quiet assurance with which he kissed her cheek and took her arm surprised her.

They were silent as he snaked the Bentley through the

evening traffic. Ruby realized that at the tips of her long tapered fingers, within touching distance, was a fortune such as she had never before allowed herself to dream about. She was deadly afraid. A wrong move, even a wrong word might drive that fortune beyond her grasp for ever. She would never have a chance like this again, and she was afraid to move, almost paralysed with fear. The decision she knew she would have to make very soon would be fateful. Must she encounter his advance with withdrawal, or must she meet it as frankly as it was made.

She was so deeply involved with her thoughts that when the Bentley came to a standstill she looked up with surprise. They were parked in a mews outside an expensive-looking flat.

Benedict came round and opened her door, and led her without protest into the flat.

She looked about her curiously, recognizing some of the art works on display in the entrance hall. Benedict took her through into the long lounge and settled her solicitously into the tapestry-covered chair which dominated the room like a throne, and suddenly her fear was gone. She felt queenlike in her control. She knew with certainty that this would all be hers.

Benedict stood in the centre of the room, almost a petitioner in his attitude, and he began to speak. She listened quietly, her expression showing no hint of the triumphant surge of her spirits, and when he stopped to wait for her reply she did not hesitate.

'Yes,' she said.

'I will be with you when you tell him,' Benedict promised.

'It won't be necessary,' Ruby assured him. 'I can handle Johnny Lance.'

'No.' Swiftly Benedict crossed to her chair and took her hands, drawing her to her feet. 'I must be there with you. Promise me that.'

Then it became suddenly evident to Ruby that the strength of her position was unassailable. Benedict needed her not for any physical reasons – but merely because she belonged to Johnny Lance.

Looking steadily into Benedict's eyes she determined to test her intuition.

'He does not have to know about you,' she said. 'I could arrange a divorce with him.'

'He *must* know about me. That's what I want, don't you see?'

'Yes, I see.' She was secure.

'It is agreed?' He could barely conceal his anxiety.

'Yes,' she nodded. 'It's agreed.' And they smiled at each other – each completely satisfied.

'Come.' He led her almost reverently into his bedroom, and Ruby stopped in the doorway with a little cry of delight.

The double bed was a mountain of glowing fur in a score of shades ranging from soft pinkish cream, through beige and oyster, pale smoky blue to midnight and jet glossy black.

'Choose one!' he ordered her. 'To seal our bargain.'

She moved like a sleepwalker towards the bed, but as she reached the centre of the Khedive carpet Benedict called out softly.

'Wait.'

She stopped obediently and he came up behind her. She felt his hands on the back of her neck, and she lowered her chin, shaking her hair forward so that he could unhook the clasp and draw down the fastening of her dress.

She stepped out of the dress as it dropped around her ankles, then waited passively as he carefully removed her brassiere.

'Now,' he said. 'Try them on.'

In her stockings and high-heeled shoes she went to the bed, subtly emphasizing the lilt of her movements, and took up the first fur.

Benedict was sprawled in the wing-back chair across the room as she glanced back at him. His face was gloating and flushed, so that his features seemed swollen and coarsened as he stared at her. She understood now that this was a form of ritual in which they were engaged. Like a victorious Roman general, Benedict was conducting his own personal triumph, reviewing the spoils and the plunder. It had no basis in sexual or physical desire, but was rather a service of worship to Benedict himself. She was the priestess of this rite.

Yet, knowing this, Ruby felt no resentment. Rather, she found herself excited by the cold perversity of the pageant. As she paraded and postured, turned and swirled and flared the skirts of a wild mink, she was very conscious of his eyes upon her body. She knew it was perfect, and his scrutiny stirred her physically for the first time in her life. She felt her blood quicken and pound, felt her heart flutter within its cage of ribs like a captive bird, and her loins tighten like a clenching first. For her also the ritual was narcissistic — satisfying her own deep emotional need.

As she discarded each of the coats she dropped it in the centre of the floor, until there was a knee-high pile of precious fur.

At last she faced him, hugging the soft creamy cloud tightly about her body. Then she opened her arms, and the coat also, standing on tip-toe to tighten and highlight the hard muscle in her legs and flanks.

'This one,' she whispered, and he came out of the chair, picked her up in his arms and laid her, still wrapped in mink, on the great pile of furs.

Ruby woke in the double bed to a feeling of excitement and enormous well-being such as she had not experienced since she was a schoolgirl on the first morning of a holiday.

The morning was far advanced, pale sunshine in a square shaft poured through the open window like a stage effect.

Benedict in a yellow silk dressing-gown stood beside the bed watching her with an unfathomable expression which changed immediately he realized that she was awake.

'My man has collected your luggage from the Lancaster. Your toilet things are in the bathroom, your clothing in the dressing-room.'

He sat down carefully on the edge of the bed, and leaned forward to kiss her forehead and then each cheek.

'We will breakfast when you are ready.' He sat back and watched her eyes; clearly he was waiting for her to say something important. Immediately she was on guard, wary of making a mistake, seeking a clue in his expression.

'Last night,' he asked. 'Was it as good for you, as it was for me?'

Understanding washed over her in a warm wave. He wanted assurance, a comparison between himself and Johnny Lance.

'I have never in my life – ' She placed the emphasis carefully. ' – experienced anything like it.'

He nodded, relieved, pleased – and stood up.

'After breakfast we will go to town.'

This morning, Edmund, Benedict's man, chauffeured the Bentley. When they alighted at the north end of Bond Street and walked arm in arm along the pavement, Edmund tailed them at a dignified crawl, steadfastly ignoring the abuse of other drivers.

The morning was cool enough for Ruby to wear her new cream mink, and the looks of admiration and envy she drew from the other strollers delighted Benedict. He wanted to impress her, he wanted to flaunt his wealth.

'The wife of a diamond man must have diamonds.' He spoke on impulse as they came up to an expensive-looking jewellers. Ruby squeezed his arm and turned to look into the window.

'Good Lord,' Benedict laughed. 'Not here!' And Ruby looked at him with surprise.

Mockingly Benedict began reading the signs in the window.

'"Paradise Jewellers. A large selection of blue-white gems. Certificate of flawlessness with every diamond. Perfect flawless stones at bargain prices as advertised on T.V. and in the national Press. Small deposit secures your ring now. A diamond is forever – show her you really care."'

'But they are such a well-known firm. They have branches all over the world – even in South Africa!' Ruby protested, and bridled a little as Benedict smiled patronizingly.

'Let me explain about diamonds. They are bought for two reasons by two different types of people. Firstly by rich men as investments that will not erode and can only increase in value. These men buy notable stones on the advice of experts, the best of the gem diamond production goes to them. So when Richard Burton buys Liz a £300,000 diamond he is not being extravagant – on the contrary he is being ultra-conservative and thrifty with his money.'

'That's the kind of meanness I like,' Ruby laughed, and Benedict smiled at her honesty.

'You may find me as thrifty,' he promised.

'Go on,' she said, 'tell me more about diamonds.'

'Well, there is another type who buys diamonds. Usually just one in his life, luckily for him – and he very seldom tries to resell it again or he would get a nasty shock. This type is Joe Everybody – who wants to get married. He usually goes to somebody like Paradise Jewellers.' Benedict poked a derisive finger at the sign in the window. 'Because he has seen it on telly and he can get a ring on the instalment plan. In many cases the deposit covers the dealer for the cost of the stone – the rest goes on advertising, finance charges and, of course, profit.'

'How do you know Paradise Jewellers are that type?' Ruby's attention was wide-eyed and girlish.

'You recognize them firstly by the big advertising splurge, then by their language.' Again he studied the notices in the window. '"A large selection of blue-white gems" – of every thousand stones of jewellery quality produced only one is fine enough in colour to be termed blue-white. It is unlikely they have a large selection. "Gem" is a special term reserved for a diamond which is in every way superb. "Flawless stones at bargain prices" – the lack of flaws in a diamond is only one of many factors governing its value. As for bargain prices – there ain't no such animal. Prices are maintained at the lowest level by fierce competition among expert and canny dealers, and there are no "sales" or special prices for anyone.'

'But where should a person buy a diamond?' Ruby was impressed and dismayed despite herself.

'Not here.' Benedict chuckled. 'Come, I will show you.' And before she could protest he had taken her arm and swept her into the shop, to be greeted with enthusiasm by the manager who must have noticed Ruby's mink and the attendant Bentley, which was causing a small traffic jam outside the shop.

'Good morning, madam and sir. May I be of service to you?'

'Yes,' Benedict turned to Ruby, as they settled down in the manager's office with a tray of diamond rings in front of them. 'You cannot examine a diamond properly in its setting.'

He selected the biggest diamond, took from his pocket a

gold-plated penknife fitted with a special tool and prised open the claws of the setting to a chorus of horrified squeals from the staff.

'I will make good any damage,' he snapped, and they subsided as Benedict took the loose stone and laid it on the velvet-covered tray.

'Firstly, size. This stone is about one carat.' He looked for confirmation to the manager who nodded. 'Let us say the value of this stone is £500. Ten similar stones will be worth £5,000, right? However, a ten-carat stone may be worth as much as £75,000. So the price per carat rises sharply as the total weight of the stone increases. If I were investing I would not touch a stone under three carats.'

The staff were listening now with as much attention as Ruby.

'Next, colour,' said Benedict, and glanced at the manager. 'A sheet of clean white paper, please.'

The manager scratched in his drawer and laid a sheet of paper in front of Benedict who placed the stone upon it, bottom upwards.

'We compare the colour it "draws" from white paper in good natural light.' He looked up at the manager. 'Switch off the fluorescent lights, and open those curtains, please.'

The manager obeyed with alacrity.

'This is a matter of experience. The colour is judged by a standard. We forget about the fancy rare colours like blue and red and green, and take our top standard as blue-white. A stone so white as to appear slightly blue, after which the distinctions drop to "fine white", and "white". Then stones which "draw" a yellowish tinge which we call "Cape" – in different shades, then finally stones which "draw" a brown colour – which will reduce the value of a stone by up to eighty per cent.'

Benedict fished in his fob pocket and pulled out a guinea case which he opened.

'Every expert carries a special diamond which he uses as

a gauge for colour by which to judge all other stones. This is mine.'

The staff exchanged apprehensive looks as Benedict placed a small diamond beside the other. He studied them a moment then replaced his gauge in the case.

'Second Silver Cape, I'd say,' he grunted, and the staff looked suitably abashed. 'Now we consider the stone's perfection.' He looked at the manager. 'Please lend me your *loupe.*'

'*Loupe?*' The manager was mystified.

'Yes, your jeweller's glass.'

'I—' the manager was deeply embarrassed.

'You sell diamonds – yet you do not own a *loupe.*' Benedict shook his head in disapproval. 'No matter, I have my own.'

Benedict took the glass from his inner pocket and placed it in his eye.

'Imperfections can be almost negligible – a "natural" at the girdle, or a bubble or pinpoint of carbon in the stone, on the other hand they can be gross "cracks", "clouds", "ice", or "feathers" which will ruin the value of the stone. But this one is flawless – so when the certificate of flawlessness is issued there will be no misrepresentation.' Benedict closed the glass and tucked it back into his pocket. 'However, in order to produce a flawless stone, the cut has been squeezed.'

He held up the stone between thumb and forefinger.

'The cut or "make" of a stone is the fourth and final decider of its value. The "make" should conform closely to the "ideal". This stone has been cut to exclude a flaw, and in consequence it is badly proportioned – heavy and out of round. I would prefer to see a graceful stone which includes a slight imperfection rather than a grotesque little cripple like this.'

He put the diamond down on the desk.

'The asking price by Paradise Jewellers for this stone is

£500 – which would be fair and correct for a gem. However, the colour is poor and although it is flawless it is of ungainly make. Its true value would be about – ah, let's see – £185 approximately.'

There was another chorus of protest from the assembled staff, led by the manager.

'I assure you, sir, that all our stones have been most carefully appraised.'

'How long have you been with Paradise Jewellers?' Benedict demanded brusquely. 'Four months, isn't it?'

The manager gaped at him.

'Before that you were a salesman in the showroom of a large firm of embalmers and undertakers.'

'I, well – I mean.' The manager fluttered his hands weakly. 'How did you know that?'

'I like to know about all my employees.'

'Employees?' The manager looked stunned.

'That's correct. My name is Benedict van der Byl. I own Paradise Jewellers.'

Ruby clapped her hands and cooed her applause.

'What a bundle of surprises you are!' she exclaimed.

Benedict smiled in acknowledgement and inclined his head.

'Now,' he said, as he rose and helped Ruby to her feet. 'We will go and buy some real diamonds.'

Aaron Cohen sold them two fine white twin marquise-cut brilliants, and Ruby chose the mounting for a pair of white-gold earrings from a leather-bound catalogue.

Benedict gave Aaron his cheque for twenty thousand pounds, then turned to Ruby.

'Now,' he said. 'We'll have lunch at the Celeste Grill-room. The food is bloody awful – but the decor is stupendous. We had best phone and reserve a table – it isn't really necessary but they get terribly hurt if you don't.'

As they settled back in the lush upholstery of the Bentley, Benedict instructed the chauffeur.

'Go past Trafalgar Square, Edmund. I want to pick up the newspapers from South Africa House.'

Edmund double-parked outside the Ambassador's entrance, and the doorman recognized the car and hurried inside to fetch the bundle of newspapers.

As they pulled away around the square towards Haymarket, Benedict selected a copy of the *Cape Argus*.

'Let's see what's happened at home.' He glanced at the front page, and stiffened perceptibly.

'What is it?' Ruby leaned towards him anxiously, but he ignored her. His eyes were darting across the page like the shuttle of a loom. She saw the colour fade from his face, leaving it white and intent. He finished reading, and pushed the paper towards her. She spread the page.

'VAN DER BYL DIAMONDS WIN VALUABLE CONCESSION.
APPEAL COURT SUPPORTS KAISER'S MINERAL GRANT.
LANCE GETS THUNDERBOLT AND SUICIDE.
Bloemfontein, Thursday.

'In an urgent application by the Central Diamond Mines Ltd, to prevent Van Der Byl Diamonds Ltd prospecting and mining a concession area off the South West African Coast, Mr Justice Tromp today dismissed the application with costs stating in his judgment: "The original concession granted by German Imperial Decree in 1899, and subsequently ratified by Act of the Union Parliament in Act 24 of the 1920 must hold good in law, and will take precedent over any subsequent grant or concession purporting to have been made by the Minister of Mines to any other party."

'The area in dispute covers 100 square kilometres surrounding two small islands lying some fifteen miles south of Cartridge Bay and five miles offshore. The islands are known as Thunderbolt Island and Suicide Island, and at the turn of the century were the site of considerable exploitation by a German guano company. Mr John Rigby Lance, the General Manager of Van Der Byl Diamond Co. Ltd, acquired the rights to the concession when he took over the inoperative guano company.

'In Cape Town today Mr Lance stated: "It's the opportunity I have waited for all my life. All indications are that Thunderbolt and Suicide will prove to be one of the richest marine diamond fields in the world."

'Van Der Byl Diamond Co. had a diamond-dredging vessel nearing completion in the United Kingdom, and Mr Lance stated that he hoped to begin recovery operations off Thunderbolt and Suicide Islands before the end of the year.'

R uby lowered the paper and looked at Benedict. What she saw was an intense physical shock.

Benedict had crumpled down in the seat. Gone was all the assurance and *savoir faire*. His face was deathly pale, but now his lips trembled and with disgust she saw that his eyes were swimming with tears. He hunched forward over his hands, shaking his head gently and hopelessly.

'The bastard,' he whispered, and his voice was soggy and muffled. 'He does it every time. I thought that I had him at last but – Oh God, I hate him.'

He looked at her, his face soft with self-pity. 'He does it every time. Often I've thought I had him, but he just—'

She was mystified by his reaction.

'Aren't you pleased? Van Der Byl Diamonds will make millions—'

'No! No!' he cut in savagely, and then the years of hatred and frustration and humiliation began pouring out. Ruby listened quietly, slowly beginning to understand it all, marvelling at the accumulation of pain and hatred that he exposed for her. He remembered conversations from twenty years ago. Small childhood episodes, innocent remarks that had festered and rankled for a decade.

'You don't want him to succeed, is that it?' she asked.

'I want to crush him, break him, humiliate him.'

For ten seconds Ruby was silent.

'Well, what are we going to do about it?' she asked flatly.

'Nothing, I suppose.' Benedict's tone irritated her. 'He always comes out on top, you just can't—'

'Nonsense,' Ruby snapped. She was angry now. 'Let's go over it carefully, and see how we can stop him. He is only human, and you have shown me enough to prove you are a brilliant and successful businessman.'

Benedict's expression changed, becoming trusting and animated. He turned to her almost eagerly: he blinked his eyes. 'Do you really believe that?'

The bunk was too narrow, Sergio Caporetti decided, much too narrow. He would have one of the carpenters alter it today.

He lay on his back, wedged in firmly, with the blanket-covered mound of his belly blocking his view southwards. He lay and assessed his physical condition. It was surprisingly good. There was but a small blurred pain behind his eyes and the taste of stale cigars and rank wine in the back of his throat was bearable. The leaden feeling in his lower limbs alarmed him until he realized that he was still wearing his heavy fisherman's boots. He remembered one of the girls complaining about that.

He hoisted himself on one elbow, and looked at the girls. One on each side of him, jamming him solidly into the bunk with magnificent hillocks of pink flesh. Big strong girls both of them, he had chosen them with care, neither of them an ounce under twelve stone. Sergio sighed happily – it had been a wonderful weekend. The girls were snoring, in such harmony that it might have been a rehearsed stage act. He listened to them with mild admiration for a few minutes, then crawled over the outside girl and stood in the centre of the cabin, clad only in his heavy boots. He yawned extravagantly, scratching the thick black wiry curls that covered his chest and belly, and cocked an eye at the bulkhead clock. Four o'clock on a Monday morning, but it had been a truly memorable weekend.

The table was hidden under a forest of empty wine bottles, and dirty plates. There was a congealed mass of cold spaghetti bolognaise in a dish and he picked it up. As he clumped out of the cabin on to *Kingfisher*'s bridge he was scooping up spaghetti with his fingers and cramming it into his mouth.

He stood at the rail of the bridge, a naked hairy figure in tall black boots clutching a dish of spaghetti to his chest, and looked around the dockyard.

*Kingfisher* was in stocks undergoing the modifications that Johnny Lance had ordered. She was standing high above the level she would attain when she was launched. Although she was a vessel of a mere 3,000-ton displacement, she appeared black and monstrous in the floodlights that illuminated the ship-builders' yard. It was obvious from her unusual silhouette that she was designed for a special purpose. Her superstructure was situated well aft like that of an oil tanker, while her foredeck was crowded by the huge gantry which would control the dredge, and by the massive storage tanks for the compressed air.

At this hour of the morning the shipyard was deserted, and wisps and tendrils of sea mist drifted about *Kingfisher*'s bulk.

Standing fifty feet above the dry dock, still wolfing cold spaghetti, Sergio urinated over the rail – deriving a simple honest pleasure from the long arching stream and the tinkle of liquid striking the concrete far below.

He clumped back into his cabin, and looked down fondly

on his two sleeping Valkyries while he finished the last of the spaghetti. Then he wiped his fingers carefully on his chest hair and called to them gently.

'Come, my kittens, my little doves, the time for play she has passed – the time for work she commences.'

With Latin gallantry he bundled them into a taxi at the dockyard gates, pressing on to each of them a lusty kiss, a banknote, a bottle of Chianti, protestations of deep affection, and the promise of another party next Friday night.

He picked his way back through the dockyard jungle of machinery and buildings, lighting a long black cigar and inhaling smoke pleasurably until he came in sight of *Kingfisher* and halted with surprise and annoyance. There was a big honey-coloured Bentley parked near the gangway that led up to *Kingfisher*'s deck. He resented visits from the Company bosses, especially this one, and especially at this ridiculous hour on a Monday morning.

T he hose spiralled down into greenness, and they followed it down holding hands. Tracey was still a little nervous. This was not like the Mediterranean, a warm blue friendly embrace of waters to welcome the diver – it was the wild Atlantic, coldly menacing, green and untamed. It frightened her, and Johnny's hand gave her comfort.

Their Draeger demand valves repeated their breathing in a singing metallic wheeze, and icy leaks and rivulets kept finding their way into the cuffs and neck of Tracey's rubber suit.

Sixty feet below the surface Johnny paused, and peered into the glass window of her mask. He grinned at her, his mouth distorted by the bulky mouthpiece, and she gave him a thumbs-up sign. They both looked upwards. The surface was silvered like an imperfect mirror, and the black cigar shape of the boat was lapped in strange light. The hose and anchor chain pierced the silver ceiling and hung down into the shady green depths.

Johnny pointed downwards, and she nodded. They put their heads down, pointed their flippers to the surface, and still hand in hand they paddled steadily towards the sea bed.

Tracey was aware of a crackling hissing sound now, and from out of the greeny blackness below them scudded clouds of silver bubbles twisting and writhing towards the surface. She strained her eyes downwards, following the line of the hose, and slowly out of the murk materialized the black rubber-clad forms of the two men working at the end of the hose; they appeared weird and mystical like black priests performing a satanical mass.

She and Johnny reached the sea bed and hung just above it, a little way off from the two men on the hose. Johnny indicated the depth gauge that he wore like a wrist watch. It showed a depth of 120 feet. Then he turned and by a hand signal showed her the direction of the reefs.

They were in a valley between these long peaked underwater ridges of black rocks, the same reefs that Tracey had seen from the air. There was a distinct pull of water as the current drifted at right angles to the direction of the reefs.

Johnny squeezed her hand, and then pulled her down. They lay on their bellies on the floor of the sea, and Johnny scooped a handful of the white sand, washed it quickly so that the smaller particles were carried away in a cloud on the current, then he showed her the coarse gravel which remained. Again he grinned, and she returned his smile.

Still leading her by the hand, he swam slowly towards the two men working on the hose, and stopped to watch them.

Attached to the end of the hose was a rigid steel pipe two inches in diameter, and twenty feet long – although now only half of its length was visible above the sand bottom. The two divers were forcing it down through sand and gravel to reach bedrock. The hose itself was attached to a compressor on the deck of the boat which was generating a vacuum in the hose and sucking up the sand and gravel as the steel pipe was forced downwards.

They were prospecting the Thunderbolt and Suicide field. Taking these two-inch samples at 500-foot intervals to ascertain the depth of water, the thickness of the overburden, and the content of the gravel beds. They were also mapping and plotting the reefs, so that by the time *Kingfisher* arrived they would have a fairly clear picture of the topography and aspect of the field. They would know where to begin dredging, and roughly what to expect when they did.

So far the results had endorsed Johnny's most optimistic expectations. There was a good thick catchment of gravel in all the gullies between the reefs. As he had expected, the heavier gravels had been laid down in the gullies closest to the gap between Thunderbolt and Suicide, and the smaller and lighter gravels had been carried further. In some of the gullies the gravel beds were fifteen feet deep, and the types of stone present were all highly promising. He had isolated garnet, jasper, ironstone, beryl chips and titanium dust.

However, the conclusive and definite proof had also come up through that two-inch hose out of the depths. They had already pulled the first diamonds from the Thunderbolt and Suicide fields. When you considered the odds against finding a stone in a two-inch sample at 500-foot centres and that payable gravel contained one part diamond in fifty million, it was exciting and encouraging that they had already recovered four diamonds. Small stones, to be sure, not one of them more than half a carat, but diamonds for all that, and some of them of excellent quality.

One of the men on the hose turned and gave Johnny a flat-handed cut-out sign. The pipe was on bedrock. Johnny nodded and jerked a thumb upwards, and drawing Tracey with him, started for the surface.

They climbed the ladder over the survey boat's counter, moving clumsily under the weight of the air bottles strapped to their backs, but there were willing hands to help them aboard and strip off the heavy equipment, and unzip the clinging rubber suits.

Tracey accepted a towel gratefully from one of the crew, and while she tilted her head to dry her sodden mane of hair, she looked across half a mile of green sea to the two white whale-backed islands with their attendant clouds of seabirds. The wave bursts on the cliffs sounded like distant artillery, or far thunder.

'God, this is a wild and exciting place.' Her voice bubbled with excitement as she scrubbed at her hair. 'It makes one come alive.'

Johnny understood her feelings, it was the forbidding restless sea and the harsh land that promised danger and adventure. He was about to reply, but the two hose men came aboard at that moment, the taller of them spitting out his mouthpiece and letting it fall to his chest.

'We'll move up to the next point, if it's okay by you, Mr Lance?' The man pulled off his mask and hood, exposing white-blond hair and a sun-broiled face.

'Fine, Hugo,' Johnny agreed, and watched approvingly as Hugo Kramer gave the orders to get the anchor and the hose up before taking *Wild Goose* seawards to her next prospecting point. Johnny had been reluctant to charter *Wild Goose* as the prospecting vessel and as the service boat for *Kingfisher*. He did not know Hugo Kramer, and Benedict van der Byl's insistence on the man had made him suspicious.

However, it was natural that they should use a skipper from the van der Byl fleet and Johnny was now prepared to admit he had been wrong. Kramer was an intelligent and willing worker, resourceful and trustworthy, a fine seaman who handled *Wild Goose* with all the skill it would need to bring her alongside *Kingfisher* in a heavy sea. His unfortunate physical appearance Johnny hardly noticed any more, although the original shock of that pink face, white hair and those blind-looking eyes had been considerable.

Tracey was not so charitable. The man made her uneasy. There was a wild-animal ferocity about him, a barely controlled violence. The way he looked at her sometimes made her skin prickle. He did it now; turning back from issuing his orders he ran his eyes over her body. In the black silk costume her good round breasts showed at their best, and Hugo Kramer looked at them with those white-fringed bland eyes. Instinctively she covered them with the towel, and it seemed as though his lips twitched with amusement as he turned to Johnny.

'They tell me this dredger of yours is something special, Mr Lance?'

'She is, Hugo. Not like the other half-baked barges and bastardized conversions that have been tried by other companies. She's the first diamond recovery vessel designed expressly for the job.'

'What's different about her?'

'Nearly everything. Her hose is operated off a gantry on the foredeck, it goes out through a well pierced through her hull.'

'What kind of hose?'

'Eighteen-inch armoured woven steel with rubber liner. We can get it down to a hundred fathoms, and it has a compensating section in it to stop it plunging with the wave action of the hull.'

'Eighteen inches is pretty big. How will you build up vacuum?'

'That's the point, Hugo. We don't suck – we blow! We evacuate water from the hose by purging it with compressed air, the inrush of water into the opening of the hose sucks in the gravel.'

'Hey, that's neat. So the deeper you work the more effective it will be!'

'Right.'

'What about the actual recovery? Are you going to have the usual screening, ball mill, and grease table arrangement?'

'That's what killed the other companies – trying to separate by the old methods. No. We've got a cyclone to start with.'

'Cyclone?'

'You know a cream separator?'

'Yeah.'

'Same principle. Just spin the gravel in a circular tank and float off everything with a specific gravity of less than 2.5. Take what is left, dry it, spread it on a conveyor belt and run it under an X-ray machine which pinpoints every single diamond. As you know, diamonds fluoresce under X-rays and they show up crisply. The X-ray machine reports the diamond to the central computer. . . ' Johnny's voice and whole attitude was charged with enthusiasm which was impossible for his listeners to resist. Tracey was carried along with him, watching his eyes and his mouth as he talked, smiling when he smiled, her lips following his faithfully.

'T his is the cyclone room,' Benedict van der Byl explained as, with a hand on her elbow, he helped Ruby Lance down off the last rung of the ladder. 'I explained to you how it worked.'

'Yes.' Ruby nodded, and looked around the room with interest. The roughly riveted and grey painted plating of *Kingfisher*'s hull formed a square metal box, in the centre of which stood the cyclone. It was also painted battleship grey, a ten-foot-high cone-shaped circular tower.

'The gravel is blown in through here.' Benedict indicated the eighteen-inch pipe which entered the cyclone room through the forward bulkhead, then connected to the bottom of the cyclone. 'Up it goes.' Benedict flung his hand upwards. 'And round it goes.' He made a stirring motion. 'The heavy stuff is thrown off and led away through that.' A smaller pipe emerged from the shoulder of the cyclone and disappeared through the farther bulkhead. 'While the lighter stuff shoots out through the top and is sprayed overboard again.'

'I understand. Now, where is the weak spot?' Ruby asked.

'Come.' Benedict led her across the room, picking their way among the litter left by the workmen who still swarmed through *Kingfisher*. They reached a steel door in the bulkhead.

'Watch your head.' They ducked into a long passageway with doors at both ends. On their right hand was an enclosed tunnel that ran the length of the room.

'This is the conveyor room,' Benedict explained. 'The concentrated gravels fall through a hot air draught from an electric furnace to dry them. They are gathered on a conveyor belt, concealed in that tunnel, and carried through into the X-ray room.'

'This is where you will fit it?' Ruby asked.

'Yes. In the conveyor tunnel. It will mean moving that inspection hatch back twelve feet to give us the space.'

Ruby nodded. 'The man who will do the work – can you trust him?'

'Yes. He has worked for me before.' Benedict did not add that the same man had designed the electronic equipment for the balloons used by the Ring, and had flown out from Japan to convert the ASDIC equipment on *Wild Goose*.

'All right.' Ruby seemed satisfied. More and more she was becoming the driving force in the alliance, bolstering

Benedict's resolution when he showed timidity or when he tried to evade the actions which must, in time, lead to a confrontation with Johnny Lance.

'Let's see the X-ray room.'

It was a tiny cupboard-like compartment. The floor, roof and all four walls were clad with thick sheet lead. Suspended from the roof was the X-ray machine, and under it a circular table the surface of which was covered with a honeycomb-patterned stainless steel sheet.

'The concentrated gravel spills on to the table, and the table revolves under the X-ray machine which fluoresces each diamond and the computer picks it up and reports its size and exact position on the table. The computer then commands one of those – ' Benedict pointed to a forest of hard plastic tubes, each attached to a metal arm, ' – to swing out over the table exactly above the diamond and suck it up. The computer selects the correct diameter of tube for the size of the diamond – and, after the tube has obeyed the computer, the table passes under a second X-ray machine which confirms that the diamond has been collected. If, by chance, the tube fails to suck up the stone, then the computer automatically sends the table on another circuit. If, however, the diamond is safely gathered then the waste material is scraped from the table and it swings round to pick up more gravel from the cyclone room – and repeat the whole process. The system is 100 per cent effective. Every single diamond is recovered by it. Even stones as small as sugar grains.'

'Where is the computer?' Ruby asked.

'There.' Benedict pointed through the small leaded glass window which overlooked the X-ray table. Beyond it was another small compartment. Ruby flattened her nose against the glass, and peered in. The computer occupied most of the room, a huge glossy enamelled cabinet not unlike a refrigerator despite the switches and dials. Benedict peered in beside her.

'The computer runs the entire operation. It controls the flow of compressed air into the dredger pipe, it regulates the cyclone, runs the X-ray machine and the table, it weighs and counts the diamonds recovered before depositing them in a safe, and it even navigates the *Kingfisher* and reports to the bridge her exact position over the sea bed, it checks the lubrication and temperature of the engines and power plant and on request will make a complete and immediate report of the whole or any part of the operation.'

Ruby was still peering into the computer room.

'What happens to the diamonds once they have been picked off the revolving table?' she asked.

'They are sucked through an electronic scale which weighs each stone, then they are carried through into the computer room and deposited in that safe.' Benedict pointed out the steel door set in the bulkhead. 'The safe has a time and combination lock. So the system works without a diamond being touched by human hand.'

'Let's go and talk to the Italian peasant,' suggested Ruby, and as she turned from the window Benedict slipped his arm about her shoulders and hugged her possessively.

'Not now,' snapped Ruby irritably, shrugging off his arm, and she led the way out of the X-ray compartment, passing the locked door of the computer control room opposite the door to the conveyor room. She was impressed with the ingenuity of the system – but the fact that it had been constructed by Johnny Lance made her angry.

Her loyalties had changed completely, going to the highest bidder.

Sergio Caporetti felt a small twinge of pity when he looked at Ruby Lance. So thin, and with a backside like a boy. She would be little comfort to a man on a cold night. Sergio worked the cheroot from one corner of his mouth to other, anointing the stub with saliva in the process. Also she was cold-blooded, he decided. Sergio had a very sensitive intuition when it came to judging the temperature of a woman's passion. Cold like a snake, he decided, his pity giving way to revulsion. He repressed a small shudder as he watched her settle on to the day couch in his cabin, and cross her long golden legs precisely. Just like a snake, she would eat a man as though he were a little hopping frog. Sergio had admiration for Johnny Lance, but – he decided – not even he would be safe with a woman like this.

'You like my ship?' he asked, an attempt at friendliness. 'She is *very* fine ship.'

Sergio actually used a more forceful adjective than *very*, one that suggested *Kingfisher* was capable of procreation, and Ruby's lips curled with disgust. She ignored the question and lit a cigarette, swinging one leg impatiently, and turned her head to stare through the porthole.

Sergio was hurt by the rebuff, but he had no time to brood on it for Benedict van der Byl came to stand in the centre of the cabin with his hands clasped lightly behind his back.

'Mr Caporetti—' he asked quietly. 'How much do you like money?'

Sergio grinned, and pushed the grubby maritime cap to the back of his head. 'I like it pretty good, I like it better than mother – and I love my mother like my life,' he said.

'Would you like to become a rich man?' Benedict asked, and Sergio sighed wistfully.

'*Si!*' he nodded. 'But it is the impossible thing. There is too much *vino*, too much lovely girls, and the cards they are cruel like – ' Sergio paused to find a suitable simile and glanced at Ruby, ' – like a thin woman. No. Money she does not stay long, she comes and she goes.'

'What would you do for £25,000?' Benedict asked.

'For twenty-five thousand – ' Sergio's eyes were dark liquid and lovely as those of a dying gazelle or a woman in love, ' – there is nothing I will not do.'

K*ingfisher* sailed for Africa on the 4th of October. As the representative of the owners, Benedict van der Byl drove down from London to bid her *bon voyage*, and he spent an hour behind locked doors with Sergio Caporetti before the departure of the vessel.

*Kingfisher* made good time southwards on her first leg of the voyage, but the unscheduled delay of ten days at the island of Las Palmas infuriated Johnny. His urgently cabled enquiries from Cape Town elicited the reply that there were teething troubles in *Kingfisher*'s engine room which were being attended to in the Las Palmas dockyards. The voyage would be resumed as soon as the repairs had been effected.

The Japanese gentleman who welcomed *Kingfisher* to Las Palmas was named Kaminikoto. This was too much for Sergio's tongue, so he called him 'Kammy'.

Sergio's crew was sent ashore with the excuse that the work on *Kingfisher* was dangerous. They were installed in the best tourist hotel and liberally supplied with intoxicating liquor. Sergio did not see them for the next ten days that he and Kammy were busy on the modifications to *Kingfisher*'s computer, and recovery equipment.

During those ten days Sergio and Kammy discovered that despite physical appearances they were brothers.

Kammy had mysterious packing-cases brought on board and they worked like furies from dawn until after dark each day. Then they relaxed.

Kammy was half Sergio's size with a face like a mischievous monkey. At all times he wore a Homburg hat. On the one occasion that Sergio saw him in his bath without his headgear he discovered that Kammy was as bald as St Peter's dome.

Kammy's abundant tastes in women were identical to Sergio's. This made the hiring of partners an easy matter, for what suited the one suited the other. Sergio took south with him fond memories of the little Japanese clad only in his Homburg hat, uttering bird-like cries of encouragement and excitement, while perched like a jockey on top of a percheron mare.

When at last Sergio shepherded his debauched crew back aboard *Kingfisher* the only obvious sign of their labours was that the inspection hatch on the conveyor tunnel had been moved back twelve feet.

'It is my best work,' Kammy told Sergio. Already he was sad at the prospect of parting. They were brothers. 'I signed my name. You will remember me when you see it.'

'You good guy, Kammy. The best!' Sergio embraced him, lifting him off his feet and kissing him heartily on each cheek while Kammy clutched desperately at his Homburg.

They left him standing on the wharf, a forlorn and solitary figure, while *Kingfisher* butted out into the Atlantic and swung away southwards.

Ruefully Johnny Lance glanced over at the mountain of empty champagne bottles beyond the barbecue pits. The bill for this little party would be in the thousands, but it was not an extravagance. The guest list included all Van Der Byl Diamond Company's major creditors and their wives. Johnny Lance was showing them all what they were getting for their money. To appear prosperous was almost as reassuring to a creditor as being prosperous. He was going to stuff them full of food and champagne, show them over the *Kingfisher* and fly them back home, hoping sincerely that they would be sufficiently impressed to stop badgering him for a while – and let him get on with the business of taking the Company out into the clear.

Tracey caught his eye. Her humorous roll of the eyes was a plea for sympathy, for she was surrounded by a pack of middle-aged bankers and financiers whom champagne had made susceptible to her charms. Johnny winked at her in reply, then glanced around guiltily to find Ruby, and was relieved that she was in deep conversation with Benedict van der Byl in a far corner of the marquee.

He made his way out of the crowd to the edge of the dune, and lit a cigarette while he looked back across Cartridge Bay.

The chartered Dakotas that had flown the guests and caterers up from Cape Town were standing on the airstrip beyond the buildings.

The marquee was situated on the crest of a sand dune overlooking the narrow entrance to the bay. The dune had been bulldozed to accommodate the tent, the laden tables, and the barbecue pits around which white-clad servants were busy, and the spitted carcasses of three sheep and a young ox were already browning crisply and emitting a cloud of fragrant steam.

Tracey watched Johnny standing out on the edge of the dune. He looked tired, she thought. The strain of the last few months had worn him down. Looking back on it now she realized that every few days had thrust a crisis upon him. The terrible worry of the court case that had won them Thunderbolt and Suicide had barely ended before Johnny had faced the delays in the construction of *Kingfisher*, the bullying of creditors, the sniping of Benedict and a hundred other worries and frustrations.

He was like a prize-fighter coming out to the bell of the last round, she thought tenderly, as she studied the profile of his face now staring out to sea. His stance was still aggressive, the big jaw pushed out and the hand with the missing finger that held the cigarette balled into a fist, but there were blue shadows under his eyes and lines of tension at the corners of his mouth.

Suddenly, there was an alertness in Johnny's attitude, he shaded his eyes with a hand before turning back towards the marquee.

'All right, everyone!' he called, stilling the babble of their voices. 'Here she comes.'

Immediately the uproar was redoubled and the whole party trooped out into the sunlight, their excitement and the shrillness of their voices enhanced by the Pommery they had been walloping back since mid-morning.

'Look! There she is!'

'Where? Where?'

'I can't see her.'

'Just to the left of that cloud on the horizon.'

'Oh yes! Look! Look!'

Tracey took a second glass of champagne from one of the waiters, and carried it across to Johnny.

'Thanks.' He smiled at her with the ease that now existed between them.

'It's taken her long enough to get here.' Tracey picked out the faraway speck on the green ocean that was *Kingfisher*. 'When will she begin working?'

'Tomorrow.'

'How long will it be before we know – well, if it has come off?'

'A week.' Johnny turned to her. 'A week to be certain, but we'll know in a day or two how it's shaping up.'

They were silent then, staring out at the gradually approaching speck. The crowd lost interest quickly and drifted back to the liquor, and the fragrant steaming platters of golden-brown meat that were coming from the barbecue pits.

Tracey broke the long friendly silence at last. She spoke hesitantly, as though reluctant to bring up a painful subject.

'How long has Ruby been back now – ten days?'

'About that,' Johnny agreed, glancing at her quickly. 'I haven't seen much of her,' he admitted. 'But she seems to be a lot more relaxed – and at least she's kept off my back.'

'She and Benedict seem to have become very pally.' Tracey glanced across to where the other couple were now included in a boisterous circle of revellers.

'She bumped into him in London,' Johnny agreed, sounding offhand. 'She tells me they had lunch a couple of times.'

She waited for him to continue, to express some suspicion or reservation, but he seemed to have no further interest in the subject; instead he began running over the day's further arrangements with her.

'I'm relying on you to take charge of the wives when we go aboard. Keep an eye on Mrs Larsen particularly – she's up to her gills in bubbly.'

For the next two hours that it took *Kingfisher* to make her approach and enter the channel of Cartridge Bay, Johnny hardly took his eyes from her unusual silhouette. She was not a pretty vessel but the white lightning insignia of Van Der Byl Diamonds on her funnel gave her a special beauty in his eyes. As she passed below them and entered the bay, Larsen proposed a toast to her successful career, then they all descended the dune and climbed into the waiting Land-Rovers and drove round the bay to meet her. By the time they arrived *Kingfisher* had made fast alongside the jetty, and Captain Sergio Caporetti was waiting to welcome them aboard.

He stood at the head of the gangway, and sensible to the importance of the moment he was decked in his finest and best; a double-breasted suit with a cream and lilac pinstripe set off the tomato-red silk tie, but his two-tone black and white crocodile skin shoes drew attention to his large feet and his gait was that of an emperor penguin. A liberal application of a hair pomade with a penetrating smell of violets had flattened his black hair into a shiny slick, bisected by the ruler-straight line of white scalp which was his parting. However, the aroma of the pomade was at odds with the particularly stinky cheroot of a brand which Sergio reserved for weddings, funerals and other special occasions.

His beautiful gazelle eyes became passionate and dark as they lit on Fifi Larsen. Mrs Larsen's tight-fitting slacks moved as though they were full of live rabbits and her pink sweater was straining its seams. Her eyes were sparkling with champagne and she giggled without apparent reason, flushing under Sergio's scrutiny.

The tour of *Kingfisher* began, Sergio Caporetti taking up an escort position directly behind Mrs Larsen. They had hardly descended the first ladder when Mrs Larsen let out a small squeak and shot about eighteen inches into the air, before coming back to earth with all her plentiful woman-hood aquiver.

'My dear Fifi, whatever is wrong?' Her husband was all solicitude, while behind her Sergio Caporetti wore an expression of cherubic innocence. Johnny felt dizzy with alarm, for he had seen Sergio's great hairy paw settling comfortably on to those majestic buttocks. Mrs Fifi Larsen had been thoroughly goosed.

In relieved disbelief Johnny heard her reply, which was preceded by another giggle.

'I seem to have twisted my ankle. Perhaps there is somewhere I could sit down.'

Johnny looked around frantically for Tracey to get Mrs Larsen out of Sergio's clutching range, but before he could signal her, Fifi was limping away on Sergio Caporetti's arm, bravely declining all offers of help.

'Please don't let me spoil your fun. I'll just sit in the Captain's cabin for a few minutes.'

Quickly Johnny moved up beside the silver-haired Larsen

and resolved to stay close beside him. Even if he could not prevent Fifi visiting Sergio's quarters, he was going to make good and sure that the husband didn't join the party.

'This is the explosives locker.' Johnny took Larsen's arm and led him away. 'We keep a store of plastic explosives for underwater blasting—'

Larsen's concern at his wife's injury dissolved and he became immersed in the tour of *Kingfisher*. Johnny followed the line of production for him from the moment the gravel was sucked in through the dredge.

As they left the cyclone room Johnny preceded him, holding the steel door open for Larsen.

'From the cyclone the concentrates pass through here into—' He stopped with surprise as they entered the narrow compartment beyond the cyclone.

'What's wrong, Lance?' Larsen demanded.

'No. It's nothing,' Johnny assured him. After the surprise of finding that the inspection plate in the conveyor tunnel had been moved he realized that it was as well from a security angle. Probably the marine architects had ordered the modification. 'The concentrates are carried through into the next compartment to the X-ray room. This way, please.'

As Johnny led the way to the next door he resolved to check with the architects. Larsen asked a question and he replied and the conveyor tunnel was forgotten. They went through into the X-ray room.

'He noticed it.' Benedict puffed quickly and nervously at the cigarette cupped in his hand. 'He doesn't miss a thing. The bastard.'

'He noticed it, yes. But he accepted it.' Ruby was definite. 'I know him. I was watching him. He was disturbed for a second then he rationalized it. I could almost see his mind work. He accepted it.'

They stood together on the exposed angle of *Kingfisher*'s bridge. Suddenly Ruby laughed.

'Don't look so worried,' she warned him merrily. 'We are being watched by your sister again. She's down on the foredeck. Come.'

Still smiling she led him around the angle of the bridge house, and out of sight she was immediately deadly serious again.

'That sister of yours is getting suspicious. We must keep away from each other until you tell Johnny.'

Benedict nodded.

'When are you going to tell him?' she demanded.

'Soon.'

'How soon?' Ruby would not be able to rest until it was out in the open, until Benedict had committed himself, yet she must not push him too hard.

'As soon as *Kingfisher* runs the Company under. I will pick the moment that he is beaten financially, then I will tell him. I want it to be the *coup de grâce*.'

'When will it be, Benedict darling? I am so anxious to be with you – without all this subterfuge.'

Benedict opened his mouth to reply and froze like that, his expression changing slowly into that of a man who doubts the evidence of his own eyes. He was staring over Ruby's shoulder.

Ruby turned quickly. The curtain across the Captain's porthole behind her was open a chink. She looked in upon a spectacle of such whole-hearted rubicund magnitude that it should have occurred only to Olympus between Jupiter and Juno.

In the cabin Fifi Larsen was receiving treatment for her sprained ankle.

'Well, you've got your toy now. Let's hope for all our sakes you can do something with it,' Benedict smiled pleasantly as he came across to where Johnny stood with Larsen under the great gallows-shaped gantry on the foredeck of *Kingfisher* that would raise and lower the dredging head.

'Toy, Mr van der Byl?' Larsen's white eyebrows bristled. 'Surely you have no doubts? I mean, now that you've got this Thunderbolt and Suicide concession?'

'Oh, I wouldn't say doubts, Mr Larsen. Reservations perhaps, but not really doubts. Mr Lance has been the champion of this venture. His enthusiasm has carried it – in the face of all opposition. Even that of my late father.' Benedict turned to Larsen smoothly.

'Your father opposed the scheme? I didn't know that!' Larsen was perturbed.

'Not opposed it, Mr Larsen.' Benedict smiled reassuringly. 'Not really opposed it. But you will notice that he was prepared to risk your money – not his own. That will give you some idea of how he felt.'

There was a chilled silence, before Larsen turned to Johnny.

'Well, Lance, thank you for an interesting day. Very interesting. I'll be watching your progress with attention – close attention.' And he turned away and strode to where a subdued and demure Fifi was waiting with a group of the other wives.

'Thanks.' Johnny gave Benedict a bleak grin.

'Don't mention it.' Benedict smiled that charming boyish smile.

'At the end of this week I'll take that little speech of yours, roll it into a ball and ram it down your throat,' Johnny promised him softly, and Benedict's expression changed. His eyes slitted and his grin showed his teeth and tightened the soft line of his jaw.

'You're pretty slick with your mouth, Lance.'

They glared at each other, the antagonism so apparent, as elemental as a pair of rutting stags, that they were suddenly the centre of all attention. The guests stared curiously, aware of the drama but not understanding it.

Ruby started forward quickly to intervene, taking Johnny's elbow, her voice sugary.

'Oh, Benedict, do you mind if I talk to Johnny a moment? I have to know if he's returning to Cape Town with me this evening.'

She led him away, and the tension dissolved. The disappointed guests began drifting to the gangplank and filing down on to the jetty.

In the confusion of embarkation aboard the two Dakotas, Johnny managed to exchange a last word with Tracey.

'You'll stay here until you know?' she asked. He nodded.

'Good luck, Johnny. I'll pray for you,' she whispered, then followed Ruby Lance up into the fuselage of the Dakota.

Johnny watched the two big aircraft taxi down to the end of the strip, turn in succession and roar away into the purple and red sky of evening.

After they had gone it was very still, and the silence of the desert was complete. Johnny sat in the open Land-Rover and smoked a cigarette while the night came down around him.

He was uneasy, aware of a deep-down tickle of apprehension and foreboding which he could not pin down.

The last glow of sunset faded from the western sky, and the desert stars were bright and hard and close to the earth, silvering the dome of space with the splendour that the city-dweller would never guess at.

Still Johnny hunched in the seat of the open Land-Rover trying to explore the source of his uneasiness, but with so little success that at last he must attribute it to the strain and fatigue of the last few months, his involvement with Tracey, his steadily worsening relationship with Ruby – and the latest clash with Benedict.

He flicked the stub of his cigarette away, watching morosely the explosion of red sparks as it struck the earth, then he started the Land-Rover and drove slowly down towards the jetty.

*Kingfisher*'s lights were smeared in paths of yellow and silver across the still waters of the bay. Every porthole was lit brightly, giving her the festive air of a cruise ship.

Johnny left the Land-Rover at the head of the jetty, and walked out to her. The muted throb of her engines cheered him a little, the knowledge that the vessel was preparing for the morrow.

On deck he paused beside the gigantic compressed air tanks, each the size of a steam locomotive, and checked the pressure gauges. The needles were moving perceptibly around the dials, and his mood lightened a little.

He went up the ladder to the bridge, and into the chart-room where Sergio and Hugo were drinking coffee.

'Not my fault, Mr Lance,' Sergio began defensively. 'I am a gentleman – I cannot refuse a lady.'

'You'll dig your own grave with that spade of yours one day,' Johnny warned him grimly, as he went to the chart table and hung over it.

'Now let's get cracking.' Johnny's sense of dread lifted completely as he looked down at the large-scale Admiralty chart. The twin humps of Thunderbolt and Suicide were clearly marked. 'Hugo, have you got the prospecting schedules?'

'There, on the table.' Hugo and Sergio came to stand on each side of Johnny while he opened the bound file of typewritten sheets.

'The soundings we made differ from the Admiralty chart. We'll put in our figures, before we plot the dredging pattern.'

The three of them settled over the chart with dividers

and parallels to begin marking in the path that *Kingfisher* would follow through the maze of reefs and gullies.

It was long after midnight before Johnny made his way wearily to the guest cabin below the bridge. He kicked off his shoes, lay on the bunk to rest a moment before undressing and fell into a deathlike sleep of exhaustion.

He was awakened by one of the crew with a mug of coffee and he pulled on a windbreaker before hurrying on to the bridge.

*Kingfisher* was just passing out through the channel of Cartridge Bay into the open sea, and Sergio grinned at him from where he stood beside the helm.

Dawn was only a lemon-coloured promise over the desert behind them, and the sea was black as washed anthracite, kicked into a chop by the small morning wind. They stood on the darkened bridge and sipped steaming coffee, cupping their hands around the enamel mugs.

Then they turned and ran south, parallel to the desert which was now touched with hot orange and violet. The seabirds were up, a flight of malgas turned to glowing darts of fire by the early sun as they winged swiftly across the bows.

With a dramatic suddenness the sun came up over the horizon, and highlighted the chalk-white cliffs of Thunderbolt and Suicide far ahead so that they shone like beacons on the cold green sea. The curtains of spray that burst on the islands flashed and faded as they shot into the sky and fell again.

*Wild Goose* was waiting for them lying under the lee of the islands, but she came out to meet them, staggering and plunging theatrically over the short uneasy sea that hooked around the islands or boiled through the gap between them.

The radio telephone began crackling and squawking as the sighting reports from Johnny's watchtowers on the shore started coming in, cross-referencing to give *Kingfisher* her position over the ground. There were short exchanges between Sergio and Hugo on *Wild Goose* as they came together, and the little trawler worked in close, ready to give assistance with the laying of the cables if she were needed.

But standing in the angle of the bridge, Sergio Caporetti had the situation under his control. The grubby marine cap pushed to the back of his head and a long black cheroot stuck in the side of his mouth, he stood balanced on the balls of his feet, his eyes darting from judging the set of the sea surf to the repeater of the computer which was feeding him his soundings and position – yet attentive to the R/T reports from shore and from *Wild Goose*.

Johnny was contented with his choice of man as he watched Sergio at work. *Kingfisher* crept slowly up into the lee of Suicide Island, half a mile from the pearly white cliffs, then she hung there a moment before Sergio punched one of the buttons on her control panel.

From forward there was the harsh metallic roar of an anchor cable running out, and as *Kingfisher* backed away leaving a yellow-painted buoy the size of a barrage balloon bobbing under the cliffs of Suicide so one of the massive deck winches began automatically paying out its six-inch steel cable.

*Kingfisher* backed and crept forward, drifted down on the current or butted up against it while she went through the laborious but delicate operation of laying her four anchors at each point of the compass. Chained above each anchor floated the huge yellow buoys, and from each buoy the steel cables led to the winches on *Kingfisher*'s deck. On instructions from the computer the winches on each quarter would pay out or reel in the cable to hold *Kingfisher* steady over the ground while she worked.

It was mid-afternoon before *Kingfisher* was ready, pinned down like an insect to a board, and the computer reported that she was directly over the gully that Johnny had selected as the starting point. She had twenty-five fathoms of water under her – and then the thick bank of gravel.

'All is ready.' Sergio turned to Johnny, who had stood by quietly all this time – not interfering in the task of positioning. 'You will begin the programme now?'

'Yes.' Johnny stirred himself.

'I would like to watch,' Sergio suggested, and Johnny nodded.

'All right, come.' Sergio handed over the bridge to the helmsman and they went down to the armoured door of the computer room.

Johnny opened the lock. There were only two keys to this compartment. Johnny had one and Benedict van der Byl had the other. He had insisted on having the duplicate, and Johnny had reluctantly agreed not knowing that the key would be used in Las Palmas.

The heavy steel door swung back, and Johnny stepped over the coaming and seated himself before the console of the computer. Covered in cellophane and suspended on a clip above the keyboard of the computer were the cards containing the various programme codes.

Johnny selected the sheet headed: PRIMARY OPERATION: DREDGING AND RECOVERY, and began feeding the code into the computer, punching it on the keyboard.

'Beta, stroke, oh, oh, seven, alpha.'

And within the enamelled console, a change of sound heralded the beginning of the new programme, the hum of her reels and the click of the selectors, while on her control panel the lights blinked and flashed.

Now the computer's screen began to answer the instruction, spelling out her response like a typewriter.

'New programme.'
'Primary Operation. Dredging and Recovery.'
'Phase One.'

'Initiate safety procedure:—
a) Report air pressure . . . 1
b) Report air pressure . . . 2'

Johnny leaned back in the padded stool and watched the exhaustive check that the computer now made of *Kingfisher's* equipment, typing out the results on the screen.

'What she do now?' Sergio asked curiously, as though he had never spent ten days in this compartment assisting his Japanese friend. Johnny explained the procedure briefly.

'How come you know this so good?' Sergio enquired.

'I spent a month at the Computer Company's head office in America last year while they designed this machine.'

'You the only one in the Company who can work it?'

'Mr Benedict van der Byl has done the course as well as I.' Johnny told him, then he leaned forward again. 'Now she is set.'

The screen on the computer reported itself satisfied.

'Phase One Completed.
Initiate Phase Two.
Lowering and siting of dredge head.'

Johnny stood up. 'Okay, let's get upstairs.'

He locked the door of the computer room and followed Sergio up to the bridge.

Johnny went to stand beside the repeater screen on the bridge, which was relaying the computer's signals exactly as they were printed on the main screen in the compartment below. He could see out through the windows of the wheelhouse, and he watched the automatic response of the heavy equipment on the foredeck.

The gantry swung forward, and the steel arms picked the dredge head from its chocks, and lifted it with the armoured suction hose dangling behind it. Then the gantry swung back, and with a jerky mechanical movement lowered the head through the square opening in the deck. This well pierced the hull, and through it the hose began to snake – a monstrous black python sliding into its hole. The huge reels that held the hose revolved smoothly, as the dredge was lowered to the sea bed.

'Head on bottom.'

The computer screen reported, and the hose reels stopped abruptly.

'Phase Two Completed.
Initiate Phase Three.
Cyclone Revolutions 300.
Vent dredge pump.'

There was a rising high-pitched whine now, like the approach of a jet aircraft. The sound reached a peak, and steadied – and immediately another sound overlaid it. The dull roar of high-pressure air through water, a sound of such power and excitement that Johnny felt the hair on his forearms prickle erect. He stood still as a statue, his expression rapt and his lips set in a small secret smile. That sound was the culmination of two years of planning and endeavour, the sweet reward of the driving dedication that had made a dream into reality.

Suddenly he wished that Tracey was with him to share this moment, and then he knew instinctively that she had deliberately left him alone to savour his moment of triumph.

He grinned then, as he watched the thick black hose engorge and pulse with internal life, like a great artery – pumping, pumping, pumping.

In his imagination Johnny could see the rich porridgy mixture of sea water and mud and gravel that shot up the hose into the spinning cyclone, he could imagine the steel head on the sea bed below the hull surging rhythmically to stir the sand and pound loose any gravel that pressure had welded into a conglomerate.

From the waste pipe over *Kingfisher*'s stern poured a solid steam of dirty yellow water mixed with the sand and gravel that had been rejected and spun out of the cyclone. It stained the green sea with a cloudy fecal discharge, like the effluent from a sewage outlet.

For three days and two nights *Kingfisher*'s pumps roared, and she inched forward along the marine gully like a fussy housewife vacuuming every speck of dust from her floor. As the third evening spread its dark cloak over her, Johnny Lance sat on the padded seat in front of the computer console. He sat forward on the stool with his elbows on his knees and his face in his hands for a full hour. He sat like that in the attitude of despair.

When he lifted his head, his face was haggard and the lines of defeat were clearly cut into his features with the cold chisel of failure.

From the meagre recovery of small diamonds that *Kingfisher* had made in the last three days it was clear beyond reasonable doubt that despite all the indications the Thunderbolt and Suicide field would not support the running costs of the vessel, let alone cover the overheads, or the interest charges and capital repayments on the loan account.

Van Der Byl Diamond Company was finished – and Johnny Lance was financially ruined beyond any possibility of ever finding redemption.

It remained only for the jackals to assemble and squabble over the carcass.

Sergio Caporetti leaned over the railing of the bridge, blowing long streamers of blue cheroot smoke from mouth and nostrils to help foul a morning which was already thick and grey with sea-fret. The islands of Thunderbolt and Suicide were blanketed by the mist, but the surf broke against their hidden cliffs like distant artillery and the seabirds' voices were plaintive and small lost souls in the void.

*Wild Goose* came bustling up out of the mist, swinging in under *Kingfisher*'s side to hover there under power with two of her crew fending off.

Hugo Kramer stuck his white blond head out of the wheelhouse window, and shouted up at the deck.

'Okay, boss. Come on!'

Sergio watched the tall figure on *Kingfisher*'s deck rouse and look around like a man waking from sleep. Johnny Lance lifted his head and looked up at the bridge, and Sergio noticed that he was unshaven, a new beard darkened his jaw and emphasized its prominence. He looked as though he had not slept, and he hunched into the windbreaker with the collar turned up against the mist. He did not smile, but lifted one hand in farewell salute to Sergio – who noticed incongruously that the index finger was missing from the hand. Somehow, that pathetic little detail struck Sergio. He was sorry, truly sorry. But there is always a loser in every game, and twenty-five thousand pounds is a lot of money.

'Good luck, Johnny.'

'Thanks, Sergio.' Johnny went to the rail lugging his briefcase and swung over it; he dropped swiftly down the steel rungs set in *Kingfisher*'s hull and jumped the narrow gap of surging water to *Wild Goose*'s deck.

The trawler's engine bellowed, and she pulled away, rounding on to a course for Cartridge Bay. Johnny Lance stood on her open deck looking back at *Kingfisher*.

'He's a good guy.' Sergio shook his head with regret.

'He's a boss,' the helmsman grunted. 'No boss is any good.'

'Hey, you! I am also a boss,' Sergio challenged him.

'Like I said.' The helmsman suppressed a grin.

'I kiss your mother,' Sergio insulted him with dignity, then changed the subject. 'I go below now, take over.'

Sergio opened the door to the control room with the duplicate key. He closed the door behind him, seated himself at the console and took from his pocket a sheet of paper headed: KAMINIKOTO SECONDARY RECOVERY PROGRAMME.

Ten minutes later he came out of the control room and locked the door.

'Kammy, I love you,' he chuckled as he closed off the watertight doors that isolated this deck from the one above. He wound the locking bars into position to ensure that he was not interrupted by one of his own crew.

From the tool cupboard on the bulkhead he selected a pair of set spanners and went through into the conveyor room. It took him twenty minutes to unscrew the heavy, deeply threaded bolts that secured the hatch. It had been designed to resist easy entry – a deterrent to casual investigation, but at last Sergio could lift the steel plate off its seating.

He eyed the small square opening with distaste, and reflexively sucked in his pendulous belly. The hatch had not been designed to afford passage to a man of his dimensions.

He took off his cap and jacket and hung them on the cock of one of the pipes, then he ground out his cheroot under his heel and brushed back the hair from his forehead with both hands, checked that his flashlight was in his pocket, and committed himself to the hatch.

He wriggled and kicked, and grunted and built up a heavy sweat for five minutes before he had squeezed through into the conveyor belt tunnel. He squatted on his haunches, panting heavily and flashed his torch along the tunnel. Above his head the conveyor belt carrying the gravel ran smoothly, but the residual heat from the driers made it unbearably hot. He began to crawl rapidly to the end of the tunnel.

From the inside it was impossible to tell, without measuring, that the conveyor belt tunnel was shorter by twelve feet than the external length.

The end of the tunnel was false, and beyond it was a secret cubicle only just large enough to house Kaminikoto's equipment through which all the gravel passed on its journey to the X-ray room.

The Japanese genius for miniaturization was demonstrated by the equipment in this secret cubicle. It was an almost exact copy of the sorting equipment in the main X-ray compartment – except that it had been scaled down to one tenth of the size without affecting its efficiency; in addition, this miniature plant could discriminate in the diamonds it selected. It would not allow a stone over four carats to pass through, and it screened out fixed percentages of the smaller stones – allowing only a proportion of the smaller and less valuable diamonds to proceed through into the main X-ray room.

It was an amazing piece of electronic engineering, but Sergio was unimpressed as he lay on his side in the cramped hot tunnel and began laboriously to unscrew another smaller plate in the false bulkhead.

At last it was open, and he reached through the opening; after a few seconds of fiddling and groping and heavy breathing he brought out a stainless steel cup with a capacity of about two pints. There were clamps on the cup to hold it in position below the chute under Kaminikoto's machine.

The metal cup was heavy, and Sergio placed it carefully on the deck beside him before propping himself on an elbow and shining the flashlight into the cup and took something out of it, stared at it a moment then dropped it back.

'By the blood of all the martyrs!' he gasped with shock, and then immediately contrite for his blasphemy he crossed himself awkwardly with the hand holding the flashlight. Then again he shone the torch into the cup, and shook his head in disbelief. Quickly he pulled a canvas drawstring bag from his pocket, and lying on his side he carefully poured the contents of the cup into the bag, drew the string tight and stuffed it back into his pocket where it made a big hard bulge on his hip like a paper sack of rock-candy. He clamped the stainless steel cup back into position, screwed the coverplate over the opening, and backed away down the tunnel on hands and knees.

He very badly needed a cheroot.

Four hours later Hugo Kramer shinned up the ladder on to *Kingfisher*'s deck while his helmsman took the trawler down to leeward to wait for him.

Sergio shouted down from the bridge.

'Johnny he has gone?'

'*Ja!*' Hugo shouted back. 'He should almost be in Cape Town by now. That Beechcraft is a fast plane.'

'Good.'

'How did it go with you?' Hugo countered.

'Come up – I'll show you.'

Sergio led him into his cabin behind the bridge and locked the door carefully. Then he went to each of the portholes and drew the curtains across them, before crossing to his desk and switching on the reading lamp.

'Sit down.' Sergio indicated the chair opposite the desk. 'You want a drink, or something?'

'Come on,' Hugo grated impatiently. 'Stop mucking around, let's have a look.'

'Ah!' Sergio looked at him sadly. 'You Germans, you are always too much hurry. You cannot rest, enjoy life—'

'Cut the crap!' Hugo's pale eyes were on his face, and Sergio was suddenly aware that this man was dangerous, like a tiger-shark. Coldly dangerous, without malice or passion. Sergio was surprised he had not noticed it before. I must be careful with this one, he thought, and he unlocked the drawer of his desk and took out the canvas bag.

He loosened the drawstring and poured the diamonds on to the blotter. The smallest was the size of a match head – perhaps point one of a carat, and the poorest quality was black and granular-looking, ugly little industrial stones, for Kammy had been careful not to take out only the best and so distort the *Kingfisher*'s recovery as to arouse suspicion. There were hundreds of these tiny crystals and chips which would fetch a few pounds in the industrial market; but there were other stones in the full range of quality and shapes and sizes – as big as green peas, or as marbles, and a few bigger than that. Some of them were perfect octahedron crystals, others water-worn, chipped or amorphous in shape.

They formed a dully glittering pile in the centre of the blotter, in all perhaps five hundred diamonds, yet all of these were dwarfed by one single stone that lay in the centre of the pile, rising out of it the way Mount Everest rises from her foothills.

There are freak diamonds so large or unusual that they become legend. Diamonds who have their own names and whose histories are recorded and invested with romance. The great 'paragons' – stones of the first water whose cut and finished weight exceed one hundred metric carats.

Africa has produced many of them: the *Jonker Diamond*, a 726-carat rough cut to a brilliant of 125 carats that hangs about the throat of the Queen of Nepal; The *Jubilee Diamond*, a superb 245-carat cushion of unearthly fire fashioned out of 650-carat rough – then the biggest of them all, a monstrous rough stone of 3,106 carats, the *Cullinan* which yielded not one, but two paragons. The

*Great Star of Africa* at 530 carats and *The Cullinan* II at 317 carats. Both these stones grace the Crown Jewels of England.

Now on Sergio Caporetti's desk lay a rough stone which would add yet another paragon to the list.

'Have you weighed it?' asked Hugo, and Sergio nodded.

'How much?'

'Three hundred and twenty carats,' Sergio said softly.

'Jesus!' whispered Hugo, and Sergio crossed himself quickly to dissociate from the use of names.

Reverently Hugo Kramer leaned forward and picked up the big diamond. It filled the palm of his hand, the cleavage plane that formed its base was smooth and clean as an axe-stroke. There were bigger diamonds in history, but this diamond had a special feature which would set it in a niche of its own and endow it with peculiar value.

Its colour was the serene blue of a high summer sky.

This stone could pay half the total bill for *Kingfisher*'s construction – if it were ever used for that purpose.

Hugo replaced the blue diamond on the desk and lit a cigarette without taking his eyes from it.

'This field – it is bigger – richer, far richer than we had guessed.'

Sergio nodded.

'In three days we have taken diamonds that I hoped to see once in five years,' Hugo went on as he began picking out the larger diamonds from the pile and laying them in a line across the desktop in approximate order of size, while Sergio opened his desk drawer and took out a box of his special occasion cheroots.

'We must tell the boss,' Hugo decided. He began arranging the diamonds in a neat circle about the big blue, thinking deeply. 'He must know how rich it is before he talks to Lance. He must make arrangements. He will know what to do – he's a clever one.'

'What about these?' Sergio indicated the treasure on the desk. 'Are you going to take them off?'

Hugo hesitated. 'No,' he decided. 'We could never get rid of this big Blue through the usual channel, it is too big, too distinctive. We will keep it aboard. When the boss takes over the Company again – then we will just declare it all nice and legal. No trouble.' He stood up. 'Look after them. I must hurry if I am to get a message to Cape Town in time.'

'The Company bears my father's name, Mr Larsen. It's as simple as that.' Benedict's voice was husky with emotion, and he looked down at his hands. 'I have a duty to my father's memory.'

'My boy, well—' Larsen came to lay his hand on Benedict's arm. 'Well, I just don't know what to say. Honour is a rare and precious thing these days.' With his free hand he was groping almost frantically for the bell on the desk behind him. He must get this signed up solid before the youngster changed his mind.

'I tried to warn you, Mr Larsen. My father and I never had any faith in this marine recovery scheme. Lance pushed it through—'

'Yes, quite so,' Larsen agreed, and turned to his assistant who came into the office at the trot in response to the bell. 'Ah, Simon. The Van Der Byl Diamond loan. Will you have an agreement made out immediately – Mr van der Byl will take over the capital amounts, and the outstanding interest as well.' By rolling his eyes Larsen tried to convey to his assistant the deadly urgency of the situation. The young man understood and fifteen minutes later laid the Agreement on Larsen's desk. Larsen unscrewed the cap of his pen and handed it to Benedict.

149

Larsen and three of his young men ushered Benedict out through the glass doors of the bank and across the pavement to where the Rolls stood in the reserved parking bay in Adderley Street.

Benedict settled into the back seat, acknowledged the bank official's farewells, and tapped on the chauffeur's window. As they pulled away, Ruby Lance slipped her hand through his arm and squeezed it.

'Did you get it?' she asked.

Benedict grinned happily. 'I frightened five years' growth out of old Larsen. He almost broke his neck in the hurry to give it to me.'

'Now you've got it all.' Ruby snuggled a little closer to him on the soft leather upholstery. Benedict nodded, and checked his watch.

'The meeting is set for fifteen minutes' time. I'll go up the front way, but I want you to go up in the private lift from the basement garage, and wait in my office. We will be in the Board Room. I will ring you at the right moment.'

The Rolls picked its way slowly down around the Heerengracht and double-parked outside the building. The chauffeur came to open the door, but before he alighted Benedict smiled into Ruby's face.

'This will be one of the high moments of my life,' he said softly. 'This time I've got the bastard cold.'

'I'll be waiting for you,' Ruby said, and he climbed out of the Rolls. He waited until it had turned into the entrance ramp of the basement garage, then he crossed the pavement into the main lobby of the skyscraper. He strode to the elevator with long eager strides, and his mouth kept pulling into a small excited smile.

The Board Room was set high, and the picture windows looked up at the great squat mountain, whose sheer cliffs dropped directly to the wooded slopes up which the first buildings of the city straggled.

Johnny Lance stood at the head of the table. He had lost weight in the last few days, so that his shoulders appeared bony and gaunt under the white silk shirt. He had discarded his jacket, and pulled the knot of his tie down an inch. The bones of his cheeks and jaw made harsh angles that were accentuated and not softened by the deep shades of fatigue that darkened his eyes. His hands were thrust deep into his pockets, and he spoke without reference to the sheaf of paper that lay on the table before him.

'Our working costs are as close as dammit to a hundred pounds an hour; right Mike?' And Michael Shapiro nodded. 'Well, we worked the Suicide main gully for sixty-six hours, and we recovered a princely 200 carats of the lousiest pile of junk I've ever seen. If we get a thousand quid for the lot we'll be doing well. This for an expenditure of six and a half thousand.'

Johnny paused, and looked around the table. Michael Shapiro was doodling on his note pad with fierce concentration, Tracey van der Byl was pale, her eyes never left Johnny's face and her expression ached with pity and helpless compassion; Benedict van der Byl was looking out of the window at the mountain, he was slumped comfortably in his chair, smiling a little and listening politely.

'The Suicide main gully is one of the five most likely parts of the entire concession. It's no good, so the rest of the field may be useless. We have the two other concessions, the original fields, to try. However, it will take three or four days to get *Kingfisher* moved up the coast.' Johnny paused, and Benedict swivelled his chair, still with the small smile on his lips.

'The interest payments fall due on the 30th – three days'

time. Where are you going to find one hundred and fifty thousand Rand?'

'Yes,' Johnny nodded. 'I think I can persuade Larsen to extend for a few weeks; he will bloody well have to if he wants to protect his—'

'Hold on,' Benedict murmured. 'Larsen has got nothing to do with it.'

Johnny was silent, watching him warily. 'Explain,' he invited.

'I've taken over the loan from Larsen,' Benedict told him. 'I'm not interested in extending.'

'Larsen wouldn't have negotiated without warning me.' Johnny was stricken, his disclaimer was wrung from him in pain.

'Shapiro?' Benedict turned to Michael Shapiro for confirmation.

'Sorry, Johnny. It's true. I've seen the documents.'

'Thanks, Michael.' Johnny's voice was bitter with accusations. 'Thanks for letting me know.'

'He showed me a few minutes before the meeting, Johnny. I swear I didn't know.' Michael's expression was distressed.

'Right.' Benedict straightened up in his chair, his voice was brisk. 'Let's get down to first principles. You've ruined my father's Company, Lance – but, thank God, I may be able to retrieve the situation. Call it sentiment or what you like, but I want your shares and yours.' He turned to Tracey and nodded at her.

'No,' said Tracey sharply.

'Right.' Benedict smiled at her. 'Then I'm going to hammer Johnny Lance for his full obligations. That way I get the Company anyway, but I'll make damn sure he remains an unrehabilitated bankrupt for the rest of his life.'

Tracey lifted her hand to her throat, and turned her eyes to Johnny. Waiting for him to set a lead. There was a long stark silence, then Johnny Lance dropped his eyes.

'I've still got three days.' His voice was gruff and tired.

'Three days you have.' Benedict grinned coldly. 'And you're welcome to them.'

Johnny picked up his papers and put them under one arm; he took his jacket off the back of the chair and swung it over his shoulder.

'Wait,' ordered Benedict.

'What for?' Johnny's grin was twisted. 'You've had your fun.'

Benedict lifted the receiver of the telephone on the table and dialled swiftly.

'Come through, please, darling.' He spoke into the mouthpiece and smiled at Johnny as he hung up. Then as the door opened he went to meet Ruby Lance, and kissed her on the mouth. The two of them stood, arm in arm, and looked at Johnny.

'The Company is not the only thing I've taken from you,' Benedict said softly.

'I want a divorce.' Ruby looked steadily into Johnny's face. 'Benedict and I are going to get married.'

They were all watching Johnny, and they saw him flinch. He looked from one face to the other, then his mouth tightened and his forehead furrowed.

Tracey saw his anger mounting, and her eyes flicked to Benedict's face. He was leaning forward expectantly, his lips quivering with expectation, his eyes alight with triumph. Tracey wanted to scream out a warning to Johnny, stop him falling into the trap that Benedict had set so carefully.

Johnny took a pace forward, coming up on to the balls of his feet. He was about to make his defeat total and ineradicable. Then Benedict spoiled it for himself, he goaded once more.

'Game, set and match, Johnny Lance,' he crowed.

The effort of will that Johnny made to recover his reason was not shown on his face, he made the step forward seem natural and he continued towards the door.

'The house is in your name, of course, Ruby, so would you please send my things down to the Tulbagh Hotel,' he asked quietly.

He stopped in front of the couple and spoke to Ruby.

'You'll want to protect your reputation, of course, so I'll not sue for adultery. We'll call it desertion.'

'You're eating your guts out,' jeered Benedict. 'Lance can't keep his woman. Van der Byl took her away from him. Go on, sue for adultery – let the world hear it.'

'As you wish,' Johnny agreed.

And he walked out of the Board Room to the elevators.

Johnny flopped on to the bed fully dressed, and rubbed his closed eyes with his fingertips. He felt confused and off-balance, the edge of his mind which usually slashed quickly and incisively through a problem was dulled. This problem was so multiplied and tangled that he felt like a man in a thicket of African ebony trying to cut his way out with a blunt machete.

Without opening his eyes he groped for the telephone, and the girl on the hotel switchboard downstairs answered. He gave her a number in Kimberley.

'Person to person, Mr Ralph Ellison.'

'Fifteen minutes' delay, Mr Lance,' the girl told him.

'Okay,' Johnny replied. 'Ask room service to send me up a Chivas Regal and soda.' He suddenly needed liquor, something to dull the pain. 'Make that a double, honey – no, make it two doubles.'

He had drained both glasses by the time his Kimberley call came through.

'Ralph?' Johnny spoke into the receiver.

'Johnny, how nice of you to call.' There was an echo like distant laughter beneath those cool ambassadorial tones in Ralph Ellison's voice and Johnny knew instantly that the word was out. Damn it, he was slow – of course Benedict would have blocked him.

'Are you still interested in a deal on the Thunderbolt and Suicide Concession?' Johnny loosed a despairing long-range shot.

'Of course, you know we are always interested,' Ralph replied.

'The price is two million.' Johnny lost interest and lay back on the bed, closing his eyes again. He knew Ralph was having his revenge – you didn't take this boy to court and win without sowing yourself a minefield to retreat over.

'Two million,' Ralph murmured. 'Now that's a little high – for a field that's yielding 200 carats of small industrial diamonds per 10,000 loads, that's definitely on the high side. Of course we wouldn't want that battleship of yours either – we are not starting our own navy.' Ralph chuckled juicily. 'We could talk around fifty to a hundred grand – no more than that, Johnny.'

'Okay, Ralph.' Johnny spoke wearily. 'Thanks all the same. We'll have a drink together sometime.'

'Any time, Johnny,' Ralph agreed. 'Any time at all. You call me.'

Johnny dropped the receiver back on its hook and looked at the ceiling. He had heard that a gunshot wound was numb at first – he felt numb now. All that energy had seeped out of him, he had lost direction.

The telephone shrilled and he picked it up. The girl on the switchboard asked politely:

'Are you finished, Mr Lance?'

'Yes,' said Johnny. 'You might say that.'

'Is there anything else you require?' The girl sounded puzzled.

'Yes, honey, send up the hemlock.'

'I beg your pardon?'

'Two more big fat whiskies, please.'

He drank them in the bath, and while he dried himself

the doorbell tinkled. He wound the bath towel round his waist and went through to open the door.

Tracey stepped into the bedroom and closed the door behind her. They stood looking at each other for a long moment. Her eyes were big and dark, reflecting his agony faithfully.

'Johnny—' Her voice was husky, and she reached out and laid the palm of her hand on his cheek. His shoulders sagged, and he moved close to her, his forehead sinking on to her shoulder. He sighed, a ragged broken exhalation of breath.

'Come,' she said, and led him to the bed. Leaving him there she went to the windows and closed the curtains.

It was warm and safe in the half dark of the curtained room, and they held each other as they had done long years before. Clinging together, so their breathing mingled, and it was not necessary to speak.

When they became lovers it seemed that they had waited all their lives for that moment.

Afterwards he lay in her arms and he felt strength flowing back into him, drawing it from her. When he sat up in the bed the bemused, almost dazed expression had gone. His jaw was out and his eyes were bright.

'We've still got three days,' he said.

'Yes.' She sat up beside him. 'Go, Johnny. Go quickly, don't waste another moment.'

'I'll pull *Kingfisher* out of the main gully. I'll find those diamonds. They are there. I *know* they are there. I'll take her right down into the jaws of Thunderbolt and Suicide, I'll find those bloody diamonds – damned if I won't.' He swung his legs off the bed, reached for his clothes, glancing at his wrist watch as he did so. 'Four o'clock. I can get to Cartridge Bay a few minutes after dark. Will you call the communications office, ask them to radio Cartridge Bay and have a flare path set for me, and *Wild Goose* standing by to run me out?'

156

'I'll phone them from here. Then I'll take a bath – you go on. Don't waste time.' Tracey nodded eagerly, and Johnny let his eyes drop down over her body. He reached out and touched one big white breast almost diffidently.

'You are beautiful – I hate to go.'

'It will all be here, waiting for you, when you get back.'


'It wasn't the way I'd planned it. It wasn't good the way I'd dreamed about it.' Benedict paced angrily over the floor of the Old Man's study, swinging towards the windows and pausing to stare out at the mountain across the valley.

'You hurt him. You crushed him.' Ruby moved restlessly in her chair across the room from him, curling her long golden legs defensively under her, sitting like a cat in the big chair. She was worried, and it showed in the tiny crows' feet at the corners of her eyes and the way she held her lips pursed. She should have anticipated this reaction from him, she should have known that this moment of triumph could never match his anticipation of it – and that revenge must always be followed by sour distaste and a feeling of disappointment. She realized that her safest course was to leave him alone now, she should never have returned with him to the old house on Wynberg Hill. She stood up.

'Darling.' She crossed to him. 'I'm going home now. I want to pack his clothes and get rid of them. I want to wipe out every memory of him. From now on it's you and I – together.'

She stretched up to kiss him, but Benedict turned his face away.

'Oh! So you're going, are you?' His expression was petulant, his lips pouting spitefully.

'We're both tired, darling. Let us both rest a while – and I'll come back later this evening.'

'So now you're giving the orders, are you?' He laughed nastily.

'Darling—'

'And cut out all the darlings. We pulled a deal and it didn't work out. You were meant to be a club to break his skull – and do you know something? He didn't give a damn. I was watching him, he was pleased – yes! He was bloody well delighted to get rid of you.'

'Benedict—' She stepped back.

'Listen.' He stepped close to her, and pushed his face towards hers. 'If you're so bloody anxious to go, why don't you bloody well go – and keep going. If he doesn't want you – then I sure as hell don't want you either.'

'Benedict,' she whispered. The colour faded from her face, leaving it washed white as beach sand. She stared at him in horror, as her dreams began to fall into ruins around her. 'You don't mean that.'

'I don't? Is that so?' He threw back his head and laughed again. 'Listen, you got some nice diamonds and a mink coat. You got a big house in Bishopscourt – now, that's pretty good pay for a whore.'

'Benedict—' She gasped at the insult, but he wasn't listening.

'I proved I could have you, didn't I? I proved I could take you away from him – and that's what it was all about. Now, why don't you go on home like a good girl.'

'The machine. I know about that thing in *Kingfisher*.' It was a mistake. Until then she still had a chance. His face changed shape and the blood flooded into it. His voice when he spoke was unsteady, thick with rage for his lips seemed to have swollen.

'Try it,' he whispered back at her. 'Go on, try it. They'll give you fifteen years in a woman's prison, my beauty. And think about this also—' He showed her his hand, holding it like a blade before her eyes. 'I'll kill you. I swear before

158

God, I'll kill you with my bare hands. You know I'll do it – you know enough about me now.'

She backed away from him, and he followed her still holding his hand at her throat.

'You've been paid. Now get out.'

A few seconds longer she stood before him, and he was not too far gone in rage to see the fear in her eyes mingle with something else that made her eyes slit and drew her lips back to show the little white teeth.

'All right,' she said. 'I'll go.' And she walked from the room, stepping daintily, the long yellow hair swinging against her shoulders.

Ruby drove slowly for her vision was blurred with her tears. Twice other drivers hooted at her but she kept both hands clenched on the wheel and stared ahead, following the De Waal Drive around the lower slopes of the mountain. Before she reached the University she swung off the road and drove up through the pine forests until she reached the car park behind the Cecil Rhodes Memorial. She left the car and walked down on to the wide paved terrace below the Greek columns and stone steps where the mounted statue eternally searched the horizon with one hand lifted to shade his eyes.

She went to the parapet and looked across to the far blue mountains of the Helderberg. She hugged herself about the shoulders for the wind through her silk summer dress was as cold as her misery.

Now the tears broke over her lids and slid down her cheeks to fall unheeded on to the silken front of her dress. They were tears of self-pity, but also the tears of an anger as searing cold as dry ice.

'The swine,' she whispered through lips that trembled.

Near her two young students sitting on the parapet, kicking their legs over the drop beneath them and hugging each other in the abandon of first love, turned to glance at her.

The boy whispered to the girl, and she giggled in unthinking cruelty – but looked away as Ruby directed a long venomous glare at her. Then in embarrassment the couple scrambled off the parapet and moved away, leaving her alone.

Never for one moment did she consider standing aside. Benedict's threats meant nothing – her only concern was to take the action which would injure him most severely. The consequences to herself were not part of her calculations. She wanted only to select the swiftest and most terrible vehicle of retribution. As the dark clouds that fogged her reason slowly cleared, the means came to her readily.

Johnny was staying at the Tulbagh Hotel.

She turned and ran back to her car, the long yellow banner of her hair floating behind her like the pennant at the tip of a cavalry lance. She drove fast until she hit the downtown rush-hour crowds. The tears dried on her face as she crawled, fuming with impatience, along the slow river of traffic.

It was after five when she parked in a loading zone outside the entrance to the Tulbagh and ran into the lobby.

'What room is Mr Lance in?' she demanded of the girl at the desk.

'Mr Lance checked out an hour ago.' Curiously the girl examined Ruby's ruined make-up.

'Did he say where he was going?' Ruby snapped at her, feeling the sickening slide of disappointment within her.

'No, Madam.' The girl shook her head. 'But he was in a hurry.'

'Damn! Damn!' Ruby swore bitterly. She turned from the desk undecided where next to look. Perhaps Johnny had gone back to the office.

Across the lobby the elevator doors slid open and Tracey

Hartford stepped out. Even in her impatience Ruby recognized in the glow that seemed to emanate from her that Tracey was a girl freshly risen from the bed of the man she loved. There was not a vestige of doubt in Ruby's mind as to the identity of that man.

The shock of it paralysed her for a moment. Then she felt the urge to cross the floor and claw that smug smile from Tracey's face. She fought it down, and instead she stepped into her path as Tracey started for the glass outer doors.

'Where is Johnny?' she demanded, and Tracey came up short. Her little gasp of guilt confirmed Ruby's suspicion.

'Where is he, damn you!' Ruby's voice was pitched low but brittle with emotion.

'He's not here.' Tracey recovered herself, quickly masking her expression.

'Where has he gone? I must see him.'

'He's flown up to Cartridge Bay.'

'When did he leave? It's important – terribly important.'

'An hour ago. He'll be airborne already.'

'Can you get a message to him?' In her impatience Ruby caught Tracey's wrist, holding her in a grip that marked the skin.

'I can radio him—' Tracey pulled her hand free.

'No,' Ruby cut in quickly. She could not have her message shouted across the ether for all to hear. 'Can you follow him – charter plane?'

Tracey shook her head. 'They won't fly to an unscheduled airfield after dark.'

'Then you must follow him – by car. You must drive up there.'

'Why?' Tracey stared at her, puzzled by this strange insistence, noticing the dried tears and the wild look in Ruby's eyes. 'It's an eight-hour drive.'

'I'll tell you. Can we use Johnny's room?'

Tracey hesitated, remembering the unmade bed. Then

the hotel manager came into the lobby and Tracey turned to him with relief.

The Beechcraft bucked suddenly and dropped a wing, instinctively Johnny corrected the lunge with stick and rudder then glanced quickly at his instrument panel for an explanation. There was none to be found there, so he looked over the wing and for the first time noticed the dust on the great plains below him; it was moving low against the earth in long streamers like mist, and the setting sun turned it to mauve and old gold. With a prickle of alarm he scanned the horizon ahead, and saw it coming down from the north like a great moving range of blue mountains. Even as he watched it, it rolled across the low sun, turning it into a sullen red orb. The light in the cockpit changed to a weird glow as though the door to a furnace had been thrown open.

Again the Beechcraft crabbed awkwardly as another gust of high wind hit her, and at the same moment the radio crackled and came alive.

'Zulu Sugar Peter Tango Baker this is Alexandra Bay Control, come in please.'

The voice of the controller was almost unintelligible with storm static. Johnny reached for the transmit switch of the radio, then stopped his hand. He thought quickly. He could guess they were trying to reach him to cancel his flight approval. That was a big northern boiling down out of the desert. They would abort his flight, and divert him out of the path of the storm.

He checked his wrist watch. Twenty minutes' flying time to Cartridge Bay. No – he was flying full into the eye of the wind, say twenty-five or thirty minutes. Quickly he searched the coast on his port side and saw the long white lines of surf stretched ahead into the thickening purple gloom. The coast was still clear, it might stay that way for another thirty minutes.

'Zulu Sugar Peter Tango Baker this is Alexandra Bay. I say again – come in. Come in. Zulu Sugar Peter Tango Baker.' The agitation in the controller's voice came through over the static.

There was a fair chance of getting in to Cartridge Bay, racing the storm and winning. He could edge out to the westward and come in from the sea, pick up *Kingfisher*'s riding lights as a beacon and sneak in under the leading edge of the dust clouds. If he missed he could turn and run with the wind for home. The radio was hissing and crackling angrily now, the controller's voice sometimes lost in the interference, sometimes coming through strongly.

' – Cancelled. I say again: your flight approval is cancelled. Do you read me, Zulu Sugar Peter Tango Baker. Come in, please. – Beaufort force seven. – visibility in the storm area – I say again, there is nil visibility in—'

The norther would roar for days now and with it would blow away his last chance of working the gap at Thunderbolt and Suicide.

Johnny switched off the radio, cut off contact with Control and immediately it was strangely quiet in the cockpit. He settled himself down into the bucket seat, and eased open the throttles, watching the needles creep up around the dials of the rev counters.

Now he was down to an altitude of three hundred feet and the Beechcraft was leaping about like a hooked marlin. He was flying her on instruments for outside the cockpit it was completely dark. He could not see his own wingtips, but above him the stars still showed. He was riding the vanguard of the storm, and the dust clouds were ahead, racing to meet him and blanket the flare path at Cartridge Bay.

Every few seconds he darted a quick glance ahead, hoping to pick up the lights, then his eyes flew back to the instrument panel.

'Now,' he thought grimly. 'It should be now. I should be over the grounds. Thirty seconds more and I'll know I've missed her.'

He looked up again, and there was *Kingfisher* dead ahead. All her lights were ablaze, a burning beacon of hope in the darkness. She appeared to be riding easily, for the wind had not yet had time to thrash the sea into a frenzy.

He flashed over her, seeming to graze her superstructure in passing, and now he was searching anxiously for the glow of the flare path on the land beyond.

It came up as a path of lesser darkness in the absolute blackness of the night. He steadied on course towards it, watching it change to a long double line of oil-burning flares that smoked and fluttered in the wind.

He flew her in fast, high above the stall and the shock of touchdown threatened to tear the undercarriage off her.

Then he was jolting and trundling down the earthen runway with the flares flashing past his wingtips.

'Lance, old man,' he murmured thankfully, 'that was a very shaky do!'

The wind hum against the body of the car, and the snarl of rubber on tarmac as the Mercedes snaked through the bends of the twisting mountain road were sounds to match the racing of Tracey's blood and the hammer of her heart.

She drove with an inspired abandon, watching the bends leap out at her out of the darkness, sensing the massive crags and cliffs that hung over the road and blotted out half the night sky.

The silver sheet of Clanwilliam Lake reflected the stars,

and then was left behind. Down from the mountains she went and over the Olifants River to make a brief fuel stop at Vanrynsdorp and scan the road map anxiously in the light of the gasoline pumps. She read with a sinking feeling the mileage figures printed along the little red ribbon of the road, and knew that for her each mile would be multiplied by her own urgency.

Then once more behind the wheel she faced the vast emptiness of Namaqualand – and sent the Mercedes flying across it.

' – There is some type of machine, I don't know how it works, but it filters out the diamonds. Benedict had it installed at Las Palmas—'

The headlights were puny little white shafts, and the road a long blue smear that went on endlessly. Tracey lit a cigarette with one hand, hearing Ruby's voice again in her ears.

' – There is one diamond amongst them. He called it "The Big Blue". Benedict says it's worth a million—' Tracey was not sure she believed it. It was the enormity of the treachery and deceit that she could not accept.

' – The Italian, the Captain, be careful of him. He works for Benedict. The other one also – Hugo – they are all in it. Warn Johnny.'

Benedict! Weak, spoiled Benedict, the playboy, the spendthrift. Could he have planned and carried this through?

A gust of wind hit the car from the side, taking her unawares, pushing the Mercedes off the tar on to the gravel. Tracey fought to hold the skid. Dust and gravel roared out in a cloud from under the wheels. Then she was back on the road, hurtling northwards.

'Warn Johnny! Warn Johnny!'

B enedict van der Byl sat in his father's chair, in his father's house, and he was alone. His loneliness ate deep into the fibres of his whole being. Before him on the stinkwood desk stood a crystal glass and a decanter. The brandy was no comfort, its warmth in his throat and belly seemed only to accentuate the icy cold of his loneliness. His fantasy showed him as a hollow man. He thought of himself as a husk, filled only with the cold of melancholia.

He looked about the room with its dark panelled woodwork and he smelled the musty dead smell. He wondered how many times his father had sat in this chair alone and lonely. Lonely and afraid as the cancer ate him alive.

He stood up and moved listlessly about the room, touching the furniture as if he were trying to communicate with the man who had lived and died here. He moved across and stood in front of the curtained windows. The rug was new. It replaced the other that they had been unable to clean.

'The Old Man had the right idea.' He spoke aloud, his voice sounding strange in his own ears.

Then on an impulse he crossed quickly to the cupboard that flanked the massive stone fireplace, and tried the door. It was locked.

Without passion he stood back and kicked in the panel. The wood splintered and he kicked again, smashing the door from its hinges.

The oblong leather case was on the top shelf, and he took it down and carried it to the desk. He sprang the catches and laid back the lid.

He lifted out the blue metalled double barrels of the Purdy Royal, and the gun oil was greasy on his hands.

'Jacobus Isaac van der Byl.' He read aloud the name in gold inlay set into the steel among the engraved pheasants and gundogs.

He smiled then.

'The old devil.' He shook his head smiling as though at some private joke, and began slowly to assemble the shotgun. He weighed it in his hands, feeling the sweet pure balance of the weapon.

'The old bastard made his own decisions.' And still smiling he carried the gun across to the new carpet. He placed it butt down between his feet with the barrels pointed at the ceiling and leaning slowly forward he opened his mouth and placed the muzzles between his lips, then reaching farther down he placed a thumb on each trigger and pushed them simultaneously.

Click! Click!

The firing pins fell on the empty chambers, and Benedict straightened up and wiped the taste of gun oil from his lips. He grinned again.

'That's the way he did it. Both barrels in the back of the throat. What a cure for tonsilitis!' he chuckled, and glanced across at the shattered cupboard door. The square packets of cartridges were on the second shelf.

He tucked the gun under his arm and went to the cupboard again, moving more purposefully now. He snatched down a packet of SSG and broke it open. Suddenly his hands were shaking and the fat red cartridges spilled on to the floor. He stooped and picked up two of them.

With mounting excitement and dread he broke open the shotgun and slipped the cartridges into the blank eyes of the breeches. They slid home against the seating with a solid double thunk, and he hurried back to the spot in front of the window.

His eyes were bright and his breathing quick as he pushed the safety catch on to 'Fire' and placed the butt between his feet once more.

He took the muzzles in his mouth again, in an obscene soul kiss and reached down for the triggers. They were cold and oily. He caressed them lightly, feeling the fine grooving in the curves of metal, thrilling to the touch and feel of them as he had never thrilled to the feel of a woman's body.

Then abruptly he stood up again. He was gasping for breath.

Unsteadily he carried the weapon back to the desk and laid it on the dark polished wood.

As he poured brandy into the crystal glass his eyes were fastened with perverse fascination on the beautiful glistening weapon.

T he steam had fogged the mirrored walls of the bathroom, so her image was dewed and misty. Ruby Lance dried herself slowly with one of the thick fluffy towels. She was in no hurry; she wanted Tracey to have a start of at least four hours on her journey to Cartridge Bay. With a deep narcissistic pleasure she noticed in the mirrors how her whole body glowed with soft pink highlights from the hot waters of the bath.

Wrapping herself in the towel she went through into the dressing-room and picking up one of the silver-backed brushes began stroking it through her hair, moving across to the open wardrobe to select a dress for the occasion. It must be something special, perhaps the unworn full-length Louis Feraud of daffodil satin.

Still undecided she went back to seat herself at the dressing-table and began the complicated ritual of applying her make-up. She worked with meticulous care until at last she smiled at her reflection with satisfaction.

She dropped the towel, went back to the wardrobe, and stood slim and naked before it. Pouting slightly with concentration she decided against the Feraud. Then suddenly she smiled, and reached for Benedict's mink.

She wrapped herself in the pale cloud of fur, fluffing up

the collar to frame her face. It was perfect. Just the fur and a pair of golden slippers, pale gold, a perfect match for her hair.

Now suddenly she was eager to go. She ran from the house to where her car was parked in the driveway.

She switched off the headlights as she turned into the driveway that curved up to where the old house crouched on the top of Wynberg Hill. The whisper of the engine was unobtrusive and blended with the whimper of the night breeze in the chestnut trees that flanked the driveway.

She parked in the courtyard, and saw that Benedict's Rolls was still in the garage and a light burned in the window of the study, a yellow oblong behind the curtains. The front door was open. Her slippered feet made no sound along the gloomy passages, and when she tried the door to the study it swung open readily. She stepped into the room, and closed the door behind her. She stood with her back to the dark panelled wood. A single shaded lamp lit the room dimly.

Benedict sat behind the desk. The room was heavy with the smell of cigar smoke and brandy fumes. He had been drinking. His face was flushed, and the top button of his shirt was undone. On the desk in front of him lay a shotgun. Ruby was surprised at the presence of the weapon, it disconcerted her and the words she had prepared were forgotten.

Benedict looked up at her. His eyes were slightly unfocused and he blinked slowly. Then he grinned; it twisted his mouth and his voice when he spoke was slurred.

'So you've come back.'

Instantly her hatred returned in full flood. But she kept her face impassive. 'Yes,' she agreed. 'I've come back.'

'Come here.' He swivelled his chair to the side of the desk. Ruby did not move, she leaned back against the door.

'Come here.' Benedict's voice was stronger now, and suddenly Ruby smiled and obeyed.

She stood in front of him, huddled in the fur.

'Kneel down,' commanded Benedict, and she hesitated.

'Down!' his voice crackled. 'Down, damn you!'

Ruby sank to her knees in front of him, and he straightened up in the chair. She knelt in front of him in the attitude of submission, with her head forward so the golden hair hung like a curtain over her face.

'Say it,' he gloated. 'Ask me to forgive you.'

Slowly she lifted her face and looked up at him. She spoke softly.

'Tracey left for Cartridge Bay at five-thirty this evening.'

Benedict's expression changed.

'She has a start of four hours – she is half-way there already.'

He stared at her with his lips parting, soft and red and slack.

'She is going to Johnny,' Ruby went on. 'She knows about the thing in *Kingfisher*. She knows about the big blue diamond.'

He began to shake his head in disbelief.

'By dawn tomorrow Johnny will know also. So you see, my darling, you have lost again – haven't you? You can never beat him, can you, Benedict? Can you, my darling?'

Her voice was rising, ringing with triumph.

'You?' he croaked. 'You?'

And she laughed, nodding her head in agreement, unable to speak through her laughter.

Benedict lunged clumsily out of the chair, his hands going for her throat. She went over backwards with him on top of her. Her laughter died gurgling in her throat.

They rolled together on the floor. Benedict's hands locked on her neck, his voice rising in a scream of fury and despair. Her long legs kicking and thrashing, clawing at his face and hands, she fought him with the strength of a cornered animal.

They rolled back suddenly and Benedict's head struck

the solid leg of the desk with a crack that jarred his whole body. His grip on her throat loosened and she tore herself free with fresh breath hissing into her open mouth. She rolled away from him and in one fluid movement gained her feet, reeling back from him with the front of the mink torn open and her hair tangled across her face.

Benedict dragged himself up the desk on to his knees. He was still screaming, a high keening note without form or coherence, as Ruby spun away from him and stumbled to the door.

Blinded by her own hair, fighting for strangled breath, she fumbled for the door handle with her back turned to him.

Benedict reached up and lifted the shotgun off the desk. Still kneeling beside the desk he held the weapon across his hip. The recoil was a liquid pulsing jolt in his hands and the muzzle blast was thunderous in the confines of the room, the long yellow flame lighting the scene like a photographer's flash-bulb.

The heavy charge caught Ruby in the small of her back. At that range there was no spread of shot and it went through spine and pelvis in a solid shattering ball. It tore out through the front of her belly, spinning her sideways along the wall. She slid down into a sitting position, facing him with the mink flared open about her.

On his knees Benedict swung the gun to follow her fall and he fired the second barrel; again the brief thunder and flame of the muzzle blast flashed across the room.

At even closer range than the first charge it struck her full in her beautiful golden face.

B enedict stood in the garage with his forehead pressed against the cold metal of the Rolls-Royce. The shotgun was still in his hands, and his pockets were crammed with cartridges that he had picked up from the floor before leaving the study.

He was shivering violently, like a man in high fever.

'No!' he moaned to himself, repeating the single negative over and over again, leaning against the big car.

Abruptly he gagged, remembering the carnage he had created. Then he retched, still leaning against the Rolls, bringing up the brandy mingled with his horror.

It left him pale and weak, but steadier. Through the open window he threw the gun on to the back seat of the Rolls, and climbed shakily into the driver's seat.

He sat there bowed over the steering wheel, and now his instinct of self-preservation took hold of him.

It seemed to him there was but one avenue of escape still open to him. *Wild Goose* had the range to take him across an ocean – South America perhaps, and there was money in Switzerland.

He started the Rolls and reversed out of the garage, the spin of tyres against concrete burning blue smoke into the beams of the headlights.


T he Mercedes crawled through the thick sand, the headlights probing ineffectually into the bright orange fog of dust that whipped endlessly over the track ahead. The hot gritty wind buffeted the car, rocking it on its suspension.

Tracey sat forward in the driver's seat peering ahead through eyes that felt raw and swollen with fatigue and mica dust.

From the main road to the coast this Jeep track was the only land access to Cartridge Bay. It was a hundred miles of tortuous trail, made up of deep sandy ruts and broken stone where it crossed one of the many rocky ridges.

The radiator of the Mercedes was boiling furiously, over-heating in the searing wind and the slogging low-gear grind through thick sand. In places Tracey followed the track only by driving through gaps in the stunted knee-high growth of desert bush. Every few minutes a tumbleweed, driven by the wind, would bowl across the track like a frightened furry animal.

At times she was sure she had missed a turning and was now grinding aimlessly out into the desert, then reassuringly the twin ruts would show up in the lights ahead of her. Once she did drive off the road, and immediately the Mercedes came to a gentle standstill with its rear wheels spinning helplessly in the soft sand. She had to climb out of the cab and, with her bare hands, scoop away the sand from behind the wheels and stuff bundles of tumbleweed into the depressions to give the wheels purchase. She almost wept with relief when the Mercedes pulled back sluggishly on to the trail again.

The slow dawn broke through the dust clouds and Tracey switched off the headlights and drove on until suddenly, and quite unexpectedly, she reached Cartridge Bay. The depot buildings loomed suddenly before her, and she left the Mercedes and ran to the living quarters. The foreman opened the door to her insistent hammering, and stared at her in astonishment before ushering her in. Tracey cut off his questions with her own.

'Where is *Wild Goose?*'

'She took Mr Lance out to *Kingfisher*, but she's back now lying at the jetty.'

'Hugo Kramer – the Captain?'

'He's aboard, holed up in his cabin.'

'Thanks.' Tracey left him, pushed the door open against the wind and ran out into the storm.

*Wild Goose* lay at her moorings, secured by heavy lines

to the bollards, but fidgeting and fretting at the push of the wind. There was a gangplank laid to her deck, and lights showed at her portholes. Tracey went aboard.

Hugo Kramer came to the doorway of his cabin in a suit of rumpled striped pyjamas. Tracey pushed past him.

'You took Lance out to *Kingfisher*?' she accused him, her voice sharp and anxious.

'Yes.'

'You idiot, didn't you realize there was something up? Good God, why otherwise would he fly in through this weather?'

Hugo stared at her, and instinctively she knew that what Ruby had told her was true.

'I don't know what you're talking about,' he blurted.

'You'll know all right when we are all sitting behind bars – we'll have fifteen long years to think about it. Lance has tumbled to it, you fool, I've got to stop him. Take me out to *Kingfisher*.'

He was confused – and afraid.

'I know nothing about—' Hugo started again.

'You're wasting time.' Brusquely Tracey brushed his protests aside. 'Take me out to *Kingfisher*.'

'Your brother – where is he? Why didn't he come?'

Tracey had anticipated the question. 'Lance beat him up – badly. He's in hospital. He sent me.'

Suddenly Hugo was convinced.

'*Gott!*' he swore. 'What are we going to do? This storm – I may be able to get you out there, but I won't be able to leave *Wild Goose*. My crew can't handle her in this sea. What can you do on your own?'

'Get me out there,' said Tracey. 'Get me aboard *Kingfisher* and you can come back. The Italian, Caporetti, he and I will take care of Lance. In this storm a man can be washed overboard very easily.'

'*Ja.*' Hugo's face lit with relief. 'That's it. The Italian!' And he a reached for his oilskins hanging on the bulkhead.

As he pulled them on over his pyjamas he looked at Tracey with new respect.

'You,' he said. 'I didn't know you were in it.'

'Did you think my brother and I would stand by and let a stranger take our birthright from us?'

Hugo grinned. 'You're a cool one, I'll say that for you. You had me fooled.' And he went out on to the bridge.

Johnny Lance and Sergio Caporetti stood shoulder to shoulder on *Kingfisher*'s bridge. The ship was taking the big green seas over her bows, solid walls of water, and the wind whipped spray that spattered the armoured glass windows of the bridge house.

*Kingfisher* had slipped her moorings the previous evening, leaving the big yellow buoys floating on their anchor cables and she was working free of her fetters. She was on computer navigation, holding her position over the ground against the swells and the wind by use of her engine and rudder.

'She is no good.' Sergio spoke morosely. 'We come too close to the rocks. I get sick in my heart looking at them.'

The dust clouds did not carry this far out to sea despite the vicious screeching of the wind. The visibility was a mile or more, quite enough to show the brooding twin hulks of Thunderbolt and Suicide. The storm-crazed swells burst against them, throwing white spray two hundred feet into the gloomy sky, then surging back to expose the gleaming white rock.

'Hold her,' growled Johnny. Twice during the night they had changed position, each time edging down closer on the gap between the two islands. *Kingfisher* was battling gamely to hold her ground against the insidious sucking current that added its pull to that of the swell and the wind.

Johnny was not attempting to work any one of the gullies extensively, he wanted only to sample as much of the field as possible in the time that was left to him. The storm would not stop him – for *Kingfisher* was constructed to work in worse weather than his. Her compensating hose section was keeping the dredge head on the bottom despite the lift and fall of her hull.

'Calm down, Sergio.' Johnny relented a little. 'The computer is foolproof.'

'The goddamned computer she no got eyes to see those rocks. Me, I got eyes – and it gives me a sick heart.'

Twice during the night Johnny had gone down into the control room and ordered the computer to report its recovery of diamonds. Each time the reply had been consistent – not a single stone over four carats, and a very precious few of any others.

'I'm going through to the plot. Watch her,' Johnny told Sergio, and staggering against the pitch and roll he went through the door behind the bridge.

He paused behind the repeater screen of the computer, and at a glance saw that *Kingfisher* was holding her primary operation and all departments were running normally. He passed the screen and leaned over the chart table.

The large-scale chart of the South West African coast between Luderitz and Walvis Bay was pinned down on the board. The *Wild Goose* soundings were pencilled in, and the pattern of *Kingfisher*'s sweeps were carefully plotted around the islands of Thunderbolt and Suicide.

Johnny picked up a pair of dividers and stared moodily at the chart. Suddenly a surge of anger rose in him against those two names. They had promised so much and delivered so little.

He stared at the names Thunderbolt and Suicide printed in italics among the maze of soundings, and his anger turned to blind red hatred.

With the points of the dividers he slashed at the chart, ripping the thick linen paper once, and twice, in a ragged cross-shaped tear.

This small act of violence dissipated his anger. He felt embarrassed, it had been a petty childish gesture. He tried to smooth the edges of the tear, and through the gap he felt another loose scrap of paper which someone had slipped under the chart. He probed a finger through the tear in the chart and wormed the scrap out. He glanced at the scribbled title and the lines of figures and numbers that followed.

The sheet was headed: KAMINIKOTO SECONDARY RECOV-ERY PROGRAMME.

He studied it, puzzled by the title but recognizing the numbers as a computer programme. The writing was in Sergio Caporetti's pointed continental style. The easiest way to resolve the mystery was to ask Sergio. Johnny started back for the bridge.

'Boss,' Sergio called anxiously, as Johnny stepped through the door. 'Look!'

He was pointing ahead into the eye of the wind. Johnny hurried to his side, the paper crumpled and forgotten in his hand.

'*Wild Goose*.' Sergio identified the small craft that was staggering and plunging towards them out of the gloom.

'What the hell is he doing here?' Johnny wondered aloud. *Wild Goose* was lost for long seconds behind the walls of green sea, then again she was lifted high into unnatural prominence, showing the red lead of her bottom as she rode the crests; water poured from her scuppers, before she shot down the steep slope of the next wave to bury her nose deep in frothing water. She came down swiftly on the wind, rounding to and beginning to edge in under · *Kingfisher*'s counter.

'What the hell is he playing at?' Johnny protested, and then in disbelief he saw a slim figure dart from *Wild Goose*'s wheelhouse and run to the side nearest *Kingfisher*.

'It's Tracey,' shouted Johnny.

She reached the rail just as another swell burst over the

bows and smothered her. Johnny expected to see her washed away, but she was still there clinging to the rail.

Thrusting the page of paper into his pocket, Johnny went out through the wing of the bridge and swarmed down the steel ladder to the deck, jumping the last ten feet and running the instant he landed.

He reached the side and looked down on the drowned-kitten figure of Tracey.

'Go back,' he yelled. 'Go back. Don't try it.'

She shouted something that was lost in the next smother of spray, and when it cleared he saw her poising herself to jump the gap of surging water between the two vessels.

He flung himself over *Kingfisher*'s side and climbed swiftly down the steel rungs.

He was still ten feet above her as she gathered herself for the leap.

'Go back,' he shouted desperately.

She jumped, missed her hold and fell into the murderous stretch of water between the hulls. Her head bobbed below Johnny, and he was aware of the next swell bearing down on them. It would throw *Wild Goose* against the steel cliff of *Kingfisher*, crushing Tracey between them.

Johnny went down those last ten feet and hanging outwards by one arm he got his other arm around her, and with a heave that crackled in his muscles and joints he plucked her from the water just as the two vessels dashed together with a crunching impact that tore splinters from *Wild Goose*'s planking, and left a smear of alien paint on *Kingfisher*'s steel plating.

*Wild Goose* swung away, and with her diesels bellowing went bucking off into the wind.

With puddles of sea water forming around her feet from her sodden clothing, Tracey stood in the centre of *Kingfisher*'s guest cabin. Her dark hair was plastered down her face and neck, and she was shivering so violently from shock and the icy water that she could not talk. Her teeth chattered together, and her lips were blue with cold.

Desperately she was trying to form words, her eyes never leaving Johnny's face.

Quickly he stripped off her clothing and throwing one towel round her shoulders he began roughly to chafe warmth back into her with another.

'You little idiot,' he berated her. 'Are you stark staring bloody mad?'

'Johnny,' she gasped through her chattering teeth.

'Christ – that was so close,' he snarled at her as he knelt to rub her legs.

'Johnny, listen.'

'Shut up and dry your hair.'

Humbly she obeyed him, her shivers became controllable as he crossed to the locker and found a thick jersey which he pulled over her head. It hung almost to her knees.

'Now,' he said, taking her roughly by the shoulders. 'What the hell is this all about?'

And she told him in a rush of words that poured out like water from a broken dam. Then she burst into tears and stood there forlornly in the voluminous jersey with her damp hair dangling about her shoulders, sobbing as though her heart was breaking.

Johnny took her in his arms.

For a long minute Tracey revelled in his warmth and strength, but she was the first to pull away.

'Do something, Johnny,' she implored him, her voice still thick with tears. 'Stop them. You mustn't let them get away with it.'

He went back to the locker, and while he ransacked it

for clothing that might fit her, Johnny's mind was racing over the story she had told him.

He watched her pull on a pair of blue serge trousers and tie them at the waist with a length of cord. She folded back the cuffs and tucked them into thick woollen socks, before thrusting her feet into a pair of sea-boots that were only a few sizes too large for her.

'Where do we start?' she asked, and he remembered the sheet of paper. He fished it out of his pocket and flattened it on the table beside the bunk. Quickly he ran his eyes over the columns of figures. His first guess was right – it *was* a computer programme.

'Stay here,' he ordered Tracey.

'No.' Her response was immediate, and he grinned.

'Listen, I'm just going up on to the bridge to keep them busy there. I'll come back for you, I promise. You won't miss anything.'

'How is she, boss?' Sergio Caporetti's concern was genuine. Johnny realized that he must be worrying himself into a frenzy trying to guess the reason for Tracey's arrival.

'She is pretty shaken up,' Johnny answered.

'What she want – that was big chance she takes. Nearly fish food.'

'I don't know,' Johnny said. 'I want you to take over up here. Keep *Kingfisher* working. I'm going to get her to bed – I'll let you know what it's all about as soon as I find out.'

'Okay, boss.'

'Oh, and Sergio – keep an eye on those rocks. Don't let her drift down any closer.'

Johnny chose a powerful incentive to keep Sergio up on the bridge.

Johnny left him and went below, stopping only at the guest cabin.

'Come on.'

Tracey followed him, lurching unsteadily with *Kingfisher*'s antics in the high sea.

Two decks down they reached the computer control room and Johnny unlocked the heavy steel door, then locked it again behind them.

Tracey wedged herself against the bulkhead and watched as Johnny seated himself at the console and clipped the rumpled sheet into the board.

Reading from the sheet he typed the first line of figures on the keyboard. Immediately the computer registered a protest.

'Operator error,' it typed back. Johnny ignored its denial and typed the second line. This time it was more emphatic.

'No procedure. Operator error.'

And Johnny typed the next line of figures. He guessed that whoever had stored this programme in the computer's memory would have placed a series of blocks to prevent accidental discovery. Again the denial flashed back at him.

'Operator error.'

And Johnny muttered, 'Thrice before the cock crows,' striking an incongruously biblical note in the tense atmosphere of the control room.

He typed the last line of figures and the denial faded from the screen. The console clicked like a monstrous crab, then suddenly it started to print again.

'KAMINIKOTO SECONDARY RECOVERY PROGRAMME. INSTALLED OCTOBER 1969. AT LAS PALMAS BY HIDEKI KAMINIKOTO. DOCTOR OF SCIENCE.
TOKYO UNIVERSITY.'

The little Japanese had been unable to resist autographing his masterpiece. Tracey and Johnny crouched over the screen, staring at it with awful fascination as the computer began spelling out its report. It began with the number of hours worked, and the weight of gravel processed during that time. Next it reported the weight of concentrates recovered from the cyclone and finally, in a series of columns, it printed out the weights and sizes of all the diamonds won from the sea. The big Blue showed up in the place of honour, and wordlessly Tracey touched the figure 320 with a forefinger. Johnny nodded grimly.

The computer ended by giving the grand total of carats recovered, and Johnny spoke for the first time.

'It's true,' he said softly. 'It doesn't seem possible – but it is.'

The click and hum of the computer ceased, and the screen went blank.

Johnny straightened up in the chair.

'Where would they put it?' he asked himself, as he ran quickly over the line of recovery. He stood up from the chair and peered through the leaded glass peephole into the X-ray room. 'It must be this side of the cyclone, this side of the drier – ' He was speaking aloud. ' – Between the drier and the X-ray room.'

Then there bobbed to the surface of memory the modification in design which he had meant to query, but which he had forgotten.

'The inspection plate on the conveyor tunnel!' He punched his fist into his palm. 'They moved the inspection plate! That's it! It's in the conveyor tunnel.'

His hands were frantic with haste as he unlocked the steel door of the control room.

Sergio Caporetti paced his bridge like a captive bear, puffing so furiously on his cheroot that sparks flew from its tip. The wind howled hungrily around the wheelhouse, and the swells still marched in from the north.

Suddenly he reached a decision and turned to the helmsman.

'Watch those goddamn rocks – watch them good.'

The helmsman nodded and Sergio shambled through the chartroom to his own cabin. He locked the door behind him, and crossed to his desk. Fumbling with his keys he opened the bottom drawer of his desk and reaching under the pile of cheroot packets he brought out the canvas bag.

Weighing it thoughtfully in his hand, he looked about the cabin for a more secure hiding place. Through the canvas he could feel the nutty irregular shape of the stones.

'That Johnny, he a clever bastard,' he muttered. 'It better be good place.'

Then he reached a decision. 'Best place where I can watch them all a time.'

He opened his jacket and stuffed the bag into his inside pocket. He buttoned the jacket and patted the bulge over his heart.

'Fine!' he said. 'Good!' And stood up from the desk. He hurried back, unlocking the door into the chartroom, and headed for the bridge. He stopped in the middle of the chartroom, and his head swung towards the repeater screen of the computer. The buzzer was going like a rattlesnake, and the red bulb that warned of a new procedure was blinking softly.

Fearfully Sergio approached the screen and stooped over it. A single glance was enough, and he rushed from it to the chart table. He saw the cross-shaped tear in the chart.

'Mary Mother!'

He ripped back the thick crackling paper and searched under it. He stepped back from the table and hit himself across the chest.

'Fool!' he said. 'Idiot!' He spent ten seconds in self-castigation, then he looked about for a weapon. The locking handle of the cabin was a twelve-inch steel bar with a heavy head. He pulled out the pin and worked it loose. He slipped it into the waistband of his trousers.

'I'm going below,' he told the helmsman curtly, and clambered down the companionway. Swiftly he moved through the ship, balancing easily to her roll and pitch.

When he reached the lowest deck he became more stealthy, creeping silently forward. Now he carried the steel bar in his right hand. Every few paces he stopped to listen, but *Kingfisher*'s hull was groaning and popping as she worked in the swells.

He could hear no other sound. He crept up to the door of the control room and cautiously peered through the small armoured glass window. The control room was empty. He tried the handle, and found it locked.

Then he heard voices – from the open doorway of the conveyor room behind him. Quickly he crossed to it and flattened himself against the jamb.

Johnny's voice came muffled and indistinct:

'There's another hatch in here. Get me a half-inch spanner from the tool cupboard.'

'What's a half-inch spanner look like?'

'It's a big one. The size is stamped on it.'

Sergio glanced one-eyed around the door jamb. The cover was off the inspection hatch in the conveyor tunnel, and Tracey's head was thrust into the opening.

It was clear that Johnny Lance was in there, and that he had found the secret compartment.

Tracey drew her head out of the hatch, and Sergio ducked back and looked down the passageway. The tool cupboard was bolted to the bulkhead under the stairs from the deck above. He turned and darted around the corner of the passageway. Tracey came out of the conveyor room, and went to the cupboard. She opened the doors on the glittering array of tools, each clipped securely to its rack.

While she stood before the cupboard, completely absorbed in her search for a half-inch spanner, Sergio came from around the corner and crept up silently behind her.

He lifted the steel bar over his shoulder and came up on his toes, poised to strike.

Tracey was muttering softly to herself, head bowed slightly, handling the spanners -- and Sergio knew the blow would crush her skull.

He closed his mind to the thought, and aimed carefully at the base of her skull. He started the blow, and then checked it. For a second that seemed to last for a long time he remained frozen. He couldn't do it.

With an exclamation of satisfaction Tracey found what she was searching for. As she turned away from the cupboard Sergio shrank back behind the angle of the bulkhead, and Tracey hurried back into the conveyor room.

'I've got it, Johnny,' she shouted into the hatch.

'Bring it to me. Hurry, Tracey. Sergio will be getting suspicious,' he shouted back, and Tracey hitched up her voluminous trousers and wriggled into the hatch.

On hands and knees she crawled up beside him. It was cramped and hot in the narrow tunnel. He took the spanner from her.

'Hold the flashlight.' She took it from him, holding the beam on the panel while he unscrewed the retaining bolts and lifted off the cover.

Lying on his side he peered into the opening.

'There's a container of sorts,' he grunted, and reached in. For a minute he struggled with the clamps, then slowly he lifted out the stainless steel cup.

At that moment *Kingfisher* reared and plunged to a freak wave and the cup slipped from Johnny's fingers, and from it spilled the diamonds. They cascaded over both of them, a glittering shower of stones of all sizes and colours. Some lodged in Tracey's damp hair, the rest rolled and bounced and scattered about them, catching the light from the torch and throwing it back in splinters of sunshine.

'Yipes!' gasped Tracey and laughed at Johnny's whoop of triumph.

Lying side by side they scrabbled and snatched at the treasure scattered around them.

'Look at this one,' exulted Tracey.

'And this.' They were crazy with excitement, hands filled with diamonds. They hugged each other and kissed ecstatically, laughing into each other's mouths.

Johnny sobered first, 'Come on. Let's get out of here.'

'What about the diamonds?'

'Leave them. There'll be plenty of time later.'

They crawled backwards down the tunnel, still laughing and exclaiming, and one after the other emerged into the conveyor room. While they straightened their clothing, and regained their breath, Tracey asked, 'What now?'

'First thing is to get young Sergio safely under lock and key, his crew also.' Johnny's face hardened. 'The bloody bastards,' he added angrily.

'Then?' Tracey asked.

'Then we'll pull up the hose, and sail *Kingfisher* back into Cartridge Bay. Then we'll call up the police on the radio. There's going to be an accounting with the whole gang of the bastards – your darling brother included.'

Johnny started for the door, asking as he crossed the deck:

'Why did you close the door, Tracey?'

'I didn't,' she replied as she hurried after him, and Johnny's expression changed. He ran to the heavy steel door and threw his weight on it. It did not move, and he swung round to face the door that led into the cyclone room.

It was closed also. He charged across the room and grabbed the handle, heaving at it with all his strength.

He stood back at last, and looked wildly about the long narrow cabin. There was no other opening, no hatch or porthole – nothing except the tiny square peephole in the centre of the steel door that led into the cyclone room beyond. The peephole was covered with three-inch armoured glass that was as strong as the steel that surrounded it. He looked through it.

The tall cyclone reached from floor to roof, dominating the room. Beyond it the steel pipe that carried the gravel from the sea bed pierced the roof from the deck above, but the cyclone room was deserted.

Johnny turned slowly back to Tracey and put an arm around her shoulders.

'We've got problems,' he said.

After closing and locking both the doors that led into the conveyor room, Sergio climbed quickly back to his bridge. The helmsman looked at him curiously.

'How's the lady?'

'Fine,' Sergio snapped at him. 'She's safe.' And then with unnecessary violence, 'Why you no mind your own business, hey? You think you Captain for this ship?'

Startled, the helmsman quickly transferred his attention back to the storm which still raged lustily about them. Sergio began to pace up and down the bridge, balancing easily and instinctively to her exaggerated motion. His smooth baby face was crumpled into a massive scowl, and he puffed on one of his cheroots. With all his soul Sergio Caporetti was lamenting his involvement in this business. He wished that he had never heard of *Kingfisher*. He would have traded his hopes of a life hereafter to be sitting on the seafront at Ostia, sipping *grappa* and watching the girls go by.

Impulsively he pulled open the storm doors at the angle of the bridge and went out on to the exposed wing. The wind buffeted him and set his soft hair dancing and flickering.

From inside his jacket he pulled the canvas bag.

'This is the trouble,' he muttered, looking at the bag in his hand. 'Bloody little stones.'

He threw back his arm like a baseball pitcher, set to hurl the bag out into that hissing green sea below him, but again he could not make the gesture. Swearing quietly to himself, he stuffed the stones back into his jacket, and went back into the wheelhouse.

'Call the radio operator,' he ordered, and the helmsman reached quickly for the voice tube.

The radio operator reached the bridge still owl-eyed with sleep and buttoning his clothing.

'Get on to *Wild Goose*,' Sergio told him.

'I won't be able to raise her in this,' the man protested, glancing out at the storm.

'Call her.' Sergio stepped towards him threateningly. 'Keep calling until you get her.'

*W*ild *Goose* staggered and wallowed through the turbulence at the entrance to Cartridge Bay, then fought her way into the sanctuary of the channel.

Hugo relaxed perceptibly. It had been a long hard run back from Thunderbolt and Suicide. Yet there was an uneasy feeling that still persisted. He hoped that the girl was able to handle Lance. He was a tough cookie that Lance, he wished that he had been able to go along with her and make sure of the business. Fifteen years was one hell of a long time – he would be almost fifty years old at the end of it.

Hugo followed the channel markers that appeared like milestones out of the dust clouds, until ahead he made out the loom of the jetty and the depot buildings.

There was a figure on the jetty, crouched beside the mountain of dieseline drums. With a prickle of alarm, Hugo strained his eyes in the bad visibility.

'Who the hell is it?' he puzzled aloud. The figure straightened and came forward to stand on the edge of the jetty. Bare-headed, dressed in rumpled dark business suit, the man carried a shotgun in one hand – and it was another few seconds before Hugo recognized him.

'Christ! It's the boss!' Hugo felt alarm flare in his stomach and chest, it tightened his breathing.

Benedict van der Byl jumped down on to the deck of *Wild Goose* at the moment she touched the jetty.

'What's happened?' Benedict demanded as he barged into the wheelhouse.

'I thought you were in hospital,' Hugo countered.

'Who told you that?'

'Your sister.'

'You've seen her? Where is she?'

'I took her out to *Kingfisher*. Like you said. She went out to deal with Lance.'

'Deal with Lance! She's with him, you idiot, she's not with us. She knows the whole deal. Everything!'

'She told me—' Hugo was appalled. But Benedict cut him short.

'The whole thing's blown up. We've got to clear out. Get your crew to load those drums of dieseline into the hold. How are your water tanks?'

'Full.'

'Food?'

'We are stocked up.'

189

'For how long?'

'Three weeks – at a push, four.'

'Thank God for that.' Benedict looked relieved. 'This storm will blow another three days – we'll have that much start. They'll never find us in this. By the time it clears we'll be well on our way.'

'Where to – Angola?'

'God, no! We have to get well clear. South America.'

'South America!'

'Yes – we can do it, carrying extra fuel.'

Hugo was silent a moment, becoming accustomed to the idea.

'We can do it,' Benedict repeated.

'Yes.' Hugo nodded. 'We can do it,' he agreed thoughtfully. For the first time he examined Benedict closely. He saw that he was in an emotional and physical mess, his bloodshot eyes were sunk into deep plum-coloured hollows, dark new beard covered his jowls, and there was a gaunt hunted look to him – like some fugitive animal.

He was filthy with dust, and there was a streak of something that could have been dried vomit down the front of his jacket.

'But what do we do when we get there?' For the first time since he had known Benedict he felt in control. This was the time to deal, to make bargains.

'We'll get ashore on some deserted spot, and then we split up and disappear.'

'What about money?' Hugo spoke carefully. He glanced down at the shotgun. Benedict's hands were fidgety and restless on the weapon.

'I've got money.'

'How much?' Hugo asked.

'Enough.' Benedict blinked cautiously.

'For me also?' Hugo prodded him, and Benedict nodded.

'How much for me?' Hugo went on.

'Ten thousand.'

'Pounds?'

'Pounds,' Benedict agreed.

'That's not enough.' Hugo shook his head. 'I'll need more than that.'

'Twenty.' Benedict increased his bid, but he knew he was playing from weakness into strength. Ruby was lying mutilated in his study, the net was probably being spread for him already.

'Fifty,' said Hugo decisively.

'I haven't that much.'

'Who are you kidding, Buster!' Hugo snorted. 'You've been stacking it away for years.'

Benedict let the barrels of the shotgun swing towards Hugo's belly suggestively.

'Go ahead,' Hugo grinned at him, screwing up his pale albino eyes. 'That'll leave you to paddle this canoe – you want to try it? You'd pile her up on the bar at the entrance – that's how far you'd get.'

Benedict swung the barrels aside.

'Fifty,' he agreed.

'Right!' Hugo spoke briskly. 'Let's get the hell out of here.'

*W*ild *Goose* was clear of the land, and of the towering blinding dust clouds. The following seas came sweeping up under her stern urging her on her westward flight, while the high-pitched shriek of the wind in her rigging cried to her to hasten.

'Why don't you get down below and grab some sleep?' Hugo said. He found Benedict's restless haunting presence in the crowded wheelhouse disconcerting.

Benedict ignored the suggestion. 'Switch on the radio,' he said.

'What for? You'll get nothing on the set.'

'We are out of the dust,' Benedict replied. 'We might pick up a police message.'

The image of Ruby was so clear in his mind. He wanted to know if they'd found her yet. He felt his gorge rising again. That head – oh God – that head! He crossed quickly to the radio set and switched it on.

'They won't be on to us yet,' said Hugo, but Benedict was manipulating the dials – searching the tortured radio waves. The static wailed and gibbered and shrieked like a maniac.

'Turn it off,' snapped Hugo, and at that moment a voice cut in on them.

' – *Wild Goose*,' said the voice from the loudspeaker quite clearly. Benedict crouched eagerly over the set, his hands busy on the dials, and Hugo came up beside him.

' – Come in, *Wild Goose*. This is *Kingfisher*. I repeat, come in *Wild Goose*—'

Benedict and Hugo looked at each other. 'Don't answer,' said Hugo, but he made no move to intervene as Benedict lifted the microphone off its hook.

'*Kingfisher*, this is *Wild Goose*.'

'Stand by, *Wild Goose*.' The answer came back immediately. 'Stand by for Captain Caporetti.'

'*Wild Goose* standing by.'

Hugo caught Benedict's shoulder and his voice was angrily uncertain.

'Leave it, don't be a fool.'

Benedict shrugged off the hand, and Sergio's voice boomed out of the speaker.

'This is Caporetti – who dat?'

'No names,' Benedict cautioned him. 'Where are your guests?'

'They safe – battened down nicely.'

'Safe? Are you certain? Both of them safe?'

'*Si*. I have them safe and sure.'

'Stand by.' Benedict crouched over the set, and his mind

192

was racing. Johnny Lance was in his power. This was the last chance he would ever have. Plans began to form, gelling quickly in his mind.

'The diamonds. Caporetti has the diamonds. That big Blue is worth a million on its own,' said Hugo. 'If Caporetti has taken care of the others – it would be worth the risk.'

'Yes.' Benedict turned to him, he had been puzzling how he could make Hugo turn back. He had forgotten the diamonds. 'It would be worth it,' he agreed.

'Just a quick pass alongside *Kingfisher* – pick up Caporetti with the diamonds and we'd be on our way.'

'I have to go aboard.' Benedict qualified the suggestion.

'Why?' Hugo asked.

'Wipe out the reel on the computer that carries the programme – it's got the Jap's name on it. They could trace him. I paid him on my Swiss bank. They'll find the account.'

Hugo hesitated. 'No killing – or anything like that. We've got enough trouble without that.'

'You think I'm crazy?' Benedict demanded.

'Okay, then,' Hugo agreed.

'*Kingfisher*,' Benedict spoke into the microphone. 'We are coming to you. I'll be coming on board to finalize matters.'

'Fine.' Through the static they could hear the relief in Sergio's voice. 'I'll be standing by.'

It took nearly two hours for *Wild Goose* to slug her way back to where *Kingfisher* lay beneath the ghostly white shapes of Thunderbolt and Suicide, and it was after midday before Hugo began manoeuvring *Wild Goose* into the big ship's lee.

'Don't waste time,' Hugo cautioned Benedict. 'The sooner we get on our way – the better for all of us.'

'I'll be about half an hour,' Benedict answered. 'You lay off and wait for us.'

'Are you taking that bloody shotgun?' Benedict nodded.

'What for?' But Benedict did not reply, he looked up at the sky. The sun was merely a luminous patch of silver light through the ceiling of sea-fret and wind-driven mist, and still the storm hunted hungrily across the sea.

'It will slow you up on the ladder.' Hugo harped on the shotgun. He wanted very much to part Benedict from it, he wanted it over the side – for its presence aboard would prejudice the plans that Hugo had been forming during the last few hours – plans that took into account the ready market for diamonds in South America, and the undesirability of sharing the proceeds with two partners.

'I'll take it.' Benedict tightened his grip on the stock of the weapon. Without it he would feel naked and vulnerable – and it was part of his own private plans for the future. Benedict's brain had also been busy during the last two hours.

'Suit yourself.' Hugo resigned himself to Benedict's refusal; there would be an opportunity later, during the long passage across the Southern Atlantic. 'You better get up for'ard.'

This time Hugo's approach was neatly executed; in a lull between the colossal swells he touched *Wild Goose*'s bows to the steel side of the factory ship. Benedict stepped across the gap and was up the landing ladder and standing at *Kingfisher*'s rail before the next wave came marching down on them.

He waved Hugo off, then hanging on to the rail, made his way aft to *Kingfisher*'s bridge works.

'Where is Lance?' he demanded of Sergio the moment he stepped on to the bridge, but Sergio glanced significantly at the inquisitively listening helmsman and led Benedict through into his cabin.

'Where is Lance?' Benedict repeated the moment the door was locked.

'He and your sister they are in the conveyor room.'

'The conveyor room?' Benedict was incredulous.

'*Si*. They find out about Kammy's machine. They open the hatch and go inside. I close both doors. Lock them good.'

'They are in there now?' Benedict asked to gain time to reconstruct his plans.

'*Si*. Still there.'

'All right.' Benedict reached his decision. 'Now listen, Caporetti, this is what we are going to do. The whole thing has blown up on us. We are going to wipe out as much of the evidence against us as possible, then we are clearing out. We are going to run for South America in *Wild Goose*. You have got the diamonds – haven't you?'

'*Si*.' Sergio patted the breast of his jacket.

'Give them to me.' Benedict held out his hand, and Sergio grinned.

'I tink I look after them. They keep my heart warm.'

A frown of annoyance narrowed Benedict's eyes, but he let the moment pass.

'All right.' His tone was still friendly. 'Now, what you have to do is get down to the control room and wipe out Kaminikoto's programme. Get his name off that reel. He showed you how to do that?'

'*Si*.' Sergio nodded.

'How long will it take?'

'Half an hour, not longer,' Sergio answered, and Benedict checked his wrist watch, sure that this would give him time enough to do what he had to do.

'Good! Get cracking.'

'Boss.' Sergio hesitated at the cabin door. 'What about my boys, my crew? They good boys, no trouble for them?'

'They're clean,' Benedict pointed out irritably. 'I'll get

them together now, and explain that you have to go ashore. They can keep *Kingfisher* hove to waiting for you to come back. After the storm blows out they are bound to radio base and find out we have disappeared. They'll be all right.'

Sergio nodded his satisfaction.

'I'll call them all to the bridge now. You talk to them.'

T he five crew members were gathered on *Kingfisher*'s bridge, and Sergio had disappeared down below.

'Any of you speak English?' Benedict demanded, and two of them affirmed that they did.

'Right,' Benedict addressed them. 'You will have been wondering about all the coming and going in this weather. I want you all to be ready to leave the ship. I want you to get all your valuables – now!'

Quickly they translated to the others, who looked apprehensively at Benedict. He was a strange wild-eyed figure with the shotgun tucked under his arm.

'Right – let's go.' And there was no dissent from any of them as they trooped to the companionway.

Benedict followed them along the passageway towards the crew quarters, and glanced quickly at his wrist watch. Seven minutes had elapsed. He looked at the men ahead of him.

The backs of their heads formed a solid target. He had shot guineafowl like that in Namaqualand when they were on the ground running away from him in a thick file, down on one knee and aim for the thicket of heads, knocking down half the flock with both barrels.

He knew he could take all five of these men with two shots. Just let them get a little further ahead so the shot could spread. But he remembered Ruby and his stomach heaved. The other way was just as sure.

'Stop!' he commanded as the five men came level with

the paint store. They obeyed and turned back to face him. Now he held the shotgun so that there was no mistaking its menace. They stared at the gun fearfully.

'Open that door.' He pointed at the paint store. Nobody moved.

'You.' Benedict picked on one of those who spoke English. Like a man in a trance he went to the steel door and spun the locking handle. He pulled the door open.

'In!' Eloquently Benedict gestured with the shotgun. Reluctantly the five of them filed into the small windowless cubicle, and Benedict slammed the door on them. He spun the lock, throwing all his weight on the handle to set it.

Now he had a clear field, and his wrist watch gave him another twenty minutes. He hurried for'ard, he wanted to keep well clear of the control room and Sergio Caporetti.

Using the forward companionway he dropped down to the working deck, fumbling out his duplicate set of keys.

WARNING. EXPLOSIVES. NO UNAUTHORIZED ENTRY.

He unlocked the door, and laying the shotgun flat on the deck he lifted a twenty-five pound drum of plastique down from its rack.

In his haste he tore a fingernail on the lid of the drum, but hardly felt the pain. He uncoiled a six-foot length of the soft dark toffee-coloured material and slung it around his neck. Next he selected a cardboard box of pencil time fuses. He read the label.

'Fourteen-minute delay. That's about right.'

Blood from his torn nail left brown blotches on the cardboard as he took four of the pencils from the box, picked up the shotgun and hurried aft. The jet engine whine of the cyclone mounted deafeningly as he came closer to it.

Tracey was curled on the bare steel plating of the deck with Johnny's jacket folded under her head. She was in a fatigue-drugged sleep, so deep as to be almost deathlike.

Every few minutes Johnny interrupted his restless patrol of the conveyor room to stand over her and look down on her unconscious form. His worried expression softened a little each time he studied her pale lovely face. Once he stooped over her and tenderly lifted a strand of dark hair from her cheek, before resuming his pacing up and down the narrow cabin.

Each time he reached the door of the conveyor room he glanced through the tiny window. The glass had resisted his attempts to smash it with one of the spanners. He had wanted to open the window to call for help, but his efforts had not marked the thick armoured glass.

There was no way out of the cabin. Johnny had tried every possible outlet. The apertures for the conveyor system were guarded at one end by the furnace, and at the other by moving machinery which would ferociously chew to tatters anyone who became entangled in it. They were caged securely, and Johnny paced his cage.

Again he stopped before the peephole, but this time he flung himself at the door with clenched fists. The steel plate smeared the skin from his knuckles as he hammered on it and the pain sobered him. He pressed his face to the glass and through it watched Benedict van der Byl enter the conveyor room and, without glancing at the window, cross to the cyclone.

Benedict laid aside the shotgun he carried and for a moment stood looking up at the thick steel pipe that carried the gravel down from the deck pumps above. As he lifted the thick rope of plastique from around his neck, Johnny knew exactly what he was going to do.

He watched in fascination as Benedict mounted the steel ladder up the side of the cyclone. Hanging with one hand to the ladder, Benedict reached out with the other and clumsily tied the rope of plastique around the gravel pipe. It hung there like a necklace about the throat of some obscene prehistoric monster.

'You bastard! You murdering bloody swine!' Johnny shouted, and again he beat on the steel door with his fists. But the thickness of the door and the whine of the cyclone drowned his voice. Benedict showed no sign of hearing him – but Tracey sat up and looked about her blearily. Then she came to her feet and staggering to the roll and pitch of the ship she went to Johnny and pressed her face to the window beside her.

Benedict was sticking the time pencils into the soft dark explosive. He used all four fuses, taking no chances on a misfire.

'What's he doing?' Tracey asked after she had recovered from the surprise of recognizing her brother.

'He's going to cut the pipe, and let *Kingfisher* pump herself full of gravel.'

'Sink her?' Tracey's voice was sharp with alarm.

'She'll pump water and gravel into herself at pressures that will tear away all the inner bulkheads.'

'This one?' Tracey patted the steel plate.

'It'll pop like a paper bag. God, you have no idea of the power in those pumps.'

'No.' Tracey shook her head. 'He's my brother. He won't do it, Johnny. He couldn't murder us.'

'By the time he's finished – ' Johnny contradicted her grimly, ' – *Kingfisher* will be lying in 200 feet of water. Her hull will be packed so tightly with gravel that it will be like a block of cement. We, and everything in her, including his little machine, will be so flattened as to be unrecognizable. It would cost millions to salvage *Kingfisher* – and no one will care that much.'

'No, not Benedict.' Tracey was almost pleading. 'He's not that bad.'

Johnny interrupted her brusquely. 'He could get away with it. It's a good try – his best chance. Encase all the evidence against him in concrete, and bury it deep.'

'No, Benedict.' Tracey was watching her brother as he climbed down the cyclone ladder and picked up the shotgun. 'Please, Benedict, don't do it.'

Almost as if he had heard her, Benedict turned suddenly and saw the two faces at the window. The shock of guilt held him rigid for a moment as he stared at them – Tracey's pale lips forming words he could not hear, Johnny's eyes burning with accusation.

Benedict dropped his eyes, he made a gesture that was indecisive, almost pathetic. He looked up at the fused and charged rope of explosive – and then he grinned. A sardonic twitching of the lips, and he stumbled out of the cyclone room and was gone.

'He'll come back,' whispered Tracey. 'He won't let it happen.'

'I wouldn't bet on that – if I were you,' said Johnny.

B enedict reached *Kingfisher*'s rail and clung to it. He looked out to where *Wild Goose* bobbed and hung on the swells. He saw Hugo's face as a white blob behind the wheelhouse window, but as the little trawler began closing in for the pick-up Benedict waved it away. He glanced at his watch again, then looked back anxiously at the bridge.

The long minutes dragged by. Where the hell was the Italian? Benedict could not leave him – not while he still had that diamond; not while he could stop the dredge pumps and release the prisoners locked below.

Again Benedict checked his watch, twelve minutes since he had set the time pencils. He must go back and find Caporetti. He started back along the rail, and at that moment Sergio appeared on the wing of the bridge. He shouted a question at Benedict that was lost in the wind.

'Come on!' Frantically Benedict beckoned to him. 'Come on! Hurry!'

With another last look about the bridge, Sergio ran to the ladder and climbed down to deck level.

'Where my boys?' he shouted at Benedict. 'Why nobody at the con? What you do with them?'

'They are all right,' Benedict assured him. He had turned to the rail and was signalling *Wild Goose* to come alongside.

'Where they?' Sergio demanded. 'Where my boys?'

'I sent them to—' Benedict's reply was cut off as *Kingfisher*'s deck jarred under their feet. The explosion was a dull concussion in her belly, and Sergio's jaw hung open. Benedict backed away from him along the rail.

'Filth!' Sergio's jaw snapped closed, his whole body appeared to swell with anger.

'You kill them, dirty pig. You kill my boys. You kill Johnny – the girl.'

'Keep away from me.' Benedict braced himself against the rail, leaving both hands free to use the gun.

Not even Sergio would advance into the deadly blank eyes of those muzzles. He paused uncertainly.

'I'll blow your guts all over the deck,' Benedict warned him, and his forefinger was hooked around the trigger.

They stared at each other, and the wind fluttered their hair and tore at their clothing.

'Give me those diamonds,' Benedict commanded, and when Sergio stood unmoving, he went on urgently, 'Don't be a hero, Caporetti. I can gun you down and take them anyway. Give them to me – and our deal is still on. You'll come with us. I'll get you out of here. I swear it.'

Sergio's expression of outrage faded. A moment longer he hesitated.

'Come on, Caporetti. We haven't got much time.' It may have been his imagination, but to Benedict it seemed that

*Kingfisher*'s action in the water had altered, she was sluggish to meet the swells and her roll was more pronounced.

'Okay,' said Sergio, and began unbuttoning his jacket. 'You win. I give you.'

Benedict relaxed with relief, and Sergio thrust his hand into his jacket and stepped towards him. He grasped the canvas bag by its neck, and brought it out held like a cosh.

Sergio was close to him, too close for Benedict to swing the shotgun on to him. Sergio's expression became savage, his intentions blazed in his dark eyes as he lifted the canvas bag and poised himself to deliver a blow at Benedict's head, but he had not reckoned with the extraordinary reflexes of the natural athlete he was facing.

As Sergio launched the blow, Benedict rolled his shoulders and head away from it, lifting the butt of the shotgun as a guard. Sergio's wrist struck the seasoned walnut, and he grunted with the pain. His fingers opened nervelessly and the canvas bag flew from his grip, glanced off Benedict's temple and flew on down the deck, sliding to stop against one of the compressed air tanks thirty feet away.

Benedict danced back, dropping the barrels of the shotgun until Sergio looked into the muzzles.

'Hold it, you bastard,' Benedict snarled at him. 'You've made your choice. Now let's see what your guts look like.'

Sergio was hugging his injured wrist to his belly, crouching over it. Benedict was backing away to where the bag lay against the tank. His face was flushed and hectic with anger, but he kept darting side glances at the canvas bag.

At that moment *Kingfisher* took another wave over her bows, and the water came swooshing down the deck, picking up the bag and washing it towards the scuppers.

'Look out!' Sergio shouted. 'The bag! It's going.'

Benedict lunged for it, sprawling full length. With his free hand he grabbed the sodden canvas as it was disappearing over the side. But he was thirty feet away from Sergio, and he still held the shotgun in his other fist. Sergio could not hope to reach him without getting both charges of buckshot in his belly.

Instead Sergio spun round and sprinted back along the deck towards the bridge.

Benedict was on his knees frantically stuffing the bag of diamonds into the side pocket of his jacket and shouting after Sergio.

'Stop! Stop or I'll shoot!'

Sergio did not look back nor check his run, and Benedict had the bag in his pocket and now both hands were free. He lifted the shotgun, and tried to balance himself against *Kingfisher*'s wallowing motion as he aimed.

At the shot, Sergio stumbled slightly but kept on running. He reached the ladder and went up it.

Again Benedict aimed, and the shotgun clapped dully in the wind. This time a spasm of pain shuddered through Sergio's big body, and he froze on the ladder.

Benedict fumbled in his pocket for fresh shells, but before he could reload Sergio had begun climbing again. Benedict broke the gun and thrust the shells into the breech. He snapped the gun closed and looked up just as Sergio disappeared through the storm doors – and the two shots that Benedict loosed after him merely pockmarked the paintwork and starred the glass of the wheelhouse.

'The stupid bastard.' Hugo watched from the wheelhouse of *Wild Goose*. 'He's gone berserk.'

Hugo had heard the explosion and seen the shooting.

'Fifteen years is enough – but not the rope as well.'

He swung the wheel and *Wild Goose* sheered in towards

*Kingfisher*'s side. Peering through the spray and salt-smattered windows, he saw Benedict drag himself to his feet and start after Sergio along the deck.

Hugo snatched the electric loudhailer from its bracket and pulled open the side window of the wheelhouse, holding the hailer to his lips.

'Hey! You stupid bastard, have you gone mad? What the hell you doing?'

Benedict glanced down at the trawler, then ignored it to give all his attention to reloading the gun. He kept going back along the deck, following Sergio to finish him off.

'You'll get us all strung up, you fool,' Hugo called through the loudhailer. 'Leave him. Let's get out of here.'

Benedict kept scrambling and slipping towards *Kingfisher*'s bridge.

'I'm leaving – now! Do you hear me? You can stew in your own pot. I'm getting out.'

Benedict checked and looked down at the trawler. He shouted and pointed at the bridge. Hugo caught one word: 'Diamonds.'

'All right, friend! Do what you like – I'll see you around,' Hugo hailed, and hit the trawler's throttle wide open. The roar of the diesels and the churning of her propeller convinced Benedict.

'Hugo! Wait! Wait for me, I'm coming.' He scampered back to the ladder and started down it.

Hugo throttled back and brought *Wild Goose* in neatly under the ladder.

'Jump!' he shouted through the hailer, and obediently Benedict jumped to hit the foredeck heavily. The shotgun flew from his hands to fall into the water alongside. Benedict cast one longing glance after the gun, then crawled to his feet and limped back to the wheelhouse.

Already *Wild Goose* was plunging away into the wind, but as Benedict entered the wheelhouse Hugo turned on him with his pink albino face set in a snarl of rage.

'What the hell have you done, you bastard? You lied to me. What was that explosion?'

'Explosion – I don't know. What explosion?'

Hugo hit him a stinging open-handed blow across the cheek.

'We agreed no killing – and you put us all on the spot.' Hugo's attention was focused completely on Benedict who had backed into the furthest corner of the wheelhouse. He massaged the dark red finger marks that stained his cheek.

'You set scuttling charges in *Kingfisher* – didn't you, you dirty son of a bitch. God, I hate to think what you've done with Lance and the girl.'

Outside the storm was nearing its climax. A rain squall swept down on *Wild Goose* – a sure sign that the wind must soon drop.

Automatically Hugo switched on the rotating wipers to clear the rain from the screen, as he continued to harangue Benedict.

'I saw you trying to murder the Italian. Christ! What for? He's one of us! Am I next on your list?'

'He had the diamonds,' mumbled Benedict. 'I was trying to get them from him.'

And Hugo's expression changed; he turned away from the wheel and stared at Benedict.

'You haven't got the diamonds? Is that what you're saying?' His tone was almost hurt.

'I tried – he wouldn't—'

And Hugo left the wheel and was across the wheelhouse like a white leopard. He grabbed the front of Benedict's coat, and screamed into his face.

'You left the diamonds! You stick my head in a noose – and I get nothing out of it.'

He was trembling with rage and his pale eyes bulged from their sockets.

Looking into those eyes Benedict realized his own danger. In the time it had taken him to leave *Kingfisher*'s deck and reach the wheelhouse of the trawler he had decided to let Hugo think that Sergio still had the diamonds. Squeamish as Hugo appeared to be about drowning Johnny and Tracey, despite his repeated demands for 'No killing', Benedict knew intuitively that Hugo had no intention of splitting a million pounds' worth of diamonds with him.

Once Hugo was certain that Benedict had the stones on board, Benedict knew there was no chance that he would reach South America alive.

The crossing might take weeks, the crew of the trawler were in Hugo's pay and loyal only to him. Benedict must sleep, and they would take him in the night.

On the other hand, of course, Benedict had no intention of splitting a million pounds' worth of diamonds with Hugo Kramer. He let his voice whine as he cringed in Hugo's grip.

'I tried. Sergio had them. He wouldn't – that's why I shot him.'

Hugo drew back his hand to slap Benedict again. Benedict twisted slightly, and drove his knee into Hugo's crutch, sending him staggering back across the wheelhouse, clutching himself between the legs and whimpering with the pain.

'Right, Kramer,' Benedict spoke softly. 'That's a little lesson for you. Behave yourself, and you'll get your fifty grand on the other side of the Atlantic.'

They stared at each other. Hugo Kramer weak and pale with agony, Benedict standing tall and arrogant again.

'Treat me gently, Kramer. I'm your meal-ticket. Remember it.'

Hugo gaped at him. The positions had reversed so swiftly. He pulled himself upright and his voice was thick with agony, but humble.

'I'm sorry, Mr van der Byl, I lost my temper. It's been a hell of a—'

'Skipper! Ahead!' The warning was shouted by the coloured crewman, Hansie.

Hugo stumbled to the untended wheel, and peered out into the storm.

*Wild Goose* was shooting down another slope of green water, and just ahead of her bows Hugo saw one of the huge yellow buoys that *Kingfisher* had laid down and then abandoned. It was held captive in the trough of the swells by the anchor cable. The cable was drawn as tight as a rod of steel across the trawler's bows, lifted just above the surface of the water; shivering drops of water flew from it under the tension of the buoy's drag.

'Oh God!' Hugo spun the wheel and threw *Wild Goose*'s engine into reverse – but she was racing down the swell, and her speed was unchecked as the cable scraped harshly along her keel.

Then came the harsh banging and clattering of the drive shaft as the cable fouled the propeller – followed by a crack as the shaft snapped. *Wild Goose*'s engine screamed into overrev as the load was lifted from it.

Hugo shut the throttle, and there was silence in the wheelhouse. *Wild Goose* swung beam on to the seas which came boiling in over her deck. Without her propeller she was transformed from a husky little sea creature to a piece of driftwood at the mercy of each current and the whim of the wind.

Hugo's head swung slowly until he was looking down-wind to where the massive shapes of Thunderbolt and Suicide just showed through the rain squall.

'Cover your ears – tight!' Johnny Lance pressed Tracey against the bulkhead as far from the cyclone room as they could get. 'There are twenty-five pounds of plastique in there – it will blow like a volcano. He will have used short fuse, fourteen minutes. We won't have long to wait.'

Johnny set Tracey's shoulders squarely against the steel plating, and crouched over her – trying to shield her with his own body.

They stared into each other's eyes, teeth clenched, the heels of their palms jammed hard over their ears and they cowered away from the blast that must come.

The minutes passed, the longest minutes of Tracey's life. She could not have borne them without screaming hysteria except for that big hard body covering her – even with it she felt her fear mounting steadily during the molasses drip of time.

Suddenly the air lunged at her, driving the breath from her lungs. Johnny was thrown heavily against her. The blast sucked at her eardrums, and burst in her head so that bright lights flashed across her vision and she felt the steel plates heave under her shoulders.

Then her head cleared, and although her eardrums buzzed and sang, she found with a leaping relief that she was still alive.

She reached out for Johnny, but he was gone. In panic she groped, then opened her eyes. He was lurching down the long conveyor room, and when he reached the locked door at the far end he pressed his face to the peephole.

The fumes of the explosion still filled the cyclone room, a swirling bluish fog, but through them Johnny could make out the shambles that was the aftermath.

The huge cyclone had been torn from its mountings, and now sagged against the far bulkhead – crushed. It was worth only a single glance before Johnny froze into rigidity at the true horror.

The gravel pipe had been severed cleanly just below its juncture with the upper deck. It protruded for six feet, but now the force of the jet through it was flicking and whipping it about as though it were not steel but a rubber garden hose.

The jet was a solid eighteen-inch column, a pillar of brown mud and yellow gravel and sea water that beat against the steel plates of the hull with a hollow drumming roar.

In the few seconds since the explosion the cyclone room was already half-filled with a slimy shifting porridge that rushed from wall to wall with the movement of the ship. It was like some monstrous jelly fish which each second gathered weight and strength.

Tracey reached Johnny's side and he placed his arm around her shoulders. She looked through the armoured glass and he felt her body stiffen.

At that moment the yellow monster spread over the window, obscuring it completely. Johnny felt the first straining of the steel plates under his hands. They fluttered and bulged, then began to protest aloud at the intolerable pressure. A seam started, and a fine jet of filthy water hissed from the gap and soaked icily through Johnny's jersey.

'Get back.' Johnny dragged Tracey away from the squeaking, groaning bulkhead. Back along the narrow conveyor room they stumbled, moving with difficulty for the deck beneath their feet was slanting as *Kingfisher* began to lean under the increasing weight in her belly.

Still holding Tracey, he reached the locked door and resisted the futile desire to attack it with his bare hands. Instead he forced his brain to work, tried to anticipate the sequence of events that would lead to the final destruction of *Kingfisher* – and all those aboard her.

Benedict had left the other entrance to the cyclone room wide open. Already that viscous mass of mud and water must be spreading rapidly through the lower levels of the hull, following always the avenue of least resistance – finding the weak spots and bursting through them.

If the walls of the conveyor room held against the pressure, the rest of the hull would be filled and they would be enfolded in the tentacles of that great yellow monster – a small bubble of air trapped within it and taken down with it when it returned to the depths from which it had come.

Would the bulkheads of the conveyor room hold? The answer came almost immediately in the squeal of metal against metal, and the crackle of springing rivets.

The monster had found the weak spot, the aperture through the drying furnace into the conveyor, ripping away the fragile baffles, bursting through the furnace in a cloud of steam, it gushed into the conveyor room bringing with it the sewage stench of deep-sea mud.

*Kingfisher* made another sluggish roll, so different from her usual spry action, and the mud came racing down the tunnel in a solid knee-high wall.

It slammed both of them back against the steel door with a shocking strength, and the feel of it was cold and loathsome as something long dead and putrefied.

*Kingfisher* rolled back and the mud slithered away, bunched itself against the far bulkhead then charged at them again.

Waist-deep it struck them, and tried to suck them back with the next roll.

Tracey was screaming now, nerves and muscles reaching their breaking-point. She was clinging to Johnny, coated to the waist in stinking ooze, her eyes and mouth wide open in terror as she watched the mud building up for its next assault.

Johnny groped for some hold to anchor them. They must keep on their feet to survive that next rush of mud. He found the locking handle of the door and braced himself against it, holding Tracey with all his strength.

The mud came again, silently, murderously. It burst over

their heads and punched them with stunning force against the plating.

Then it sucked back once more, and left them down on their knees, anchored only by Johnny's grip on the locking handle.

Tracey was vomiting the foul mud and it filled her ears and eyes and nostrils, clogging them so that it bubbled at her breathing.

Johnny could feel her weakening in his arms, her struggles becoming more feeble as she tried to regain her feet.

His own strength was going. It needed his last reserve to drag them both upright.

The locking handle turned in his fingers, spinning open. The steel door against which he was braced fell away, so that he staggered backwards without support but still clutching Tracey.

There was just a moment to recognize the big, reassuring bulk of Sergio Caporetti beside him and feel an arm like the trunk of a pine tree steady him before the rush of mud down the conveyor room hit them and knocked all three of them down, sending them swirling and rolling end over end before its strength dissipated in the new space beyond the conveyor room door.

Johnny pulled himself up the bulkhead. He had lost Tracey. Dazed but desperate he looked for her, mumbling her name.

He found her swilling aimlessly in the waist-deep mud, floating on her face. He took a handful of muddy hair and lifted her face out, but the mud had hold of his legs, pulling him off balance as it surged back and forth.

'Sergio. Help!' he croaked. 'For God's sake, Sergio.'

And Sergio was there, lifting her like a child in his arms and wading to the ladder that led to the deck above. The mud knocked Johnny down again, and when he surfaced Sergio was climbing steadily up the ladder.

Despite the mud and water that blurred Johnny's eyesight, he could see that Sergio's wide back, from shoulders to hips, was speckled with dozens of punctures as though he had been stabbed repeatedly with a knitting needle. From each tiny wound oozed droplets of blood that spread like brown ink on the blotting-paper of his sodden jacket.

At the head of the companionway Sergio turned, still holding Tracey in his arms; he stood like a Colossus looking down at Johnny wallowing and slipping in the mud below.

'Hey, Lance – go switch off your bloody machine. She drown my ship. I sail her myself now – the right way. No bloody fancy machine.'

Johnny steadied himself against the bulkhead and called up at him:

'Sergio, what happened to Benedict van der Byl, where is he?'

'I think he go with *Wild Goose* – but first he shoot the hell out of me, not half. Fix your machine, no time for talk.'

And he was gone, still carrying Tracey.

Another rush of mud carried Johnny down the flooded passage and threw him against the door to the control room. Already his body seemed to be one aching bruise, and still the battering continued as he tried to unlock and open the control room door.

At last, using the suck of the mud to help him, he yanked it open and went in with a burst of yellow slime following him and flooding the compartment shoulder deep.

Clinging to the console of the computer he reached up and punched the master control buttons.

'Dredge Stop.'

'Dredge engines Stop.'

'Main engines manual.'

'Navigation system manual.'

'All programmes abort.'

Instantly the roar from the severed dredge pipe, which

had echoed through the ship during all their strivings, dwindled as though some vast waterfall had dried. Then there was silence. Though only comparative silence, for the hull still groaned and squeaked at the heart-breaking burden it now carried and the mud slopped and thudded against the plating.

Weak and sick, Johnny clung to the console. He was shivering with cold, and every muscle in his body felt bruised and strained.

Suddenly the ship changed her motion, heaving under his feet like a harpooned whale as she swung broadside to the storm. Johnny roused himself with alarm.

The journey back through the flooded passages to the companionway was an agony of mind and body – for *Kingfisher* was now behaving in a strange and unnatural way.

The scene that awaited Johnny as he dragged himself on to the bridge chilled his soul as the icy mud had chilled his body.

Thunderbolt and Suicide lay less than a furlong off *Kingfisher*'s starboard quarter. Both islands were wreathed in sheets of spray that fumed from the surf that was breaking like cannon-fire on the cliffs.

The maniacal flute of the wind joined with the drum of the surf to produce a symphony fit for the halls of Hell, but above this devil's music Sergio Caporetti bellowed, 'We got no power on port main engine.'

Johnny turned to him. Sergio was hunched over the wheel, and Tracey lay on the deck at his feet like a discarded doll.

'The water, she kill port main.' Sergio was pumping the engine telegraph. Then abandoning the effort, he looked over the side.

The reeking white cliffs were closer now, much closer – as though you could reach out a hand to them. The ship was drifting down rapidly on the wind.

Sergio spun the wheel to full port lock, trying to bring *Kingfisher*'s head round to meet the sea and the wind. She was rolling as no ship was ever meant to roll, hanging over at the limit of each swing, so that the wheelhouse windows seemed but a few feet from the crests of the green waves. She hung like that as though she meant never to come upright again. Then sluggishly, reluctantly, she swung back, speeding up as she reached the perpendicular and the great mass of mud and water in her hull shifted and slammed her over on her other side, pinning her like that for eternal seconds before she could struggle upright again for the cycle to be repeated.

Sergio held the wheel at full lock, but still *Kingfisher* wallowed down towards the cliffs of Thunderbolt and Suicide. The wind had her the way a dog carries a bone in its teeth. Under half power and with her decks awash *Kingfisher* could not break that grip.

Johnny was a helpless spectator, held awe-bound so he could not break away even to succour Tracey who was still lying on the deck. He saw everything with a supernatural clarity – from the dribbling little shot holes in Sergio's back, to the ponderous irresistible rush of the white water up the cliffs that loomed so close alongside.

'She no answer helm. She too sick.' Sergio spoke now in conversational tones which carried with surprising clarity through the uproar of the elements. 'All right then. We go the other way. We take the gap.'

For a moment Johnny did not understand, then he saw it. *Kingfisher*'s bows were coming up to the narrow opening between the two islands.

A passage less than a hundred yards wide at its narrowest point, where the vicious cross-currents met head-on and leapt fifty feet into the air as they collided. Here the surface was obscured by a thick froth of spindrift that heaved and humped up as though the ocean were fighting for breath under the thick cream-coloured blanket.

'No.' Johnny shook his head, staring at that hideous passage. 'We won't make it, Sergio. We won't do it.'

But already Sergio was spinning the wheel from lock to lock, and unbelievably *Kingfisher* was responding. Helped now by the wind she came around slowly, seeming to brush her bows across the white cliff of Thunderbolt, and she steadied her swing and aimed at the gap. It was then Johnny saw it for the first time.

'Christ, there's a boat dead ahead!'

The steep swells had hidden it up to that moment, but now she bobbed up on a crest. It was a tiny trawler, flying a dirty scrap of canvas as a staysail at her stubby mast, and struggling piteously in the granite jaws of Thunderbolt and Suicide.

'*Wild Goose!*' roared Sergio, and he reached for the handle of the foghorn that hung above his head.

'Now we have some fun.' And he yanked the handle. The croaking bellow of the foghorn echoed off the cliffs that were closing on either side of them.

'Kill my boys – hey? Shoot me – hey? Trick me – hey? Now I trick you – but good!' Sergio punctuated his triumphant yells with blasts on the foghorn.

'Christ, no! You can't do it!' Johnny caught urgently at the big Italian's shoulder, but Sergio struck his hand away and steered directly for the trawler as it lay full in the narrow passage.

'I give him plenty warning.' Sergio sent another blast echoing off the cliffs. 'He no give me warning when he shoot me – the bastard.'

There was a group of men on the trawler's foredeck. Johnny could see that they were manhandling an inflatable escape raft, a thick mattress of black rubber, towards the nearest side of the trawler. But now they were frozen by the bellow of *Kingfisher*'s foghorn. They stood looking up at the tall cliff of steel that bore down on them. Their faces were pale blobs in the gloom.

'Sergio. It's murder. Turn away, damn you, you can miss them. Turn away!' Again Johnny lunged across the wheel-house and grabbed at the wheel.

Sergio swung a backhanded blow that cracked against Johnny's temple and sent him reeling back half-stunned against the storm doors.

'*Who* Captain for this bloody ship!' There was blood on Sergio's lips, the shout had torn something inside him.

*Kingfisher*'s bows were lifting and swinging down like an executioner's axe over the trawler. They were close enough now for Johnny to recognize the men on the trawler's deck – but only one of them held his full attention.

Benedict van der Byl cowered against the trawler's rail, gripping it with both hands. His hair fluttered, soft and dark, in the wind. His eyes were big dark holes like those of a skull in the bone-white face, and his lips a pink circle of terror.

Then suddenly the trawler disappeared under *Kingfisher*'s massive bows, and immediately after that came the splinter-ing crunching sound of her timbers shattering. *Kingfisher* bore on down the passage between the cliffs without a check in her speed.

Johnny fumbled with the catch of the storm doors, and the wind tore it open. He staggered out on to the exposed wing of the bridge and reached the rail.

He stood there with the storm clawing at his clothing and looked down at the wreckage that dragged slowly along *Kingfisher*'s hull, and then was left behind.

There were human heads bobbing among the wreckage, and the wash from *Kingfisher*'s propeller pushed them towards the cliffs of Suicide.

A wave picked up one of the men and carried him swiftly on to the cliff, sweeping him high and then swirling back to leave the body stranded on that smooth white slope of granite.

The man was still alive, Johnny saw him clawing at the

216

smooth rock with his bare fingers, trying to drag himself above the reach of the sea.

It was Hugo Kramer; even through the fog of spray there was no mistaking that head of pale hair and the lithe twisted body.

The next wave reached up and dragged him back over the rock, tearing the nails from his hooked fingers as he tried to find a hold.

He was swirled and flung about in the turbulence below the cliff before another wave lifted him and hurled him on to the granite. One of his legs was broken at the knee by the force of the impact and the lower part of the leg spun loosely like the blade of a windmill as the water tugged at it.

Once again Hugo was left stranded but now he made no movement. His arms were flung wide, and his leg stuck out at a grossly unnatural angle from the knee.

Then from among these mighty waves there rose up a mass of green water which dwarfed all the others.

It reared up with slow majesty and hung poised over the granite cliff before it fell on Hugo's broken body with a boom that seemed to shake the very rock.

When the giant wave drew back, the cliff was washed clean. Hugo was gone.

The same wave that destroyed him came down the passage between the cliffs and, in contrast to its treatment of Hugo Kramer, it was tender as a mother as it lifted *Kingfisher* and carried her out into the open sea beyond the reach of those cruel cliffs.

Looking back into the gap between the islands, the last trace that Johnny saw of the *Wild Goose* was the black rubber escape raft tossing and leaping high on the turmoil of broken water and creamy spindrift.

'They'll have no use for that,' he said aloud. He searched for a sight of any survivor, but there was none. They were chewed to pulp in the jaws of Thunderbolt and Suicide, and swallowed down into the cold green maw of the sea.

Johnny turned away and went back into the wheelhouse. He lifted Tracey from the deck and carried her through to Sergio's cabin.

As he laid her on the bunk he whispered to her, 'I'm glad. I'm glad you didn't see it, my darling.'

At midnight the wind still howled about the ship, hurling sheets of solid rain against the windows of the bridge. Forty minutes later the wind had veered through a hundred and eighty degrees and become a light south-easterly air. The black sky opened like a theatre curtain, and the full moonlight burst through so brightly as to pale the stars. Though the tall black swells still marched in martial ranks from the north, the gentle wind was soothing and lulling them.

'Sergio, you must rest now. I will take the con. Let Tracey dress your back.'

'You take the con!' Sergio snorted scornfully. 'I save the ship – and you sink her for me. Not bloody likely.'

'Listen, Sergio. We don't know how badly you are hurt. You are killing yourself.'

The same argument spluttered and flared intermittently during the long night hours while Sergio clung stubbornly to the helm and coaxed the labouring vessel back towards Cartridge Bay. He insisted on detouring far out to sea to avoid the islands, so that when the bright dawn broke, the land was only a low brown line on the horizon and the mountains of the interior were a distant blue.

An hour after dawn Johnny made radio contact with the very agitated operator at Cartridge Bay.

'Mr Lance, we've been trying to raise you since yesterday evening.'

'I've been busy.' Despite his fatigue Johnny grinned at his own understatement. 'Now, listen to me. We are coming into Cartridge Bay. We'll be there in a couple of hours. I want you to have a doctor, Doctor Robin Sutherland, flown up from Cape Town – also I want you to have the police standing by. I want somebody from both the Diamond police and the Robbery and Murder squad – have you got that?'

'The police are here already, Mr Lance. They are looking for Mr Benedict van der Byl. They found his car here – they have a warrant . . .' The operator's voice broke off and Johnny heard the mumble of background voices, then – 'Mr Lance, are you there? Stand by to speak to Inspector Stander of the CID.'

'Negative!' Johnny cut in on his transmission. 'I'm not talking to anybody. He can wait until we get into the Bay. Just you have Doctor Sutherland ready. I've got a badly wounded man on board.'

Johnny leaned over the radio set and shut off the main switch, then he stood and made his way slowly back to the bridge. Every muscle in his body felt stiff and bruised, and he was groggy with tiredness, but he took up the argument with Sergio where they had left off.

'Now listen to me, Sergio. You must lie down. You can take us in over the bar; but now you must get an hour or two's rest.'

Still Sergio would not relinquish the wheel, but he consented to strip to the waist and let Tracey examine his back.

In the expanse of white muscle were little black holes each set in its own purple bruise. Some of the holes had sealed themselves with black clotted blood, from others fluid still oozed – clear or pink in colour – and there was a faint sweetish smell from the wounds.

Johnny and Tracey exchanged worried looks before Tracey reached into the first aid box and set to work.

'How she look, Johnny?' Sergio's jovial tone was belied by his face which was a lump of bread dough touched with greenish blue hues.

'Depends if you like your meat rare.' Johnny matched his tone, and Sergio chuckled but cut it short with a wince.

Johnny put a cheroot between Sergio's lips and held a match for him. As Sergio puffed the tip into a glow, Johnny asked casually, 'What made you change your mind?' And Sergio looked up at him quickly, guiltily, through the cloud of cheroot smoke.

'You had us cold. You could have got away with it – perhaps,' Johnny persisted quietly. 'What made you come back?'

'Listen, Johnny. Me, I've done some damned awful bloody things – but I never killed a man or a woman – ever. He said no killing. Fine, I go along. Then I hear the plastique blow. I know you two in conveyor room. I think the hell with it. Now, I climb off the wagon – but she's going too fast. I get bum full of buckshot.'

They were silent for a while. Tracey was absorbed in patching the shot-wounds with adhesive tape.

Johnny broke the silence. 'Was there a big diamond, Sergio? A big blue diamond?'

'Si.' Sergio sighed. 'Such a diamond you will never see again.'

'Benedict had it?'

'Si. Benedict had it.'

'Did he have it on him?'

'In his coat. He put it in his coat pocket.'

Tracey stepped back. 'That's all we can do for now,' she murmured and caught Johnny's eye, shaking her head slightly and frowning with worry. 'The sooner we get him to a doctor the happier I'll be.'

A little before noon Sergio took *Kingfisher* in through the entrance to Cartridge Bay, handling the mud-filled ship with all the aplomb of the master mariner, but as they approached the first turning in the channel he sagged gently to the deck and the wheel spun out of his hands.

Before Johnny could reach the helm, *Kingfisher* had yawed wearily across the channel. She had so little way on her that when she went up on the sand bank there was only a small jolt and she listed over a few degrees.

Johnny pulled the engine telegraph to 'STOP'.

'Help me, Tracey.' He stooped over Sergio and took him under the armpits. Tracey grasped his ankles. Half dragging, half carrying, they got him through to his cabin and laid him on his bunk.

'Hey, Johnny. Sorry, Johnny,' Sergio was mumbling. 'First time I put ship on bank – ever! Idiot! So close – then *wap*! Sorry, hey, Johnny.'

The motor launch left the jetty and came down the channel towards the sand bank on which *Kingfisher* lay stranded. The launch was crowded, and the whine of the outboard engine raised a storm of water fowl into a whirlwind of frightened wings.

As it drew closer Johnny recognized some of the occupants. Mike Shapiro and with him Robin Sutherland, but there were also two uniformed policemen and another person in civilian clothes who stood up in the launch as it came within hail and cupped his hands about his mouth.

'I am a police officer. I have a warrant for the arrest of Benedict—'

Mike Shapiro touched the man's arm, and spoke softly to him. The officer hesitated and glanced up at Johnny again, before nodding agreement and settling back on to his seat.

'Robin, get up here as quick as you can,' Johnny shouted down at the launch, and when Robin came over the side Johnny hustled him towards the bridge, but Mike Shapiro hurried after them.

'Johnny, I must talk to you.'

'It can wait.'

'No, it can't.' Mike Shapiro turned to Tracey. 'Won't you take care of the doctor, please? I must speak to Johnny before the police do.'

Mike led Johnny down the deck and offered him a cigarette, while the three policemen hovered at a discreet distance.

'Johnny, I have some dreadful news. I want to break it to you myself.'

Johnny visibly braced himself. 'Yes?'

'It's about Ruby—'

Johnny made his statement to the police inspector in *Kingfisher*'s guest cabin. It took two hours for him to relate the full story, and during that time one of the uniformed policemen discovered the crew locked in the paint store below decks. They were half poisoned with paint fumes but able to make their statements to the police.

The inspector kept them waiting in the next-door cabin while he finished his interrogation of Johnny.

'Two more questions for now, Mr Lance. In your opinion was the collision between the two ships accidental or deliberate?'

Johnny looked into the steel-grey eyes and lied for the first time.

'It was unavoidable.'

The inspector nodded and made a note on his pad.

'Last question. The survivors from the trawler, what were their chances?'

'In that storm they had none. There was no hope of effecting a rescue with *Kingfisher* almost disabled, and considering the condition of the surf in the passage between the islands.'

'I understand.' The inspector nodded. 'Thank you, Mr Lance. That is all for the present.'

Johnny left the cabin and went quickly to the upper deck. Tracey and Robin were still working over Sergio's bunk, but Robin looked up and came immediately to Johnny as he stood in the doorway.

'How is he, Robin?'

'He hasn't a chance,' Robin replied, keeping his voice low. 'One lung has collapsed, and there appear to be perforations of the bowel and intestine. I suspect a massive peritonitis. I can't move him without risking a secondary haemorrhage.'

'Is he conscious?'

Robin shook his head. 'He's going fast. God knows how he has lasted this long.'

Johnny moved across to the bunk and placed his arm about Traccy's shoulders. She moved closer to him and they stood looking down at Sergio.

His eyes were closed, and a dark pelt of new beard covered the lower part of his face. His breathing sawed and hissed loudly in the quiet cabin, and the fever lit bright spots of colour in his cheeks.

'You magnificent old rogue.' Johnny spoke softly, and Sergio's eyes blinked open.

Quickly Johnny stooped to him.

'Sergio. Your crew – your boys are safe.'

Sergio smiled. He closed those dark gazelle eyes, then opened them again and whispered painfully, 'Johnny, you give me job when I come out of prison?'

'They won't have you in prison – you'd lower the tone of the place.'

Sergio tried to laugh. He managed one strangled chuckle, then he came up on his elbows in the bunk with his eyes bulging, his mouth gaping for breath. He coughed once, a harsh tearing sound, and the blood burst from his lips in thick black clots and a bright red spray of droplets.

He fell back on the pillows, and was dead before Robin reached his side.

Tracey was asleep in the bedroom next door. Robin had sedated her heavily enough to keep her that way for the next twelve hours.

Johnny lay naked on the narrow bunk in the second guest room of the Cartridge Bay depot, and when he switched on the beside lamp his wrist watch showed the time as 2.46 in the morning.

He looked down at his own body. The bruises were dark purple and hot angry red across his ribs and flanks from where the mud had battered him against rough steel plating. He wished now that he had accepted the sleeping pills Robin had offered him, for the ache of his body and the whirl of his thoughts had kept him from sleep all that night.

His mind was trapped on a nightmare roundabout, revolving endlessly the two deaths which Benedict van der Byl must answer for in the dark places to which he had surely gone.

Ruby and Sergio. Ruby and Sergio. One he had seen die, the other he could imagine in all its gruesome detail.

Johnny sat up and lit a cigarette, seeking a distraction from the tortured images with which his overexcited brain bombarded him.

He tried to concentrate on reviewing the practical steps that would be necessary to clear up the aftermath of these last disastrous days.

He had spoken that evening by radio to Larsen, and received from him a promise of complete financial support during the time it would take to clear the mud from *Kingfisher*'s hull and recover the diamonds in the conveyor tunnel, and to tide over the period of salvage and repair before the dredger was ready to begin once more harvesting the rich fields of Thunderbolt and Suicide.

A salvage team would fly in tomorrow to begin the work on *Kingfisher*. He had cabled IBM requesting engineers to check out the computer for water damage.

Six weeks, Johnny estimated, before *Kingfisher* was ready for sea.

Then his unruly imagination leapt suddenly ahead to Ruby's funeral. It was set for Tuesday next week. Johnny rolled restlessly on his bunk, trying to shut his mind against the thoughts that assaulted it – but they crowded forward in a dark host.

Ruby, Benedict, Sergio, the big blue diamond.

He sat up again, stubbed out his cigarette and reached across to switch out the bedside lamp.

He froze like that, as a new thought pressed in on him. He heard Sergio's voice in his memory.

'*Such a diamond as you will never see again.*'

Now he felt the idea come ghosting along his spine so that the hair at the nape of his neck and on his forearms prickled with excitement.

'The Red Gods!' he exclaimed, almost shouting the name. And again Sergio's voice spoke.

'*In his coat. He put it in his coat pocket.*'

Johnny swung his legs off the bunk, and reached for his clothes. He felt the pounding of his heart beneath his fingers as he buttoned his shirt. He pulled on slacks and sweater, tied the laces of his shoes and snatched up a sheepskin jacket as he ran from the room.

He was shrugging on the jacket as he entered the deserted radio room and switched on the lights. He crossed quickly to the chart table and pored over it.

He found the name on the map, and repeated it aloud.

'The Red Gods.'

North of Cartridge Bay the coast ran straight and featureless for thirty miles, then abruptly the line of it was broken by the out-thrust of red rock, poking into the sea like an accuser's finger.

Johnny knew it well. It was his job to find and examine any such natural feature that might act as a barrier to the prevailing inshore currents. At such a place diamonds and other seaborne objects would be thrown ashore.

He remembered the red rock cliffs carved by wind and sea into the grotesque natural statues which gave the place its name, but more important he remembered the litter of ocean debris on the beaches beneath the cliff. Driftwood, waterlogged planking, empty bottles, plastic containers, scraps of nylon fishing-net and corks – all of it cast overboard and carried up by the current to be deposited on this promontory.

He ran his finger down the chart and held it on the dots of Thunderbolt and Suicide. He read the laconic notation over the tiny arrows that flew from the islands towards the stark outline of the Red Gods.

'Current sets South South-West. 5 knots.'

Above the chart table the depot keys hung on their little cuphooks, each labelled and numbered.

Johnny selected the two of them marked 'GARAGE' and 'LAND-ROVER'.

The moon was full and high. The night was still and without a trace of wind. Johnny swung the double doors of the garage open and switched on the parking lights of the Land-Rover. By their glow he checked out the vehicle; petrol tank full, the spare five-gallon cans in their brackets full, the can of drinking-water full. He dipped his finger into the neck of the water container and tasted it. It was clean and sweet. He lifted the passenger seat and checked the compartment beneath it. Jack and tyre spanner, first aid kit, flashlight, signal rockets and smoke flares, water bottle, canvas groundsheet, two cans of survival rations, towrope, tool kit, knapsack, knife and compass. The Land-Rover was equipped to meet any of the emergencies of desert travel.

Johnny climbed behind the wheel and started the engine. He drove quietly and slowly past the depot buildings, not wanting to awaken those sleeping inside, but when he hit the firm sand at the edge of the lagoon he switched on the headlights and gunned the engine.

He cut across the sand dunes at the entrance to the bay, and swung northwards on to the beach. The headlights threw solid white beams into the sea mist, and startled seabirds rose on flapping ghost wings before the rush of the Land-Rover.

The tide was out and the exposed beach was hard and shiny wet, smooth as a tarmac road. He drove fast, and the white beach crabs were blinded by the headlights and crunched crisply beneath the tyres.

The dawn came early, silhouetting the mystic shapes of the dunes against the red sky.

Once he startled a strand wolf, one of the brown hyenas which scavenged this bleak littoral. It galloped, hunchshouldered, in hideous panic for the safety of the dunes. Even in his urgency Johnny felt a stir of revulsion for the loathsome creature.

The cold damp rush of the wind into his face refreshed Johnny. It cooled the gritty feeling of his eyes, and eased the throb of sleeplessness in his temples.

The sun burst over the horizon, and lit the Red Gods five miles ahead with all the drama of stage lighting. They glowed golden red in the dawn, a procession of huge half-human shapes that marched into the sea.

As Johnny drove towards them the light and shadow played over the cliffs and he saw a hundred-foot tall figure of Neptune stooping to dip his flowing red beard into the sea, while a monstrous hunchback with the head of a wolf pranced beside him. Ranks of Vestal Virgins in long robes of red rock jostled with the throng of weird and fantastic shapes. It was eerie and disquieting. Johnny curbed his fancy and turned his attention to the beaches at the foot of the cliffs.

What he saw started his skin tingling again, and he

pressed the accelerator flat against the floorboards, racing across the wet sand to where a white cloud of seabirds circled and dived and hopped about something that lay at the water's edge.

As he drove towards them a gull flew across the front of the Land-Rover. A long ribbon of something wet and fleshy dangled from its beak, and the gull gulped at it greedily in flight. Its crop was distended and engorged with food.

The seabirds scattered raucously and indignantly as the Land-Rover approached, leaving a human body lying in the centre of an area of sand that was dappled by the prints of their webbed feet, and fouled with dropped feathers and excreta.

Johnny braked the Land-Rover and jumped out. He took one long look at the body, then turned quickly away and braced himself against the side of the vehicle.

His gorge rose in a hot flood of nausea, and he gagged it back.

The body was nude but for a few sodden tatters of clothing and a sea boot still laced on to one foot. The birds had attacked every inch of exposed flesh – except for the scalp. The face was unrecognizable. The nose was gone, the eye sockets were empty black holes. There were no lips to cover the grinning teeth.

Above this ruined face the shock of colourless albino hair looked like a wig placed there as an obscene and tasteless joke.

Hugo Kramer had made the long voyage from Thunderbolt and Suicide to the Red Gods.

Johnny took the canvas groundsheet from under the passenger seat of the Land-Rover. Averting his eyes from the task, he wrapped the corpse carefully, tied the whole bundle with lengths of rope cut from the tow line, then laboriously dragged it up the beach well above the high-water mark.

The thick canvas would keep off the birds, but to make doubly certain Johnny collected the driftwood and planking that was scattered thickly along the high-water line and piled it over the corpse.

Some of the planking was freshly broken and the paint on it was still bright and new. Johnny guessed this was part of the wreckage of *Wild Goose*.

He went back to the Land-Rover, and drove on towards the Red Gods which lay only a mile ahead.

The sun was well up by now, and already its heat was uncomfortable. As he drove he struggled out of the sheepskin jacket without interrupting his search of the beach ahead.

He was looking for another gathering of seagulls, but instead he saw a large black object stranded in the angle formed by the red stone cliffs.

He was fifty yards from it before he realized what it was.

He felt his stomach jar violently and then clench at the shock.

It was a black rubber inflatable life raft – and it had been dragged up the beach *above the high-water line*.

As he climbed out of the Land-Rover Johnny felt his legs trembling beneath him, as though he had just climbed a mountain. The hard knotted sensation in his chest shortened his breathing.

He went slowly towards the raft, and there was a story to read in the soft sand.

The smooth drag mark of the raft, and the two sets of footprints. One set made by bare feet; broad, stubby-toed and with flattened arches, the prints of a man who habitually went barefooted.

These tracks had been made by one of the coloured crew of *Wild Goose*, Johnny decided, dismissed them and turned his whole attention to the other set of footprints.

Shod feet, long and narrow, smooth leather soles; the

imprints were sharp-edged suggesting new shoes little worn, the length of the stride and the depth of prints were those of a tall heavily built man.

Johnny realized with mild surprise that his hands were shaking now, and even his lips quivered. He was like a man in high fever; light-headed, weak and shaking. It was Benedict van der Byl. He knew it with complete and utter certainty. Benedict had survived the maelstrom of Thunderbolt and Suicide.

Johnny balled his fists, squeezing hard and he thrust out his jaw, tightening his lips. Still the hatred washed over his mind in dark hot waves.

'Thank God,' he whispered. 'Thank God. Now I can kill him myself.'

The footprints had churned the sand all about the raft. Beside them lay a thick piece of planking which had been used as a lever to rip the emergency water container and the food locker from the floor-boards of the raft.

The food locker had been ransacked and abandoned. They would be carrying the packets of iron rations in their pockets to save weight, but the water container was gone.

The two sets of prints struck out straight for the dunes. Johnny followed them at a run and lost them immediately in the shifting wind-blown sands of the first dune.

Johnny was undismayed. The dunes persisted for only a thousand yards or so, then gave way inland to the plains and salt flats of the interior.

He ran back to the Land-Rover. He had his emotions under control again. His hatred was reduced to a hard indigestible lump below his ribs, and he contemplated for a few seconds lifting the microphone of the Land-Rover's R/T set and calling Cartridge Bay.

Inspector Stander had the police helicopter parked on the landing-strip behind the depot buildings. He could be here in thirty minutes. An hour later they would have Benedict van der Byl.

Johnny dismissed the idea. Officially Benedict was dead, drowned. No one would look for him in a shallow grave in the wastes of the Namib desert.

The crewman with him would be a complication; but he could be bribed and frightened or threatened. Nothing must stand in the path of his vengeance. Nothing.

Johnny opened the Land-Rover's locker and found the knife. He went to the raft and stabbed the blade through the thick material at a dozen places. The air hissed from the holes, and the raft collapsed slowly.

Johnny bundled it into the back of the Land-Rover. He would bury it in the desert; there must be no evidence that Benedict had come ashore.

He started the engine, engaged the four-wheel drive, and followed the spoor to the foot of the dunes.

He picked his way through the valleys and across the knife-backed ridges of sand.

As he descended the last slope of the dunes he felt the oppressive silence and immensity of the land enfold him. Here, only a mile from the sea, the moderating influence of the cold Benguela current did not reach.

The heat was appalling. Johnny felt the sweat prickling from the pores of his skin and drying instantly in the lethal desiccating air.

He swung the Land-Rover parallel to the line of the dunes and crawled along at walking speed, hanging over the side of the vehicle and searching the ground. The bright specks of mica in the sand bounced the heat of the sun into his face.

He cut the spoor again where it came down off the dunes and went away on it, headed arrow straight at the far line of mountains which were already receding into the blue haze as the heat built up towards noon.

Johnny's progress was a series of rushes where the spoor ran true, broken by halts and painstaking casts on the rocky ridges and areas of broken ground. Twice he left the Land-

Rover to work the spoor through difficult terrain, but across one of the flat white salt pans he covered four miles in as many minutes. The prints were strung like the beads of a necklace, cut clearly through the glistening crust of salt.

Beyond the pan they ran into a maze of black rocks, riven by gullies, and guarded by the tall misshapen monoliths.

In one of the gullies he found Hansie, the little old coloured crewman from *Wild Goose*. His skull had been battered in with the blood-caked rock that lay beside him. The blood had dried slick and shiny, and Hansie stared with dry eyeballs at the merciless sky. His expression was of mild surprise.

The story of this new tragedy was written in the sandy bottom of the gully. In an area of milling, confused prints the two men had argued. Johnny could guess that Hansie had wanted to turn back for the coast. He must have known that the road lay beyond the mountains, a hundred miles away. He wanted to abandon the attempt, try for the coast and Cartridge Bay.

The argument ended when he turned his back on Benedict, and returned on his old tracks.

There was a depression in the sand from which Benedict had picked up the rock and followed him.

Standing over Hansie, and looking down at that pathetic crushed head, Johnny realized for the first time that he was following a maniac.

Benedict van der Byl was insane. He was no longer a man, but a raging demented animal.

'I will kill him,' Johnny promised the old white woolly head at his feet. There was no need for subterfuge now.

If he caught up with Benedict and did it, no court in the world would question but that it was self-defence. Benedict had placed himself beyond the laws of man.

Johnny took the deflated rubber raft and spread it over

Hansie. He anchored the edges of the rubber sheet with rocks.

He drove on into the dancing, shimmering walls of heat with a new mood on him; murderous, elated expectation. He knew that at this moment in time he was part animal also, corrupted by the savagery of the man he was hunting. He wanted payment in full from Benedict van der Byl in his own coin. Life for life, and blood for blood.

A mile farther on he found the water container. It had been flung aside violently, skidding across the sand with the force of its rejection; the water had poured from its open mouth, leaving a dried hollow in the thirsty earth.

Johnny stared at it in disbelief. Not even a maniac would condemn himself to such a horrible ending.

Johnny went across to where the five-gallon brass drum lay on its side. He picked it up and shook it, there was the sloshy sound of a pint or so of liquid in it.

'God!' he whispered, awed and feeling a twinge of pity despite himself. 'He won't last long now.'

He lifted the container to his lips and sucked a mouthful. Immediately his nostrils flared with disgust, and he spat violently, dropping the can and wiping at his lips with the back of his hand.

'Sea water!' he mumbled. He hurried to the Land-Rover and washed out his mouth with sweet water.

How the contamination had occurred he would never know. The raft might have lain for years in *Wild Goose* without its stores being checked or renewed.

From that point onwards Benedict must have known he was doomed. His despair was easy to read in the blundering footsteps. He had started running, with panic driving him. Five hundred yards further on he had fallen heavily into the bed of a dry ravine, and lain for a while before dragging himself up the bank.

Now he had lost direction. The spoor began a long curve

to the northwards, running again. It came round full circle, and where it crossed itself, Benedict had sat down. The marks of his buttocks were unmistakable. He must have controlled his panic here because once more the spoor struck out with determination towards the mountains.

However, within half a mile he had tripped and fallen. Now he was staggering off course again, drifting southwards. Once more he had fallen, but here he had lost a shoe.

Johnny picked it up and read the printed gold lettering on the inner sole. 'BALLY OF SWITZERLAND, SPECIALLY MADE FOR HARRODS. That's our boy Benedict, all right. Forty-guinea black kid,' he muttered grimly, and climbed back into the Land-Rover. His excitement was climaxing now. It would be soon, very soon.

Farther on Benedict had wandered down into the bed of an ancient watercourse, and turned to follow it. His right foot was lacerated by the razor flints in the river bed, and at each pace he had left a little dab of brown crumbly blood. He was staggering like a drunkard.

Johnny zigzagged the Land-Rover through the boulders that choked the watercourse. The gully deepened, and spiky cockscomb ridges of black rock hedged it in on either hand. The air in the watercourse was a heavy blanket of heat. It seared the throat, and dried the mucus in Johnny's nostrils brick hard. A small noon breeze came off the mountains, a sluggish stirring of the heavy air, that provided no relief but seemed only to heighten the bite of the sun and the suffocating oppression of the air.

Scattered along the river bed were bushes of stunted scrub. Grotesque little plants, crippled and malformed by the drought of years.

From one of the bushes ahead of the Land-Rover a monstrous black bird flapped its wings lethargically. Johnny screwed up his eyes, uncertain if it was reality or a mirage of the heat and the tortured air.

Suddenly the bird resolved itself into the jacket of a dark

blue suit. It hung in the thorny branches, the breeze stirring the folds of expensive cloth.

'In his coat. He put it in his coat pocket.'

With eyes only for the jacket, recklessly he pressed down the accelerator and the Land-Rover surged forward. Johnny did not see the knee-high boulder of ironstone in his path. He hit it at twenty miles an hour, and the Land-Rover stopped dead with the squeal of tearing metal. Johnny was flung forward against the steering-wheel, the impact driving the breath from his lungs.

He was still doubled up with the pain of it, wheezing for breath, as he hobbled to the jacket and snatched it out of the bush.

He felt the heavy drag of the weighted pocket.

Then the fat canvas bag was in his hands, the contents crunched nuttily as he tore at the drawstring. Nothing else in the world felt like that.

'Such a diamond as you will never see again.'

The drawstring was knotted tightly. Johnny ran back to the Land-Rover. Frantically he scrabbled in the seat locker and found the knife. He cut the drawstring and dumped the contents of the bag on to the bonnet of the Land-Rover.

'Oh God! Oh sweet God!' he whispered through cracked lips. His eyesight blurred, and the big blue diamond glowed mistily, distorted by the tears that flooded his vision.

It was a full minute before he could bring himself to touch it. Then he did so reverently – as though it were a sacred relic.

Johnny Lance had worked all his life to take a stone such as this.

He held it in both hands and sank down into the scrap of shade beside the body of the Land-Rover.

It was another five minutes before the hot cloying smell of engine oil reached the conscious level of his mind.

He turned his head and saw the slowly spreading pool of it beneath the Land-Rover chassis. Quickly he rolled on to his stomach and, still clutching the diamond, crawled under the vehicle. The ironstone boulder had shattered the engine sump. The Land-Rover had bled its lifeblood into the hot sand of the river bed.

He wriggled out from under the body of the Land-Rover and leaned against the front tyre. He looked at his wrist watch and was surprised to see it was already a few minutes after two o'clock in the afternoon.

He was surprised also at the conscious effort it required to focus his eyes on the dial of the watch. Two days and two nights without sleep, the unremitting emotional strain of those days and nights, the battering his body had taken, the long hours in the heat and the soul-corroding desolation of this lunar landscape – all these had taken their toll. He knew he was as light-headed as in the first stages of inebriation, he was beginning to act irrationally. That sudden reckless charge down the boulder-strewn river bed, which had wrecked the Land-Rover, was a symptom of his present instability.

He fondled the great diamond, touching the warm smooth surface to his lips, rubbing it softly between thumb and forefinger, changing it from hand to hand, while every fibre of his muscles and the very marrow of his bones cried out for rest.

A soft and treacherous lethargy spread through his body and reached out to numb his brain. He closed his eyes for a moment to shut out the flare, and when he opened them again with an effort the time was four o'clock. He scrambled to his feet. The shadows in the gully were longer, the breeze had dropped.

Although he moved with the stiffness of an old man, the sleep had cleared his mind and while he wolfed a packet of biscuits spread with meat paste and washed it down with a mugful of lukewarm water he made his decision.

He buried the canvas bag of rough diamonds in the sand

beneath the Land-Rover, but he could not bring himself to part with the big blue. He buttoned it securely into the back pocket of his slacks. Into the light knapsack from the seat locker he packed the two-pint water bottle, the first aid kit, a small hand-bearing compass, two of the smoke flares and the knife. He checked his pockets for his cigarette lighter and case.

Then without another glance at the radio set on the dashboard of the Land-Rover he turned away and hobbled up the gully on the spoor of Benedict van der Byl.

Within half a mile he had walked the stiffness out of his body, and he lengthened his stride, going well now. The hatred and hunger for vengeance which had died to smouldering ash since he had found the diamonds now flared up again strongly. It gave power to his legs and sharpened his senses.

The spoor turned abruptly up the side of the gully and he lost it on the black rock of the ridge, but found it again on his first cast.

He was closing fast now. The spoor was running across the grain of the land, and Benedict was clearly weakening rapidly. He had fallen repeatedly, crawled on bloody knees over cruel gravel and rock, he had blundered into the scrub bushes and left threads of his clothing on the hooked red-tipped thorns.

Then the spoor led out of the ridges and scrub into another area of low orange-coloured sandhills and Johnny broke into a jog trot. The sun was sliding down the sky, throwing blue shades in the hollows of the dunes and the heat abated so that Johnny's sweat was able to cool him before drying.

Johnny was intent on the staggering footprints, beginning to worry now that he would find Benedict already dead. The signs were those of a man in extreme distress, and still he was driving himself on.

Johnny did not notice the other prints that angled in from the dunes and ran parallel to those of Benedict, until they closed in again and began overlaying the human prints.

Johnny stopped and went down on one knee to examine the broad dog-like pug marks.

'Hyena!' He felt the sick little flutter of revulsion in his stomach as he spoke. He glanced around quickly and saw the other set of prints out on the left.

'A pair of them! They've smelt the blood.'

Johnny began to run on the spoor now. His skin crawled with what he knew could happen when they caught up with a helpless man. The filthiest and most cowardly animals in Africa, but with jaws that could crunch to splinters the thigh bone of a full-grown buffalo, and their thick stubby fangs were coated with such a slime of bacteria from a diet of putrid carrion that their bite was as deadly as that of a black mamba.

'Let me be in time; please God, let me find him in time.'

He heard it then. From beyond the crest of the next dune. The horror of the sound stopped him in mid-stride. It was a shrill giggling gibbering cry that sobbed into silence.

Johnny stood listening, panting wildly from his run.

It came again. The laughter of demons, excited, blood-crazy.

'They've got him.'

Johnny flung himself at the soft slope of sand. He reached the crest and looked down into the saucer-shaped arena formed by the crescent of the dune.

Benedict lay on his back. His white shirt was open to the waist. The blue trousers of his suit were ripped and shredded, exposing his knees. One foot was a bloody lump of sock and congealed dirt.

The pair of hyenas had trampled a path in the sand around his body. They had been circling him for hours, while greed overcame their cowardice.

One hyena sat ten feet from him, squatting obscenely

with its flat snakelike head lowered between humped shoulders. Brown and shaggy, spotted with darker brown, its round ears pricked forward, its black eyes sparkling with greed and excitement as it watched its mate.

The other hyena stood with its front paws on Benedict's chest. Its head was lowered, and its jaws were locked into Benedict's face. It was leaning back, bracing its paws on his chest, tugging viciously as it sought to tear off a mouthful of flesh. Benedict's head was jerking and twitching as the hyena worried it. His legs were kicking weakly, and his hands fluttered on the sand like maimed white birds.

The flesh of his face tore. Johnny heard it distinctly in the utter silence of the desert evening. It tore with the soft sound of silk – and Johnny screamed.

Both hyenas bolted at the scream, scrambling over the far crest of the dune in horrible clownish panic, leaving Benedict lying with a bloody mask for a face.

Looking down at that face Johnny knew he could not kill him now, perhaps could never have killed him. He could not revenge himself on this broken thing with its ruined face and twisted mind.

He dropped on to his knees beside him, and loosened the flap of the knapsack with clumsy fingers.

Benedict's one ear and cheek were hanging over his mouth in a thick flap of torn flesh. The teeth in the side of his jaw were exposed and the blood dribbled and spurted in fine needle jets.

Johnny tore the paper packaging off an absorbent dressing and with it pressed the flap back into place. Holding it there with the full pressure of his spread fingers. The blood soaked through the dressing, but it was slowing at the pressure.

'It's all right, Benedict. I'm here now. You'll be all right,' he whispered hoarsely as he worked. With his free hand he stripped the packaging off another dressing, and substituted it neatly for the sodden one. He maintained the pressure on the clean dressing while he lifted Benedict's head and cradled it in his lap.

'We'll just dry this bleeding up, then we'll give you a drink.' He reached into the first aid kit for a piece of cotton wool and tenderly began to clean the blood and sand from Benedict's nostrils and lips. Benedict's strangled breathing eased a little but still whistled through the black lips. His tongue was swollen, filling his mouth like a fat purple sponge.

'That's better,' Johnny muttered. Still without relaxing pressure on the compress dressing, he got the screw top off the water bottle. Holding his thumb over the opening to regulate the flow, he let a drop of water fall into the dark dry pit of a mouth.

After another ten drops he propped the water bottle in the sand, and massaged Benedict's throat gently to stimulate the swallowing reflex. The unconscious man gulped painfully.

'That's my boy,' Johnny encouraged him, and began again feeding him a drop at a time, crooning softly as he did it.

'You're going to be all right. That's it, swallow it down.'

It took him twenty minutes to administer half a pint of the warm sweet water, and by then the bleeding was negligible. Johnny reached into the kit again and selected two salt and two glucose tablets. He placed them in his own mouth and chewed them to a smooth thin paste then he bent over the mutilated face of the man he had sworn to kill and pressed his own lips against Benedict's swollen dry lips. He injected the solution of salt and glucose into Benedict's mouth, then straightened up and began again dripping the water.

When he had given Benedict another four tablets and half the contents of the water bottle, he stoppered it and returned it to the knapsack. He soaked the compress with bright yellow acriflavine solution, and bandaged it firmly into place. This was a more difficult task than he had anticipated and after a few abortive attempts he passed the bandage under the jaw and over the eyes, swathing Benedict's head completely except for the nose and mouth.

By this time the sun was on the horizon. Johnny stood up and stretched his back and shoulders as he watched the splendid gold and red death of another desert day.

He knew he was delaying his next decision. He reckoned it was five miles to where he had abandoned the Land-Rover in the gully. Five miles of hard going, a round trip of four hours – probably five in the dark. Could he leave Benedict here, get back to the vehicle, radio Cartridge Bay, and return to him?

Johnny swung round and looked up at the dunes. There was his answer. One of the hyenas was squatting on the top of a dune watching him intently. Hunger and the approach of night had made it unnaturally bold.

Johnny shouted an obscenity and made a threatening gesture towards it. The hyena jumped up and loped over the back of the ridge.

'Moon rise at eight tonight. I'll rest until then – and we'll go in the cool,' he decided and lay down on the sand beside Benedict. The lump in his back pocket prodded him, and he took the diamond out and held it in his hand.

In the darkness the hyenas began to cackle and shriek, and when the moon rose it silhouetted their evil shapes on the ridge above the saucer.

'Come on, Benedict. We're going home. There are a couple of nice policemen who want to talk to you.' Johnny lifted him into a sitting position, draped Benedict's arm over his shoulder and came up under him in a fireman's lift.

Johnny stood like that a moment, sinking ankle deep into the soft sand, dismayed at the dead weight of his burden.

'We'll rest every thousand paces,' he promised himself, and began plodding up the dune, counting softly to himself, but knowing that he would not be able to perform that lift again without a rock shelf or some support, against which to brace himself. He had to make it out of the sandhills in one go.

' – Nine hundred and ninety nine. One thousand.' He was counting in his mind only. Husbanding his strength, bowed under the weight, his shoulders and back locked in straining agony, the sand hampering each pace. 'Another five hundred. We'll go another five hundred.'

Behind him padded the two hyenas. They had gobbled the bloody dressings that Johnny had left in the saucer, and the taste of blood was driving them hysterical.

'Right. Just another five hundred.' And Johnny began the third count, and then the fourth, and the fifth.

Johnny felt the drip, drip on the back of his legs. Benedict's head-down position had restarted the bleeding, and the hyenas warbled and wailed at the smell.

'Nearly there, Benedict. Stick it out. Nearly there.'

The first cluster of moon-silver rocks floated towards them and Johnny reeled in amongst them and collapsed face forward. It was a long time before he had regained enough strength to shift Benedict's weight off his shoulders.

He readjusted Benedict's bandages, and fed him a mouthful of water which he swallowed readily. Then Johnny washed down a handful of salt and glucose tablets with two carefully rationed swallows from the water bottle. He rested for twenty minutes by his watch, then using one of the rocks as an anchor he got Benedict across his shoulder again and they went on.

Johnny rested every hour for ten minutes. At one o'clock in the morning they finished the last of the water, and at two o'clock Johnny knew beyond all possibility of doubt that he had missed the watercourse and that he was lost.

He lay against a slab of ironstone, numb with fatigue and despair, and listened to the cackling chorus of death among the rocks nearby. He tried to decide where he had gone wrong. Perhaps the watercourse curved away and he was now moving parallel to it, perhaps he had already crossed it without having recognized it. That was possible, he had heard of others stumbling blindly across a tarmac road without realizing it.

How many ridges had they climbed and descended? He could not remember. There was a place where he had stumbled into a scrub thorn and ripped his legs. Perhaps that was the watercourse.

He crawled across to Benedict.

'Brace up, bucko. We're going back.'

Johnny fell for the last time a little before dawn. When he rolled his head and squinted sideways at his wrist watch it was light enough to read the dial. The time was five o'clock.

He closed his eyes and lay for a long time, he had given up. It had been a good try – but it hadn't worked. In an hour the sun would be up. Then it was finished.

Something was moving near him, soft and stealthy-footed. It was of no interest, he decided. He just wanted to lie here quietly, now that it was finished.

Then he heard the sniffing, the harsh sniffing of a hungry dog. He opened his eyes. The hyena was ten feet away, watching him. Its bottom jaw hung open, and the pink tongue lolled loosely from the side of its mouth. He could smell it, a stink like an animal cage at the zoo, dung and offal and rotting carrion.

Johnny tried to scream, but no sound came from his mouth. His throat was closed, and his tongue filled his mouth. He struggled on to his elbows. The hyena drew back, but without the ludicrous panic of before.

Leisurely it trotted away, and then turned to face him again from a distance of twenty yards. It grinned at him, slurping the pink tongue into its mouth as it gulped saliva.

Johnny dragged himself to where Benedict lay, and looked down at him.

Slowly the blind bandaged head turned towards him, the black lips moved.

'Who's there?' A dry husky whisper. Johnny tried to answer but his voice failed him again. He hawked and chewed painfully, working a trace of moisture into his mouth. Now that Benedict was conscious Johnny's hatred flared again.

'Johnny,' he croaked. 'It's Johnny.'

'Johnny?' Benedict's hand came up and he touched the bandages over his eyes.

'What?'

Johnny reached across, lying on his side, and untied the knot at Benedict's temple. He peeled the bandages from his eyes, and Benedict blinked at him. The light of dawn was stronger now.

'Water?' Benedict asked.

Johnny shook his head.

'Please.'

'None.'

Benedict closed his eyes and then opened them, staring in terror at Johnny.

'Ruby!' Johnny whispered. 'Sergio! Hansie!'

A spasm of guilt twisted Benedict's face, and Johnny leaned closer to him to hiss a single word into his ear.

'Bastard!'

Johnny rested on his elbows, swallowing thickly, then he spoke again.

'Up!' He crawled behind Benedict and pushed and dragged him into a sitting position.

'Look.'

Twenty yards away the two hyenas sat expectantly, leering idiotically and bright-eyed with impatience.

Benedict began to tremble. He made a mewing whimpering sound. Johnny worked him slowly backwards until he had him propped against a rock.

He rested again, leaning on the rock beside Benedict.

'I'm going,' he whispered. 'You stay.'

Benedict made that mewing sound again, shaking his head weakly, staring at the two slobbering animals ahead of him.

Johnny slung the knapsack about his neck. He closed his eyes and called upon the last reserves of his strength. With a heave he got to his knees. Darkness and bright lights obscured his vision. They cleared and he heaved again and he was on his feet. His knees buckled and he grabbed at the rock to steady himself.

'Cheerio!' he whispered. 'Have fun!' And he went lurching and staggering away into the wilderness of black rock.

Behind him the mewing whimper rose to a bubbling scream.

'Johnny. Please, Johnny.'

Johnny closed his mind to that cry, and staggered on.

'Murderer!' screamed Benedict. The accusation checked Johnny. He leaned against another rock for support, and looked back.

Benedict's face was convulsed, and a thin line of bloody froth rimmed his lips. The tears were pouring unashamedly down his cheeks to soak into the blood and antiseptic stained bandages.

'Johnny. My brother. Don't leave me.'

Johnny pushed himself away from the rock. He swayed and almost fell. Then he staggered back to Benedict and slipped down into a sitting position beside him.

From the knapsack he took out the knife and laid it on his lap. Benedict was sobbing and moaning.

'Shut up. Damn you!' whispered Johnny.

The sun was well up now. It was burning directly into Johnny's face. He could feel the skin of his cheeks stretching to bursting-point. The veils of darkness kept passing over his vision, but he blinked them away. The flutter of his eyelids was the only movement he had made in the last hour.

The hyenas had closed in. They were pacing nervously back and forth in front of where Johnny and Benedict sat. Now one of them stopped and stretched its neck out, sniffing eagerly at Benedict's blood-clotted foot, creeping inch by inch closer.

Johnny stirred and the creature jumped back, bobbing its head ingratiatingly, grinning as if in apology.

The time had come to fall back on their last line of defence. Johnny hoped he had not left it too late. He was very weak. His eyes and ears were tricking him, his vision jumped and blurred and there was a humming sound in the silence as though the desert was an orchard filled with bees. He spun the cog-wheel of his cigarette lighter and the flame lit. Carefully he applied it to the fuse of the smoke flare, and it spluttered and caught.

Johnny lobbed the flare towards the hyenas, and as the clouds of pink smoke spewed out, they fled in shrieking terror.

An hour later they were back. Slinking out of the rocks, cautious again. Johnny saw them only in flashes, between the bursts of darkness in his head. The insect drone in his ears was louder, it was confusing, making it difficult for him to think clearly.

It took him ten minutes to light the second flare. His throw was so weak that the flare pitched only a few inches beyond his own feet. The pink smoke spread over them.

Johnny felt the blood humming in his ears as the swirling pink clouds engulfed him. The sulphurous bite of the smoke in his throat choked him. The sound in his ears became a drumming roar, a rushing clattering hissing bellow. Then there was a wild wind in the stillness of the desert. Miraculously the smoke cloud was ripped away by the wind.

Johnny looked up into the sky from which the great wind came. Twenty feet above him, hanging on the glistening dragon-fly wing of its rotor, was the police helicopter.

Tracey's face was framed in the cabin window of the helicopter. He saw her lips form his name before he fainted.